Birthrights

Book One of the Last Son of the Feromage Saga

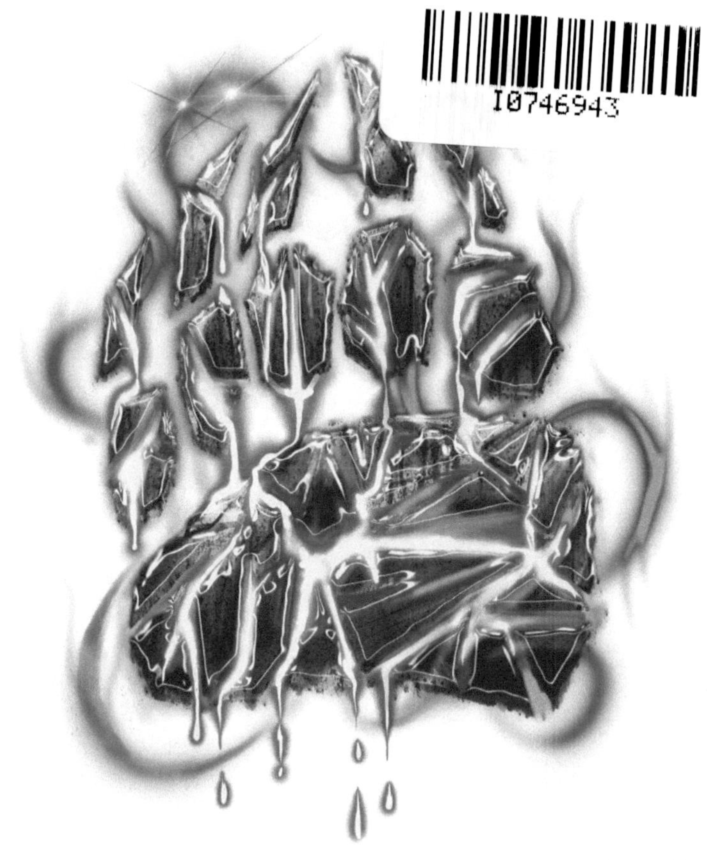

Written By David Trotter

TABLE OF CONTENTS

Copyright Page

Registration Number TXu 2-277-767

Effective Date of Registration:
September 02, 2021

Registration Decision Date:
September 20, 2021

This book is dedicated to my beautiful wife and my children, the three that walk this earth with me and to the three who have gone on before me.

To Oliver, I love you and your adventurous heart. You encapsulate everything I find fascinating and wild about this world.

To Lily, who has always been my little girl. You are more precious to me than all the fame and fortune this world has to offer.

To Theodore, your tiny smile lights up my world. You will grow into an amazing young man one day, and I look forward to discovering what you will become.

And to my amazing wife, Heather, whom I love and adore with my whole heart. Without you, none of this would have been possible. You have been my rock and my high place, my joy and my boon. You held me up when the darkness sought to overtake me. You brought me cheer and warmth in my bleakest hours. This book if as much yours as it is mine, even if you can't pronounce half the names in it.

I love you all more than words can ever express; and to my children, I am proud to be your daddy.

Love,

~David A. Trotter~

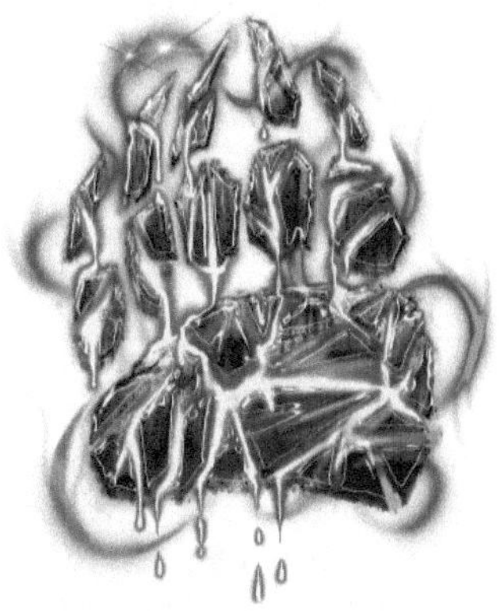

PROLOGUE: THE FINAL NIGHT

Wailing cries of dying men, mixed with the harrowing howls of dark beasts, filled the cold night air, bitter and unforgiving. Harsh winds shook the tall pines of the forest, casting drifts of snow onto the thick, black hair of a lone warrior. He was tired, so tired. However, the acidic hatred and determination boiling within his veins urged him forward.

Slowly, the warrior, Denathurias, climbed the ruined mountainside, using the broken trees to support his battered body as he pressed forward. A crimson crescent moon loomed in the night sky, dimly lighting the man's steep path. Blood stained the ground behind him as he limped onward, dripping blood from the chainmail-covered animal hide that wrapped about his body. That seemed trivial to him, the loss of his lifeblood, compared to what he had faced.

Wounds heal, death is eternal.

The battered warrior ran a calloused thumb over an untarnished ring of silver, roughly hewn and embellished with a single pawprint of a bear. The thick ring harnessed an unnatural light about it, faint and fading, but still present. The moonlight could no longer aid him, for he had already drawn upon her light far too long during this bloody night. He trudged forward, climbing slowly upward. And with every step, searing pain emanated from the wound on his side, which did not seem to heal as others had in the past, and his golden eyes slowly dimmed.

Ahead, at the peak of the twin mountains, past where the trees could grow, two figures could be seen talking. One was a tall Morrean male, the high priest of their dark cult. He had unnaturally white flesh and long, pronounced features. His head was shaved, save only a single black braid of hair that hung off the back of his scalp. This was covered by a helmet formed from the skull and horns of some dark beast spawned by his master. Red tattoos veiled the man's lean but muscular body, running like rivers of blood over his face, torso, and extremities.

"Diabhail." A mix of disgust and rage formed in his bosom at the appearance of his foe.

The other was a woman in a long black dress of Turish design. It was slim and sleek, flowing majestically over her slender features. A three-pronged crown of icy steel sat nobly upon fiery hair of crimson. Her flesh, too, shone bright white in the moonlight, enhanced by an otherworldly sheen. The warrior had never actually seen Mireya before this moment, but he knew exactly who she was.

The Blood Queen, as she was known among the tribes of men, practiced the darkest form of magic: blood magic. She was at one time the most powerful sorceress the land of Ethrea had ever known. But now, at the end of this Great Desolation, this last and terrible war, the dark queen was depleted. Seemingly abandoned by her corrupted gods, the Fallen Ones, dark deities who lent her demonic abilities, Mireya was but an empty hull abandoned by all but her most loyal servant.

Queen Mireya was the first to see the bleeding warrior making his way slowly up the mountain pass towards them. She quickly turned towards her high priest, Diabhail, muttering something to him. A gaze that could pierce the night was the last thing the warrior saw from Mireya before she hurried out of sight.

The tattooed man took up a crude stone hammer from the earth and rushed furiously towards the warrior. The two clashed, and the wounded man fought with all his might against his colossal enemy. Hot blood spewed across the snow as blows were traded in a ferocious duel. Despite Diabhail's towering size, the warrior's skills gained him the upper hand. The warrior forced the hammer from Diabhail's icy fingers. He then knocked the tattooed man to the earth with a powerful blow from the haft of the stone hammer.

Still breathing, the warrior thought to himself, noting Diabhail's heaving, bony chest. Morreans were such unnatural creatures. Perhaps they were once human, but no longer. They were pale as seashells, boney, and dark veined. The strained rise and fall of his chest was the only thing moving on Diabhail's otherwise lifeless body. Better than he deserved. Hate was an unusually powerful feeling for the warrior, but he truly hated Diabhail for what he had done to him and his people, to his father.

However, he did not have time to squander on Diabhail or his personal vendetta. No, both would have to wait. His purpose had just fled across the top of the mountain, sending her dark priest to forestall her impending doom. For years the Blood Queen had escaped the warrior and his fellow Feromage. As the leader of the Morreans, a cruel and perverted tribe who slew and sacrificed others to their fallen goddesses, Mireya had caused much death and grief upon the lands of Ethrea. The warrior grunted as he lifted the black obsidian dagger from the tattooed man's broken body.

Poetic, the warrior thought as he looked over the long, black blade. His eyes then turned northward to where Mireya had retreated. *To die by the same blade that slew my father.*

As the lone warrior crested the mountaintop, he spotted the woman draped in a black ceremonial dress. *She's beyond beautiful*, the warrior thought. Almost as beautiful as the great Ellitheor, the old gods. It was even said she was Half-bound, having the Aethereal of the Fallen Ones tethered to her being. Mireya's scarlet hair and purple irises were an unusual trait, even amongst her people. The Morreans were known for having wild eyes of dark browns and greys, and coarse hair that was black and rough like horses' manes. Moreover, Mireya was altogether different from her people. She was both terrible and magnificent, past the thoughts of man's imagination.

The Blood Queen stood next to a black stone altar, which had crude runes etched into it. The table was stained with blood, and crystalline sickles of crimson lined its rough edges. The center of the obsidian slab was hewn out, and a black hole sunk into the nothingness beneath it. Mireya screamed out a terrible cry that chilled the warrior to the bone.

But it did not break his resolve.

No, she would not escape him this time, not if it killed him. He gritted his teeth, the last steps towards her nearly unbearable due to the pain of his injuries.

"Ordan, strengthen me," the warrior muttered weakly as he stared at his foe, "one last time."

"Your false gods will not save you," Mireya hissed in a voice both cruel and intoxicating.

Mireya struck first, casting a spell of black mist from her hands. He rolled swiftly out of its path, popping up right in front of the Blood Queen. Forcefully, he plunged the dagger towards her stomach as he rose from the snow. Mireya's eyes flashed with crimson light, runes forming around her body, deflecting the strike and knocking the dagger from his hand. Her face strained; she was weak.

The warrior reached for the dagger as Mireya attempted to flee. He rushed towards her, hurling himself against her stonelike flesh. He heaved in pain as they collided and tumbled to the ground. The two fought wildly for a few moments. And then, before Mireya could muster another spell, he overpowered her, casting her weary body against the stone table. He took the obsidian knife into his bloodstained hand and cried out, "For my father!" and plunged it deep into her heart.

Everything went dark.

First Movement

The Warrior, the Priest, the Chief and the Thief

CHAPTER 1: AWAKENING

It was dark and dank within the deep catacombs of Tur'Mor. The smell of decay and once burning incense clung to the stifling air. High columns of white marble held up the vaulted ceiling that told the tales of gods, known by the Ordiatians as the Ellitheor. In the back of the massive sanctuary, past marbled floors and painted ceilings, were the stone tombs of a time long gone. Inside an ancient casket lay a lone body, wrapped tightly in thin white linen. Long forgotten was this lair, as was the man who inhabited it. None visited; none remembered. Here, in a world that had forgotten him, awoke the mountain of a man.

With a furious motion, the bands that swaddled his body burst. A loud thud rang out as his hands crashed against the stone lid, scraping the skin off his knuckles. Heaving, the man pushed the stone cover off the dusty casket that encased him. Through deafening thumps of his beating heart, he sat upright, trying to gain his bearings as his head pounded in agony.

Weakened eyes could barely distinguish the wall from the floor, yet they could make out blurry forms of other stone caskets that cluttered the small room. Panic struck first, crashing over him like a wave battering the cliffside. Then came confusion.

Where am I? What happened? He tried breathing slowly to calm his jolted nerves, but the stifled air gave little reprieve.

His calloused hands felt colder and feebler than he remembered. He questioned why he had struggled so greatly to remove the lid that enclosed him; such a task should have been effortless. With a shaking hand, he pulled a golden veil off his face in the hopes of making it easier for him to see. It did not.

After an ineffective attempt of decerning his surroundings, the man placed his hands on the edge of the coffin to support his body as he swung his legs over the thick, cold lip. The weight of his body collapsed under unsure legs. He fell, limp like a rag doll, to the floor, narrowly missing the edge of the casket which had previously encased him. He did, however, manage to catch himself on the lip of his tomb with his right hand before falling flat on his face. Pain surged through his cramping leg muscles, yet that slight discomfort was barely a tickle compared to the unnatural burning sensation that emanated from his bosom.

Fire!

A feeling, like that of molten iron being poured onto the center of his chest, burst forth. Wildly, he flung his head back in agony and let out a ferocious howl. Through the pain that seared his body, an even more powerful sensation overtook him, strangling his consciousness. Try as he might, he could not force-down the overwhelming feeling. All light faded from his eyes.

***

Snowfall surrounded him. Looking about, he realized he no longer stood in the tomb. Wind that chilled him to the bone blew wildly. Dark trees and stony mountain peaks began to take form, not around him, but beneath. The man's perception seemed to hover in space, as if he were seeing from the sky above.

A figure came into view, appearing from nothingness, and to his astonishment he could clearly see his own personage crouched over a bloody woman dressed in black. He could see that it was he who had plunged the dagger into her heart. His own hands were red with blood, and he remembered the burning hate that filled his eyes as he looked upon her. This was no dream, but some sort of vision from his memory. Somehow, he was not seeing it from his own point of view.

Something caught his eye. The woman, in her last breath, thrust her hand to his chest while muttering something indiscernible. His body fell lifeless to the earth as a white fire burned his consciousness.

***

The man jerked awake. He was lying vulnerable upon the cold floor, his eyes looking upward without seeing. Panic ensued. No coherent thought could form in his clouded mind. He felt like a fly caught in a spider's web, helpless and unable to move. A surge of energy ran through his body, followed by a primeval urge to escape that utterly consumed his mind.

A dim ray of light crept through the darkness of the crypt, seeping out from under the door ahead, capturing his attention. The man pulled himself awkwardly across the floor towards the light. Slowly, he struggled to his feet, hobbling on legs still trying to find their strength. His heightened sense of smell and hearing also began to return. Though there was nothing to be heard but the sounds of creeping things scuttling across the floor, the smell, on the other hand, was quite revolting. Musty rot and decay hung in the stale, dank, and dusty air.

The door from whence the light crept was plain and old, very old. With a solid push, it swung open violently and slammed into the white plaster walls of the main sanctuary. A mighty thud echoed throughout the catacombs as the door burst in twain, causing the man to freeze in alarm, the sound deafening to his ears.

The vaulted ceiling's slotted windows let in pale rays of silver moonlight, illuminating the grey and black checkered floors, though it felt as blinding as the sun to the disoriented man's aching eyes. Pressing forward, he passed several rows of intricately crafted marble tombs, each bearing a carving of the likeness of those who rested beneath the heavy lids. His troubled mind did not allow him to stop and admire the workmanship. He continued forward towards a large flight of stairs at the far end of the room that led up to an ornate door.

A stone arch outlined the door of polished timber and golden embellishments. It touted a large brass handle, and a small stained-glass window was positioned in the center. The man reached out his hand and took hold of the knob, trying to turn it, but the door would not budge.

Blast! He huffed in frustration. He then lifted his leg and kicked the door, stumbling backwards upon connection with the heavy wooden aperture. It rattled violently but did not give an inch. In a craze of pure determination, he took a few steps back, lowered his right shoulder and ran forcefully towards the door. Followed by a jarring thud and the sound of snapping steel, the internal bolt holding the door shut gave way to his weight.

The freezing night air rushed over his face, feeling as if he had just jumped into a mountain lake in early spring. He stumbled out of the large marble catacomb and into an open cemetery. Drawing in deep breaths of fresh air, he looked about the quiet resting ground. The dead grass was dusted with a light snow, barely covering the endless rows of headstones that uniformly lined the vast graveyard. He was still.

Taking stock of himself, he looked down at his hands in the pale moonlight, examining every crack, scar, and callous as if to make sure they were really there. While doing so, the feeling of pain in his chest persisted even stronger. The man burst the strings that held the top of his faded tunic shut, tearing the fabric all the way down to the middle of his abdomen. A white scar seared into his broad chest in the form of a hand gleamed like the scales of a great dragon in the moonlight. Fear and confusion rushed over him as he struggled to catch his breath once more. *What is this?*

Turning swiftly, glaring into the stained-glass portion of the door, he studied every aspect of his body, as if to assure himself he was not dreaming again. The reflection that met his gaze was comforting and familiar, yet pained and weary. It was that of a younger man in his late twenties, in whose bright eyes honey-yellow irises glistened. He had a powerful jawline that bore a thick, black beard, and a nose that appeared to have been broken time and time again, touting a small scar on the left nostril. The face held a hollow look for one so young, one that had seen far too much evil and death for ten lifetimes, let alone twenty-something short years. Thick, straight, black hair was pulled tightly back behind his ears, every strand appearing to be brushed and oiled to perfection. A golden chain was wrapped about his beard, which bore an unnatural looking silver streak that ran from the base of his lip to the tip thereof.

With a pounding heart, he moved trembling fingers over the flesh of his face. He closed his eyes and took short breaths, attempting to calm himself. Other than the shimmering scar on his chest, everything else seemed normal. However, something was off on the inside – he could feel it. As he tried to unravel what that irregularity was, a chilling sensation began to crawl up his spine, like a spider closing in on its prey. A blackness began to well within his eyes, muddling his sense of reality. His reflection in the window seemed to fade, replaced with something grim.

In front of him stood a towering and muscular man, whose ghastly pale skin blended unnaturally with his snowy surroundings. The man's body was tattooed in cruel tribal markings of blood red. He had an angular face that was covered with a helmet in the form of a skull, with two ram's horns curving downward. He hefted a large stone hammer from the earth.

He knew this man.

Diabhail, the tattooed man, yelled out in an unknown language. He rushed forward across a bloodstained field, wildly swinging a stone hammer over his head, an evil fire burning in his dark eyes.

"Halt!" a voice called out from the dark, wrenching the dreamer back into reality.

Turning quickly and staring in the direction of the noise, he could barely make out the form of two men approaching from the far end of the cemetery. As they drew closer, he noticed that both men were wearing some kind of black body armor with a silver star on their chest. He also realized that they were rushing towards him with furious, intimidating determination.

"You there!" shouted the larger, more muscular one of the two. "Don't move a muscle!"

The guards looked more annoyed than angry, most likely due to the hour and the temperature. They were both in their middle years, yet the larger had flecks of grey forming in his hair. Black gambesons with silver embroidery and buttonholes poked out from behind their breastplates, hanging down to their knees. Both held unusual looking instruments of metal and wood. Besides the weapons they were holding, long nightsticks hung from their belts, and one of them held an iron torch in his hand.

"Don't move!"

Growling lowly, the young man's eyes locked upon the guards who pressed ever closer. He stepped back, his back brushing the cold stone of the building. *Trapped!* The word formed in his mind, animalistic and raw.

The guards reached the bottom of the steps, eyes blazing with hate. The big one raised his mysterious weapon into the air and pulled the trigger.

BOOM!

The sound from the peculiar weapon split the sky as a burst of flame leapt from the metal rod. The blast echoed, and while the guards seemed unbothered by the loud noise, the stranger's ears rang furiously. Instructing the man not to move, the taunting guards moved up the steps. Confusion struck the man, and in his panic, he fell to the earth. Using the soles of his feet, the man pushed his crumpled body against the walls of the catacomb.

The smaller guard reached him first and, while grasping at a pair of iron shackles, boasted, "Caught us another grave robber. Up then, thief! To your feet now!"

"By the gods," the second snarled, curling his nose in disgust as he stared down at the scared man, huddled against himself on the stonework. "He smells like gutter rot!"

"And what is this you is wearing?" the first questioned, poking at the young man's chest with the hot end of his strange metal tube.

"Things do seem to be getting worse around here," the second replied. "I moved my family to Tur'Mor to get away from the crazies out there."

"Come on, Rauel." the first chided as he chained his prisoner's hands behind his back. "Tur'Mor may not be perfect, but it is the best place in all the Republic to live."

"True. . . and still, we gotta clean up trash like this. Can't leave well enough alone and stay to his own place." Rauel pushed the barrel of his gun into the face of the prisoner, lifting his chin. "Looks like a filthy Dane to me. Bunch of brutes. I'm surprised Mayor Adelmo ain't totally outlawed his kind by now."

"Ah! You know the Holy Council would never let that happen, Rauel." The first laughed at the other. "I say, let 'em serve their purpose in the coal mines. We need the work, and the gods know I don't want to do it. Besides, he looks ter be big an' strong; he should have no trouble swingin' a pickaxe. A'right then. Let's get 'em down to the station."

"You, boy, get up now. Give us your name, then!" Rauel spat. "Ain't got all night."

Bewildered, no words escaped his mouth. He silently met the guard's questions and taunts with only a blank stare. Anger, confusion, and panic boiled under his skin. Yet, weak and facing the unknown, he just bowed his head in submission.

"Got ourselves a mute then, aye?" Rauel rose to his full height. "Up you go then, swine!"

When Rauel attempted to lift the man by the shoulder, he was met by unexpected resistance. His prisoner dropped to the ground and retreated to the wall.

"Come along nice and there won't be no beatings, you hear, thief? You don't want to get clever with ole' Brue here!" A nervous chuckle escaped Rauel's breath. "He's been known to take a man down a notch or two for misspeakin' on the name of the uniform!" Rauel said as he tapped the silver star at his chest.

Thief? I took nothing...? questioned the bearded man in his head as he stared blankly at Brue and Rauel. His eyes narrowed. *Fight, flee, break free...* His head ached and his vision blurred as he tried to find a way to escape his captors, to flee over the far wall that ran around the cemetery. His legs burned with fatigue from just crossing the catacombs, and his lungs felt as if they could burst. And what of those things, those strange weapons? *It is too risky... far too risky.*

"You may be a big'n, but you don't want a scrap tonight. I ain't in no mood, thief," Brue said as he tightened the grip on his short blunderbuss. His black leather gloves creaked under the tension as a large vein in his neck bulged. "Last chance before things get interesting."

Mind far too cloudy, memory blurred, the man did not argue, nor did he attempt to scoot away as he had before. Bowing his head in submission, not willing to try anything, he surrendered. He could not escape, not yet. The odds were not in his favor.

Brue lifted his prisoner to his feet without any resistance. Seemingly satisfied with the apparent acceptance of the situation, Brue motioned for his companion to lead on. Rauel gave a final glare, and then marched forward. Brue walked close behind the mute, occasionally ramming the buttstock of the gun into his back if he slowed or stepped out of line.

The three followed a long trail that led to the other side of the cemetery. As they headed down the sloping terrain, the prisoner looked back past the tomb to the top of a domed hill. At the top sat a large temple, with towering spires that reached up into the heavens. The temple was majestic and beautiful, with decorative carvings etched into the marble arches and walls. No ordinary man could make out those details from this distance, especially not in the darkness of night, but he could, perfectly. Turning his attention southward, past the iron gate that separated the two sides of the stone wall, a small village known as Templetown lay drawn-out and half-mooned about the bottom of the hill. Further in the distance, the sounds of the ocean beating on the cliffs of the western border of the land became apparent, signs that his hearing was returning to him. A colossal lighthouse had been erected upon a jagged rock, protruding out of the black, foaming water of the Great Sea. On the mainland, directly across from the lighthouse and the drawbridge that connected them, rose a great city with high stone walls.

The group walked towards those rising walls of white. The spectacle was breathtaking. Battlements and massive, black guns lined the top of the granite wall composed of huge stones that gleamed in the moonlight. Yet all this was nothing compared to the city. Even in the dark of night, the city looked as if ten thousand stars lit it from within. Several grand buildings climbed into the air, yet one stood out among all the rest.

An ancient tower rose in the middle of Tur'Mor, both beautiful and ornate. Even from a distance, the likeness of three carved personages could clearly be seen at the top of the tower. A single orb of polished stone sat upon the backs of the three beings. One of the men had a large brass shield and helmet upon his head, his eyes looking down at the city. Another had a large beard, and a tartan was wrapped around his waist an d draped over his left shoulder. In his right hand, he held a war hammer, pointing it northward. The last figure was a beautiful woman in a flowing dress. She had long, wind-wisped hair that seemed to be blowing westward. A bronze crown rested on her head and jewelry adorned her body. A bronze seagull was perched on her westward-pointing hand and with the other hand, she too held the stone upon her shoulder.

The two guards rambled back and forth as they led their prisoner through the place they called Templetown. As Rauel and Brue talked, they would often refer to their prisoner as Skunk, due to the silvery stripe in his beard and the dank odor coming from his body. A repugnant scent the man himself could not deny as he tilted his haggard face to one of his pits, and unwisely sniffed.

The walk from Templetown was long and winding, leading them down a vast hillside. At the base of the town sat a small wall with an iron-barred carriage, which Brue forced the man into. Once inside, they rode for hours until they reached the gates of Tur'Mor. During the ride, the once weakened prisoner began to feel strength return to his legs, arms, and eyes.

Despite the return of some of his forgotten strength, the animalistic urges were still ever-present. The compulsion to strike, to attack, were hard to subdue. And making matters worse were the feelings of utter confusion as to where he was, how he had gotten there, and most terrifyingly, who he was. Somehow, he could understand the words of Brue and Rauel, but they were unnatural to his ears.

Who am I? The terrifying thought crashed in his mind like waves on the white cliffs that edged the city to which he was being hauled. Images of blood and death assaulted his memories, though it was little more than blurs and fragmented pieces of an unknown puzzle.

Who am I?

At the North Gatehouse of the massive city, there was a gathering of black-clad guards standing around a small flame. A stack of halberds leaned together behind them in a circle. The men, who had been jesting with one another around the firelight, rose to their feet as Brue and Rauel approached, having left their carriage behind.

"What do you got tonight, then? Another drunk in the street?" One of the guards laughed.

"No, got us an oddy here. Broke into the Royal Crypt trying to get himself some loot." Rauel laughed. "Couldn't smell no drink on him, but something else sure reeks."

"Odd? That's one way to put it," scoffed Brue. "Skunk here looks like a damn deranged street dog! Won't say a word, but'll stare at you like the last piece of meat on a bone."

The men around the fire laughed at Brue's remark until one stepped forward. He was clearly the leader, for he had a golden star on his chest and his helm had a yellow plume. The men referred to this one only as "Captain." He was an imposing man with a thick neck and a thicker beard, which was curly and well-trimmed in a square. His coat, for he did not wear a gambeson like the rest of his company, had a high-collar with stiff shoulders, that were adorned with seemingly endless knots of golden cords, and the split tails fell to the top of his polished boots. And his trousers, unlike the matching black of the City Guard, were white with two black stripes running up the sides of either leg.

"Looking to take him to the precinct 'til mornin'," Rauel said. "Maybe a few days in the hole will get him to say something useful."

"All right boys, I'll have 'em lower the gate," the captain said as he walked over a wide drawbridge, which spanned a dry moat and led to the gate.

Captain rang a large copper bell that hung by the towering wall doors. Thrice in sequences of two he pounded the bell with a mallet that hung by a chain. After the noise from the dull bell faded away, the low sound of doors moving open on the inside of the wall began to slowly grow louder. Next, the sound of a gate raising rumbled as chains clanked together over a great spindle. Lastly, the outer doors that faced the drawbridge groaned open slowly as two guards manually pushed them open.

"She don't get called the safest city on Ethrea for noth'n, do they?" Rauel chuckled wickedly as he pushed his prisoner forward. "Unfortunately for you. But I didn't force ya to be break'n into royal property."

A sharp pain shot up the prisoner's back as Brue drove the stock of his weapon forward, shouting, "Move, Skunk!" to urge him across the drawbridge.

After crossing the drawbridge and entering Tur'Mor, the outer doors were pulled shut and the iron gate was lowered. Fascination and wonder captivated the mind of the prisoner as he beheld the sheer size of the city. The multitude of buildings, markets and roads seemed to be little more than a blur to him as they marched forward hastily. Fountains and statues graced the courtyards and streets, lending a feeling of architectural grace to the city. The streets were straight and true, with the buildings in clean and orderly rows. Though the city was relatively quiet, everything was illuminated by iron lamp posts that lined the streets.

With his mind racing and wonder blossoming, the realization that shackles were around his wrists escaped the prisoner's mind. He began to walk toward a large fountain in the middle of a massive entry courtyard when a rough hand grabbed his shoulder, pulling him backwards. Brue stared at him with a smirk and said, "Ain't no time for sightsee'n. It'll be to the dungeon with you." Brue then led the group away from the courtyard towards a long, dark road.

This backstreet was dark and cold. It did not house the same wonder as the beautiful courtyards did. No, it held a looming sense of dread. The cobblestone backroad led to what looked like a mineshaft with an iron barred gate that protruded from the side of the wall. Brue unlocked the iron door and pushed the prisoner forward into the dark tunnel. The place they now tread lay below the ornate city of Tur'Mor. Here in the underground was where those who broke the law, rioted, or due to some form of civil unrest, were locked away.

The dank smell of still water and old earth filled the dungeon. The walls were created of stacked stones and were lined with iron bracers. Chains and shackles hung from crude hooks, and there was a stockpile of weapons locked behind an iron gate near the front of the dungeon. At the far end of the large corridor was a stone building which protruded out of the wall. Upon drawing closer, a man could be seen sitting behind a small window, a large book resting in front of him. A small fire burned brightly in a blackened stove. The Bookkeeper was a burly, fat man with a long beard braided tightly under his heavy chin and smelled of beef and sweat. He wore a leather vest with the same silver star on the chest, but no shirt on his body. The hot flame behind him caused his body to perspire heavily.

"Desecration of graves, breaking and entering, thieving and resisting arrest!" said Rauel to the Bookkeeper. Then, looking over the man, he continued, "And public indecency. Wearing not but a pair of worn trousers that look to be one step away from tearing."

"Aye," said the Bookkeeper. "Let me see the hand."

Rauel unchained the prisoner, grasping his right hand. When he pulled it to the light, a strange metal ring with a rough etching hewn into it could clearly be seen. It had the image of a bear's paw surrounded by a winding form of runes. After forcing the man's hand toward the Bookkeeper, Rauel went to remove the ring, during which time the Bookkeeper began speaking. "Prisoner 3257, that will be your name here," then turned to the small fire behind him, pulling out a hot iron in the shape of a circle with a line through it. "You've earned your mark, and you shall wear it with shame for your crimes."

The Bookkeeper's face, for only a moment, appeared to change.

His skin went pale as a ghost, and a helmet of bone materialized upon his head. Dark blood markings were painted around black eyes of death. The fire in the stove was gone and the chill of winter flooded over the prisoner. A stone hammer lay broken on the snow and a knife of black obsidian was in the bloodied hands of the ghoulish giant man. A fierce spark of rage lit within the warrior's heart as he stared into the face of the tattooed man.

The prisoner moved with such speed and force that no one in the room had time to react. He threw Rauel with his left hand into the wall of the Bookkeeper's office, rendering him limper than wet socks. With a powerful swoop of his massive paws, he latched onto the beard of the Bookkeeper, pulling his head straight down into the countertop. Blood spewed in an outward arc like a fountain. This was followed by a hollow thud as the fat man fell silently to the floor.

"I am not your prisoner," the man said shakily. The words were filled with both shock and fortitude. He might not know his own name, but he knew, deep down, he would be no man's slave. Not now, not ever.

Something blunt crashed against his skull with a sickening thud. The blow brought him back into the reality of the moment with brutal force. Brue, with all his might, had driven the buttstock of his gun into the back of his head. Yet, much to Brue's dismay, this action had little effect upon the prisoner. He turned around and faced Brue, looking him dead in the eye, unwavering and cold.

Brue lifted the gun again, but not quick enough. Like a bolt of lightning and with hands like iron, the prisoner grabbed the weapon and tore it from Brue's hands. Enraged, he grasped an iron chain from the wall and then wrestled Brue to the floor. He wrapped the chain around the guard's struggling arms and torso, binding him tight. He then lifted Brue off the floor like a rag doll and hung him from one of the hooks on the wall, leaving him dangling helplessly. He could smell the dangling man's fear, his perspiration, his anxiety. He shook his head – his senses were coming back, and like a feral hound, he had the urge to tear into the hanging man's flesh.

Wide eyed, the man suddenly stepped back, as if alarmed by his own actions. The rage in his eyes dissipated as quickly as it had overcome him. It was replaced with what could only be described as guilt, guilt for his actions. A sensation of shame overtook him, and his shoulders fell. He knew these men were only doing their duty, regardless of their own flaws. He shook his head, as if he could fling the anger that boiled in his veins from his body.

Flee! The urge redoubled in his mind.

With heart pounding and eyes focusing, he scanned the room. Half a dozen other guards had witnessed the brief struggle and were now making their way swiftly towards him. And though part of him sought to go and check on the Bookkeeper, he knew that there was no time for that. The prisoner took the set of keys from Brue's belt, breaking the loop from which, they hung. He let out a sigh of regret, looking over the mess he had caused. He forced back the urge to help the men he had just beaten. He had to flee, now!

With no time to think, instinct kicked in. Years of training found themselves in his sinew and muscles. He saw the room, he smelled the oncoming men, he heard their footfalls. Everything seemed to slow. Like an angel in grace and a demon in speed, he rushed towards the iron gate at the far end of the room. With shaking hands, he fumbled to grab the correct key, the tarnished skull key Brue had used earlier. After heaving the door open and slipping through, he slammed the iron door shut, breaking the key off in the lock. Out of the tunnel he fled as the yells of the guards slowly faded from earshot.

He had escaped his prison. But what to do now, he did not know.

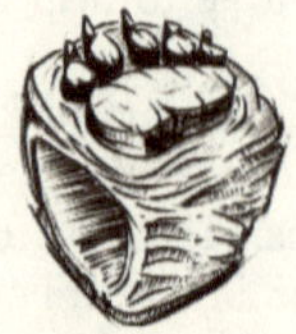

CHAPTER 2: JUST A PIECE OF BREAD

Frigid wind licked the face of the dark-haired man. Perched high above the reddish clay rooftops of Tur'Mor, he peered out from a towering belfry. Though even from this vantage point, the escapee could not see even the smallest sector of the massive walled city state of Tur'Mor. No, he could see only a few tightly packed blocks running like streams away from the central courtyard below. The man must have been forty or fifty measures high, though that was nothing compared to some of the soaring buildings which rose above the walls of Tur'Mor.

He had not slept the whole night, having run a good portion of it in an attempt to flee his pursuers. A ping of guilt stung him, almost as bitter as the wind, for how he had assaulted Brue and Rauel. *They had it coming anyways*, he thought to himself, shoving the concern away in annoyance. But they hadn't, and he knew that.

His back was stiff as a board and his legs throbbed. Not only did this discomfort dampen his morale, but he found he could not adjust himself adequately, either. A large brass bell hung close by, taking up much of the open-faced tower top. And he himself squatted atop the trap door so as to keep any potential pursuers away. What was worse than the physical pain and discomfort was the feeling of confusion that weighed upon his mind. For hours, he racked his brain, trying to remember anything. However, all was a blur, fractured memories cluttered his mind, and he could not make sense of any of it. Not where he was, how he got there, or what was going on.

There he sat, watching the sun rise slowly over Tur'Mor. The stars were fading from view, all save two very bright stars, one casting vibrant purple light and the other silvery-blue. The Two Sisters, as he knew the stars, were smaller than the pale moon, but far larger than all the rest. "Ellindeal, Talendeal," the man said, kissing the ring which sat on his right middle finger, showing respect to the hallowed stars. "Guide me home, far ones..." Wherever that might be.

Morning light cast away the night, along with much of the frost that sat atop the buildings. Cold normally didn't bother him, but what was normal about any of this? He shook his head, drawing his wandering mind back into focus. His stomach growled. *Hunger*. The thought was primal. Turning his gaze downward to the streets below, he searched for any signs of food.

The city beneath him was expertly laid out, everything organized and linear. The buildings all had a whitish coloring to them, most of which were plastered with a thick stucco and bordered with intricate paintings of yellow and purple glyphs. The shorter buildings had rusty red shingles of clay, while some of the newer looking, tall buildings, had metal and glass domed roofs. These were far less common near where he was, in the more southward area of the city. Alongside the many shops and buildings ran a complex network of cobblestone roads, leading away from the Grand Courtyard in which the Sanctuary sat.

With the rising of the sun came the many sounds of life. Birds chirped, horse-drawn buggies groaned and creaked, and the faint voices of the people below began to fill the morning air. The man stared out in wonder. The people, from this height, looked no larger than ants. And there was something different about them, though he could not make out what that was.

Then, it hit him. The sweet, savory smell of food wafted high into the air, wholly capturing his attention. *Bread! Fresh, warm bread*, the man thought, his eyes almost watering with a euphoric glee as he drew in a deep breath through his nostrils.

Without a second thought, the man slid over, opened the hatch, and scurried through the square hole. There was a wooden ladder, about sixty rungs long, bolted to the stacked stone of the belfry. This ladder led down to a spiraling staircase, steps the man took in twos and threes, his legs seeming to forget their soreness as his stomach led them forward. At the bottom of the angular steps was a small wood door with no adornment. A broken slat of wood lay on the floor. The shattered plank had fallen victim to his foot, having kicked the door in the night before in his hasty attempt to conceal himself.

He had not noticed the grandeur of the chapel the night before, which caused him to halt in his flight. His eyes widened in astonishment, taking a full pause to examine the elegantly crafted pillars, arches, and hand-painted, vaulted ceiling. It was breathtaking. The floor was polished marble, checkered like the catacombs. A long, emerald-green carpet ran from the open-air archway at the front of the building to a raised platform near the center of the vast room. On either side of the jeweled toned carpet sat rows of stone benches, which were covered with white silk sheets, piped with a matching green trim.

Atop the raised portion of the room sat a marble altar of pure white, unblemished. It was one measure deep and two measures long, and the height was roughly half a measure. Behind the altar was the grandest sight in the whole building. Two statues rose nearly to the ceiling, a circular glass skylight pouring light atop their radiant heads. One was of a powerful man, draped in regal robes and holding a hammer, whose haft was the length of his own leg. He had a glorious beard and bald head, upon which a golden, jewel-studded crown was adorned. The other statue was that of a divine woman, beyond beauty, captured perfectly in the glistening white marble. She had flowing hair which hung to the small of her back, blowing motionlessly in still wind. Her eyes were filled with compassion, just as the man's were filled with wisdom.

The black-haired man fell to his right knee, dropping the weight of his body on to his left arm, which rested upon his left leg. He placed his ringed hand to his forehead. "High Father. Life Mother." He did not move for a time but just knelt there, perfectly still. When he arose, he did not look back to the statues and turned away swiftly, eyes to the floor. He exited the sanctuary with his head held down in reverence.

The light of the sun illuminated the courtyard, which was far vaster than he had remembered or seen from the towering heights of the belfry. He did, however, note the chipped and worn steps which led up to the sanctuary. These things fled from his mind as another waft of bread drew his attention. Several men with carts were out selling bread, drinks, and other such sustenance to the masses who gathered and traversed the courtyard.

Now he knew what was so bizarre about these people. From a distance, even with his keen eyes, he could not properly make out what they were wearing. *What are they wearing?* he wondered. Never before had he seen the styles or mannerisms of these people of Tur'Mor.

The men wore vibrantly colored, lavish overcoats, many of which were embroidered with silver and gold stitching. Some wore flowing undercoats with tails, while others wore snug-fitting undercoats around the waist, studded with brass or golden buttons. Most men dressed in pressed shirts with a wide variance of lace, stiff or high collars and sleeves, along with a mixed assortment of vests that varied in color, cut, and style. There was a plethora of trousers as well: plaid, pleated slacks, tight leather riding pants, and fitted britches worn with knickers. Some of the men had arming swords or sideswords fastened to their belts. Many sported heavy leather boots with brass, cog-like bracers for buckles. Others wore long stockings with polished shoes with thick wedge heels. The men seemed to wear hues of either deep blues, rich purple and vibrant greens, or shades of amber, rusty-red, and orange, their clothing adorned with metal buttons, lapel pins, and various chains and pendants. An occasional man, appearing to oversee a collection of carts and their tradesmen, could be observed walking about pompously adorned in heavy fur coats and peculiar circular hats that rose high into the air, with silk bands tied about them and a round brim resting on the forehead. A majority of the men wore odd beards or strange mustaches and long sideburns, many of which ran together, while others had rolled mustaches and sharp, pointed beards of curly hair.

As for the women, they wore equally elaborate cloaks with hoods, which were either drawn over their hair or fell to their shoulders. Many wore colorful dresses and blouses, tight around the bust and cinched at the waist by corsets. Most wore long gloves, while some of the exceptionally wealthy also wore golden jewelry. Those who did not wear the more elegant dresses wore a variety of garments. Some touted loose tops with vests and riding trousers with boots ranging from mid-calf to over the thigh. Others wore cutaway dresses with long trains in the back and an open front to reveal fitted britches of fine fabrics and classy footwear. While the women did not seem to carry swords, an occasional dagger could be spotted. Many of the women wore their hair done up in elaborate patterns of curls, knots and buns. However, there was something even more peculiar than their styling – all those wild colors! Dyed hair formed a sea of hues and stood in stark contrast to that of the typically curly, black or brown, straight hair of the men. As a final measure of ostentatiousness, the women wore layers of vibrant makeup and carried folding fans of either feathers or brass and colored paper, which they flashed about like birds dancing.

These more colorfully dressed citizens all seemed to move in packs, snubbing their noses to those few who dressed in dull colors and simple styles, such as long overshirts and dull trousers or flat dresses and bonnets. Many of the colorful folk rode about the crescent market in horse-drawn carts the man had never seen. Decently carved buggies, with large wheels constructed of metal spokes and strange, shimmering windows, carried passengers swiftly down the roadways. And though he could tell there were people inside, he couldn't quite make them out as they moved past due to the nearly opaque gleam of the glass.

The courtyard, though he had stared at it from above, was so much larger than he thought. The edifices of the Ellitheor sat atop a grassy hill, though the grass was brown and dead in winter's cold. Hundreds of stands with bright awnings opened around him, forming an arc of merchants and tradesmen, all clamoring for attention.

Tradesmen, who sat behind their carts and produce, only called out to the upper-class citizens, turning their eyes away from the meager and simple. The man had not noticed the commoners from the belfry; his eyes had only been drawn to the plumes and feathers of the upper class, and their alluring carts of breads and the savory smells of meats and cheeses.

Across from where he stood, a strange spectacle was taking place. An old man, wispy haired and dressed in muddy rags, whose forehead had an ash-drawn symbol upon it, had drawn a crowd of colorfully clad men and women, who appeared to be jeering at him. He was near screaming at the top of his lungs about the end of days and that there was a great evil lurking in some place called Ranok Forest. He rang a large bell in his left hand and used his right to help project his voice. Several of the crowd laughed, but there were a few who tossed old fruit at the man, who in turn seemed not to even notice the inconvenience. When the old man said something about witches and black magic, the crowd roared with laughter, many of which used this moment to turn away from the doomsday speaker. It did not deter the man but sent him into a fit of flailing and yelping, shouting about the end of times and of dark beasts that would consume their souls.

Unable to make heads or tails of the sight, and his hunger ever pressing at the forefront of his mind, he began to rummage through empty pockets. There were no stone chips of blue or red for payment, but he did not care. He was hungry, and these strangers would give him bread. It was the way of the Code, to give to those in need and protect those who could not protect themselves. So, without a second thought, he walked determinedly across the lawn, straight to the nearest tradesman.

"Bread," he croaked out gruffly, his throat dry and voice low. For some reason forming words was still a struggle for him.

At first, the tradesman did not even look up, tending to his loaves with head down, whistling a tune as he worked. The hunger continued to gnaw at the confused man, and the utter lack of response from the tradesman brought on further frustration. So, he called out a second time, a little louder, a little clearer.

"Preposterous," the tradesman scoffed in disgust as he ran beady eyes up and down the other's haggard body. The tradesman was a short, fat man with mutton chops and a balding head. His skin was copper toned, and his sparse, curly hair was slicked back and oily. "I bet a dirt-scraper like you ain't even got a siglat to your worthless name. Flaming cutpurse."

"Bread," the man retorted gruffly. "By the Code, I hunger and request bread."

"Code? There is no code 'cept the Code of Health. One which you are in severe incompliance with," the fat tradesman spat. "Now piss off!"

"You are without honor." The man drew closer to the cart, glaring at the tradesman, a mix of frustration and shock apparent in his wild eyes.

"And you are without coin, beggarworm. Now, piss off before I call the guards." He seemed less sure of himself as he looked about for any sign of aid.

"Come now, man," a sophisticated voice called out from behind. One of those round-hatted 'gentlemen' was making his way forward. He wore a long, purple tailcoat and had a black cane with a silver studded handle, which smooth hands gripped until the knuckles turned white in contrast. No sword hung from his satin belt; in its place was a brass watch on a golden chain. His silken trousers were tight, bunching right below the knee and bright yellow, finely embroidered with ivy of white. Long stockings of purple to match his coat covered his calves and crept into shiny black shoes with a small heel. Everything about the man told of one who was used to being listened to, not enforcing his own words but relying upon others to do so. He had a stench about him, that of the worst kind. Pride. Twisting at a thick, white mustache with his free hand, he added nonchalantly, "Why not go to where your kind belongs?"

"My kind?"

"Yes, you beggarworm," the tradesman cut in. "They have bread houses in Southend, away from the decent folk. Made just for your kind of filth."

"Yes, that would do," the pompous, mustached man continued, placing the head of his cane on the tradesman's shoulder, shooting the other a fierce glance. "Your kind is... bad for business. I mean, look at you. Torn shirt, tattered britches from the gods know when. They look worse off than my Grand's, rest his soul."

"You have bread to spare," the hungry man interjected, pointing at several loaves of round, cracked bread.

"I have *none* to spare," the tradesman drew out every word. "I have bread, two loaves for a single gram, that's what I have. I pay my rent, I pay the baker, and I have a family to cover. Ain't nothing for free. My lord here told you where to find 'free' bread. Now piss off!"

Shocked, the hungry man just turned away, his fingers fidgeting. His blood boiled; animalistic rage burned inside. He wanted to reach out and grab the fat weasel, but he knew better than to draw any more attention to himself. Several of the nearby citizens were already looking at him. He was a head taller than most, two more than others. He was also built like an ox and of much fairer complexion than those around him.

Drawing a deep breath, he ran his thumb over the silver ring on his hand. He then turned his head and looked about, having no clue where or what "Southend" was. His expression of confusion must have been apparent because the tradesman called out, "Oy! You great oaf, get on out. Ain't you know where Southend is? Or are you so damn drunk you can't find up from down?"

"Go down past the Sanctuary there and follow the loose dirt roads until you smell the aroma of piss," the lord said as he rolled his mustache. He then turned a sharp hazel eye to the man and sneered. "And if you don't know what that is, sniff yourself. That should help guide you. Now, off with you! You have ruined enough of my business!"

Not looking back, he drew in a deep breath. His fidgeting fingers ceased and then pulled into a tight fist. He swallowed the hot spit that was salty on his tongue. *Don't strike, it's not worth it*, he reassured himself as he began to walk away, angry, hungry, but peaceful.

"Maybe he'll get knifed in the streets." The tradesman laughed to the lord, out of earshot of a normal man.

"Filthy Danesman. Did you see the way he was built? I bet even Mikel would struggle with that lad's size," the lord replied.

The response given by the tradesman was inaudible over the bustle of the massive courtyard, which was now filled with hundreds upon hundreds of people. It was hunger that drove the man forward, but it was pride that kept him from turning back and leveling the spineless man to the earth. He could not understand why he had been treated so rudely. All he had done was ask for food. What was so wrong with that? He was lost and hungry. Was it not the duty of a man to help those who were in need?

What is wrong with this place?

These thoughts and many others circled about his mind as he passed the large, circular Sanctuary. The belfry rose high above the building near the front right portion. Three other towers rose up, forming a square. A single spire, plated with gold, rose from the center of the dome, which was comprised of four plates of rounded stained-glass. This was what let in the light that bathed the statues of the High Gods, Ordan and Gallea, the Ellitheor.

Once on the far side of the Sanctuary, another series of streets and shops came into view. They were butted up against a shorter dividing wall. Three archways were carved into the stone, allowing for traffic to flow easily through. There were gates and gatehouses, but they were open and unguarded. This lower wall ran from the high outer walls of the city to a round, central wall, which surrounded the glistening tower at the center of the city.

The man made his way through one of the arches, plain, greyish, stacked stones held together with some form of yellowed cement. He felt his footing change gradually as the road transitioned from the fine cobblestone style to an earthen, well-trod series of paths. The paths wound tightly through closely stacked houses, three to five stories apiece. There were also several open-faced shops, smitheries, tanneries, forges, glass smiths, and unique buildings filled with trinkets and small statues he did not recognize.

The tradesman was right about one thing; this part of town did have a lingering smell of piss and waste. And along with those scents, the smell of tanning solutions, burning fires, and molten metal turned the air into a cacophony of nearly unbreathable fumes. These only grew stronger the further inward the man journeyed. The main source of the rank smell was coming from strange, circular discs of iron that lined the alleyways. The sound of water could clearly be heard flowing beneath these discs, though it was very deep. The man stopped and marveled at the implications, if only for a fleeting moment, before the pains of hunger drove him forward.

Pressing onward, through crowded streets, the man searched for signs of hospitality. The people that surrounded him seemed to part uneasily as he lumbered forward, their eyes perpetually downcast. Unlike the men and women who flaunted about near the merchants' stands, these citizens wore dull colors and simple designs. No feathers plumed from satin caps or velvet top hats, nor were there extravagant vests and coats upon the men. The women wore equally drab dresses, plain bonnets or hats, and simple lace covered their hands. Their clothing seemed more practical, the fit seeming true and the stitchwork expertly crafted. The people were not dirty, at least, most of them were not. Some of the men that roamed about, however, were covered in black ash or spattered with some strange liquid that stained their heavy cotton shirts, shirts that buttoned up the left half of their torsos. These men all wore a patch on their right shoulder, either a hammer striking an anvil or a plow pulling dirt.

Despite the frustration of being turned away, the man's hunger drove him forward. He did not know where this 'bread-house' was, but he figured if he followed the earthy paths, he would find it eventually. Every settlement he had ever entered, every town or stronghold, had places of refuge. He just needed to find the right path.

The man walked for hours, searching for signs of the elusive bread-house. The dirty roads wound in and out of shops and side streets, some down darker alleyways and others to public bathhouses and small decaying gardens.

Down one path, he saw another intriguing sight. Dozens of long buildings, supported by steel beams and housed in glass walls, were constructed in straight rows. They sat behind a locked gate of iron at the far side of Southend. They butted against another wall, similar to the one with the arches he had passed through earlier in the day. High stacks, formed of brick with iron tubes, bellowed black smoke, casting an acrid darkness into the air. The man had no idea what such buildings were, but what fascinated him more were the metal rails that ran along the roadside with carts set atop them. It was here near the gate where he came across a few men, dirty and exhausted, bearing the patch of the hammer and anvil, that the answer to his desires for food were finally met.

"Another damn day in that place and I may keel over," said the taller of the two. He had black soot on the leather apron he wore. His scarred hands were also blackened, and his brow was beaded with sweat, though it was quite chilly. He wore strange pants that came up over his chest, fastened with straps that rested on his shoulders, and looked so different from the lavishly dressed merchants.

"Ain't nothing you can do elsewise, just be thankful you ain't sent to the mines," the second replied. He was equally skinny but a head shorter than his companion. Neither wore beards, and their shoulder-length hair was pulled tightly back behind their heads, tied off with black string.

"Ordan knows that's the truth. Bless their souls," the first replied, his face growing even more grim.

"I wonder if it'll be potato soup and sour bread?" the second piped up after a brief moment of silence. "That's me favorite!"

The first laughed in response. "I'd prefer a long loaf. I'd shove it up the master's arse!"

The two laughed together as they took off their aprons, folding and then placing them into wooden cubbies. Others were leaving in long rows, their faces soot-stained and eyes downcast. They wore dull greys and blues, though the thick ash and grease that caked their bodies obscured most of their features. However, despite their worn demeanor, there was an obvious camaraderie between them, some supporting others while they walked, others talking in hushed tones.

A loud steam whistle sounded, causing the two who were talking to look up from their conversation. The taller one spotted their onlooker first, his grey eyes searching him from head to toe.

"Oy, you look'n for work? The master is out this until Ordae," the tall man called out, his voice a little weary, but kind.

"No." The man struggled with his wording. He took a breath and continued, "I heard you talk of bread. Do you know of this bread house?"

"You ain't from around here, are ya, big fella?" the shorter man questioned. His voice was more pleasant than the other's.

"No."

"Came across some Uppers then?" the short one continued.

"Uppers?"

"You know, them fancy suits, with their curtsies and top hats," the tall one said with a fake laugh as he performed an overly exaggerated bow.

"Name's Marlique," the shorter man said, nodding his head politely.

"I'm Caulfric," stated the other and gestured the same.

The man stared at the two. *My name?*

The smell of Tur'Mor's factories dissipated and the two men who stood talking before him faded from view.

Trees, thick and dark, gathered in their place. The sounds of water running over rocks and down gurgling falls filled the evening air. A large fire lit the grove where a dozen or so men sat, each dressed differently than the other, save three. One sat on either side of the black-haired man with the silver ring. They too had silver rings, wore furs and had long hair. However, one had snow-white hair and his beard was braided tight. His eyes were two tanzanite fires encased in glass-like orbs that peered out onto each of those who sat about the camp. The other man had a bushy brown beard, braided with iron rings, and a strong but merry face. A great bearded axe sat on the log next to him. His arms were bare despite the bitter cold, showing rippling muscles. He had topaz eyes that danced in the firelight.

Behind each of the other nine were banners of varying colors with insignias of houses and tribes of men. There were two men representing those from the far eastern plains. They were those who came on horseback and slept in round tents, wore colorful clothes and carried bows that were short and powerful. There was a horse over a lake on one banner and the other was just the head of a horse with crossing arrows behind it. Then there were four men who looked nearly the same, though each had their own banner. They had curly black beards and wore breastplates of bronze, and their helms were plumed with feathers or horsehair. Lastly, there were three women, all in long robes of varying shades of blue. One, however, stood out above the rest. She was a regal woman, hair crimson, and eyes green as fields of clover. Her jaw was strong but beautiful. A silver crown sat on her head and a single-handed blade hung from her slender waist.

They were gathered, the tribes of mankind, to face the common enemy: the Morreans. Those who had sailed from their island and wrought death and destruction where they went.

The white-haired man stood, using a thick, gnarled spear for support, and began to speak, "The time has come to put them down. They cannot be compelled but by force, and too many of our peoples have fallen."

One of the men in bronze stood next. He had removed his helm, placing it on the tip of his own short spear. Besides his breastplate, which was formed to look like a muscular man like he was, he wore bronze greaves and a leather skirt studded with bronze. "I speak for the House of Tur under the Banner of the Rising Star. We have suffered much. Our men cannot continue to propel these endless hordes of both man and beasts of darkness."

"If we wish to strike a blow true, we must strike for the heart." The voice was that of the silver-crowned woman. "Lord Tarish, long have our peoples been united in this. Shall we not go and cut out the heart? Take the fight to their cursed Isle and crush them under our foot?"

"Lady Aoibhinn is right – together we can destroy them once and for all," Lord Tarish said triumphantly. "What say you?" His eyes turned to the Horsemen of the East.

"Death has taken a mighty toll upon our people, but these pale demons do not come our way, and we have been too far from our women for too long," a short man said forcefully. "The men of Kyn'do will not fight this war anymore. We are safer away from this. The blood of too many has spilled. We leave on the morrow to our home."

"Inkar," Lord Taresh protested, "we are on the cusp of victory. How can you leave now?"

"I will send one hundred archers, but no more," Inkar replied coolly, "We are done in this war. We return home."

"And what of you, Angenthor? Will yours stay and fight?" Lady Aoibhinn asked of the white-haired man.

"It is not mine to command," Angenthor said softly. "There are but three of twelve. We grow too close to the grave. Our sons have not walked in the light and must take the Journey, or all will be forgotten."

"No," the black-bearded man said as he rose. He met the eyes of every leader of every land known to mankind: The Tur of the Riverfolk and the Glistening Sea, The Kyn'do of the East, and lastly, The Ladies of the Far Islands. "We will fulfill our oaths, as will each of you, or ruin will surely come. We will set sail to Kunri, the Isle of Morr, and there we will meet our common foe."

"Darius?" Angenthor said in shock, staring at him in the eyes. Darius, it was the name he himself had chosen to be called. It sounded strange

coming from his old friend's mouth. "You know as well as I what we risk by going."

"I know more what we risk by staying," Darius replied sorrowfully, hiding the pain he felt well within. "We set sail at first dawn. Those who wish to leave us, we will not force. But I have said my word. My brethren will go forth and end this blight of Morr."

"Darius," Angenthor said with a bow of his head.

"Darius." The name rolled clumsily out of his mouth. It was not his True Name, *Denathurias,* but it was a name, his name, nonetheless.

Caulfric and Marlique were both staring at him, confusion riddling their faces.

"What is it?" Darius inquired as he rubbed his head.

"Well, ya kind of just went stiff as a board there, mate," Caulfric said. There was apparent concern in his voice. "Are you okay? Ya ain't got the fever, do ya?"

"I am just hungry." Darius's voice was as short as his reply. His head was still spinning. *How long did I just stand there? I must have looked like a gods-cursed fool!*

"Darius?" Marlique replied with a furrowed brow as he looked him over, if only for a moment. He then relaxed with a shrug of his shoulders and said, "Ain't a common name, but ain't nothing wrong with that."

"Where are you from, friend?" Caulfric inquired as he wiped his hands on a rough, greyish rag, trying to turn the conversation away from their awkwardness.

Friend? Darius eyed the man carefully, his response stiff and guarded. "Northward."

"Well, got us a real talker here, don't we?" Caulfric laughed.

"Anyhow, you said you was look'n for supper then?" Marlique inquired. He had already wiped his hands and was pulling over a long brown coat of wool.

"Yes."

"We're head'n down to Ranun's Place. Won't you come along then?" Marlique stated hurriedly as he finished pulling a pair of woolen gloves over his hands, for he too was hungry.

"Always an open table there," Caulfric added. He too pulled a coat about himself, though his was short, not longer than his waist, and grey with thin stitches of blue.

Darius nodded and the band walked on. Caulfric and Marlique talked amongst themselves, having given up trying to talk with Darius. They spoke of hard days of labor in a thing called a 'factory'. They spoke of smelting iron, of odd things powered by boiling water, and of coal and steel. It seemed like sorcery to Darius's bewildered mind, but he kept his mouth closed. He allowed no word to escape in question, but he listened intently to the whole of the conversation.

What is this place?

It took a good long while to get to Ranun's Place. Once inside Tur'Mor, none could tell the whole city was formed in a circle – it was far too vast for that. To make it even more confusing, the streets seemed to twist and turn forever, splitting off into hundreds of paths. Worn and dull signs hung just above eye level. Some had writing etched into them, though most were just images notating what was inside: bottles, hammers and anvils, brooms, books, and such. Every so often they would pass by an open courtyard, though they were not elaborate or colorful as the ones in the first part of the town Darius had entered. Most were barren, with only a small fountain and circular white stone paths around it.

It was on the far side of one of these courtyards that Ranun's Place was stationed. It was a three-story building, each floor looking oddly perched atop the one below. The first floor was of stone, the next two floors of wooden beams and worn plaster. Wooden shingles, painted forest-green, roofed the building, and a large painting of a golden hammer decorated the outer wall of the third floor. Canopies of faded green and gold extended out over the large, open-fronted bottom floor, blocking the rays of sun for those who would stand in long lines outside.

There was already a line beginning to form. The sun was well past high noon and would not stay up much longer during the cold season. Darius did not mind the cold season; as a matter of fact, he greatly preferred it to the rainy season or hot season. The rain made his feet wet. He hated wet feet. As far as heat went, well, he just did not like to perspire. The cold did not bother him; no, he liked it. *One can always put on another layer. There are only so many you can take off.* A phrase his father always said, one which he held to be true.

Caulfric and Marlique continued to ramble on as they waited in line. Darius just looked forward, eyes in a daze. His mind raced with the many strange things he had seen this day and the night before.

The night before... What happened? Where was he? How did he come to this place?

"Son, what will you have?" an elderly voice called out to him. They were now at the front of the line. The man was heavyset, with dull, blue-grey eyes and a shiny bald head. Gold-rimmed spectacles sat at the end of his button nose. He had a thick, white mustache that fell in braids past his triple chin. His voice was tranquil and methodical, like a gentle river running through the meadow. He was wrapped in long robes of green, a white apron tied about his waist bearing the image of Ethra, Ordan's golden hammer.

Darius looked up blankly at the kindly man. He shook his head, gathering his thoughts, as if being pulled from a dream. "Just a piece of bread."

Chapter 3: Ranun's Place

Ranun handed a circular loaf of bread to Darius with a smile. The bread was light, warm, and had a crack across the top. The rich smell comforted Darius, drawing him back from his daydreaming.

"I have not seen you here before, Son. What draws you to a place of His Omnipotence?" the heavyset priest inquired.

Darius stared back at the kindly man. His mind was a fog of confusion and turmoil. Unsure how else to answer the priest, he awkwardly muttered, "Bread."

"Most men are these days. But there is more to life than bread alone," Ranun said with a smile as he fetched a small wooden cup and ladled in fresh water. "Sit anywhere you like; all are welcome here."

Darius nodded politely and then continued into the open building. He spotted Marlique and Caulfric sitting together, along with several other men, all laughing and talking as they dined. Darius walked past them; he wanted to be alone right now. He lowered his eyes as he passed by, heading towards a small wooden table near the back of the room. A tall, cream-colored candle sat atop the lone table, whose dim light offered little illumination.

He sat for hours, watching people come and go as he ate. Despite the feeling of comfort and nourishment that the hot stew and bread brought him, Darius's mind was uneasy. He felt the crushing weight of confusion and ignorance bearing down on his anxious mind. He had no clue as to how he had come to be in this place. Well, he knew he had been captured and brought here in a carriage, then escaped. But this place. He did not understand any of it. It was so vastly different than anything he had ever seen or known. And, as if to spur the thoughts of disorientation even deeper into his mind, as he sat pondering, he caught several sidelong glances from the other patrons, who in turn diverted their eyes when they met his.

A brightly clad man with a strange five-stringed instrument stood playing and singing tunes about grand battles and brave warriors, of Sages past, and those who would come again to herald in the last days. Another man sat at an odd instrument, ornate in construction, with a small box filled with wires, so that when the musician pressed ivory keys, small plucking sounds were made. They both played their songs well into the evening, while people filed in and out of the bread-house, talking and chattering about their days and struggles.

Frustrated and unbalanced, Darius tried his best to block out the voices of the other patrons. He did not despise or hate the people for their raucous behavior. No, it was not that at all. It was just that his sense of smell and hearing seemed to wax and wane so often that it made him feel nauseous. Jarring screams of children, who ran and played while their weary parents tried to eat, sent tremors down his spine. And the plucking of the odd musical device, when his senses seemed to heighten inexplicably, made his skin crawl with apprehension.

When the bread-house known as Ranun's Place finally emptied, the once tall candle was reduced to little more than a stub of wax. Darius arose and walked out into the night. A sea of purple and orange light danced across the star-speckled sky that shone over the city. It was a beautiful sight, though Darius hardly even noticed it. Nor did he pay any mind to a group of men that were walking about the streets, lighting the iron lamps that dotted the alleyways. He did, however, take notice of the kind priest named Ranun, who was outside taking down the green canopies from the front of his house.

Darius watched on as the old man struggled with one of them, trying to roll it up, huffing and puffing in strenuous bouts. Something stirred within Darius – a memory, perhaps? It was not of any particular event in time. No, it was an instinct, a desire, to help. He felt that something pull at his consciousness, and before he knew what had happened, he had reached the priest. Without a word, and to the apparent surprise of the priest, he knelt down and began to roll the cloth alongside the old man.

"Thank you." The words did not come easily, though not from a lack of gratitude. Darius was thankful, but he had to admit his gruff voice sounded more prepared to fight than to offer aid. He sighed, and then added, "The bread was good, and the soup warm. Thank you."

"Oh, think nothing of it. And your kind service is much appreciated, my son. Though you owe nothing for the food. That is provided by the goodness of Ordan to his children from the offerings of the devout," Ranun said, his wrinkly smile returned to his ruddy cheeks. He adjusted his spectacles, which had fallen crooked in his jump.

In reply, Darius hoisted the three rolled canopies to his shoulder with ease and asked, "Where to?"

This action seemed to cause Ranun a great bit of surprise. The canopies were not small objects. Most men would have struggled to lift a single sheet, yet Darius easily lifted three. If Ranun had reservations, he did not voice them but directed Darius to the back of the building, past a freshwater well and a few wooden benches that lined the side of the structure. The kindly priest fumbled around with his keys as he attempted to unlock a wooden box that was designed to store the canopies. When he finally got it opened, Darius quickly dropped them inside, letting out a low grunt of relief.

"Much appreciated, Son!" Ranun said graciously through huffs of air, his breath a little short like himself. He had walked much faster around the building than usual in an effort to keep up with the younger man.

"There is no need for thanks," Darius replied with an unexpectedly eloquent bow of his head, bringing his right hand to his heart in his flourish. "I only returned good for good."

"Pray tell me, Son, have you a place to rest this evening?" Ranun inquired as they turned away from the box and began to walk back to the front of the building.

"No." Darius's response came slowly, almost sounding embarrassed. But why should he be embarrassed? He did not choose to be here. He did not even understand where 'here' really was.

"Well, you do tonight," Ranun said gently, placing a soft hand on Darius' shoulder. "This house is open to you for as long as you need to get back on your feet, young traveler."

Traveler? He was not a traveler, was he? Something inside of his mind stirred, memories of blood and violence. *Not a traveler...a fighter. A warrior!* The thought filled his being, consumed his consciousness. He ran his thumb across the silver ring, he felt the urge pulling at him. He saw the dark mountainside, the bloody dagger in his hand. His golden eyes quivered, and his mouth went dry. *I have to get back!*

"Son," – Ranun's voice cut through the fog of confusion that consumed Darius's mind like a hot knife through butter – "are you alright?"

Darius shook himself. He was not standing on a mountainside in the snow. He was at a bread-house in the middle of a city he did not know. He was with a mere stranger who had taken him in during his time of need. And he had just been two seconds away from doing something that he knew he would have regretted.

His hard eyes softened, though they were now filled with uncertainty. He fumbled to find the words. "Apologies, I . . ." His focus slipped. How could he explain what he could not even comprehend?

Ranun smiled a tender, understanding smile. He bid Darius to follow. The old priest led him silently back into the house. They headed up a wooden flight of stairs, each step creaking under their weight. On the second floor, there were a series of green doors. The paint of each was fading and chipped, showing the age of the building. Ranun continued past several of these, all closed, until he came to one which was slightly ajar.

"I can provide you with this room, Son," Ranun said as he pushed the door open wide, again adjusting his spectacles. "Just promise to not break anything," he said with a chuckle as Darius stepped through the door.

The room was plain, but clean. A small, flat, straw bed sat against the wall atop thick wooden beams. A wool blanket lay on top of the mattress, pulled tightly about, not a wrinkle in sight. A simple stand with a candle sat beside the bed and a hand-painted image of Ordan above. The room smelled of bread and old cloth, along with a hint of cedar wood from which the bed and stand were crafted. The only other thing in the room was a circular rug, hand-stitched and worn, on the center of the floor.

"It is not much, but it will keep the cold off and allow for safe sleep," Ranun said kindly, patting Darius on the back.

"I have no coin for my stay," Darius said as a small frown of shame was drawn across his face.

"I owe you for the rolling, stacking, and storing of those canopies. That work would have taken me an hour. So that is two copper siglats, which is the cost of your stay," Ranun said with a wink as he pulled at the long ends of his white mustache. "Besides, I am a host! It would be most unbecoming if I turned you away. It would bring me bad will from the Ellitheor, resting it on my head until next Ellitheal, or until I can make a penance offering at the temple."

Darius stared back at Ranun blankly, unsure what to say. For all Darius was concerned, Ranun could have been speaking a foreign language, and he would have understood that just as clearly. He was tired, exhausted really. His limbs were heavy, and his mind was cloudy with lack of sleep and confusion. Thankfully, Ranun seemed to understand. He turned away from Darius, stepping out of the simple room.

The priest paused in the doorway, turning back to face his new tenant, and asked, "Have you a name, Son?"

"Darius," the young man replied. A simple but genuine smile slunk crossed his tired face.

"A strong name. One befitting the man who carries it," Ranun stated assuredly. "I pray that you rest well and find peace in the night. May Gallea guide your dreams."

"Likewise," the younger man replied as the priest closed the door.

Darius turned away from the door and sat on the bed. He stared up at the ceiling, wishing for dreams to take him away. Dreams. . .What if this was a dream? It was more of a hope than a question. Something in him felt hollow, as if a piece of him were missing. Darius, that was a name, but not his true name. Could he even remember his true name? Did it matter? Yes, it had to matter. He was something, something more than this... this stranger in a strange land.

Perhaps when he laid his head to rest, he would wake far from this odd place, returned to the home he knew. He removed the paper-thin slippers from his feet; they were no more useful than silk stockings. He pulled the worn tunic from his torso, tossing it upon the nightstand. The threadbare pants he kept about him just in case he needed to flee in the night, the memories of being taken hostage still fresh in his mind.

However, Darius had only seen a single set of guards in Southend, and they walked right past him without a care.

Maybe they didn't get a good look at me? It is a big city. Darius found little comfort in the thought, but he was hopeful that, just maybe, nobody cared about a lone man in such a vast place. He had not done anything wrong, not really. He had only defended himself. He hadn't meant to hurt anyone. Resting the thought, he crawled into bed and closed his eyes, swiftly drifting into the realm of dreams.

***

Cold winds engulfed Darius's body. He lay under a starlit sky, peering up at a silver crescent moon, which cast beams of radiant light over a battered landscape. The mountainside upon which he lay was cracked, as if it had been struck by a massive bolt of lightning. Veins of char ran through the snow laden stone. Trees were scattered about, as if shattered by some unnatural blast of energy. Darius's body was the focal point of the scar on the earth, as if somehow, he had made the strange markings.

The scene was familiar to him yet held an eerie sense of dread within it.

Slowly, Darius arose and looked about himself as he gathered his composure. Strange robes of white were wrapped about his body and his feet were shod with golden sandals.

He looked at his hands, which seemed to smoke with a vaporous white light. Darius gasped in astonishment at the sight. And while he studied his nearly translucent figure, tiny wisps of light danced from his glassy flesh.

He felt strangely powerful, and with each heartbeat, something in his bosom surged.

Darius began to walk by the light of the moon and his own pulsating essence, looking, searching, seeking for any signs of where he could be. It looked familiar, but was warped, as if looking into a black mirror whose reflection could not be trusted. He searched for what seemed like hours, scanning the mountainside. Yet he found nothing. He was alone.

Then, in the distance, a terrible sound arose, ringing in the back of his mind. Sickening screams and harrowing cries filled his ears. Though they seemed so far away, they were somehow right next to him. No, they were coming from inside of him.

Darius turned to look about, searching for the source of turmoil. He saw nothing but the broken trees and burnt rock. He was utterly alone on the mountainside. But those screams... They seemed to echo throughout the forest and penetrate his very soul.

A feeling of dread began to creep upon him. His breath stifled as he tried to clear his mind, but to no avail. He felt as if the very stars in the sky were weighing on him. And then it happened. A voice of thunder echoed out, indiscernible at first, though growing louder and clearer with each repetition:

"Find them!"

Darius searched the sky, his eyes darting from star to star, seeking out the source of the voice.

"Find them!"

Darius jumped. The voice seemed to come from behind him. He whirled around. But he was still alone.

"Find them!"

The voice seemed to shake the very earth under Darius's feet. It was grand and beautiful, terrible as a storm and majestic as the falls. A lump grew in his throat as Darius fell to his knees. Tears welled in his eyes, though he knew not why. Powerful emotions flooded over him as he racked his mind for the meaning of the words. He tried to call out and ask what the voice meant, but he could not. His lips were sealed by some unknown force. He felt every soul, every pain, every hurt that had ever afflicted him. He heard every cry, every tormented scream, every dying breath he had ever heard. His father, his brother, his friends, and his companions. All extinguished only by the silent touch of death. There was no escape, there was no boon to ease his sorrows.

"Find them, or blood shall rain!" the thunderous voice called out one final time.

***

Darius shot up from his slumber, panting heavily, eyes darting about wildly. *Where was I? What was that place?* His hands felt soft cloth. *Am I in a bed?* Sweat rolled from his brow. *How did I get here?* It began to come back to him. *I was at that man's inn, the kind one...Ranun? Yes, Ranun was his name.*

Darius drew in a breath and closed his eyes, grounding himself. He felt cold sweat running from his brow and the sticky feeling of perspiration on his soaked back. And though his heart was pounding and his mind ached, Darius continued to take measured breaths until he could focus again. He tried to recall the dream, but it was a blur in his mind. The only thing remaining were those cryptic words and that thunderous voice echoing in his ears. *Find them.*

Darius bent over to grab his shirt from the nightstand when he noticed that the rays of light, which were slipping under the door, were blocked by something. Darius slowly staggered across the small room and opened the door. A square object lay on the floor, butted against the doorway. The parcel was unwrapped, revealing a simple wooden crate, open and filled with a bundle of clothes. A pair of boots and fresh stockings of grey wool were also inside. Darius's brows wrinkled in confusion as he stared at the opened box. He looked to the left and the right, and seeing no one moving about, took the box into the room.

Darius removed each item from the crate, one by one. He laid them out on his bed and studied each article with intrigue. Never in his life had Darius expected clothing to be something that confused him, but in this city, people wore such strange garments. Simple tunics and woven trousers, held up by a rope, were what he had worn his whole life. Those and perhaps a heavy fur cloak for warmth in the winter. Here, his eyes looked upon something totally foreign. There was a light grey shirt which had buttons running down the front and a stiff, folded collar. A double-breasted vest, grey and black plaid with silver buttons, laid underneath. Next were a pair of heavy britches made from a thick material, one Darius did not recognize, with leather knee patches sewn into them. The boots were sturdy and well-made, far better than the paper-thin slippers he had been wearing. Large cogs of brass ran up the calf-high, black leather boots, used to tighten the laces in a turning motion. These cogs were much more intuitive than the odd buttons that lined the vest and shirt, which he had considerable difficulty maneuvering with his untrained fingers. The insides of the boots were soft, and much to Darius's surprise and gratitude, fit perfectly, just as every other article of clothing had.

Once dressed, Darius looked in a polished mirror of metal that hung on the wall, which was no bigger than his own upper torso. *How did Ranun know?* Darius thought as he ran his eyes over the new clothes that covered his body. In doing so, he noticed a small golden brooch in the likeness of Ethra, Ordan's hammer. The golden head had a single emerald stone set in it. Darius had sworn fealty to Ordan, High Father of the Three Realms, but had never worn emblems of the High Father before. His actions were his banner, his honor to the Oaths his mark. Only the silver ring that sat upon his finger marked him and what he was. However, he did not intend to be rude to the man that had fed, sheltered, and clothed him, so he left the pendant on the vest.

Darius stood in front of the mirror for quite some time, losing sight of his reflection and drifting into memories. Questions crashed upon him like waves of the sea. Firstly, how did he come to this place? He remembered that fateful night when he slew the Queen of the Morreans, yet he could not recall anything past that, save the blinding white light of a curse. He figured that he must have lay unconscious, and a soldier presumed him dead, taking his body to their burial. That would explain the odd tomb and the strange city. *It must have been one of those of Tarish's men*, he concluded. That made sense in his mind.

Mireya is dead, I killed her, but was it enough? Surely it was, or else I would not have been taken to such a burial place. We must have won that night, but at what cost? Do any of my men remain? There was so much death, scores of men had fallen. . . I must go back. I need them to know that I survived. They must know that a Guardian still stands.

Darius turned from the mirror and left the small, sparse room. He headed down the stairs, each step creaking loudly under his weight. Across the open floor, at the entrance of the house, he spotted Ranun serving a few passersby the leftovers from the night before. Darius was truly beginning to admire this man greatly, though he barely knew him.

"Ah! Darius, I see you found the clothes to your liking," Ranun said brightly.

"You did not have to –" Darius began courteously.

Ranun cut Darius off before he could continue, "Oh, I did. For you will have to earn them around here. Help is hard to find, and I could use some assistance with running the place." Ranun's eyes twinkled with delight. The idea of helping a stranger seemed to give the old man such joy. "Unless, that is, you have somewhere more important you need to be?"

"No," Darius replied, though in his mind he knew what needed to be done. He would show gratitude to the old priest by helping during the day, and then he would leave in the night to return to his people.

"Ah! Chin up, my boy! It is a blessed life in the service of the High Father Almighty!" Ranun said as he cleaned the table he was standing behind. "Anyway, you think you could help me set the poles and canopies this morning?"

"Sure," Darius said, lifting his gaze back to meet Ranun's twinkling eyes.

"Has anyone ever told you that you have peculiar eyes?" Ranun questioned Darius, peering into his eyes with intensity. There was something there, though the older man did not say what.

"Not particularly, no..." Darius replied. But that was a lie. He didn't like to talk about himself; it made him uncomfortable. "The poles and canopies, why put them away each night? The sky is fair."

"Ah, but the Great Sea blows mighty winds and storms, sometimes quite suddenly," Ranun stated as he reached for the key in his pocket. "Better safe than unprepared, you know!"

"That, I believe," Darius responded resolutely. He then followed Ranun, doing as the man did. Pulling out the poles and the sheets, setting them up. Then, to the tables, cleaning and straightening. Ranun worked him most of the day, all the way until Midfall, the sun being two thirds of the way across the sky.

"Lad, you got a back like an ox and the legs of one, too!" Ranun was sitting admiring the house – it had not looked this clean and organized in years. He motioned for Darius to come sit by him on the wooden bench.

Darius obliged silently and walked over to the kindly man. He sat next to Ranun and looked over the place. It felt good *to do*, to make himself useful, but he still felt hollow. There were so many questions running through his mind, though the work kept him busy and relaxed. Part of him longed to return to his home in the mountains, but his mind was still unsettled, and he needed to understand how he came to this place before he left it.

"I need to go to the market, get yesterday's unsold bread," Ranun said after a moment of silence. "Would you fetch me my satchel? It is in my room, the only room on the top floor."

"I can," Darius replied with a slight nod of his head.

The third floor of the house was smaller than the second, and the second smaller than the lowest, open floor. Ranun's chambers were at the far side of an open sitting room, enclosed by a thin wall of plaster. The sitting room was decorated with old tapestries which hung from the walls, lit by the dimming sunlight, the soft beams leaking through painted windows in the form of teardrops. There was a couch and a sitting chair on either side of an octagonal table of cherrywood. The door to Ranun's room was simple. Green paint and a brass handle were all that adorned the meager planks.

Darius pulled the door open slowly, as if unsure what to expect. It was not latched and creaked in a shrill whine as it moved. Inside the large, square room was a four-poster bed with faded green curtains trimmed in gold hanging about it. A dark, wooden bookshelves ran the length of the far wall and a chandelier set with candles hanging from the ceiling, forged from dull metal and rudimentary in form. A desk cluttered with papers, books, pendants, ink, and quills was stationed across from the foot of the bed against the far wall. It was upon the chair of the desk – a high, wingback seat – that Ranun's satchel lay. Though, it was not alone. Several coins and small bars of silver and gold lay about the desk and chair.

Darius huffed as he looked upon the handful of money, unsure of its value. He had never seen such coinage but was sure it was the currency of Tur'Mor. Undeterred, Darius took the leather sack and left the room untouched. He shut the door behind him and headed down the stairs to the bottom floor where Ranun was joyfully humming as he cleaned.

"Priest," Darius called out, announcing himself. "I fear you may have been had."

"What makes you say so?" Ranun said, turning his eyes up from the countertop he was wiping.

"Your desk looked riffled through and there were several coins about your chair and floor," Darius replied apologetically as he handed the old man his bag.

"I appreciate your concern," Ranun said with a weak smile that housed embarrassment. "Though I must admit, it was my own doing. I overslept this morning, and when I reached for my offering beads, I spilled the contents of my satchel. As for the desktop. . . Well, tidiness is not my strongest suit."

Darius looked at the man, then to the rag in his hand and the nearly reflective countertop, and then back to Ranun. Ranun's eyes lowered. There was something he was not saying, but Darius could not tell what.

"Regardless," Ranun stated sharply, straightening the green apron about his waist. "I must go get bread from the market. Would you like to come along?"

"What about the house?" Darius inquired, his voice a mixture of uncertainty and worry.

"Eh, what about it? She doesn't have legs. Figure she'll be here when we get back," Ranun said with a laugh. He walked across the barren lawn to a simple horse-drawn cart made of wooden slats nailed together, braced with a few iron bars.

"I would rather stay," Darius replied, showing little emotion in his tone. Though, on the inside, he just needed time alone to think.

"Suit yourself, Son," Ranun said with a smile. He then climbed onto the flat bench and clicked his tongue as the cart creaked off.

***

Darius looked out the window of his room. The moon was high in the sky and there was not a soul in sight. He had scanned the empty courtyard three times over, just to make sure no guards were patrolling. This was it. He would sneak out of the window and through Southend, find a portion of the wall that was not heavily guarded and scale over. From there, he would head northward by starlight until he saw the peaks of Iarainn rising above the Glistening Lake.

The plan was sound, and without delay, Darius slunk through the window and down the side of the wall. He dropped a few measures from the ground, his new boots splashing in the mud. He looked about one more time and disappeared into the city. Darius ran swiftly and silently, the thought of returning to his people pushing him onward, though it took hours to reach his first destination: the Outer Walls. Excitement to see his home and his kin was building with each step. He did not know how far away he was, nor how long it would take to get home, but that did not matter. He was homeward bound.

Darius rushed towards the Outer Walls without detection, a feat remarkable enough on its own. And though few guards patrolled Southend, the more prosperous sectors of Tur'Mor were far better guarded. He looked to the wall, staring at the endless line of mounted cannons, each gleaming in the moonlight. Soldiers carrying towering halberds marched two by two, each with large plumes atop their polished helms and purple cloaks fastened over steel breastplates bearing the Stars of Tur'Mor. Under their plate, they wore crisp purple uniforms with high collars and golden trim, and staunch, white breeches with knee-high boots, black and polished to a shine. At their hips were beautiful, curved swords with golden baskets around the handles, and a star for the pommel.

The regal display only halted Darius for a few moments before he began searching for a place to ascend. He slunk up to the wall, creeping between shops and low gates, hiding in the shadows. Yet, as he drew closer to the towering outer wall of the city, a whiff of something strange pulled at his senses, something gruesome and rotting. He could smell...

Lightning struck from a clear sky.

Reality warped and consciousness faded.

Darius's skin turned to glass and his eyes to fire.

Once again, he stood on a mountainside, scarred and devoid of life. The trees lay broken about, and his skin glowed with transfixing light. He whipped his head around in shock, wondering how he had come again to this place.

A low wind blew, warm and consuming. Darius felt a pulsating sensation of power in that wind. It washed over him. Consumed him. The world opened before his mind's eye. And at the edge of that jagged mountain peak, the eternities filled his gaze.

He saw men of all ages, wandering and battling. Civilizations rising and falling. He heard the songs of life and the drums of war. Creation and destruction, illumination and darkness. It swirled in a great mist, rivers of light feeding the scene.

In the sky above, heavy clouds of brilliant radiance filled the horizon. Darius fell to his back and stared up from the earth. In the heavens he beheld the image of a man's face, larger than the span of time. It could not be, but yet it was.

"Your duty is here. You have taken the Oaths. You must find them! One is near."

The voice was the thunder, and the words were hurricanes demolishing the world.

Darius gazed into the being's star-formed eyes and felt as if he would burst into flames just standing in the presence of such an awesome entity. He tried to form words, but he had not the strength to even move his tongue.

"Find them!" the thunderous voice rang out.

The ground rushed towards Darius's eyes. A single tree, gnarled and drooping, clung to a grimy boulder of massive proportions. A fissure split stone, opening into the maw of some horrific cavern.

"Find them!"

Louder and longer the words hung in the air, bringing Darius to his knees. The surge of energy that rushed through his body was all consuming. Fires scorched his veins and his heartbeat magma in his chest. He had no eyes, but flames blazed from within his sockets, eternal and unyielding. All images of greenery and nature, however menacing, vanished.

"Find them, or blood shall rain! This is your duty."

A bolt of lightning flashed through the sky. Three stars flickered.

And all went black.

***

Darius lay on his back, eyes streaming golden light, like effervescent tears mixed with molten glass running down his cheeks. He did not understand what the voice meant but could not deny the vision a second time. There was a purpose rekindled now that had been extinguished before. It was a calling, burning deep within his soul, that he could not refute.

He would not leave this strange place. He had to find them. Who, or whatever, they were? Darius attempted to stand, but all strength failed him. Darkness overtook him once again as he lay solitary in the streets of Tur'Mor.

CHAPTER 4: FELIK'S CREW

Thunder rolled across a cloudy night sky as warm rain pelted the ground outside the abandoned three-story building that was once known as the Academy. A bolt of lightning cast a silhouette of a rising tower in the eastern wing of the building. The building seemed to stand, like many of the older establishments in Southend that were built before dividing walls, as a hallowed memory of better days.

Southend was the basest of the base. Once, before the walls had been erected, Southend was not the slums of Tur'Mor, but where hundreds of shops, apartments, brothels, markets, and courtyards bustled with life. An open view of the Potamae Canal and straight road to Harbortown had attracted tens of thousands to the area. True, they were not the noble or ruling class of citizens, but they were valued members of society.

A change in governmental hierarchy, three brutal wars, the last ongoing, and the dreaded White Fever had left Southend nearly in ruins, rundown and impoverished. The people who had either been quarantined or sequestered here, had never truly recovered, with many of them being forced to work long hours in either the factories or, worse, the mines of the north.

Originally, the separating walls of Tur'Mor had been built to maintain security, if one of the four outer gates were to fall in a siege. But that was ludicrous, for who would ever attempt to besiege the unsiegable city of Tur'Mor? With an entire section of the city dedicated to crops and livestock, and another with shops, factories and storehouses, and a standing army of over three hundred thousand strong, not counting the men-at-arms who could be called upon at any time, Tur'Mor was invulnerable.

Those walls now housed something far more dangerous than enemy forces or terminal plagues. Yes, in the underbelly of Tur'Mor, factions of low-class citizens crawled like ants. Forced to spend their days in mindless labor, toiling away, the people of Southend had become hardened and vile. True, not every person sequestered was a lowlife thug, but they were all keenly aware of their situation and the vast distinction between 'they' and 'them'.

A small flame cast beams of light that danced across the inner walls of the old academy building where long, tattered tapestries hung. The flickering firelight illuminated the faces of five individuals who sat hunkered around a circular stone pit for warmth, directly in the middle of the large room. An odd choice, as there were no less than four large fireplaces lined against the walls. They sat here, burning scraps of wood, not out of necessity but out of tradition.

The five were an odd group, each differing from the other in size, shape, fashion, and nationality. The oldest looking of the group was a man with short hair and a well-kept beard, who sat tall above the rest. He was clearly Ordiatian by birth; the tight curls in his black hair and beard gave that away. He was a handsome man, looking to be in his early thirties, with light olive-golden skin and strong features. Handsome indeed, save for a series of nasty scars on his left cheek, and another large one across his eyebrow. He dressed in dark shades of browns and blacks, wearing a tight-fitting gambeson and an uncharacteristically lavish cloak. All in all, he had a commanding presence that, along with his rather expensive attire, gave off the sense of a lord or a wealthy nobleman.

"What's the damage?" he asked, his voice firm but smooth.

"Ain't much luck today, with the rain and all, Felik," said a soaking wet, pale-skinned lad with straw-like hair of about seventeen or eighteen years of age.

"The Uppers don't move about in weather like this, too afraid of ruining their knickers." The voice was as cold and sharp as the young woman it came from.

Tomokorash, or Tomo, as her friends called her, was from the island nation of Zau'fi and looked to be in her mid-twenties. Tomo had chopped, shoulder length hair, black as midnight with a bold blue streak running from scalp to tip on the right side. Her skin was like porcelain, though she did not show one speck of fragility. Her eyes were the deepest shade of brown, nearly black, and were hard as steel. A long, red-wrapped and golden-hilted Di'kha hung from her waist. The pommel of the sword was a hoop cast in gold, and the guard a twisting dragon. The slightly curved, single-edged blade stood in stark contrast to the sleek, purple, split-front and thigh-length, Garen-style tunic she wore. Besides the sturdy blade at her side, a slender boot knife was tucked into her calf-high, ash-grey riding boots.

"The Wet-drunk Upper's have their britches in a wad any time the sky ain't spewing sunshine and birds about chirpin!" scoffed a heavyset man with dark skin, a long beard, and shaved head. His thick accent sounded as if he was trying to talk around his tongue and was filled with harsh stops in unnatural places. The fat man rubbed a brand on the side of his head as he stoked the fire. He had earned the paired dragon's wings on either temple in a failed attempt at escaping from a Tuawtia slaver when he was young. When he was recaptured, he was forced to watch the beheading of his own mother and father, and then was seared with the markings of the Hakkandhar, or Unfaithful of Uuradan. However, the dragons on his temple looked much different than the one that formed the guard on Tomo's blade. Hers was more like a serpentine great cat, while his markings were of a bold and terrible creature with great wings extending upwards.

"A merry lot of good y'all do then, eh?" Felik said angrily as he rolled his eyes at his companions. "Guess we'll be eat'n bad dreams for dinner then, huh?"

"Easy, Felik, not like we wanna be hungry, all right then?" The Zau'fi girl sneered, "Besides, what did you bring to the table?"

"Two grams and a loaf of wheat bread," Felik said, flicking two small silver coins onto the ground and pulling a battered loaf of bread from his sack.

"Ah, wet wheat, my favorite," the branded Tuawtian laughed as he rubbed his round belly.

"How you even get so fat, Folehme?" Tomo jested.

"Watch it, Tomo!" Folehme replied with a false air of hurt. But then added jovially, "It is a sign of great respect to be well rounded in my culture."

"I am sure that is what is meant." Tomo laughed, and the rest of the group joined in on the ruckus.

Tomo, Folehme, Tornak, and Belthazer. Felik thought, counting his crew in his head, though using his fingers to keep track. He stopped and looked about just as the old door crashed open against the wall, a cold wind blowing in. *Where is –*

Through the doorway walked a lean silhouette. A hood was pulled over her head, dripping with warm rain. Steam emanated from her mouth and nostrils with each breath she took. As the fire cast its light upon her face, hard grey eyes pierced from underneath. Pale skin and rosy lips became apparent next, her flesh almost blending in with her white garments. Silver vambraces were latched about her forearms and a series of small throwing knives were strapped to her boots. Another set of daggers, curved and worked in silver, were hiding behind her cloak, her favorite weapons. In her hand was a small sack, sagging from rainwater and something else inside.

"I think Ordan himself is take'n a piss out there," Aellia scoffed, turning her head back to the doorway. "It's miserable."

"I take it you were as successful as the rest then?" Felik sighed halfheartedly.

"Nine years and you still don't trust me?" Aellia said as she threw the bag to Felik with a sly smile.

The bag jingled as Felik snatched it from the air with quick reach hand, like a viper striking its prey. His face lit with glee as the sound of coins clinking together filled his ears. As Aellia took a seat next to the fair-skinned Tornak, Felik dumped out the contents. Four grams, thirteen siglats and, to everyone's amazement, a bar. A bar was a gold coin, if you could call it that, that was worth a full day's labor for an Upper. It was about half the width of a palm and solid gold, bearing the image of a regal man's face upon it.

"How in Ordan's beard did you get a bar?" Felik asked, both fear and amazement on his face. "Please tell me you didn't kill anyone."

"Oh, come on! The siglats came from actual honest work!" Aellia replied with a false tone of hurt in her voice. "I helped an Upper carry some fruit to a dinner party. They were short on help, and I volunteered. Right thankful they were, but stupid as most Uppers are. They had a few sitting in a box in their ballroom, as decoration. So, I figured they wouldn't even notice one missing. About lost my composure as they handed me the siglats for my 'honest work'."

"Well, well, Crew," Felik called, "looks like we'll be visiting Lady Phaedra at the Twisted Stool tonight!"

The gang cheered with excitement and clapped Aellia on the back. Felik rose and took a bucket of raindrop water and poured it onto the fire, extinguishing it with a hiss. He quickly scooped the mismatched coins into his pouch with a smile.

"I still want that bread though, Felik!" Folehme said with a raise of a meaty finger.

"Eat your heart out!" Belthazer said, throwing the loaf at his companion. He too was from Tuawtia, but from the northern part, and his skin was more tan than dark. The Tuawtian had not adopted the Ordiatian style as his near kinsmen had but wore loose-fitting linens of sandy tones and had on shoes that curled up at the toe.

Folehme said something back, indiscernible to the group, in Tuawa, yet all knew it was clearly unkind. Belthazer and Folehme began arguing so fast it would make one's head spin even if they could understand what they were saying.

"Enough!" Felik said, placing a firm hand on Belthazer's shoulder.

"Piss off!" Belthazer shouted angrily, slapping away Felik's hand.

This did not settle well with him, and while Belthazer was taller and Folehme larger, Felik was the only one of the Crew who had real military training, save maybe Tomo. If she did, she never talked about it, though she was quick with her single-edged blade and sharper with her laminated bow of bamboo, wrapped and lacquered to a black sheen. Felik twisted Belthazer's arm quickly and placed a boot in Folehme's chest, knocking one to the ground while overpowering the other.

"We are all going to go to the pub and get drunk and laugh," Felik breathed through his clenched teeth as he bent Belthazer's wrist back, "or, Ordan help me, I will slit each of your throats tonight."

"Not mine," Tomo said with a laugh as she got up from the ground, walking over to Aellia and placing a hand on the small of her back, "or hers."

Felik laughed as he rolled his eyes. "Alrighty then, are you two done?"

"Uurdan burn it all, I just wanted bread!" Folehme said, rubbing his gut with a grimace.

"Dirty dragon worshiper," Belthazer snarled as he pulled his arm back to himself.

"Oy!" Felik yelled. "Religion's off-limits, you know that!" He thumped Belthazer on the back of the head with his palm. "You two need to grow up."

"You're only a few years older, don't act so high and mighty," Belthazer sneered, turning his deep brown eyes hatefully towards Felik.

"Ten years older than you," Felik said, a smile beginning to form on his face as he hesitated. "And I have the money," he finished as he jingled the little bag of coins.

"I get first drink then," Belthazer said indignantly, squaring off with Felik.

"Like damnation, you will! I got the coin; I get first drink. You probably didn't even go out." Aellia's face was riddled with shock and disgust. "See, your clothes aren't even wet!"

"That is enough!" Felik shouted, all humor out of his voice. "We're all going, and we're going to behave. We don't want the Stars onto us, do we?"

Everyone stopped and just looked at the ground, save Aellia. She walked to Felik's side silently and planted herself firmly. Tomo had been with Felik the longest of the group, though Aellia came shortly thereafter, and Felik had taught her many things. Felohme and Belthazer found their way in by happenstance, replacing a burly Dane who had gotten himself arrested for smashing in the head of a city guard in a bar fight. Many others had come and gone over the years, leaving Tornak as the newest addition to the Crew.

"All right, then. Get your coats or whatnot and let's go. You have five minutes," Felik ordered, his voice sharp and straightforward. He was used to commanding people – he had earned the rank of Sergeant in the Ordiatian Army before he deserted. Of course, that was years past now, and he did not like to think of it much.

The group gathered, each wearing more traditional Ordiatian garb so as to blend in at the tavern and left for the Twisted Stool. The rain had not subsided, and the walk was long and cold. By the time the small group had made it to the Twisted Stool, it was pitch black out, save the oil street lamps.

The multi-level brothel was warm and cramped, a favorite of the lower class of Tur'Mor. Though tonight, it seemed especially busy, with several groups filling most of the tables, yammering about, laughing and drinking. Madam Phaedra was near the front, talking to a couple of totally inebriated men, who were not only drunk upon the liquor. She was a plump rosy thing with breasts like melons and curly red hair. A tight corset, white with roses, exaggerated her already pronounced features. No self-respecting Upper would ever find themselves in such a place, and that was the way Madam Phaedra, and Felik for that matter, liked it.

"Phaedra!" Felik called loudly as he entered through the blue-chipped wooden doors.

"Felik!" Phaedra replied loudly, in a throaty, sensual voice. "Come on in! Oy! Missy, get their coats now and bring up a table for our guests!"

Two girls, probably in their early twenties and very pretty, hurried over to help Felik's Crew to their seats. Both Belthazer and Folehme looked down at the ground as they entered. They did not agree on much, but the dress, and the occupation, of these women they found quite inappropriate. Tornak and Tomo, on the other hand, did not mind the view in the slightest. As for Aellia, she simply did not care; she just wanted a drink and something to eat.

As they walked through the loud tavern, music, giggling and swearing filled their ears. Several people were singing along to folk tunes as a small band played on a lute and strings. Everyone in the Twisted Stool seemed to be uninterested in the diverse little group, as many people from different lands were common in Tur'Mor, and even more so in the lower-end bars and taverns. No, their interests were elsewhere, fully focused on food, booze, and pleasure.

The two girls led the group to a table near the back – there was only one left big enough for all of them to sit around. Felik called for an order of drinks and some hot bread and stew, tossing a siglat to each girl, which they tucked into their blouses and then left with a wink.

Suddenly, Felik rose, his eyes staring across the room at the door that had just opened. A middle-aged man had just walked in. He had a ruddy look about him, a thick neck and heavy eyebrows that met over a bulbous nose. The man had a long purple cloak with a golden seal of Ordiatea clasping it together. A beautiful sidesword hung from his belt, and a large-brimmed hat with a yellow plume sat on his head. Two lackeys walked in behind him, each wearing heavy hooded trench coats to keep off the rain, only just covering the rapiers at their sides. The strange man had a presence about him, and though no one in the Twisted Stool looked in his direction, everyone acknowledged his presence.

"I'll be back," Felik said quickly to his comrades.

"Watch yourself, all right," Aellia said, grabbing Felik's arm as he began to walk towards the newcomers.

"Hey," Felik said with a smirk, "it's me, I'm always careful."

Aellia gave him a stubborn look. Felik just moved on to greet the man across the room. The two talked in hushed whispers for a moment and then walked up the wooden staircase to the inn portion of the Twisted

Stool. The two lackeys hung behind at the base of the staircase, arms crossed.

"Well, let's hope he doesn't die," Aellia said to the table. "Felik took the money with him."

"I will not wash dishes," Folehme grumbled.

"He'll be fine, won't he?" Tornak asked, looking at Aellia.

"He better be," Aellia replied, eyes following Felik up the stairs.

***

"Felik," the fat man barked, his voice booming in their secluded room, "I thank you for meeting with me." His voice held little in the way of thanks, more like disgust.

"Midcouncillor Aldorian," Felik replied with a slight bow, but snarled his lip in disdain while doing so, "always a pleasure."

"It is never a pleasure to mix with your kind," Midcouncillor Aldorian spat, letting it sit heavy in the air. He had a thick Upper accent, proper and boastful, and laced with venom. "But that is neither here nor there. I have a business deal that needs to be brought to fruition."

"And what business is that?" Felik replied carefully as he forced back the derision.

"Do I sense a hint of unpleasantness from you? Perhaps you forget your place, traitor." Midcouncillor Aldorian leered as he ran his hand over the pommel of his sword. "Or maybe I should alert the City Guard as to where you are?"

"Of course not," Felik replied. "How can I assist you then, Midcouncillor?"

"As you know, the King's Jewel is being moved from Un'Mor's coffers to the Valamour in the Parade of Patriarchy in just a few weeks." The midcouncillor had a wicked, greedy look in his eyes.

Felik glared at the large man with absolute shock, and he felt a tinge of fear crawl up his spine as he did. Midcouncillor Aldorian had often asked for small things to 'go missing', but never something of such great importance.

"I think you understand what is requested," the midcouncillor leaned close to Felik as he spoke. His breath smelt rank with aged beef and ale, an unpleasant scent that caused Felik's stomach to turn. "Don't you, traitor?"

"What I think?" Felik scoffed, unable to conceal his utter disbelief and arrogance of the fat midcouncillor. "I think you're a damned fool who'd be better off asking me to find Fenron's Lost Blade than to try and steal the blasted King's Jewel!"

"That stone has been in the royal coffers for generations," Aldorian said, turning his thick back to Felik, admiring his face in a polished sheet of metal that hung upon the wall as he spoke. "It was crafted for High Lord Tareth during the first age of our people. And it has been over one

54

hundred fifty years since that monarchy had been disbanded, and only a few relics of the Old Monarchy remain. The King's Jewel was the most prized possession of the Court and the High Seat of the Republic. It is a symbol of the foreordination of the House of Tur's right to govern. Even to this day, the Rising Star, the very Head of the High Seat, Sarean Hal-Tur, is a direct descendant of the House of Tur."

"And what does that have to do with anything?"

"Everything, boy!" Aldorian laughed at his reflection, shaking his head as if Felik was stupid. "The whole lineage, the Line of Ancestry, all of it, with its pomp and circumstance, is a charade. A charade that they will pay dearly to keep."

"You can't think you could sell it even if I got it?" Felik scoffed. "Even you aren't that dense."

"Watch your mouth, traitor!" Aldorian whirled his mass about, stepping so close to Felik that his belly rubbed against the other's. Pointing a sausage-like finger violently into Felik's chest, he continued, "I do not mean to 'sell' it back to them. I mean to bribe my way into their inner circle. Close-minded twats. They sit in their high mansions within the Inner Walls of the Valamour while we, the true leaders of the people, are forced to live amongst...your kind."

"By Ordan's beard! You are insane!"

"Insane? Insane? I am owed this!" Aldorian's thick neck veins were pulsating, and his face was a burning red. His voice lowered, a seething hiss of venom spewing from his purple lips. "You will get me that stone, traitor, or the whole world will know what you did. Do you understand me?"

Felik's eyes fell.

"I understand," he whispered.

"Good then. We shall meet back here in four weeks. I'll expect you to have the package." He slapped Felik on the back with a heavy hand, eyes glinting with hate and greed. "Oh and do mind yourself. I've been told that stone messes with the minds of those who touch it. But that is no more than a child's story. All such things are heresy under the Church."

Before Felik could respond, the fat midcouncillor disappeared through the doorway without another word, the sheath of his sword clanging against the wood in his hasty retreat.

Felik's knees buckled, and he slid, his back having been forced against the wall by the raging midcouncillor, down to the ground. Dropping his head into his hands in terror, he wept.

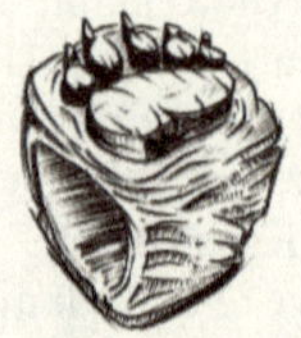

CHAPTER 5: A SIGN

Darius awoke to the sound of two or three men talking, though he could not quite make out what it was that was being said. Everything sounded as if he were listening through a conch shell. He had a splitting headache, and his eyes saw nothing but blurs of fuzzy light.

"What happened?" he groaned.

The men stopped talking. Footsteps grew closer, coming his way. He cocked his head to try and focus but could only make out the outline of a short, portly man in green robes. Two other men followed him, both in black with something on their chest.

"By Ordan's beard, Son!" Ranun said, his voice unsteady and fraught with worry. "What in the realms were you doing last night?"

"I went out for fresh air." Darius's lie was almost as weak as he was.

"We found you belly-up in the streets near Midtown," one of the men snarled. "Damn lucky you was wearing the mark of the Church, or you'd be in shackles right now, I'd tell ya!"

City guards, Darius thought with scorn. He tried his best not to snarl but felt his lip turn.

"And we are ever grateful you brought him to us!" Ranun called out, cutting off the guard from getting too close. "May Ordan watch over you and bless you! He just came from Daneland, an emissary from the Northern Church. He is not learned in our customs, or he would have known it ill advised to stroll out so late at night." Ranun's last words were not so sweet, and Darius could hear the displeasure in the priest's voice towards him.

These words seemed enough to suffice the guards. They gave a final glare at Darius's disheveled body, lying haphazardly on a couch in the center of Ranun's Place. "Keep your kind in their place. The Church ain't what it once was, you hear?" And with that, the two guards left, clunking away in their heavy boots.

Darius felt like he had been knocked over the head. His mind was fuzzy, his memories skewed. *What happened last night?* And then it began to come back – the voice, the vision, and the feeling of purpose. *I must find them!*

"Upstairs, right now!" Ranun's voice was uncharacteristically stern and sharp.

"What?" Darius inquired, still dazed.

"You and I are going to talk," Ranun said with a lower voice. He looked around, making sure there was no one else around. "Upstairs, right now."

Darius followed the old priest to his room on the third floor. He had only been in this room once before, but it was noticeably cleaner this time. There were no papers about, and everything was well-dusted and organized. Ranun sat in his chair and then pointed to a large wooden chest, motioning for Darius to sit. He did so silently.

"By the grace of Gallea, I have lied for you, and for what?" Ranun started, both worry and frustration swirling across his animated face. He tugged at his mustache again and again. "Well? Say something!"

"Why did you lie for me?" Darius asked earnestly. "You had no reason to, nothing to gain."

The question caught Ranun off guard. His expression changed. The frustration seemed to melt away from his face, and contemplation replaced it. Ranun snorted and stood. He walked behind his armchair and grabbed the back, eyeing Darius intently.

"Darius, Son," Ranun said pointedly, "I have known many men in my life, and yet none have perplexed me the way that you do. You come out of nowhere and aid me with no thought of coin. And then, without a farewell or warning, you just take off in the night. Why?"

"There are things about me that I cannot discuss," Darius stated firmly, meeting Ranun's eyes with his own, piercing, yellow and unyielding.

"If you are to stay under my roof, I will not have you running about the streets after nightfall," Ranun retorted, seeing that Darius would not expound on his endeavors.

Darius raised an eyebrow.

Ranun held his breath for a moment, and there was a stifled silence. The old priest let out a sigh and said, "You still need a place to stay, right?" A smirk slipped across his lips. "Anyhow, if you do stay in my house, you will abide by my rules. No drinking and no late nights in the city. It is too risky; I won't have you arrested! You are the best help I've gotten in over ten years!"

"Why do you care what time I am about?" Darius inquired. Such restrictions on his abilities to search would only complicate matters further. *Complicate?* Not even knowing where to begin, Darius's mind raced. *Who is the "them" that I am supposed to find? Patience. I need to be patient right now. Answers will come, won't they?*

"Darius." Ranun's voice was gentle yet firm. "There is much going on at this time in this city. Now, I do not know where you are from. And I understand if you do not want to share your past with a stranger, but how have you not heard of the war?"

The war? Of course, he has heard of the war! He was fighting in the war when he was struck by some light-forsaken curse. It was the very event that made him end up in this strange place! Again, he felt it best to not share that. People did not take kindly to those that were cursed. Darius growled, "I know of the war."

"Then you must understand why they patrol the streets so diligently," Ranun said, voice exasperated. "Five years we have been fighting this godless scum back from our borders, Ordan forgive my tongue. They sneak through the streets, worm their way into places of power and politics. They would turn everything to rubble and ash. Though, I will say, I am not surprised it is of little concern to you."

"I care," Darius said passionately, eyes flashing up from the floor. "I would see every one of these vile men eradicated from existence." His countenance grew dark. Just thinking of the Morreans made Darius's blood boil. To learn that they had come as far southward as these borders and had such a hold on these people's lives angered him even further. *How could they live? Did I not slay their queen? Shouldn't they be gone?*

"Well, Son," Ranun said, slightly shocked as to the stark shift in Darius's demeanor. "I do not believe Ordan's will is death and wanton destruction. I simply pray that they would return to their own lands and leave us be. The war is taxing on our people, draining many of their dignity and class."

"Ordan did not *will* them," Darius snarled. It was Mireya and her damned priest, Diabhail. They were the cause of this death and destruction, not the gods, not even the High Father Himself.

"Darius, guard your tongue," Ranun snapped. "No ill will of the Ellitheor will be spoken in this house. Now, do I have your word you will not go running out in the night? I do not think I will be able to keep you from the dungeons again."

"I will not leave in the middle of the night again," Darius replied. However, if he was called, what else was he to do? Not respond? And if it was the High Father calling to him, he must obey. That was his sacred duty. A duty he had sworn his life to, as his father before him and so on to the dawn of mankind.

"Good," Ranun said with a sigh of relief. "Such things of worry are no good for an old man's health. Anyhow, let us talk of duties." He turned his attention to the needs of his bread-house.

"What of them?" Darius replied confusedly. He was still pondering the words of the High Father.

"Well, do you have any knowledge of timbers and carpentry?" Ranun inquired. "There are many boards and panels that need replacing in the house, and I am too old to do them."

"I have spent a good many years working stone and wood," Darius said, glad for the turn in topic.

"Excellent!" Ranun clapped. "You'll start with the stairs then. There are supplies in the back. Hammers, nails, and boards. I have to go see an old friend. I will be back by Evenfall but must first stop by the baker's and grab the bread for the night's meal."

"I can fix your stairs," Darius replied with assurance. "It is the least I can do for the help you have provided me." For both shelter and raiment, and now protection.

"Ah, don't worry yourself, Son," Ranun said with a smile. He then raised an eyebrow. "The guards did say you looked quite a lot like someone who had broken into the Royal Catacombs a few nights back. I assured them it couldn't be you, as you are part of the Parsonary. I hope last night was the last time you do go out, and I mean it."

Darius looked like a scolded child, in trouble for sneaking dessert before dinner. He attempted to speak, but Ranun just cut him off. "I do not want to know. The less, the better. I see goodness in you, and while there are bound to be misunderstandings, I do hate to lie. And I would not have you thinking I am a tired old fool," Ranun said pointedly as he pulled a faded, hooded cloak from a brass knob near the door. "Now, I must be off. Good day to you. I look forward to a rather eventless day filled with work and servitude."

***

Darius's back was damp with sweat despite the cool air that flowed through the open-fronted bread-house. He poured over the words of the vision while he labored diligently to fix the staircase. The old staircase was near the top of Ranun's list of things that needed fixing. It was at the top of Darius's list; the blasted thing squeaked and moaned every time he stepped on it. It made slipping out into the night far too challenging. Therefore, he cleared his mind and began to work.

Throughout the day, the poor and the haggard filed in and out of the bread-house, men and women alongside small children, dirty-faced and hungry. A small staff of monks helped feed and care for those who entered, though the crowds had dispersed, and the flow was much gentler. Darius overheard conversations about the costs of iron, wine and seed. He heard many of the people talking about the new mayor, Lord Xander of House Adelmo, and how the new laws he proposed were much more favorable than those of the previous mayors of Tur'Mor. Many times, he overheard the patrons speak of how he would be 'reforming Southend' and would 'bring down the overbearing aristocracy' so as to help raise the wages of those who toiled in the factories and shops.

Darius did not understand the socio-political landscape of Tur'Mor, but he did understand one thing. An unhappy people, who were destitute and starving, were a liability to any city or group. And his short run-ins with the wealthier Uppers of Tur'Mor had taught him that they were little more than useless sacks of fabric and gold. Pretty to look at, soft to the touch, but utterly useless in things of merit. They had no knowledge of how to lay a stone, plow a field, snare a beast, or skin a fowl. But these, the beggars and street urchins, toiled in the factories, manufacturing the goods that brought the wealth to this city.

Darius brushed such thoughts aside. *This is not my tribe, these are not my people,* he thought as he laid another plank of wood down firmly. *These are not my concern, not my purpose.* He struck at the iron nails with his hammer. *My duty is to protect from the shadow-spawned and soulless, to destroy evil and guard the land.*

He closed his eyes and breathed out, hearing the words of his father in the back of his mind, lecturing him. *We do not interfere in the ways of other tribes. We can only protect them from the evils that they cannot defend against. Our duty is beyond ourselves, but our ways of life are our own. Do not presume to think you know what is best for another people, especially a people whose ways you do not know.*

Darius sighed. His father had always been so wise, so strong. He seemed to know things, the right things at all times. Darius looked at the stairs he had been working on. They were completed, every step perfectly aligned and mounted. His father knew how to rule, how to lead, how to act with purpose. Darius knew how to build and to fight, but he seemed to struggle with every other aspect of leading his tribe. A pang of guilt struck at his heart; the desire to return to them was strong. But in his heart, he knew he was where he should be, but where he should be and what he was to do were two very different things.

Darius arose, both mind and body completely exhausted, and retired to his room to recover. Once on the bed, vest and boots removed, he took in a deep breath and stared up at the ceiling. Try as he might, something felt abnormal, as if he were not truly there. He closed his eyes and took in a second breath. A rotting smell, carried upon winds of bitter cold, blew across his face. Darius inhaled deeply. The terror struck. The scent of wrongness was the last thing his conscious mind gleaned.

***

Blackness engulfed him, and his mind faltered.

The air had become thin and cold.

Darius moved his hands slowly, his fingers dragging through something sticky and wet. He looked down at his fingertips. They were red with blood. He looked at the ground on which he knelt. There, too, was a pool of red, shimmering in stark contrast to the white snow.

Dazed, he tried to move. A sudden jolt of pain erupted from his side, causing him to double over in agony. Grabbing at the wound with his left hand, he looked away from the blood-soaked snow to the puncture in his flesh.

He knew this moment. He knew this place. This was one of the darkest days of his life.

The landscape began to form around him. Hills of stony peaks rose from the earth. Blankets of snow covered the ground, tucking away the rock and dead vegetation for the winter. And there, looming before him, was a gnarled tree atop a gaping boulder.

This vision was lucid, not like the one in the catacombs. He was there, present and feeling, not watching from above. Though he could not do anything to change the actions of himself, as if he were stuck in a prison of his own body, he knew what would happen next.

A dark figure moved from the shadows. It had an eeriness to it that unsettled Darius to the bone. The being was not human. It was vapor and death. It smelled of putrid rot and decay. Six eyes of firelight stared out from a long face of unnatural make, shar, yet somehow translucent and flowing. A forked tongue of liquid blackness licked the air. A singular metal horn protruded from its forehead, surrounded by what appeared to be carved runes in its scalp.

An Itheanam.

Darius looked at the creature dead in the eyes and snarled. His wound was fresh, but already seemed to be closing itself, as if the sinews of his flesh were reaching out to each other and pulling themselves together. Though the process stung terribly, there was an oddly satisfying sensation as well.

The creature's form vibrated unnaturally, as if its own skin was crawling off itself. It lowered its head, horn pointing to Darius, and dropped onto all fours. The beast's front limbs were much like that of human arms, though its fingers were long and claw-like, and the rear more like that of a bull.

Darius rose slowly, tightening his fists. He knew what needed to be done.

The beast lunged at Darius, mouth gaping open, revealing rows of yellowed teeth and black smoke. Darius raised his left forearm to block the beast and thrust his right hand back as if to prepare to strike. He opened his mouth and began to yell out a war cry.

A voice like rolling thunder called out to him, shattering the illusion of the beast.

"Find them!"

***

"Darius!"

Darius's eyes opened suddenly. He was no longer in the snow but laying face up on the floor of the small room at Ranun's Place. A man crouched over him; terror engraved on the round face. It was Ranun. Darius then heard the sound of his own heart. It was pounding rapidly. This was accompanied by the heaving of his own labored breaths. His legs felt fatigued and sore. Sweat dripped down from his forehead, the salty beads stinging his eyes as he lay prostrate on the cold, hard floor.

"You're awake!" Ranun said with a sigh of relief. "Thank Ordan's grace, you're awake."

"What – what happened?" Darius muttered through labored breaths.

"I came back from the market and found you here, convulsing on the floor, screaming and calling out '*Ie thacayn nahan! Prypi natavro itharthema*'," Ranun replied with concern. He stared with uncertainty at what was going on. "What does it mean? What happened to you?"

Darius continued to lay motionless, mind racing. *What has happened to me?* And then the cold struck him. He felt like a spider's cold, spiny legs were creeping up his spine, sending chills across every nerve in his body. Darius shuddered and went pale. Nausea struck next, then came claustrophobia. His labored breathing turned into sharp breaths that drew no reprieve.

"Are you okay?" Ranun inquired wearily.

Darius ran a trembling hand over his sweat-drenched face. His calloused fingers swiped down from flesh to beard. The sensation calmed him. He drew in two more breaths, each slower than the one before. His finger curled and he pressed the back of his knuckles to his lips. The cold metal of his ring stood in stark contrast to that of his warm flesh. It calmed him. The ring seemed to reassure him, ground him in reality.

"I am fine," Darius answered gruffly after another few moments of silence as he raised his body to a seated position. His face did not look fine, nor did it look inviting. He did not want to talk about it. "Just a bad dream, demons that haunt me from my past."

Ranun wanted to protest and press the matter, but then changed his mind. He smiled a not-so-reassuring smile at Darius as he rose to his feet. He extended a hand. saying, "Perhaps I will not work you so hard tomorrow."

Darius smirked. A sly yet understanding smirk. He took Ranun's hand, and rising, said, "Thank you for not pressing."

"We all have demons from our past we wish to keep buried," Ranun said with compassion, "but some demons we must confront to destroy. I rely on the strength of the High Father and the grace of the Life Mother to get me through."

Darius wanted to tell Ranun what happened, of the visions and those words. Yet, something sealed his tongue, as if a power from beyond held him bound. Dejected, Darius walked to his bed and sat down, hands falling onto his knees.

Ranun perceived that Darius would not say more. Yet, he knew something was wrong. He eyed the young man who sat across from him, face buried in his hands, hiding those yellow eyes. *It is not natural.* Ranun shuddered. *Ordan, forgive me! It is not my place. A thousand apologies.*

"Darius, Son," the priest said softly, "I am going to serve the guests of the house. You are welcome to come down. But I understand if you need space to breathe." And with those words, he left Darius alone in the room, shutting the door behind him.

***

The next three days went on much like those before. Ranun would have Darius perform several tasks, ranging from the routine setting and dismantling of the canopies and cleanings, to repainting the doors and fixing many of the tables and chairs of the bread-house. Darius found the work calming – it kept his mind steady – though he often pondered over the visions and what they meant. Even though he was desirous of returning to his own country and people, he dared not leave – the message had been clear enough for that. All there was to do was work, wait, and pray for another vision to bring more clarity.

After his tasks were completed for the day, Darius would set out to explore the city as best he could. He had promised Ranun that he would not go near the Outer Walls at night, but he had never said that he would keep himself entirely secluded. Darius was a man of action and duty, not one to sit idly twiddling his thumbs when there was something that needed doing. Despite his daily walks, the whole of Tur'Mor seemed far too large to traverse even in a month's time, much less a couple of evening jaunts. He did try, though, to see as much as he could, searching for any signs of what the voice had commanded him to find. However, this always led to a frustrating walk back to Ranun's Place, more perplexed than the day before.

Despite the infuriating lack of enlightenment around the meaning of the visions he received, Darius had begun to notice, more so than before, the divide of the people of Tur'Mor. Whether tall or short, plump or lean, dark complected or fair, only one thing seemed to truly segregate the peoples of Tur'Mor, and that was wealth. The lords and ladies in lavish regalia or pristine ensembles and dresses would not spare a moment's notice of any that were perceived beneath their station. The merchants and tradesmen fared not much better, though they were more colorfully adorned than their regal counterparts. Neither of these groups ever made it near the southern gates which led to Southend. As a matter of decorum, they would seldomly venture as far southward as the Sanctuary, where Darius had hidden himself his first night in the city.

63

It grated upon Darius to see men, women, and even worse, *children* in the streets, starving and clinging to so little. It burned his soul to witness the hardships that beset the people of this strange city. How could so many possess such things he could never have dreamt of while others were forced to live in squalor? He longed to do something to aid and assist them, but besides helping at the bread-house, what more could he do? Besides, he had those visions to attend to, regardless of the lack of answers surrounding them.

When Darius had tried confronting Uppers, or aiding the paupers for that matter, they would each retract from him, looks of stupefaction upon their faces. At first, he had thought it was his abnormally large size, or perhaps his long, straight beard with the silver stripe that drew their gazes. They all seemed to stare at him, merchant, lord, or pauper, with indignant eyes. Though, where the poor would then cast their faces down and shuffle away, the Uppers would curse and shout lewd comments toward him, threatening him with shackles and the lawmen.

"It's your eyes, you know," Ranun said to Darius as they rode in the cart back from the market with several loaves of bread. The priest had noticed the way the people stared at Darius, for he too had been captivated by Darius's unnaturally yellow eyes. "You have very...unique eyes."

"How so?" Darius inquired stiffly, not turning to meet Ranun's gaze.

"Come now, Son." Ranun laughed knowingly. As a matter of fact, Ranun knew quite well why there was no one with brightly colored eyes as Darius's were. Everyone in Tur'Mor had either black, brown, dull grey, or hazel eyes. Not even his own bluish tinged eyes had any shimmer of brilliance to them. Darius's eyes, on the other hand, shone like two radiant stars in the sky.

"What?" Darius said dryly, still not turning his head. "You have two, don't you?"

"By the Holy Ellitheor themselves, was that a joke?" Ranun sounded overly shocked, though some of it was real.

Darius huffed a muted laugh. "I guess it was."

"A poor attempt, but maybe I have helped you in some small way," Ranun said proudly. bouncing in his seat merrily, the path bumpy from last night's rain. Showers and thunderheads were a common occurrence in the coastal city, even in the winter months. While the storms did not affect the northern or central sectors of Tur'Mor, they turned Southend to a boggy swamp of cold and muck that smelled of rain-wash and human waste.

Darius nodded his head; a small but genuine smile crossed his sealed lips. A soft drizzle of warm rain began to fall in the cool of the evening as they rode together. Ranun had told him a few things about the city and Ordiatian culture, but it did not seem like Darius was truly opening up to him. Despite his best efforts to pry, he could not get the younger man to reveal much more of his past than the fact that he had been some kind of worker-turned-warrior in this horrible war that was plaguing the nations.

When the two arrived at Ranun's Place, the young man quickly unloaded the groceries and set out the poles for the pavilions without so much as a single word of command. Ranun sat watching for a moment, wondering about the feats of strength Darius presented rather casually before he headed to the kitchen to prepare for the night's crowds. Ranun was sure it would be a busy night; it always was when a storm was brewing.

With the fall of the evening came more grey clouds, though darker than the night before. A heavy wind blew from the sea, warm and unsettling. Something was off this time. An eerie green tinge veiled the usual vibrant orange and pink twilight. Ranun could smell the rain on the heavy air, thick and wild. Thunder crashed and winds howled. Heavy downpours of hot rain pelted the people as they scurried to find shelter in the open room of Ranun's Place. The canopies were blowing wildly, tearing from the gales of the storm. Parents and children darted madly; the commotion was suffocating. Great bolts of lightning tore brilliantly across the dark, bluish-green sky.

Ranun was out in the courtyard, hurrying all that he could inside, dodging the debris that littered the air. He saw Darius too helping an elderly couple into the house when he heard a terrible crash. The hairs on his arm and the back of his neck went erect. A twinge ran down his spine as he heard the lightning strike. A large, metal-edged wooden sign atop an adjacent building had been struck by the bolt, splintering the wooden supports. To Ranun's horror, amid the pounding rain, a small child could be seen huddled against the side of the building where the damaged sign hung by bent nails and splintered wood.

It all happened in a moment.

The secondary support failed under the strain of the winds, and the sign dropped from above.

Ranun's heart seemed to stop as he stared out in horror, caught halfway between the house and the building across the courtyard, with no way to save the girl. He was too far away; there was nothing he nor anyone could do.

Ranun cried out in agony, bemoaning the imminent loss of the small girl.

Yet, to his pure astonishment, he witnessed an event that could only be described as a miracle.

He clearly saw, through the pounding rain, something span the distance in a blur of yellow light. Never before had he seen anything move so swiftly, streaming light like an angel. The water turned to steam as the figure ran, distorting his view. Another bolt of lightning flashed, illuminating the scene once more. A terrible crashing noise rang out as the sign fell through an upper balcony and then what sounded like a hollow thud of wood against flesh. Ranun tried to lift himself, but his strength had failed him. His limbs ached from the fall upon the slickened stone. Yet, from his prone position he saw a sight that was beyond anything he could ever imagine. Darius stood, his body bent over the girl, holding the sign flat in his hands, with stone and shingle alike littering the ground around him.

"By the gods..." No one heard Ranun's remark over the sounds of the violent storm, nor could anyone make out the scene he had just witnessed due to the blackened rain and hazy mist. But he had seen what he had seen, and he was sure of it. Even now, Darius stood like a god among men, holding the sign with his bare hands, having snatched it from its descent out of mid-air and using it as a shield to protect the child. Darius cast the massive sign to the side with a shrug and then fell to his knees, water splashing upwards and swirling into mist around him.

What happened next stirred something in Ranun's soul that he had not felt in a very long time. He saw Darius grab the child, pulling the small girl close to him, and then rock her back and forth as she wept. However, touching that was, it was not this that moved Ranun so. No, he saw something, something he could not explain. Darius's honey-yellow eyes leaked lustrous torrents of light. The very rain around the brilliant streams turned to steam, wisping away into the storm. Those blazing eyes then went dim as Darius sealed his eyelids, hiding the incandescent blaze as he stroked the young girl's hair, whispering something indiscernible to her.

After a few moments of calming, Darius scooped the young girl up from the ground and walked her across the courtyard to Ranun's Place. The rain was pounding so hard that Ranun believed himself unnoticed by Darius. He stared at the young man as he walked by, no longer appearing mortal, but something else. Something grander.

Who is this man? Ranun thought in awe as he watched Darius take the little girl to her weeping parents and then disappear into the crowds. Though the rain soaked Ranun's body, and the storm raged on, he took no notice of these things, focusing all his attention on the radiant-eyed stranger named Darius.

CHAPTER 6: THE PLOY

Felik's face was a maze of scars and worry. Wrinkled skin from furrowed eyebrows met the deep gashes on his flesh. He sat alone in that room for nearly half an hour after the midcouncillor had left. Though he felt sick, he knew he had to hide the worry that ate away at him. It did not matter if it was death or not – it had to be done.

A curse flew from his lips as he looked at the door.

No sense spoiling the Crew's night. *Just breathe, and we'll talk tomorrow*, Felik thought, attempting to push his anger and fear down. He took a discarded washrag from atop the adjacent nightstand and used it to wipe his face. Then, with another deep breath, he left the upper room.

As soon as the door opened, the sounds of the Twisted Stool filled his ears. There was laughter and cursing. Drinking and merriment. The sounds of vagabonds' stories and fools' tales were accompanied by lutes and harps as bards sang their songs of grandeur. The rooms around him sounded of subdued moans of passion from those who had paid Matron Phaedra to employ one of her barmaids.

Felik walked down the steps, drawing in a deep breath and forcing a smile to his troubled face. The smell of cooked food helped with lightening his steely features. Food always helped calm him, bringing focus and ideas. And he would need ideas this night.

"Phaedra," Felik called out to the matron, "a bowl of stew and the hardest drink ya got...It's been a day."

"And should I ready a room for you?" the woman asked with a raised eyebrow as she walked closer to him.

Felik's eyes shot around the room and landed on Aellia. He winced as he looked at her. She was talking with Tomo, the two laughing and drinking, seemingly detached from those around them. A pained smile pushed across his lips. *She deserves to be happy, if only for a little while.* "No, not tonight. I think I'll take a walk after my meal though. I'll settle everyone's tab at my table now, if you don't mind?" He slipped a bar and two siglats from his pouch.

"That's more than enough, far too much!" Matron Phaedra said with a cocked eye as she gazed hungrily at the coins.

"The night is not done yet." Felik sighed. "Best take it to be sure."

"I won't give up coins that are given," Phaedra said with a smile as she tucked away the money. "Business isn't too good these days." Her smile faded some as she looked over her inn. She quickly wiped her hands on her apron and said, "I'll see one of the girls to your table. Go and sit down. And remember, the room is always open to you if you need it."

"Thanks," Felik said with a nod.

The table where Tomo and Aellia sat laughing had an open seat, the others taken by a sulking Belthazer and a plump Folehme. Felik pulled up the vacant chair and sat with a false smile, tossing the coin bag onto the table. "Food and drink is covered for the night. Already seen to it."

Folehme smiled a grey toothy grin. "May Uurdan fly ever high!"

"And what of the rest?" Aellia inquired with a smile. "Tornak will run you a room's rate."

"Ehm, well, I'll make sure all is settled," Felik said with a roll of his eyes. He couldn't blame Tornak though. The drive was always present in his mind, though he had learned to better control his urges years ago as a soldier. Tornak was still young. *Let the boy have his fun... He may not get another chance.*

"Boys," Tomo said dryly with a roll of her eyes. "Can't make it a moment without sticking their noses where they shouldn't be."

"I don't think it is the nose that Felik was worried about." Folehme laughed through a mouthful of food.

"Guard your tongue!" Belthazer hissed as he slapped Folehme upside the head. "Have you no shame?"

Aellia laughed, a beautiful, sweet laugh. She seemed to captivate all around her when she did so, especially Felik. Tomo touched Aellia's shoulder softly. "Not you too?" Her eyes, though, did hide light amusement.

Matron Phaedra brought food and drink. Felik dug in with haste, thankful for something to occupy his mind. A barmaid with a very low-cut blouse came by often to wipe the table and refill drinks. Tornak did not show his face the rest of the night, and Folehme and Belthazer both left after a few hours of eating. That just left Tomo, Aellia, and Felik.

"So, what does the midcouncillor want?" Aellia asked after a long silence.

"Not tonight." Felik attempted to brush away the conversation, but he knew he had missed his chance to leave unimpeded.

"You know how this goes," Tomo said flatly. Her voice was as cold as ice, strong as steel, and sharp as a razor.

"You know I would tell you if I could," Felik said as he looked into his mug. "I just don't know enough yet."

"By the look in your eye," Aellia said as she leaned over the table, "I'd say you know too much."

He could smell her; it was intoxicating. Well, he was already intoxicated, and that did not help his resolve either. "Listen, you two. I will let you know in due time. Everyone together. But not tonight."

Uncharacteristically, Aellia pulled back. She smiled a curt smile and rose. "Tomo, I am going back to the Loft." The Loft was the name the Crew called the abandoned academy where they gathered.

Tomo raised a thin eyebrow.

Felik ground his teeth.

Aellia walked away, a curt smile directed at Felik as she left. The smile cut at him, but tonight, he had more than longing on his mind. The King's Jewel... He shuddered.

"Dammit," Tomo said after Aellia stepped out into the rain.

"What?" Felik replied in confusion, Tomo's voice having jarred him back to reality.

"You know good and well *what*," she tossed back as she leaned back into the now vacant bench, crossing a long, slender leg over a sharp knee. She raised a wooden mug and took a long drink, eyes never leaving Felik.

"You don't understand," Felik started.

"She likes you, you know," Tomo said with a twisted smile. "I mean, not like that. But she does like you. She often says you're the only reason she stays here."

"What does that have to do with anything?" Felik said defensively.

"Half the time you treat her as the child you found, helpless and alone. Then, you treat her as you would have her in your bed at night and by your side in the day," Tomo said as she set her drink down firmly. Not a drop splashed out.

"Tomo –" Felik began but was quickly cut off.

"You know you'll have her at your side as a lover, but you could have her at your side as an equal. Only she rivals you in swordplay. And somehow, she can even find ways to sneak up on me," Tomo said those last words with a distance that was unsettling.

"She is special," Felik said with a sigh, "there is no doubt there. But what would you have me do? I can't put one above another – it is not our way."

"Our way?" Tomo raised a finger to her eye and rubbed it. "We don't have 'a way', Felik. Halfak! Only Aellia and I have been around more than a few years. And how many have we buried in shallow graves?"

"It is not an easy life; everyone knows that before they join."

"And yet you have one who has followed you for so long, and why do you think that is? Do you think it is the money? The conversation?" Tomo pressed. "No, it is because she sees something in you. Something deeper. Gods know I don't know what it is. But if she sees it, it must be there. She has a way about her. She can do things, see things others cannot."

"So, what do I do?" Felik asked in earnest.

"Let her lead, let her take the reins," Tomo answered bluntly. "Let her take the knife's edge while you run the rope. Every time it must be you, but you can't always be the one to risk it all and expect her to stay. She needs to be seen as an equal...and we both know she is more than either of us."

"You're lucky," Felik said as he raised his drink to Tomo and took a long drink.

A slight movement of what could have been a smile flashed in Tomo's eyes. She wrapped her hands together on the table. "You know you could have any girl in this bar tonight."

"I don't want any girl," Felik said as he rose from the table with a small smile.

"All men want what they can't have," Tomo said as she too rose. "But that does not mean that they can't have something as great that they don't yet know."

"Tomo," Felik said with a nod, "always a pleasure to talk."

Tomo laughed dryly, shaking her head slowly and answering. "We never talk."

"Then this is hopefully the first of many pleasures." He blushed when he said it. "Too many drinks. I need to walk to clear my head."

Tomo did not seem to take offense; she just nodded. They both grabbed their cloaks from the wall, bid Matron Phaedra farewell, and left in opposite directions into the rain.

***

Morning's light brought little comfort. Felik arose with a pounding headache and sore feet. He had walked about Southend for hours into the night, mulling over Midcouncillor Aldorian's demand. No plan formed. No bright ideas illuminated his mind. But the team had to know now. The jewel would be coming through in just a few days, and they had to take it. *I have to take it.*

Felik walked down to the lower floor where the smell of salted pork sizzled in a cast-iron skillet, along with a few peppers and eggs. Folehme was cooking again. Belthazer was ridiculing everything his kinfolk was doing. Well, they were not really kin, but close enough. Very few people came to Tur'Mor from Tuawtia, so few that these were two of the five that Felik had met from the Drylands.

"I guess that is where your earnings went then?" Felik asked with a jovial voice. He needed everyone to be in good moods to take the news. They began to talk together over the fire about last night.

Tornak walked in not two minutes later. *I know he'll be in a good mood.* Felik chuckled to himself. Tornak flashed a wide, toothy smile at Felik. He then sat next to Belthazer and Folehme, talking about this and that. Belthazer seemed to be in a much better mood today. *That is good. Tomo and Aellia should be down by now... Blast, I wish I would have left*

70

before Tomo cornered me...though she does have a point. Agh! Where are they anyways?

"Pork, Master Felik?" Folehme asked in his happy, deep voice. "I have made green peppers, red peppers, and even purple peppers from Fi'Yan! Tomo will like that."

"If she gets around in time; it's alre–"

"I do like Juena peppers, very thoughtful," Tomo said, seemingly appearing out of nowhere. "Though they are a little spicy."

Felik jumped at her appearance and Folehme boomed a bellowing laugh. Belthazer jabbed the fat Tuawtian in the ribs, and Tornak wiped grease from the pan. Felik threw off his shirt, the same shirt he had worn the night before. Tomo mocked the whole lot of them, pleased that her entrance caused such a scene. Aellia was behind her, wearing a loose robe of white, tied about the waist with a cord. Her icy white hair was spiked back, as if blown by the wind and frozen in place, and her eyes lit brilliantly as she laughed at her friends.

"Well, I am glad I brought a good mood to the morning," Felik said in frustration as he wiped cooking grease from his short brown boots and loose-fitting grey trousers.

"That you did," Aellia said as she sat next to Tornak. "I see you had a good night."

The young man ran his hand through his long, straw-like hair and blushed. "It was fine," he muttered to the floor. "I am fine."

"His smile was as bright as Uurdan's Flame this morning, Miss Aellia! You should have seen his walk." Folehme laughed. "A man of high courts he looked to be!"

"All right! Enough is enough," Felik broke in, "let the boy be."

"Men," Aellia said seductively as she ran a finger across his leg.

Tornak jumped as bad as Felik had, then blushed even harder. Aellia laughed and, to everyone's surprise, so did Tomo. She stopped quickly and sat next to Aellia. Her intertwined fingers were stationed perfectly still on her lap. Her poise was remarkable, as if she had spent her whole life in the high courts. No one knew, not even Aellia. She never talked about it.

"If we could stop acting the fool, I have a new target." Felik's voice was commanding now.

Everyone stopped laughing, turning eager faces to hear the news. Even Folehme set his plate down and rested his hands on his crossed legs in an attempt to focus, which was quite a feat for the large Tuawtian.

"Target?" Aellia questioned. "Is that why you were meeting with that snake last night?"

"The bounty will pay well," Felik replied, "well enough that we can all find a nice spot and disappear. No more shadows and squalor'n in the muck of the Uppers. We could be made free of this." He drove his finger into the dusty floor as he spoke. His face was alight, and his countenance beamed. He had this way about him when he spoke, so that others would do more than simply listen; he could command them. And all would seem to willingly follow.

"And what's the bounty for?" Tomo inquired, eyes drawn in, on the edge of her seat.

"The King's Jewel leaves Un'Mor in two weeks and comes into Tur'Mor," Felik began explaining, but was cut off by a chorus of dumbfounded gasps. Felik rolled his fingers out from fists as he let out a long exhale, and then began again, "The King's Jewel leaves Un'Mor in two weeks, or so they say. I heard that it comes in three days, and there is going to be a big party at the Mayoral Residency, where all the prim and proper can gawk and stare at it up close and personal for a price. And that is where we relieve them of it." There it was. It was out there. Felik's half-baked plan was made bare. Now, he was ready for the ridicule.

"HA!" Felohme bellowed out.

"What?" Felik snapped, unusually defensive.

"It sounded as if you had said we were going to try and steal the Jewel of your Kings..." Felohme was wiping away a tear as he spoke, but no one else was laughing. "But then I remembered I put rare mushrooms in my dish, and I am hallucinating! They are good mushrooms!"

"I don't think he's joking, Felohme," Belthazer inserted, eyes hardening as he stared at Felik, as if searching for something unseen.

"It wasn't mushrooms, Felohme." Tomo seemed more angry than surprised. "Unless you gave some of them to our fearless leader last night."

"If you would jus-" Felik began but was abruptly cut off by Tomo.

"Because only someone who was higher than a Zau' kite would say something that absurd!"

"Just listen to m-"

"It is death our ever-victorious leader seeks, and great glory in the Cavernous Pits of Uuradan's Flames!" Felohme blurted out through laughter.

"Hey! Why don't you shut it and listen to what he says?" Aellia snapped at the group. "Or perhaps you would all rather go back to where you were before he dragged you out of the gutters?"

No one laughed at that.

"Well?" Tomo asked, breaking the uncomfortable silence.

"Tornak was raised in Northend, where the High Merchants live, weren't you?" Felik asked, beginning to build back some of his lost confidence.

The shaggy, red-headed lad looked up and spoke for the first time in the argument. "Ya, I was. A push-cart boy, ain't no properness in me. What'd you have of me, then?"

"I need something from each of you," Felik said, turning his eyes about the group. "Each of you possesses talents that will be required if we are to pull this off. Of you, Tornak, I need two things. I need you to forge us an invite to the Mayoral Residency, under false names of course, and on to the viewing party. You've seen plenty of official seals, haven't you?"

"Aye, I can make forges fine and all, but that viewing party, I don't know if my sources can find out what those would be like. Ain't been nothing like that in a long time, and I'm sure they're all held secret and whatnot."

"I don't need excuses, lad, I need those papers," Felik said with finality. He then turned to Belthazer and Felohme. "Felohme, see if you can't swipe a cartman's rights. Shouldn't be too hard, just permissions to drive lords and ladies onto the premises. Belthazer can help you with that."

"And what about me?" Tomo asked indignantly. "I don't see how my talents are any good here."

"Oh?" Felik said with a sly smile and a cock of his eyebrow. "You and Aellia have a very important task."

"By the gods, no..." Tomo groaned.

"Come on, Tomo," Felik prodded. "I need you two."

"Halfak!" Tomo spat. "I hate clothes shopping!"

"We *need*" – Felik heavily emphasized the word – "to look the part, Tomo! We can't show up in these rags. There's no way, barring an invitation for the Rising Star himself, that we'd be allowed in."

"And what is it you get to do while we spend hours in the market haggling with sag-chested coin-whores?" Aellia scoffed, stepping up next to Tomo, grey eyes equally filled with frustration.

"Maps," Felik said with a finality. "I have to get the maps. And the gods know it ain't gunna be easy."

"Don't bring the gods into this, you pig!" Aellia snorted. "You get to go play adventurer while two of us have to figure out how to be slaves and the other two have to go dress shopping. And then, to top it off, you let Tornak do forgery?"

"Can you compose letters in Proper Ordiatian?" Felik countered. "Or have access to seal-breakers? Don't belittle Tornak, we need him."

The lad seemed to glow with the compliment, however backhanded it was towards the others, though he had enough sense about himself to not pipe up. Aellia and Tomo just rolled their eyes and shook their heads; Felik knew that they knew he was right. Besides, Felohme loved talking to people, especially the poor caste. He had often caught the fat Tuawtian dicing with beggars when he was supposed to be snatching coins from merchants or Uppers.

"Then, it's final?" Felik asked the group. "We know our tasks?"

The Crew nodded in agreement, solemnly but affirmatively. Despite their constant bickering, they were all each other had as far as friends and family went. They would do what they needed to do. And they knew, however dangerous it was, that if Felik had a plan, he would somehow find a way to pull it off, just like he always had before.

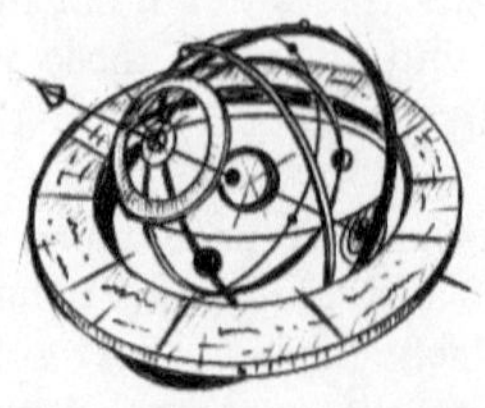

CHAPTER 7:
BENEATH THE BLUE LIGHT OF TRUTH

The once heavy storm was almost over; only specks of rain splattered onto the muddy street that Ranun walked, alone and in the dark. The iron streetlamps were burnt out, and the stars were covered with clouds. It was as close to pitch black as possible. However, Ranun dared not remove the fragment-infused steel torch from under his robes. Revealing such things were strictly forbidden by the Church. Fascinating devices, though, Fragtorches were. They could light up an entire alleyway if one removed the cover from the sapphire stone. They were crafted by the Asterivians in their tower under strict guidance by the High Patriarch himself, Orrum. Ranun often marveled at such things that Ordan had blessed His own with. Though, they didn't do a lot of good if you weren't ever allowed to use them.

And people think that there is no High Father? Preposterous! Even at the mere thought of denial of the Supreme Beings, Ranun touched his fingers to his lips then forehead three times. "Apologies on High! I didn't even mean to question!" Yet, he could not shake the unease of the Church dealing with the Asterivians. Such an odd lot. Godless and calculated. Strange rituals and ideals. *Best be thankful for what they've given and avoid them as much as possible.* A shudder ran down his spine.

The sandstone-colored monastery was not far now. Ranun could see it from a distance, several of the rooms still lit by candlelight. Elcon had requested him to come have another discussion about the strange man with the yellow eyes. Originally, Ranun was surprised at how eager the high priest was to learn about this stranger. Yet now, in lieu of recent events, he could hardly contain his desire to delve into all of the oddities.

This truly was after hours. *If it was any more after hours, it would be before hours!* Ranun snorted at his own thoughts as he wiped his spectacles free of warm rainwater. The heavy grey cloak kept most of the rain away from Ranun, but the winds often whipped droplets across his ruddy face, which then trailed into his grand mustache. His body was not the only thing the cloak concealed. A simple arming sword with a dull grey basket hilt hung at Ranun's side. And while he was no swordsman, he was also no fool. It was unwise to walk around Southend at this hour alone and unprotected.

When Ranun reached the gated monastery, he did not go to the main gateway, but made his way around to the side where the walls were much higher and thicker. There was little vegetation here, save some sprigs of dried weeds and shoots, which crunched under his rain-sodden shoes as he ran his hand along the smooth wall.

Ah! Ranun's fingers found a loose stone in a mural on the painted wall. This particular image was of Ordan crafting the mythic city of Vialhael. It was a vast city of legend, where Ordan reigned with Gallea by his side over the free peoples of Ethrea before the Great Desolation. The stone sunk in ever so slightly when Ranun applied pressure to it. The rock beneath slid into the stone below and a circular apparatus formed by dozens of bronze cogs and wheels appeared. Ranun removed the Fragtorch from his belt. It clinked against his arming sword, causing the elder priest to jump and look about.

Upon seeing he was alone, Ranun removed the cover from the head of the device. Iridescent blue light flooded the area where Ranun stood. The Fragtorch did not shine like light from a flame, but moved like smoke, clinging to the air around him. Ranun drove the device into the bronze apparatus and then twisted the silver torch a quarter of a turn to the left and then a full turn to the right.

The whole section of the wall shook as the rock bed upon which he stood began to open in front of him. A pathway, lit by the same smoky blue light, opened up. It led down beneath the wall and under the monastery. Ranun took the Fragtorch from the wall and walked forward. Almost immediately after removing the device, the apparatus began to spin and click, starting the process of sealing the pathway beneath. Ranun had not made it ten steps forward before the opening sealed itself shut.

Ranun hurried along the tunnel, all the while whistling a tune. The path was not dark nor foreboding, but clean and very well maintained, with a Fragtorch mounted on the wall every ten measures. Fragtorches were metal objects woven into intricate, almost living, patterns and set with an infused blue stone that cast radiant light. These mystical objects were mounted to the walls in silvery containers of masterful design. The floor of the hallway was crafted of simple sandstone, swept and unadorned, a suitable path for any to travel and standing in complementary contrast to the whitewashed walls painted with orangish-red images of times long past.

Ranun had just finished his tune when he reached the wooden door at the opposite end of the hall. Two statues of Aluth stood on either side of the door. Both their swords were crossed, one in the left hand and the other in the right, blocking the entrance. The arms that did not wield swords were extended straight outward, perpendicular to the entrance. Their outstretched palms were open wide, and in each was a unique carving. One bore the Eternal Eye, a singular open eye with three curving lines etched beneath it. The other bore the image of Ordan's hammer, Ethra.

Ranun held forth his hand, which now bore a signet ring, one which he did not often wear, that had the Eternal Eye formed onto it. He pressed the ring into the palm of the statue's hand. There was a low rumble of grinding stone as the arms of the two statues, which held the blades, lowered slowly out of the door's way. He cheerfully walked past the two statues, nodding to the one on the right and saying, "Thank you kindly!" This made him chuckle a deep belly laugh that echoed through the hall. He wiped away a tear from his eye and moved forward into a large, well-lit study.

"I would've known it was you even if we were not set to meet, my friend," Elcon said pleasantly as he looked up from the high-backed chair that he was reading in. Elcon was not in his traditional robes, but a rather dapper looking blouse of silver with a black collar and seams, fitted britches and a well-polished pair of shoes. He also wore a long evening jacket with drooping sleeves and a pillbox night-hat, each with matching silver applique needlework.

"You look well, Master Elcon," Ranun said with a bow as he entered the room. He then removed his cloak and hung it on a pegboard near the entrance.

"I see you carried your sword," Elcon noted with a raised eyebrow.

"You know the streets are no place for old men at night."

"One could once say that the streets were no match for you," Elcon said as he placed the book he had been reading onto an open lectern.

"I am an old man now, my friend" – Ranun laughed as he slapped his belly – "and far too fat."

"Ah, to be young again." Elcon sighed as he looked over his portly friend. "We were not always so, were we?"

"Well, I have always been fat and happy, so I guess not much has truly changed," Ranun said as he moved to a chair across from Elcon. It was another high-backed chair, wooden with a velvet seat. There was a circular table between them of a peculiar design, like several wheels and gears fused together in an unnatural way that made a perfectly level and flat surface. Atop the strange table was a brass globe of moving parts and pieces, circular rings at all angles forming a layered sphere.

This device was of Elcon's own making, outlining the cosmos as he had come to observe, both the Terral or physical and the Aethereal. It showed at the center, Kharnathar, home of the continent Ethrea. Then on the next set of rings were two small objects denoting Ynazranal and Ephranden, the Far Stars. The third ring held the Moon. The fourth ring held the floating isle of Vanherran, cast in gold, the home of the Ellitheor.

Then, there was at the base of the same ring, below Ethrea and on the same ring as the sun, Halfak, which was cast in lead. Then, there was a silver ring with nothing, representing the Aethereal plane and the Falls of Life. This was where all men pass when they died, either rising to Vanherran or falling to Halfak for eternity. There were three more series of bronze rings, each bearing several lesser stars. And the last ring, at the top of the device, was a flat disc of gold which represented the sun.

"I call it Yyhanzmar," Elcon said as he saw Ranun studying his workmanship. "The Cycle of Life."

"By Ordan's beard! It is magnificent," Ranun said in hushed tones as he gawked at the device.

"The members of the Asterivae have been very generous and allowed me unfettered attendance in their observatory. Well, mostly unfettered," Elcon added quickly with an exasperated raise of his eyebrow. A sigh escaped Elcon's lungs, and he added rather solemnly, "But that is not why you are here, is it?"

"By the High Father's throne! Elcon, why would you muddle yourself with those Asterivians?" Ranun looked shocked.

"My studies are for my own sanctification," Elcon replied firmly, running a finger over the table as he eyed his odd globe. "I have long studied things which the Church has thought lesser, though I fear their judgments little."

"I mean no disrespect, High Priest," Ranun said with a shifted bow of his head.

"You do not need to speak to me in such a way, old friend," Elcon said with a halfhearted smile. "Now, you came here to speak of sensitive things outside the walls of the Sanctuary, things you know I can lend an ear to, did you not? About that yellow-eyed young man from the streets, correct?"

"No," Ranun said with a sigh, his mood shifting to match his worried face. "I mean, yes. Well, I do not rightly understand what I am to say."

"Mysterious are the ways of Ordan, my friend."

"Yes, but the records state that only those Blessed by the Divine shall know the Touch of the Everlight," Ranun said in a hurried torrent of words. "And yet this boy, or young man, Darius, well, he has eyes that spark with such light as I have never before seen. Brighter even than the Sisters. Yes, bright, but wrong."

"Ranun, my friend, it does not do well to the soul to question the ways of Ordan," Elcon said calmly as he ran a finger over the arm of his chair in contemplation. His eyes drifted over to the portion of the room where a small bookstand held an open book. "Perhaps you were mistaken?"

"Elcon, I tell you, I saw something. Something incredible," Ranun said in a mixture of eagerness and concern, his gloom dissipating for a moment. "This young man did something that defied the laws of nature. It was as if he was endowed by the High Father with great strength."

"Come, friend, say what you mean to say," Elcon said, his nonchalant posture now turning stiff.

"Elcon, he saved a girl..." Ranun's voice was pained as he struggled to say the words. He then added lowly, looking to the floor, "High Father, forgive my blasphemy."

"You speak no blasphemy here, friend." Elcon's eyes lit with intrigue as he leaned forward. "Please, continue."

"Well, you see, he moved with the speed of a diving hawk, he did. And he caught a broken sign that fell from Master Haemon's shop with his bare hands!" Ranun choked on his last words, and then winced. He lifted his fingers from lips to forehead thrice over.

Elcon did not speak for a measure of time. He just sat there, hands folded, pondering the words of Ranun. He stroked his naked chin with wrinkled fingers. Breath after breath he drew, thoughts flooded in, but words did not come out.

"Father above, Elcon, his eyes practically spewed golden light," Ranun blurted out. His hand shot to his mouth and fear manifested in his eyes for what he had said.

After a few more moments of silence, Elcon sighed. He then drew up himself and began to speak, "Ranun, my old friend, you were wise to come to me with this. I thank you for your trust in the Parsonary. But what you speak, it does bring a great weight with it, and I would encourage you not to let these words fall on another's ears. That could become...problematic."

"You believe me?" Ranun sounded utterly surprised, yet deeply relieved. "But how could he be capable of such things?"

"Not a word to anyone, Ranun. There are forces at work that seek to destroy the sanctity of our faith," Elcon said as he rose, beckoning Ranun to do the same. "But I do trust you, of that be sure. These are perilous times indeed." The last seemed more for himself than for Ranun.

"Anointed of Light, know that I would never do anything to jeopardize the Church," Ranun stuttered hurriedly.

Elcon extended a gentle hand and placed it on his friend's shoulder. "You did no wrong, my friend. Though, I would like to meet this young man. He sounds... most intriguing."

"As you wish, High Priest!" Ranun said with a slight bow of his head, formality etched deep in his voice. "I could bring him to the services, on the morrow! I am sure he will come if I press. Though, Darius is not one for crowds."

"A strange name, Darius," Elcon said as he walked with Ranun towards the door. "An old name." He seemed to drift in thought for a moment, but then continued, "Did you happen to see the young man carrying anything odd with him? Perhaps a small rod of silver with a stone beset in it?"

"No," Ranun said as he twisted his mustache, trying his best to recall any such thing. "He had not but meager rags when he came to me. No coat or purse, only worn trousers and a tattered shirt. Not a copper gram to his name."

"Interesting," Elcon said with a distant look.

Ranun moved as if to ask more, but then retracted. There had been too much for one night, too many questions. Too many indeed. His face grew weary, the late hour of the night taking hold of his consciousness. He had had a long and eventful day, and it was showing.

"You need rest, my friend. You look tired. Besides, tomorrow is the High Father's Day, praise to his name and throne forever. We must prepare for services." Elcon's voice was still kind, but there was a hint of concern lingering about.

"He has terrible dreams, the boy," Ranun said with a sorrowful voice. "Talks of his brother and father, as if they died in some terrible manner. He is still so young." Ranun looked up into his friend's eyes; they were just as tired, and doubly concerned. A thousand mysteries seemed locked behind them. "We have seen spectacular things in our days, haven't we?"

"And they have all led us closer to the High Father and the Holy Mother, blessed be," Elcon replied with a tired yet comforting smile. "Now, travel safely, and may the grace of Gallea guard your step and the goodness of Ordan take you home."

Elcon pulled a lever on the wall near the wooden door. The sound of stone moving could be heard from the outer hall; the Aluth statues were mechanically lowering their swords.

Ranun, looking as if he just remembered something suddenly, drove a hand into a pouch on his belt and retrieved a single silver gram. He handed the bar to Elcon and said with a pip in his voice, "For services tomorrow. Ordan bless the Sanctuary and those who keep it."

"And may Mother Gallea watch over those who feed and shelter her people," Elcon responded. He then paused, his brows furrowing in contemplation. "Old friend, I may need to ask for this stranger to stay closer, perhaps here in the monastery. If what you speak of is true, it would be of great interest to the Church to understand how he is able to have the Touch of the Everlight." *If that is what he is doing...*

"Of course, High Priest," Ranun said with a final bow. "Oh, and one other thing. In his sleep, the boy speaks gibberish, most of which is utter nonsense. However, there is something he does say, repeats it over and over. 'Find them', he says, over and over, and something about blood. I don't know what to make of it, but I thought you should know." And with that, Ranun departed through the hallway of blue light.

The door slid shut behind him.

***

By the Gods on high! Elcon let all the calm serenity he had held fall away as he hurried across his study to the lectern where he had set the book he had been studying. First, whispers of darkness rising in the forests of Ranok. People claiming to have visions of death and shadows. Small children speaking randomly in the Old Tongue, babbling about the return of the Fallen. It was all blasphemy – it could not happen.

Elcon stared at the small, aged book, closing the yellowed pages and staring at its worn cover. It was an odd work, filled with writings of strange prophecies, most of which were paradoxical and stood in stark contrast to that of the teachings of the Church. The old priest ran a wrinkled finger over the leatherbound work, an upside-down eye with a red iris branded on the dull grey cover. His body shuddered as he outlined the ancient symbol, the once-called Eternal Eye.

Gently, he lifted the ancient text from its resting place and began to thumb through the pages, looking for something he had read a few nights back. A voice echoed in his mind, his own, softly saying, *Careful. Guard your thoughts. Above all is the High Father. Remember.* He pushed the thought away, redoubling his efforts to sift through the runes and drawings that littered the pages. This was no ordinary novel or scripture. These were secret works, hidden from the minds of men, and buried somewhere in these pages was –

Elcon stopped and stared at a drawing. A diagram covered the span of two pages, so that if you held the book vertically, you could clearly see the image. Three spheres formed an inverse triangle, with the tip pointed downward. The two that were on the top were shaded very differently. The left was drawn to appear as a circular cut gemstone. *Ria'Elahm* was penned in gorgeous handwriting with looping letters and a flowing hand. The right appeared barely touched, almost translucent. *Aetora* was written in the same loose script beneath it. The bottom sphere, however, was a solid mass of black ink with no shadow or highlight. Under it was written with little care, *Iodaba.*

Seven stars surrounded the spheres, forming a diamond. Between each star, seven lines flowed, a single line connecting each star to another. Above six of the seven stars was a symbol, each symbol representing one of the Universal Elements: air, water, fire, earth, spirit and awareness. Above the highest star, the one forming the top of the diamond, was the ancient symbol of Governance.

Elcon studied these markings with such intensity that his eyes began to burn from lack of blinking. Two weeks ago, he happened upon this curious text during one of his trips into the Asterivae's library. In truth, Elcon was not sure what had drawn him to this book in particular. It was as if it had called to him somehow. In a dream, perhaps, he had seen the shelf it was concealed in. Two weeks ago, he had delved through the wealth of secrets that laid hidden throughout these long-forgotten pages. The more he studied the aged work, the more his mind wondered. This symbol, or diagram, was the second most alluring of the findings he had uncovered in his studies.

The design was part of an ancient prophecy. A prophecy that had long been hushed by the Line of Patriarchs, for the 'ease of the public mind' and 'the betterment of the human condition'. Elcon's intensive studies had led him to this book, and up to this point, he was not sure why. It was becoming clearer. The Blessed, those women of the True Line of Ancients, were the only ones who could harness the powers from beyond. But in this diagram, it spoke of an order more ancient than all simply called the Seven Sages. Seven beings called and chosen to seal the realms and bind natural law. Each could control an element, commanding it, binding the source to their will. These Seven Sages were foretold to herald in the last days, and by their hand, the very order of nations would crumble, and the True King would sit upon a throne of glass and gold to rule and heal the lands.

Ranun must have seen something. He had no reason to lie. Elcon looked up at the walls above the towering shelves. Paintings lined the upper walls, each depicting one of the many High Priests and Priestesses of Tur'Mor. For hundreds of years, it had been the duty of the Church to protect and guide the people. *Does it become our generation that must bear witness to so much death? Is it ours that will be shortened, and in our nights that the endless shadow is cast?*

Elcon snapped the book shut and placed it back on the stand and began pacing, eyes downcast and hands locked behind his back. *And what of his connection, this Darius? Ranun saw no amulet, no stone to bind or stave to hold. How could he Touch the Source without a medium, some source to harness? Unless...*

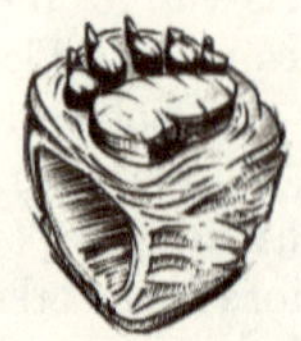

CHAPTER 8: SANCTUARY AND HERESY

Darius awoke early in the morning, well before dawn. He had made it a habit to do so years ago, for his mind was clearest at this time. He was alert and refreshed, usually. When those cursed dreams came upon him during the night, they muddled his mind in the strangest ways, leaving him confused and anxious. Luckily, they hadn't come upon him last night.

Darius had also picked up the habit of doing stretches and exercises in an attempt to calm his nerves. He had never dealt with such anxieties as these before his awakening, as both Ranun and he were now calling it. And though debilitating at times, he knew he needed to get them in check, for he did not like being out of control. Next would come a morning run, as in days past, down the cobblestone streets to a nearby public bathhouse. There he would bathe in warm water that was heated below the floors by networks of pipes running over coal fed fires. These bathhouses amazed him, one of the few absolute positives he found in this strange city of metal, mechanics, steam, and coal.

After his bath he would walk back to Ranun's, taking different paths each day, observing other parts of Southend. He would not go to the other sections of Tur'Mor until after Evenfall, when people were about for evening meals. Once back at Ranun's Place, he would then spend the morning continuing whatever tasks the priest asked of him. But not this day; this day was different.

"Darius, I would invite you to come to services with me this Ellitheal," Ranun said as he met Darius at the entry to his house. Ranun was dressed in his holy garb. This consisted of a long green robe hemmed in gold, a white apron with a golden hammer, a flat, three-cornered hat of stiff green material with a golden tassel, and lastly, a set of white penance beads which hung from his thick neck.

"There is work that I could do here, in preparation for the needy," Darius objected, speaking much more comfortably now than in days prior. Though that was not the reason for his rejection. No, he did not like the idea of being around that many people doing strange things he did not understand.

"Darius, I would invite you to come." Ranun's voice, a little more firm than usual, held a sense of command and determination. "I did not press last Ellitheal; you were new and in a strange place. But as a guest in my house, being a House of the High Father, I must insist that you come with me on this day of worship."

Darius did not protest a second time, much to the contentment of Ranun, but consigned himself to the request of the older man. Ranun smiled a toothy smile to Darius and nodded understandingly, the folds of his neck bulging while doing so.

"So, I have placed fresh shirt and clean trousers on your bed. Please change quickly and anoint your beard and hair with the plum oil on your nightstand. The fragrance is pleasant to the Ellitheor," Ranun said hastily, leading Darius to the bottom of the stairs.

As Darius walked up the stairs, he pondered, *why is Ranun acting so odd? Why does it matter to him if I go to the* Sanctuary *or not?* Darius stepped across the hallway; it no longer creaked and moaned, thanks to his handy work. He reached the now vibrantly painted door that led to his private room. He opened it and found a crisp white shirt laying on the bed. A pair of grey trousers lay there as well, pressed and without a wrinkle, with small red pinstripes forming squares. A vest matching the pants was also present, well cut with two rows of black buttons.

Darius changed quickly. He then brushed through his hair and pulled it back with a golden cord, as was more common among the Ordiatians. *A strange practice*, he thought, as he normally would leave his straight hair free after a good brushing. He dabbed the plum oil into his beard and brushed through it, using a polished piece of tin as a mirror to guide his hands. A small pair of black shoes, each with a silver buckle on one side, lay on the floor. He laughed at the sight of the shoes and then grabbed his heavy boots and shoved his feet into them, unwilling to wear such silly things.

He stared back at his reflection. It was like seeing another man. It looked like him, but then again, it did not. Where were the armor and furs? Where were the cries of battle? The blood and gore? Darius sighed in anguish of soul. *Why am I still here and what is it I am to find?* The image of a man's face, cruel and tattooed, flashed across his mind, drawing a snarl to his lip. But he knew Diabhail would be long dead, just like the rest of them.

His reflection gave no answer to his troubled mind. Despite the days of quiet contemplation, the hours of conversation with Ranun about the city he was in and people who surrounded him, he felt no closer to any of his answers. Darius's time in Tur'Mor was short, he knew it. He could not continue on this way. He needed to get back home, he needed answers.

Darius shook his head and grabbed his overcoat, pulling the door shut behind him as he left his room. Several other patrons, those whom Ranun had taken in, were also stepping out of their rooms, each wearing the best of what they had. The men wore simple button-down shirts and pressed trousers, and they all seemed to have oiled and parted their dark, curly hair. The women wore plain dresses, bonnets or caps, and had long gloves that covered up the length of their forearms.

Ranun was at the base of the stairs talking to a few people when Darius reached him. Ranun looked like a proud father seeing his son come back from his first successful hunt. Those eyes glowed with a warmth that moved Darius's heart. He smiled back and nodded his head to say thank you. Thank you for the clothes, for the hospitality, for the warmth, and most importantly, thank you for caring for a man whom he did not know nor had any obligation to care for.

A large wooden wagon harnessed with two horses sat in the front. It had two long rows of rough-hewn benches and a driver's box. Ranun took his seat at the front of the wagon and took hold of the reins. The rest of his patrons crouched into the back, huddled closely together for warmth, all but Darius. He sat at the very end, two hands' lengths away from the next rider. Ranun popped a whip and the wagon crept forward through the streets.

The ride was long and cold, the skies still grey and bleak from last night's storm. It seemed to take hours to finally reach their destination. Darius had grown stiff and anxious on the ride. He did not know what to expect at the service, but once he saw the four spires rising over the wall, his mind grew even more uneasy.

Ranun pulled through the largest of the three archways, into the circular courtyard where the Sanctuary sat atop a domed hill on a raised platform. Darius looked upon the building in wonder. Despite his trepidation, he still found it in himself to marvel at such a finely crafted structure. The grey clouds seemed to break as they circled around to the front of the building, allowing the sun's golden rays to bathe the Sanctuary in effulgent light. The beams danced off the walls, glass, and metal parts of the chapel. The bell let out a long, low ring, far deeper than Darius would have expected it to be.

Clusters of worshipers were making their way out of the ornate building, each wearing vibrant colors. Their large hats and cloaks were the peak of fashion. The women's dresses had large bows on the back and patterned corsets. Others wore hoops in their dresses, accentuating their womanly features. All had hair varying in color from powdered white to vibrant shades of blues, greens, purples, and every other color in between. The men wore a wide array of suits and stockings, some having large puffy sleeves and ruffles on their collars. They laughed and talked to one another, speaking in a low buzz that Darius could not quite, nor cared to, make out. Several coaches sat outside the courtyard in a large stable a few measures away. These were not like the old wagon that Ranun drove but were elaborate carriages made for the taste and whims upper echelon of Tur'Mor.

Ranun did not pull closer, nor did any of the meagerly-clad citizens from the wagon approach the Sanctuary, until all the Uppers had left.

Several of the wealthy turned their noses up at the wagon as it pulled forward, tsking as they shook their heads in dismay. Darius peered back at that group, his eyes burning equally with derision. The Uppers dropped their gaze and hurried away shocked, as if they had never received a glare of disdain before. *It's your eyes.* Darius recalled Ranun's words as he continued to scowl at the cowering Uppers.

"Ho!" Ranun called out as he pulled the wagon to a stop. "Alrighty then, best be heading inside while the sky is lit!"

The wagon emptied quickly, Darius helping a few of the elderly and women down with a sturdy hand. They all smiled at him as he did so. *They don't seem to mind my eyes,* Darius thought as he helped the last elderly woman down. She was wearing a dull grey dress and had her salt and pepper hair pulled in a tight braid.

Ranun turned over the reins to a stable boy, who then took the wagon away from the courtyard. After a quick straightening of his robes, he led the small group up the worn marble steps into the Sanctuary, the veins of which were like rivers of speckled black and gold cutting through a field of white. The pillars leading to the open-air doorway were as wide as a man around and had deep grooves carved into them, the tops thereof floral in design.

Darius walked at the back of the group yet kept close enough so as not to mingle in with the masses of other folk who were making their way into the Sanctuary. Inside, the air smelled sweet with burning incense. Long, silver chains, extending from hooks attached to the curved walls, held shimmering thuribles, the source of the incense. The stone seats at the front were beginning to fill with worshipers, so Ranun led his party to a middle section, placing himself nearest the aisle.

Low kettle drums began to echo throughout the open room. The tonal thuds were rhythmic and serene, yet somehow primal and jarring. Each thud drove to the core of Darius's chest, his heart finding its own beat intertwined with the pounding. Men in long green robes and hoods, each waist wrapped about with a golden sash, began to walk forward chanting in low tones that matched the drums. Darius felt drawn in by the sensation of the rhythm.

A tall priest stepped to the front of the altar, taking his place behind a lectern that had been set out and draped in gold and green cloth. He held a long staff of gold, the head in the form of a hammer, though not much longer than a hand's length. He wore layers of robes, far more intricate than any of the other priests. His head was not covered by a hood. A tall, green hat of sorts sat on his head, covering his thinning white hair.

"May the Holy Ellitheor watch us this day," he said loudly, his elderly voice still powerful and captivating. It had a strength to it that ran deep, a knowingness, both obvious and mystical.

The congregation replied in unison, chanting solemnly, "May the gods be with us."

"Let us pray," the priest added purposefully as he drove the staff's pommel into the ground, making a solid thud. "High Father above, hear our words. We have come on your day to this sanctuary of men to worship thee and thy House. Bring our minds in focus with thee that we may return to the Mountains of Ellin and ever stand in thy golden halls of Vanherran. Mother of the Living, giver of life, prepare our fields in this season, so they may produce that we may live. Grant our youth strength and our elderly knowledge. This we ask of thee. Amen"

"Amen," echoed the chorus of worshipers, heads bowed low, palms up towards the statues of Ordan and Gallea.

"It is man's desire to be enlightened. It is my desire, as High Priest of Tur'Mor, to aid in this endeavor. My father, when he named me Elcon, gave me that name as a reminder of my heritage. It was the name he bore, and his father before him. Our heritage is the source of pure enlightenment. When we search our past, we may often find truth and purpose beyond what we currently see. Today, on this Ellitheal, we show our respect to our ancestors by continuing the faith in the great gods, the Ellitheor, who gave us this land as a blessing. A blessing with a promise." Elcon dragged out those last few words, leaving them hanging in the air before he continued, "It is said that worship of the Ellitheor is all that is required to return to the Halls of Or and serve in the Eternal Courts on High. But I would challenge this. I would look to our forefathers. They were not asked to simply worship at the feet of the High Father alone but serve him in all things. They fought alongside our gods, standing with the Ancient Sages, and helped to seal away the Fallen Ones into darkness everlasting.

"It was after this showing of valor that Ordan himself gave us the Blessed. Those who would watch over and guide His people after His Ascension back to Vanherran until the return of the Promised, the Sages of Times Past, who will usher in a new and glorious age. Our Blessed are the most gifted of all mankind, given divine abilities over the senses and elements, each in their own sphere, to guide and help our people find their own Ascension. Blessings of visions, blessings of healings, and blessings of the Light itself, passed down from generation to generation. The Gift. The Truth."

The drums began to beat again in low, steady thuds. The hooded priests began to chant as they brought forth bundles of wood, drenched in oil, and laid them upon the altar. Darius watched unblinking as a sense of unease began to spread. His eyes darted around the room. He searched for what could happen next. What he knew would happen next. A priest then brought a steel torch forward. He was followed by two other priests who carried a sealed wooden box ornamented with gold.

Elcon took the torch from the priest, who had walked to the high priest and knelt before him. Next, Elcon motioned to the priests carrying the wooden box. Darius grew even more uneasy as the box seemed to jolt and move. Something was alive within the box. The priests set the box before Elcon, who held the torch in one hand and the golden staff in the other.

"Many years have we come before the High Father in prayer and humble laudation, offering the best of our increase. And so, we offer up this, the first of the new flock." The priests opened the box to reveal a young lamb, its feet bound with cords. They raised the beast to the altar as the drumbeats intensified. Elcon turned his head to the domed glass skylight and began to chant something Darius could not make out. It was not common tongue, but something old and forgotten to men, save the Devout of the Church of Ordan.

The beating of the drums was now almost frantic, the chants of the priests loud and long. Darius's heart raced, and he watched in silence as one of the two priests produced a dagger from his belt. The other held the lamb by the head, as if to shield its eyes from the inevitable. The knife cut was swift and true, so swift that the beast did not even bleat. Elcon lowered the torch to the oiled wood, which burst into flames as a single drumbeat sounded. And all went silent.

The smoke reached up into the ceiling and then traveled through the building. The smell was sweet at first, and then became dark with char. Darius had seen sacrifices before. He had performed sacrifices, both of adoration and for the hunt, living sacrifices, and sacrifices of grain or earth, but never had he witnessed such a display as this. The drums, the chanting, it was all so overwhelming, driving him to the edge, literally. Darius looked about; people were staring. He was at the edge of his seat, fingers drawn into tight fists and eyes locked ahead. His chest was heaving, and his nose flared.

Quickly, Darius released his fingers, realizing his current stance. He then slid to the back of the pew and measured his breathing. Ranun too was looking in his direction. Though it was not concern upon his face; no, it was something different. Something was altogether different with Ranun today. His attitude, his demeanor, and his tone when he spoke to Darius. *Why does he want me here? What was his motive?* Darius wondered as he eyed the mustached priest carefully. Ranun turned his gaze away from Darius swiftly and back to the altar where Elcon stood.

"Followers of the High Father, come and cast upon the altar the offerings you bear," Elcon said after he turned about to the congregation, having handed the torch back to the priests.

Steadily, one by one, people began to stand and make their way to the center of the room to the raised platform. They took what appeared to be rolled pieces of parchment up to the altar and dropped them onto the flames. They lit quickly, whipping into the air and dancing upon the streams of heat. During this ordeal, many knelt on small benches on the ground in front of their pews, offering silent prayers to their deity. Darius did not move his body but searched about with his eyes vigorously. He then noted that after the devotee would cast their parchment, they dropped a coin or two into a basin at the side of the altar after touching the coin to their lips and forehead three times over.

The progression went on for several dull moments, the only sounds being the stifled movements of those proceeding to the altar and the steady plinking noise of coins falling into the brass vessel. Darius had relaxed, though his eyes still moved about the room steadily. He then looked up at the paintings, admiring the intricate designs. Beautiful imagery of Ordan and Gallea, their two sons, Fenron and Theallan, and their journeys upon the continent of Ethrea. Then, something stuck out to him. Or rather, the lack of something.

Darius studied the depictions, those of which told of the descent of the High Father and his holy family. The forming of Vialhael, the First City, and many other things. Yet there were a great many things missing. Where were the Daulkaefar, the Elder Elves who ferried the Ellitheor from Vanherran to Ethrea in their great Silver Skyships? Where were the Iarathor, the Arcane Dwarves of Kranhalla who forged the Ellitheor's silver into powerful totems, which were endowed with powers from on high? There was a depiction of the casting down of the Fallen Ones, yet it seemed too clean, hollow even. Furthering his wonder, he could not find a single image of the Guardians of old, those whom the High Father had called, who fought alongside the Ellitheor. None of these things were depicted, only diluted acts of Ordan and Gallea. The romanticized scenes lacked the dark and terrible truth that Darius had been taught as a youth. True, their two sons were by their sides, and there were men basking in their greatness, but this was not all that had been. There had been slaughtering among the nations; wanton destruction had plagued the land before Ordan had chosen to cast down his daughters.

Darius was caught away in thought, so much so that he did not hear Elcon continue his sermon. He did not hear the words of the high priest, but pondered over the images above, studying each and every scene. He had heard many of these tales as a child. His father, being the tribe's chief, was a devout man of Ordan. He had taken it upon himself to teach Darius at a young age of devotion and honor. Fond memories, seemingly lost, had been found. Darius could almost hear the deep voice of his father teaching him as they sat around a campfire, cooking what they had hunted that day. He could almost feel the wind pull at his hair and seemed to catch whiffs of the smells of his childhood home.

The time passed rapidly, Darius not noticing that Elcon had now stopped speaking. The beat of the drums drew his mind back from thought to reality. He looked forward and noticed that Elcon was staring directly at him. Their gaze only locked for the briefest moment before the old man turned his head to the rest of the congregation. The look had not been one of dismay or animosity, but of curiosity and wonder, as if he were seeing something beyond what Darius could comprehend.

When the drumbeats finally fell silent, all arose as one. Darius remained seated. Ranun stepped to the aisle, letting the people who had traveled with him depart from their pew. He then walked to Darius, silently yet smiling. Something was on his mind. Elcon, too, walked towards the stone seats where Darius was positioned, fixed in his seat.

"Darius," Ranun said with a reverent, but friendly voice, "I would like you to take a walk with me."

"Sure," Darius said, thumbing his ring in an attempt to calm his nerves.

"High Priest Elcon would have a word with you and I," Ranun said with a smile. He leaned in closely to the lad, though Darius was a head taller than him, and whispered in his ear, "It is a great honor."

Elcon gestured towards Darius and Ranun, touching his forefinger and thumb together, then pressing them to his lips then forehead. Darius had noticed this was how everyone greeted one another inside the Sanctuary, though he did not know what it meant. He simply nodded and arose in silence. Ranun let out a sigh of what could have been described as relief but was more of just acceptance of Darius's more standoffish nature.

"High Priest," Ranun said quietly, "I thank you for taking the time to meet on this holy day."

"Of course, Ranun," Elcon said with a kind smile. The old priest was in no way intimidating. He had soft features, a long and crooked nose, a toothy smile, and gentle eyes of dull grey. But there was something about him, something deeply concealed. Perhaps it was his eyes – they seemed to be so deep with years of understanding and mystery, both captivating and intriguing. "But let us now move to a more secluded space," Elcon said with a raise of his eyebrow when he caught Darius's stare.

"Agreed," Ranun said understandingly. Turning to Darius, he said, "I know in your days in Tur'Mor you have been burdened with a great many questions. I hope to help you find answers and have enlisted the guidance of Elcon in doing so."

"Perhaps it's best if I speak with young Master Darius alone," Elcon replied firmly, eyes turning to Ranun for only a moment before they turned back to Darius.

"Yes," Ranun answered sheepishly. "Of course, Anointed One."

"Just a few words." Elcon's voice lightened. "I do not want to overbear, my son. That is all."

Darius shot a glance at Ranun, who smiled and urged him to follow. However, Darius could not miss the momentary disappointment that the kindly man quickly hid. Despite the odd nature of the greeting, Darius nodded his head in compliance and followed the elaborately clad high priest.

Elcon led Darius to a small study in the back of the circular, domed Sanctuary. Three large tapestries hung from the wall, draping onto the polished floor. Darius did not take notice of the brilliantly colored cloth, nor the symbols imprinted on them but kept a steady eye on the high priest. There was something about this man, something that seemed to pull at Darius's subconscious, though he could not puzzle out what. Then, there was the reason for this strange meeting. Darius had wondered why Ranun had been so adamant – that much was at least clear now. But why would one not want the other to listen?

Darius was in mid-thought when Elcon began to speak. "Darius, my son..." He was holding back one of the tapestries and propping open a small door that had been concealed. Darius walked past him into the small room, circular and well kept. There was a wooden table, a high-backed chair on one side where Elcon moved to, and two plain sitting chairs on the other.

"Kindly Ranun has told me many things about you." Elcon took his seat.

Darius did not sit. "I hope they are all good. He has been most kind to a stranger."

"A stranger? I was told you were an Emissary of the Church in Dane, is that not correct?"

Darius's eyes widened. That was the story Ranun had told the guards who had found him. Now, he had just sold out the very man who had sheltered and cared for him.

"Be at peace, young Master Darius," Elcon said with a subtle laugh, raising a hand in doing so. "No need to go running out. I am aware of your desire to remain, how should I say, secluded?"

"I am just trying to find something," Darius responded, perhaps with a touch too much gruffness in his voice. "Then I'll be gone from here."

"And what is it you seek, my son? Perhaps I can aid you."

Darius's eyes fell to the floor. He sighed and brought a large hand to his chin and pulled at his beard. With the thumb of his other hand, he spun the ring about his finger in agitation. He was not upset with Elcon; he had no right to be. He was not even upset with Ranun for bringing him here; the old man was only trying to help. But he was frustrated. He was frustrated with himself. He was frustrated with these visions and the voice that seemed to call out in the back of his mind. Worst of all, he was frustrated that he had no idea where he was, how he got there, or why he was there. And the fact that he was not one step closer to answering any of those questions boiled his blood.

"And what help can you offer me?" Darius's awkward words were little more than a murmur.

"Ranun tells me that you are quite handy with a hammer?" Elcon said in a calm voice, as if he did not hear the bitterness in Darius's words. He slid a book that was sitting on the lacquered mahogany table in front of himself and flipped through the pages.

Darius blinked. There was a moment of silence. Elcon stopped on a rather inconspicuous page, and his eyes began to narrow.

"A traveler from afar, searching in a city he does not know for something he cannot see?" Elcon continued after seeing Darius would not answer.

Darius did look up now.

"Perhaps what you are searching for is not so far away," Elcon said smoothly.

"How do you know of such things?" Darius's voice was quick and sharp. His hands gripped the front of the table as he leaned forward to stare at the old man.

"Darius, I am a man who values knowledge," Elcon said calmly. "And I have been blessed by Ordan on High to have lived long enough to gain a considerable amount of such. Yet, my search never ends." A finger tapped a page of the book, resting on a strange series of twisting lines.

"And what do you know of dreams?" Darius asked, releasing the table abashedly.

"Dreams? I know a good many things about dreams. It is thought, among some, that dreams are merely incoherent thought built by the subconscious mind to entertain." Elcon cocked a smile. "Others theorize that some dreams are when the Aethereal meets the Terral and the essence of a man is free to experience the eternities, walk paths unknown, and see things beyond time and space."

Whatever answer Darius was hoping Elcon would have given, that was not it. He was more confused than before asking his question. Not only was he confused, but somewhat concerned as to what this high priest was passing off as 'knowledge'.

"But I do not think it is dreams that bring you here, my son." Elcon continued, cutting off Darius's reply. "Ranun tells me you have a unique gift."

"A gift?" Darius's face was a picture of perplexity. He felt truly lost now.

"This is a safe place. I promise I am not here to report you to the authorities," Elcon said with a laugh, hand still on the book, eyes locked on Darius.

"And why would I fear the authorities?"

"Come now, Darius. Surely you know that professing the ability to use magic or conjure spells is heresy in all of Ordiatea and goes strictly against the ordinances of the Church."

"I professed neither." Darius replied.

"But you did save a child, did you not? That night in the storm."

"Yes," Darius answered, eyes narrowing. "I don't see what that has to do with anything."

"Darius, Ranun said you were able to catch a sign mid-fall with your bare hands."

Darius's lips drew into a thin line, and his back stiffened.

"My son, you have no reason to fear. This I swear on the High Father's throne." Elcon seemed to be trying to encourage trust. He did not know Darius.

"What I do, it is not for laud or glory," Darius answered curtly.

"I am not suggesting such. Only trying to ascertain how it is that you were able to save that child."

"Being so well-protected has weakened this land's spine. Too far from the dangers of the wilds. Mireya and her hordes slaughter by the thousands, and you draw concern from those who were called as Guardians to protect this land." Darius's voice was hot, but level. He outstretched his right hand, revealing the silver ring with the paw etched into the cold metal. "I am what I am, and I serve Ordan High Father. It is my calling and my duty, and I do as I am commanded."

Elcon's face went pale. The pages of the book shuffled as his hands fell to his side. Shock riddled his eyes, and Darius could sense the old man's heartbeat quicken. The high priest licked his lips and stammered, "My son..."

"I did not mean any disrespect." Darius sighed, and then muttered under his breath, "This is why we keep to ourselves."

"I, uh," – Elcon cleared his throat – "I must attend to certain matters of the Church."

Darius thrust his hands into the deep pockets of his long, tawny trench coat. His feet shuffled in his heavy boots. But his eyes, his eyes focused on Elcon, a bit of regret hidden behind the crystalline yellow orbs.

"Darius." Elcon rose quickly while speaking. "You misunderstand me. I do not mean to push you away, but there are certain limitations I must look into. I will come to you again as soon as I can. There is much we need to discuss."

He hurried past Darius to the door of the small room, the book still sitting on the table, upside-down red eye staring at the ceiling. Elcon urged Darius to follow him into the main corridor of the Sanctuary. Darius did so without complaint. As they stepped out, the brilliant light from the glass dome bathed them both in effulgent rays. Elcon stared at Darius's eyes, which caught and refracted the light.

"Darius, my son," Elcon said, taking Darius by the arm as Ranun approached, "don't talk about your...unique ability...to anyone. I will come to you as soon as I can, I promise. But you cannot mention this to anyone, do you understand?"

"I understand," Darius said, though he turned his eyes away from the man. He did not like the way he stared up at him. There was an urge; he could feel it crawling up his spine. The ring felt cold, and the rays of sun were tugging at his will. He just needed...

"Good," Elcon spoke, severing the urge from Darius's subconscious. He then turned on his heels and hurried away from Darius, leaving him there to be intercepted by a jolly-looking Ranun. However, as the high priest walked away, Darius heard him mutter, "There is more at play here than I could have ever known... I need time, more time."

93

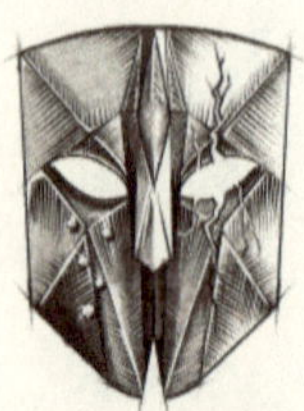

CHAPTER 9: MASKS AND GOWNS

Warm flesh pressed against Aellia, fragrant and soft, smelling sweetly of spice and sandalwood. Dark, straight hair with a thick streak of blue flowed lazily over her bare arm. The scents of warm spices and sandalwood were subtle, but the mixed fragrances were quickly becoming Aellia's favorite smell. Tomo was nearly a hand and a half taller than Aellia, but she seemed to fit perfectly next to her in the large bed, the bed that had once been clustered with pillows, now bare of all but the two of them and a silk sheet. Aellia gazed at Tomo's slender neck where a winding tattoo, that of a wingless dragon with a lion's mane and two large fore-claws, ran from the nape of her neck to the small of her back. She traced a finger down the ink, gently caressing Tomo's body.

"It is too early," Tomo grumbled in a flat voice.

Aellia bit her lover's ear playfully and then swung out of the bed. She had always been the early riser of the two. A white robe of silk, embroidered with golden vines running along the hem, lay over her nightstand. Aellia pulled it over her bare body and walked to the wash basin to scrub her teeth with soda and comb back her short, frosty-white hair.

Tomo sat up after a few moments and looked to Aellia, eyes narrowing with frustration, surely from being awakened before she had wanted. As she sat up, the sheet fell from her, revealing a large burn mark on her right ribcage, the only thing blemishing her porcelain flesh. She was far more ample than Aellia was, her body seemingly constructed of perfect curves. Curves that sometimes-caused hints of jealousy in Aellia, her own body being more angular and sharper, like carved marble, though etched in scars. She shook her head as the Zau'fi woman rose. Every man and woman seemed to gawk and stare at Tomo, and while some did glance Aellia's way, the jealousy was there. Despite this, Aellia could not repress a smile as she looked at her with those ever-deepening, dark eyes.

"I hate you," Tomo muttered in a frustrated, howbeit, playful manner. She snatched up a night-gown of black silk, embroidered with silver serpents throughout, from the ground and pulled it around herself. It clung to her curves just perfectly and flowed in all the right places.

"I know." Aellia smiled back at her in the mirror. "You made that very clear last night."

Tomo blushed and looked away. She had never been comfortable talking about sex or intimacy, even with Aellia. Custom dictated this in Ja'una, and Tomo, being from a small Jou'khay, a fortified settlement loyal to a local feudal lord, had been raised in the utmost ways of propriety. Tomo slid on a pair of slippers and started for the door as she hastily tied the night-gown shut around her waist. Aellia rushed over and grabbed Tomo's hand, pulling it away from the doorknob, spinning her about to face her in one, swift motion. Despite being far shorter than Tomo, Aellia was just as strong, and when she wanted something, she could be quite forceful. That being said, this was not a motion of anger but of affection. Though, as Aellia had to admit, it could be hard to differentiate between the two when she acted.

"Yeshka-na, Mirano'ko!" Tomo gasped, dark eyes locked onto Aellia's hard, grey eyes. A smile flashed across her pink lips, a smile filled with life and desire.

"You will not escape me that easily, Ko'Zau," Aellia whispered, rising to her tiptoes and pressing her lips to Tomo's ear.

Tomo laughed and said, "Your Yun Zau is improving, but the Ko is to succeed the proper noun. To say 'my dragon' is Zau'Ko, Aellia. But your pronunciation, that is very nice. You are becoming very proper. Perhaps one day I can take you to the emerald lakes of Na-yan and see the Yexhu Xar."

Tomo did not talk about her homeland often, but she always got the same distant look in her eyes. Aellia did not believe the stories about her departure from Ja'Una and Zau'Fi, the Land of the Dragon. Tomo had told the crew her family were fishermen and that she was sent to learn of the ways of the West. However, Aellia suspected differently. On the sparse occasions where Tomo did talk about the razor-like rock formations of the Yexhu Xar, the Spine Peaks, capped with green and rising high into the misty mornings or upon the glistening lakes of her home province, she spoke wistfully, mournfully.

"I would go, you know," Aellia said comfortingly, running her fingers along the silk night-gown. "I would follow you, leave all of this behind."

"Nahye, Mirano'ko," Tomo said softly. "Your home is here, and these are your people."

"But what about your people? Your home?"

"My heart is with you, and that is all the home I will ever need."

A call from below broke the intimate moment. Felik's voice boomed, "Aellia! Tomo! Report!"

Aellia rose quickly on her tiptoes and stole a kiss, then whispered, "Best be getting back to your room and get dressed," into Tomo's ear.

"Sounds like Felik is in one of his 'commanding moods', Aellia," Tomo said with a roll of her eyes. "Try not to embarrass the poor man again."

"What makes you think I'd do something like that?" Aellia said with a sly smile.

Tomo did not answer, just turned away and opened the door to leave. Aellia swung her hand, spanking Tomo on the backside. A satisfying slap echoed loudly.

Tomo sniffed in response, shaking her head in exasperation. But Aellia could see the color rising in her cheeks as she walked away.

Now, what to wear? Aellia thought as she walked to her wardrobe. She picked out a rather audacious outfit, quite different than her normal tight leather outfits of white and silver. Today's activities were not about sneaking and acrobatics. No, today she would be performing her least favorite activity, that of acting like a proper lady.

The dress she settled on had a fine corset of golden latticework, extenuating her rather small chest, which was made bare near the top with an oval cutout and lined with lace. The high neck of the purple dress was also laced in gold, and the long sleeves covered the back of her hand, with finger strings looping around her middle fingers on either hand. The front of the dress was split to show off her high heeled boots, which sparkled with thousands of tiny stones, and laced up the back. There seemed to be at least four or five layers of fabric as the skirts of the dress, each with their own unique color and patterns, the top of which was pleated. A wooden hoop was built into the dress, just above her seat, so as to enlarge her hindquarters.

After working herself into the dress and boots, Aellia pulled a cap over her brushed back hair and donned a wig of soft blue, whose ringlets and curls towered atop her head. A string of pearls wrapped around the false hair, matching the set she was now stringing about her neck.

Aellia looked herself over in the mirror. A chill ran through her being, and she felt almost as if she would puke. The woman she stared at was not Aellia of Livithia. No, it was everything she hated about this place. The pomp and pride, the utter lust of material things over the lives of those less fortunate than oneself. She caked on face powder and blush, even working her lashes with makeup, all the while repressing the feelings of disgust.

In frustration, Aellia turned from the mirror with a curse. She stomped over to her wall of knives and daggers and took two from their stands. The first was a straight blade of pattern forged steel, an ivory handle, and an orange stone set in the butt. The blade was almost the length of a court sword, but the tang and hilt were made in the manner of a knife. This she fastened about her side in a sleek scabbard that was wrapped in dyed leather and tipped with steel. The second blade was only a hand's width long, bearing a slight curve with a single edge. This, she sheathed on her thigh under the layers of her dress. She would only ever use this one in the worst of cases.

Feeling more herself now that sharp blades of danger were fastened to her body, Aellia drew in a deep breath and sighed in relief. She was not a lady of Tur'Mor. No, she was far from it. She turned from her wall of weaponry and crossed her room confidently. After a quick glance around the room to make sure all was where it needed to be, she left, closing the door behind her.

"You mule-headed ditch weed!" Felik's voice echoed throughout the Loft. "How could you not secure two simple things?"

"Felik, I –" Tornak began, muttering sheepishly as he stared at the floor.

"Of all the goat-brained things," Felik shouted in frustration, turning away from the red-haired lad. "Ten hours! We have ten hours!"

"Leave the boy alone, Felik," Tomo said from the opposite staircase as Aellia. She was now wearing a long, black dress with vibrant blue pleats, matching her hair. Silver roses wound up the sides of her dress and a huntsman's sword hung from her hip. Her dress was tight-fitting, leaving little to the imagination, though she only had a corset, no hoops or padding to enlarge herself. They were clearly unnecessary. Her dress, however, was cut more after the style of the Islanders to the East, the neck of which tied all the way to the chin and the sleeves hung long and loose about her slender wrists. Bright blue gloves that were missing the tips of the fingers covered her hands, matching her black boots' back-lacing, which rose over the top of her calves.

Felik shot Tomo a stare that could have frozen fire.

Aellia glanced from Tomo to Felik and found it hard not to laugh at the sight of her commander. He stood there, angry as a scorned lover, in a stiff white overcoat, adorned with pink roses and golden petals, that fell just below mid-thigh. His powdery-pink shirt had a high and ruffled collar and an ascot tucked behind a vest that buttoned down the left side of his torso. Puffy white britches were tucked into yellow stockings just below the knee, and polished white shoes with pink laces were tied at his feet. A lord's sidesword hung from his hip, the knuckle-bow crafted from fine silver and the scabbard crusted with gemstones. To top it all off, a white wig sat atop his head, pulled it back with a pink lace in a bow and holding it right below the nape of the neck. A satin top hat of soft pink and yellow sat atop the powdered wig.

"May the gods have mercy on us!" Aellia bellowed. "How far up your arse is your cane, Lord Felik?"

"Careful, my lady," Felik snapped back, "one such as yourself should not debase another. It isn't proper."

"Proper?" Aellia said as she walked down the stairs, her train flowing behind her. "Acting proper is for the useless and gorged, those too weak to defend themselves."

"Ah, you two do go on like two Hunukaru fighting over whose son will marry the village's first daughter!" Felohme called out from his position leaning over a stove frying eggs and pork belly, sweat forming on his thick brow.

"Watch it, Felohme!" Felik snarled at the fat man. "Best remember what your duty is today."

"Oh, yes yes, my lord. I am to wear the sackcloth and scrummage," Felohme said in a sarcastic, lowly voice. "A humble servant of the great Lord Sparkle-Shoes!" He then rolled his hand in an ostentatious manner and bowed mockingly.

Tornak cracked a smile at that remark but quickly dropped his eyes from Felik, who turned bright red around the neck and cheeks. In the moppy-haired lad's hand were two envelopes, sealed with royal purple wax and an insignia Aellia could not make out from the distance. Tomo had made her way to the end of the staircase and was fixing her dress in a stand mirror, purposefully ignoring the squabbles of the rest of the Crew. She had a knack for that, Tomo did. Starting something, then walking away and leaving the rest of the Crew squabbling like unruly children of Harvest Night's Feast.

"You abase yourself, Felohme." Belthazer sighed as he walked into the room, rolling his eyes at his near-kin of Tuawtia. Belthazer did, however, continually remind the Crew that he was of the Blackridge Qyari, not of the cultist tribes of the north where Felohme hailed from.

"I only baste the chicken before I cook it, ha!" Felohme slapped his rotund gut as he laughed.

"All of you, what is your problem?" Felik roared, though it was more exasperation than domination. "We have one last chance to secure admittance into the Valamour to secure that blasted jewel, and if the lot of you blunder this due to your abundant stupidity and arrogance, I will personally skin your hide and hang it over the balcony!"

The Crew went silent, each of them looking down at their feet or off to one thing or another. Felik's eyes were a fire of frustration and stress. Aellia could feel the exertion this had taken on the man. She had become accustomed to him always being in control, dealing out short means of confrontation with a level head, not lashing out in such a manner as this.

"Now," Felik continued, after a few moments to steady his breathing, snatching the two envelopes from Tornak's trembling hand. "If we could each, please, do the part we were asked to do, we should have no trouble securing our way into the Regalia of the Jewel tonight. It is the most high-profile event this city holds, and I do not think there is any way to slip in unnoticed. This requires a different approach, one which I do believe none of us are overly comfortable with. That being said, I do expect each of you to play your part well."

The room seemed to take a collective breath, all relaxing and gathering near Felik, even Felohme, though he did take his eight eggs and three slices of hog's belly with him. They moved across the central area of the Loft to the Study, a narrow room with three chandeliers hanging from the ceiling and a large brick fireplace at the far end. The dilapidating walls were lined with gold and white wallpaper, which reached the vaulted ceiling. The Crew gathered around a blocky, wooden table that did not seem to match the room, Felik sitting at the head and the others on opposite sides. The chairs were all of different makes and styles, some high-backed and lavished with ornate gilding, others fashioned after chaise-like lounges with tubular cushions and floral print. Felik's chair, however, was neither gilded nor cushioned. It was lacquered black and had sharp angles and a woven back.

Felik placed the two envelopes along with several sheaves of paper on the table, having retrieved them from a locked box on a stand next to his chair. He looked over each piece of parchment with a steady eye, studying them as if to make sure they were without blemish or flaw. After a few moments of silent contemplation, he looked up.

"Tonight, is the Commemoration of the Kindred." Felik's voice drew in the room, captivating those that sat about as he began to lay out his plans. Aellia often wondered where the man had learned to speak in such a manner, and the older she grew, the more subtleties she noticed in her commander that set him apart from other men. Even now, as he spoke in his pompous, downright ridiculous outfit, it somehow suited him. "We have secured two invites to this masquerade that will be held at the Mayoral Residency within the heart of the Valamour, though we were unable to obtain acceptance into the private viewing of the jewel." Felik shot a paling Tornak a fierce glare.

"I told you," Tornak protested, face flushing red yet again. "There was no way to forge the bloody invitations. According to my sources, each were sealed with the bloody House they were intended for! No way to fake a house that doesn't exist, no way to have two of one house arrive."

"Your sources need to be vetted better next time," Felik growled, "if there will even be a blasted next time. Halfak's fiery gates, this a mess!"

"Leave it, Felik. We'll make do," Tomo interjected. "We always do."

Felik steeled himself, forcing down the frustration that welled within. He imagined himself alone and in the forest, seeking out the tranquil flow of the stream. Slowly, calmly, he bridled his emotions the way he had been trained to do all those years ago. In his heart, he knew that his crew deserved to know why they were doing this. Not just because he had asked or that there was pressure from Aldorian for simple greed. No, the honest truth. That, if they failed, Felik would be revealed as not just a simple soldier, but a disgraced Captain of the Ordiatian army. A man wanted with a price on his head for what had come to be known as the Folly of the Fourth. He had abandoned his post, let his men die, and forsook the entire army. He could not tell them that. It was his burden to bear.

"You are right, Tomo." When he spoke, his voice was level and exact. He forced his emotions away. It was time to act, and they had to do it with what they had. "We will find a way."

"We got invitations," Aellia said, looking at the floor plans of the mansion. It was enormous. "And I'm sure that wherever the private party is, it shouldn't be too hard to pick out. We'll just divide and grab it. Once the jewel is secured, we'll each leave at different times so as to not draw attention."

"Just grab it?" Belthazer laughed, pointing to the red circles placed sporadically over the map, each representing a guard. "If a whiff of something wrong were to happen with that stone, the whole place will be locked down tight. There won't be a prayer for us if we are spotted."

"It will just have to do," Felik answered, though there was little confidence in his voice.

***

Ordiatian parties, especially amongst the Upper caste, were a thing of lavish splendor and more often than not led to rampant debauchery. Wine flowed freely and those present cared little for anything other than their status, and those were fermented by the simple act of arriving at such a party. Ball gowns of exquisite construction, layers upon layers of silk, silver and gold adorned the women, who used the hoops and corsets to over-exaggerate their features. Men too wore luxurious clothing, with bulbous enhancements in the tight britches to show off their girth. They were all a prideful lot, gluttonous and without care for those who suffered and hungered.

Aellia walked with her hand draped in Felik's crooked arm up the cascading marble steps of the Mayoral Residency. Two dozen men in voluminous trousers, striped purple and gold, lined the steps on either side. They wore polished breastplates and metal caps, each with oversized plumes flowing from the tops. The guards held poleaxes that were nearly as ornate as their chest plates, causing Aellia to question their true functionality. Jewel-crested sabers hung from their waists, those she did not doubt, for they were surely sharp. Atop the bulwark of the mansion, several dozen gunners stood at attention. These dressed nearly the same as the guards, save they wore a surcoat embroidered with the Stars of Ordiatea instead of a breastplate and had a powder horn and satchel slung over their shoulders.

"Breathe," Felik whispered into her ear as they walked up the steps. His breath was stale, though he had tried to chew mint leaves on the carriage ride. He was afraid as well, she could tell. The feathers on his ridiculous mask brushed her cheek, causing her to jump slightly.

"Damn these blasted masks to Halfak and back!" Aellia swore under her breath. "And damn Aldorian for putting you up to this. I'll mount his fat nose over my headboard for this."

"Smile, my lady," Felik said as he placed a lace-gloved hand on hers, eyes straight forward. "We are guests here."

Aellia grimaced. This was no place she ever wanted to be a guest at. And, to make matters worse, hundreds of lords and ladies from all across the Republic were pouring into the mansion. Aellia felt a spike of claustrophobia as fancily clad individuals and couples made their way into the Residency. She had never before seen such a display of wealth and propriety before, nor such a diverse gathering of peoples. True, Tur'Mor prided itself in being multicultural, but amongst the poor, all seemed to be the same. Downtrodden men and women of Ordiatian lineage who lacked the good fortune to be born into a family of wealth.

"Invitation," a thin-lipped man with a sharp mustache asked, white-gloved hand extended, eyes not even appearing to notice the two.

"Ah yes, good sir," Felik answered, sliding his hand into his stiff outer coat and retrieving one of the two sealed envelopes Tornak had procured. He then handed the parchment to the doorman with a haughty upward tilt of his chin.

"Sir Tingwood?" the doorman asked in his snooty voice, looking from parchment to Felik. "Lady Elphandra?" He turned his olive eyes to Aellia.

Aellia wanted to reach out and slap that ridiculous mustache and sour smirk of the pompous doorman's face. Instead, she curtsied, ever so slightly, never taking her eyes off the spindly man.

"You have quite the appearance, for a Highblood of Tarnfields, of course, Sir Tingwood," the doorman said as he looked at Felik's powdered face, the deep scars clearly blemishing his face.

"It was a hunting accident when I was a younger lad," Felik answered, though he could not keep his hand from settling on the pommel of his sword.

"Quite unfortunate," the doorman replied. Then, turning his crooked nose towards Aellia, he continued by saying, "At least you have secured a good woman to birth a child, and perhaps his features will fare better."

"I think that is quite enough," Felik snarled as he snatched the envelope from the doorman's gloved fingers. He only barely held them in his dainty hands.

"Good evening," the stiff-backed man said with a slight bow, his back and legs staying straight.

"Even the doormen speak with arrogance," Aellia cursed under her breath as they walked into the grand Mayoral Residency. "I hate the whole lot of Uppers. Bunch of tight arsed f-"

"Aellia!" Felik snapped in a sharp whisper, tightening his hand on hers. "We are them tonight. Behave yourself!"

Aellia turned her icy eyes on Felik, glaring at him with a coldness that could have frozen the very flaming gates of Halfak. "Yes, Sir Tingwood. But of course, I will behave."

Felik grimaced, and Aellia knew that she had struck a chord. This argument was not over. Only postponed.

The masquerade was overly lavish, with every bit of the Mayoral Residency decorated with flowing bouquets of flowers set in ornate vases. Hundreds of prim Uppers colluded around endless tables of foods and exotic beverages, indulging themselves. There were strange silver pipes connected to glass jars that burned intoxicating aromas men and women alike would breathe in and then laugh and act a fool. Bards played songs as men and women danced about with hands held stiffly and motioned in flowery exactness. It was all so much. Aellia had never seen anything like it.

Hours seemed to pass, and despite her unwillingness to accept it, Aellia found herself beginning to enjoy the ebb and flow of it all. Laughter rang through the Residency, along with a feeling of unbridled euphoria that she had never felt before. The wine had been strong, and those blue-green jars that housed that wonderful aroma, seemed to be pulling at the back of her mind, tearing her away from reality. Aellia lost herself. She could barely even remember the procession of the mayor and the announcement of the King's Jewel.

It did happen, right? She was beginning to question everything. Where was Felik? Aellia looked at her hand. It seemed to sift in color, from pink to green and blue and then silver. She held a goblet in that hand, golden with red wine inside, though nearly drained. *Why does my hand shake?*

"Aellia," a familiar voice whispered in her ear. "Aellia, we have to go, now!"

"Wha – why?" Aellia murmured. When did her eyes get so heavy?

"Aellia, what is wrong with you?" the female asked. She had drawn in close. She smelled amazing. And her skin, it was so soft.

A sea of shifting steps unfurled before Aellia's eyes. They were not solid, but a viscous mass of melting marble. She brought her hand to her chest. *Where are my gemstones?* The nice smelling lady with the soft skin took her by the arm and began to lead her down the swirling steps.

"I am going to be sick." Aellia laughed as her head rolled to the side. She saw the face of a beautiful woman, and was that blue in her hair?

"Aellia," Tomo said as kindly as she could, though there was a seriousness to her words. "I think you've been poisoned. I am getting you home."

"I feel great." Aellia's contradicting words slurred in her mouth. Her tongue was growing oddly heavy. Also, she could smell things now, though it was all oddly pungent. *They are so sour.* She emptied her stomach into a shrubbery pruned to look like a woman holding a vase on her head.

"Aellia!" Tomo sounded shocked. "What has come over you?"

"What about Lord Sparkle-Shoes?" Aellia asked with a hiccup. "He is in need of a lady tonight."

"Did you take anything from anyone?" Tomo inquired, brushing aside Aellia's comment.

"Just wine, that's all for me," Aellia slurred. And then slumped over.

***

Felik ambled through the massive Residency, nonchalantly climbing stairs and sliding past people. *I look ridiculous. And I can't move in this gods-forsaken suit. And who in Ordan's name wears these things?* He looked at his shoes, the rhinestones glittering in the chandeliers' light. This was all supposed to be the pinnacle of modern fashion. He looked like a damned peacock, with the emphasis on the –

A set of guards moved ahead. Felik slid behind an ornately carved column of marble gilded with gold. The two men in breastplates and plumed helms walked past him without taking a second look, their faces showing a lesser desire to be at this place than Felik. He understood. Soldiers did not want to guard wine and paintings, they wanted to fight for glory. Or at least, that was what they thought they wanted.

Dark memories of blood and gore flashed through Felik's mind. He breathed in sharply, grabbing the hilt of his sword. He was not in war; he was not on the battlefield. No, he was safe. He was in a mansion with a bunch of prudes. He was fine. Felik released his grip, letting out a long sigh.

"Ah yes, the King's Jewel. The showing is taking place as we speak," a thick-faced man with a beauty mark on his bulbous nose said.

"A pity you have so little status to your name," a spindly little man in tight green trousers said. His codpiece looked absolutely ridiculous in those britches. "Mother was right."

"Come now, Andras, can we not en-"

Felik quit listening. So, the time was now. He had learned of where the King's Jewel would be shown, but not when. The problem now was how to get into the most secure room of the mansion, with men, women, and guards parading around like ants, without being noticed? And what was more, how to escape with the bloody rock once he had gotten his hands on it.

***

Belthazer Haadura looked at the aberrations of man with horror. Such gluttony and lasciviousness was damnable in the Eternal Eye of Uuradan, the Eternal One. A covered hand touched the amulet that lay against bare flesh, under the layers of silken cloth. He could not see the twisting form of

103

the Eternal One, the Great Dragon, Uuradan. But to feel its touch, that was enough to steady his racing heart. If the zealot of the Great Dragon knew anything, it was that all present were full of immorality, unclean beings whose souls were lost to the endless flames of desolation. They deserved the fate that they doled out for themselves.

"Tuawtian," a low-voiced man in a knee-length green coat called, lace seeming to burst from every opening. "Bring me wine."

"I am not a servant here," Belthazer answered in his best Ordiatian, trying his best to keep his lip from snarling.

"I did not ask for your tongue, dust licker." The man turned a cheeky smile towards Belthazer. "I asked for wine."

"Manuel, leave the pests alone," a woman scoffed, tugging the green-coated man off to the side, measuring Belthazer with demeaning eyes. "It is unbecoming."

"Dare you offend?" Belthazer snarled, stretching his hand out to take hold of the man Manuel's arm.

Three others that were standing near turned, each placing thick hands on their sideswords. Belthazer did not wear a sword at his side, but carried an ebony cane with a silver handgrip, molded in a perfect sphere.

"What's this?" another voice called out, an uncomfortably familiar voice. Belthazer's face paled and eyes widened as he saw Midcouncillor Aldorian approaching, six armored guardsmen in tow. "Cousin, is that you?"

The man Manuel smiled greasily. "Ah, dear cousin Arrius, how timely is your arrival."

Belthazer stood frozen, not knowing what to do. Things could not possibly get any worse.

***

Tornak looked at the display with amazement. Here in the Retainer's Lodging, an oval room on the second floor with a balcony overlooking the great hall of the Mayoral Residency, he could easily watch for the sign Felik had given. And it had to come any minute now. It had been hours now. The other attendants and retainers all wore tailcoats that had high, stiff collars, starched shirts of varying colors, and knee-high stockings that covered the bottoms of tight trousers.

Tornak's attire mirrored theirs but seemed less fine. Well, that was to be expected when you had taken them from a man who looked old enough to have seen the first stone being crafted by Ordan's hammer. It also had a smell to it, something he could not wash out. That smell, mixed with the tonic used to paste his hair back made his stomach uneasy. He held a lace handkerchief to his nose as he looked over the party. He wanted to be down there, drinking and mingling. But, yet again, he was on lookout duty. He was always doing the worst of jobs. Well, nearly the worst.

***

Felohme chuckled a hearty laugh that rippled through his belly. "I win again!" He reached out and picked up the dice from the stable floor where he and other men in drab clothing sat in a circle on the hay.

"Y'er too damn good at this, Farleum," a gap-toothed man with sparse, greying hair bemoaned as he drunkenly watched Felohme pick up two copper siglats from the floor.

"F-el-O-h-ma, Charne, Felohme!" Felohme replied as he placed the dice back into a wooden cup. He had always enjoyed a pleasant game of dice, something his father had taught him before he was killed off by the slavers. He had not known this game before the start of the night, having lost five siglats, but now, now he was on a roll. He laughed again, thinking of the pun.

"What's so funny, Tuawan?" a grey-clad man with a missing eye patched with a leather strip asked. Felohme guessed he was the driver of a lesser house.

"Life is too short to be upset all the time, my friends. Look at us, all from different places, but here now. We have food and are allowed out of the cold and rain to live and enjoy."

"We are in stables dressed in rags, while our lords and ladies drink wine and listen to the best music in the Republic. Why should we be so happy?" a shallow-faced woman, whose hair was tied back in a tight bun, scoffed.

"Well," Felohme said as he rubbed his rotund gut, "I ate this morning, I'm playing dice now with new friends. I do not mine for saltpeter nor coal, I have not been whipped today. I have good shoes, and I know I will sleep tonight with a roof over my head."

The group stared at him incredulously, most people did. Felohme's smile widened, soft and warm. "Well now, friends, shall we dice again?" The cup began to rattle in his hand.

***

The Mayor, Xander Adelmo, arrived in full regalia. Two dozen men and two dozen women walked in a column behind him. He wore the very best of the best, from his false, powdered hair in rising ringlets down to his red, heeled shoes which were studded with gemstones. A masterfully crafted saber hung from his side and a gold inlaid cane tapped in perfect beat upon the marble steps as he walked. He was a handsome man in his middle years, well loved by the people for his progressive stances on re-unifying Tur'Mor. He was also loved by the lord and ladies of this place, for his expansive taxation to fuel factories, schools, and industry. Most everyone loved Adelmo.

105

Behind the double column of men and women walked another man, whose face nearly mirrored the Mayor's, though his build was slighter than his younger brother and his nose was more beak-like. Alec Adelmo was Deputy of the City, whose duty was the protection of its people. He enforced the will of his younger brother with an iron hand. Many feared him and his judgment, though his brother spoke highly of him and his effectiveness in demolishing the once rising tide of crime that had plagued the city.

Trumpeters in voluminous britches sounded their brassy horns as the mayor and his entourage climbed the steps. People parted ways as they made their way into the Residency, the mayor waving and nodding to those in attendance with a mesmerizing smile. Tornak watched with awe. The man had such a presence, he seemed to emanate grandeur and command. Everyone cheered as the man walked up the steps to the second story of the house, though they all grew silent as he outstretched his hands.

"People of Tur'Mor!" His voice was captivating, strong yet kind. "Tonight, we celebrate the unity of the Republic by the Carrying of the King's Jewel, a national treasure. Though, it is not the jewel we celebrate, not truly. But it is each of you. Your contributions and loyalty to the greater good of the Republic have helped ensure a lasting legacy. And for that, I give my most humble thanks."

The room erupted into cheers and applause. Men clapped hands above their heads and women waved kerchiefs. Musicians strummed chords and trumpeters blared their horns. Mayor Adelmo raised his hands again, quieting the room. A slender woman wearing an elegant dress, far more beautiful than any woman Tornak had ever seen, walked up beside the mayor, holding a satin pillow with a bejeweled mask atop it.

Mayor Adelmo leaned over and kissed the woman, causing a second eruption of cheering and laughter. Adelmo took the mask from the pillow and placed it on his face. "Well then," he called out loudly, "Are we not here to celebrate? Let the wine flow freely. Enjoy yourselves; you have earned it!"

The music and trumpeting carried away the words of the mayor, though he was no longer addressing the whole group, but the few that surrounded him. He walked from person to person, extending a gloved hand and shaking those that met him. He laughed and hugged, talked and pointed to murals or artifacts that adorned the Residency.

Felik knew this was his only chance to act, while everyone was caught up in the thralls of the mayor's entrance, less attention would be placed on the vault. The maps of the Residency, so far, had proven accurate to the baseboards. Felik ran his hands along the elaborate paper that covered the walls. It was smooth, but he knew that if he kept... *click.* A door opened inward; the seams hidden in the decor of the paper.

Ducking to fit through the secluded, square opening, Felik skulked through the narrow passageway. The Mayoral Residency was over three hundred years old, renovated and updated through time, but the bones were nearly ancient. This passageway was a remnant of a time when Tur'Mor was not the massive city state it was today, a necessity from a time when wars abounded in the land, before the Outer Walls had been erected and when monstrosities lurked in the shadows. At that time, this was the Keep of the Kings, not a mayor's mansion. Cold, grey stones and bars of blackened iron formed the walls, dirtying the lace of his shirtsleeves as he used his hands to guide him down the pitch-black path.

***

"It is quite fitting, brother," Mayor Adelmo's smooth baritone voice punctured the ruckus of the evening's festivities.

"How so?" questioned Alec in his sure, though raspy voice. He drank sweet wine from a silver goblet, though his dark grey eyes found no pleasure in the moment.

"These parties, this frivolous behavior. It is quite fitting that a relic such as the King's Jewel be paraded about, further showing the division of this city."

"You know as well as I that appearances are most important, brother." There was a bite to his words, a hint of disdain, though covered by a false sense of adoration.

"So true," Xander answered wistfully. "I would have us unified, elder brother. I would have us a glorious people, united in purpose and brotherhood. No more divisions, no more petty squabbles over names and titles."

"Xander, you speak lunacy." Alec did not hide the spite in his voice this time, and his sharp motion caused wine to spill over the sleeve of his coat.

The mayor looked at his brother and wondered, yet again, how he could be so cold. Yes, it was a boot knife that had taken his sister-in-law from this life, wielded in the hands of a beggar. But could Alec not see that not all were such? Alec had once been a happier man, a good man. He had hardened. Turned distant and cold.

"I speak of hope, my brother," Xander said as he placed a hand on Alec's shoulder. "I speak of hope and a better tomorrow. To heal the wounds of the past and pave the way for a brighter future. Look about you, my brother. See you not the glories of the day? Steam and coal, powder and steel! It is no longer swords and lances that change the lands, but that of science, ingenuity and mathematics."

"I agree that there are marvelous inventions, dear brother. But I do question your understanding of who funds these things. Know you not that it is them that put the gold in our coffers, them that fund the guilds that

107

produce, and the taxation of this populace that turns the wheel of enlightenment?" Alec waved his hand over the crowds of masked dancers that laughed and moved in fluid motions to the rhythmic music.

"Not so true, brother," Xander said with a shake of his head. "It is such that cast the great cogs, but it is the low-born who crank the grinding wheel. It is their backs that have hauled the burden of progression, their flesh that has felt the whip of modernization. And they are the ones who bear the brunt of change. Do we drink new wine? No, but vintage stock from our grandfathers, while those who hovel around pit fires drink polluted water from troughs and gutters."

"Lesser folk will always accumulate in lesser places."

"Perhaps. But I seek to make Tur'Mor a place of total prosperity."

"I commend your vision, little brother. But you are painfully deceived. Such folk as those will not become great, they don't wish the burden of it. They have chosen their station. They could save and better themselves. They could work their way out of the squalor they so love but chose to stay. We provide factories and plants for them to work in, shops and managers to guide. The Guild Masters and Tinkerers employ thousands, and the wheel turns onward and must not be halted."

"Perhaps."

"Gentlemen!" a booming voice called out as a heavy-footed man made his way around the stairs railing. He wore a wide-brimmed hat with a large plume and had a Tuawtian man behind him, escorted by two guards in silvery breastplates. "I do believe there is an attempt at a robbery this very evening."

"That is a bold claim, Midcouncillor," Alec said with a snarled lip as he looked at the Tuawtian man, who looked oddly calm.

"It is my duty, good sir, as the Midcouncillor over the territories of Southend Tur'Mor, to keep a watchful eye." Aldorian's face drew into a cruel smile as he motioned the guards to bring Belthazer forward. "And this man is a known smuggler and counterfeit. And I know he does not work alone."

***

Aellia's eyes opened. She gasped in air, as if her head had just been pulled out of early spring water. "What in the name of the Second Son of Ordan happened?"

"I think you were poisoned," Tomo whispered. "That or drugged by a small-peckered flop looking for an easy night with you."

"No." Aellia rubbed a clammy finger across her brow. "No, there was something in that house..."

"What are you talking about?"

"Tomo, I felt something unlike anything I have ever felt before. And then the wine...the wine took a hold on me like I was a child."

“I think you’re still drunk.”

“We need to go back.”

“And what good would you be? You couldn’t stand up straight two seconds ago.”

“I’m telling you, something in that house isn’t right! I could feel...it. Whatever it was.” A deep furrow of concern crossed her pale face.

“Aellia, you are worrying me. This isn’t like you!”

“I was in an open room, and there was a case of glass.” Aellia squeezed her eyes shut. Her head was pounding now, and the images of her memory were swirling blurs. “There – there was something else in there. Something...living.” Her voice trailed off, uncertainty abounding. An insatiable need was clawing its way to the forefront of her mind.

Aellia began to run towards the Residency, Tomo rushing after her.

CHAPTER 10: CONSUMING NEED

Muffled voices barely penetrated the thick, plastered wall that separated Felik from the Uppers on the other side. Sweat beaded on his brow, and though the powdered wig and stiff overcoat had been discarded, the passageway was still stifling. The jewel-encrusted hilt of his sword felt too light in Felik's hand, and he found himself wishing for his rapier and sword breaker. What he would do next would require all the luck and finesse he could muster; two things he did not feel he had ever really possessed. But the stakes were too high, far too high for him to back out now. His heart pounded so loudly that the already-muffled voices dissipated in his ears.

Click!

The sounds of heavy cogs turning revibrated through the air.

Creak!

A steel door was being opened, the hinges straining under the weight.

Gasps!

Felik drove his heels into the plaster. Something soft met his feet as they breached the wall. A fat noblewoman crashed into the floor. Men swore and women screamed as halberdiers fell into place, pointing weapons towards the hole in the walls, eyes wide with surprise. Felik's eyes darted across the room in a singular moment of surveyance – this was the only time allotted to gather his wits. The moment of truth was now.

***

"Madam!" a gloved butler exclaimed from in front of the Mayoral Residency. "You cannot – ulgk!"

Aellia struck hard and fast, her hand catching the unsuspecting butler in the throat just under his pointed chin, sending the man crumpling to the steps upon which he stood. Two guards, who had not been paying much heed rushed forward, but Aellia had already slipped into the mansion before they could intercept her. Tomo, on the other hand, was not so lucky. Aellia heard her struggling but did not turn from her goal.

Once through the double-doors, Aellia melted into the populace, pulling her mask back on to conceal her face. She twisted and turned through the crowded room, the smell of wine and perfume nearly overpowering her. The sensation, that of weakness and nausea, was foreign to her, but she shoved back the urge to vomit. That pulsating need that gripped her mind forced her onward. It was the only thing she could focus on.

Aellia, after several minutes of weaving through the throngs of masked Uppers, feeling that she was no longer being followed, began making her way back towards that large room with the...need inside. She did not know what it was she was after, but the absolute need was undeniable. The curving marble staircase seemed to climb upwards for eternity, and every step she took elevated her heart rate ten times over. It felt as if her heart would explode from anticipation, from need.

Towering doors to the right marble steps and a muscular man in a polished breastplate wielding a shiny polearm, barred Aellia from her final goal. Whatever it was that consumed her psyche lay concealed on the other side of those damned doors.

"Halt!" the guard commanded as he lowered his halberd to a defensive position. "None may enter here!"

Aellia placed a gloved fingertip to the tip of the weapon, eyeing the thick-jawed man with a sensuous gaze. "Good man, is this not a party? And why do I feel so alone? Would you not come with me to enjoy the night?" The false innocence in her sultry voice was as alluring as she could manage. The breathiness was a mixture of false intent and all-consuming need that ate at her.

The hard grey eyes of the man narrowed, though his demeanor shifted slightly, his grip lessening on the shaft of the halberd. He cleared his throat gruffly, muttering, "Madam, best be about your way. This room is off limits to all guests."

"Oh, is it now?" Aellia said as she slid her hand down the shaft to meet his own. "And does that mean no one would be disturbing this room?"

The guard's hand was warm to the touch and trembled as she ran a finger over it. His grip slipped on the weapon, letting it clang clumsily to the floor. Aellia gave a slight chuckle as she bent over to grab the halberd, doing so in such a manner as to reveal as much cleavage as possible. As she rose, she blushed, meeting his eyes, which no longer seemed to focus on anything but her.

"You did say that room is off limits to anyone?"

"Uh, erm."

Aellia wrapped her slender fingers around his, placing the shaft against his palm and closing his fingers around the rod, and placed another hand on his chest, leaning so close she could smell the scent of wash soap and shaving cream. By the vein protruding in his neck and the sweat forming just below his steel cap, she knew it was working. Now, just to get him inside tha-

"Thief! Thief in the hall!"

The booming voice shook the guard back to his senses. Aellia's sensual smile turned sour. The moment had passed, the ruse was up. Aellia sighed. *Oh well*, she thought, *violence is better than petty sex. But damn it, couldn't Felik have waited two more bloody minutes?* The guard ripped his hand from Aellia's and began trying to leverage the polearm against her, but she had backed him too close to the door. The butt of the weapon hit the door, and Aellia swiftly placed the edge of her hand against the shaft near the head, turning it away from her. The guard's eyes widened in surprise. Aellia winked.

Dropping to the floor in a fluid motion, Aellia spun on her back, placing one foot behind his right knee, the other on his shin. The popping sound of a dislocation rang out as the guard yelped in agony. Next, Aellia drove her heel into his groin, doubling the man over as she slid backwards across the polished marble floor away from him.

From her current vantage point, through the banisters, she could see a very disheveled Felik running from a dozen or so men with weapons drawn. His scabbard held no blade, and his hands were empty. Six other men in breastplates were rushing up the steps towards Aellia. The night was a bust. Necessity told her it was time to escape. Need would have to wait, despite her biting teeth of desire.

Aellia flung herself from the upper balcony, landing on a fat man who was lounging on a triclinium of floral print. The triple-chinned man let out a yelp of pain as she crashed into him, bloodying his upper lip, mustache, and nose where his silver goblet slammed into his unsuspecting face. Despite his girth, Aellia, too, let out a grunt of pain. The upper balcony was much higher than she had expected, but what else was she to do? Besides, hurting another Upper was worth it, and the look on his teary-eyed face made her laugh as she stumbled to her feet.

"Apologies," Aellia said, reaching up her skirts to retrieve her concealed dagger. "That was not so ladylike of me." She hurled the weapon, taking the guard nearest Felik in the face just as he was about to grab his arm. Two other guards stumbled over his crumpling body.

"Run, damn it!" Felik cursed, snatching Aellia's arm as he rushed towards the entry doors.

Belthazer swung a wooden chair into another guard as he met the two fleeing crew members, bursting out of a side corridor. His bare chest was far more toned than Aellia would have guessed. From the side room, Aellia made out the face of a very flustered midcouncillor holding onto what was once Belthazer's outer garments. Two other men lay on the floor, the upward facing boots blocking their features, though Aellia guessed they were those lackeys that always seemed to follow Aldorian around.

"Belthazer," Felik exclaimed, a jolt of relief in his voice, though his eyes fixated on the nearing doors that led out of the Residency.

"Damn this place," Belthazer swore through gasps of breath.

The moon was high and bright, clearly illuminating the courtyard in front of the Mayoral Residency. Two guards lay sprawled out on the marble steps, along with a seated butler who was holding a bloodied nose and swearing. People were running about, this way and that, while gunners and archers fired shots towards a fat man atop a stolen carriage. Arrows thudded as they struck the carriage, and lead shots splintered wood upon collision, though most missed. Guns were not nearly as reliable as arrows or swords, howbeit far more intimidating. But if, by some misfortune, a lead shot was to take you, it would tear limbs away or blast cavities through the flesh, and what was far more dangerous were the infections if not treated properly.

Aellia did not focus on these things but upon the open door of the already fleeing carriage. The three crew members dodged and swerved through screaming Uppers until they lunged into the carriage, slamming the door shut behind them. More shots echoed, more arrows struck, the heads of some penetrating the ride.

"About blasted time." Tomo looked more relieved than frustrated. A single cut was leaking crimson blood on her pale cheek.

Aellia stared at the wound, thinking not for the first time how beautiful she was. Reality did not allow for many moments like this, and Aellia could not help the sly smile that slid across her trembling lips.

"And what in the name of the Fallen One's own damnation caused you to go back into the cluster of a mess?" Tomo snapped, catching Aellia's glance, her flushed cheeks going red.

"Damn it all!" Felik screamed, kicking the carriage. "We are royally f-"

Boom!

The deafening explosion upended the carriage, tossing each of the members of Felik's crew around like ragdolls. A series of rolls, accompanied by splintering wood and grinding stone, disoriented Aellia in a way she had never felt before. Colors whirled about her as glass windows shattered and screams filled the night air. An eternity seemed to pass in those few, terrible moments.

When the carriage finally came to a jarring halt, Aellia's body ached, and her ears rang in sharp agony. A shard of carriage, a blood-soaked splinter of lacquered wood, protruded from her thigh. Raising her head up tenderly, she began searching around the wreckage for her friends. Lights seemed to meet in odd streams in her field of vision, both fracturing and swirling together, like a trickling mountain stream that met a raging river of muddied water.

"Tomo?" Her voice was raspy, and her lungs burned as she tried to call out.

The moon, bright and silvery, hung heavily in the night sky. Aellia could almost feel its gentle beams caress her flesh. She shook her head, driving away the disorientation. She would not be taken captive in a state of delusion.

"Felik?" she croaked as she drew herself up to a full stance. Her thigh screamed under the weight of her body, and in a moment of pure idiocy and against her better knowledge, she yanked the shiv of wood from her leg, sending a stream of blood spurting from the open wound. A scream of pain reverberated through the night, and for the first time, Aellia realized she could hear again.

Men's voices were calling out commands as other voices were screaming in terror and confusion. Heavy footfalls were moving this way and that, pouring out from the twisted iron bars of what was once the gates of the Mayoral Residency.

Did they fire a cannon at us? Aellia thought in horror as she looked at the warped gates and smoldering spit of roadway just outside where the carriage had been struck.

Run!

Aellia remembered that she was one of those these men were searching for, and if they had been willing to fire a cannon on them, what would they do if they caught her? Reflexively, she pulled a few cords around the waist of her dress, allowing both the fabric and the wooden hoops to fall away from her, leaving her in naught but her corset and small clothes. After sloppily binding her leg with a torn cloth from her skirts, Aellia darted off into the night, not taking a second look back for her friends.

***

Felik flung open the doors of the Loft with his free hand, the one that had only been saved from the flames by those stupid gloves he wore. Those stupid, lifesaving gloves. With the other arm, he supported a bloodied yet living Felohme. Worried, hollowed eyes darted about the room, searching for anyone who could have made it out alive. He was less than hopeful to find anyone; that explosion had been gruesome and totally unexpected. Having been flung through one of the carriage's glass windows during the initial blast, Felik had watched in horror as the carriage, filled with his team, his crew, turned end over end. Felohme had been driving the cart, and he, too, had been tossed away with the initial impact, and having struck one of the horses, managed to walk away with little more than a head wound and a bruised back.

Concern began to manifest itself in the form of hate. Dark, bitter hatred. It was Aldorian's fault; he was the one who had forced Felik into

114

this. He was the one who had placed this impossible task on them. It was he who was to blame…it was he. Felik.

Felohme steadied himself, slowly walking away from Felik's embrace, as if he was answering Felik's own guilt with his actions.

It was Felik's fault, and he knew it. It had been his pride that had got them mixed up with the midcouncillor in the first place. It had been Felik's own pride at hiding his past from the Crew, even at the worst costs. They weren't trained professionals. They had no way to pull off something like this. It had been one thing to steal and scavenge from the upper crust of the Ordiatian lords and ladies. But such a feat as this was asinine.

"I never saw Tornak."

The words cut through Felik's self-loathing like a hot knife. He had seen Aellia and the others in the carriage and had Felohme next to him right now. But Tornak, young, innocent Tornak, he had not seen him either. Not since the beginning of the night.

Felohme's round face was drooping in weariness, muddled with dirt and ashes. "Maybe the young fay'ak made it okay. Better than us even." He feigned a small smile, but it vanished quickly.

"I failed us," Felik bleated as his back hit the wall. He slid to the floor in grief, muttering, "I killed them. I killed them all."

"Felik," Felohme said with tenderness in his deep, gentle voice. "This was not your doing. You did not kill them, my friend."

"How can you say that?" Felik answered, lifting his eyes to meet the Tuawtian man's own. Tears streamed down Felik's once hardened face. "I forced this upon you, the Crew. And they are dead. It was my insatiable need that drove us to this."

"Then, my friend," Felohme said as he placed a meaty hand on Felik's shoulder, kneeling down to face him with an untimely smile. "Then, we are haunted by ghosts, and we need to pray to Uuradan for His Holy Flames to cleanse us."

"What?" Felik asked, his voice more biting than he meant.

Felohme's eyes darted to the still open doors, and a twinkle of delight danced in them. Felik shot up from the ground, dragging his shirtsleeve over his eyes to dry them. Felohme rose next to him, placing his hand on Felik's back as they peered out into the night.

Belthazer was just coming into view, as no streetlamps had remained lit this evening, carrying Tomo in his arms. Tomo, however, seemed to be conscious, for she clung to his neck with sure arms.

Felik rushed out into the night towards the two of them, taking no thought of his appearance. He grabbed Tomo under the left arm as Belthazer lowered her.

"I am fine," she muttered. "Just dizzy. I couldn't see well enough for a moment, and then Belthazer wouldn't put me down the rest of the way, even though I told him I was fine." Despite the reproof in her voice, she could not totally mask the adoration.

"Did either of you see Aellia?" Felik asked, not letting go of Tomo as they walked back into the doors of the Loft.

Tomo's dark eyes closed tight, grief striking her features.

"No," Belthazer answered. "No, we did not. Nor Tornak. I fear they did not make it."

"Do not give up hope, zealot," Felohme chided, though there was no true scorn in his words.

The remaining Crew members made their way back into the Loft's oaken doors, faces somber and eyes downcast. True, there was an air of thankfulness for those who had survived, but a dark shadow of death was cast upon their minds, and the bitter feelings of loss for Tornak and Aellia hung heavy in the air.

Felik helped Tomo to a chair while Felohme and Belthazer gathered kindling and logs to start a fire in one of the many hearths that lined the large, open room, all of which were scorched and unkempt. Silently, the two worked until warm flames cast beams of dancing light across the dusty floors and hangings that reached from the ceiling downward, like spiderwebs of multicolored fabrics.

Time passed slowly, unnervingly so, and despite the crackling flames, a deafening silence filled the corridor with an unnatural heaviness. It was Belthazer that broke first, turning from the kneeling position he had taken in front of the flames where he had been praying to his god, Uuradan the Dragon.

"What does that midcouncillor hold over your head?" he asked quietly, not much more than a whisper, though the words shattered the silence like broken glass, cutting Felik to the core.

Felik did not answer, but stared absently into the flames across the room, straight through the now rising zealot.

"He was who you met with in the tavern," Belthazer continued, his voice growing harder. "He was the one who put you to this. Why?"

More silence.

"When you found me, I was near death and owed you my life. I have paid that debt this night. It was he who betrayed us. And I want to know why! I demand to know why!"

Tomo and Felohme both glared back and forth between the two as Belthazer neared Felik, unsure what to make of the confrontation. Their watchful eyes did not dissuade Belthazer in the slightest. He hovered over Felik, dark eyes burning with questions.

"Will you not answer me?"

"I am sorry..." His words were less than a whisper, a fragile plea.

"I do not seek an apology," Belthazer answered coldly. "I need an answer. I need it! I need to know why, Felik. Why?"

"Need..." Felik muttered, raising his eyes to meet Belthazer's. There was a fire in those grey eyes, a burning, seething hatred that had not been there before. "Need is why, Belthazer. Need drove me to this."

"You speak straight to me, friend of my past." Belthazer pointed a long finger to his bare chest, directly over his heart. "You answer me now!"

"All of this was from need!" Felik barked out, far louder than expected. This caused Belthazer to stumble back in surprise. Felik drew himself up to his full height. "Each of you, you came to me under need. But my need, my need was deeper. I have lied to you all. I have lied because I must lie. But I will speak the truth now, for we are no more after this night. My need is dead. I am dead."

"What does the midcouncillor have to do with you?" Belthazer pressed, regaining his bearings. "With us now?"

"I was a captain in the Ordiatian Army, commander of men," Felik answered, every word dripping in bitterness.

The Crew looked baffled. They had guessed he had been a soldier, perhaps even a squad leader, but a captain? Felik met each of their eyes in sequence, affirming his words with a hollow stare that did not lie.

"It was under my banner that the battle known as the Folly of the Fourth took place. One thousand and twenty-one men died that day, Marcel Moretriov with them."

The Folly of the Fourth Regiment was perhaps one of the greatest blunders in Ordiatian military history. It was supposed to have been the battle that ended the Calun Conflict. It had turned into a bloodbath where Ordiatian troops were slaughtered by the hundreds and thousands. It had tipped the Conflict into full out war and lost the ground of a hundred years of negotiations and treaties.

A young captain had spit in the eye of decorum. He pressed too hard against a foe strung far too tight, a foe ready to strike back with a terrible vengeance. His foe's unaccounted forces had lain hidden throughout the fractured and stony Dreadridge Mountains, awaiting a chance to fall upon the prideful and unprepared. One thousand lances rushed a force of footmen. A dream to crush the rebellion and end the conflict turned into a nightmare of untold proportions.

"By Uuradan's Eternal Flame!" Belthazer swore, an uncommon thing for the once holy man to do. He drew crossed palms over his chest in a swift motion, and then brought the tips of his fingers to his lips to offer a silent prayer of protection.

"Aldorian found me out last harvest season," Felik continued, face dead and emotionless. "His father had been a Knight, and he had seen me in numerous War Councils. His father fell among the dead. He was seventy-three. Andelor was my advisor and confidant; he was my friend. He should never have placed that lance in his hand that dark day."

"By the gods," Tomo muttered.

"No. There are no gods out there," Felik spat. "There is nothing but death. All I wanted was to be left alone. To be forgotten until I die in peace."

"But you are not alone," Belthazer countered. "You have dragged us all into this. I do not wish to die; I have no such aspirations."

"You should have told us, Felik," Tomo cut in, betrayal on her face. "You should have let us know. We trusted you."

"Let you know what? That I am disavowed?" Felik snarled the response, though it was more at himself than towards Tomo. "If word got out that Captain Marcel lived, then I would face a fate worse than the death I deserve. To the world, Marcel was carried captive into Calun and slain by their bloody king."

"And what of us, then?" Tomo continued. "This Aldorian knows that we are connected, tied together under you. Theft is one thing, but I won't dangle from the gallows for your pride."

"It is too late for that," Felik scoffed. "Did you think we would ever be free after stealing the King's Jewel?"

"You said we were to use it to buy our way away from this place. We were going to escape and live a life away from the running and hiding."

"You've doomed us to a fate beyond prisons and gallows," Belthazer interjected. "My people are not so warmly welcomed in this place. We will be made an example for all to see, beaten and tortured."

The door to the Loft slammed open, wood crashing against the stone wall. A figure stood in the doorway, the firelight mixing with the moonbeams that cast shadows that darkened her face, but there was no mistaking Aellia. Her body was covered by nothing but her small clothes, her frosty-white hair disheveled and caked with mud. Blood besmirched her face, and her left leg was red from the wrap wound around her thigh.

"I will kill them," Aellia swore. "I will kill every last one of them!"

The Crew looked stunned, eyes bulging with a mixture of fear, excitement and confusion. Tomo moved first, rushing away from the group and throwing her arms around Aellia. She smelled worse than she looked. Acrid smoke had clung to her clothes, choking Tomo as she held her close in her arms.

Aellia, startled by the uncommon display of affection, placed an awkward arm around Tomo. She was crying. Why was she crying? She had almost died a dozen times, why would Tomo find this one any different?

The other members of the Crew did not rush to meet her. They did not even move. Felohme had an unusual gravity to his face and Belthazer looked livid. Felik, the always stoic leader of the Crew, looked utterly defeated. She could see that he was relieved by her arrival, but there was a darkness in his eyes that had not been present before.

"What in the name of Ordan's sons is going on here?" Aellia asked, pushing Tomo to the side, limping towards Felik.

"Felik," Belthazer said the name with hesitation. "You should answer her."

Aellia stepped closer, eyes darting between the two men. One hot with rage, the other dead and cold. "What happened?"

"Aldorian sold us out," Felik answered.

Tomo was behind Aellia, close by. Felohme looked so crestfallen that it nearly caused her heart to break without reason. Belthazer was so angry. She had never seen him this way. She had never seen any of them this way. Confusion gnawed at her.

"Aellia," Felik continued. "I am not who you think I am."

"What are you talking about?"

Belthazer shook his head, rubbing his forehead with his hand.

"Unless you plan on telling me that you stole that jewel, I don't really give a damn who you are or what you've done," Aellia stated. "I don't give a damn about any of your pasts. Is this what this is? We get knocked down and we need to sit around moaning about who we are? What have we done?"

"Aellia," Belthazer interrupted, "he is a liar and a fraud. No, he was a captain and an Upper who betrayed his vows!"

"Vows?" Aellia's hardened eyes could have cut steel as they flashed to meet Belthazer's. "You speak of vows and breaking vows?"

Belthazer looked as if he had been slapped in the face. Aellia's words had struck true.

"He's not wrong." Felik sighed. "I am what he says. If you would jus-"

"Just what? Hear another's history from another man? Felik, you took me in, I was sick with the White Fever." She grabbed her hair as she said it, the only residual effect that the plague had left upon her. "So, you betrayed a bunch of soldiers who seek gain to off others? So what? What does it matter?"

"She is not wrong," Felohme said, stepping between Belthazer and Felik, placing a hand on both their shoulders. "We are all who we are."

"So, that is it?" Belthazer questioned. "We just let this go?"

"No..." Felik said slowly. "No. I let you all down. I will turn myself in, I will bargain for your lives with my own."

"On Gallea's name, you will not!" Aellia snapped. "That jewel gets put under lock and key for the next year, ain't no question there. Not one thing we can do once it rests after the parade."

"What are you suggesting?" Felik asked, his watery eyes appearing somewhat perplexed.

"If we are all dead anyways," Aellia scoffed, "why not give them Uppers one last middle finger? We'll get that stone. We'll take it out from under their prideful noses. We'll do it, not 'cause it will help us, but because it will be a final slap in their faces."

"We can disperse, we can hide," Belthazer argued.

"No," Felohme said with a shake of his bald head, "too many saw our faces. There will be warrants out for all of us. And I do like a good insult."

"And how do you propose we do that?" Belthazer questioned combatively.

"The parade," Felik answered. "We take it at the parade. We'll take it, because the last place they would think we would be is out in the open, in the eyes of the public."

"And what's in it for us?" Belthazer asked scornfully.

"While I like the idea of the middle finger," Felik said, shooting a subtle smile to Aellia, "other than that, the bloody thing could be a right nice bargaining chip. We could use it to buy passage out of the port and off to Galacia in secrecy."

"We would be arrested on the spot."

"No, Tomo, we wouldn't be. The prize for returning the jewel would pay the dockmaster a fortune and could be used as hush money to quiet the embarrassment."

"You put too many eggs in one basket, Felik," Belthazer ridiculed. "If one were to break, then we're all dead."

"Do you not think Aldorian knows where we are? I will watch the doors tonight, but if we do not act fast, we will be dead by nightfall tomorrow."

"I doubt the fat blowhard knows we're here, not yet. Though he'll be looking for us. That being said, I believe we can hold out a week or two." Felik's voice was growing with resolution. "We can make it to the parade."

"You have not answered how we will take the jewel," Tomo scoffed, with arms now folded. Though, her eyes did shine with the light of desire.

"A distraction, within a foil, within a play," Felik said with a smile that was quickly widening. "I do not ask you all to forgive me, nor to like me, but I am asking you to trust me."

"If it is death or chance, I do like to gamble." Felohme laughed a full belly laugh. "I will follow again, my friend."

"I want to kill that hook-nosed prick, Aldorian," Aellia spat. "I want that, and I am in."

"I don't like the odds," Tomo added reluctantly, moving her eyes from Aellia to Felik. "However, odds of escape are better than certainty of death."

"One last time." Belthazer sighed with resignation. "If we escape, I will take my leave from this company. I am done with this."

"Understood," Felik answered the Tuawtian. Then, turning about to face them all, he began to unfurl a plan forming before his very eyes. "First, we will need eyes in high and low places alike. Secondly, I'll need my steel and an old cloak. And lastly, we'll need a distraction. A very big distraction."

Aellia's eyes lit with fiery hatred and glee. She would get her revenge on these Uppers. She would get her revenge at last.

CHAPTER 11: FRAGMENTS OF TRUTH

The sun was still hiding, the moon's light the only source of illumination, when Darius awoke the next morning. Darius had not slept well, his mind still heavy with the discussion from the day before. To make matters worse, his dreams were that cursed mountain and blasted forests, and of the unnatural, thunderous voice calling out, commanding him to *Find them! Find them! Find them, or blood shall rain!* That place, and of the snowcapped mountains of Morr, where he had fought for his life against Diabhail and the Blood Queen. He was forced to relive every painful memory, unable to force himself awake. The dull throbbing of a battered body, the sharp pain of an obsidian dagger tearing his side, and the searing sensation of the curse that Mireya had left branded upon his chest. All berated his body, his mind, his entire essence, until he jolted awake.

Darius rolled out of bed and crouched on the floor, beginning his morning routine of stretching and exercise. His body moved seamlessly through the advanced motions of what looked like a surreal dance. He was powerful, yet graceful, each movement exact and pristine. He lowered to his hands, lifting the weight of his whole body into the air with ease, pressing himself several times, until beads of sweat began to roll down his brow.

Exercise always made him feel better. It grounded him, allowing him to focus. It was real, tangible. It was his body that proved to his mind that he was in control. Subconsciously he began to hum an unfamiliar tune. It was the melody the priests were chanting the day before. He dropped his feet to the floor with perfect fluidity, the bare skin silent against the wood paneling.

His chest, patched with black hair save for the white handprint, protruded a little more than normal due to the heightened blood flow. His torso was firm, every bit of him built powerfully. He looked like one of the statues in the courtyards, if not so lean. Yet, there was a difference between him and the marble figures. His body was covered with a myriad of scars and markings. His flesh had become a tapestry of war, of violence and pain, though none stood out more than the white, shimmering handprint burned into his chest.

Darius grabbed a cotton towel he had set out the night before and wiped the sweat from his forehead, taking in measured breaths to steady his pulse. Next, he took up the folded clothes from the nightstand and placed them in his satchel, turning the brass clasp to protect them from the light drizzle outside. Darius pulled on his boots and threw a loose-fitting tunic over his body, keeping his lounging pants on.

Darius left his room as quietly as he could, shutting the door gently. He then took the familiar path through the backstreets to the public bathhouse. He ran swiftly, his long black hair fluttering behind him. Darius hated to run. But it brought such clarity, and he found a sickening vigor to it. Running was the closest thing to a fight he could find, for he truly struggled at every breath after only a few measures of distance. He always pushed himself, and today would not be the exception.

There were no other patrons at the bathhouse when Darius arrived. He smiled through the huffs. Another bonus of an early rise. Darius had nothing to be ashamed of, but he did not enjoy bathing naked with other men. Plus, the water would be much cleaner at this hour than near the end of the day when most bathed.

The bathhouse was an open-fronted villa, the nicest building in all of Southend. It had a circular entryway, large columns of marble holding up a stone eave, not so dissimilar to the one at the Sanctuary, though far less grandiose and decorated. From the entry, the hall forked into two. The men to the left and the women to the right. The baths were large rectangular pools, each with a fountain in the center thereof. Aqueducts fed fresh water to Tur'Mor from the north, and a series of underground pumps and pipes pushed the water through the city. This thing fascinated Darius, and despite his many qualms with the attitudes and traditions of the Ordiatians, their plumbing was not one of them.

Darius slunk into the warm water and stared into the starry immense, the sky open above him as there were no roofs directly over the baths themselves. He drew in a deep breath and plunged his head under the surface of the clear liquid. Bubbles ran past his cheeks as he pushed the air from his lungs.

His mind raced as he swam. Lap after lap, he pounded deeper to the words of Elcon. *"Don't talk about your...unique ability...to anyone. I will come to you as soon as I can, I promise. But you cannot mention this to anyone, do you understand?"*

And what of them? he wondered as he swam. *Why is everyone here so against people who can Bind or Touch? Surely there must be others here? This place is massive! I have never seen half as many people in my life.* The questions rushed past him as the bubbles of air did, rising to the surface and popping away.

The sky was turning a majestic purple hue, the sun beginning to rise above the glistening walls, when he reluctantly left the bath. There was a basin near the pool, which was filled with strange liquid that, when rubbed together, would form suds. Darius had seen other men use this to wash their hair, so he did the same. It had a smell of lye and lavender, though the sharper undertone was overpowered by the floral notes. He rinsed quickly and then toweled himself off.

A small group of robed men walked into the pool area, but when they spotted Darius, they turned into one of the many open rooms, continuing their conversation. Darius did not seem to mind and dressed himself in fresh clothing, placing the lounging britches and dull tunic into the leather satchel. He then left the bathhouse, walking back to Ranun's Place feeling much better, mind sharpened and body honed. He needed to apologize to the old priest; he had been too harsh with him the day before. That was the first thing he meant to do when he arrived back.

When Darius did arrive, he found Ranun out front, cleaning tables after morning meals. He was almost to the old priest when a horse-drawn carriage came rushing down the muddied street. Four large horses, all of which were pearly white, though now spattered with brownish globs of mud, pulled the elaborate carriage. The carriage was small, only large enough for two or three people on the inside, a driver donning a large-brimmed hat with a golden plume seated in the front box. It had large wheels with wooden spokes, gold trim, and white paint. It was a quaint ride with purple curtains pulled over glass windows, which acted as a barrier, blocking the view of who was inside.

The carriage came to an abrupt stop, parking in between Darius and Ranun's Place, blocking Darius from reaching his destination. The single door swung open, revealing an interior of green fabric with gold-colored seats. A man sat on one of the two benches, legs crossed, reading what appeared to be a large book, leatherbound of an amber hue. He wore flowing green robes, far more vibrant than the faded looking interior of the carriage. Darius could not make out the man's face but could tell by his long features and wrinkled left hand bearing a signet ring of gold with a large emerald, that this was Elcon.

Elcon put down his overly large book, which revealed a silent companion sitting next to him. The man was dressed in all white, face wrapped with cloth, save his eyes, and a hood pulled over his head. He wore a leather jerkin of grey, the only non-white article of clothing on his body, which split below the belt and rested on his thighs. His legs were covered in tight white pants and calf-length boots. He did not turn his head when Elcon arose but sat motionless as the high priest stepped out of the carriage.

"Young Master Darius," Elcon called out as he stepped into the courtyard from his carriage, "your timing is impeccable."

"High Priest," Darius answered with a slight nod, eyes still searching the white-clad man, his sword holding Darius's attention.

"It is good you have been made ready for the day," Elcon said as he brushed the front of his finely stitched emerald robes, the needlework of gold producing an ivy pattern running down the hems and sleeves.

"Anointed," Ranun called out with an air of reverence to the title. "I did not expect you so soon. I would have prepared a meal."

"Ranun, old friend," Elcon said with a warm smile as he walked to the portly man, nodding his head in a bow. "You honor me too much with your kindness. Though, it is for the best you had not. I do not have time to linger, I am afraid. Our emissary from the north needs to accompany me as quickly as possible."

"Accompany?" Darius asked as he stepped towards the two priests. "And to where, exactly, am I going?"

"To the Sanctuary, of course," Elcon answered with a cock of an eyebrow, as if to question Darius. "Is this not why you came to our fair city?"

"Ah! Yes, yes!" Ranun said, wiping his hands on his dirty apron. "Young Master Darius's chor- duties, that is, can wait for another time."

"Well then, Priest Ranun can take your wash-bundle, Master Darius, and you can accompany me. There is much work to be done."

Darius looked rather confused, but before he could come up with an answer, Ranun had taken his laundry and bid him a good day. Elcon was already climbing into the carriage when he turned about, and the driver was holding the door to usher Darius inside.

Once inside, Darius took his seat across from Elcon and the white-clad swordsman. Elcon had already picked up his book and crossed a leg over his other knee. There was a smile on the old priest's face that puzzled Darius. It was not a cynical smile, nor was it mischievous or malicious. No, it was a smile of knowing. The man knew something, and Darius was sure of it.

"Why the show?" Darius asked flatly. "You could have just called me to the carriage."

"Master Darius," Elcon returned in a smooth, level voice. "You are to be seen as an emissary from our Northern Chapel, not a street rat to be bundled away with a sack over your head. Presentation is everything. This city thrives on precedence and procedure. You can no longer act as a vagabond, but as a man of the Parsonary. I had thought Ranun had explained more of this to you? No matter... Well, just sit back and enjoy the ride, Master Darius. There are a good many things that we need to discuss, though this is not the time nor the place to do so. Remember, appearances are often more so the truth we want others to see, than the reality we intend."

The carriage started forward, moving far smoother and much faster, than Ranun's wagon had the day before. Neither spoke the entire ride. Darius would have normally been thankful for this. Under current circumstances, it left him feeling nervous and vulnerable. The carriage came to a stop as the driver called, "Whoa," out to the horses. The slender man in the wide-brimmed hat jumped down and lowered the steps, and then opened the door with a bow. Elcon motioned for Darius to exit first, and then he followed behind. They were back in front of the Sanctuary of Ordan, her four spires glistening in the midday light.

"Come now, Darius," Elcon said as he rose, "there is much to discuss, and time is far spent."

Darius eyed the old man, if only for a moment, searching him over before stepping forward. He could tell there was sincerity in the high priest's voice, another perk of his unique abilities. He could sense the rise in heartbeat or rush of blood if someone were lying. Elcon was as tranquil as a mountain lake. Darius climbed out of the carriage and followed Elcon up the stone steps and into the Sanctuary of Ordan. The white-garbed man filed out silently behind, never more than a step away from Elcon.

Elcon led the party to the three hanging tapestries in the back. The right tapestry was purple with golden trim. The central and largest of the wall hangings was crafted from white silk and had green embroidery around the entire panel. In the center thereof was a depiction of an island in the sky with three mountains rising from its heart, and waterfalls flowing down to a river on either side. That river ran through a massive continent, that of Ethrea, and then drained into a great pit at the base thereof. The last was a blue cloth with a sickle striking a stone of white, three rings above it, one of red, one of blue and the other of black, each interlaced and twirling about the other.

"I have given my whole life to the study of the Church and its sacred teachings. What I am about to show you could change everything..." Elcon said slowly, drawing out the words as if he felt unsure whether or not he should say them. "Darius, I am going to show you something sealed beyond the span of time, kept away from all but those of the Holy Council of the Church. I implore you to keep an open mind and to not judge too harshly."

Elcon drew back the curtain, though there was no door as before, just a smooth wall formed from cold marble. Elcon pulled out a necklace from underneath the neck of his robes. It had an amulet in the shape of Ordan's hammer, formed from gold, with a sapphire set in the head of the hammer. However, there was something strange about that sapphire – it shone with vibrant light. Real light, just as the flames of a fire.

"You have magic?"

"My son, there is no such thing as magic."

"Then, what is that?" Darius said, pointing a finger at the sacred emblem about Elcon's neck.

"This is a Ra'el Aund. A divine instrument imbued with Everlight, drawn from the Source. It is not magic, my son; it is a sacred tool that allows the Anointed to perform small miracles."

"What do you mean?"

"You talk of 'magic' as if it is mundane," Elcon answered with a subtle smile. "Surprised I had access to it, but not that such things existed."

"I understood that such things are banned in Tur'Mor. That people claim them a myth, no more than folktales," Darius returned, "but I never said I disbelieved in it."

"Magic is far too limited a term for what we have access to," Elcon answered. "Magic is curses and spells. This is true and holy power. Gifted only to the chosen and the Blessed. The people see it and know that it is of the gods, and it fortifies their faith."

The high priest pressed the amulet against the wall. Blue light flooded from the hammer bleeding across the large marble blocks, sinking into a series of once imperceptible crevasses. They creaked and moaned, light dripping from what now appeared to be a small door of intricate design, protruding from the marble. Elcon then opened the door, revealing a downward spiral of steps, the walls studded with small blue gemstones casting out faint, wisping light. Darius gaped in awe at the glistening gemstones.

"Come now, there is still so much more to discuss."

Elcon headed down the spiral, Darius following close behind, neither saying a word. There was a reverent silence to the air as they walked down the steps, descending ever deeper into the Sanctuary. At the bottom of the stairs stood a second door, one that had no handle or knob, only a small grate and a knocker of brass.

Thrice Elcon tapped the knocker, allowing the sharp pings to resonate in the small room. He then gave a heavy knock after a brief moment of silence. The metal plate behind the brass lattice slid open, though nothing was visible save a stream of yellow light.

"Speak truth..." The words came from behind the door.

"And let the earth hear it," Elcon responded.

"And let all bear witness," both spoke in unison.

The sound of gears turning filled the confined space. Bolts moved up, followed by the low creaking of metal and stone. Darius stiffened. His fingers curled into tight fists and his nostrils flared. As he drew a deep breath, his eyes caught Elcon's. The high priest returned the glare with a droll smile. He then placed a gentle hand on Darius's shoulder and winked.

The door began to open slowly. However, it did not swing outwardly or inwardly, but slid down into the granite floor. The room which opened to view was not a large room. On the left side of the room was an unusual apparatus with cogs and chains. This device was what raised and lowered the trick door, a door that was over a foot thick and composed of both wood and metal layered together. Four polished torches lit the room, illuminating a solitary man dressed identically to Elcon standing across from the doorway.

Two men besides the priest were standing in the room. They wore tightly-wrapped white clothes. A thin cloth was pulled over their faces and covered their hair, allowing only their eyes to be visible. They wore all white, save a padded vest of ashy grey and leather gauntlets with steel plating. The vests had protruding, stiff shoulder pads and a simple, stitched emblem of a hand over the left breast. Across their backs were two single-edged swords, such as Darius had never seen. Their eyes seemed fixed on Darius, unflinching.

"The Aluth," Elcon whispered in Darius's ear while nodding towards the two men with swords. "They are the servants of Orrum His Superior, executors of His holy will. They are friends here; there is no need to fear."

"I fear no man," Darius replied with hushed confidence as he locked eyes with one.

"Well, these are more than men. They are Blessed, endowed with grace, and commissioned to fulfil the Holy Mouthpiece's commandment. They guard the monasteries and the temples of the land, charged with keeping truth and protecting the humble servants of Ordan and Gallea," Elcon explained as he and Darius crossed the small room. Elcon bowed his head in respect towards the two guards as he passed them.

As Elcon approached the second priest, he extended his left hand, taking the left hand of the other. They then touched the other's mouth with two fingers and then their own foreheads. The priest stepped through the doorway, bowing his head, and turned up the stairway. One of the Aluth stepped up and started turning the large wheel, pulling the door up slowly. The other turned and faced Elcon. The Aluth touched both of his eyes, using his first two fingers, and then lowered his hand into an open palm waist high. Elcon bowed in response to the Aluth's gesture, who then in turn nodded as a reply.

"The Aluth have taken a vow of silence. They have no name, no voice, and no other will save that of the Superior," Elcon stated as he rose gingerly to his feet. "There are no men more honorable than those of the Aluth. They have guarded my family and this land for twelve generations."

Turning towards the other Aluth, who had finished sealing the first door, Elcon gestured to the wall behind them. Both Aluth pulled their swords from their backs. The blades were masterfully crafted, yet not after the manner of normal blades. The swords had ridges along the edge of the blades, unique patterns that looked almost key-like in design.

The Aluth drove their swords into the small slits in the wall. They slid in perfectly. The soft grate of metal sliding across stone was the only audible sound in the room. In unison, they turned their hilts. Then, to Darius's continued astonishment, the wall cracked along the stonework, revealing a second hidden door.

Elcon used the same key used to open the first door and placed it into a secret keyhole that had appeared in the crack.

"This way," Elcon said as he walked through the opening passage. "I believe I have found at least one answer here."

Darius followed Elcon into a cavernous room, crafted out of what appeared to be an underground cave. The columns that held up the ceiling were not crafted of marble but rather formed from stalactites and stalagmites that fused together. A series of small streams ran through the cavern floor, draining into the unknown. Man-made bridges linked several paths together, allowing for ease when walking by the small waterways. These paths led through a gallery of statues, artifacts of gold and precious metals, pottery of what seemed to span several cultures and times, all of which were in neat rows. There were dozens of wood shelves, each full of leatherbound books bearing ornate etchings and calligraphy.

Past these, in the center of the perfectly square room, rose a round pedestal illuminated by pallid green light. The platform was unnaturally smooth and formed from what looked to be radiant glass. Atop the rounded dais was a lone podium with a single, golden book atop it. The light which bathed the edifice came from a vent in the lofted ceiling, carved straight up through the rock. The vent had a large, flat, glasslike emerald placed over it. The gem seemed no thicker than a sheet of parchment, refracting the light from above into shimmering green.

"This is a sacred place. Few have ever stepped foot in this holy room," Elcon said as he used the candle to light a large pyre. Rising flames licked the musty air, light illuminated the dark corridor. "These are all that remain of the great city Vialhael, her towers cast into the sea in the Great Desolation. Those men who lived there would come to be known as our forefathers, the Ordiatians of old. They entered into a covenant with Ordan to be true to him evermore; thus, this great city was established atop the ashes of the lost."

"Why bring me here?"

"Because I believe you are more than meets the eye," said Elcon as he walked towards the center of the room. "At first, I believed you to be a drunkard, or perhaps deceived. But then you said something . . . something that has been lost to the memories of mankind."

"And what is that?" Darius queried.

Elcon did not respond but just walked forward. The two stepped up onto the circular dais where the book of golden pages, linked by four brass rings, sat atop a pedestal of white marble with gold veins. Elcon walked solemnly over to the sacred text, admiring the glyphs that were hewn into the plates. The symbols were ornate and well crafted. It was apparent that much care had gone into preserving this sacred work.

"This is *Prymus Naan Zya*, The First Account of Man. It is the only text left from Vialhael, the City of Ordan," Elcon said in a reverent tone as he delicately flipped through the book. "This recants the Journey of the Ellitheor: their coming down from Vanherran with the ancient Daulkaefar. Their journey over the great sea of the sky. The transformation of Ethrea from an unlivable wilderness inhabited by wild dragons and beasts to a rich and prosperous land. It also tells of the betrayal of Ordan by his own flesh. His two daughters, Morgana and Moranna, the Fallen Ones, sought a way to rival Ordan's Everlight and fell into darkness. The final battle where Ordan used Ethra to drive open the Dimdreal, casting his own daughters into this pit. Ending in the ascent of the Ellitheor back to Vanherran with the remaining Daulkaefar, never to be seen by man since."

"Yes, I know this story . . . how could one not know?"

"Such things are not spoken of... not anymore," Elcon replied, voice heavy. "And those who do talk of it believe it only to be a child's tale. Yet, what's more intriguing is that you know of the Morreans, those who followed the Cursed One, Mireya."

"How did you-"

Elcon raised a finger. "You talk in your sleep. But that is no matter, for you do know of them, do you not?"

"What are you getting at, priest?"

"I, myself, am a man of understanding, a 'seeker of truths,' if you will. I have spent my life seeking out all truths. Some even that would be deemed unholy in certain circles. Not for the sake of practice, but for the gain of knowledge, obviously. A lifetime of learning, searching for even the smallest fragments of understanding. And then I hear of you, a man who knows and speaks of things long forgotten. Of a people forgotten to time and of a world lost to the ages."

Darius did not answer. His mind raced with a thousand questions. His eyes locked onto Elcon as the high priest fingered the pages tenderly. The man would not look at Darius but studied the book with intent. Darius stepped closer. He felt the priest's heart jolt, he could smell the sweat beginning to form around the old man's brow.

Elcon pointed to a passage on the golden pages and began reading.

From the Records of the Lords of Ordiatea, the House of Tur

Entry 33:

> *The Ellitheor are gone from this land. They are no more. They do not hear our pleas, and they do not come to our aid. Gone are our gods and hope in them is faded. For foul creatures and wicked men have begun to come down out of the seas to the West. Their skin is pale and dead. They wear the bones of their enemies. Death is their welcome, and destruction is what they take delight in. We are unable to continue here alone, and we fear we will face our decimation at the hands of our foes. Where is the Key Bearer? And from whom do we seek refuge? To what ends do we face our fate?*

Entry 48:

Those who are called the Morreans, for they are those who come in the night from the Isle of Morr, have taken hold of the land south of the river Unra and infest the land. We have lost Thran and Iaur in battle, and the city Gath has fallen. It has been four cycles, and there is still no hope of escape. The Great Desolation is upon us again. Songs sung of old had told of Sages past. But there is no boon from the gods. We have survived in the stronghold of the people of Ordia and hid deep in the earth, fortifying our people for what we fear to be our last stand.

Entry 53:

We have received communication from a tribe in the east from a people who call themselves Kyn'do. They mount horses and shoot darts from bows. They have driven the Morreans from their lands and have joined forces with us. For the first time, there is hope. We will meet at the near side of the Red Marsh, as we have come to call it due to the swamp oaks and red maples that grow. Tales of fallen creatures of the land infest those regions, taking our men in fear, but we press on.

Entry 57:

We were victorious in driving back the Morreans with the help of the Kyn'do. Their horses and arrows combined with our shields and spears pressed the Morreans away from our lands. Our people are weary, but their spirits are raised. We have raised a stronghold at the edge of the Red Marsh. Her walls are high and strong. Zargareth will stand as a testimony to the strength of men. The men of the east have returned to their homelands across the grasslands of Eduth. Many have fallen, but we will ever be thankful.

Entry 73:

My father has fallen to our Mother Earth and has gone away from this world. I, Tarish of Tur, begin my record in this book of Lords of the House of Tur. My people have grown strong, and our once small city has become a haven for many across the land. We welcome all who would be free. Yet, we hear accounts of the Morreans again, this time to the north. We have sent emissaries to the east for Kyn'do to join us. We have heard tales of the north and of those who would oppose the Morreans there. We will take men and go there to seal the fate of the wicked.

Entry 74:

> *We travel north into the wild of the mountains. I have taken two hundred strong men and my own son, Tareth, to destroy the Morreans once and for all. For they seek not peace nor land, but to worship a false goddess, whom they call Mireya, the Blood Queen. We will join with people who possess those lands, of whom we are unfamiliar, and the Kyn'do people one last time. There is a presence to these lands, and I think that something ancient slumbers in these hills, something ancient indeed.*

Entry 78:

> *Red lightning splits a black sky. Men weep and their strength fails them. We cannot stand against this foe. Death is in the air. Blood in the skies. Evil is about. And the rain is fire and damnation. We cannot stand against this. We will fall but will not falter. This will be my last record. I seal it with my own blood. Tarish of House Tur. Last of the Sons of Men. I leave my crown to my son, my shield and my spear. I go into that endless night. I go proud, and I go free.*

Entry 79:

> *I, Tareth, in my nineteenth year, return with only fifty and three souls of my people. For two seasons, we pursued the Morreans into the mountains of cold. We fought valiantly alongside the Kyn'do people and the Sea Maidens, and our newfound ally who call themselves Iaraininns or those of the Iron Mountains. They are a blessing from the High Father. A last remnant of a covenant long-forgotten, true guardians of the land. We bring their bodies back on our shields. Their homes are no more, burned by the Morrean survivors. They were valiant in life and died with honor. They will be laid to rest with my forefathers. And when I lay to rest at the end of my days, so shall I rest with them. The last of their kind. Our Saviors.*

Elcon looked up from the golden-leafed pages, meeting Darius's pained stare. Only one word escaped Elcon's lips before Darius's body faltered.

"Guardian."

Darius fell limply to the stone floor.

***

Twilight embers had burned away the last glisten of day, and the dark of night was settling in. Darius was alone. He stood, again, in a scar of

131

charred earth, clothed in the white robes and golden sandals from prior visions. The wisps of white light were drifting from Darius's pellucid flesh, casting a dim luminescence about him. There was a peace about this place, and yet, there was still that haunting feel of dread. As if nothing in this place was natural and all things were anomalous.

Darius tried to look about, grasping for any sense of why he was seeing this place or what it meant. The stars looked to be the same as he had always known. The moon was there, along with Ynazranal and Ephranden, the great stars of the north that hung nearest to the moon. However, the air seemed less like air and more like fluid. And his body seemed less like flesh and more like smooth crystal.

Through the silence, the voice came once more. It started as a distant rumble, creeping slowly over the mountainside. Quietly at first, then growing ever grandiose.

"Find them!"

"Who? Find who?" Darius could not speak aloud, yet the words swirled in his mind as if he were calling from a hole or some dark cavern.

"Find them!"

"Why am I here? What does this mean?" Darius cried out into the void of his mind.

The stars glowed so vibrant in the sky it was almost blinding. There was Ynazranal, flame ever-reaching blue. Ephranden, glistening green, like an emerald set in the heavens. And then a third star, one that had been hidden, one that Darius did not know, seemed to appear. It was, to his mind, black as midnight, though a harsh scarlet light oozed from its depths. The stars seemed to spin, slowly at first, increasing in speed. They were connected, but all separate still.

"Find them, or blood shall rain!"

***

"Darius! *Darius!* Can you hear me?" Elcon pleaded as he shook the shoulder of Darius's lifeless body.

Gasping for breath, Darius jolted awake in a panic. His eyes were muddled with both confusion and dread. Elcon was hunched over, looking pale as a ghost, pressing on his shoulder as beads of sweat dripped down from his brow. He took deep, long breaths, and a shudder ran down his spine. Darius called out in delusion, his voice raspy and strained, "Do you hear the voice? It calls!"

"Voice?" Elcon replied with a quaver, his trembling hand still on Darius's shoulder. "There was no voice other than your own."

A long moment of silence ensued, wherein neither dared to move.

Darius's raging heart eventually slowed, along with his labored panting and wheezing. Never had an episode overtaken him so violently before. He ran a hand over his forehead, wiping sweat from his brow. The

132

wild, distant look seemed to fade from his eyes. Despite these small factors, Darius's mind still felt clouded and ached with a steady throb. After two more breaths, he began to speak again, his voice strained, as if he had just exerted an extreme amount of energy.

"I knew the man called Tarish. He was a great leader; he fought with honor to the last breath."

No answer came from Elcon. For some reason, the high priest was just staring down at him, confusion marking his face.

"What is the matter, priest?"

"Incredible..."

"Tareth, the son. Is it he who rules this city? Perhaps it was he who ordered my body brought back after the fall of Mireya. He must not have realized that I lived." Darius's eyes were frantic, and his voice trembled as he muttered, "He must not have known that I can heal..."

"My son," replied Elcon, his voice barely above a whisper, "Tareth is dead. All of those from that battle have long since passed."

"What happened? How?" Darius felt as if he were about to get sick. He had just been on that mountain no more than a few weeks ago. How could they all have fallen? How could this priest know they had fallen? Darius's heart beat as if it were about to burst, and he felt his failing hold on reality slip further from him.

Elcon dropped down in front Darius and placed a hand on the young man's shoulder. He stared into Darius's eyes, as if to make sure that something was there, really there. After a long moment of silence, Elcon cleared his throat and spoke. "Darius, Tareth is dead. His ascension to the Fields of Vanherran from this world happened almost twenty-nine generations ago."

Utter disbelief overtook Darius. His chest tightened so that he could not draw breath. Reality and panic took turns pulling at his mind, causing him to feel as if he were about to lose the slight grip he held on sanity.

Elcon, realizing that Darius was unable to speak, continued, "The Abandoned Ones, the ones you named Mireya and Diabhail, were destroyed somewhere near a thousand years ago. No one has spoken their names since the Fall. At first, Tareth had that name stricken from every scroll, book and record before his death. He then began to believe that even saying their names gave her power, so he ordered every bit of their existence concealed. They became less than myth, and the Church has long since held this, the only record mentioning the Abandoned Ones by name hidden from the world. Such knowledge could dispel hundreds of years of law and order."

The haunting, yet now so obvious truth, was becoming crystal clear. Darius began to feel a swarm of emotions berate him. It made sense, but how could it? The crypt he had found himself in, the strange and towering buildings, the unfamiliar clothing, even the city of Tur'Mor itself. It was all like nothing he had ever seen before because none of it ever existed until long after his demise. Darius had thought, up to this point, that he could not have been asleep for more than a few days, maybe a week or so. Fear came first, then frustration and confusion. And then, all emotion was replaced with the creeping sensation of dread. Darius buried his face in his hands as his mind raced. *It cannot possibly be true! How could it be?*

"You...you lie!"

"What does it benefit me to lie to you?"

"It cannot be! I was there! We stormed the Ashen Sands of Morr. Hundreds died before the iron gates of the Black Fortress of Mireya. I watched as my blood brothers fell around me, hacked, hewn, and melted. I saw where their blood stained the very snow where they lay! I was forced to witness the fall of even my own brother, soul torn from his chest as he wept for our mother."

Darius rolled to his side, knocking away Elcon's helping hand. He could no longer look at the high priest. He stared into the nothingness that he felt drawing ever closer. His soul felt hollowed, and his mind lost to the endless expanse of nothingness. It could not be true...it must be true. How? How could it be? But he did hold on. He fought against the cascading emotions that battered away at him. He found resolve in his actions, and that terrible night played out in his mind in crystal clarity that brought tears to his eyes.

"I alone climbed that mountain. As good men fought to their last breath in that godforsaken hole of blood and carnage, I climbed. I bested the bastard, Diabhail. And I, alone, drove the obsidian blade through the very heart of the Blood Queen, Mireya. I finished it..."

Despite the pain of truth and realization, Darius found strength in those words as well. It was primal rage from within. The power that was endowed upon him by the High Father seemed to bubble in his veins. The green light seemed to bend towards him; it was distilled, but there. With trembling hands and knees that shook, he began to bring himself to full stance. His eyes began to radiate yellow light from his irises.

However, during his attempt to stand, a searing pain overtook him. Darius yelped in agony and fell to one knee. His chest felt like it had burst into flames. He tore open his shirt, revealing the glassy handprint, which shone with blazing light.

"By Ordan's Throne!" Elcon gasped, stepping back suddenly in fright, pressing his hand to his lips and forehead again and again.

"What? What is this?" Darius barked out in pain as he looked down on the mark. "What is wrong with me?"

"You may have slain the Blood Queen," Elcon said as he glared at the shimmering handprint, "but you have been cursed with a dark curse. And I fear it is far from over for you, my son."

Darius faltered; the light left his eyes, and he fell, writhing on the ground. He felt like his body was atop shards of fractured glass, slicing into the very essences of his being. The vivid memories of Mireya, tainted with seething hate, festered the wound. Though it always hurt with a dull pain, this was excruciating. Darius could see her face, those red eyes flashing before him. She was beautiful; she was terrible. It was like she was reaching through the void of nothingness, attempting to touch him. Shadows began to crawl around his mind.

"Darius, stay with me!" Elcon commanded as he placed his hand back on Darius's shoulder.

Elcon was holding the amulet in his hand as azure light cascaded from it. Darius's eyes were clouded with tears of agony. His chest still burned with blazing heat, causing sweat to form around the scar. However, something strange happened, something Darius could not even comprehend in his current state. The blue light that radiated from the amulet seemed to drift towards Darius, drawing closer with each labored breath. However, the streams of light evaporated before reaching him, fading away into mist.

Amazed and perplexed by the transfer of light, the high priest gathered his robes and sat next to Darius. The light had all but left the amulet; only a dim pulsating glow remained. Elcon, folding his wrinkled hands in his lap, stared up towards the green stone which illuminated the room. "Darius, my son," Elcon began out loud, though he was sure that the young man was quite unconscious, "I know you do not know what this means...for any of us. But I promise to do all that I can, all that is in my power, to help prepare you. Something is out there, and you may be the only thing that can stand in its way."

First Caesurae:
Betrugyn, Assassin of Cogadh

Blood dripped from the tip of a silver blade. A woman lay face down in the street, drenched in her own gore. The shrouded assassin looked over her body, examining his work. She wore a purple dress with long sleeves and a low back. A necklace of fine gold was about her neck and her black hair was pulled up into a tight bun, save a single lock of wavy hair that fell about her spine.

The assassin wiped the long, straight-edged dagger on a neckerchief he had pulled from the deceased damsel. He then tossed it from his grip as if it were poison. Turning about, he stepped over one of the many puddles of dirty water that littered the well-trodden earthen street, marred with ruts and ridges.

Betrugyn grimaced as he sheathed his favorite dagger. The flamberge slipped silently into its place, strapped onto knee-length, Cogadh-style boots. Despite his detestation for his own people, everything the assassin wore was of traditional Cogadh clothing.

Betrugyn wore a long sleeved, split-front tunic of forest green that came down past the center of his thighs. The tunic had what appeared to be the stitching of a golden snake slithering from the base and winding up to the shoulders. His long and muscular arms were outfitted with leather vambraces with intricate golden patterns of arcane runes and tribal knots. A short cloak with a large hood was fastened around his neck and drawn up over his head, concealing his face. A thick brown belt was tied about his waist, crafted from layers of heavy cloth. The stiff collars of his earth-colored shirt covered the high cheekbones of his clean-shaven face. He wore a silver brooch which bore the emblem of a diving hawk.

Betrugyn would be considered both ugly and shameful amongst his people. He had unnatural eyes, one vibrant green and the other a bluish hazel. His blond, choppy hair was unkempt and bespeckled with red. A sign of impure lineage, as 'true' Cogadhars had only blond hair.

Betrugyn did not know what this woman had done to deserve the wrath of his master, but that did not matter. He could not dwell on such things; he had no stomach for it. He simply did as assigned. Each of his 'assignments' came the same way. The assassin was Oathsworn to a vile man, a man who commanded Betrugyn's every move from the shadows. For ten years he had been bound, and he had never even seen his master's face.

With a sigh of remorse for his actions, Betrugyn left the woman lying face down, as instructed by his master. He then placed a single silver turin on the bare skin of her back. He stared at the coin. The image of the High King of the Danes was stamped on it, proud and smug. He seemed to mock the assassin, almost jeering at him. Betrugyn turned his head and walked away.

In the distance, the sounds of people approaching became apparent. Betrugyn touched the brooch on his left shoulder. The diving hawk's eye, which was formed from a polished black stone and had veins of silver swirling about like a tempestuous storm, was placed upside down and had strange markings at the base and seven lashes. As his fingers ran across its smooth surface, sparks of energy seemed to jump from the pendant to his flesh. His green eye flashed with a bright light, and Betrugyn the Assassin vanished from sight.

Second Movement

The Guardian and High Priest, the Disavowed and Disgruntled, and the Hunt

CHAPTER 12: A NEW NORMAL

Six sets of dark, hardened eyes focused on Darius as he rose from the ground, the rest of their faces concealed behind tightly-wrapped white cloth. Only the eyes of the Aluth were visible, focused with an unwavering exactness. Sweat dripped off Darius's face, falling freely to the wood-plank floor. The smell of iron, perspiration and blood hung in the room. His ears rang terribly. Something had struck him hard in the side of the head, knocking him to the floor.

Six Aluth stood around Darius, each holding a different weapon, each dressed somewhat differently than their counterparts, though all wore the face covering called the Lo'Phandrak. In Darius's own hand was a rod, two hand-widths longer than his own height, held in low guard. He eyed his opponents wearily. He was exhausted, and there was no natural light here for him to draw upon for aid, not that he would have done so, but the reassurance would have been nice.

A gong was struck, and two Aluth stepped forward in perfect harmony. The first one came at Darius swinging in fluid sweeps, stepping like a dance; Aesuna Stance it was called, Motion of Waves. The other moved, twisting the blade in a sharp movement known as Ka'ral, lunging and jabbing with both hands on his sword's hilt. Their feet were wrapped in white cloth and bound with cords, as were Darius's. He wore white sleeveless tunic and loose trousers, tucked into the white binding. The only source of protection he had were the white cloths bound about his forearms. A green band was wrapped around his forehead, matching several of the other Aluth, as the sign of a Pupil.

Darius raised his staff to block Ka'ral with a loud crack. With a quick flurry of the sweat slick rod, he blocked the fluid motions of Aesuna with the center of his staff, then caught the heel of the other Aluth, who was attempting Ka'ral, with the other end, flipping him over to the hardwood floor.

Another gong strike sounded. and two more moved towards him. One held a pair of Nakau Nahu, dark wooden clubs from the Western Isle, though this had the jagged stones removed from the striking edge. The other a short spear, tip blunted, with a red tassel hanging from the top of the shaft. The lead struck with Hunu'a, wildly flailing the Nakau Nahu about himself; the other floated in Tau'le, spear tip dancing about Darius's head. He bobbed and dodged each strike, using the haft of the rod with heavy arms. He took a blow to the thigh from the Aesuna form, forcing him to one knee. He swung his staff out in a wide sweeping motion. Tau'le's fluid motion, like a viper striking, met his right shoulder, causing him to drop the rod. Twin Nakau Nahu stopped at the flesh of his neck, moving slightly as he swallowed.

A dark smile crossed Darius's lips. *Four this time. A good fight.* He did not speak the words, he dared not utter a single word while wearing the green band about his forehead.

The gong struck twice in sharp succession, ending the Phar'ais, or 'practice fight'. All of the Aluth came to attention, those with green bands in the front. Darius rose as quickly as he could, leaving a salty pool where he had knelt. It had been Elcon's idea for him to train with the Aluth, and Darius was extremely thankful for it. Though his muscles were sore, and his body felt battered, he was beginning to remember his old strength. That being said, he had never fought or trained with an opponent quite like the Aluth before. They were mastered in more martial arts and weaponry than Darius had ever dreamed existed, and it seemed to him they were trying to have him be just as proficient within a few short days. His increased strength and speed helped him stand against them, but their years of practice and patience always led them to victory.

Days had passed now, at least fifteen, maybe seventeen or more. Darius had had continual problems with his memories and blacking out, even after Elcon had led Darius beneath the Sanctuary, revealing to him the most terrible truth he had ever had to confront.

He was no longer living in a time he knew, and everyone he had ever known and loved were gone. The words etched into those plates cut like a knife's edge, slicing his very soul to the quick, making bare the basest of all emotions: fear and loneliness. His mind often contemplated the words of that manuscript, trying to form the truths therein in some semblance of reality. Yet, acceptance came hard to him, though he could see little other means by which all could be explained.

Elcon had sent for Darius's belongings, meager as they were, after that fateful revelation, relocating him to the monastery, assuring him that it was for the best. Elcon had said he wanted to keep an eye on him in case he had further episodes. Darius knew that it was more so to remove him from the ever-watchful eyes of those who could have seen his actions during that storm. The Church and her followers were not too keen on the idea of anomalies. And Darius, he was the greatest anomaly of all, and not even Elcon seemed to have fully come to understand just how different he truly was.

That first night, Darius had not slept at all, but lay motionless in his bed, contemplating his existence. The day following the sleepless night was a barrage of questions and comments, a haze only broken by a short episode, an oddity, in that Darius remembered nothing therein when he had awoken. The days that followed were similar, lessons and studying, lectures and trials.

A sharp gong sounded.

A stern woman with brassy flesh and hard eyes stared at the practice ring. She stood atop a short tower, observing the Aluth. She had long grey hair, braided tightly down her back. Two Aluth accompanied her, standing just behind her on either side. She wore a white uniform, golden epaulettes at her shoulders and a series of aiguillettes on the right arm. Two rows of large golden buttons outlined her torso, stitched from the top of her high collar to the bottom of the coat, and a green sash draped from left to right across her chest. An officer's saber, pommel adorned with tassels of green and white, hung from her belt, hilt brushing against her knee-high, white leather boots.

"Form up." Her voice was as hard as her eyes and twice as commanding.

All in the room stopped and turned their attention to the commanding deck to listen, for she was their Only Voice. The Avajan'Aluth was the only Aluth that was ever allowed to speak, for they were never permitted to swear the Oath of Silence. Each Avajan was picked at a young age, trained in every aspect of the Aluth, but never allowed the oath. Avajan'Aluth would serve until they could no longer stand, and then the mantle would be passed to the next.

Twenty or so Aluth moved into a straight line. None wore the traditional Aluth garb that Darius had seen worn by those under the Sanctuary, but each donned the attire of the form they were practicing in. Though, regardless of style, they were all adorned in white, save for the green Pupil bands on about a dozen or so. Darius had realized on the first day that he did not train with any full-fledged Aluth; those who had passed the rigors of the Avajan'Aluth's tutelage were made to swear the Oath of Silence. Though, every Pupil practiced the Art of Silence in preparation.

"The night is far spent," the Avajan'Aluth called out. "Bathe and to your quarters!"

The gong sounded once more, and all moved in one accord. Weapons were neatly stacked in their holding racks and large mats where Pupils and Aluth practiced hand to hand combat were rolled and put away. Darius always tried to help clean up, but each time he was shooed out of the way. To make it even more awkward, several of the Pupils would swarm him and help him out of his training garb. The first time they had begun doing so, he had resisted, but this was met with a firm lecture from the Avajan'Aluth.

"You are a man of the Parsonary now, a Robed One," she said firmly. "It is an Aluth's duty to serve. Do not dishonor them by denying them their rights."

Darius had wanted to argue, but Elcon had made it very clear that he would continue with the guise Ranun had established for as long as he was in Tur'Mor. He was to be an emissary from Daneland, come to Tur'Mor to deliver a message to the Holy Seat, and who sought to further his studies in the art of masonry. And 'study' he did.

While Darius's evenings had been filled with the rigorous, and somewhat painful, training sessions with the Aluth, his time spent during the light hours of the day were altogether different. Elcon had him laboring for hours on end laying stone and repairing the worn-down and crumbled sections of the Sanctuary and repairing the grounds about it. Elcon had advised this so that other monks and priests would not question why this stranger, Darius, was residing with them in the monastery. Elcon had been careful, painstakingly so, about Darius's past, noting the younger man's desires to rise in the Parsonary from lowly Envoy to Holy Architect, Sealed to the Order of Creation under the Commune of the Ordan's High Architects. It was a daunting task, concealing Darius's past and providing means for an increasing education, a task that Darius himself was quite grateful for.

After the Aluth Pupils had finished removing the bindings from Darius's feet and forearms, they untied the green band from him. The latter action held more ceremony – they held the band carefully, always above the heart. They placed the shimmering cloth atop a shelf where several others lay. Darius noted that the Pupils never removed their own bands; it was a sign of great honor to have the band removed from their head. An honor they had not yet received. For Darius, it was a sign of brotherhood. For as long as he wore the green band, he was one with the Aluth, and they treated him as such...save for helping him at the end of their sessions to undress.

Once down to naught but his loose-cut pants, the sleeveless tunic tossed aside, the Pupils finally let him be, though a slight reddening on the back of his neck and cheeks had already begun to form. Darius was not sure how many of the Aluth were male and female, their tight bindings making it hard at times to tell the difference, though neither sex seemed to mind changing before the other in the gymnasium. That being said, some were more obvious than others, and one of these two was certainly female. Darius always felt uncomfortable with anyone helping him undress, and females more so than others.

In his life, Darius had not had many times to enjoy leisure or love. He had barely reached adolescence when he was called before the Council of Chiefs and told of the duties and oaths he would have to fulfil. At twenty-two his father had died, forcing him to take up the mantle of chief of his own tribe, being named the Black Paws of Iarainn. Five years of war had placed him far away from his home and any chance of finding a *ghaehan*, a wife. It was during this time that he had taken the Oaths of the Feromage. The first oath granted him his abilities to Bind the light of the sun to his essence, channeling its currents through his ring and fusing its rays to his being, increasing his strength, speed and stamina. And then he had fallen at the Two Peaks of Morr to the curse of Mireya, Blood Queen of the Damned, only to find himself awakened in this place.

Darius pondered these things as he walked from the gymnasium into the bathhouse located in the bottom chambers of the monastery. Large furnaces beneath the tiled floors heated the mosaic, circular bath, making it a most enjoyable place to sit and relax. Steam clung to the air, hovering into the domed ceiling, distorting the paintings there and mixing with the sweet smells of incense, which delighted his senses. Darius sunk beneath the water and gazed up at the vented domed ceiling. Like many of the other rooms in the monastery, the walls were sandstone and plain. However, the ceilings all seemed to be adorned with masterful works of art, each painted with steady hands and expert precision. Darius marveled at each, knowing that such artistry was far beyond his talents. No, the hammer was what his hands were called to swing, the hammer in work and the axe or club in war. He was no artist, but he did enjoy the fruits of their labors.

Staring up at the paintings, body soaking in the hot water, Darius's mind drifted into thought. On his first day with Elcon, the high priest had Darius recount his days in Tur'Mor, listing the failed attempt to flee the city, a rather frustrating detail that Ranun had told, and the subsequent vision that had stayed his flight. Next were the days of laboring and searching about; Elcon was quite amused at Darius's attempts to find information by stalking the streets of the city. Yet when he asked the younger man why he did not seek out a library, Darius just stared in confusion. He did not know how to read; he was never taught. Darius had told Elcon that the histories and chronologies of the Iarainn Tribes were passed down by *Bechimahn*, soothsayers, who recanted the tales by memory. After learning this, Elcon carved out hours a day, after his stonework and before his time with the Aluth, to the study of characters, letters, and numbers. Darius much preferred katas and exercises of the body to the strain of the mind brought upon by the study of letters and figures.

Rising from his bath, Darius walked the familiar path to his room on the top floor of the sandstone monastery. The building was four stories, the walls smooth and the hallways narrow, though the many chambers and studies were large and open rooms with little furniture other than wooden chairs and small tables, and rows upon rows of books, scrolls and shelved parchment. Besides these small amenities, the only other thing the rooms bore were edifices of Ordan and Gallea, set atop precipices of marble and surrounded by flickering candles at all times. Darius walked the halls quietly, as most of the monks and priests who inhabited the monastery were long since asleep, adopting the phrase: *rest well in the night, so that thy mind is prepared for the light.*

Once at his room, a small hovel separated from the hallway only by a thin curtain hanging from a rod of iron, Darius removed the towel that was about his waist and used it to dry his long hair. After many pleas from Elcon, Darius had agreed to trim back his burly beard, but he refused to cut his hair, saying it was dishonorable to do so, nor would he totally remove his beard, as all the monks had done. As a matter of fact, Ranun was the only member of the Parsonary that had any sort of facial hair. When Darius questioned Elcon about it, the high priest simply dismissed the inquiry with a change of topic. After his hair and body were dry, Darius pulled over a loose, white shirt of soft cotton and donned a pair of baggy trousers. Despite his affinity for the cold, the night air would still plummet near the seashore, so Darius conformed to the wearing of shirt and trousers to bed.

The four-poster bed that he slept upon was old, the wood looking as if it were about to give way any day. The coverlet was worn and faded, though held a certain warmth to it. Darius was growing quite accustomed to sleeping on a soft mattress, beneath smooth sheets that did not itch or bother. He chuckled as he blew out the candle near his bed and drifted into sleep.

And so ended another day.

At dawn's first light, Darius was awakened to the Chant of the Rising, a solemn, harmonious melody that would be recanted, monotonically, every morning by green-cloaked monks, both male and female. Hundreds of monks lived in the monastery, both called and named after what their function entailed. Priests and priestesses also dwelt in the complex, though Darius ascertained that the majority lived outside the sand-colored walls. He also found himself an anomaly once more, for he was neither monk nor priest. He was a stranger, a foreigner, granted the right to bathe, eat, and sleep amongst the others, but not wholly integrated into their society. This latter fact did not, however, bother him all that much.

Beyond the titles, Darius had noticed something else in his time living in the monastery, and that something was becoming more and more discriminate. There was a separation here, amongst the monks and priests. And though he was not clearly certain as to what positioned the monks to their station or the priest to theirs, one thing was crystal clear. The monks were beneath the priests in the hierarchy of the Church. And nothing highlighted this distinction more than the ceremonial robes of green, along with the white aprons bearing the image of Ethra, that the monks always wore. The priest and priestesses were more diverse in their accoutrement, often wearing three-pointed hats, long overcoats with fine trousers, or split-front dresses with long sleeves and high necks that were the foremost in fashion.

Darius rolled out of bed and dropped to the floor, beginning his morning routine of stretches, push-ups, and katas. Sweat began to form on his back, sticking to the fabric of his nightshirt as he went through the various motions. It was a dance, like the flow of a river that turned to a gale storm of fury near the end. Veins bulged, and yellow, crystalline eyes shook as he pushed himself harder, harder, harder. His mind was filled with images of blood and snow, of cracked-fleshed Morreans with blood-red tattoos, and of death. Memories of loss and hurt rushed through him, a torrent of pain and despair. Harder, harder, harder he pushed himself. The thoughts of failure and frustration worked out of his mind as he worked his body. He fought for the serenity of peace that came only from the pain of the body, for pain was real and pain grounded him in reality.

Chest heaving, he placed trembling palms on the floor as he knelt, focusing his attention on his breathing. Steady, slowly. In through the nose and out through the mouth. Feeling the flows of air, releasing the hurt with every exhale.

His eyes twitched and his body shuddered. A flash of the vision he was plagued with burst in his mind's eye. Translucent skin of crystal leaked yellow light. A blasted, barren spit of rock, charred as if by a bolt of lightning, filled his view instantaneously. And then, as quick as it had come, it vanished. It had been since his visitation with Elcon to the underground chamber that he had been taken from reality to the vision. Days now had passed since he had gleaned any more from the mysterious words if what he had actually gleaned was anything at all in the first place.

He exhaled. It was time to get ready for the day.

Darius took a large brass basin of water and a porous sponge and began to clean himself. Next, he brushed out his hair, pulling it into a rather sloppy ponytail, tufts of hair parting at his brow. His hands trembled slightly as he worked his thick, dark hair and his stomach felt tight, and try as he might, he could not push aside the unusual feeling of fatigue.

He dressed quickly. First came a pair of thick, dark trousers with reinforced patches that fit rather snugly, though not too tight. These bland pants kept his knees free from scrapes and bruises as he worked stone with hammer and chisel. The more fashionable knee or shin-length britches, tight and colorful, did not suit his taste, much to Elcon's chagrin. That old priest always had a head for the finer things in life, but Darius preferred sturdy and plain, just like himself. On the plus side, he had to admit, button-down shirts were not nearly as challenging for him anymore. His calloused fingers moved deftly around each wooden circlet that fastened up the center of the starched white shirt, sliding them into place with ease. Next was his vest, Darius's favorite part of his ensemble, a double-breasted piece with fine pinstripes of blue and red set against a deep grey wool. Darius had procured two other vests, using his meager earnings on them, for he had no true need for money at the time. One was a bright blue piece, embroidered with silver swirling patterns and lined with a single row of brassy buttons, which he only wore on Ellitheal, the

Ordiatian holy day. And the other vest matched his current one, a redundancy of sorts.

After donning his dark, heavy boots, brassy cogs pulling the laces tight up to the base of his calves, Darius set out of his room, taking his overcoat in hand on his way through the curtain that separated the room from the hallway. He slid his arms through the coat sleeves as he walked past a row of monks in the narrow hallways, both parties having to turn sideways to pass. The monks bowed their heads and touched fingers to lips and forehead in succession. Darius returned the gesture, though only performed it once, not the customary three.

Once through the hallways of the monastery, Darius made his way to the back courtyard, which was walled on three sides and hedged with a towering row of evergreen shrubbery. The courtyard itself was set up in two levels, the top being a well-manicured garden with a central fountain and mosaic deck. White stone steps led down to the lower half of the courtyard where, in the springtime, there would have been tight rows of green grass. Now, it was rather dead and brown, though still well maintained. A large marble sundial sat in the middle of the grass, circled by a path of matching stonework.

Darius walked down the steps, eyes adjusting to amber rays of warm sunlight that bathed the courtyard. Normally, he would have felt a sense of peace and bliss in the dawn hours of the day. Of late, he could not seem to shake the feelings of weakness that had been plaguing his body. Darius had never been the strongest of his kind at Binding the Light, the first ability of the Feromage. However, the feelings of nausea and exhaustion he was experiencing of late were a whole new low for him.

Thirteen days now, Darius had demonstrated the process of how he was able to Bind the rays of the sun to High Priest Elcon. The last three days, he had held the flows for as long as he could, allowing Elcon to take note of how it affected his body. Each day, it seemed to take a greater toll on his body.

At first, Darius had been hesitant to show how his abilities functioned. However, the old high priest was a convincing man. He had laid out clearly his intentions to help the young man. He had taken him to places of study to recant past tales and lore. And after a few days of prodding, explaining that he would be far more helpful if he could see what Darius was capable of, Darius finally conceded to demonstrating the First Oath. The same that he had used to save that little girl. The same that had been the catalyst to all that he currently faced.

On the other side of the sundial, several items lay out on the lawn. There was a stone, roughly the size of a large man's torso, a single-edged backsword with a brass knuckle-bow, and a series of iron bars with globes of solid metal affixed to both ends. These were set out to test the abilities Darius possessed. Elcon had not made his way to the courtyard yet, and Darius was feeling a bit more apprehensive than usual. He made for the backsword, the curved blade sheathed in a leather scabbard. The wire-wrapped hilt felt cold in his hand as he drew the sword from its sheath. A chill ran up Darius's spine, but he had to know; the question burned more than he knew the process of finding the answer would. Cupping his left hand, Darius drew the sharp edge across his palm. Flesh separated and warm blood flowed downward. The blade slid easily; the sensation burned as icy fire. A shudder ran through his body as blood breached the surface of his palm. Wincing, Darius sheathed the sword with a reverence that the Aluth taught him to show to all weaponry.

Rising slowly, clearing his mind, Darius began the process of Binding the energy from the sun to his personage. The silver ring went ice cold as the veins in his body began to dilate, allowing the flows of molten light to surge throughout his being. Drawing in a deep breath, Darius's eyes burst into yellow flames. Golden rays began to pulsate around the stream of crimson that dripped from Darius's palm and down his forearm. The blood, in a rather unusual manner, began to flow backwards, against gravity, slowly at first, then steadily increasing in speed, until all was back into the wound. The beams of light then seemed to stitch the cut together, using flesh and sinew as thread. After a few painful moments, the wound was mended, leaving only a slight scar on Darius's hand.

"So long," Darius muttered to himself, though not inaudible, as he stared at his hand, inspecting every inch of minded flesh.

"Fascinating!" Elcon exclaimed. "I would not have expected it to happen so quickly!"

Darius whirled around; blazing eyes filled with alarm. He was unused to being caught unawares. However, when he saw the high priest, the flare dwindled in his eyes.

Elcon was strolling leisurely towards him, a faded green book in his hand. He wore a gold-embroidered, emerald-green coat, with the buttons opened across the torso and tails hanging down the back. He had a white ascot tied at the neck and ruffled cuffs were poking out from the ends of his ornamented coat sleeves. His trousers matched his coat, save they plumed wide at the thighs and were tucked into his knee-high stockings. Darius shook his head at the sight of the high priest and began preparing himself mentally for the onslaught of questions that were sure to follow, just like they did every morning.

"Good morning, Darius."

"Morning."

"Did you rest well?" Elcon asked wryly. "You look rather worse for wear."

"Well enough," Darius answered slowly. The acetous taste of sunlight rippled across his tongue as he spoke, and wisps of golden light drifted from his lips when they parted. "No dreams, if that is what you are digging at."

"Unfortunate." Elcon sighed, taking out a strange-looking metal device from his inner coat pocket, then notating something in his book. He had called his quill-less contraption a mechanical pen. "Anyhow, are you prepared to begin?"

Darius removed his heavy coat in silent answer, then threw it over a lectus and walked over to where the massive sundial stood, facing the hedges with his hands behind his back. Elcon followed, continually jotting notes with his mechanical pen, watching. From this angle, no prying eye could see what was happening from a balcony in the monastery. It was also less than rare for a monk or priest to be about at this hour, for it was time for their morning services. Elcon had picked both this time and this place for those exact reasons. Elcon had no desire for their private meetings to be observed, and he made it very clear to Darius that he thought it best to keep his abilities to himself for the time being.

"Your hand." Elcon paused for a moment, looking up from his writing, and continued, "Will you be able to perform the tasks?

"The deeper the cut, the longer the heal," Darius answered gruffly as he ran his right hand over the thin, white scar. "This was minor. I'll be fine. Broken bones take longer; a puncture to the gut or lungs isn't guaranteed, and you risk burning yourself trying to heal those types of injuries."

"And what of head or heart?"

"If you die, you die," Darius answered flatly; though a hint of agitation flared. "There is no healing death."

Darius stepped up to the stone, which must have weighed at least two hundred kilograms, and took hold of the rough-hewn stone. Sparks flared from his eyes as he moved from a near seated position and rose upright, stone held securely in his muscular arms. He held the boulder for the time it took all the sand to drain from the top of a strange-looking glass object Elcon had produced to the bottom chamber. At Elcon's command, Darius dropped the great stone. It fell to the lawn with a solid thud.

Drawing in deep breaths and more flows of light, Darius walked to the bars of iron. He lifted the first with ease, high over his head. The next went up as quickly. It was the third that caused him to struggle, the bar bending under its own weight, forming a bow as Darius hoisted it over his head with a grunt. The Binding, as always, was beginning to take its toll on Darius. Beads of sweat were forming on his brow and an itch was lurching along his nerves; the first sign of burnout. Darius knew if he went on much longer, he would feel nausea settle in, then the ecstasy would overtake his mind and he would give in to the light, allowing himself to be utterly consumed until nothing but ash remained. At the sound of Elcon's order, Darius released his grip on both the bar and the Binding. The light faded from his eyes as the iron weights fell to the earth. Doubling over, Darius emptied his stomach in exhaustion.

"Nearly ten minutes this time," Elcon said as he wrote in his little book.

"I can go longer when I need to," Darius panted. He did not sound as if he could have lasted another three seconds.

"Yesterday you only lasted eight and a half minutes," Elcon returned as Darius slowly stood. "I presume it has to do with the tasks."

Darius nodded in agreement.

Elcon made two or three more notations, and then asked, "How do you feel?"

"Hungry," Darius snarled, it was always harder to temper his mood after letting go. The desire to pull in the light was so strong, and he craved binding its flow of energy. "And tired," he added more meekly, upon hearing the harshness of his own voice.

"And the urges, do you feel them even now?"

"Always." Darius was running his thumb across his ring absentmindedly. It was no longer icy cold, though it seemed to tingle ever so slightly as he drew his thumb over its rough-hewn pawprint.

"What would you say your increase in strength is, from unbound to bound?"

"Hard to tell," Darius answered through measured breaths. "Sometimes I feel that I can draw in more than at others, and it's always easier on a clear day like today."

"What does it feel like?" Elcon asked, lowering the pen and looking at Darius with intrigue, his elderly face sharp and grey eyes focused.

"It is ecstasy," Darius answered wistfully, his eyes looking through the old priest. "It's pure elation. I feel invincible when the flows are rushing through my veins; I practically am. I heal faster, run faster, jump further, see clearer. Though, the closer I get to the Burning Point, my focus begins to shift, and everything becomes a blissful blur."

"The Burning Point?"

"If you hold on to the flow too long, it can cause a burnout," Darius said as he rubbed his neck, squinting his eyes as he realized he felt totally recovered from the evening's activities and morning exercise.

"As in, you would no longer be able to Touch the True Source?"

"Not the 'True Source', as you have explained," Darius answered for what seemed like the hundredth time. "I don't draw upon this Aethereal Everlight, some remnant of the god's own power, as your Blessed do. I Bind direct sunlight. There is no store, no secret source or well of power, but infinite energy to Bind. Hold on too long or Bind too much to your being, and you will literally burn up."

"This is fascinating, Darius. It must have been centuries since anyone has had such abilities," Elcon mused. "Who knows what else people are technically capable of?"

"I thought the point of these sessions was to help get to the bottom of how I was receiving these cursed visions," Darius grumbled, "not theorize on how to move water with your mind, melt stone, or some other wild theory of yours."

"Darius, my son," Elcon said with a tsk and a smile. "You know I am not going to pass on a chance to learn something new, like how when you Bind the Light in full sun, as today, your eyes burst with light. Though, on a cloudy day, they more or less pool with light. I wonder if the Binding has more to do with clarity of skies or distance from you to the rays."

"I can't Bind sunlight in a building or cave, unless there are windows or openings," Darius answered. "I need to be able to draw direct sunlight into myself."

"And what of other celestial bodies?"

Darius's face fell for a moment, eyes shooting downward. However, he recovered quickly, answering, "The sun is a living and ceaseless source of energy; the moon is merely a reflection, as are stars. Kind of like a shift from one reality to another. Only a reflection of something else."

"Ah." Elcon sighed, jotting down another few notes in his book. "Too bad."

"I can still hear," Darius said. "Even without Binding."

"I just would have assumed something would come from the other," Elcon said, snapping his book shut.

"The Blessed, how is it they Bind?" Darius questioned, turning the attention from himself.

"It is not really 'Binding' that they do, not really," Elcon said, eyes filling with excitement to share his understanding. "The Blessed are born with the Spark, a hereditary trait we have found, passed from mother to daughter. And while it has been cataloged that the trait can skip generations, we have clearly surmised that it cannot, unfortunately, pass genders."

"That did not answer my question....."

"Well, patience, Darius," Elcon said with a twinkle in his eye. "For one so stoic, you have little patience when timing does not suit you."

"Apologies, Elcon," Darius said with a slight bow of his head, color rising in his cheeks.

"Now, as far as the Blessed go, what they do is called Touching. The Blessed cannot control the True Source but open themselves up to the flows thereof, allowing the Everlight to direct Itself in the way Its conduit allows, being either to heal or to reveal."

"But the Everlight, that is not of this realm," Darius stated in confusion. "I must see the light, feel its warmth to Bind it to me. How are the Blessed able to Touch if they cannot see nor feel this True Source?"

"There are places, sacred places, where the Everlight's presence is close to the tapestry of this Terral Realm. It is in those places that radiant flows can be harnessed in what are called Ra'el Aundreal. Perfect gemstones of pure crystal, mined only from the heart of the Northern Mountains; the more exact the cut, the longer they can hold the light.

These crystals will diffuse slowly, the more impure the faster, and in time, go dull. Therefore, it is the duty of the Blessed to make a pilgrimage to holy sites to reinfuse their Ra'el Aundreal so as to always have a reservoir of the True Source to Touch."

Darius stared at Elcon, confusion etched deep in his face.

"Not the mind of a scholar." A small chuckle slipped. "Not all find pleasure in the pursuit of understanding. I will try harder to dilute my language, my son. I do not mean to offend."

"Have you learned anything more about dreams?" Darius asked gruffly as he walked past Elcon, not meeting the high priest's eyes. He grabbed his coat from the lectus and pulled it about himself to block the wind. He had sweated during his Binding of the light, and the bitter wind chewed at his damp back.

"Nothing yet, my son." Elcon sighed. "But do not lose hope. The ways of Ordan are above our own. We can only submit our will to him and trust in his path."

"For one so studied and calculated, I would not think you so religious."

"Ordan, the great High Father, is a god of order and law, my son. Do not confuse faith with foolishness. One can be both educated and devoted. I believe the Eternal Architect would have us come to knowledge as close to his as possible. I have dedicated my life to the service of the High Father, and through my studies I have found so much more than blind belief and simple prayer. But I must say, seeing you here, what you are, it does cause contemplation."

"It is hard for me, you know," Darius said, looking at the back of his hand, studying the silver-worked ring as he spoke. "For me to accept that your people just don't know...know of my people, of magic and the Fallen."

Elcon placed his hand to his bare chin, staring at Darius with a face that seemed to have instantly gone weary. "Darius, Son, there is no such thing as magic, not as you speak of. There are holy ordinances, gifted from the Ellitheor, bestowed upon the chosen few. These things, as I have explained, are holy, and only the Blessed are able to Touch the Source."

"Elcon." Darius's voice grew firm as his eyes turned upwards. He extended his hand to the side as the light around it began to grow distorted. He pulled his fingers together into a fist, grasping at the light of the sun, pulling it into his being. Flows of scorching heat surged through him again, causing sweat to bead across his brow. "I am the proof. I have seen Darkness, stood in its bleakness. And it was for that purpose that I was called. To stand where others could not, to be a light in the shadows."

"If there are gods, then logic would say that they have an opposite," Elcon answered. "I do not deny your words, but your memories, perhaps, are clouded. Were their ancient Guardians called after the Holy Order of the First Son? Yes. Are you a miracle, a survivor, most likely the last of these? It seems so. But are there witches, goblins and trolls? Black magic and demons? Darius, those are children's stories; they have no place in our society."

Eyes crackling with golden light, Darius stared at the high priest. "My mother always said, 'To every myth there is a truth'. Elcon, there is more to this. I can feel it."

"I believe that the Fallen Ones are locked away behind the Eternal Gates of Halfak. I do believe there was a holy war, where your kind stood with the Ellitheor against the wicked and vile of Ethrea. But, Darius, that is all long past. There are no such things anymore," Elcon answered as he met Darius's blazing eyes. "I am sorry, Darius. I am sorry for your confusion. I cannot begin to understand your loss. That being said, I cannot have you going about speaking blasphemy."

"Blasphemy?"

"What would you call it? To speak against the teachings of the very High Father and Holy Mother? To say that their sacrifice of Sealing away their own daughters to damnation was in vain and that now there are such evils in the world?" Elcon shook his head as if in dismay. "Darius, the corruption of the heart is the only true evil in this world, and the words of the Ellitheor are our path to salvation."

"Then, why did I awaken? Why am I here?" Specks of liquid light spewed out of Darius's mouth as he shouted the words with a passion that was absolutely foreign to his more reserved demeanor.

Elcon did not answer; he could not. He stared at Darius, quivering eyes showing the true terror at the display he was witnessing.

Darius, realizing how far he had gone, let go of the Binding. His skin steamed away the energy of the sun's rays, trailing wisps of shimmering light. As the heat flowed from him, so did the anger and agitation. It had always been so, the more light bound within, the more intense the emotions. Nausea struck, along with a proverbial punch to the guts as Darius realized he had yelled at the high priest. He had lost his temper and yelled at a man who had taken him in, fed him, clothed him, and more importantly, had been helping him find answers to questions neither of them could have even comprehended mere days ago. A taste of rancid salt filled his mouth, and his tongue grew heavy.

"Son, are you okay?" Fear had turned to concern in the old man's dull eyes as he rushed to Darius's side, catching him before he slumped to the ground.

"I am sorry..." Darius groaned weakly.

"Darius, there are so many things we just don't know yet. That does not mean we will cease our search for truth," Elcon said in a consoling voice. "I just ask that you guard your tongue. There is a balance to this world, and it is the responsibility of the Church to maintain that balance. Do you understand, Son, the situation you put me in?"

"I understand," Darius answered. And he did understand. But he also knew that there was more. There had to be a reason for his awakening, for his being in the place that he was. He was unsatisfied with the ideas of simply 'adhering to the will of a greater deity'. That being said, there was nothing more to add to this conversation. It was time to go about his daily labors.

***

The steady clink of Darius's hammer filled his ears as he worked on the walkway around the base of the mounded hill the Sanctuary sat atop. Other than the sound of metal on stone, clearing grout from between pavers, the bustle of the city was beginning to swell. Merchants in their finery were calling out to fanciful citizens to come see their wares and produce. Lords and ladies were about, overseeing their goods and talking about politics and other such things that consumed the minds of nobles. Carriages rolled and bards sang; all was alive in Tur'Mor.

Darius consigned himself to the work. He would not give up. He would find answers, whether this day or the next, he would discover where this path was leading him. He would not sit here forever, pounding away at stone and rubble. There was a darkness in this world, an oozing wound that the priests and politicians of this strange land had hidden away from sight, but he could feel it. It was there, out lurking beyond the borders of this city, he could feel its corruption.

No, he would not stay long in this place, hidden away safely behind walls and towers while others were consumed by creatures of shadow and demise. He had a calling, and he did have a purpose. He was a Guardian, the Last of the Feromage. Now, all Darius needed was a plan.

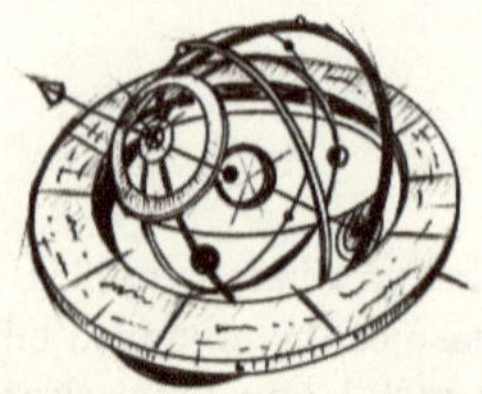

CHAPTER 13: A SINGLE COG

Elcon poured wine, purple in color, into a silver chalice of curious workmanship. The cup was a Galacian artifact, or at least a copy of such, which harkened to the Unka'Pala'Hununoo Dynasty, a time before the Ordaitian colonization of the Western Isles. Images of men holding wriggling eels and worshiping their forlorn, pagan gods adorned the silver vessel. Elcon breathed in the fumes of the pungent wine, closing his eyes and taking in the aroma. It was an old stock, from the lower vineyards, nearly eighty years old. A smile pursed his lips. He was nearly eighty years old; in fact, he was older.

"When in Ordan's holy name did I get old?" he mused to himself as he took a small sip of the aromatic wine. It was sweet for his taste in wine, only a small hint of the bitterness that aged alcohol carried. He sighed in contempt, allowing the refreshing flavors to dance in his expert palate. Elcon did not feel old, and many would not place the man's age near to what it was. Keen eyes and a mind filled with knowledge did, however, betray his years, for no one truly could see as he did without witnessing so much raw history.

The high priest pulled at the cream-colored ruffles of his sleeves, adjusting them so that they protruded perfectly out of his tailored waistcoat. Rings clinked together as his aged fingers moved deftly at his cuffs. Those hands were once the hands of the most revered swordsman in all of Ordiatea. Now they were the hands of her most renowned high priest. Elcon had never settled for second best, not in wine, not in fashion, not in anything life had to offer.

A knock at the study door drew his attention.

"Come in."

The door opened outwardly, making no sounds at all, revealing the ever stern-looking Avajan'Aluth. The stately woman's left hand was resting on the pommel of her sword, thumb caressing the weapon. Two other Aluth stood behind her, neither moving a muscle. The Voice of the Aluth made her way into the room and shut the door behind her, leaving her guards outside.

"Thank you for joining me, Micaela. Would you care for a drink of wine? The vintage is quite nice, and I do believe your lineage is much to thank for that."

"Do you call me in to patronize me?"

"By Gallea's mercy, no!"

"Then please, Holy Father, refrain from calling me by that name."

Elcon's lips turned up into a smile. Micaela was a beautiful woman, so very bold and commanding. Her features were not tarnished by her years, but refined, just like a fine wine. Elcon had been married, happily, for forty years. He had raised a son with Elyna, but he had lost both Tanish and his precious wife in the selfsame year, one to battle, the other to the White Fever. For Elcon, Micaela was the fruit he could not pluck, but that did not dissuade him from coquetting with her.

"For what reason did you call me here?" the Avajan'Aluth asked forcefully, placing emphasis on the words *did* and *here.*

"I wanted an update on the boy," Elcon asked with a sigh, setting the silver chalice on the scrollwork desk. "Though, I'll admit, I was hoping for a less formal meeting, Avajan."

"My duties do not allow for a lax in formality, Holy Father," the hard-eyed woman returned, placing her hands behind her back as if she were at parade rest. "As for the boy, ask and I shall answer.

"Master Darius is strong, and oddly talented for one so young. He has many skills with the blade and picks up on others with an uncanny swiftness. He won his first Phar'ais just last night. I'll admit, he has surprised me greatly."

"And his episodes, has he had one while in combat?"

"He was struck in the head, hard, and convulsed on the floor for five or six seconds but recovered quickly."

"And did he happen to speak in his fit?" Elcon asked, turning his back on the Avajan'Aluth, and running a long finger across the spines of books stacked neatly on their shelves, looking for one in particular.

She cocked her head, narrowing her eyes at the old priest. "No. Nothing of the sort. He hasn't said two words. It's almost as if he has taken the oath."

Elcon removed a book from the shelf, a large, black bound book with golden glyphs on the front and golden-leaf pages. He turned back, facing the woman, staring at her with tired eyes, as if all that spry youthfulness had been drained from his soul. "Micaela, the darkness creeps within the land. Can you not feel it growing ever colder?"

"Holy Father, I have ask –"

"*Yyahn'ghan*, Micaela, *Nu'farbaet!*" Elcon commanded, waving two fingers of his upturned left hand, the right hand still gripping the black book with golden markings.

The woman, eyes widening in shock, fell to one knee, turning both palms upwards, and replied with a trembling voice, "I live only to serve."

"The Days of Darkness must never return, Micaela," Elcon said firmly as he placed the book upon his desk, next to the silver wine chalice. "For this cause have I commanded you to train the boy. For this cause have many things been set in motion. It is the sole duty of the Aluth to protect the Patriarch of the Church, so that the truth is ever established, is it not?

"From the time of the Fall to the day the Books of Judgment are unbound and the Sages usher in the Restoration of All Things that once were, so shall the Voiceless serve the Holy Order.

"And you, Voice of the Voiceless? To whom is your allegiance?"

"I live as those who lived before me, as a proxy for those who have sworn the Sacred Vows."

"Halfak's very gates begin to bend under the strain, Micaela." Elcon's voice cracked under the strain of admittance. He was so tired. How had he ever been able to hold the ruse of confidence with such knowledge, such damning knowledge?

"What would you have me do, Great One?"

"You must make sure the boy is ready to fight," Elcon answered with a near plea in his voice. "There is a darkness that is corrupting the Forests of Ranok. Merchants dare not travel there unless by force. Men have harbored hatred towards their brethren, and the division between the Three Nations is at a tipping point. The underbelly of the Republic is showing her gruesome refuse, robbers with secret combinations, masked terrorists who seek to overthrow the government, and zealots of the corrupt faiths of the Fallen Ones spreading propaganda and disarray. Long have I stood at the precipice, standing in defiance of all that is wrong, but I am old now and someone must soon take my place."

"Great One, you concern me with your words," the Avajan'Aluth said as she stepped forward, placing a hand on the desk's lacquered surface.

Elcon did not meet her eyes but glared at the pages of the large book as he shuffled through them. His answer came after a long stint of silence, the subtle sounds of turning pages filling the uncomfortable void. "I care not for myself nor the concerns of others, Micaela. I care only for the preservation of our species. For three hundred years, Tur'Mor and the entirety of our nation has been kept safe from the evils of this world, protected by the Divine Light and the Blessed who wield Its glory, called by the Hand of the High Patriarch. Healing Blessed to mend the wounds of our people, and Vision Blessed adjust the memories of those who have seen beyond what they should. The entirety of our civilization is built upon the one terrible truth, one terrible lie. We are not chosen, we are not holy, and we are not alone."

"And the boy?" the Avajan'Aluth asked. "What is he to this truth?"

"The boy," Elcon said with a hollow laugh. "The boy, he is the tipping point, the piece of the puzzle that completes the most terrible picture that could ever be rendered. He is the truth, the truth which we have sought, Micaela. A relic and a vision for a better tomorrow.”

“How?”

“I do not know yet, Micaela.” Elcon turned the book around as he spoke, placing a finger on a series of small glyphs. The images were of twelve tiny men pulling on rays of sunlight, as if opening the blazing orb. From behind the luminescent orb, nine stars glistened, made from strokes of paint of green and blue. “But I believe it has something to do with this.”

“My priest, I do not understand the meaning of this.”

“The Unfolding of the Realms, Micaela. A pagan prophecy, one not well regarded amongst the Church.”

“And what does it mean?”

“It speaks of beings, sealed away for their transgressions against Ordan and Gallea by the Holy Blade of Fenron, and of their imminent return to Ethrea before the coming of the Fallen Ones.”

“But Holy One, that is blasphemy!”

“Did I not say these were pagan prophecies?”

“Yes,” the Avajan'Aluth replied abashedly, casting her eyes away from the book as if disgusted by it.

“It is well that you question falsehoods,” Elcon said kindly, shutting the book. He then drew himself up, clearing his throat and continued, more resolutely, “But, as High Priest of the Holy Church of Ordan, it is my duty to stand as a barrier, a shield between the falsehoods of the world and the children of Ordan. And I cannot rightly do so unless I know what the minds and intents of the Fallen are.”

“And what does all this have to do with that boy?”

“My good Avajan'Aluth,” Elcon said with a sly smile, “I do believe it all hangs upon his shoulders, that he is the precipice of a mount that separates two different worlds. The more I study him, the more I come to realize just how little we know about this world or that of the Aethereal and Beyond. The very Silver Gates of Vanherran are a mystery to those who live, and yet here is a man who could help unlock these secrets.”

“And what would you have me do, Holy One?”

“I would have you train him. Push him. Guide him. He is to be crafted into a tool for the Hands of Ordan and his Holy Church. He is a cog in his system, one that we must find its use.”

“As you command, Holy One,” the Avajan'Aluth said with a bow, placing her hand across her chest and leaning over low to the ground. She strained and turned for the door, knowing that this conversation was over.

“Oh,” Econ called out, causing the Avajan'Aluth to stop in her place, though she did not turn her head to meet his gaze. “I think this should go without saying, but do not speak of this evening or these things to anyone. I would hate for the Sisterhood to need to visit you.”

“Understood,” she replied, her voice cold and hard.

"Good," Elcon answered. "You may go."

* * *

"Of course, Lord Mayor," barked a monocle-wearing man with thick, curly, black chops. His voice was proper, if not slightly arrogant and stuffy. "I completely understand the issue."

"Do you now?" mused Lord Mayor Xander Adelmo as he pulled white gloves over muscular hands. He wore an exquisite coat of velvety-red with golden scrollwork covering nearly every inch of fine fabric.

"I take my duty very seriously, my lord!" the high detective replied as he folded the leather cover over his notepad. He proceeded to then tuck the pad away into the breast pocket of his long overcoat, which was black and marked by a silver star.

"And what do you think of the current predicament?"

"If my lord does inquire, I feel it my obligation to state that there are many inconsistencies. Far too many inconsistencies for my liking."

The mayor rested his hand on the pommel of his sidesword and looked over his balcony. There were no people there now, all was empty in his Residency. All was quiet but the two of them. That eerie, noiseless calm did not aid Adelmo's nerves nor bring clarity to the current situation. Something had happened at his masquerade. Something strange. And yet, for the life of him, nor apparently any of his patrons, he could recall no such oddities. It was as if he had drunk too much wine and there was nothing but blurs. But the wreckage of his gates — something had caused that, something he did not understand.

"And no witnesses have come forth as of yet?"

"No, my lord mayor," the detective answered, thick brows furrowed. He had been there that night, hidden amongst the guests, observing the events of the night. And he too was drawing a concerning lack of remembrance.

"And nothing was taken? No culprits captured?"

"The only thing I did find, my lord mayor, was a servant boy, found dead where a cart had struck a lamp and burned," the detective scowled. "Damnedest thing I ever did hear. Doesn't sit well, my lord, doesn't set well at all."

"Any family or kin come and claim him?" Mayor Adelmo inquired. His face showed the slightest signs of weariness as he glared down the empty hallway.

"None, my lord. Sat for three days before we had him taken to be buried. Your brother oversaw that, he did. Said he did not want the house to start stinking, and I have to agree with him there. An unsightly business and all."

"And the family who owned the carriage?"

"No word, sir."

160

"This is not right, Hallock." Adelmo sighed, turning back to face the other. "There is too much that is unanswered. Too many holes in this story. I would have you dig a little deeper."

"Of course, my lord," the detective replied with resounding surety. "Though, I would require Permissions of Writ, naturally."

"Naturally." Adelmo grimaced. A dirty work, to dig deeper. Best left to the professionals. Xander had never much cared for the harder work, but he had always cared for the results. Effective, if not brutal. "I will have my secretary draw them up by evenfall."

"I'll be needing my boys, you know. Scal and Tin."

"I expected as much," Adelmo replied as he cracked his knuckles.

"This is no savory business, my lord. But we'll get to the bottom of it all. You can rest assured."

"And of the women?" the mayor asked, almost fleetingly. "Any word? The High Priest Elcon has pestered me about this numerous times."

"That is bleak business, my lord. We've caught wind of seven ladies, one knife wound in each. Each face down. Each no older than your own daughter, Lord Mayor."

Adelmo snarled. "Permissions of Writ will be drawn to include the findings of such dead ends."

Detective Aurelius Hallock nodded in agreement, hazel eyes hard. There was no malice nor was there joy in his face. Just a somber steadiness. The detective clicked his heels together and made to leave the balcony when Adelmo called out one last command.

"Detective." His voice was ice. "I want this cleaned up before the election. I want this cleaned up and done. No more whispers in the streets. No more citizens fearing for a knife in the back by some invisible assassin. We have enough real problems to worry about, what with the war and the unrest caused by those damned Kh'ar. Bloody lot of bastards."

"Understood," Hallock answered in a huff. "And no need to worry about my coming and goings; Scal and Tin are the typification of professionalism. We'll find out what is happening in the shadows. We'll get to the bottom of this. That much I promise."

* * *

The twilight hours in Tur'Mor were a spectacle beyond comparison. At times, powerful storms would rage from the Southwestern Sea, producing clusters of ominous green clouds capable of producing lightning, tornados, and hailstones. During the calmer nights, a sea of stars painted the skies. Ynazranal, the Greatest Star, shone with a deep purple light and Ephranden, the Second Star, glistened with hues of blue.

Elcon starred up into the night sky, eyesight amplified through the powerful telescope atop the domed Asterivae, pondering the heavens and the infinite possibilities the cosmos held. The moon hung close to the surface world, full and vibrant. Elcon wished he could spend eternity looking into the skies for its mysteries, but he was old now, and his time was far spent. And still, he looked upward, ever upwards to the great beyond. He turned a series of levers, which engaged cogs that cranked slowly, amplifying even further the magnificent Star Gazer. This was a night of perfect clarity.

The Star Gazer rested atop a marble pillar, wider than the outstretched arms of ten men, with a spiral set of gold-inlaid steps leading up to the gazing platform. Dozens of cogs, lenses and bronze tubes formed the telescope, along with levers and knobs for adjusting distance and clarity. Three tables of cherry wood sat in the chamber of the Star Gazer, along with three chairs of the same behind each. Each table was set with parchment and inkwells, ready for notating any findings.

"Holy Priest of the Eternal Ellitheor," a stately, howbeit timid voice called out, breaking Elcon's concentration.

Elcon let out an exasperated sigh and, while rubbing his brow, turned away from the massive telescope. "I presume you have a need?"

"Holy Priest," the librarian said while adjusting his bottle-thick glasses with his free hand, the other clutching a sheave of parchment in a leather case. "It is well past observing hours. I'm afraid I must close the observation deck for the night and ask you to leave. Would you have me call a carriage? I dare say, it is most vile out on the streets now. I would be besmirched if I allowed one such as yourself out without a proper carriage. If only I had known earlier of your visit, I would have had a retainer to take you back to the monastery."

"It is quite all right, High Steward," Elcon said to the plump man as he ambled down the twisting marble steps. "My visit was supposed to be kept in silence, as I expect it to remain."

"Of course, Holy Priest!" the little man said in an overly reassuring way, bobbing his head so that his large, beaded necklace, from which a silver star hung, swung to and fro. "The Master of the Tower has made it abundantly clear that no name of any who has ascended to the Apogee be uttered outside of her golden doors."

"Good," Elcon answered with a nod. It would not do his reputation well for those inside his conclave to know of his dealings inside the Asterivae. Only two others had ever known of his studies outside of the Church: his lifelong friend, Ranun, and the Avajan'Aluth. For very different reasons. However, now there was a third, one with even a more complex reasoning as to why they needed to know. Darius, the young man with a thousand secrets. Maybe as many secrets as he had himself. "Gather my notes from the table. Burn the replicas."

* * *

Starlight illuminated the sky and flickering flames from lampposts lit the streets, casting wavering beams of yellow onto the cobblestone path. Elcon had not expressly forbidden Darius to go out at night; he had only asked him not to try to escape the city. Apparently Ranun had told his superior far more than Darius would have liked. That frustration aside, Darius could not be kept stuffed up in that monastery any longer.

True, the bouts with the Aluth were invigorating. The baths and studies inside the monastery were welcoming, and Elcon's tutelage was needed, pressing further on his abilities than he had done even in the time before his awakening. But Darius was not a man to be confined. The drab walls of the monastery had turned into a cell, and the ever-pressing thoughts on his mind needed an outlet. Something new. Something helpful, if not a little brash.

The idea had come to him two nights before, though he had been unsure how he could go about it until now. There were hundreds of thousands of people who lived inside Tur'Mor, maybe even more, and as far as Darius could tell, only a handful of City Guard regiments. And of those, he felt less than impressed with their zeal in protecting any who were unadorned with silk and finely woven linens. Darius had also witnessed firsthand the brutish mannerisms the City Guard took in doling out so-called justice. And during his time in Southend, he had observed dozens of examples of the poor and needy being neglected and abused by those who held authority.

So, Darius came up with his own plan. If he could not leave Tur'Mor, then he would do his best to make it a better place for those who stayed within. He would have to be stealthy, keep to the shadows, but he was no stranger to the darkness of night.

Darius stopped by an old storage shed near the gatehouse along one of the dividing walls that separated Southend from the open market sector of Tur'Mor and slunk inside. Darius had noticed that several of the sheds stacked against the dividing walls were used by merchants to store their goods, but a select few had been vacant for what appeared to be quite some time. Darius had selected one that was nestled between two larger sheds, obscured from view by the city guards who watched the triple gates, and stashed away a few items for this very night.

Darius quickly moved an old rug from the center of the floor, and then dropped to his knees to pry open the floor paneling with a small hammer he wore at his waist. This revealed a small space wherein laid that selfsame crate that Ranun had given him his first change of clothes. However, this time, the contents looked much different.

Excitedly, Darius removed a strip of white cloth and began to wrap it around his head after the same manner as the Aluth. Two wraps of the wide cloth over the mouth, then over the ears and under the chin, and then around the forehead until all hair and flesh, save the eyes, were covered. Next, he retrieved a circular brimmed hat of dark brown leather and placed it on top of the white wrappings. After that, he took off all but his thick trousers and boots, folding his shirt, coat and vest into a neat pile. Darius pulled out a thick shirt of spun wool, dyed black, with a swoop-neck and enforced seams that he had bought from a blacksmith, along with a pair of leather gloves that were well-worn.

After neatly placing his own clothes inside the crate, Darius lowered the box into the opening. Lying on the earthen floor, next to where he had set the crate, rested a rod of sorts, wrapped tightly with grey linen at one end. The cloth formed a handle, two hand-widths long, and trailed bits of cloth where he had tied the bindings. Darius hefted the rod, a tamping iron that had been used well past its prime, only a little longer than an officer's backsword. He had filed away the pointed tip of the octagonal bar, Darius did not want to kill anyone tonight, or any other night for that matter. It was heavy in his hands and would have been far too unwieldy for a normal man. Darius was no ordinary man though. That was why he had made this decision.

He was tired. Tired of sitting around waiting to find answers to questions he did not understand. He was tired of doing nothing while he knew others were hurting. Only once since his awakening had he felt any measure of fulfilment – that evening during the storm. The storm that had begun his journey towards discovery, revealing both his cursed slumber and his unnatural abilities. But not only was he tired; he was restless. Countless nights of anxiety and stress plagued him. Corrosive feelings of remorse for those he had left behind, for those he had lost to the hands of fate and time. He knew he needed to act, or else he would give up that last part of his soul, that feeble part of him that dared to go on, to hope for purpose.

Rising slowly, the iron rod gripped tightly between gloved fingers, Darius found that for the first time in a long time, he had a purpose. "I will always fight to preserve those who walk in the light of truth, to protect the weak and guide the lost." The Second Oath of the Feromage rang out in the back of Darius's mind, validating his course of action. *I may not know what these visions mean, and I don't know how I am to 'find' what I cannot see. But I do know how to do one thing*, Darius thought as he rested the heavy rod onto his shoulder, a wry smile forming at his lips as confidence began to replace feelings of self-doubt. *I know how to fight, and I will protect the weak. Even if I cannot do much, I can do that.* And with those thoughts, Darius left the shed into the dark of Tur'Mor.

Three hours passed as Darius patrolled the back alleys of Southend, having climbed over the wall that separated it from the Mercantile Courts. Few were out at this hour, and those that were ambled about drunkenly. Darius was beginning to second guess his decision to go out, for these people did not appear to need or want saving, when he heard a cry of fear. The pleading screech reverberated through the alleyway and Darius did not hesitate to rush towards the sound.

"Merciful Gallea, please!" cried the woman from her knees, her azure and scarlet dress tattered and soiled by muck, and her hands grasping golden prayer chains with the seal of the Sisterhood of the Graced.

The woman did not appear to be one found in Southend – her clothing was far too ostentatious and her pleas too proper. Laying in the dirt next to her was a man in green monk's robes, blood pooling on the cobblestones from a head wound. Four men, dressed in dark greens, browns and blacks, circled the fair woman, faces hidden behind cruel masks that portrayed anguished faces of demons. One of the men, a massive brute with a thick neck and back, held a cleaver that was nearly as long as his own forearm, while the others wielded cudgels.

"You'll be comin' with us now, pretty," the thick man snarled in hateful glee as he stretched out a hand to take the woman. "Your goddess won't sa-"

A bone-splintering crack rang out as Darius slammed the iron rod into the man's extended wrist.

"AH!" the brute bellowed, dropping his cleaver and grasping his dangling arm, just above a fractured bone protruding from the flesh.

"What in the name of –" a second called out.

But he was silenced immediately by a blow to the chest with the heavy iron bar.

Darius raised his leg and kicked the first away from the dumbstruck woman, sending his body tumbling across the stones. The thrill of the fight boiled beneath Darius's skin. This was not a bout with an Aluth, wearing training garments and using blunted weapons. No, this was a real fight, and he reveled in it.

Taking a firm stance, planted directly between the kneeling woman and the remaining two robbers, Darius slapped the bar into his left hand. He then raised the bar, left hand forward, end directed towards the closer of the two, assuming Ka'ral, the stance of Stone Breaker. This was the best form he had learned from the Aluth, a powerful series of lunging and slamming of blunt weapons common amongst the peoples of Galacia. Or so he had been told.

The two robbers rushed him at once, cudgels raised in a wild, untrained manner. Darius blocked the first blow with his rod while simultaneously raising his right leg shockingly high, kicking the second in the teeth, bloodying his face and sending him to the ground with a grunt. Wood on iron cracked loudly as the rod and cudgel connected. Darius used the momentum of his raised leg to twist himself around the robber as he brought it down, catching the unsuspecting man around the neck with his own rod, and sending him flying over his now turned back.

Rising victoriously to full stature, Darius twirled the rod about himself in an ostentatious flurry of motion, then snapped it under his armpit with an exactness that could only be acquired from practice. He had learned the art of warfare from a young age, having trained his whole life with the

spear and the axe, primitive weapons nowadays. However, he had always
had a gift for picking up forms of violence and combat and had learned
quickly under the tutelage of the Aluth.

The robbers, beaten and broken, scuttled away like spiders into the
night, fleeing from their better. Darius glared at them though, standing
between where they had lain and the young woman whom they had
attacked. He had not been able to Bind during the night hours, but that
need had never been there in the first place.

"Yhunfree!" a trembling voice called out.

Darius turned to see the maid huddled over the monk's battered body,
sitting upon her knees, hands still grasping the golden chain. She was a
slim woman, beautiful by Ordiatian standards, young and fair of skin. And
she had bright eyes, blue, like two sapphires set into marble flesh.

Darius dropped the iron rod to the ground and rushed towards the
lifeless monk. He stopped mid stride and witnessed something amazing.

The maiden opened the locket about her neck, revealing a vibrant blue
stone that shone with a light that filled the alley. She took a deep breath
and sucked in the light. Her eyes burst with a light not so different from
Darius's own eyes when he performed a Binding yet azure instead of
yellow.

"By the Grace of Gallea, my Light to your soul," the maiden chanted.
Her voice did not quiver now, but was deep and strong, like that of a
rushing river over a bed of shallow rock. "Be ye healed."

And then she blew out the Light. It washed over the monk, coating
him in a translucent film of energy. It rested upon him for a matter of ten
heartbeats, and then sunk into his clothes and flesh.

The maid's flesh dimmed to a pale, nearly grey coloring, and she fell
forward weakly, barely catching herself with her outstretched hand. The
amulet, which was held in the other hand, had dimmed greatly, though
there was still a pulsating light to it that seemed to match the woman's
own eyes, ebbing and flowing with bursts of azure.

The monk seized, body drawn into an upright sitting position, as if it
had been pulled by an outside force that Darius could not see. The young
man gasped a great breath of air, letting out tiny wisps of evaporating blue
light. The wound at the side of his head had healed, and no blood
remained on the street nor his garments.

Darius was dumbfounded, absolute and utterly shocked. He stood
there, still as a board and gaped at the scene. Questions assaulted his
stupefied mind. Bindings could only affect one's own self. Light could not
be stored in stones. How could she pass her Bindings to another? How was
she able to Bind without the sun? True, Elcon had talked about such
things, but to witness them? The scene shook Darius to his core.

"May the Goddess Gallea bless your soul," the maiden said tenderly as
she rose to her feet.

"What?" Darius muttered distantly, still gawking at the two.

"You saved me and my Guide," the woman continued, pulling back her blue hood with red trimming from her head. She had such yellow hair as Darius had never seen. It was not golden; it was not blonde – it was yellow. And not only that, but it was also intertwined and braided with chains of silver and gold, sapphire gemstones laced throughout.

"Don't mention it," Darius mumbled, trying to take it all in. The yellow hair and her stunning beauty were not helping his mind become at ease.

"We were most blessed to have you come to our aid," the monk Yhunfree said in a shockingly low voice. He had brown eyes, a neatly trimmed beard of curly hair that was midnight black, and dark skin. "But Blessed Auna must be delivered to the Sanctuary as quickly as possible."

"Why did they attack you?" Darius asked, trying to make sense of everything as quickly as he could.

"I assume it was her garments," Yhunfree said as he pulled the hood back over the young Blessed's head. "They know that the Blessed carry sacred things, things that can fetch a great deal of money." His eyes darted to the amulet and then back to Darius, hardening instantly. "What do you mean by coming to these streets? You wrap your face with the Lo'Phandrak of the Oathkept, but you do not wear their arrayments, nor apparently take their Oath of Silence. Do you mean to steal from the Blessed?"

Darius raised his hands, opening them to show he meant no harm. "I only came because I heard her screaming."

"I must get her to the Sanctuary," Yhunfree stated. "Your help was appreciated, but we must go. She is weak now, and we cannot afford to wait."

"I can trail you to the gatehouse," Darius offered. "But I cannot draw too close. I am not exactly supposed to be out tonight."

"Well," Yhunfree said with a hint of exasperation, eyeing the bowed head of the Blessed. "That makes two of you. Anyways, by Ordan's hammer, we should find safety once we are outside of this wretched part of the city. I told her it was unsafe." The disgruntled monk seemed to be muttering those last words more to himself than to Darius or the Blessed.

Yhunfree then waved Auna to follow him forwards, towards the gatehouse. Darius, still unsure of what he had just witnessed, stayed true to his word, though even more questions were mounting up in his mind.

Darius followed the two, though he stayed out of sight. It took a little over an hour to reach the gatehouse, and there were no other signs of struggles. However, Darius had a feeling that there would be consequences to the actions he had taken this day. Though, what those consequences were, he could not even begin to understand.

Tired and confused, Darius decided it best to call it a night. There would be other chances to get out. For now, he needed sleep. Because tomorrow, tomorrow he would get answers.

CHAPTER 14: TASKS

"Darius, are you alright?" Elcon asked, placing his mechanical pen down and rising from his couch on the lawn.

"Why does it weaken the Blessed?" Darius asked, undoing the Binding and releasing the flows of sunlight. Golden streams of light melted from his eyes, then dimmed into nothingness.

"Pardon?"

"To use their powers. Why does it weaken them?"

"I do not understand what you mean by that?" Elcon looked troubled.

"I Bind the very sun's rays to my being, absorbing the flows directly into my essence," Darius said whilst studying the back of his hand, the silver ring still pulsating from the light it had just relinquished. "What is it that they do?"

"What a peculiar question, Son," Elcon said, rubbing his chin with ringed fingers. "What is prompting such an odd question?"

"It should be a simple answer." Darius's voice was perhaps a little too curt, but it frustrated him how the old priest would so often dance around his questions. "Why do they weaken?"

"Well," Elcon snapped as he eyed Darius closely, as if studying him for some unseen issue. "Perhaps the Aluth are not keeping you busy enough, or at least they have not taught you proper respect."

Darius's shoulders fell. He had not meant to be rude. It was just that he could not get the events of last night to settle in his mind. The Feromage were the Order of Guardians. They were granted their powers through the High Father Himself, Ordan, to Bind Heavenly Light. During his first life, before his awakening, Darius had only known of one other group of people able to access any form of power – the Blood Queen Mireya and her accused witches, who pulled their dark powers from the black souls of the Fallen Ones through blood rites. How had so many other forms come into existence? And where were they actually drawing their power from?

"It seems, that despite pretenses, we are both on edge this morning," Elcon said with a sigh, his face softening and lips drawing upwards into a kindly smile. "I had a late night."

"Oh?" Darius asked, thankful for the shift in the mood.

"Yes." Elcon chuckled. "When one gets to be my age, late nights are rather more tedious the following day, and the mornings far less forgiving."

"I guess." Darius shrugged.

"Anyways, where were we?" Elcon mused, "Ah yes, we were discussing the celestial bodies and how they interact within the infinite systems."

Darius rolled his eyes. *I guess Elcon won't be answering that question*, Darius thought to himself. Elcon had not held back at any other time discussing the Blessed. He had gone into great lengths about their divine calling, their intricate role within the Church that they played, and how they were Touched by the Ellitheor, granted gifts to aid others in their journey back to the Glistening Gates of Vanherran, and on to the eternities. Blessed. Ordan and Gallea's Anointed servants. Females granted the priesthood of the Ellitheor, sent to guide the faithful, each a direct descendant of the First Patriarch, or so it was told. And none of whom were male.

Elcon blabbered on for what seemed like hours but couldn't have been much longer than thirty minutes, describing the stars, moon, sun, and planets that hung in the endless sky. Darius usually paid better attention, and despite his outward act, usually found such topics far more interesting. Today, however, he could not. He needed to find answers. He was tired of finding more questions.

Darius was certain that Elcon was upset with his lack of attention during their discussion, though the high priest had sent him about his masonry duties without any further chiding. And as Darius rode towards the Sanctuary in a simple carriage, he began to feel a small twinge of regret for losing his temper. However, the feelings of frustration would not abate.

When he finally arrived, thanking the driver for the lift, Darius stared up at the monolithic building in a renewed light. How long must it have taken to build the great domed structure and her four towering spires? The eave that jutted out from the open doorway, intricately carved and displaying the heroic tales of the Ellitheor, must have weighed thousands of pounds. Perhaps one of these so called Blessed had the ability to move stone or craft architecture with a single breath of light and an uttered word as that maiden had done the night before when she healed the dying monk.

"A beauty isn't it, my son?" a familiar voice asked.

Darius swirled about, caught off guard in his wondering stupor.

"Ranun!" he exclaimed with excitement. He had not seen the portly priest in days, though somehow, it felt like far longer.

"By the grace of Gallea and the strength of Ordan, look at you!" Ranun beamed brightly as he stared upward at Darius. "You look like a new man! Hair brushed and beard clean cut. And these clothes, much finer than any I could afford you."

"Ranun." Darius could not hold back an equally beaming smile. "You offered me something of far greater merit than clothing. It is good to see you again. How goes the bread-house?"

"Just as well as ever," Ranun said as he rubbed his rotund belly. "And we seem to have even more guests and tithes than usual, thanks to a rumor that an angel had graced us at one time."

There was a twinkle in Ranun's eye, directed at him, that Darius could not mistake.

"I thought we were keeping that secret?" Darius questioned with a lowered voice.

"A secret that you can do miracles? Of course," Ranun said slyly. "A secret that Ordan, through his infinite grace and wisdom had blessed my establishment, no. That, I am unabashedly unafraid to admit, I cannot do. You see, Ordan moves in ways beyond mortal thought. And the poor need food. Besides, no one there saw you that night, leastwise, saw and could make out anything."

"So why bother hiding my abilities anyways?" Darius grunted, kicking a small rock with his boot.

"Abilities?" Ranun raised a hand in objection. "I have been counseled to avoid any such conversation. The Church sees fit to keep such miracles close to heart. If everyone saw every mercy of Ordan and Gallea, they would have no need for faith or trust in the eternal mysteries." Darius raised an eyebrow, but Ranun simply shook his head and chuckled. "It was so good to see you again. But, alas, I must gather the bread and prepare for the evening meal. Ever since my help ran off to join the order of the Anointed, I have been quite busy." And with a pat on the shoulder, Ranun hurried off towards the bakeries to bid for yesterday's bread.

Darius shrugged his shoulders and laid out his tools to get ready for the day's labors. *I guess I won't find the answers about the Blessed amongst the priests. But why so secretive? Elcon had been open about their particular gifts and how they accessed the Everlight of the Ellitheor. But of their weaknesses, oddly defensive. Why?* Unperturbed by his questions, and hopeful for peaceful clarity of honest effort, he began working the stone.

***

"Your stance is weak," the Avajan'Aluth said, slapping a long rod into the back of Darius's thigh.

He was standing, well, squatting, shakily, atop two separate pillars, arms tucked in, eyes forward. The strike stung, but he barely flinched. He drew in a long breath and tightened his stomach. Sweat dripped from his bare torso, falling two full spans to the matted floor.

"Tighten your core, find your center," she barked, moving on to the next trainee, pointing the long, white stick at the soon-to-be unfortunate recipient of another sharp crack.

This evening's session was not focused on sparring and dueling but was a night of muscle development and practice of the forms. Darius was not sure just how many different forms the Aluth were trained in before they were full-fledged Aluth, but Darius had been introduced to at least five separate forms of violence. Each unique. Each painful to understand. These martial arts were not so much dance-like, as he had seen from some training gymnasiums in the city, but were practical and deadly, made to inflict pain and maim your enemy. Darius enjoyed sparring; this kind of training, not so much. Sure, he saw the merit in it, but that did not make it enjoyable.

"Enough!" the Avajan'Aluth commanded.

The Aluth in training came to attention, dropping from pillars, rushing from blocks or the trapeze and rising from planks and holds on the floor.

"You are all dismissed," she yelled loudly, though measured and controlled. "To the baths!"

Darius walked towards the exit, removing the green band from his forehead, but stopped when a rod firmly popped him on the shoulder.

"You, young man, are not excused," the Avajan'Aluth stated flatly.

Darius turned, and to his surprise, saw that she had removed her green sash and high-collared overcoat. She wore a long white gauntlet that flared at the ends and held a helmet with a mesh face-covering under her steady arm. Two Aluth were stationed to either side of her, though a step behind. One held a pair of white gloves that matched the Avajan'Aluth, along with another mesh-covered helm. The other held two rapiers with blunted edges and rounded tips.

"You are in need of swordplay, young Master Darius," the white-haired woman said, measuring Darius up and down with hardened eyes that did not waver in the slightest.

"Avajan'Aluth," Darius said, bowing himself in respect. "I am not worthy to train with you."

"Do you disobey your Avajan?"

"No, of course not!" Darius answered fervently.

"Then, take up your steel," she commanded. "Make yourself ready to face me."

Darius, unsure what else to do, as it was very improper for anyone to address the Avajan'Aluth, much less spar with her, pulled on the long, white gloves and donned the helm. The Avajan'Aluth was much smaller and shorter than Darius, but she stood with a poise that he had never possessed. True, he was a warrior, but his foe was an artist.

"Sword to the ready!" she snapped clearly, bringing her blade directly in front of her face, hilt level and arm firm.

Darius awkwardly mimicked her.

"Stance!"

She stood forward, placing the tip outwards towards Darius's face, and raised her free hand above her head. Again, Darius tried to do the same.

"Two for the head, one for the body. Nothing below the belt." Her voice was like steel, cold and focused. "This might hurt."

The Avajan'Aluth moved with speed such as Darius had never before witnessed. He felt the sharp crack of steel on his forearm, shoulder and the side of his head before he even realized what had happened.

"You have to move to win a fight, Darius," she scoffed, clearly happy with herself. An emotion Darius did not think she regularly felt or showed.

"Sword to the ready!" she commanded, blade whipping upright. "Stance!"

Pain!

Darius hadn't even the time to react before a flurry of sharp stinging sensations bit at his body. A trickle of blood formed on his forearm, just above the glove where a welt burst. This was going to be a very painful lesson indeed.

Bout after bout, Darius felt the sting of the Avajan'Aluth's slender blade, rounded tip bringing no comfort as it struck his unprotected flesh. His legs ached from holding the unusual pose and his arms burned; his own sword felt like it weighed dozens of pounds of lead. That being said, he was beginning to understand the basic motions of the blade, the melodical way in which it sung in the air, turning and twisting with a deadly exactness.

And then it happened.

He deflected one of his Avajan's blows, parrying the strike and lunging forward with his own counter. He failed miserably. His legs were jelly and his core loose. She easily sidestepped the tip of his weapon and brought her own to his thigh, the same she had stuck earlier with the white rod.

"Enough!" he gasped, finally breaking under the strain, every breath burning in his lungs. He was on all fours, his own practice blade a few feet away, abandoned in his humiliating fall.

"Do you command this gymnasium?" the Avajan'Aluth scoffed, handing off her practice steel to one of the observing Aluth.

"No, Avajan," Darius said, abashed. He rose from the ground, tenderly rubbing welts and bruises.

"They don't stay on you," the Avajan'Aluth noted.

"What?"

"Your bruises," she said pointedly. "You have been training here for weeks, and no cut remains, no bruise or marking. Though your body is riddled with such terrible scars."

Darius turned from her, walking over to where his blade rested.

"Do not think we do not notice such things, young Darius."

The Avajan's voice was far less demeaning and authoritative than normal. And when Darius turned, her helm now removed, he saw that her eyes were inquisitive, not angry or upset as he would have expected.

"You have no reason to fear here," she continued. "You are safe within the walls of the monastery. Ordan's own watches out for you."

"Why?" Darius asked, handing the blade to an Aluth. "Why do you continue to allow me to train? Why do you, yourself nonetheless, take up the sword to teach me? What am I to you?"

"You are a boy in need of guidance," the Avajan'Aluth answered, puffing her chest up in pride. "It just so happens that I am quite adept in providing...guidance." She smiled at that last word, not a kind smile, but a rather menacing smile.

"You are the best blade-master I have ever met," Darius blurted out frankly, not sure of how to answer her previous statement.

"As a woman, I have to pick my bouts wisely," the Avajan'Aluth answered with a nod of her head. "To wrestle or box, you would utterly destroy me in the ring. But, with dexterity and training, I can best most anyone. This is a game of the mind more than the body; therefore your advantage is void, and my skill reigns supreme."

"Clearly." Darius laughed, rubbing his stiff muscles.

"The Master of the House has requested I train you to the best of my abilities," she continued. "You need little work of the physical body, sure, your stance is weaker than desirable, but it is your mind that is weakest. You second guess everything. You question yourself. You doubt your abilities. Such doubt can be catastrophic."

"I don't understand though." Darius's bushy eyebrows furrowed.

"I don't expect you to understand," the Avajan'Aluth stated bluntly. "I expect you to grow. There seems to be a great investiture in your wellbeing, young Darius. Best focus on how to improve than daydreaming on what could be."

Darius did not respond. His mind raced; despite his weariness, he could not halt the onslaught of questions. Now there was, yet again, another question. Why, why were the Aluth being drawn into this? He had figured Elcon had just allowed him this time to work out the restlessness. But was he being trained for something specific?

"Darius." The Avajan's call took him away from his thoughts. "This time tomorrow, come prepared for another bout of swordplay. I do not expect you to miss your regular training, but I will continue to work with you in these things. As for now, though, we are done. I take my leave."

The Avajan'Aluth left, coat draped over her left arm, right hand resting on the pommel of her tasseled saber. Darius watched her leave, standing bare chested and drained. He shook his head. This whole day had been a constant daze of motions, moving in fractures throughout. He walked to the lockers where his own clothes hung and retrieved them, not even bothering to dress himself before heading to the baths.

Soaking in the lukewarm water, the fires beneath had been extinguished much earlier in the night, for it was well into the dark hours. Darius scrubbed his body with a lathered sponge. His eyelids felt heavy; he was utterly exhausted. Without the golden rays of the sun, Darius had no way to draw in extra energy to soothe his battered and weary body, the split portions of his flesh having only barely sealed themselves within the hour.

"I am in no shape to go out tonight." Darius sighed to himself, looking up at the domed ceiling. *Blast it all, I'm just too tired.*

***

Aellia kicked a rock as she walked through the market, the rock skidding across the cobblestone out of sight. She swore under her breath. The last few days had been miserable; she hated every bit of them. She raised a gloved hand, trimmed with pastel green lace, to scratch at the vibrant red wig that covered her short, white hair. Aellia hated wigs, but concealing her identity was of the utmost importance.

Three days had passed since the fiasco at the Mayoral Residency, and Midcouncillor Aldorian's men had been constantly scavenging the city in hopes of finding Felik's Crew. Much to their surprise, Felik more so than any of theirs, the pompous prick did not know of the Loft or, at least, he did not know where it was located. *The one perk of living in such a massive city,* Aellia thought to herself as she moved down the street, *was the ease of concealing oneself. You could probably assault an officer, and no one would even take more than a day or two to search before forgetting about the whole thing.*

Two women with veiled faces and blue robes, hoods drawn over their heads, trimmed with burning red, walk past, causing Aellia to pause. This was the fifth time she had seen women dressed in such a strange manner, and all since the night of the failed heist.

"Lilane," Tomo called out, walking away from a street vendor selling large spools of cloth.

Aellia did not even notice at first, eyes still following the hooded women. They stood out so vividly, unfashionable, yet graceful.

"Lilane, perhaps you would care to look at these for your wedding to Duke Talmund?" Tomo's voice was a little louder than the call before and carried an edge with it.

"Oh, right!" Aellia returned, twirling about, causing the pleated dress to swish and clink, the brass rings and chains ruffling together.

Tomo, unlike Aellia, was dressed in trousers and a topcoat with long tails. She had a small velvet hat atop her tightly done-up hair. She was portraying a master butler, her coat a loud orange with white trim, and

174

trousers starched and equally bright white. In her lace-covered hand was a pocket-clock, the small cogs and springs ticking quietly, keeping perfect time.

"This good lady, Madame Marhallae, is saying she has the finest silks from Ja'una." Tomo's voice seemed skeptical as she announced her so-called lady to the merchant.

"Do you have leathers by chance, Madame?" Aellia asked as she looked over the shopkeeper's assortment of lavish cloth.

"My lady," Madame Marhallae said, aghast. "Leathers have not been fashionable for quite some time. Surely you wouldn't go galivanting around in such? How about a fine silk chinoiserie? Or a dazzling damask in velvet for the late winter nights?"

"I like leather," Aellia answered, not looking at the woman. "It is exciting and bold. Besides, I don't have much of a chest, and leather makes my ass look good."

Tomo went as red as a blazing sunrise. The shopkeeper brought a hand to her large breast, doubly aghast, and her makeup-caked face too went red. Aellia smiled, catching both their reactions from the corner of her eye as she thumbed through patterns. This had been a hard week – she would take whatever slight moments of joy she could get, even if it was fleeting and at the expense of others. She scoffed. *Especially* if it were at the expense of others.

"Perhaps the lady would be interested in these?" the fat merchant said, regaining her poise and pointing to the back of her shop.

Aellia and Tomo followed the merchant from the outer portion of her shop, which was just a large canvas awning with shelves set out on display, into a wooden structure that made up the storage portion. All the merchant's shops were made that way. Massive mobile boxes that were set down at their designated spot at the beginning of the day, wheels removed from the sides and horses taken to stables. Spools of thread and cloth hung from the walls, and small windows let in drab light. At the back, there were four or five small roles of leather, all brown or black, upon stands.

Aellia sighed and Tomo spoke, "My liege, Lady Lilane of House Arastese, only likes white."

The merchant's eyes almost bulged out of her head. The Arastese were third in houses to the Adelmo and Tur houses, their family having a mansion and gardens inside the Valamour. The Arastese were also well known for having large families, so it was harder to keep track of who was who. The diving dove, forged of gold and eyes set with sapphires, the emblem of House Arastese that rested on Aellia's collar, drew Madame Marhallae's eye, causing her to nearly faint.

"Tis' an absolute honor!" Marhallae nearly doubled over as she tried to bow ostentatiously in the confined space.

"Is it?" Aellia said in an airy voice, trying her best to mimic the haughty and aloof Uppers she had seen at the masquerade.

"But of course! Anything, anything at all I can assist you with, please, anything, just ask," the fat woman stuttered, unwilling to look Aellia in the eyes again. All pretenses had left her.

"My stable boys could use some mucking clothes. Surely you have drab clothes for hired hands?" Aellia said, turning her nose up.

"My lady." Marhallae's voice broke, and she sounded as if she would cry. But she did move forward, taking them to some grey patterns that were bunched in crates lining the wall.

"Very good," Aellia announced. "I'll take the lot." She retrieved a golden bar from her purse, one she had lifted not so long ago when she was 'helping' another Upper and handed it to a wide-eyed and scarlet-chested Marhallae. "Talla, take the box. Good day."

"You're insufferable!" Tomo hissed as they walked away from the baffled merchant.

"I seem to recall you liking the leather," Aellia teased.

"We're just lucky Tornak made those befo-"

"Don't say it," Aellia snapped, whirling her head around and stopping in the market. There was a wildness behind her eyes, a fury she had been hiding for so long, that was creeping out more and more.

"It wasn't your fault." Tomo raised a hand, consolingly, as she spoke.

"Put your damn hand down!" Aellia hissed through clenched teeth. "Do you forget you are my servant today?"

"I was only trying to..." Tomo did not finish. She could see the hurt in Aellia's eyes, eyes she deeply loved. She had tried so hard to get Aellia to see that it was not her fault Tornak had died. Aellia always countered with "had I not been so drunk" or "had I been more x or y" or whatever her excuse was.

"I know." Aellia sighed, turning away from Tomo's searching stare. "I don't need your comfort. I'll kill'm. I'll put a knife right through Aldorian's fat gut."

"And what of Felik," Tomo mused, trying to lighten the mood. "I'll reckon he'll want to skin the fat bastard."

"Let'm," Aellia scoffed, shooting Tomo a thankful glance. "But not till I run him through first."

"I thought you were on distraction duty? How are you even going to get close to the shite?"

"I'll find a way," Aellia said, snatching an orange yapa fruit from an unwary vendor, and taking a bite from the juicy, tangy fruit. "Besides, it's a bloody parade. It's gunna be wild."

"By the stars!" Tomo laughed out loud.

"What?" Aellia asked.

"Look who made the Communique!" Tomo pointed a finger at a large bulletin board near the triple-arch gateways.

Dozens of black and white illustrations of faces and likenesses were nailed to the board. In the middle, slightly covered by sheaves upon sheaves of pictures, were the faces of Belthazer, Felik, and Aellia.

"They never get my eyes right, you know," Aellia said, studying her own picture with a smile.

Across each of their foreheads were written the words: *Armed and Dangerous. Three Bars for Information, Five for Bodies.*

"Best not to get too close," Tomo said worriedly. "They didn't do you justice, but I wouldn't want people taking a double-glance at you."

"What about that guy!" Aellia said with excitement. "He looks right terrible."

Not only in the very middle of the Communique, but in several other places as well, was a drawing of a wild man. He had frizzled hair that was unkempt and fell to his shoulders. A matted beard hung to his neck, a grey streak through the center. And in every single picture, the artisans had taken the time to paint his irises with yellowish ink. *Murderer! Do Not Engage! Contact Authorities Upon Sighting! VERY DANGEROUS!*

"Someone must have offed a lord," Tomo said, shaking her head in bewilderment as she studied the wild man in the picture. "He looks like a werewolf."

"Tomo?" Aellia laughed. "Werewolves? Are you a schoolgirl?"

"Where I am from," Tomo said with a hint of dismay. "Such things are not taken so lightly."

"Well, let's be sure not to be out in a full moon then."

"You can sleep on your own tonight."

"But what about the lack of clothing I bought myself today?"

"By the gods, Aellia, do you ever stop?"

"Do you want me to?" Aellia mused.

They had so many things that hurt, and only had each other for happiness. And so, for today, they laughed together as they made their way back to the Loft.

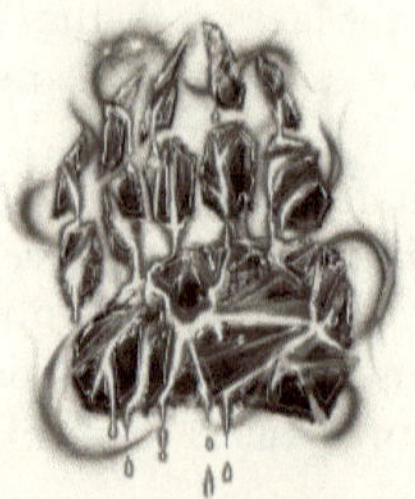

CHAPTER 15: DISCUSSIONS

"Focus, Darius," Elcon snapped as he dropped a leatherbound tome onto the desk, causing Darius to jolt.

"Sorry," Darius mumbled, wiping at his bloodshot eyes.

"Do I bore you so badly, Son?"

"No," Darius stammered, "I am just tired. It seems the Avajan has taken extra notice of me."

"I thought you could use the light to replenish yourself?" Elcon asked with a slight smile. He had been trying to get Darius to break for three days now.

"Limitations, Elcon," Darius grumbled while rubbing his forehead. "I'm still a man."

Ah, but are you? Elcon wondered silently. "You have been pushing yourself too hard, Son. You lack focus."

Darius sat up straighter, fixing his eyes on Elcon. "I need to find out what this means."

"The episodes?" Elcon urged, trying his best to contain his excitement. He had studied Darius closely for weeks but had still not got the boy to open up entirely. *What secrets is he holding? What truths lie in the recesses of his mind?*

"Visions, priest." Darius's voice was flat and unamused.

"Only the Holy Patriarch can receive direct contact from the High Father," Elcon countered as he sat across from the bleary-eyed youth of over a thousand years of age. *Does he feel the age, the ceaseless years? Does it hurt him? What mysteries has he beheld?*

Darius snorted.

"This is a house of worship, Darius. I will not have you speaking against the teachings of the Church," Elcon asserted, sliding the tome towards Darius as he lectured. "I am open to helping you find purpose and meaning in all of this, as is my duty. But I will not have you speaking against the precepts of my faith."

"Why are you doing this?" Darius looked into his eyes. The boy looked utterly exhausted.

"You yourself have claimed that you were called to a higher calling. Sworn by oaths to the will of the High Father," Elcon began, again. "I too have sworn oaths, though mine less violent. I am responsible for every soul that walks within this city. And in truth, for every soul on the face of Ethrea, as my higher calling of Member of the Holy Council dictates."

"So, you are concerned for my soul?" Darius laughed dryly.

"Do you not understand what you could mean for this people? For the Church?" Elcon questioned. "You hold secrets far greater than you could possibly imagine."

"So, that is what I am to you? A puzzle to work out."

"Darius!" Elcon proclaimed. "How could you say that? I have taken you in, provided and guided you, without request or demand, save you do not proclaim yourself to this world until we understand what you are truly capable of."

"I am sorry." Darius shrugged. "I didn't mean to seem ungrateful. I am just tired."

"I know these days must be hard on you." Elcon softened his voice, attempting to sound far more consoling than he felt. "I cannot imagine what burdens you must bear. Learning the fate of your people, finding yourself alone in a foreign world. But you must not give up hope, Son. You must not question the will of the Church. I am only here to protect and aid you. Help you find your full potential. That is all I seek to do."

"You have been helpful." Darius sighed.

There was something on that boy's mind. Elcon shook his head. *I really should stop thinking of him as a boy. Even if it weren't for his true age, he is nearing his thirties. He would be but a few years younger than my own son. My son. If only...*

"Are you all right?"

Darius's voice caught Elcon off guard.

"Ah, yes. Sorry," Elcon stammered.

"Looks like I'm not the only one who needs sleep," Darius said with forced joviality.

"So it seems," Elcon sighed. Though he did not rise to retire, he flipped open the book and began fluttering through its pages to find the place he had notated in his mind. "So it seems."

The place where Elcon stopped looked no different than the other yellowed pages of the tome. Many of the pages had large, scrollwork handwriting, while others had tight, cramped writing. The one thing they all had in common that separated this book from many of the others Elcon had forced Darius to read was the commonality of glyphs and images transcribed on the pages. Nearly every page was inked with some form of image, graph, or chart. On the page that Elcon finally rested was the image of a large sword.

Elcon touched the depiction of the two-handed blade, inked in gold. The sword took up most of the page, and on the page across from it were several other depictions of the blade, each at a different angle with cramped writings alongside them.

"Do you know the Folly of Fenron the Honorful?" Elcon asked, not looking up at Darius as he spoke.

"First son of Ordan?"

"Yes."

"I know little of him, other than his role in sealing the Dimdreal alongside his father, casting away the Fallen Ones to their doom. My people held only a rudimentary faith compared to yours."

Elcon could not help but smile as he heard Darius speak. "You are learning swiftly. Careful, Son, you begin to sound like a scholar."

Darius blushed slightly, a small smile appearing as he stared down at the page, studying the text. That boy could not decipher letters a few weeks ago. Now he could understand the complexities and differentiations between sects and religions.

"Fenron, the Holy Knight of Honor, from whom our own Order of Knights are called, was known amongst the people of Tur as a beloved hero. Even after the time of the Great Fall, he was known to show himself in his divinity, to inspire and encourage the hearts of men," Elcon stated wistfully. "After the High Father sealed away his own daughters, having cast them into the Dimdreal and using his own power to lock them away for all eternity, the Ellitheor were never heard from again. It is thought, amongst the scholars of the Church, that Ordan sacrificed something to seal away his daughters that barred his entry into this realm of existence."

"You talk in circles, Elcon." Darius sighed. "Say what you mean to say. I have not left you yet."

"What I was getting at, Darius," Elcon said with a hint of reproach as he looked over his nose at the younger man. "There were many records of a man in glistening white armor who wielded a great sword of pure gold, who did walk amongst the people. It was said that he slew wicked beasts and dark creatures that had remained after the Fall."

"So?" Darius asked.

"Was it not your purpose to do this? Were not your people called to stand as 'the iron that strikes the hardest'?" Elcon asked, quoting Darius's own words back to him.

"Yes, but what does that have to do with a legend of a demigod?"

"Demigod?" Elcon cocked an eyebrow in question.

"The High Father is God Almighty, and Gallea the Holy Mother," Darius said nonchalantly. "Their offspring are lesser beings. From what I've studied, demigod is as good a description as I can think of."

"They are the heirs!"

"Heirs of immortal, unceasing beings?" A smirk ever so slightly touched Darius's face.

Elcon scoffed, but then scratched his head. At first, Darius thought he was annoyed. But then a smile began to form across his lips. "You are getting very sharp, young man. Very sharp indeed."

"But I did not come here to discuss my findings," Darius said in reply, suppressing a swell of pride in seeing the old priest's reaction. "I came because you found something of worth. Or so you said."

"Ah, yes. Well, hmm." Elcon cleared his throat. "Fenron the Honorful was documented, not only on Ethrea, but also the Western Isles, fighting against various forms of evil and such. Well, it was years afterwards, I assume; we don't have great collections from the ages of yonder. Of the time before the collapse and subsequent rise of Tur, very little of recorded history survived."

"Elcon, you're rambling again."

"I am not rambling, Darius. I am setting the scene. Now, excuse me as I continue to relay the information that I have discovered for you, through many painstaking hours of study," Elcon chided. "Now, we do not know what caused the disappearance of Fenron from Ethrea. Some rumors say he went to slay the last dragons, while others speculate more sinister motives. And though I cannot prove either true or false, I have another theory. A theory that directly involves you, Darius. Or at least, your tribes of Feromage."

Darius did not answer but looked on with a burning intensity. He was drawn in now and had to hear what the old priest had to say.

"You have told me that your ring was crafted by the High Father, using Ethra the Life-Forger, correct?" Elcon asked, prompting only a nod from Darius in agreement.

"And you are certain it was done in this manner? Without a shadow of doubt?" Elcon asked.

"It is as the forefathers have spoken; from the first of the Feromage to my own father, such history is passed. It is the heritage of my people. There is only one way to forge Ellindahl, Ellitheor's Silver," Darius said as he rubbed his ring with his finger. "The blood of a god, the blood of a man, and the Silver of the Heavens. All are forged together, bound by oaths and sealed blood. It is the only way."

"But you did not say that the hammer Ethra must be used, Darius. Are there three requirements, or four?" Elcon pressed the question intently.

"It is as the story goes, Elcon," Darius said flatly. "I do not profess to know more. Already, my life has been many strange paths."

"There is no mention of the Guardians until after the Fall, not even until after the disappearance of Fenron from our records," Elcon continued. "What if you were not granted your gifts by the High Father, but by Fenron, to stand in his place. The sword that strikes true," Elcon said as he placed a finger onto one of the phrases under the golden blade.

Darius felt a jolt of panic. A surge of fear. And a rise of frustration. This went against everything he had ever been taught, everything he had known. He had been called as the Hand of the Ellitheor, made to strike down evil. This thought caused him pause. Did it change anything, his calling being from one Ellitheor or another? No, that wasn't it. It was the principle. It was another thing that Darius felt like he was losing. Another connection to his already distant and fleeting past that was being severed.

"Are you all right, Darius?" Elcon asked carefully. His grey eyes were focused on Darius, gentle and concerned.

"I am fine, Elcon. Just −" Darius breathed slowly. "I will be fine. Please, continue."

"All right," Elcon said as he crossed his leg over his knee. "You had to obtain your abilities somehow, and your methods of Binding seem somewhat primitive. That is, the results of overindulgence are. The hidden writings tell that the Guardians of olden times were established, as you have said, to be a sword against evil. That you were granted your abilities through the conduit of the gods to stand in their places and dole out justice and vengeance."

Elcon paused, seeming somewhat uncomfortable. The high priest was scratching at his chin, a nervous tick that Darius had noticed the old man fell on when he was trying to hold back something. However, Darius could tell that his eyes were unfocused, not staring through him as he often did when he did not want to say something in particular.

"What are you saying?" Darius asked.

"There are many things we just do not understand as of yet, Darius," Elcon said, trying his best to put on an air of confidence. "But I was wrong to try and withhold some from you. Something very important, and I am afraid our time is far spent."

"What is it?" Darius inquired. All the fatigue and weariness drained from his body. He felt a rush of excitement. A surge of hope. And oddly, a pang of frustration. If Elcon had discovered something, why had he withheld it from him? What could possibly be so important, or divisive, that the high priest would conceal it from him?

"Darius, what I am about to tell you, this secret, it is more valuable than my life, for it is not mine to tell." Elcon's emotions twisted within him as he spoke. He knew he did not have the right to tell this boy what he was about to, but he also knew he could never find the answers he himself was searching for if he did not unveil, at least in part, some of his knowledge.

A heavy silence hung in the air. Long moments passed with only the clicking sound of a brass clock that hung from the wall to break the stillness. Neither seemed to want to be the one who broke the silence, but Darius, in all truthfulness, had nothing to say. So, after a few more painstaking seconds, Elcon sighed in submission.

"In the days before dawn's light touched the realms, there existed only the True Source," Elcon explained. "This Source was infinite, a power that knew no bounds nor could be measured in any calculable way. It was known as both Consciousness and Sentience. Little is known of such things, but what we do know is that it was from this power that Ordan, first of the Ellitheor, our Gods, was created. From this power was Gallea, the Holy Mother, formed, a perfect companion to our God. And of them, five sons and three daughters were born, two of which would come to be known as the Fallen Ones.

"Morgana and Moranna. The Cursed Ones, those who let evil abound and sought to corrupt all their father had created. They harnessed some form of darkness unlike anything known to mankind or God alike. With this darkness, they could drain the very life from those who sought to oppose them. You yourself have seen the touch of such unholy evil," Elcon said, pointing to Darius's chest, to the scar that laid tucked away behind shirt and vest.

"I already know about these things," Darius answered, sounding confused. "We've talked about this at length."

"Patience," Elcon replied. "To understand is to first hear, and then accept."

Darius's eyebrows furrowed as his head tilted at Elcon's words.

"Well, to put it in your words, bluntly, that is, our God is just as confined as the Fallen Ones," Elcon said brashly, exasperation heavy in his words. "Doomed by his own hand, a prison forged to seal away his own daughters, fashioned from his own essence."

Darius looked stunned by the high priest's confession.

"Our First Oath is to the High Father, to serve him. The first of our Holy Order, Patriarch Al'Endar, was granted foresight and charged with admonition to proclaim the day of his return. Such task has befallen every first son of the line of Al'Endar, from his death even to this day. High Patriarch Orrum holds that very admonition, the charge to be the Watcher of the Fates, Proclaimer of the Keyholder," Elcon pronounced uneasily. He felt the weight of his own words pressing down upon him, condemning him as he spoke.

"So, it was at the Fall that the first Blessed was pronounced?" Darius asked, breaking the flow of Elcon's words. "Granted his powers from the High Father?"

"Darius, you are missing the point." Elcon sighed. "Yes, this is the first recorded instance of a Blessed. But we have clearly discussed that no Blessed existed when your tribes guarded the land. We have records now, that I have discovered, that preach of the First Son of the High Father walking the earth after the Fall and subsequent Sealing."

"So, what am I missing?"

"When we first met, Darius, I promised that I would help you find the purpose of your visions. I promised you I would not cease until we found truth and meaning in all of this," Elcon's eyes grew unsteady, almost ashamed. "Despite this promise, with every discovery, a dozen new questions arise. The only thing there is, is more searching. Endless circles."

Darius looked to Elcon, studying him. He did not speak swiftly but tried his best to form a comforting response. Words failed him again. And when he finally spoke in a broken voice, all he could mutter was, "I believed I was searching for something, someone... good. Not another fight. I thought I could be more."

"Darius," Elcon answered as he leaned forward, placing a reassuring hand on Darius's shoulder. "You must not lose faith. You can do much good in this. A purpose of seeking out and destroying darkness is not a bad thing. You are a hero. Godsent to save these people."

"Like my family?" Darius asked bitterly.

The words seemed to cut Elcon deeply, for his facade shattered and his hand fell.

"I have fought against the darkness, Elcon," Darius continued coldly, not allowing the old priest to form an answer. "I have lost my father, my brother, and my mother. I lost my whole tribe to the darkness. I have been scared, broken and bruised by the darkness. And now, I have been called back, to stand against it once more. I just had hoped..." He looked down. "It doesn't matter what I wanted."

"Son," Elcon said slowly. "Many have given their all to the greater good. I promised I would help you find meaning and purpose. I did not promise it would be what you wanted."

"Thank you, Elcon," Darius answered, crestfallen. "For all you have done for me. If the Ellitheor want me to be their sword, so be it."

Darius rose from his chair, the legs scraping the stone floor as he pushed himself backwards. His hands hung open and his shoulders bore a slight droop. It was a stance that Darius rarely took. And for the first time since his childhood, Darius couldn't maintain the outward image of strength he had cultivated for so long. Something in his soul seemed to break.

"Do not lose faith, Darius," Elcon said tenderly as the boy turned to walk away. "You are perhaps the only hope our people have."

"The world has forgotten. The Ellitheor have gone silent, and the new gods are silver and steel, machinery and steam. People have forgotten the horrors of the past, but I have not." Darius opened the door and disappeared into the monastery.

Darius shoved his hands in his pockets as he walked down the hallway. Candelabras cast a dim, flickering light down the drab corridors. His eyes saw clearly enough, though they always did. Darius breathed in; he could smell the food that was cooking, salty and savory meats being placed in stewpots. He could hear the monks shuffling about, conversing in low tones, one with another, about topics of religion and faith. All the noise, the overwhelming sensations, the immutable racket of the seemingly quiet monastery wracked Darius's brain, harrowing at his insides. He rushed out of the building, feeling the walls closing in around him.

The cold, blustery wind licked his cheeks, biting away the claustrophobia that had crept over him. Darius drank in the openness, breathing in heavy, unsteady breaths. His thumb ran around the edges of his ring, soothing his troubled mind. His skin crawled. It was all just too much.

Darius had feared this from the moment Elcon had first taken him to that place below the Sanctuary, revealing to him the fate he had suffered. He had dreaded this one thing more than anything. He slumped against the outer wall of the monastery, looking down over the city streets. Thousands of people walked about. Nightfall had just begun to wean away a beautiful, red-pink sunset fading over the ocean. Darius looked out, seeing life and motion. People living, going, doing. They were free, unfettered by a sense of duty and command. Tears formed in Darius's eyes. He had never known such a life.

"*Darius,*" a voice called him from the past. It was his father's voice. And though he knew that his father was not truly beside him, it did not diminish the lucidity of words that filled his mind. "*What is the First Oath of the Feromage?*"

Darius looked up, eyes bleary and unfocused. He had half-expected to see his father standing before him, so strong and certain of himself, as he always was. He would have his thick, black beard braided down the front of his chest, with stones and metal ringlets woven throughout. He would be resting one of his burly hands on the head of his great axe, her half-moon blade razor sharp, the haft wrapped in deer hide. His golden eyes would catch the moonlight, just as Darius's did. He would have a stiff back and squared shoulders, but his face would be warm and filled with light. But he was not there. There was nobody there.

"I will always be faithful to the High Father who grants me strength," Darius recanted out loud, still gazing outward, not focusing on anything in particular. The words seemed to comfort him, carrying a certain solidity within them.

And then, to his even greater surprise, came his father's voice again, clear as crystal: "*And what is the Second Oath, my son?*"

"I will always fight to preserve those who walk in the light of truth, to protect the weak and guide the lost."

"*You are never truly alone as you live by your oaths, my son.*"

Darius's heart nearly stopped. That was not a voice from the past. Darius jumped up, looking about himself. He was alone. But he did not feel alone. He could feel a heartbeat, low and rhythmic. He could sense someone was truly there, watching over him.

Maybe I am destined to spend my entire life in conflict, but I am not giving up that easily. There is something else out there, something or someone I must find. I may not know why yet, but I cannot give up now. I must continue to search.

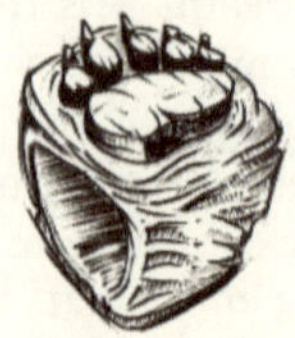

CHAPTER 16: BLOOD AND DUST

The night wind was blowing hard now, so Darius drew his overcoat closer to him. Luckily, the wrappings around his face, plus his natural affinity for colder weather, kept him comfortable enough. That being said, his arms and legs still stung from the evening bouts with the Avajan'Aluth, and his body was continually feeling weaker and weaker, the Binding lasting for less and less time each day, sometimes only a moment or two before he had to release it.

The last two nights, no one had needed his assistance as the 'Masked Marauder', as he called himself. Or at least, nobody that he could find. That was the problem. Tur'Mor was just too big. The world was just too big. But tonight, tonight he was not out for them, not really. He was out for himself, to prove he could be more than just a sword against the darkness. He could help. He could do actual good.

Darius had a reinvigorated determination to *find them*, thanks to the comforting words of his father. He refused to question the reality of the lucid conversation but held to the feeling of determination that had been seared into his soul. And while he didn't know who or what he was searching for, he still felt the need, that consuming purpose to find those whom he was commanded to seek out. True, his conversation with Elcon had not brought the answers he had been searching for. However, those words, spoken to him in his mind by his father, rung true. He knew he could not just give up, give in. He needed to keep going, to keep pushing.

Darius had left the monastery hours ago, having gone to his secluded shed and donned his night attire, and then set out to scavenge the city for those in need. He felt bad for skipping his lesson with the Avajan'Aluth, but tonight, tonight he needed this. Whether as a distraction or as a fulfilment of purpose, he could not decide just yet. All he knew was that he would not give up on his hope that he might be more than just a tool swung wildly at an incomprehensible darkness.

Hours continued to pass as Darius meandered across rooftops in the darkness. Smoke rose from chimneys, casting plumes of grey ash into the air that stung Darius's eyes. Without the distractions of a fight, feelings of longing for his home began to creep once again into his mind. He missed the smells of nature, the touch of wild clover and the smell of rising pines.

He longed to be free from this city, back in his homeland. Yet, he could not deny the need to be here, nor the command he had received to search out and find. That damned, elusive command.

Darius lifted his head suddenly. A strange scent caught his attention. Distant, but strong. A part of him wished that he could use his Binding to seal light into gemstones and then use that reserve at a later time, and that part was practically screaming right now. He was tired, but he would not leave people helpless at the hands of miscreants and robbers. True, he had not saved anyone the past two nights, but he had helped several on other nights, and had even begun to grow somewhat of a name in the underground. Darius liked to think of himself as the Masked Marauder. He was called the Shadow.

Using a tool he 'borrowed' from the Aluth, Darius latched the edge of a grappling hook to a chimney and turned a spring-loaded coil mechanism that was attached to his belt and strapped across his chest and back. Three clicks, and then he jumped off the edge of the four-story building. There was a subtle whining noise as Darius ran down the side of the building, the mechanism slowing his descent, though only slightly. When he landed, he yanked the rope and the hook fell down, reeled in at an incredible speed.

Running, Darius unsheathed his rod from the makeshift scabbard at his back. It was not a practical place to keep it for fighting, but it was out of the way, and he could finagle it back in after the fight was over.

Two men stood over an old man. They weren't in the dark green and black clothes of those strange, masked men he had encountered the first day. No, these were just street thugs trying to take advantage of the weak. This was not going to be a profitable night for them.

Darius made short work of the two men, using his rod more for deflection that attack. These were not trained men, and they were overcome easily. The old man, much to Darius's relief, was only pushed down, not badly hurt.

"It's you!" the old man exclaimed through gasping breaths with widening eyes. "You're the one called Shadow!"

Darius slid the iron rod back into its sheath, then squatted down and extended a gauntleted hand to the wispy-haired man. The man took Darius's hand with an air of adoration upon his face, as if he were idolizing him. Darius nearly shuddered. The look unsettled him.

"You do not speak?"

Darius shook his head in answer, the wide brim of his hat and the wrapping totally concealing his features. He did, however, point a finger away from the alley, gesturing for the old man to leave the scene. Darius had made it a point to keep his promise to Elcon. There would be no hint of who he was or what he could do. He could not speak, for his accent, though blending more and more with the Ordiatian phonetics, was still vastly different. His eyes, brilliant yellow, stood in stark contrast to the dull greys, browns, and hazels of Ordiatian men and women. Only his size could truly be seen, though there were several people from other nations who had expatriated into Tur'Mor who equaled him in stature.

"May the grace of Gallea watch over you and the strength of Ordan attend," the man said in a final bit of praise before hobbling away, a wide smile upon his wrinkled face.

Darius tied up the two miscreants and carried them both, one over each shoulder, to a nearby crossroad. A City Guard precinct was located not too far from the place where he lay them, clearly visible by light emitted from a series of iron lampposts.

As Darius walked away from the thugs, he sighed. He had truly hoped he would find something, or someone tonight. He just felt like it should have happened by now. He had heard his father's voice. He had felt that consuming need to find. He shook his head in dismay. All that was left to do now was to go back and try to get a few hours' sleep before dawn broke.

***

Darius pulled his heavy overcoat about himself, leaving the heavy brass buttons undone so that his tweed vest and high-collared shirt were clearly visible. He tied a whitened leather apron, which had two deep pockets near the beltline and a gold-stitched emblem of Ethra over the right breast, about himself. It was a stonemason's apron, handy for holding tools and supplies.

Against the bed frame rested a basket-hilted broadsword that had been gifted him by the Avajan'Aluth, having earned it after competing in twenty-four individual Phar'ais, though he had only won seven. The blade was simple, forged from dull steel and lacking any of the pompous frivolity that 'gentlemen' searched out. However, it was sharp and true. The only thing on the blade that stood out was a green band hanging about the hilt. Darius had no real use for a sword, other than its intrigue as a token of honor. It was unheard of for a member of the Parsonary, someone who worked for the Church, to be attacked or threatened. As a matter of fact, Elcon expressly forbade him from carrying the sword, despite Darius's numerous requests.

The high priest always replied the same way: "Swords are weapons of war and instruments of death, Darius. You are now a bringer of peace. Go now and spread the peace of the High Father, and He will guard you well." Darius would always return the sword to his room in obedience, though often would mutter to himself about just wanting to wear it because he liked the way it looked.

During Darius's childhood, he had never even seen such a weapon as these modern blades. Even those first Southern men he had met, those of the Tarish army, had worn bronze armor and wielded short, bronze swords and spearheads. These new swords were forged of sturdy steel, with hard edges and long blades, some curved and single-edged and others

188

straight with fullers and two sharp edges. The hilts were also finely crafted, and the handles protected by baskets, cages or swept hilts.

Darius thought he looked rather dashing in his long overcoat, a polished blade at his side, and his hair pulled back tight. However, Elcon would give him a glare if he voiced such thoughts, a knowing sort of look that would make Darius laugh and then do as asked.

Darius left his room with a chuckle at the thought, taking up his masonry hammer and a leather satchel of supplies for the day, leaving the sword against the bed. He headed down the broad steps of the outer portion of the monastery and out the back gate, passing through the chest-high stone wall that encased the convent. Darius kept to the side streets and back alleyways as he traversed the massive city. He still distrusted the city guards in black armor, considering them vile and cruel, often exercising their authority in unjust ways and harsh brutality.

Cool, salty wind licked Darius's rosy cheeks, which protruded sharply, adding additional color to his rather pale flesh. His now neatly-trimmed beard and tightly-bound, shoulder-length hair, did not keep back the wind quite as well as when it was longer and unkempt. However, the Ordiatian style was very handsome on Darius, and it helped to better show the strong youthfulness of his face, save the bright and strikingly unusual silver streak through the center of his beard. Despite all Darius's frivolous attempts, Elcon was beginning to turn him into a proper gentleman.

The brisk air, though definitely still cold in the mornings, was steadily warming day after day. Three weeks had passed since Darius had moved into the Monastery, and the feel of Tur'Mor was steadily normalizing to him. The smell of salt was growing stronger and the sounds of birds migrating back to their homes was becoming more common. Darius walked with a light step and a smile. He was happy to be about his day, for he had no dreams of that mountainside nor heard the voice of thunder calling to him the night before. His morning had gone well, and he had even managed to win a duel against one of the Aluth last night.

Darius gazed upon the magnificent structures that dotted Tur'Mor, and while he was becoming more accustomed to the city, the sights were still fascinating. However, the sights that brought him the most satisfaction, or cynicism, were the higher-classed citizens strutting in their fancy garb, bowing and snarked over little tiffs and disagreements. The very best moments were when two men would square off and challenge each other to a duel for "honor's sake". And while Darius could not deny that many were quite skilled, it was all for show, as no one ever really got hurt and most ended swiftly in a draw. Though this did not stop the women from swooning over their champions of valor.

The streets of Tur'Mor were crowded, more so than normal. Darius had heard of some artifacts of days long past being brought into the city to be taken to the Valamour, one in particular which was of great importance: the King's Jewel. Apparently, it had sat in Un'Mor in the

Cathedral of Sages for the last several years. Now it was time again for the jewel to be brought back over the Potamae River that flowed into the Western Sea, separating Un'Mor from Tur'Mor.

Thousands of people from across the nation were gathered. There were vibrant costumes and dancers, jugglers and acrobats, and bards singing about tales of yonder years. Darius found it hard to move even from the Monastery to the Sanctuary, a relatively untraveled path in normal times. It, too, was filled with mothers and fathers taking young ones to see the presentation of the King's Jewel, for when it was locked in the Cathedral of Sages or the Valamour, the common folk would have no access to see such an important relic of the past. Other than the jewel, the High Seat of the Republic would be there, greeting the crowds with great ostentation, along with delegates and leaders from across the northern portion of Ethrea and the Isles of Galacia.

By the time Darius finally reached the Sanctuary to begin his day reworking the steps of the beautiful building, the tradesmen were already out and selling everything from fresh produce to vibrant accoutrements. Darius paid them little heed. He was still bitter towards the lot of them for the way they had treated him in his need for bread all those many weeks ago. Selfish hypocrites, the lot of them!

Darius walked up the raised portion of earth upon which the Sanctuary sat and laid his tools down where he would begin his labors. He looked up to the depictions of events long passed, etched into the massive eave of the Sanctuary that was supported by towering pillars of marble, truly studying them for the first time. Darius had always believed in the Ellitheor. He viewed them as he believed they were: gods, divine beings, the very creators of life and matter. He had always followed them devoutly, faith being a key principle in the access to his ability. The oaths and honor were required, and though he did not understand all, that much was evident. Not only had his father taught him these things, but life had also painfully reinforced them time and time again. However, in the back of his mind, a feeling of uncertainty began to lurk. Perhaps it was these strange visions, or maybe it was the curse that had cast him from home and family, but he had grown distant in his trust of the Ellitheor. Not to the extent of abandoning his principles, but to question them. He would be a fool not to, right?

Elcon had said that faith was lacking among the followers of Ordan in Ordiatea, and, therefore, the people needed to provide sacrifices to the Ellitheor so that they would continue to protect and sustain the Republic. Darius felt that there was an underlying tension between the Church of Ordan and the High Seat of the land, though Elcon would not condone such talk. He had tried to press the high priest, at first tactfully and then more forcefully, but Elcon would always evade or change the subject.

Darius began to carry large, flat stones to the steps from a nearby pile. They were extremely heavy and would have taken two normal men to carry, but Darius moved them just fine on his own. He did not care that people would occasionally point at him, mainly children whose parents would hastily pull them to their sides and tell them it was rude to point.

Darius knew Elcon was only trying to protect the sanctity of the Church and its strained relationship with the governing body of the land. But why? Everyone knew that the Ellitheor drew their power through the faith and offerings of their people, and it just seemed odd to him that Elcon would not condemn those who would try to twist the Words of the High Father for their gain.

Darius laid down the last of eight stones he had carried. He then took up his hammer and a large steel spike and began to chip away at an old, worn step. The stone chipped, flinging fragments of rock about into the air.

And what made matters even more bizarre was how Elcon had vigorously instructed him to keep his abilities secret, to not tell anyone about them. Elcon had warned him that performing supernatural feats would result in a one-way trip to the dungeons of Tur'Mor, never to be heard from again. The ideals of religion seemed to have masked the truth and shrouded the facts with mythos and legend.

Darius just shrugged his shoulders and pulled out another of the tools from his satchel: a wooden wedge about a hand's length across and not thicker than his thumb at the base. He drove it behind the step and pounded it with his hammer until the step cracked free from its mortar. Darius threw the chunks into a pile beside him. He then took one of the new slabs of marble, laying it in place of the old, and then moved on to the next step.

Elcon had explained to Darius that both sorcery and the arcane arts were taboo in Tur'Mor. And if one were to talk about such things, they were regarded as fools and mocked by the people. Only those in the Church, the Blessed, were permitted to perform any form of incantation, and their powers were directly bestowed upon them by the High Father Himself through one of His chosen disciples. What he did not say was that those that were even capable of touching the Spark were sought out and placed in 'healing halls' until they could no longer feel the Spark within them.

The one bright light to these days was the trip Ranun would make near the end of each day to buy bread from the bakers and a few ingredients from the merchants and peddlers for his bread-house. Darius would often meet his elderly friend, for truly he had become such, and talk for some time in the waning hours of the day. And those hours were soon drawing near, and he was ready to let off some steam that had built up in his mind. *Ranun will listen, he always does.*

Darius had just started working on the bottom steps, the stack of flat marble at his side down to three, when he heard a loud crash. He stood quickly and turned to see what had caused the noise. He saw that large crowds of people were parting swiftly, some even jumping to get out of the way of something. What was it? Darius could not see, but whatever it was, it was drawing closer to the open courtyard wherein sat the Sanctuary. *The procession isn't supposed to be here yet*, he thought as he peered out into the crowds of colorfully clad citizens.

From amidst a group of the upper-class citizens, a loud scream erupted.

A woman in a fine silk dress shot backwards, rolling across the ground, muddying her expensive attire. The man next to her swore loudly as he was shoved sideways, stumbling into a food cart, which knocked off his top hat.

A small figure, dressed in a sleeveless, white cloak darted past the group of angry Uppers. The individual was running at full speed, sweeping people of all different sizes out from in front of him in a remarkable feat of both strength and dexterity.

Darius chuckled lowly as he watched the oh-so-proper Uppers fall to the ground, dirtying their ever-so-precious accoutrements in such an ungraceful way. However, his ebullience was cut short, and his expression went from lighthearted glee to concern in an instant when the scene he was witnessing took a dark turn.

The white-hooded runner was followed by several other people. Three ominous-looking, black-cloaked, men in wicked masks chased after the one in white. Darius quickly realized this was no simple thief escaping with a minor score from a merchant's stand. No, this person was in grave danger. And to make matters worse, behind the black-clad men, two city guards with silver-starred, black vests gave chase.

Darius's yellow eyes sparked with light as time seemed to slow, as all became much clearer. He could smell the sweat, the dread, perspiring from the fleeing man in white. He could taste, like bitter salt and mire, the vileness of the three in black cloaks. This caused his lip to curl into a wicked snarl as he felt the heat of the sun begin to rage within his veins.

The ill-assorted cluster of men rushed through the large courtyard that separated the markets and workshops from the temple. The one in white moved with quick, dodging motions, often knocking tradesmen down as a means to slow his pursuers. However, these attempts were certainly in vain, and Darius quickly realized that death was certain if they caught their prey. He needed to act, yet he knew he could not reveal himself in front of all these people.

One of the dark-clad men turned suddenly. He had a staff in hand, and to Darius's surprise, attacked both the pursuing city guards. The robber bashed them to the ground with a mighty swing of his rod. In that same instance, another of the men jumped towards the hooded figure in white. The collision drove both into the front of a fruit seller's stand, knocking both produce and crates across the ground with a crash.

Darius moved quickly, his masonry hammer clamped tightly between whitened knuckles, his instincts kicking in. He rushed down the hill and across the courtyard, taking no thought as to the repercussions of his actions. The once-bustling crescent-shaped courtyard, vibrant with commerce and pleasantries, was now filled with panic and disarray. Something about these hooded figures terrified the people. Darius did not care. He would not allow someone to die in front of him, not without doing all he could to stop them.

"That is enough!" Darius's deep, booming voice reverberated through the courtyard, causing the black-clad men to stop and turn their heads. Their steely eyes, each hidden behind a different kind of mask, lit with rage at the sight of him moving towards them. Darius did not care; he would not allow them to continue this way any longer.

Darius wished he had taken that sword from his room. Darius wished he had his rod, mask, and hat. Darius wished a great many things, but he had none of these things. He released the Binding, letting the light seep away, and he tightened his grip on his hammer. It would have to do.

"Parson, you do not want to get involved," the red and gold masked man who had seized the one in white sneered in a raspy voice. "This is no business of the Church."

The bandit who was wielding the staff, a large burly man wearing a dark green tunic and hooded, black leather cloak and trousers, turned and faced Darius. He had a crooked nose and dull eyes, which poked and peered out from a fractured mask. His cloak was covered with intricate stitching of snakes and winding things. Darius noticed that the man's meaty knuckles were covered in blood, as well as his stave.

Darius looked to the two men on the ground. The guards who had been wrestling with the bandit were both unconscious. The robber had beaten them badly, but Darius could tell that they were still breathing. However, they were bleeding heavily and needed assistance.

Find them!

Darius's hand sprung to his head, and he winced as the voice echoed in his mind.

"You would find it in your best interest to move along." The voice of the robber was hoarse and calloused. He wore an ivory mask that just covered the top of his forehead and eyes, with silver inlaid in winding patterns. "This prick stole, and we are just taking back what is ours. Besides, you ain't looking so well, parson."

Darius did not slow his pace. He shrugged off the noise in his head; every step forward was both firm and powerful. He moved quickly, though not as fast as the night he had caught the falling sign and saved the young girl. Hundreds, if not thousands, of people were gathered in the courtyard now. *Be subtle.* His hardened yellow eyes locked on his foe, and his lip had drawn into a snarl. *I wish I had that sword.*

The bandit lunged towards Darius, swinging his quarterstaff towards him. Darius caught the rod with one hand, rolling his back across the staff in a deadly move of grace. Next, his elbow connected with his attacker's face. Bones crunched and blood sprayed upon connection. The bandit fell to his knees, gurgled a blood-thickened grunt, and crumpled into a pile on the ground.

The man holding onto the hooded figure in white let out a yelp of pain. Darius's eyes shot towards him, emotions flaring, senses heightened. The figure in white was fleeing down a side alley. The man in black held his leg, writhing in pain, a small dagger protruding out of his inner thigh. He did not take a second look at Darius but turned immediately, swearing as he staggered after the escapee.

Darius began to follow after the two, but he stopped suddenly. Time slowed around him. Not even the birds moved in the sky and the screams in the courtyard turned to a lull. A single note frozen in time. The sound of a turning mechanism reverberated through Darius's ears.

Darius snapped his head around, glancing over his shoulder just in time to see the last of the black-clad men raise a weapon to his shoulder. He had pulled a crude, wheellock rifle with bronze fittings and a dark cherry wood stock, from his back and was now pointing it at a very wide-eyed Darius.

The man turned the metal pulley on the side of the firearm, raised it to his shoulder and then pulled the trigger, releasing the flint head. Darius spun quickly to the side, flinging his hammer behind him at his opponent, right knee sliding across a patch of damp grass as his left hand grabbed at the edge of a potter's cart. The hammer collided with the fiend's chest, a hollow thud accompanying the impact. A large vase near Darius's head burst into pieces as the lead shot whizzed past his ear.

Eyes wide with the thrill of combat, Darius rose to his feet, never coming to a complete stop in motion. He took three long strides to reach the second robber. The man was kneeling on the cobblestone street, grasping at his chest with one hand and using the other to hold himself upright, struggling to draw in air.

"Coward." Darius leered as he stood over the wheezing robber. "At least your companion had the brass to face me like a real man."

Darius picked up the wheellock rifle and lifted it over his head. He then brought it swiftly down onto the cobblestone, shattering the buttstock with a splintering crack, leaving only a warped barrel and fractured wood. With a swift kick to the ribs, Darius knocked the darkly clad man unconscious. Without missing a beat, he quickly snatched up his hammer and continued to follow the wake of broken pots and overturned tables that were left behind by the escaping figure in white and the third robber.

The proximity of the buildings and markets left little room to escape left or right. Not only were the smooth stone buildings built tightly side by side, but they were also sheer and rose upwards of five stories. Darius moved swiftly, and he could see the two heading up the stairs that led to the central portion of the city. The white hood of the escapee stood in stark contrast to the blackened, muddy leather of the robber.

Atop a series of stone stairs, Darius could see that the robber had caught up to the individual in the white hood. He hurried towards them through the crowded streets, people screaming and flailing to get out of the way. But when Darius had made it to the top of the stairs, the robber had vanished, having left the hooded figure alone on the stairs.

Darius rushed to the body, which was draped lifelessly across the worn steps. His heart pounded with unexpected concern for the assaulted person. For some unbeknownst reason, Darius was drawn to a motionless being, and something deep within his soul seemed to resonate as he drew closer.

Quickly, carefully, Darius knelt over the fallen body. Yet, as he extended a hand, a sharp crackling rang in his ears. His vision blurred as a sudden flash of light distorted the air.

Darius jerked his hand back from the lifeless body. An intense sensation tingled in the palm of his hand, and the scar on his chest seemed to blaze in protest. He winced in agony. However, as quickly as the pain had assaulted his body, it faded away. And when he looked at his shaking fingertips, wisps of yellow light rose.

"What?" Darius questioned out loud as he stared at his fingers. A tingle ran down his spine and a taste of metal coated his tongue.

Shaking away the oddity with agitated motion and a rub of his brow with an unsteady hand, Darius turned his attention back to the motionless body and began searching for signs of injury. The hood fell away as he turned the body over, and he blinked in surprise. The cloth that had been wrapped about 'his' face was gone, and the face of a young female with sharp features and ivory skin now stared back at him, unblinking. Her eyes were bright blue, like the Blessed from the alley. However, much unlike the woman he had saved, these seemed to have turrets of lightning flashing within them.

What was that? Darius gasped in wonder. But as he looked back into the stranger's eyes, they were no more than a pale blue. *My mind must be playing tricks on me*, he reassured himself as he turned his gaze to her torso, checking for hurt or harm. *This day just keeps getting stranger.*

The young woman had short hair, no longer than the back of her neck, which was slicked back, as if frozen by an icy gale. Her face was fair but strong, appearing no older than her early twenties at best. A bruise on her high cheekbone stood in contrast to her pale face and rosy lips. The girl looked very different from the women of Tur'Mor; her lighter skin stood in stark contrast to the sun-kissed tan of the Ordiatians Darius had come to know. Her petite frame was covered in a long, sleeveless leather archer's cloak, which was as white as her hair and split below the belt, brushing the top of her long boots. These were also white and rose up to the mid-section of her thigh, embellished by dozens of straps and buckles. Polished vambraces of glistening steel guarded her forearms and elbows. And a small silver chain hung around her neck, slipping between her breasts.

It struck Darius, as he looked over the young woman, that this was the first time he had actually been close to a female since his awakening. Sure, he had seen women, helped them at the bread house and sat near them in the Sanctuary. But he had not been *close* to a woman, not like this, for over a thousand years. However, those foreign feelings of primal instincts that had tingled deep within him were quickly extinguished. For while he searched the young woman for injury, he felt a sudden and intense pain in his groin.

Darius let out a yelp of agony.

The intense, nauseating pain emanated from the girl's boot, ending in the connection it had made with his manhood. This was accompanied by the feeling of cold steel against his flesh. A knife rested expertly against his neck. The girl had moved so swiftly that Darius had not even comprehended what had happened until it was far too late.

"Back up there, big fella," the white-haired girl demanded. Her voice was firm and eyes unwavering. "Don't get too familiar!"

"I was trying to help," Darius groaned through clenched teeth as he fought back the taste of bitter bile that was quickly rising in his throat. He slowly raised both hands up and gingerly rose to his feet, taking a step back away from the woman.

"I can take care of myself," said the girl, slowly lowering her knife. She then grabbed quickly at her side as a sickening look of dread struck her face. "Damn it to all to Halfak's fiery gates! The bloody bastards took it!"

"Took what?" Darius inquired cautiously, gaining a more level tone to his gruff voice.

The girl gave Darius a quizzical look and then sheathed her dagger behind her back where a secondary blade was also stowed. Something about this girl puzzled Darius, and he couldn't quite tell what it was. But it, in fact, fascinated him.

Undeterred by her brash behavior, he lowered a hand towards the still-prone girl. She stared at his bulky hand for a moment, as if almost disgusted by it and Darius as a whole and cocked a white eyebrow. Her face then softened, if only slightly, and she reluctantly took his hand.

As Darius helped her to her feet, he added, "You take care of yourself then, okay?"

"What do you care?" she scoffed, shaking her head. "Forget it, I gotta get my bag back."

"You need a hand?" Darius inquired, though truthfully, he didn't have any desire to go chasing after the robber. *Whatever he has can't be that important*, Darius thought.

"From a soft-gutted parson?" the girl mocked as she raised an eyebrow in amusement, poking Darius in the gut. It was not soft.

"I am not a parson –" Darius began to retort; however, he was cut off quickly by the white-clad lass.

"It doesn't matter who or what you say you are. They are Kh'ar Robbers. The lot of them infest this city like a mess of roaches." Her voice was thick with venom towards the robbers, yet her eyes locked onto the golden hammer on his apron. "Parson," the title slipped from under her breath, mockingly. Though, she did have a strange look of surprise as she held her finger, apparently somewhat sprained from ramming it into Darius's abdomen.

"I was only offering to help," Darius mumbled awkwardly. He could feel the heat of embarrassment crawling up the back of his neck.

"I don't have time for this." The girl sighed with a shake of her head. She began moving forward, pushing past Darius up the stairs.

"You got a name?" Darius called out after her, unable to think of anything else to stall the girl as he stood there dumbfounded.

"I don't need saving. Not physically, and for damnation's sake, not spiritually," she said as she crested the top of the steps. She smirked, another flash of blue lighting her eyes. "Besides, looks like you have plenty saving you need to do for yourself." And with that, she vanished.

Darius felt a strange rush, an exhilaration, as he stared up at the young woman. He did not know what to think of her, but for the first time in weeks, he felt an unusual compulsion. No, that was not the correct word. But Darius could not think of the correct words for how he felt. There was a bond there, something he could not explain, between them. He could have sworn that he recognized the young woman from somewhere, but from where, he could not recall.

The light was fading now, and twilight was drawing near. Darius scoffed as he walked slowly down the steps, his mind racing. He wondered about the strangeness of the Kh'ar. There was a darkness about them that was unsettling, vile and unholy. *Unholy?* Darius scoffed at himself. *You have been spending too much time with Master Elcon... unholy...evil, more like it. And what of that girl? There was something...strange about her.*

At the base of the stone steps, the once-dispersed crowd had reformed. A huddled mass of peacock-like Uppers and brightly-clad merchants were gathered around something Darius could not quite make out. A low murmur of commotion was passing between the spectators, hushed whispers and stifled tears. Darius had not taken note of his surroundings and nearly ran into a short, stout woman before he looked up. What met his eyes rocked him to the core.

Darius was a head taller than most Ordiatian men, and a head and shoulders taller than the brightly colored hair of the women. It was clear to see from his vantage point that the crowds were gathered around a being, who was lying in the street in his own gore.

"He had no business getting involved," said one man, thick-gutted in a wide-brimmed hat of deep purple.

"What was he thinking?" said a spindly woman in a barrel-styled hoop dress with an enormous bow of red lace around her caboose. "A fool...still sad though."

"Sad? Eh, it was his time. Probably believed he was foreordained for it anyways, damned priests," a hook-nosed woman with sea-blue hair said scornfully as she shook her head.

"Watch your tongue, madame! He was a man of the cloth! We should not disrespect him so. Someone ought to call the guards!"

"The guards are already coming," answered another. "They were summoned when the ruckus started."

Darius looked over their heads and saw a figure on the ground, blood soaking the stone around his broken skull. Lifeless grey eyes stared with fright up into nothingness. A thick mustache of snowy white was stained red.

Darius's heart missed a beat, and his mouth went dry.

"No..." Darius bellowed out, his voice sad and shaken. His eyes filled with bitter tears and a lump caught in his throat.

"Oye! He was with them! That big man there in the duster!"

"He started all the fighting too! Him and those miscreants in the robes."

Darius saw dozens of eyes turn on him, and a dozen or more fingers pointed accusatorily in his direction. To make matters worse, several black-suited guards were heading in his direction, having been summoned to the scene. Darius, without thinking, turned his collar up and darted down a small path that led between the merchants' carts.

Moving through the tight rows of cloth-tented booths was difficult, and Darius's broad shoulders often bumped and jostled hanging fish, meats, vegetables, and other such items as he rushed forwards. He turned backwards only for a moment, looking to see if there were still guards following him. In doing so, eyes blurred with tears, he struck a large vase that was sitting on a countertop.

CRASH!

Several city guards turned quickly in the direction of the noise, but Darius had already fled. He glanced left and right as he rushed through the back alleys to find a place to hide, the whole while questioning why he was even running. Maybe it was fear that one of the guards could recognize him from his initial entry into the city, or maybe it was just a basic instinct. He heard the voices of the people jeering and pointing at him, and it felt as if the executioner's blade was coming down on his head.

The street seemed to narrow in his vision, and everything had a soft haze about it as he rushed onward. Darius could still smell the guards, hear them shouting, and he knew that they were not far behind. He could also smell the thick char of burning coal, and he knew that he was nearing the northwestern part of Tur'Mor.

The walls between the four sections were always roughly twenty measures high and well-guarded, but they seemed, in his current state of mind, to be his best chance of escape. If he stopped now, there would be no questions, he would be considered guilty for fleeing, and he would be taken to that dark underbelly once again. He would be branded, becoming a marked man, and more likely than not, strung up for crimes he could not contest.

The wall began to loom closer as Darius ran forward. He knew what he had to do. *Five breaths.* There was a tall shop near the wall. *Four.* He saw small wooden support beams protruding out of the stone building. *Three. Two.* His pace quickened into broad, bounding steps. *One.* With a mighty leap, he cleared the building's wall, landing heavily onto the red tiled roof. His eyes streamed yellow light. *It doesn't matter what they've seen anymore.* He took two large steps towards the wall, preparing to leap across the large span.

With a crack, the tile beneath his feet gave way.

Darius fell helplessly through the roof, streaming golden light, and came crashing down into an open room. *SNAP!* Something in his leg gave way to the pressure of the fall. Pain flooded through Darius's body, and he yelled out in agony. He now knew he was trapped. His leg was busted in two, bone sticking through the flesh, blood soaking into the floor. Darius's eyes, still bright with light, though fading rapidly, searched the room. There was only one way down out of the abandoned building, which he was sure was now surrounded by the guards of Tur'Mor. Agony tore across his sweat-drenched face, his face reddened with fluster and pain.

In a moment of true grit, he took the fractured bone, placed a piece of fallen wood in between his teeth, and reset his own leg. The sound was terrible, and he screamed even louder through clenched teeth, snapping the oak with his powerful jaw. He heard the downstairs doors bust open with a loud crash. Several men were rushing into the building, armor clinking and shouts erupting. There was a large dresser in the room where Darius huddled in pain, which he found the resolve to shove in front of the doorway. *Why is this happening? What does it mean?* A flash of Ranun's lifeless face flashed before his mind's eye. *No...*

Darius limped towards the window, wincing in pain in doing so.

A gruff-sounding guard yelled from downstairs, "Don't try anything stupid, we've got this place surrounded! There is no way out. Do not make matters worse for yourself!"

Darius tried to open the window, but it was latched shut and his strength was failing him – his eyes no longer emitted light at all.

The sound of half a dozen footfalls, nearly silent, overhead drew Darius's attention away from the oncoming city guards. A subtle, mechanical whizzing sounded, that of a cord unwinding swiftly over a pulley system, and then the roof gave way in several places. Before Darius could move, a rough burlap sack slipped quickly over his head, as several cords wrapped deftly around his upper body. Lastly, a set of cold, slender irons cuffed his hands in front.

Darius's thumb brushed the ring. His skin was reddened with heat from holding the Binding so long. But he would not be taken –

A hand softly pressed against his mouth and then his forehead. And though not a word was said, Darius knew exactly who had come for him. He relaxed his hand and accepted his capture. A loud thud came next, as the door Darius had shoved the dresser in front of burst open.

"What in the name of the Three Stars are you doing here?" a man yelled angrily. Darius heard three other men rush in behind the shouting man, their boots stomping wildly. "This man was seen fleeing the scene of an attack on city guards. He'll be coming with us!"

Darius saw the shadow of someone stepping in front of him from beneath the sack that hid his face. Not a word was spoken.

A sword was drawn.

"I'm warning you! We've every right to take him, Aluth! We'll use force!"

The sounds of four other blades being drawn was clear to Darius. The figure in front had taken a defensive stance. Another two figures fell from the holes in the ceiling, one on either side of Darius, let down by mechanical contraptions.

A deathly silence followed; no movement or sound could be detected. Darius tried to focus his senses but failed. What little strength he had left was being channeled into healing his wounded leg. He could feel the blood, warm and sticky, running down his leg, but he was so close to the Burning Point he could not draw upon a single sliver of light without causing more damage than was already done. Everything stood still for several, painfully long moments.

"The mayor will hear of this!" the leading guard spat. "You and your cult are losing favor in the eyes of this city. Mark my words: your time is coming to an end, filthy Aluth."

"Let's go, boss," another voice added. "Ain't worth dying over. Not for this street rat. Who knows, maybe ol' Orrum'll have him strung up."

"Bollocks!" the leader shouted angrily. "Damn that whole cult and their brainsick followers!"

Slowly, the sound of men retreating down the stairs filled Darius's ears. After the city guards had left, the Aluth sheathed their swords. Firm hands took either side of Darius's body, assisting him to his feet. He faltered, unable to support his weight on his right leg. An Aluth caught him, helped steady him, and then supported him as they left down the stairs. However, for some unknown reason, they did not remove the bag from his head nor the binds around his body as they left the building.

The Aluth walked Darius to a small carriage in front of the house. Pushed him inside firmly, giving little sign of notice to his leg. He was then hastily chained to the wooden bench inside the cart.

Once that was complete, the door was slammed shut and a lock could be heard being fixed to the door. With a crack of a whip, the horses darted forward. Darius rode in silence, yet he could tell someone was sitting across from him.

Not a word was issued.

CHAPTER 17: THE PARADE

Time: High Noon - Day of the Parade

Roaring crowds cheered, drums pounded, and silver and brass instruments blared joyous tunes. Performers, artisans and craftsmen from across Ordiatea had gathered in Tur'Mor for the showing of the King's Jewel. Thousands flooded the streets. Every courtyard was filled with colorfully clad Uppers, each donning their very best attire. Beautiful dresses and fitted suits painted a picturesque scene. Sunlight glistened off the metal buttons, chains, and gold-stitched corsets. Smells of cooked meats, hard soap and floral perfumes were heavy in the air.

Behind the crowds, the buildings seemed a blur as Felik ran. Lungs burning, face sweating, he pushed onward with a wicked smile on his face. A half dozen men in glistening armor chased after him, swords drawn and cursing at him to stop. Felik stayed a steady step ahead the whole time, for he knew if they caught him, it would be the executioner's blade. A fate only kept for the worst of criminals.

In his left hand he held a sack, the contents of which pressed jaggedly against its encasing. It felt heavy. Far heavier than it should have, and to make matters more complicated, there was an unnatural pull to the concealed treasure. Something strange he could not describe, along with a soft humming that filled his ears. At his right, a stocky short sword with a single edge that curved slightly and a basket-hilt overlayed with brass, was held within whitened knuckles.

Felik bolted behind an old bathhouse and into an alleyway he knew all too well. Three paths down and on the right was an old shop. A rusted sign with a fat man stirring a large kettle hung by one chain over a busted door. Felik nearly fell flat as he turned sharply into the building, sliding behind an overturned table. He thrust his feet into the slatted door, jamming it shut.

***

Tomo hid atop the pre-appointed tower, forcing her slender body between the bronze fixtures of the Asterivae's domed roof. Blood soaked her left leg and a bandage formed from part of her hooded cloak was wrapped around an arrow wound. Another shaft had punctured her left shoulder, the iron head of which jutted out of the crimson-stained top. Her face, while normally pale in complexion, had turned a sickly white from blood loss, and her lips had gone cold.

She turned over slowly, dulling eyes quivering in their sockets, and glanced through the glass that suspended her. Something below, in the circular corridor of the Asterivae, caught her attention. Someone that should not have been there.

Tears of pain and betrayal soaked her cheeks. But it did not matter, not now anyways. Tomo sank down and gave up her soul to the gods of her people.

***

"Dead, sir!" called a city guard as he checked the neck of a bald Tuawtian man with branded temples. "Ran through twice, with a crooked blade of sorts. They weren't clean. They were meant to hurt."

"Anything else?" the grizzled faced captain asked as he looked at the bloody mess. Four bodies lay strewn about. Three were in black and green robes, all Ordiatian by the looks of them, save only slightly darker in complexion, and each wearing a golden ring with an eye set with a small ruby.

"Just these rings, sir," the beady-eyed lieutenant said as he stood back up. "Must have been some kind of rivalry. But, if I didn't know no better, I'd say this one here has the marks of a Tuawtian slave. Ain't none of them allowed in the city. They all get kept in the border houses while their masters trade."

"Strange times, these are," the captain said with a snort. "Best get this cleaned up soon. Our good mayor does not like things out of sorts in his streets. I'll send men to check with the border houses to make sure all the Tuawtia folk are accounted for. Last thing we need is trouble from that lot... Strange men, those are. Steeped in witchcraft and darkness. Don't care what people say. There's something unnatural about the lot of them."

"Best guard your tongue, Captain. You don't know who listens about," the lieutenant said slowly as his eyes darted about. "I've seen strange things, and I don't want no more attention on me. They done locked Brue up for it. Wouldn't stop talking, took him to the asylum, they did."

"Just mind yourself, Rauel, and you'll be fine," the captain scoffed. "Your old mate went crazy saying he saw a man with the strength of ten and flames for eyes. That's nonsense. And I don't take you for a nonsensical fool, now are you?"

"Of course not, Captain! I ain't see nothing like that," Rauel replied hastily, hoping his eyes did not give it away. It had been months, but his memories were still sharp of a hulking lad with honey-yellow eyes.

***

Three men, cloaked in shades of black, green and brown, swore as they pursued Aellia through the crowds of Tur'Mor. They pushed and shoved people who could not dive out of the way in time. Glass broke, food spilled, and carts flipped. Aellia jumped, slid, and darted, always just out of the hands of her pursuers.

Aellia turned, eyes filled with...thrill! She lifted her left hand, a satchel gripped tight, taunting the men as they hurried towards her. With her right, she threw up an obscene gesture, and flashed a smile. She then drew her white hood over her head and pulled a handkerchief over her mouth and nose. Aellia's next move was to hurry into a crowd of dancers and acrobats, disappearing into the commotion.

Men and women in white uniforms of gold trimming and green vines danced and trumpeted. Dozens of shaved-headed men carried banners upon banners wearing loose green trousers and white tunics. The Rising Star of Tur'Mor, the Horned Helm of Un'Mor, the Running Golden Horse of Livitha, and the Eagle of Telnor. Other, lesser banners of the three gulls of Harbortown, the crossed swords of the Outpost of Tur'Mor, and of Ranok Outpost, the black crow on a maroon banner, fluttered in the wind. In front of the bannermen were royal guards, knights, and footmen, archers and gunmen marching behind. All wore their very best, polished, clean, and pressed.

Aellia ducked into a back alley and into a dark shop. The roars of the crowds and blares of the trumpets lessened. Aellia slid down behind the closed door, pressing her back against it. She fumbled nervously to open the sack, though it was not fear but excitement that pressed upon her. As the bindings fell away, a brilliant blue light flooded into the once dim room. A strange rod of silver, which twisted and formed around an impossibly-cut sapphire, lay alone in the sack. Aellia sighed in amazement as she stared at the scepter, which seemed heavier than expected in her hand.

The sinuous rod, not much longer than the length of her hand, looked like muscles and veins intertwined and twisting to form the slender handle and bulbous head that held the sapphire. The stone within the scepter was formed in impossible angles, casting the light in a strange manner. Her eyes settled on that stone, transfixed and unblinking. It was perhaps the most beautiful thing she had ever seen. A flow like the waves of the sea, but formed of light, moved endlessly in the spherical yet edged gem. But there were no edges nor lines, neither on the stone nor the scepter that held it. There was, however, a series of runes that ran up the short handle.

204

Aellia had never seen anything like them. One looked almost like a streaking bolt of lightning, the other an endless swirl of lines and cuts, and the last, three eye-like shapes stacked atop the other.

"*Ada'eha El-dached*," Aellia chanted as she ran a finger over the cold silver engravings. A spark jumped to her flesh from the gem as her pale fingertip drew close, and her eyes flashed bright for a moment as a flurry of heat rushed through her veins.

She jerked her finger away from the scepter. Her heart pounded furiously. Where did those words come from? What did they mean? And that power. . . what was that power? Despite her confusion, Aellia did not have time to think.

"Girly, girly, girly," a dry voice sung cruelly through the streets.

"Come on out now, little one, and give us back what is ours," a low, gruff voice called out.

Aellia shoved the silver rod into the sack and cinched it shut. Her breath caught in her chest, and her eyes closed slowly. There was no way out, nowhere to run. She forced out a cold breath and prepared for the inevitable.

- Time of Day: First Light -

Felik leaned out over the balcony of the Loft, the abandoned hideout his Crew had learned to call home. He thought about how it all started. The dishonor of abandoning his battalion on the fields of battle, the disgraced exile from his family, and the hard years of living on the streets, broken and drunk beyond recognition. Then, having found a pair of starving pickpockets, a young lad and his tiny sister, rummaging in the same street, Felik decided to make something of himself once more. He took the two in and showed them the old academy where he had been hiding alone those first years. He welcomed them into his home and promised to help take care of them.

Two grew into four, and four into seven. Each learned to rely on the other, and over the years, the small band had good times and bad. There were six now, though twelve had borne the illustrious title of Crew Member. They were those of the underground, the outcasts and unwanted. They were bizarre and deviant. Those first two had left three years back. Got real jobs, honest jobs, working in Harbortown a few miles to the west of Tur'Mor. After those, the longest-term Crew Member was Tomo Yukysa, the pale-skinned and sharp-eyed young woman from the East. She was skilled with the blade and followed some odd code that Felik truly did not understand.

Felik had often found her in a back alley on a strange mat, woven of red and green, with the face of a dragon upon it, bowed before a shrine of candles and small dragon figurines. She had been attempting to pray when

205

a couple of street thugs thought they could have their way with her. Felik had meant to save her. All he had done was get in the way.

Then there were the two Tuawtian men, Folehme and Belthazer, the latter a plump man with slave brands on his temples and the other a pompous, self-proclaimed holy man. They were an odd lot, but they kept the group grounded, providing entertainment and food. Of the two, only Folehme had actually lived in the vast sands of the Tuawtian Realm. Belthazer was raised in Calun and fled with his family to Ordiatea. To both of their chagrin, they had found Tur'Mor far less accommodating than expected.

Tornak, the wiry redheaded lad, was not forthright with where he was from but said he had been born in the port city of Westermost on Galacia. He was the youngest of the party and the newest. And while all had their quirks, they had one thing in common: they only had each other. A twinge of shame stung deep at his heart as he thought of the fate of that poor, awkward lad. Dead too soon. Perhaps they would all be joining him soon anyways.

And of course, there was Aellia. The daughter of a Livithian family, whose father assaulted a nobleman and was thus cast away into prison. Her mother and younger brother, due to poor living standards, had contracted the White Fever and died over twelve years ago. It was in the muddy streets of Southend that Felik had found the young girl with snowy hair and eyes of silver-grey. And it was under Felik's watchful eye that she had grown into a beautiful young woman, slender and alluring. Quick with a smart remark and quicker with her knives. Aellia had trained harder than anyone he had ever met in his life, save only one other, a cousin whom he had long since put out of his mind. That man had moved on to greater things, leaving the once 'Captain Felik' a vagabond and a street urchin.

Felik shoved those thoughts away, both those of the cousin he had loved and the young woman whom he now lusted after. A passion burned within him, a desire to be with her, to hold and caress her flesh. And was it so wrong? He was only ten years her elder; many Uppers married well beneath their age. And yet, Aellia did not see him in that way. She looked at him with those beautiful eyes in a respectful and subservient manner, always seeking to impress him. Her eyes were never meant for him, and he knew that to his core.

Felik shoved his hands away from the railing, bitterness pitting in his stomach. He walked back into his room, separated from the open balcony by a large red curtain. Inside was a jumbled mess of mismatched furniture and artwork, all of which were repurposed from their original owners for Felik's room. There was a large mattress with purple silk sheets. A strange lounging couch, with one high side and a long rectangular cushion all covered in leopard print. There were clay pots with paintings of warriors, and there were blown glass vases of intricate design. The most curious of all the items in the room was not kept in the open but under his bed, locked away in a strongbox.

Felik knelt and pulled out the heavy wooden box. He reached into the inner pocket of the long-tailed, blue coat with brass buttons he was wearing. From within his pocket, he produced a key. He placed the key in the lock and opened the box, revealing a breastplate of fine steel, with matching pauldrons, gardbrace and vambrace joined by a cowter, and a pair of gauntlets. All of these were atop a folded purple cape with four golden stripes at the shoulder, the markings of a Royal Captain. Next to the armor was a beautiful hand-and-a-half sword of polished steel, forge-welded and folded, forming a dazzling pattern on the blade. The pommel of the sword bore a single gemstone, a milky crystal cut round with many facets.

Felik ran his fingers over the black leather handle of his sword, memories rushing over him as they touched the cool hilt. He was once a man of renown, a man of honor. Women would have swooned as he walked by in the past. A bright young officer in the Royal Guard. Now women turned their noses at his scarred face and haggard appearance. All women except Aellia, though she did not love him. He knew how she felt for him, that of a mentor or brother. But he loved her with a passion he could not explain.

He shut the box, cranked the lock, and kicked it under his bed with the heel of his boot. Tears formed in his dull eyes as he buried his face in his hands. *What has it been? Fifteen years or is it thirteen? What does it matter anyways?* Felik rose and walked over to a dresser and wardrobe of light wood, glass broken on the door and scratch marks along the side. *A little like me, you are. A little roughed up, but still useful, right?* He removed the fancy blue coat and hung it in the wardrobe, then his ruffled collared shirt, hung neatly on a wooden hanger. Felik replaced these with a tattered tunic of grey and a brown factory-worker's vest. Next, he slipped into a pair of loose trousers of itchy material and some soft leather boots, worn on the heels and toes.

His persona was that of a street urchin, for they were practically invisible in Tur'Mor. Uppers were easy pickings. They just walked about as if none could touch them, proud and arrogant. Well, that is until they had to fend for themselves. Then all they did was snivel and plead, offering only what you planned on taking. Felik felt a sick pleasure in taking them down a notch. "Pompous pricks," he swore under his breath as he fastened a thick belt around his waist that had large pouches for holding wrenches and bolts.

He took a long look at himself in the mirror and went over the plan one more time. Felohme would walk the Southend gates, watching for any unwanted eyes. He would send a report via pigeon to the top of the Asterivae if there was need to where Tomo would be keeping an eye on the city below. The parade would make its way past that point right around noon. Belthazer would be boots on the ground near the fountains. Simple eyes watching and guarding, both ready to get the package from Felik and run if need be. Aellia would be the diversion. She would cause a scene, piss off an Upper or something, and draw away the attention of the crowds. And Felik, he would rush the guards in whatever confusion and steal the King's Jewel right in plain sight. All would see it was him, or at least the version of him he wanted to portray.

Felik took a tangled wig, salt and pepper, and placed it over his own hair. Next, he splotched grease on his face and wrapped a stained bandage around his left eye. He then took up a set of false teeth and stuck them into his trouser pocket – those would be for later. Dirty, battered, and poor. None would give a second look at him. He was ready.

At the center of the lower level, gathered around a cooking fire, the rest of the crew sat eating their morning meal. Felik hurried down the steps, having last donned a worn pair of boots. Last night's failures were behind him. Today, today he would succeed. He had to.

***

Perched at her window, Aellia looked down at the cracked and muddied street where the Loft stood, a towering edifice in an abandoned row of crumbling flat-roofed houses. Hers was a small room, walls draped with silks of reds and golds. The room was atop the old tower of the Loft. It was circular in make and had a trap door which led down a spiral stone stairway to the main floor. There was a single oval mirror, with a wooden frame painted gold, and a simple bed with several pillows. She had always wanted lots of pillows, and in her current station, pillows she had.

Aellia was not a pragmatic person. While some would call her hardheaded, and others reckless, she considered life was best lived in the moment. She had grown up with little. Her father an entertainer and her mother a seamstress, she was not accustomed to the finer things in life. Now that she was on her own, both her parents dead, if she saw something she liked, she took it. And why not? Everything she had ever loved had been taken from her. Her father, her mother, and even her younger brother. All taken, without care or consideration as to what it would do to her.

Besides her pillow-strewn bed, Aellia's second most prized possession was her collection of knives. An entire portion of her circular stone wall was covered, from head-height to knees, in a wild assortment of knives. There were broad knives and throwing knives, short, spiky knives and golden-hilted knives. She had knives from Tuawtia and Zau'fi, both cruel and beautiful, either varying from one another as the sun and moon. She had ancient knives, stolen from collection houses and museums, and brand-new knives. Aellia was sure she had enough knives to pay for her

208

own villa in the country, with two or three servants to wait on her every whim.

As alluring as those thoughts were, that was never what Aellia wanted. What kind of life would that be? Boring, lazy, good for nothing, just like the Uppers that had taken everything from her. Aellia reached out with a finger and drew it slowly down the handle of a throwing knife. Her reflection caught in the perfectly-oiled blade. Her frosty white hair seemed frozen back on her head, coming to sharp points. She smiled a sly smile back at herself, a wild glint in her eyes. No, retribution was what she wanted. She wanted them to hurt, and if she could have some fun while doing so, she would.

Aellia slid out of her silk night robe and walked to her wardrobe. She was petite yet well defined. Years of running, climbing and slinking through the streets and skyline of Tur'Mor had turned her into a masterful acrobat. Additionally, years of training with Felik had turned her into a deadly woman with the blade and her body. She was just as hard on the outside as she was on the inside. Aellia often put on airs of nonchalance and frivolousness, but she had a plan, a dark plan, and she would see it through.

She opened the doors to her wardrobe, revealing a wide array of clothing. The assortment ranged from dresses and blouses fit for the upper crust all the way to a pauper's garb. While most of her clothing varied in cut and style, they shared one thing in common: Aellia loved white. Everything she owned was either mostly white or had white accents throughout it. Only a deep purple gown with golden stitchwork and corset stood out.

Aellia smiled a forlorn smile at her collection. That purple dress came from a woman, whom she had more than her fair share of fun with before taking it and that she kept just for the memories. Memories. Some were so sweet and filled with vibrant life, and others too bitter to relive. She took out an outfit of white with a hood on it, not uncommon for her, and shut the door.

- Time of Day: High Dawn –

Trumpets blared, cymbals crashed, and people lauded the grandeur and prosperity of Ordiatea. Banners waved, horses trotted, and wealthy nobles flaunted brightly colored outfits adorned with jewels, fine cloth, and expensive wares. The hair of the women formed a sea of hues, done up in poufy curls and locks. Others wore powdered wigs which sat like towering crowns of cotton on their sun-kissed brows. Many of the men donned their highest of top hats and tightest of overcoats. Even the lower caste of Tur'Mor, and her neighboring citizens who had gathered from across the land, were dressed in the best they had.

Felik moseyed through the crowds easily. The wealthy Uppers, not wanting to be tarnished by his haggard appearance, stepped away aghast. And those who caught a glimpse of his blood-stained wrapping or crooked and stained teeth turned their heads sharply, sticking their noses high into the air. He smiled at this, a wicked smile of satisfaction. Their reactions made his actions all the more savory.

The King's Jewel and the procession of one hundred royal guards followed by three hundred men-at-arms, would be making their way up through the city soon. The irreplaceable and invaluable stone would also be accompanied by the High Seat of Ordiatea. Each member would be riding comfortably in their lectica, having their own entourage of personal guards and servants with them. A lectica was a seat or an upholstered couch set upon a four-poster box, typically with curtains and a sturdy covering, and carried by four or eight men, depending on its size or make.

Felik maneuvered his way until he was exactly where he wanted to be. The procession would make its way up the main street, and then turn tightly through the dividing wall that sectioned off the prosperous sectors of Tur'Mor, moving it to the central area known as the Valamour. This was the only choke point they would go through, save through the entry gates of the city. Hundreds of archers, crossbows loaded, lined the walls, and men in both black and silver armor patrolled the crowds.

Felik scratched at his chin anxiously. *This is suicide!* He cursed under his breath. The choke point was so well guarded that a dozen arrows would riddle his body before he could even touch the displayed stone. There was a reason no one had ever attempted to steal the King's Jewel in the history of its existence. *I'll have Aldorian's bloody head on a spit!*

The sounds of trumpets heralded the approach of the parade.

First came the jugglers, spinning their sticks of fire and shimmering balls of color. Next were the dancers and acrobats, twisting and twirling about. Fifty drummers on snares were accompanied by two hundred other drums both large and small. All wore fanciful outfits, ranging from the skintight clothes of the acrobats to the militant uniforms of gold and purple worn by the plume-hatted drummers.

Felik felt his heart rate spike. Sweat beaded at his brow; though the temperature was still cool and crisp, only the earliest signs of spring had arrived. He drew a steadying breath as the first procession passed.

Next came knights in silver riding on stallions draped in long coverings of checkered patterns, varying as widely as their style of armor and surcoats. Lances glistened in the mid-morning light. Felik's shoulders dropped in shame. At one time, he would have been with them, proudly bearing his colors. But no more. He shook his head. He needed to focus.

Men and women in white uniforms, gold trimmed with green vines running through, danced and trumpeted. Dozens of shaved-headed men carried banners upon banners, wearing loose green trousers and white tunics. Behind them were archers and gunmen walking in tight formation. These would be the last before the King's Jewel and the High Seat.

The Uppers of the crowd cheered and clapped. Some waved purple kerchiefs or golden streamers. Hundreds upon hundreds were packed together in endless rows of celebration. Though, much to Felik's liking, there were other hundreds, dressed in rags and tattered clothing, who grumbled and swore at the wealthy and prosperous. These were those who had long suffered poverty, negligence, and ridicule. These were they who would be the kindling on which Felik would soak with fuel and burn.

Aellia needs to make her move, Felik thought anxiously as he studied the cascade of color and clamor. The gates to the Valamour were opening and time was slowly running out for action. He inhaled sharply and steadied himself.

A cry of panic sounded loud above the crowd. Screams began to erupt through the crowds. Felik whipped around, searching for the source of the disturbance. People were moving, shoving and running to get away from something in the distance.

A large gong sounded from one of the many watchtowers on the inner walls of the city. This was echoed by several others. Three sharp blasts rang out, each from different vantage points.

"No!" Felik cursed. "Halfak burn it! No, no, no, no!"

This was not part of the plan. Something was wrong.

Knights pulled their swords, archers raised crossbows, and gunmen readied their firearms. Just a few measures away, Felik could see the brightly lacquered lecticas of the High Seat being circled by guards. Though, that was not what he was focused on. Right in front of the governing body of the Republic was a pedestal, set with the King's Jewel.

The gemstone was as large as a man's first, bright purple with a striking band of yellow running through it. At the core of the stone, an anomaly had formed from what looked like fractured glass. This oddity caused light to refract in an impossible way, casting wild beams in all directions. The rest of the ametrine gemstone was cut to look like a droplet of rain, wide at the base and coming to a multifaceted tip. This stone once sat in the throne of the Line of Kings, long before the formation of the Republic. It was now only ever paraded about as a reminder of things long gone.

Three knights, not wearing the emblems of any city state but bearing the image of the King's Jewel on their surcoats, surrounded the pedestal that displayed the gemstone. They held poleaxes tipped with a long spike. Their britches were strange, unlike any that Felik had seen before, save only on Knights of the Jewel. They were very baggy, with large colorful pleats in them of purple and gold. Their helmets were wide-brimmed but did not cover the face, save only a nose guard, though they did wear chainmail coifs underneath both helmet and breastplate. Along with the lack of pauldrons and vambraces, they did not wear armor about their legs, but donned long stockings of vibrant purple and polished black shoes. One might laugh if they saw these men, but they would be foolish in doing so. These were the most elite warriors in all of the Republic. Only a tenured knight could apply for commission as a Knight of the Jewel, and once accepted, it was for life.

Felik did not have time to laugh. He figured there would be Knights of the Jewel here, but seeing them only made matters worse. Frantically, he searched for any kind of opening he could take, anything. Something strange caught his eye. Was that person in grey robes wearing a mask? What was going on now?

Two more blasts sounded, the commotion in the street turning into a jumbled mess. Someone threw a rock at a knight, screaming something about not caring for the poor. Other people began to fight one with another. The parade was starting to run into itself, the back catching the halted front. Three men in dark garb jolted through the crowd, running to the back of the parade. Four others, dressed likewise, jumped a mounted knight, dragging him off his horse.

The King's Jewel and the seven members of the High Seat of Ordiatea were quickly being ushered towards the gatehouse of the Valamour. Dozens of heavily armed men pushed against the crowds, clearing a path so that they could escape the haze of violence. Felik cursed, cracked his neck, and began to rush the party. He had to make his move now, or else he was a dead man.

***

Aellia rushed across the rooftops, glaring at the snooty Uppers and their stupid clothing. She hated everything about them. She hated their wealth, their laziness, and most of all, the way they all treated those beneath them. Today, it was her turn to push back, really push back. Sure, she had stolen and taunted Uppers for years. But nothing she had ever done had truly affected them, save a small dent in their daily pocketbooks. No, she had never really gotten the chance to make them feel the hurt they had caused her. But today, today she would make them hurt.

She passed over Felohme, who was pushing a wheelbarrow in tattered rags, as she crested a red shingled building, four stories in height. The buildings were so dense she could easily run roof to roof without a struggle. Yet, every so often the buildings would gap to allow a street to pass between them. Tur'Mor was a maze of perfectly plotted buildings and courtyards. Even Southend, where the poor lived, was still laid out in lines and patterns of order. Though, it was no longer well-kept and had fallen into disarray.

She continued her path until she was deep in the Valamour, running until she saw something she should not have. The buildings here were beautiful. Formed of white marble with vast courtyards surrounded by

212

their walls and rooms, these villas were for the most elite of Ordiatea. One of these, with vine-covered walls about the outer court, was the Mayoral Residency. It was in this house, unattended, except by twenty or so city guards, that Aellia caught a glimpse of that strange looking rod, cased under a glass dome on a pillar of gold-capped marble.

Aellia licked her lips. She had no idea what that thing was, but the blue sapphire that sat lodged in the priceless silver rod was worth twice over the rod, or more. Yet, it was not the value of the rod that drew her; it was something else, something primordial. A surge of need rushed over her, an overwhelming lust for the scepter of silver seemed to consume her mind. Cause a commotion. Start something, he had said. Aellia thought with a greedy laugh, *this will start something!*

CHAPTER 18:
A HOUSE OF BLOOD, A PRIZE OF SILVER
Time of Day: Ten to Noon

The smell of fresh flowers and strong incense wafted through the halls of the Mayoral Residency. Chandeliers of thousands of crystal fixtures hung over grey and white checked flooring. The click, click of metal boots of black-armored guards, who held halberds with half-moon blades and were draped in purple and gold striped surcoats, crossed the floors in otherwise silent surveillance. While not Royal Guards of the Order of Knights, these were the best of the City Guard, esteemed even among the lesser knights in Tur'Mor. They stepped with a silent assuredness and deadly firmness. They were proud, focused, and utterly unaware of the capabilities of one, small, innocent, fever-weakened girl, her white hair a mark of such.

Aellia bounded quickly over the walls, her white archer's cloak seemingly blending in with the stonework. At the center of the courtyard was a large fountain, the water covering mosaics of blue, green, yellow, and red, with a large statue of a lordly man wearing a feathered hat and holding a rolled piece of parchment. It was Henran del'Alesuer, the first Mayor of Tur'Mor. Before him, those of the House of Tur sat as monarchs over the Kingdom of Ordiatea.

Aellia practically threw herself against the edge of the fountain to avoid being seen by two patrolling guards. She slid a slender, arrowhead-looking knife from her boot. *Don't breathe, don't move, don't even think!* The guards were only four measures away now. Three measures. Aellia's heart pounded in her chest, hand tight around the knife.

A crash sounded. Broken glass. The two men whipped around, looking upward to the source of the disturbance. Aellia, in pure instinct, struck. The brown-eyed guard would go down first. He had a slight favor in his left leg. A kick to the back of the right knee and a twist of the left sent him face first to the ground. With a leap, she landed on the back of his helmet with a thud, knocking him out cold. A cylindrical blade, slender and stained with a toxin that caused instantaneous paralysis, flashed through the air, striking the second guard in the neck between his plate and helmet. He fell helplessly to the ground with a grunt.

Across the courtyard she sprinted, taking no thought as to what could have caused the crash. Perhaps it was luck. Aellia's eyes hardened. Perhaps someone else was taking a chance at her score! Her slender body, petite, slid between the ornate, curled gates of gold like a hot knife through butter. She was in the great house now, her prize not far.

Three sets of fanning stairs led to the three separate areas of the Mayoral Residency. She rushed to the marble steps, a purple runner with golden trim covering the center of the steps and headed upward. The guards of the house were surely making their way to the same room she was headed. *Who in Ordan's creation would be dumb enough to try'n steal from the mayor?* Aellia cursed to herself as she took the steps in leaping bounds of two and three. *And why in Halfak are there so many damned steps?*

With the silvery dagger in one hand, a wide-edged curved blade in the other, Aellia fell to the steps. Three other guards rushed across the upper platform, unable to see her pushed against the heavy marble banisters, or at least did not think to look. Aellia waited until they rushed through double doors of heavy, painted wood. *Eight, maybe nine now? And then, however many of whoever else is here.*

Sounds of men shouting and armor clanging erupted. Howls of agony followed, and then bodies falling to the floor. Aellia listened intently.

BOOM!

A blast rang out, deafening in the open air. Sounds of tiny pellets ripping through wood and stone came right after the shock. White smoke, acrid and sharp, began to waft out of the open room.

BOOM!

BOOM!

Two more blasts sounded, men screaming in pain as they fell to the ground in a crash of metal on stone. All went silent.

Aellia was holding so tightly to her blades that her fingers had begun to cramp. Short breaths came and went, as silent as possible. She was trembling, teeth grinding in a dry mouth. She was not used to being scared. *Bloody guns! I have to move, now!*

Slowly, carefully, she began to inch her way forward, one step at a time. Her elbows propped her up, and her soft leather boots pushed slowly into each step. Men were laughing in the room. *Surely the guards wouldn't be doing that. But who could it be?*

A lifeless guard lay atop the staircase, body curled over backwards, blood dripping from sightless eyes and unmoving lips. His armor was peppered with round holes, blood spilled onto the white marble floor, staining it crimson. Aellia crawled over him like a spider, not allowing any part of her white clothing to touch the soiled mess. She held her breath as she moved, the thick smell of blood filling the air.

A gong rang out, loud and clear. This did not stop her; she was too far now.

Through the doorway, she could see ten or eleven men, all clad in black armor with surcoats torn or punctured. Two men in dark robes with heavy, hooded cloaks lay in their own refuse, dead eyes staring into nothingness. They were Ordiatian by look, though their garb was not common wear in the city. Four other men stood around the marble display, all eyeing the strange silver rod with the sapphire gemstone.

Massive hands, strong as a vice, closed around Aellia's neck. Her eyes flickered and light danced between strained blinks. She grabbed at a leather gauntlet that choked her, dropping both knives in doing so. The massive hand felt like steel. A cloaked man wearing an iron mask over his face hoisted her up from the ground with ease.

"Rahnaluz!" the mountainous man called out in a dry, low voice. "I caught a little cat, sneaking about with its claws out."

A slender man with a beak of a nose, thick curly hair, and sharp features turned away from the pedestal and eyed Aellia, still flailing in the brute's hand. He wore a mask over his face, though it covered only half of his oily face. It was deep red, with golden markings inlaid into it in sharp, contrasting patterns. Aellia thought she recognized him from somewhere, but the mask obstructed too much of his face for her to be sure. She tried to think, but her mind was spinning; she was going to black out.

"Drop it, Lundrek!" the man called Rahnaluz croaked, his own voice hoarse and raspy.

Aellia fell through the air, crashing hard onto a bloodstained rug. Specks of black and white light danced in her eyes. She felt dizzy, weak, and vulnerable.

"Look here, peasant," Rahnaluz sneered.

Aellia lifted her head as best she could; it bobbed and swayed on her shoulder. She brought a hand to her throat and rubbed gingerly. She could feel the indentations the gloves had made in her neck

"You are no maid nor house servant." Rahnaluz's voice was oddly refined, if not still hoarse and raspy. He began to walk; each step he took was over a body. "So, tell me then, why did you come here?"

"I," Aellia tried to speak, but the words did not form right. She cleared her throat. "I needed..."

Rahnaluz stepped right in front of her. He squatted down and grabbed her by the ends of her short, white hair, pulling it back so her eyes met his. His face was miserable, cold and cruel. "You needed what? Speak, cur, or I'll have your head in a sack."

Aellia felt the lumbering Lundrek step up behind her. The other three men who had been by the pedestal were also making their way closer. She did not like the way they were eyeing her – hungry...no, ravenous.

"Such pretty eyes," Rahnaluz snarled. "It's a pity we'll have to cut them out. Lundrek, Talfein, discard of her. We can't afford witnesses." He rose as he said it, throwing Aellia's head to the side. "Such a pity indeed."

Another lanky man stepped forward. His face looked severely burned, his right eye melted away, along with his hair and ear. His hood was longer than the others, him being the only one not wearing some form of a mask, but when he knelt on one knee and looked at Aellia, she could see all his horrid features. His good eye was grey with lines of green. His breath was hot and sour. "Little house cat, you shouldn't have come today." His voice rent steel, a breathy, gaspy noise with sharp inflection in all the wrong places. An expression that could have been a smile tried to form, twisted lips curling upwards. "I do like little ones." A tongue breached those blistered lips, licking slowly.

The room seemed to go still. The dust particles stopped floating about, hovering motionlessly in one place. Rahnaluz was walking away, bony fingers knitted together behind his lower back as he stretched, yet in Aellia's mind, he did not move. Lundrek was a step behind her and Talfein. She shuddered – Talfein's horrid face was in the perfect place.

Two curved knives under the split back of her cloak. A boot knife on the left was laced with Stingroot, the same that the guard outside had fallen to. The other two were behind her four steps. There were two other men to account for, one with a staff, the other with a long-barreled rifle on his back and a disposed blunderbuss in his hand. Like a scene from a dream, Aellia saw the room and the next moments play out.

Time was not really still. She had only breathed once since Talfein began to lean forward, taking a strained sniff through mutilated nostrils. This was a trick Felik had taught her, and she heard his steady voice echoing in her mind as she moved: "Sense the room. Know your enemy. Use anything, see everything. Breathe slowly and find the void. Then, strike!"

Aellia's hand moved with blinding speed. Two curved knives slid out of their sheaths and crossed, blood spraying, spine severing, in the middle of Talfein's neck. A confused stare of horror still gleamed in his grey-green eye as his head rolled from his shoulder and onto the floor. As the knife's blade cleaved through the man's scar-puckered face, gore spattered back across her own, a hot fountain of red nearly blinding her. The vile taste of iron, salt and sweat filled Aellia's mouth. She dropped to the floor atop the Kh'ar's lifeless body and spat the blood from her mouth. She looked up to the other men, a twisted smile on her face, accented by the crimson spittle that ran from her lips and dripped off her chin onto her white vest. Horror filled their eyes and hatred filled her own. Their end had come.

Whirling in a half circle, knives sliced the front of Lundrek's meaty thighs. She jumped up onto his torso, using the daggers as tools to climb his body. Screams of agony erupted from the big man, but a downward plunge of sharp steel through his mouth silenced him. With a hard jerk, both sides of his head flayed open.

Aellia used the momentum of Lundrek's fall to push herself out of the way of a staff that was whizzing through the air. The rod narrowly missed her face by a finger's width, the rush of wind sending a ripple across her hood. Without missing a beat, Aellia slid between the knees of her attacker and drove an armored elbow into his groin. He fell with a grunt, ivory mask clinking as his face hit the floor.

In a blur, Aellia darted across the floor, the soft leather of her boots trailing prints of red blood. Her eyes were set on the strange scepter that the hawk-nosed man was placing in a brown sack. The fellow with the rifle was still struggling to remove the knife that had skewered it. He was cursing angrily as Aellia flashed past him, catching him in the gut with a curled, silvery gauntleted fist, making him double over with a solid thud.

Something hot whizzed past Aellia cheek, then crashed into a pillar behind her, blasting away a chunk from it. The report of a pistol sounded in that same moment but seemed to lag in her ear as opaque grey smoke rose from the extended barrel of Rahnaluz's wheellock pistol. His dead grey eyes, almost black, seemed to bleed hatred.

"Die!" he hissed out as he held the smoking barrel towards Aellia. "Why don't you die?"

Aellia wiped blood from her cheek, eyes radiant with the thrill of violence. "I don't much want to, thief!"

"Thief?" the man called Rahnaluz snarled back as lowered the pistol slowly. "I am the Khall'ah Kh'ar!"

Aellia rushed forward again, spanning the distance in a moment. Rahnaluz dropped the pistol to the ground and drew a twisted dagger with a dragon's head for a guard, the blade made to look like its serpentine tongue. He thrust the dagger at her face, blade narrowly missing as she twisted out of the way. She grabbed the sack that Rahnaluz was holding and yanked it from his bony fingers. Something hard caught her eye, marring her vision. It was a ringed backhand from the enraged leader of the Kh'ar, the Khall'ah Kh'ar. The seething pain nearly caused Aellia to lose her focus, but she had come too far; her discipline was sound.

An open window, the same she had seen the strange scepter through from before, was only paces away. Instead of attacking the hawk-nosed man, she bolted for the marble opening, purple curtains hanging to either side as a covering. She grabbed onto one of the draping lengths of fabric and jumped.

***

The King's Jewel was being placed into a steel box by the colorfully clad guards when Felik burst through the crowds and into the procession. Archers that lined the walls brought their repeating crossbows, with barrel

218

drums and crank-arms, to their shoulders. However, due to the close proximity of the High Seat of Ordiatea, they could not get a clear shot. Half a dozen men lowered polearms and rushed Felik, while the others formed circles around their leaders.

With a flurry of his tattered cloak, Felik produced two short swords built after a peculiar manner. The swords, however, were not really swords but square bars that came to a needle-tip point and had wide cross-guards with notches to catch opponents' blades. The blackened estocs bore no edges but could thrust through small crevices in plate armor with an exactness that no broad or long sword could muster. Besides that, they were excellent for what Felik was about to do, and that was to block and parry bloody polearms from chopping him to mush.

Felik moved fast, stepping between falling axe heads and thrusted spear points with an exactness that came from years of training. Every motion was planned, every counterstrike moving him closer to his goal. He could see the steel box being locked and twelve or thirteen more men in polished plate rushing towards him.

A white fletched arrow struck one of the Knights of the Jewel through the back of the neck, just below the helmet. Another arrow struck one of the running men in the face plate, the shaft splintering on impact, blood spraying where the head pierced the eye-slit. The remaining two Knights of the Jewel looked towards the direction of the arrow, pausing only for a brief moment, where a figure in tight, dark clothing was loosing a third shaft.

Felik breathed out a straining, "Thank the creators, Tomo!" and used the distraction to rush past the oncoming men. The rows of archers that lined the wall fired volley after volley towards where Tomo had been, though she had already disappeared from Felik's sight. Black bolts clouded the sky and added to the madness. *Good,* Felik thought, *madness and confusion are my only chance.*

The entire High Seat, along with their retainers, were now through the gates of the Valamour and only the Knights of the Jewel and two dozen royal guards remained. Hundreds of citizens rushed about, along with street performers and musicians, all trying to escape the fighting. Yet, as Felik had expected, those who were not overly fond of the current ruling class of Tur'Mor used Felik's aggression as fuel to attack the far superior knights and footmen. As the dozens of scums and beggarworms rushed forward, Felik slipped next to the wall, dropping one of his estocs and releasing his cloak.

In a final assault, he caught a Knight of the Jewel by the back of this plate, and swung him to the side, ten or twelve dully clad commoners jumping him. The last was holding the steel box under his left arm. He pulled out his own blade and held it steady, tip pointing towards Felik's face. The next few moments happened like clockwork.

A blast near Southend seemed to rattle the ground, causing all to falter where they stood. Then, the gates swung shut, the King's Jewel left outside the Valamour; Felik guessed it was by mistake.

Felik recovered faster. The tip of his estoc rammed into the knight's right shoulder, his arm limp to the side and sword on the ground. Archers above were regaining their footing and lowering their weapons to fire. All of the knights had fallen. Felik grabbed the steel box from the dazed man and fled.

Dozens of people lay dead in the street. Men crying, women weeping, and the lifeless staring into the great beyond. Felik knew he did not have much time to get away. This was not the plan, but the plan was working, somehow.

Now, if he could just make it to the rendezvous point. He had to run. That was all that Felik could think of now; that and a haunting echo that began to creep into the back of his mind.

CHAPTER 19: INTO THE TEMPLE

After a very long and very uncomfortable ride, the carriage that held Darius captive slowed. Its four wooden wheels groaned with a low, creaking noise as the pounding hoofbeats died down. Darius sat for what seemed to be an hour or more, waiting in utter silence. The Aluth that sat across from him did not move an inch, and in the endless moments of eerie silence, Darius was not even sure if it breathed.

When did I start thinking of the Aluth as 'it'? These are just well-trained humans. That is all.

The silence was finally broken by the sound of metal clanking as the bolts were undone so that the door could be opened. Chains clanked as Darius was loosed from the bench. Two firm, but careful, hands grabbed either side of him and led him out of the carriage onto what felt like smoothed stone under his thick boots. A silent hand then led Darius up a series of steps, pulling on a makeshift leash formed from a cord tied loosely around his neck.

Darius hobbled slowly, unable to put much weight on his right leg without excruciating pain. Though frustrated at the bonds, Darius thought it best not to resist. Something within him told him to just follow along. He then heard two doors open in front of him, and he knew exactly where he was: the temple near where he had awakened. He could sense it. The smells, the sounds, even the texture of the stonework used to craft the building.

Darius was marched further forwards, and though he could not see in front of him, he could make out the beautiful emerald-colored rug that ran across the path he was led down.

Twenty steps.

No, twenty-three.

There was breathing.

What is making that noise?

Several people were in front of Darius and lining the sides of the colossal room. He sniffed the air, searching for the scent of emotion that lay on those who surrounded him. To his surprise, he did not smell fear or aggression but contemplation and awe. Darius felt a rush of relief flood over him. These were not enemies.

And then he heard something, something else. Something alive.

A heartbeat, but not of man or beast. There was a power flowing through the room unlike anything Darius had ever felt before. It was intoxicating. It overcame his mind and body.

Thud Thud . . .

Thud Thud Thud . . .

Thud Thud . . .

The noise was like that of a hammer striking stone. No, it was like the beat of the heart of a great mountain elk, strong and powerful. Or maybe it was that of a warrior preparing for battle.

Thud Thud Thud . . .

Darius tried to crane his body to find the source of the noise.

"Please, there is no more need for the cover." Elcon's voice was clear as day; however, there was a sense of regret masked behind the firm, commanding tone of his words.

The sound of Elcon's voice pulled Darius back to reality. His ears perked up as he heard the familiar man speak. But where did that pulsing go? He could have sworn he felt it...almost urging him, calling him. Darius did not dare to breathe; he stood still, listening for any hint of the pulsating rhythm.

A blade slid silently up the cords binding Darius, slicing them effortlessly. As the ropes fell off his body, the hood was also removed, letting a dull light shine over Darius's face. He looked around at his surroundings. While he did not recognize the inside of the building, he knew where he had to be – the Temple of Ordan.

Large tapestries hung down the side of the towering marble walls. Shimmering columns of marble rose majestically from the floor to vaulted ceilings. Along the walls were towering statues depicting the gods of the Ordiatians in their grandeur, standing over fifteen measures in height. The corridor had a long emerald carpet that extended from the doorway all the way to the raised platform near the center of the room. Where the carpet ended, white marble steps led up to a series of polished seats, of which the central one was raised slightly higher.

Each of the five seats had someone sitting on them, each cloaked in ceremonial robes of white and purple, save one. This man, who was sitting upon the raised seat, wore white and green, and a large crown-like cap sat gracefully upon his silver-haired head. He had a pair of half-mooned, silver-edged spectacles with a silver chain running from them around his neck. Elcon, whose face was mixed with exasperation and concern, sat immediately to this man's right, and a woman to his right, and such was mirrored to the left, a man and then a woman. None of the Holy Council looked happy to be there, and it appeared that they had been talking, rather heatedly, for quite some time.

Several Aluth lined the aisle, each one wearing a full veil over their faces. The veils had a painting of an eye, with blue flames emanating from the iris. They also had their hoods pulled over their heads, which came to a sharp point where eyes would be if not covered by the veil. Instead of swords, each of these Aluth were holding halberds. And across their chest was a banner of green with the golden hammer of Ordan embroidered upon them.

The two Aluth that had helped him out of the cart grasped both sides of Darius, helping to steady him and walked him forward towards the seated council.

"Are you hurt?" the central figure inquired, though there was little concern in his voice.

Darius, as if he did not even notice the question, looked directly at Elcon. "Master Elcon, they killed him...they killed Ranun." His voice broke as he stared at the high priest.

"We will need to have that seen to," the central man said. He then gestured with his hand to the man on his right. "Elcon here said you have caused quite the trouble today?"

"Did you not hear me?" Darius gawked in disbelief at the calmness of the man, a total lack of empathy or concern.

"A fight led to his death," the man continued, brushing aside Darius's response. "A fight, I have been informed, that *you* started."

"There was a girl. . ." Darius started, cutting off the speaker.

"Were your duties to fight, Darius? Or were they to tend to the Church as a stonemason?" the Patriarch rebutted heatedly, raising his voice so that it rang through the marble chamber.

"Patriarch Orrum, if you would hear him out," Elcon implored, eyes unwavering, barely holding back waves of emotion.

There was an uneasy pause, a bleak stillness for several moments. Darius could hear his own heartbeat, pulsing blood into his leg. And though it no longer bled, it ached to stand upon it. Though, he would not give them the satisfaction by requesting a reprieve.

"Speak swiftly," Patriarch Orrum demanded, eyes like steel that bore into Darius, "for this is your only chance to redeem yourself. We've already had to clean up your mess with the city guards not a season ago."

Somewhat shocked, and somehow even angrier at the knowledge that the Holy Council had not only known about his endeavors but were a part of them, Darius continued, "There was a girl in need, and I did what any man worth his own breath would do." He thought he should tell them of the power that seemed to emanate from her, but then he recalled Elcon's words around magic and the implications it may cause this young girl, so he simply added, "As far as my arrival to this city and those guards, well, they got what was deserved."

"Every man will answer for his own actions," Patriarch Orrum replied bluntly. The Patriarch's forthright, egotistical voice waned slightly. His dull blue eyes, which had been pointed and piercing, softened behind his silvery spectacles. An air of curiosity became apparent when he then asked, "High Priest Elcon has told us that you claim to be Feromage. Is that true?"

Darius did not answer but turned his eyes to Elcon. The high priest nodded, apparently trying his best to give a sense of reassurance. However, Darius could not let his guard down that easy, not when he was surrounded by guards and being placed on some form of trial. Yet, his eyes gave him away. Vibrant, powerful and unashamed. And brilliant yellow.

"So then, you do not refute the claim to be a descendant of a race of beings who vowed to guard the ways of the High Father and his people?" Orrum further questioned as he studied Darius intently.

"I am what you say I am," Darius replied boldly.

A hushed murmur fell amongst the Holy Council. Elcon seemed pleased, at least more so than his counterparts. They continued to quarrel in hushed tones for several minutes as Darius stood firmly in his place, doing his very best to not falter under the pain in his leg. Orrum then leaned forward, his bony elbow on his thigh and his long, hairless chin resting upon his thumb and jeweled forefinger. His eyes were focused, and he was taking in every aspect of Darius.

"We must commence in further counsel," Orrum finally spoke, looking closely at Darius, searching his face in curiosity. "Aluth, please show this man to the healer's chamber to care for his leg. We shall send for our guest when we have reached a verdict."

Two of the Aluth, the ones that had been standing guard behind Darius, touched their covered lips and then their foreheads. They helped Darius, whose leg still pained him, though not as much as before, away from the center of the temple and off to a side room.

The room to which he was led was of grey stone and sat behind a silver crested door of ash wood, which opened inwardly. Blue light, streaming from the stained-glass windows, illuminated the grey stones of the room. The walls depicted Gallea and Ordan forming parts of Ethrea. A painting of a large waterfall fell from the wall onto the floor and ran into a central basin of brass that sat upon the backs of four lions of shimmering white marble. Crystal clear water flowed from under the floor where the painting touched the edge of the basin from a natural hot spring under the temple. What looked to be hundreds of candles were flickering like starlight in contrast to the azure glow of the tinted sunlight.

Two women draped in flowing white dresses, whose flesh appeared to be nearly porcelain, were standing behind a stone table that looked like a bed of granite. The women were adorned with silver veils over their blush lips, and a crown of white and yellow flowers rested upon rivers of fiery red hair. Atop the stone bed was a golden headrest and a thin white linen. The two women moved towards Darius, their steps perfectly in sync, waves rolling across a misty seashore. There was a soft glow and a comforting warmth in their ambiance that lowered Darius's defensive nature.

"We are servants of the goddess Gallea," said the first.

"You have been hurt," continued the second. The two voices were indistinguishable from one another, both light and airy, like a dream.

"I am Alyn, and this is Brei. We are the Candius sisters," said the first, pointing with an open palm to the second. "Be at peace in thy heart."

"We shall tend to your wounds," Brei continued in a melodic tone as she stared at Darius. "Though I see that there is hurt that runs deeper than flesh and bone... Time does not conceal all wounds."

The sisters led Darius to the brass basin and said harmoniously, "There is no shame in the service of Gallea. Please, let us help you remove your pain."

They then began to remove the coat and clothes of Darius. He seemed to be in a trance, unable to stop the two sisters as they worked. When he was stripped down to his manhood, the two ran cool fingers over the many scars on his body. Yet, it was his right leg that drew the attention of Alyn. The wound, though closed, was a purple, swollen mass that stretched from the knee to the ankle.

"Many wounds from many struggles," Alyn said as she ran her fingers over Darius's leg.

Darius stood transfixed as Alyn did so, unable to form words. The euphoric feeling was odd yet comforting. In normal circumstances, he would have tried to cover himself, yet here and now, he was totally at peace, as if between a dream and reality.

"Yes, you have suffered much in your journey," Alyn continued, "a very long journey...a journey that still calls you forward."

"Come and lay upon the altar and let us tend to your leg," Brei urged in a singsong voice.

Darius turned toward the bed, candles illuminating scars across his broad back, one of which stood in contrast with the rest of the dull, white markings. Across the top of his right shoulder was what appeared to be a large branding in the form of a bear's paw, whose claws were tearing at his flesh, frozen in time. This marking drew the attention of one of the sisters, who, in a soft voice, whispered to the other, "*Cosentor da Urab.*"

"*Una la merna,*" Brei replied in an astonished voice.

"How did you come upon that marking on your back?" Alyn inquired peaceably as she ran her soft, cold fingertips across the mark, sending chills through Darius's body.

"It is the heritage of my family," Darius said as he rubbed the marking on his back, brushing her fingers away in haste. The mark was as large as his own hand, crude and raised. "I received it when I became of age, after the passing of my father."

"It is quite unique." Brei's voice was still in awe. "We have not seen a mark as such in our time."

"Only in the memories of our ancestral mother have we seen the emblems of the Guardians of Old," stated Alyn as she helped Darius onto the stonework bed. Darius's eyes lit up at the statement. Alyn, seeing his reaction, continued, "You see, we share all the memories of our ancestors. Well, Brei more so than I."

"For generations we have been keepers of the line of our First Mother, who was the handmaiden of Gallea. She was gifted with foresight and the power to heal on behalf of the goddess Gallea," Brei began to explain as she gathered several rags of white linen. "We were born twins, and thus both inherited a different divine Blessing. I was gifted with knowledge and visions. And my sister, Alyn, was granted the power to heal."

"Yes," Alyn interjected softly. "But every Blessing comes with a price. For nothing can be for naught, and what is can only be transfigured to a thing of equal substance."

"Everything has its place and mana, Terral and Aethereal. There are but few who can borrow from one and add to another," said Brei gently. "And thus, we draw our source of power from the flowing water, the burning fire, and the illuminating sun."

"They are all one in the Everlight, the greatest gift of the gods to mortals," Alyn sang sweetly.

"And what of blood-curses?" Darius asked in curiosity as his eyes fell to the marking on his chest.

"Dark is the heart of man."

"Dark are the souls of the damned."

"One can draw out the life force of another and transfuse it to their own influence. But this is wicked and corrupts the soul."

"Once one has turned to this black art, they sacrifice the light within, and serve only evil for time and all eternity."

"You carry the burden of such darkness in the marking on your chest," Alyn said mournfully.

"Yet, in your true heart, you are pure," Brei said in a comforting tone.

"What does it mean, then?" Darius questioned. "This burning that I feel?"

"Once, it was said that darkness is the absence of light."

"But we have learned through a millennium that light needs darkness. Darkness needs light. Without the other, there is none. There must be opposition in all things. Peace and pain. Love and loss. Light and darkness. There is no life without death, no tomorrow without today."

"The sun must set in order for it to rise again."

"So, you feel the pain of evil, because in you is the heart of good."

Both were silent for a moment. Alyn took the linen rags and dipped them into crystal water that filled the basin. Three times she did this, and with each submersion it seemed that some of the refracted light from the stained-glass window was absorbed by the rags. When Alyn arose, a soft glow emanated from the dripping rags. As she placed the bandages softly around Darius' knee and ankle, it felt as nothing he had ever experienced before. It was not that of a wetness, but more of a gentle breeze accompanied by the soft flow of energy through his entire leg.

"Like the damage to your leg, the curse on your body is," Alyn stated kindly. "You see that your body does not reject your leg, but only wishes to be whole."

"As now does your heart," continued Brei. "It beats with a fire of determination, even though the weight of the anguish of darkness pushes against it from all sides. You were not entirely truthful with the Council, were you?"

Darius was silent. Could they read the thoughts of his mind? Never before had he heard of such magic.

"My sister has sensed that there is more to you than you let on," Alyn said, locking her emerald eyes with her sister's matching pair.

"Yes, there is more," Darius began. "But my story is not what is important...not anymore."

"Ah...the wanderer doubts his journey, for he cannot see the path to make him a traveler." Brei shook her head as she spoke. "You see, it is not in the destination that the answers are always revealed, but oftentimes in the voyage that one embarks upon."

"I completed my journey. I did what I set out to do..." Darius said, though his voice did not echo confidence. It was pained and filled with emptiness.

"And yet here you are."

"And there you were. You saved a young woman in the market today, did you not?" Brie inquired boldly, her green eyes locking decisively with Darius's, yet they were not as they were. They were bright and flowing, almost as if her irises were a raging river of emerald light. "You need not have helped, but you did, why?"

"I...I felt like it was the right thing to do," Darius said slowly, for his tongue had become heavy and his mind began to feel weak.

"And that is why you are good," Brei said with a soft smile.

"Rest and be healed," said Alyn while she ran her tender hand softly across the brow of Darius as to fade away into slumber. "You must rest to be healed. Take deep breaths."

One, two, three, four...

The room seemed to turn to water.

Five, six, seven, eight ...

The bed was gone.

Darius seemed to hover in blank space, somewhere between reality and non-existence.

Nine.

All light faded.

Ten.

Darius slipped away from consciousness.

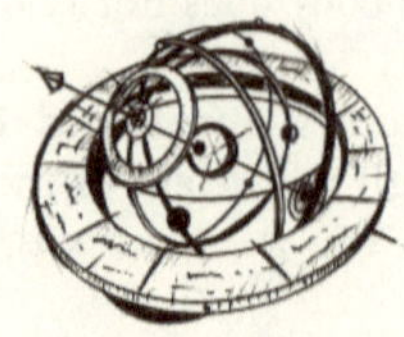

CHAPTER 20: THE GREATER NEED

Elcon, High Priest of the Church of Ordan, Shepherd of the Souls of Tur'Mor, paced back and forth, his emotions made bare on his tired face. Trepidation filled his eyes, anguish of soul crystalline. He could hear the others speaking in hushed tones behind him, but their words were no more than a dull hum in the back of his mind.

"Council of the Anointed," a voice called out, clear and crisp, drawing Elcon from his thoughts.

The door banged shut behind the Patriarch as he spoke, closed by one of the temple guards outside the secluded council room. Another two Aluth stood silently next to the door on the inside of the vaulted, octagonal room, halberds in hand. Orrum was a tall, rather unimposing man, with grandfatherly ears and a hooked nose that seemed slightly too large for his wrinkled face. A towering hat rested on his balding, curly grey hair. He had donned his half-moon spectacles, which dull blue eyes stared tiredly through. A large, ornamented amulet hung about his neck by thick golden chains. It was crafted after the likeness of Ethra and was as thick as a man's fist. Orrum wore green slippers with golden soles, which made a slight swishing sound as he walked. However, every step the Patriarch took was with precision, and his eyes never wavered from his purpose. He was the Voice of Ordan, the Watcher of Souls, the Highest of the Anointed, and he commanded respect in all things.

For the first time, Elcon noticed the others in the room, though he knew them each intimately. First was a grey-haired woman of high poise. Priestess Shanavaral's features were sharp and angular. Her robes matched Elcon's exactly, save for the emblem on her apron. Elcon's apron had Ethra in gold stitching while hers bore the image of a chalice with two handles, a flame burning within. Her eyes, too, were grey and dull, as were all who were on the Holy Council save Patriarch Orrum. Next behind her was a male, darker in complexion, though still Ordiatian by birth as all the members were. Talendeal's apron matched Elcon's, save his was purple instead of green. Lastly, there was Yemera, a shorter, black-haired woman. She was scowling and seemed as if she had been rushed from something else that she deemed more important than this meeting. Her apron bore the same image as her sister's, though the fabric was purple and Shanavaral's green.

"Talendeal, tell me you had no hand in this," Orrum said as he turned his eyes to the tall, darker high priest. His eyes shifted across the room to the high priestesses. "Yemera? Shanavaral?"

"No, Your Eminence," Talendeal said in a strong, regal voice. He was from northern Telnor and had a thick accent, every word proceeding out of his mouth both heavy and short. "I speak for the Northern Conclave; we had no knowledge of such."

"Nor the sisters of Livithia," Yemera said quietly as she dusted nervously at her apron.

"Neither us of Un'Mor, High Patriarch," Shanavaral said firmly, then clicked her tongue in disfavor as she ran her hand to smooth her flat, grey hair.

"None knew, Patriarch Orrum," Elcon said, meeting his superior's eyes firmly. "I can assure you –"

"Elcon," Orrum cut in curtly, "you cannot assure me of anything, not until you can make me understand why you would withhold such knowledge from the Holy Council."

"High Patriarch, surely you must see that there is more at stake than we could have ever realized." Elcon's voice held a certain calm to it, though his eyes never lost their intensity.

"A strange thing, this is," Talendeal's deep, rich voice cut in.

"Strange?" Shanavaral snarled. "No, not strange. Wrong! It is wrong!"

"Gentle your tones in my presence," Patriarch Orrum said with reproof. "Remember well all of your places."

Both Shanavaral and Talendeal brought fingers to their lips then forehead in quick succession. Elcon took the momentary break to step forward and began addressing the whole room, not just the High Patriarch. "We live in unprecedented times. The world changes around us daily and the faith of our followers dwindles. It was not us but our forefathers who sought to shield the world from the evils that lay beyond our borders. It was not us five that decided that it was better to walk in blindness than face the harsh light of truth. How can we continue in this way? We have already lost our brethren to the north. When was the last time a Danesman sat on the council? When was the last time any of us have traveled beyond the borders of Ordiatian soil?"

"The Church must remain singular in its teachings, Elcon," Orrum said with a shaking of the head. "You ask too much. It would uncover too much."

"Are we stunted by our own fears, or do we still seek the will of the High Father?"

"You would do well to guard your tongue, Elcon," Orrum answered sharply.

"But I have seen with my own eyes." Elcon's voice was nearly pleading. "How can I deny what I have seen? What I know to be truth?"

"My daughters have often helped the misguided find simpler truths." Shanavaral's voice was cold, the meaning of her words far colder.

"The work you and your sisterhood performs in the infirmary is integral, Priestess Shanavaral," Orrum interjected. "And the council recognizes the position it has put you in at times, but you will not speak in such a way to one of the council."

"Of course, Your Eminence," Shanavaral replied with a stiff bow of her head.

"We may not have sworn the First Entente, Elcon, but we will hold to it until the Forsworn Times," Orrum stated resolutely.

"And what are these times?" Elcon questioned, stepping forward, voice docile, not angered. "Wars rage in the Southlands. Our borders shrink to the east, and our alliances hang by a thread. Sightings of dark creatures within Ranok have increased, and those who return from battle speak of shadows with eyes of flame and of pale demons haunting the land."

"We ease the minds of the weary and afflicted," Shanavaral said with her nose turned upwards. "No word of such has spread beyond the borderlands."

"And the Huntsmen?" Elcon pressed onward, ignoring Shanavaral's biting remarks. "More and more flock to their cult. It is one thing to hide the darkness from the minds of mankind. It is another to discredit beings from myth being brought into our own cities. And what will the people say then? Do you think we can send every Ordiatian man, woman, and child to the infirmary? Do you not think they will not put two and two together?"

"Perhaps you spend too much time in the Asterivae and not enough time in your Sanctuary, preaching the true word of Ordan to his children!"

"Shanavaral! Elcon!" Orrum barked, his gentle face turning to stone. "You will stop such childish squabbles! You must learn to put petty differences aside. Why must I continue to reprove you as my own children? You have both sat on this council for decades. I would expect you to have learned to work together by now."

The silence that followed was deafening.

"Your Eminence." Yemera's voice was barely more than a squeak. "Our brother, Elcon, does speak the truth... In a means, that is, a small way." Her fingers gripped the edges of her apron so tightly that her knuckles whitened.

Elcon looked more startled than Orrum. It was not common for Yemera to voice anything contradictory to that of the High Patriarch, even in such hidden council sessions where no one else could hear. In truth, none of the Holy Council ever spoke a word out of alignment with the will of the Patriarch outside of closed doors. Behind closed doors, that was another story. Each council member was considered next to royalty in their governing city state. They were each powerful members of society, and the haughtiness that came with such prestige, even kindly Yemera, known amongst the Livithians as the Mother Healer, was openly flaunted amongst themselves.

"Speak clearly, Yemera," Orrum commanded, turning his cold eyes on her.

"There have been rumors spreading of Diju in Ranok," Yemera said as she gathered herself up to the full height of her short stature.

"There have always been Diju roaming Ranok," Talendeal interjected with a contemptuous sigh.

"I think I know my own borders, Recorder of Records," Yemera said icily. "Or perhaps you would also wish to wear the title of Guardian of Lands?"

"I meant only to say that Diju are not a new threat to the way of the Church, sister." Talendeal's words were less harsh than before. "I did not mean to overstep my bounds."

"Just continue, Yemera," Orrum said as he rubbed his brow with a tired hand.

"Of course, Your Eminence. Well, as I was saying, the Diju had never before ventured too far south in the forest. But my Aluth have seen motions as close to our lands as the Dogtooth Mountain range. They also report that, more than once, they have seen some of the Ancient Blood amongst them. The Old Ones who can whisper in the Ancient Words." Yemera shook her head disbelievingly but continued after a quick breath, "If such were spotted amongst the workers of the fields, we would be hard-pressed to conceal the spread. And I fear that even the infirmary could not handle such an influx of the burdened of mind. Not to insult you, Shanavaral, nor your healers. It could spell catastrophe."

A dark grimace etched its way across Patriarch Orrum's worn face. A sigh followed the expression, long and tired. The other council members were silent; not even Shanavaral, Watcher of the Infirmary, spoke to defend her sisterhood. If what Yemera said were true, if there were those who could Touch past the natural world and those secrets got out, everything the Church had built and protected could crumble, and every member of this council knew that.

Elcon finally broke the silence. "Darius is not of any of the Three Orders of Blessed, nor is he one of the Lifesingers of Diju, or anything I have seen before. He is something far older. Something even we have failed to keep in our records."

"The Holy Council was formed to keep the truths of this land, to preserve their integrity," Talendeal marked. "If there were such things as you speak, we would know."

"The Holy Council was founded to protect the Church and guide its followers, to prepare the world for the return of the Ellitheor, High Priest Talendeal," Elcon answered. "We have always borne the burden of truth. And at times, that has meant concealing such truths."

"You speak of the Fallen Ones and their dark cult again," Shanavaral said with a roll of her eyes.

"Was it not foretold that great wickedness would befall the lands before the Ellitheor would grace this realm once more?" Elcon asked, turning to face her. "Do we not know that the Sages of Old must once again unite to cleanse this land to usher in that great day of omnipotence?"

"There were no words of this 'Feromage' in the First Prophecies, uttered in the Dawn Time by the First Patriarch." Orrum's voice was long and drawn as he spoke, nearing what seemed like exhaustion.

"But does it not say, 'Woe be unto the world, for earth has forsaken her King! Woe be unto the seas, for the depths have disavowed their Queen. Let the beasts lament and the fowls cry, for blood shall rain from an azure sky. The dawn is coming, the day is near. When Sages return, the wicked shall fear. Return once more the Sages old, heralded in by guardians untold'?" Elcon scanned each member of the council, grey eyes unwavering. "We have long since believed it us to be the silent guardians of the truth, those that would usher in the Sages of Old. What if we were wrong?"

"You speak very near blasphemy, old friend," Orrum said wearily, though Elcon could tell his superior was considering every word that he had spoken. The Patriarch began to pace again as the others mumbled to themselves.

"I have dedicated my whole life, my everything, to the pursuit of the High Father's will," Elcon said firmly. He swallowed hard as he fought back powerful floods of emotion. "I will never have the finger of blasphemy pointed towards me, not by any man or woman, regardless of title. The days of idle watching have passed. The Calun have risen in full declaration of war. Kh'ar plague our cities, corrupting our way of life. Danesmen to the north have forsaken their faith, delighting in war and bloodshed, putting their trust in the strength of their own arm. Galacians have reverted to pagan and animistic beliefs. People speak in hushed whispers of creatures of mist and flame walking amongst the trees of Ranok, slaying beasts and man alike. And now, when a man has come forth, devout in his belief of the High Father and endowed with a gift never known in our time, you wish to send him to have his mind Cleansed. Why?"

"It is clear to us, Elcon, that this boy means a great deal to you" Orrum said firmly, meeting Elcon's eyes with a sharpness that melted almost instantly to a near watery pleading, though no less dignified than the former. "But the sanctity of our faith outweighs all else."

"Each of you knows my dedication is to this Church, and moreover, to the will of the High Father and the Holy Mother. I am ever faithful to my oaths, having never wavered from them," Elcon answered, looking each member of the Holy Council in the eyes, one by one. "But I cannot sit idly by when the world is aflame with death, deceit and destruction. Especially when one such as Darius has come forth, one who could help turn the tide back to the light."

Orrum took the amulet about his neck and held the golden emblem between his hands. The hammer was composed of several seams and gears wound within the golden outer layer. Slowly, methodically, Orrum began to move the gears and edges of the amulet, shifting them here and there, twisting some and pushing on some of the glowing gemstones.

The head of the hammer clicked suddenly, and then opened. The room ignited with a radiant blue light, fueled by the perfect sphere that was housed in the hammer's head. The azure stone seemed to swirl, as if it were liquid and not stone at all. Bursts of cobalt light flared as the High Patriarch touched his signet ring to the stone. A strange zinging noise filled the ears of those who surrounded him. The only ones who did not stare with utter shock and awe were the two Aluth.

"Do you wish for the truth?" Orrum bellowed. His voice had turned as deep as the Great Sea. Sapphire light leaked from his lips as he spoke, as if thunderheads were forming inside his bosom.

"Patriarch Orrum, ours are not ears worthy to hear the Voice!" Talendeal cried out as he buried his face in his hands.

THE DAMNED RISE. THE EARTH BREAKS. SHADOWS AND DEATH AWAKENS. MOURN FOR THOSE WHO WILL FALL. CRY FOR THOSE WHO SHALL MEET THEIR FATES.

THE SUNLESS DAY COMES. THE OATHBOUND WILL STAND AND PROTEST THE CORRUPT. BE FAITHFUL TO THE SOURCE OF ETERNAL LIGHT. RISE UP AND FULFILL YOUR OATHS.

Gusts of wind seemed to pull at the High Patriarch's robes as he chanted the words with arms thrusted outwardly. The amulet was no longer in his hands, floating in mid-air, only bound by the golden chain about his neck. A halo of light swirled about his ceremonial headpiece and pulsating flows of blue energy crackled from his eyes and mouth.

When the chanting stopped, Orrum slammed the amulet shut, driving a palm onto either side of the hammer's head until it concealed the swirling stone within. A sound like shattering glass cascading down stone steps echoed through the council chamber, and then all went silent.

It was a long silence. A cold silence, wherein none dared to speak.

In all Elcon's life, he had never expected to see a prophecy made bare. Never in his life would he have thought that he would witness the Patriarch speak with the Tongue of the High Father. However, this one moment would not, could not, change the facts that he had discovered. No. It strengthened his theories. Fueled them.

"The will of the High Father be done," Patriarch Orrum said reverently.

"Thus shall it be," Elcon found himself saying in perfect unison with the other three members of the Holy Council.

"There is no division in the will of the High Father," Orrum voiced.

"The council seeks to fulfill their duty," the others voiced. "Command us, and we shall obey. We are one."

"Then the question at hand, I lay at the feet of the council," Orrum said tiredly. "What shall we do with the boy?"

"He is too dangerous to keep in the city." The resolve was still strong in Shanavaral's voice as she spoke. "Even if one of my daughters were to Cleanse his mind, the boy has attracted far too much attention. We risk too much in letting him stay."

Shanavaral was right, and Elcon knew it. Darius was dangerous, for far too many reasons. Yet, he was also intriguing, far more so than any other Elcon had ever met. So much history, so many secrets lost to time that floated in the young man's head. However, the facts lay bare. Darius had shown himself to be more than a man, in the very city that the Holy Council convened. Such actions could not go without repercussions.

Stories could be told, seeds planted, and dissension sown in the minds of the people. Tales could be fabricated to dissuade those who had seen. But the true quandary – that Darius would continue to choose to use his powers if he felt compelled – was an absolute certainty. And for that reason alone, Darius could not stay. The bitter truth soured Elcon's weary face. He had tried his very best, done all he could, and he had inevitably failed.

Elcon relented, "We must trust in the will of the High Father and in the grace of the Holy Mother. Darius must leave this place if our peace is to remain."

"Brother Elcon," Yemera said softly, raising a comforting hand to his shoulder.

"That being said, I do not mean to send him away idly." Elcon shrugged away the wrinkled hand of the shorter priestess as he spoke. "Holy Patriarch, teach us the meanings of the words you have received. Help me to understand how to give purpose to the boy."

"If what you speak of is true, that the Dawn Times are upon us and that this Darius is such a powerful warrior, then we could use him in our services," Patriarch Orrum said with more assurance than his weary eyes gave. "But it cannot be our word that proclaims him as such. There is only one who can attest to such a claim."

"You do not mean to send him there, Holy Patriarch?" Elcon asked, aghast. "That road is beyond treacherous, and the Danesmen have come to despise our ways. They are brutish and unholy."

"Only the Apostle can divine his legitimacy," Orrum answered, raising a hand to silence the other. "Darius must travel to the Dane's capital city. It is the only way we can know the truth."

"Yemera, did you not say that there are dark creatures in Ranok?" Elcon asked, sounding a bit worried for the first time.

"Despite the attempts of my own Blessed, and at the expense of a dozen of my Aluth, many of my congregation have claimed to have seen vile things and have whispered of the innocent gone missing amongst the trees in the dead of night," Yemera said with a tired nod of her head.

"So, you send him into the forest to die?" Elcon asked.

"No," Orrum answered resolutely. "Not if what you say of him, and what he claims to be, is true. If he is, in fact, a Feromage, then the forest should be no issue for him. Perhaps, he might even be of some use there, to root out, as it were, this darkness."

"And what do we tell him?" Elcon contended. "He believes he has a divine calling to fulfill. He will not leave the city easily."

"A divine calling? What is more divine than the words of their own Anointed?" The Patriarch answered.

A hush fell over the room. None dared speak, much less argue. The High Patriarch had spoken. It was the duty of the council now to hear and obey. The will of the High Father had to be carried out.

"I do not wish to contend with you, my friend," Orrum said more softly, looking over his spectacles with understanding in his eyes. "And I would not idly send the boy away without the need to do so. Perhaps divine providence will afford us a miracle in this thing. It is not often that we are handed such a tool as this young man could prove to be. If he is indeed Feromage, confirmed by the Apostle, then we will bring him back to us and guide him along his path to fulfilling his destiny. If he is not... Well, just because something is not what it appears to be, does not make it useless."

"So, you would use him?" Elcon scoffed.

"And what have you done?" Orrum asked, turning up a grey eyebrow in questioning. "Weeks have passed since this young man has fallen into your care, and only now we have learned of him. Do not think that this is settled, not in the slightest. Darius will be sent, that is certain. But of your actions, they will be addressed at another time."

Elcon looked down, unashamed of his actions, more so frustrated in being caught out. He had not harbored intentions of deceit, not truly. He had just been so curious, fascinated by the complexities of the situation. His scholarly mind, always yearning to expand and understand, had gotten the better of him again. Darius represented a lifetime of study, a cog of truth within the mechanisms of understanding that formed everything Elcon held true, for if Darius was Feromage, then the tales and fables Elcon had uncovered, the countless hours of study and research, were not in vain. Elcon had, through Darius, found an answer, a single truth. There was more.

"Come now, Elcon. This is not to be a moment of reprimanding. No, indeed this is a moment of triumph for us as a council," Orrum said proudly, drawing himself up, eyes still shining slightly with crystalline blue light. "We must prepare the lad to go, and I think it best we send him with all the help we can. Guards, send for Blessed daughter, Sister Brei. Perhaps she can provide guidance to our newfound friend."

"Visions are reserved only for the Anointed, High Patriarch," Shanavaral replied in subtle protest, doing her best to conceal her apparent frustrations of the matter.

"Then, I will anoint him, give him my blessing," Orrum answered. "I will not indiscriminately send this boy to death and ruin, as if he had committed some grievous sin against the High Father. Do not think to forget that one of our own, Ranun, was murdered by those that Darius confronted."

"Thank you," Elcon conceded before Shanavaral could retort further.

"I myself will prepare letters of mark, sealed by my own signet, to send with the boy," Orrum stated firmly, ending further debate. "These will allow him into Dane and afford him an audience with the High King of the Danes, for surely they have not fallen so far as to ignore my own hand. It is the best I can do."

And with those words, the council concluded.

CHAPTER 21: VISIONS AND BLESSINGS

Gentle was the sound of flowing water to the ears of Darius as a warm flow of energy coursed soothingly through his veins, waking him from his dreamlike trance. His eyes slowly opened, peering upward into the vaulted stone ceiling. A soft blue light illuminated the healer's room. He knew not how long he had slumbered, but his body felt completely renewed.

A gentle pulsating sensation moved though his right leg, trickling like water over his joints. The soft sounds of the Candius sisters' singing drew Darius's attention. And though he did not understand the tongue in which they sang, certain words seemed to make sense to him. In silence he lay, soaking in the harmonious feelings of healing and the soothing sounds of Alyn and Brei's song.

"Ah, he wakes," Brei said in a singsong voice. "Alyn, your hands have not failed you, my sister."

"Strong is he," Alyn replied as she walked gracefully to Darius's side. "Many men would sleep for days under the Trance of Healing's Blessing."

"How long was I asleep?" Darius inquired groggily, struggling to form even the simplest thought.

"No more than the hours of twilight."

"See there," Brie said as she pointed to the nearly translucent, glass-like gemstone in the center of the vaulted ceiling. "Only the moon lights the world."

"Let me remove these bandages, Darius. Brei, do let the council know our guest is prepared to stand before them," said Alyn.

"Of course," said Brei with a slight nod while raising both hands to her bosom with a smile. She scampered away quickly and quietly out a back door.

"This will only take a moment." Alyn brushed her hand across Darius' cheek as she spoke.

Alyn removed the bandages from around Darius's knee and ankle with grace, her gentle hands moving in rhythmic synchronization. While the bandages were being removed, a dim light faded away from both the rag and the leg. Not only had the bone completely re-knit itself, but the purple swelling had also left his extremities. Darius stared at that light with both awe and reassurance, thankful the light was leaving but grateful for what it had done.

Alyn took the once-white bandages and placed them on a small stone slab. A marble statue of Gallea rested behind the simple altar, her arms open and a single blue gem set in her forehead. Next, Alyn poured oil from a crucible over the rags and set them ablaze. The flames that consumed the rags turned a vibrant blue and the sweet smell of incense filled the room. Alyn muttered a soft prayer to the goddess.

"You should probably clothe yourself now," Alyn said as she returned the candle she had used to its place.

Darius, having forgotten his nakedness, felt a rush of embarrassment. Brei laughed as she walked back into the room, seeing his reddening face. Alyn moved gracefully over to help him up. Her hands were so soft and smooth, but there was surprising strength in them as she guided his feet to the floor.

An Aluth, seemingly appearing out of nowhere, stepped into the light. He was carrying Darius's belongings, each item cleaned and tightly folded. The silent guardian offered the clothing to Darius with a bow and walked back into the shadow next to the doorway.

Darius dressed quickly, not only covering up his nudity but also the scars that littered his body. After he was finished, Alyn handed him a wooden comb to brush his beard and hair. He nodded thankfully and ran the comb through his hair quickly, making himself presentable. Darius then turned to the sisters, as if seeking approval for his appearance, holding his hands out and open to his sides. Brei and Alyn chuckled softly as they looked him over.

"What is it?" Darius inquired; the feeling of embarrassment having not totally subsided.

Alyn smiled and then straightened the collar of his vest and coat. She had to stand on her toes as she was much shorter than he was. "There you are then," Alyn stated proudly, "ready now to meet the Holy Council."

"I thank you," Darius said to the sisters. "I do not think I can repay you for this."

"No. No, you cannot. For it was not me, but the Holy Mother, Gallea, who has healed you. I am but a vessel," responded Alyn, who then paused and smiled. "You have a good heart; of that I am sure. But go now. Until we meet again."

Darius nodded his head in adoration and turned about, heading towards the doorway where the two Aluth stood in silence. Alyn quickly grabbed a small vial of glass and silver, a blue elixir visible inside. She handed Darius the vessel, saying, "Where you go, I cannot follow. In a moment of great despair, use this for healing blessed by my own mother's hand."

Darius accepted silently, only nodding in appreciation of the gift. These girls owed him nothing, and yet he could tell that this gift was of great worth to Alyn. He placed the unique vial in the inner pocket of his trench coat and gave Alyn his best smile. She smiled back, eyes twinkling like starlight.

One of the Aluth that stood by knocked firmly on the door three times. An iron bolt slid outside, and then the door opened inwardly. The Aluth walked out, beckoning Darius to follow him as the other walked behind him, shutting the door as they left.

The main corridor of the temple was now lit by many pyres which rested atop small stands of marble down the sides of the vast, rectangular room. The light danced on the walls and the ceiling, making the painted work almost come to life. Darius walked back to where the stone seats were. However, this time, to his surprise, they were vacant.

The temple Aluth, who were dressed in the separate garb, were still standing at attention, with the halberds' polished heads reflecting the firelight. Across the floor, the leading Aluth guided Darius past the raised platform to the back of the temple where a grand statue of Ordan stood with his great hammer in both hands. Behind this statue were three iron clad doors, each bearing a different symbol. One had an eye with three lines beneath it. The other, the center and larger door, bore the mark of Ethra. And the final had a golden sword that ran from the top of the frame to the ground.

The Aluth led him to the door with Ethra upon it. Thrice again was the knock, but this time came a response: "Show thy loyalty from the other side." And with that, a small slide opened on the door, not much larger than what a hand could fit through. The Aluth reached his hand inside this opening for a moment and then withdrew it solemnly. Again, the sounds of iron turning, and bolts being unfastened filled the room. Darius thought on the high levels of security and secrecy these rooms held, and the measures the Aluth went through to keep them secret.

The door opened inwardly, revealing a small chamber with two temple guards on either side of the room. These Aluth did not have halberds but broadswords hanging at their sides. Beyond the blades, they held peculiar crossbows, each with a revolving drum of arrows, loaded in their hands.

Straight in front was a set of double doors made of heavy oak and had gold embroidery upon them. Large brass rings were on either door with a brass plate behind them. One temple guard on each side grabbed a brass ring and pulled the doors inward once the single door behind them was closed and locked.

When the doors opened, it exposed one of the grandest rooms Darius had ever beheld in his lifetime. The room was in the shape of a diamond, with it being slightly longer than wide. There were two sets of nine stone hewn seats on either side of a green carpet that went all the way to a chest-high silver gate. On either side of the gate, a marble stonework ran wall to wall, connecting to a lit pyre on either side. A giant crystal chandelier hung from the domed ceiling. There were no paintings in the white marble room, nor any statues save one in the far back corner of Ordan, again holding Ethra firmly in his grasp.

Behind the gate, a raised platform stood. The left and right sides were at a slight angle, pointing to a high veined marble seat, grander than the other four, two of which were on either side. On these seats, in the same order, sat the Council. In front of the stand but before the gate was a circular mosaic of silver and gold depicting the entire land of Ethrea spanning from the Northern Mounts of the Danes down into the Uurdan Desert, including Galacia to the west and the Ja'una Island to the east. Atop the mosaic sat Brei, legs crossed, and eyes closed. In her lap was a bluish green bowl, thick and heavy in appearance. Thin wisps of smoke rose into the air from the dish and the room smelled of burning incense.

"Come and stand before us," Orrum commanded in a reverent tone.

Darius made his way forward through the rows of marble seats and stood before the silver gate, studying each of the council members, noting the resolution up their faces, resolution that had not been present before. Their eyes seemed firmer, and Darius could feel a sense of unity that had not been present in their encounter before.

"Darius, Son of the Iron Mountains, we beseech you now to hear the words of the Holy Council, Voice of the Ellitheor," Orrum began in a regal, self-assured voice. "For generations, we have sat as the Watchers of Ethrea, Preservers of the Noble Truth and Professors of the Divinity of the Ellitheor."

"And what does this have to do with me?" Darius asked bluntly. There was an odd feeling in the room, a sensation that he could not quite define, but it felt alive. And this feeling did not sit well with Darius at all.

"Ah, never one to mince words, I see," Orrum replied with a forced laugh before continuing his speech. "My right hand, and my dearest friend, Elcon, has said that you have spent many a night concerned as to the nature of your current state. Is that true?"

Darius looked to Elcon first, who, in turn, proceeded to give Darius a look of encouragement, as to invite him to speak. Darius just turned his gaze back to Orrum and gave a simple nod.

"In your introduction, you spoke of an age-old feud, one that has long since been forgotten by the people of this land. What is even more intriguing is that Elcon rehearsed how he found you, the visions you have experienced, and the scar that marks your body," Orrum said as he pointed his finger towards Darius's chest.

Darius met the Holy Patriarch's eyes, not wavering in the slightest. Yet as he stared at the old man, he heard something beneath the earth. A pulse. A rhythmic, living beat. It was the same sound that he had heard as he had been led into the temple. A heartbeat, but not of any living creature Darius had ever heard.

"I want to make one thing very clear," Orrum then stated, his voice softening some as he leaned forward in his chair. "You are no enemy to us here. No, quite the opposite. We see you as a great blessing."

Darius raised an eyebrow as he looked from Orrum to Elcon.

"However, unfortunately," the Patriarch continued. "Your actions inside Tur'Mor have caused great strife between the Church and the High Seat."

"Darius, when I met you in my chapel, led by Ranun, High Father guide his soul to the fields of Pallenthor upon Vanherran," Elcon said gently. "I thought you were a drunkard who had come to rest from the night's cold. But when we descended to that sacred temple of the Ancient Apostles of Ordan, where the history of the Church and its people are kept, you opened my eyes to a greater possibility."

"Speak clearly," Darius said. "What is to be my fate?"

In answer, Orrum nodded towards Brei, who was slowly swaying to and fro while inhaling the vapors of smoke. Darius had not noticed the grate in the flooring, mixed amongst the mosaic tiles. Two Aluth pulled on either side of the metal fixture, allowing a subterranean vent to open. A waft of saltwater, something very metallic, and something very sweet filled the room. The amulet around her neck seemed to lift from her flesh by an invisible string. Blue light emanated from the floor and from the jewel set within her necklace. Brei's long, crimson hair began to float about her head and shoulders. The heartbeat rang so loud in Darius's ears that it nearly caused him to double over. Brei snapped her eyes open, revealing irises that flowed as waves of the ocean, barely contained within the whites of her eyes.

Five breaths. Brei drew five breaths.

The oracle lifted gracefully from the floor, as if hoisted by an invisible cord. She glided motionlessly towards Darius, who stared dumbfounded in return. Brei raised her hand and touched Darius on the forehead. With her other she touched the glowing blue gem that hung between her pale breasts. Brei's sapphire eyes ignited with vibrant light, and she began to chant, "*One who calls himself Darius, a son of the old blood, the chosen blood, hear you the words of my vessel.*"

There was a shift of her head; her body seemed to convulse, almost dancing as a puppet on strings. Her blue eyes went white, cloudy orbs of hazy light. Her hands opened at her sides, and she began to speak in a voice as vast as the ocean, and twice as deep.

As fire forges fate, so shall perseverance establish the great.
Seven stars shall light the sky, and all mourn.
Ancient secrets, sealed in blood, emerge once more.
Mist and shadow, lurk and creep. Death takes form and heroes weep.

A sound of raging water rushing over a riverbed flooded the room. A force of energy surged, nearly knocking the Holy Council from their seats. Brei sank towards the floor, descending gently as mist while the whooshing sounds continued to batter the room. As she drifted downwards, the light that once gleamed faded from her body. Two Aluth quickly moved to seal the vent and then caught her, clutching her lifeless body from the air with gentle haste.

As the two carried Brei's body silently from the council chamber, her clouded eyes met Darius's for a short second. He felt a spark ignite in his heart. The room seemed to close in around him as something awoke inside, a feeling that Darius had not felt in an age.

Weeks of studying about the past and present affairs had not gotten him an inch closer to understanding the words of the voice. Nights spent training and roaming the streets had lent little more than frustration. But now, now there was seemingly a purpose where there had only been questions. His heartbeat quickened and his eyes widened. A determination to find whatever lay northward filled his bosom.

"Do you understand the words spoken to you?" Orrum asked as he leaned forward, eyes locked on Darius.

Darius looked up at the High Patriarch. All of the cool confidence and arrogant authority that had been there before seemed to have vanished. The old man's face was a maze of questions. Yet, behind those wrinkles of concern were eyes that shone with determination. Darius returned the stare with his own and, unable to suppress the feelings of determination, answered, "I must follow the words of the Blessed."

Orrum drew in a breath as he continued to study Darius over his glasses. The Patriarch then turned to Elcon, whose face was a picture of awe. His eyes fell upon each member of the Holy Council. None seemed to be able to form words.

"Truly you are called, and truly you must follow," Orrum stated ostentatiously, regaining his air of regal composure. "Darius, son of the past, he who is pledged in the ancient ways, I too have heard the words of the High Father and would ask that you fulfill your part in his great plan. The words spoken this day are of great importance, and I would have them delivered to the Northern Church," Orrum said. Then, adding quickly, "Seeing that you are already going in that direction, I would send you as soon as they are compiled. But I feel I must warn you; the way is dark and treacherous. There have been many claims of dark beasts in Ranok, the forest which impedes your path."

"I am no stranger to darkness," Darius answered.

"You know that the ways of the Church must be preserved," Talendeal said in his deep, rich voice. "It would be most unfortunate if certain rumors were spread."

"You fear that I will talk of your attempts to disavow magic and sorcery?" Darius questioned with a roll of his golden eyes.

"This is no light matter, young Darius," Shanavaral snapped. "We protect this land and all those who live within her borders."

"Protect?" Darius questioned. "From what?"

"Unbelief has caused the destruction of many nations, Darius." This time it was Elcon who spoke in a pleading tone, and he looked weary beyond description. "Please take this seriously. We cannot afford to lose what we have gained through our peace."

Ignorance is never peace. Darius heard his mother say in the back of his mind. The very words she had said when the men of his tribe had sought to hide his father from his eyes as the body was carried upon the shields of warriors.

An image of a young woman popped into Darius's mind, with blue eyes and icy-white hair. He remembered the feeling he had when he was near her. Something inside him, that same feeling he felt when Brei looked into his eyes. Thoughts of contending with the five in front of him vanished as he stepped forward and spoke, now respectfully, "Holy Council, I would request just one thing. I just need a day or two to prepare-"

"Prepare what, Darius?" Shanavaral asked as she stared down her nose at him. "Is not all you own given by the Church? What could you possibly need to prepare?"

"Shanavaral," Elcon censured.

"Am I wrong? Is there not greater need than material possessions at stake? Did the Blessed One not say that urgent are the needs of this man?" Her voice was sharp, yet proper, every word snapped off her tongue like a whip.

"Darius, due to your actions against the law of our city, we can no longer offer you sanctuary," Orrum voiced with empathy. "That being said, it does seem to me that your purpose draws you elsewhere, and I do believe this is a matter of great urgency."

"Then I must go," Darius acceded, but not without turning an eye to Elcon.

"You cannot go back into Tur'Mor," Elcon said with a certain pain in his voice. "Nor can you be seen as aided further by the Church until you are far from our watch."

"I understand," Darius grunted. "I can manage myself."

"Very well then. I will have the words of this vision transcribed and sealed with my own holy seal," Orrum stated as he rose, motioning to the Aluth to come forward. "You must not break the seal, for the Danes are untrusting people, and too few hold to the faith. They will need to see it intact to believe the words which are written."

"Understood."

"Show our guest back to the Hall of the Ellitheor. Have him wait until our parcel is prepared. From there, see him on his journey, but do not follow him from this temple," Orrum said as he turned away from Darius to the awaiting Aluth.

Two of the Aluth nodded and then walked to Darius's side, each placing a hand on his shoulder. The Holy Council left one by one through the door in the back until only Elcon remained. He turned and looked to Darius.

"Darius," Elcon said softly, "be careful."

"It's only trees," Darius answered. "How bad can one forest be?"

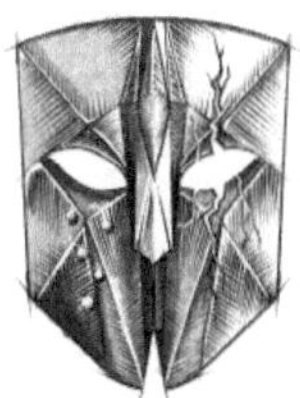

CHAPTER 22: ENCOUNTERS

Aellia ran up the stairway, the Khall'ah Kh'ar fleeing before her. Thrice today that strange scepter of silver had been in her hands, and every time, the cursed Kh'ar had managed to wrangle it from her. And despite her better judgement, something about that rod beckoned to her. She needed it, and it needed her. She could feel it. *Ada'eha El-dached.* The palm of her hand itched where she had held the scepter as she recanted those mysterious words. The yearning was stronger now; she had to find it.

The alleyway where Aellia found herself was overcrowded and narrow. Away from the main courtyards and large villas, the rising stacked style houses blocked much of the sun's light. Large signs hung from sides of buildings and patterned awnings of vibrant colored cloth shadowed markets and shops further. Stands with fruits, dyes, clothes, and ironworks butted against the endless rows of buildings, and the calls of merchants filled the air. Aellia was not one for tight crowds, but she did not let this slow her.

Where are you leading me? Aellia mused as she chased after the darkly clad man. She was like a wild mountain cat on the hunt. Her prey was fleeing, but it was to little avail. Aellia always caught her mouse, no matter how long it took.

As she continued onward, a secondary thought entered her mind. *What is it you could want with it? What is it?* She had seen strange artifacts, jewels, and ornaments in the past, but nothing like this. It had a feel to it, an essence of something beyond, something grand. The Kh'ar had long been known to the underground as those who were usurpers of power and authority, and it was no secret that they were behind many of the attempts of rebellion and anarchy in the city. And while Aellia was no proud loyalist of Tur'Mor, she hardly felt that reestablishing a dead monarchy would help anything. The more authoritative the government, the more the lower people suffered. Despite their 'all will be given as needed' mantra, Aellia had seen first-hand where the wealth really went when lords and kings had total control. But that still did not answer the question of what they needed that scepter for. Aellia had never even seen or heard of it before this day.

A crash ahead drew Aellia back into the moment. It was a problem of hers, to keep herself focused at all times, Felik had always said. "Felik!" She stopped, horror filling bright blue eyes. "The rendezvous! The plan!"

Ahead, an overturned cart with cabbages spilled into the street marked where the man called Rahnaluz had fumbled in his haste. He too was on the ground and cursing as he crawled on all fours to where the brown sack that held the silver rod lay. She could actually hear him, every word.

Aellia's eyes darted back and forth. Ahead was that strange scepter that seemed to call to her. Behind: her friend, their plan...his need. She knew what was right, what needed to be done. Another thought then jumped into her mind, unwelcome and unexpected. *And what of the stone-cutter? Who was he? And why did he stare at me like that?*

Aellia shook her head, frustrated. *What am I thinking? Felik could be in danger.* Her heart sunk as yet another thought assaulted her swirling mind. *Tomo could be in danger!* The man called Rahnaluz had already reached his prize and was quickly making his way to his feet when Aellia was able to refocus. *I can get that back and make it to Felik!* she thought as she began to run. *I can do both!* Her eyes hardened. *I have time.* A craving seemed to creep up her spine. *I need that rod.*

A torrent of rage filled Aellia. Something within her was different; she could feel it. A flash of a man's face filled her mind: yellow eyes, a strong jaw and inky-black hair. She stumbled as she moved, pressing her fingertips to her head. The pain was searing; nausea almost overtook her.

Rahnaluz was running now, appearing as a blur of meshing colors to Aellia's strained eyes. Those who had littered the streets were rushing to shelter themselves from the ensuing chaos.

The craving was so strong; the need ate at her core, tormenting her. A scream burst from her lungs, blood curdling and shrill. She thrust her hand outward and leapt forward. A sound that could only be described like cracking thunder erupted in the alleyway.

A burst of air coursed through carts and stands, upending all, emanating from where Aellia had landed. Torrents of blue light streamed from her eyes, her veins radiated like lightning were surging through them, pressing them to the surface of her skin. Azure streaks of light seared through the vambraces that covered her arms, like bolts of lightning frozen across a silver sky.

The man called Rahnaluz yelped in surprise and pain. The brown sack he held burst into flames. His eyes widened further as the silvery scepter levitated near eye level and then bolted through the sky. Aellia snatched it from the air with uncanny ease, as if it had a will of its own to return to her hand. A second rush flooded through her, and she soared up into the sky, streaming trails of blue light.

***

The man called Rahnaluz staired upward from his position on the ground, tossed like a rag doll from that unnatural surge of wind. His dark eyes filled with hate and unbridled rage. That power was supposed to be his. His blood boiled in his veins. Again, he had been shorted. Again, power had slipped from him. He wanted to scream into the sky, curse the heavens and all that were in them. He hated the feeling of lack, the emptiness of failure, but he had no time to draw further attention to himself.

Drawing his hood back over his head, he slunk away from the alleyway before those urchins would creep their way back out to sell their trinkets and trifles. Petty fools. They were worms, they were all insignificant, lords and peasants alike. So many wasted hours, planning and edging. The pieces were moved perfectly, and everything was going to work.

Curses slid from his lips as he delved ever further into darker parts of Tur'Mor. The man called Rahnaluz did not stop until he reached a corner of the city that looked unlike any other part of the city. The cobblestone alleyway, overshadowed by towering plaster-coated houses five to six stories in height, was slick with grime and rain-wash. The windows and doors of the towering buildings were covered with iron and steel. Gargoyles of granite sat on several of the roofs and eaves, staring dead-eyed into the streets below. Heavy, wrought-iron fences surrounded several of the homes and shops, baring unwelcoming spikes or barbs like fangs. The iron lamps that edged the path were blackened, and the windows of the shops were filmed or cobweb-lined.

Though the appearance of Darhdall Alley was that of abandonment, several folk were seen walking about, talking with one another in tight huddles. They all wore fine garments, fancy hats and dresses and the like, though the colors were not as vibrant as what would be traditionally worn. Deep colors of purples, blues, and bloody maroon adorned the people that walked about. These were not peasants but those of wealth sealed for generations. Older members of the monarchy before it had crumbled into a spineless democracy where commoners could raise opinions in matters they did not understand.

The other oddity of those who walked Darhdall Alley were the strange masks that covered their faces. These ranged from gaudy covers that were jewel-encrusted or held large fans of featherings to simple masks of slate grey. Some only covered the eyes, while others covered the face, looking somewhat like a skull of sorts. The man called Rahnaluz ran a finger over his own, half-covering his face.

247

These were those who were known as the Kh'ar, and even the city guards in the black armor wore masks on their faces here. If Mayor Adelmo had any knowledge of these so-called Kingsmen, as they were sometimes called amongst themselves, he did not dare make an open statement against them. Too many of them were in places of high power and influence. They were lords and ladies, chief architects, captains, and noblemen. High-ranking members of society who, despite what others might perceive, truly ran Tur'Mor.

The man called Rahnaluz made his way to a shop where two men, brawny and stone-faced, stood guard. Their large arms were folded across thick chests, and each had a morning star-headed mace hanging at their belts and steel tips on their heavy boots. They wore masks that covered their nose to the bottom of their jaws, with a symbol raised in the leather: a crown wreathed in flame. These men were called Talkers. *A sardonic term*, Rahnaluz thought as he walked between them, both a head taller than he, as these Talkers were more typically used to get someone else to talk, rather than themselves.

Rahnaluz was neither Talker, Inquisitor, nor Follower. He was the Khall'ah Kh'ar, Head of the Serpent, leader of the Kh'ar. And today, today he was supposed to have become a god, and some foolish child had stripped him of it. He would just have to settle for lesser powers, for now. He would get that back; he would drain her of every ounce of what he was due. It would be his eventually. Though he was never a man who was okay with just settling.

The man called Rahnaluz's study was as dark and brooding as he was. An iron gate with sharpened tooth-like spikes guarded a polished black fireplace, the mantle of which was of ebony and inlaid with a silver trim. The crackling fire did not seem to warm the room, a dark chill lingering. A massive hexagonal table was positioned in the center of the room, six high-backed chairs surrounding it, each of which were masterfully carved and upholstered in deep maroon fabric. Looking down at the table, it appeared to be an aerial view of Ethrea and the varying islands that lay about her borders. It was a deep table, the domed bottom of which rested on a coiled snake of brass. The imagery inside the table was formed by painstakingly crafting a detailed diorama and then pouring a clear liquid resin that set to form the smooth surface of the table. A rim of brass surrounded it, along with twelve sturdy legs. Rahnaluz was extremely proud of this creation; it had taken years to perfect, each individual piece placed by his own hand. Every carving, painting, stitching and grinding was his work.

An imposing man sat in one of those high-backed chairs, and another hooded figure stood in a dark corner. What would have been the seated man's chin was mostly covered by a tall collar of burnt red. His topcoat was exquisite, inky black with golden buttons and stitchwork of crimson running up the sleeves and down the tails. A golden pendant was fastened to the lapel, a circle forged of flames raging around an open hand whose palm bore the image of an upside-down eye, whose pupil was a single onyx gemstone. A rapier hung from his belt on one side and a breaker on the other, both of which were jewel-encrusted. A high leather riding boot was propped up on the table, another crossed over the top. Smoke from an egg-shaped pipe, long-stemmed and golden in color, drifted towards the vaulted ceiling where a small chandelier hung set with candles. His face, however, was shrouded by darkness.

"Master Edous," the man called Rahnaluz said humbly, though there was a note of disdain in his raspy voice. He totally ignored the other figure. That was his squire, and he was the last of Rahnaluz's concerns at the moment. "I was not expecting you here."

"You are not to expect me ever," the man said in an icy tone as he removed his boots from the table. "I would have thought you'd learn that by now."

"You know I serve as well as any!" Concern seemed more predominant in the hawk-nosed man's voice now, more so than obstinance.

"Serve? You think you serve?" The air rippled around Edous's face, distorting his features from view as if by the heat of flames. "You dance about this city, a strutting peacock without feathers. You have no teeth, no bite, and are of little worth to me."

"I have always served, faithfully, absolutely!" Rahnaluz croaked, falling to his knees, pleading.

"Then, do you have what I sent for?" Edous snarled at the begging man, a hardness in his voice that could snap steel. "Do you have the Tel'un Aund?"

"It – it was stolen from me!" Rahnaluz stammered. "I lost two of my best men! A girl –"

"*You lost it*?" Edous bellowed.

Rahnaluz fell on his face, hand reaching for the base of the riding boots. "Please! I was taken unawares! Please, have mercy!"

"Sobs are unbecoming of you, Khall'ah Kh'ar." Edous's voice was back to its level, icy tone, filled with cruel indifference.

Tears streamed down the man called Rahnaluz's face. He wailed for mercy as Edous drew out the jewel-encrusted rapier. The blade seemed to capture every glisten of light, catching and refracting it across the dimly lit room. Edous placed the tip of the blade under the chin of the weeping man and raised his face.

"I will come for you again to reclaim the Tel'un Aund." Edous slid the blade quickly across the flesh on the other's neck. The cut was shallow and no more than a thumbs width in length. "This will not heal, save by my command. It will continue to spread, slowly, until your wretched head is removed from its pitiful stand, unless you have what I seek. Only then will I heal you."

"I will not fail you!" the man called Rahnaluz answered, rising from the ground. "I swear, I will not!"

"You would do well to remember who you serve," Edous replied coldly. "I will not forgive your impotence again."

Edous stepped backwards. A crackling sound, much like that of breaking glass or crashing waves, formed around a fissure in the air. The black smoke enveloped Edous, and he vanished from sight.

The man called Rahnaluz raised a trembling finger to his neck, cautiously feeling the trivial wound. Yet he knew it was not a trivial thing. He had seen what that blade had done to the Khall'ah Kh'ar before him. He had been stabbed through the heart, which in turn burst into liquid flames of dark maroon. Rahnaluz had always sought such power, such authority. But this did not feel like power; it felt like cowardice.

Rising slowly to his feet, the man called Rahnaluz looked about his study, as if to make sure Edous was gone. His squire, who had remained reclusive during the exchange, continued to hold his silence. And as well he should. That little prat had cost him much in gold and sway to win over. And there he was, standing. Not kneeling. Not proffering himself on his knees, bellowing tears and swearing fealty to some corrupt being from the very pits of Halfak.

Rahnaluz pulled the mask from his face and flung it into the flames, cursing loudly as he did so. First, the girl stealing away his source of domination. Then, Edous and his cursed blade. The man called Rahnaluz was beginning to feel as if everything he had ever wanted was just ripped from his hands. Glory, power, and control. He was supposed to end this night presenting the mysterious artifact to his master, and in return, he was to be granted immortality and power. He would not give that up, not easily. He had been marked, but not defeated. Not yet.

He snarled as he slammed his hands down on the table, looking over the vastness of Ethrea. This would be his. It would all be his. One day. One day soon. He just had to find the girl in white. She was the key to everything. Or else he would die.

"Squire," Rahnaluz barked hoarsely. "Get over here. I have a job for you. And you best do it right, or this little nick I received, it'll look like roses brushing the cheek compared to what I'll heap on your worthless corpse."

The lean man stepped forward into the light, removing his hood, and answered, "I do as my Khall'ah Kh'ar commands. What would you have your servant do?"

Chapter 23: Into the Night

"What in the blazing pits of Halfak was that?" Orrum's palms pounded a table of dark stained wood.

Elcon wore an expression that was a mixture of confusion and pain, his grey eyes downcast and shoulders slumped in his regal robes. The Telnor High Priest, Talendeal, was pacing nervously and talking to himself with animated hand motions. Shanavaral and Yemera were talking in hushed whispers. All had looked up when their religious leader slapped his wooden desk.

This was beyond the will of men now, Orrum knew that. He could trust in the will of the High Father. He could believe that Darius had certain supernatural abilities. He could even believe that the boy could be a so-called Feromage. What he could not have foreseen, ironically, despite his calling as High Patriarch and seer, was the words of the oracle, Brei.

What did this all mean now? The subtle game the Church had been playing for generations just received the first unknown move from its adversary. The nation could not be opened up to such things when it was still so tender and unformed. For far too long had the High Patriarchs crafted and formed the necessary lie that led to the peace and prosperity of the Nation of Ordiatea. For hundreds of years, through slow, painstaking moves and countermoves, had the Church directed the flows of mankind. And now, there was risk where there should have been security. There were truths, ever so close, that could not be unveiled. They had to act. They had to get Darius out of Ordiatea. That was Orrum's number one concern; what lurked in the forest only came second.

"We must now come together," Orrum stated with affirmation.

"Orrum," Elcon said in a voice near timidity, "is it wise to send the boy away now, after what we just witnessed?"

"It is our duty," Shanavaral said proudly, placing an unusually kind hand on Elcon's shoulder.

"Have you no heart?" Elcon asked, whirling on the high priestess. "He is being sent as a lamb to the slaughter!"

"We do not know all things as of yet," Orrum said dryly. "But we would be fools to not prepare. No word of this may leave this chamber. We cannot afford this getting out until we can be certain."

"I agree," Talendeal said. "It would be unwise to disrupt the ways of the people until the signs have been seen. There have been many who have claimed they are the Keyholder. Yet all have been false."

"Did the man claim he was the Keyholder?" Elcon questioned quietly. "No, he did not. He claimed only to be one from days long past. You forge a destiny that may not be his, a path he might not need to walk!"

"I would have liked to have seen his Touching of the Source," Talendeal mused as he stroked his dark chin. "It seems a most interesting notion."

"He doesn't Touch the Source; he does something – oh, never mind," Elcon spat through clenched teeth. "High Patriarch, I implore. Just give me more time with the boy. Please."

"We must put our trust in him now," Orrum replied with a consoling smile. "Strange are the workings of Ordan, mysterious are his ways. You have led him well, High Priest, and the High Father will continue to do so."

Orrum produced a quill from its well on the table and took a sheet of yellowed parchment from a stack. Drawing in a breath of resolve, he began to write upon the parchment, large and looping letters, stating the unique events that he and his council had borne witness to. His heart was heavy, though his mind firmed. Resolve filled his bosom as he wrote the words of the vision. He knew it was his duty to do so, though it did not lessen the dread of what was to come if it was the time of the Sage's return. The words had been eerily familiar, detailing such certain events as most were concealed.

One by one, each of the Holy Council took their rings and dipped them into the pools of wax that sealed the parcel closed. Afterwards, the envelope was placed into a leatherbound case. Two strips of leather wrapped around it to hold it shut and a golden hammer branded the front.

Orrum went to hand the parcel to one of the Aluth, but Elcon stepped forward and placed his hand out. "I would deliver this to him and say goodbye. Allow me this."

"As you wish," Orrum said as he placed the leather envelope into Elcon's hand. Before releasing it, he added, "Not a word to him about it. If he is not the Keyholder, he cannot know of such things."

"Understood, Patriarch. I simply wish to bid a friend farewell before he sets off on his journey," Elcon said with a smile as his fingers tightened on the parcel.

"Not a word," Orrum added one last time. "You must not speak. His destiny still unfolds about him. And we cannot deny it is one of great importance, whether Keyholder or not. A burden shall rest upon him that I would not wish upon any."

***

Darius stood in front of the massive statues of the Ellitheor, eyes locked on the two proud beings. His burly arms were folded, the vest and long leather overcoat pulled tight against his muscular chest. Darius felt a sense of encouragement, a rush of motivation flowing through his veins. He took in deep breaths as he tried to calm his nerves, though he appeared as poised as the statues at which he looked. His thumb rubbed fervently across his ring, turning it around and around on his finger.

The soft, almost nonexistent, scraping of the approaching Aluth drew Darius's attention. Following carefully behind them were the careful steps of an elderly man, along with the smell of melted wax and old leather. Darius sniffed the air without turning and said, "Elcon."

"How you can do such things is beyond me, friend," Elcon replied with a smile.

"I've been with you for weeks now," Darius replied as he turned to greet the elderly high priest. "You know better than any what I am truly capable of."

"Darius, there is little time to speak," Elcon started hurriedly, his voice hushed to little more than a whisper. He had pulled Darius away from the other members of the council, and his eyes darted about as he spoke.

"What is it?" Darius's eyes hardened, and he felt an urge to pull at a weapon that was not there.

"Darius, this letter is not why you are sent," Elcon said as he handed the parcel to Darius. "There is something rising out there. A darkness. The council seeks to silence such things, but there is an evil touching this world. Just as you felt the Touch of the Everlight this night, there is an inverse to all things. Where there is good, there is always evil lurking. Where there is light, darkness. Guard yourself, and don't trust anyone."

Darius tucked the letter into his satchel, along with a few provisions the Aluth had brought along with them. A necklace with Ethra on it, two extra pairs of stockings, a field knife, a spindle of twine, and four green apples. These he placed next to his own flask and the crystal vial that Alyn had given him, which he had wrapped in a few white rags.

Turning his head up, he saw Elcon hurrying away. Darius reached out quickly and grabbed the old priest, saying, "Elcon, I am sorry about Ranun... I am sorry I could not save him."

"Do not burden yourself with that, Son," Elcon answered with a consoling smile, a smile that did not reach his tired eyes. "He was a good man who lived a good life."

"He was a good man," Darius said assuredly. The image of a blue-eyed girl with icy-white hair flashed before his eyes once more. "Elcon, tell me again, how is it that the Blessed gain their gift?"

Elcon grimaced, looking about him as if someone was about to pop out from one of the stone effigies. Quickly, he spoke, "The Blessed are called by Ordan, endowed with powers from beyond. The Blessed can

Touch the Everlight if they carry fragment pieces, which are infused with light, such as what Brei and Alyn wear about their necks. They must replenish their light often, lest it fade away and they lose their Touch. That is why the sisters stay in the temple, so they are always close to the Everlight." Elcon stopped suddenly. Too much.

"Can someone Touch without these fragments?" Darius questioned further.

"Not that is known to mankind." Elcon eyed Darius carefully, the apprehension in his voice apparent. "Why? What brings this to your mind?"

Darius stepped closer to Elcon, looking around to make sure none were close to him, and whispered, some of Elcon's trepidation wearing off on him, "I met someone, a girl, well, a young woman, when Ranun... well, I was hoping to find her before I left, but I don't see that happening now."

"I do not understand," Elcon answered slowly.

"I believe she is important," Darius said, fumbling. "Just swear to me you will find her, and tell no one of it."

"Darius, there must be over a million people who live within the shining walls of Tur'Mor. I do not-"

Darius wrapped his hand around Elcon's and stared the old man hard in the eyes, "It is important."

"How would I even know how to find her?" Elcon protested, trying his best to remove his hands from Darius's.

But Darius's grip was firm, as if his hands were forged of iron. "She walks the underbelly of the city, though I do not believe it will be hard for one such as yourself to find her. She has the..." Darius paused for a brief moment before continuing with an even more hushed tone, "The bluest eyes I've ever seen, and hair like winter's snow."

Elcon's eyes widened at the implication. "I will do my best to see it done, my son."

"See that you do," Darius replied, and he loosened his hand from Elcon's ringed fingers. "Goodbye, Elcon. I cannot thank you enough for all you have done for me."

"I only did what was right, nothing more, my son," Elcon answered, his face still somewhat startled. A look that was only deepened when he saw that Darius had placed his masonry hammer in his own hand. "What is this for?"

"Peace was never an option for me." Darius sighed as he looked down on the craftsman's tool with longing. "Try as I might to turn away from it, violence always finds me. Where I go now, that will do me little good. "But" – and a small, forced grin slid across his lips – "perhaps you'll remember me well by it."

"Darius." Elcon smiled back, a grandfatherly smile, warm and gentle. "I do not think our fates have severed as of yet, and I believe we shall meet again."

"Then keep it all the same, and maybe on that day, I will have filled my purpose and can build instead of break." Without another word, Darius nodded and turned away from the high priest.

As he walked, he gazed at the domed ceiling, admiring the ornate architecture and magnificent paintings. It seemed like just yesterday that he had stared up into the Royal Catacombs. At the same time, it felt like a lifetime ago. He was not the same; everything inside him had changed. Gone was the young man who only sought to return home to his tribe. That was gone now. They were gone. All that was left was the burden of destiny that rested on his shoulders. The voice that had called unto him, commanding him to *find them*, echoed through his being, strengthening his resolve.

At the far side of the room stood three men. Each was dressed in dark clothing and wore heavy black coats and large brimmed hats. The high lapels of their cloaks covered most of their faces, only leaving the eyes visible. Rapiers hung from the side of two of them and the third had a crossbow in his arms. Four temple Aluth, shining halberds in hand, stood two to either side of the long carpet where these three men talked.

"We are to escort you to Ranok Outpost," a lean man with a grizzled beard said in a low voice. "Name's Ironclaw. The tall one is Darkknife and the other is Billtooth."

Darius nodded as he eyed them over. Their garb was thick, and he could see links of mail under their vests. Wheellock pistols hung from inside Ironclaw's overcoat, both on the left side. He chewed on a piece of wood, his teeth crooked and yellowed. He had dull eyes and a face that looked like it could be pounded with a rock, and the result would only be broken stone. And he smelled like tanning solution and stable straw.

"We will need to bind you up tight, see. Just until we reach the forest," Darkknife said with a sly smile as he scratched at his patchy beard. "Many eyes are out tonight. You made quite the commotion yesterday in the market. I think you have plenty of people call'n for your head, boy, without a scene tonight."

Darius placed his hands in front of him calmly. The two men wielding rapiers, Darkknife and Billtooth, took cords and bound Darius's hands together. He then lowered his hands, and two iron chains were wrapped around his body and arms, binding them to his side. He eyed them sternly.

"Ain't taking no lower measures," Ironclaw grumbled. "You don't need comfort; you need to get gone. That's all we're here for."

He led the way out into the cold, crisp night. The moon was high, waxing towards a full moon, only a few nights away now. Creatures of the night could be heard singing their solemn songs. Darius took a final look at the distant city of Tur'Mor. Her lighthouse shone brightly into the Western Sea. The walls glistened in the moonlight. And the city's lights looked like ten thousand fireflies flickering in the night. Darius breathed in a final breath and boarded the iron-barred carriage.

Billtooth sat across from Darius in the carriage, his demeanor bleak. He was a short, thick man with a pointed chin and greying eyebrows. He stared as if he would burn a hole through Darius with unwavering eyes. Ironclaw and Darkknife rode on top, Darkknife driving and Ironclaw with his crossbow at the ready. With the crack of a whip, they were off. Four black stallions pulled the transport along on the long and rutty route towards Ranok Outpost on the far side of Ordiatea.

The party rode for hours before coming to their first stop. Light crept across the hilly countryside and smoke rose from cottages. Most of the land northwest of Tur'Mor was farmland, though there were several large villas with stone walls and iron-barred gates dotted through the countryside. These lavish estates were home to the wealthy elite, crop owners and lords who did not wish to live within the massive city of Tur'Mor. Vineyards, now dead in early spring, covered rolling hills where forests had once been. The farmhouses were not nearly as lavish and were surrounded by picket fences and barbed wire to keep cattle, goats, pigs, and horses within. Most of the farmhouses were made in a peculiar manner, the lower half being the barn, and the upper being the homes for the families.

Darius stared out the window at the passing scenery. He had grown accustomed to the walled city, but now that he was outside of it, even chained, he felt free. He drew deep breaths of fresh air. He had forgotten that taste. Dew, morning, flowers, and fresh earth. Too accustomed to smoke, stone and waste had he become. The feel of nature seemed to breathe life into him as he had not felt in ages. Within Templetown, the house chimneys' smoke had filled his lungs, and that town was a kernel of sand on the beach that was Tur'Mor. But this – wide skies and clean air – was freedom to his soul, even if his body was bound.

It took everything Darius had not to burst his bands and escape into the countryside. But then the words came to his mind, *find them*, and he was reminded once again of his duty. He pressed his head into the back of the carriage and closed his eyes to sleep. It had been a long, long day.

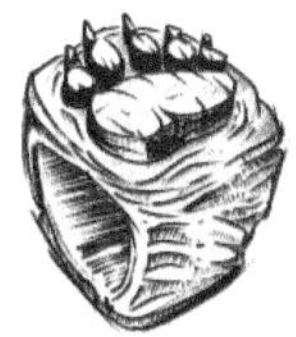

CHAPTER 24: FOURTH EYE INN

Darius had slept for several hours when the iron-barred carriage came to a halt. Billtooth stood and kicked Darius's boot, jarring him awake. Darius looked out the window, expecting to see trees. There were none. A small shack stood out with a trough of water for passing horses.

Ironclaw was down from the driver's box talking to a man in a loose-fitted white blouse and riding boots. The man had thin features and looked more handsome than many men ought to have looked, blond instead of black hair and far fairer skin than the more common olive tone Ordiatians had.

"Twelve in five I'd say," the man named Eyran said in an odd accent, nasally and fast-paced. "You'd be hard pressed, I'd say. Ought to stay down in the Fourth Eye Inn. Ask for Lylen. She'll do you nice like. Good gal, nice place. Plenty o' warm food'n all."

"We have pressing matters and would rather not be disturbed," Ironclaw said in response. "Trying to avoid prying eyes."

"O, well, well, lads. I'd go in still and stay at the Fourth Eye. Good people there, you know? Good people indeed," Eyran said as he ran his fingers through thick blond hair, pale green eyes glinting.

Billtooth had, by now, unchained Darius and was letting him out of the carriage to take a piss. Darkknife was watering the horses when Darius stepped out. Eyran stared up at Darius as he came into the light of midday.

"High Father on the throne!" Eyran gasped as he stared up at Darius. "You have the build of the mountains, grizzled as a bear, you do, don't ya then?"

"Don't mind him," Ironclaw said sharply. "Best you forgot you saw him. Again, we are trying to stay private-like, savvy?" His fingers danced on the stock of his crossbow that was propped one-handed against his shoulder.

"I'd still say stopping is a good thought for travel," Eyran said as he eyed Darius quizzically. "You're still a good day and a half ride from Ranok Wood, sirs... though I'd pity why you'd be take'n such a man into that wood, for what, you know."

"Don't worry yourself with details," Ironclaw said coldly, his eyes narrowing on the blond man. "You got any food in that shack of yours, or do we need to press on?"

"Cured meats and goat cheeses today, a few jams and such," Eyran said as he pulled his eyes back to Ironclaw and smiled. "I can go and whip up a thing or two and basket it for you, if it'd please you to do so?"

"Sounds good." Ironclaw pulled out a small pouch and handed Eyran a few silver grams.

"Ah, thank you kindly, good sir!" And with that, Eyran hurried into the wooden shop and began preparing a basket of food, all the while humming a strange tune.

"It doesn't feel right," Darkknife whispered to Ironclaw. "Ever since we left."

"I know." There was hesitance in Ironclaw's voice as he spoke, though he showed little in his leathery face.

"They said the city guards didn't know about this, but I can't shake the feeling that something isn't right."

"We keep on," Ironclaw said lowly. "We can make it to the Far Quarter by the end of the day. We'll find a rest point and make it to Ranok by tomorrow evening."

"And what of the lad?" Darkknife hissed. "Something ain't right about him."

"We were paid to get him to Ranok, no questions," Ironclaw said with a grimace. "So, no questions. We ride and deliver. That is what was asked. That is what we do. Nothing more."

Darius was sure the two could not tell that he could hear them. Billtooth obviously couldn't, not from this distance. But Darius could, clear as day. And something was off; he could feel it too. Ever since he had awoken, something felt plain wrong, as if there was something lurking behind them, but he could not make it out.

Billtooth led Darius back to the carriage, though he did not bother to chain him this time, just gave him a stern look. Something in the man's eyes told Darius that he was simply following orders, though he didn't seem all too worried about how closely those orders were followed.

"Here you go, lads," Eyran said with a glamorous smile. "Have a good evening and ride. And remember, the Fourth Eye Inn is just three or so hours on. You'll come up to a fork: right'll take you in on to Furrow's Gap and the Fourth Eye, left is onwards into the Far Quarter towards Ranok."

"Thank you, Eyran," Ironclaw said as he took a wicker basket from the blond man. As Eyran raised the basket to Ironclaw, the blouse opened at the strings to reveal a small tattoo on his right breast. It was a strange mark: an upside-down eye with long lashes and strange ink marks rising up from the base of the eye up towards his neck. Ironclaw did not seem to notice it, but Darius caught just a glimpse of it as Eyran turned, lowering his arm.

Darius did not recognize the symbol, but he didn't like it. Part of him wanted to jump out and attack the man. But he seemed so harmless and kind. He had done nothing but help. However, there was something there that Darius just did not trust.

With a loud crack of the whip, the iron-barred carriage rolled on. And it rolled on and on and on. Darius, far more comfortable now that the chains were removed, bounced up and down on the rocky path. The sun had begun to set when they came to a fork in the road. To the right, down in a valley, a few flickers of light signaled a small town. And to the left, the trail became steeper and more winding, low mountains in the distance.

"What d'ya say, boys?" Ironclaw called down into the carriage after a few hours on the road. "A night in or a night on the road?"

Darkknife spoke up after a moment of thought, and the carriage halted. "I don't know what to think. Ol' Orrum seemed to think this fellow needed to be good and gone as soon as possible. But I don't want to ride to death. Plus, the horse could use a night's rest."

"And you, Billtooth?"

"Mhh," Billtooth grunted, his eyes not leaving Darius.

"I figured as much... well, I say we take our chances at the Fourth Eye," Ironclaw said after a long pause. "Can't see how word could travel any faster than us."

"So, the Fourth Eye it is, then," Darkknife said with a grunt as he turned the horses to the right.

Darius didn't feel comfortable with the decision, but at the same time, he did not think he had any say in the matter either. So, he sat quietly as the group rode down the winding hillside into a quaint country town.

Furrow's Gap was quiet and unassuming. A few wooden shops and stone-faced buildings formed the city square, which was built up around a large fountain that gurgled up from a natural spring. Houses were loosely dotted around the town square, and iron lamps lit the packed-dirt streets.

It did not take long to spot the Fourth Eye Inn, as it was the only inn in Furrow's Gap. It had a blue wooden sign hanging from the second story of the stone-front building bearing a couple smiling widely, chipped and faded, their four eyes open wide. Two chimneys puffed wisps of white smoke into the sky and crumb-covered glass windows were filled with yellow firelight from within. A few folks stood outside the inn, talking about this and that, and when the carriage drew close, one of them stepped forward and guided them around to the back where a mostly empty stable lay.

Billtooth undid Darius's bonds, ones that had only been added right before entering the town, and gave him a sharp look as he patted the pommel of his dull rapier. Darius understood what he meant by the action: no running. And why would he? Did these men not realize that they were escorting a man willing to go where sent? Or did they believe they truly had a prisoner? They had not been so uneasy outside the temple. However, there was now an aroma of caution and concern thick in the air. Darius shrugged and stood, hunched over, his head brushing the roof.

When all three had disembarked, they were asked by the stable hand to leave their weapons inside their carriage. They did so begrudgingly. Darius was then let out, and Billtooth locked the door shut once all were gathered on the earthen road. The dusty-haired stable hand turned and faced Darius, expecting him to produce some sort of weapon.

Without thinking, Darius touched his finger to the golden pendant of the hammer Ethra on his lapel. The man blinked and shook his head, and then added, "Beg your pardon, Priest. I meant no offense."

Ironclaw cut in, "Listen, it is important that there is no word of our arrival. We need to keep this between us. This man here is an important member of..." He whispered something into the man's ear. "You understand?"

"Oh, yes! Yes, yes, yes! Right this way," he said with a bow towards Darius. "We'll go in through the back and I'll see you to your rooms." The man then hastily led them through a backdoor which opened into a small, stuffy kitchen, three or four women busy cooking evening meals and kneading bread.

From the kitchen, Darius could see into a large common room where several tables were spotted with a few patrons. The room was lit well enough, the flames from the double fireplaces providing an ambiance of tranquility, while the antler-formed chandeliers provided a majority of the light. A small platform housed a bard in patchworked britches, tight as his own skin, and a plumed vest with broad stripes. He sang loudly in a baritone voice as he played a harp-guitar with twenty-three strings, the sounds ranging from thick bass to thin, shrill plinks. The handsome bard was accompanied by a vivacious woman in a plummeting dress that left little to the imagination. Her hips swayed to the music, captivating nearly all the patrons, who sat about drinking and talking.

Darius took note, however, that there were two men in the back that seemed almost to hide in the shadows. A strange chill ran up his spine as he looked over them. They did not meet his eyes but conversed quietly, each having a long pipe dangling from twisted lips. Darius found himself reaching to his belt where there had once been a masonry hammer hanging, but no longer.

Neither Ironclaw, nor Billtooth nor Darkknife, seemed to notice the men in the corner booth. And if they did, they did not seem to mind. All followed the man, whom Darius assumed was the innkeeper now, not a stable hand, up a wooden staircase to an open room. The walls of the room were lined with wood bed frames, topped with feather mattresses and woven blankets. Between each bed was a small wooden chest and a curtain that could be drawn to divide its patron from the others. No one was in the large room as of right now, so the four men took the far corner.

"Country folk..." Darkknife muttered under his breath.

Darius plopped onto his bed, his elbows resting on his knees and his face in his hands. He rubbed his eyes, and then worked his shoulders. His whole body was sore and stiff from the long ride. And while he was not excited to stop, he was thankful for the break.

"You watch first, Bill," Ironclaw said, "then I'll take watch. Darkknife, you need to sleep. You've been driving all day."

"I won't complain there," Darkknife said as he sat in the bed next to Darius. He turned and faced him, "You ain't said a word this trip. You're almost as talkative as Billtooth here."

Ironclaw laughed and sat on the other side of Darius while Billtooth pulled up a chair. When he sat, he lifted his right leg over his knee and drew a cruel dagger from his long boot and used the tip to dig at his fingernails.

"Did you see Eyran's tattoo?" Darius asked in a very low tone, eyes on the floor.

"What was that?" Ironclaw stopped laughing and looked towards him.

"He had a tattoo on his chest," Darius continued, eyes coming up from the ground and hands falling into his lap, "a marking I have never seen."

"What was it?" Darkknife inquired as he leaned forward on his forearms, which rested on either thigh.

"It looked like an eye, but upside down," Darius answered. "You ever see anything like it?"

Ironclaw rubbed his scruff as he searched his memories. Darkknife shrugged and simply said, "Can't say that I have. But there are lots of symbols and markings out there. Best not go looking for demons where there are none... That can get you into a world of hurt."

"Darkknife's right," Ironclaw said slowly. "I ain't heard of one either. And there is enough real evil out there to not go caus'n commotion. Now, if it was the Three Crowns of Calun, well, that'd be a different story. But can't say as I didn't get an odd sense from that fellow."

"Yeah," Darius replied, unsatisfied. He reached down and undid the gears that loosened the laces of his heavy boots. He then took off his heavy overcoat, laying the leather behemoth over his nightstand. He left his trousers, shirt and vest on, and then lay back on his bed.

"I'm gunna go get a drink," Darkknife said as he stood back up.

Ironclaw eyed him but did not protest. Billtooth rose as well and followed the taller man out of the open room, sliding the blade back into his boot. Right before they left the room, Ironclaw piped up, "Take it easy tonight. No scenes. We're being paid to be discrete. And don't be too long; you need rest tonight."

"Quiet as the night," Darkknife voiced as he bowed, holding his wide-brimmed hat in his hand. Billtooth raised a scarred finger to his lips and made a shushing sound. And with that, they stepped out of the room.

***

The Fourth Eye was a cozy inn, and her dual-hearth fires were warm and welcoming. The smells of cooked meats and fresh bread permeated the low-roofed building. Dull stone walls with timber frameworks made up the inn. The two hired hands walked into the room rather inconspicuously, sticking to the back of the room, avoiding the groups of men playing dice and listening to music and the women folk who were eating and chattering about this and that.

Darkknife spoke in low tones, pointing towards an open table, and Billtooth nodded in response. Billtooth only ever nodded, having had his tongue removed years ago due to a run-in with some rough folk. Rumor had it that it took a dozen men just to floor him, and they cut out his tongue because he kept laughing and insulting them as they robbed and beat him. And what was the cause of the assault? Well, it all came about after he won a bet in a horse race against a lower lord and disgraced him publicly. After the loss of his tongue, he joined the transportation business, as keeping silent was often a prerequisite of the job. The other prerequisite, being deadly. He was both. Darkknife was a superstitious one, often taking to strange traditions such as wearing a hog tusk about his neck and keeping two silver grams in his pockets at all times. He had come into the business by birth, his father being a driver and his mother a whore, though you'd never say that to his face.

The two men had not been down in the common room of the Fourth Eye Inn more than an hour or so when a group of six men walked in. They were clad in black trench coats adorned with matching lapel pins depicting an iron spike driven through a skull, wide-brimmed hats, and tall leather boots. They wore chains about themselves, and each carried hangers, or as the Huntsmen called them, wood-knives. These were curved, short sabers with knuckle-guards around the wire-wrapped handles. The men's faces were obscured by high collars and the shadows cast by their wide-brimmed hats. Two of them had long muskets hanging over their backs, three had billhooks in hand, and one wore a coat of dark coal adorned with dull grey buttons and epaulettes to match.

"By the heathen gods of Gal, that's Tassi!" Darkknife gasped. "I'd bet my two grams on it!"

Billtooth looked over the other's shoulders and grunted in agreement. His face turned sour, a grimace forming on dry lips and blank eyes. The room grew quite as unease crawled through the patrons of the Fourth Eye like a black mist off the night sea.

So much for an inconspicuous night.

CHAPTER 25: SONGS AND CURSES

Alessandro Tassi, Head of the Huntsmen, was a connoisseur of bodies, collecting both the exotic and rare. His own body had become a tapestry of scars and deformities from his many hunts, though none of these slowed him in the slightest. Alessandro had olive-colored eyes, a crooked nose broken more times than he could remember, curly black hair and a short cut beard. His black hat bore a wicked skull that had been cast from silver with a spike driven through the top and protruding from the open mouth. Grey feathers crafted from tiny knife-blades, spanned either side of the punctured skull, wrapping around to the back of the hat. A studded gauntlet was wrapped around a long, octagonal-barreled pistol, which had a cruel bayonet attached. Heavy leather boots, with iron spikes protruding from the tips of them, thumped as he walked boldly into the firelight. Dual pistols were holstered in an X over his lower belly and a leather strap that housed two silver spikes, shot-wads, and a series of vials wound from his left shoulder down to his right hip. For protection, he wore a dull breastplate, which peered out from under his long, black coat.

Tassi's dead eyes scanned the room, and his upper lip drew up in disgust. The music stopped and the gamblers quickly scooped up their loot. Regardless of whether you were on their list of wanted individuals or not, no one wanted to deal with a Huntsman. They were known for their cruelty and their strange beliefs in otherworldly creatures, beasts, and other such folklore.

"Best get out before he notices anything," Darkknife whispered to his companion. "That common sleep'n room will find us all with a spike in our hearts and heads on stakes."

Billtooth flashed a toothy smile, but his face was covered with dread despite his best efforts to show calm. He pushed himself away from the table and fell in behind three others heading up the stairs. Darkknife remained behind, kicking his boots up on the table and lifting his mug of ale to his quivering lips.

Clump, drag. Clump, drag. Clump, drag. Clump, drag.

The sound of Tassi's limping walk filled the dead-silent room. It was said he was bitten by a *gaukal*, a shapeshifting demon hound, and that the bite broke the hound's jaw. And though no self-respecting Ordiatian would believe such tall tales, no life-preserving Ordiatian would ever argue that to Tassi's scar-torn face. It was also said that it was the reclusive Asterivians who were responsible for his mechanical leg, an engineering marvel that no regular citizen could afford. This tale was much more widely acceptable than the previous.

Darkknife could not swallow his drink, though he did not lower the mug. Tassi stopped, grunted a satisfied noise of a hideous nature, and plopped himself in a low-backed wooden chair at a recently vacated table.

"Blackberry wine!" Tassi barked at a serving girl. His voice was hoarse, coarse and crude, the sound of which caused the girl to curtsy quickly and dart away, a slight tremble to her downturned lips.

The five other Huntsmen walked to the table where their leader sat and unabashedly pulled chairs around it from other tables nearby. The ones who had carried billhooks left their polearms in a wardrobe for walking staves and shepherd's crooks. They did not remove their hats nor their coats, something that was a common courtesy in the country. And as they sat, the sounds of chains clicking and metal grinding filled the room.

"Well then, bard, sing us a song, then!" Tassi shouted to the man in tight leggings, who was shaking as he now held a golden-painted lute. "Something sorrowful to match this cursed spit of earth."

The bard nervously began to strum his lute to 'The Night I Lost My Lover', a melancholy tune of a man who returned from war to find his wife gone to another's bed. The song was slow and played in a minor key. A subtle chill seemed to fill the air. The serving girl returned with Tassi's drink, took the orders of the others along with some crude remarks about her ample breasts, and then hurried out of sight again, face flushed.

"Damnation's own pit ain't worse than this wine and hovel," Tassi cursed as he drank his wine, then slammed the cup on the table. "Serving wench, get another one!"

Darkknife noted that Tassi's speech was slurred. He breathed out a sigh of relief. Huntsmen were known for a great many things but drinking on duty was specifically against their code. *Code?* He laughed to himself mirthlessly as he actually drank from his own cup now. *Do such as them have honor or code?*

"Hey, driver," Tassi called out. Darkknife's face paled. "Oy, you daft? I said, driver!"

"Sirs," Darkknife said levelly as he turned about to face the group.

"What news from the city do you bring?" Tassi inquired curtly through gulps of wine.

"Ain't got much news, sirs," Darkknife said. "Not news that ain't been known. That being that the King's Jewel went missing a few days back during the celebration of the nation and everything."

"I heard the bloody stone was back," Tassi scoffed. "Ain't you got better news than that?"

"True, word is they found the group that stole it, all dead."

"It's the damned Church and them bright-eyed witches," said one of the Huntsmen.

"Damn witches," Tassi grumbled. A few of his men nodded in agreement, spitting out curses and phlegm alike.

"I heard it was the Kh'ar, myself," Darkknife replied as he pulled a chair over to the table. Better safe acting comfortable than nervous.

"Spineless group of pricks," Tassi jeered, "the whole lot of 'em. Just a bunch of spoiled rich twits who want more than they could know what to do with, I say! They want a revolution, so they can have a king? What bloody good would that do to get them anywhere anyhow?"

"Not much love for the Kh'ar?" Darkknife inquired, genuinely intrigued. He always figured the Huntsmen and the Kh'ar were in league with one another. He didn't care either way. He had driven people from Boren Bridge to the Eastern Shores, and all the way to the borders of Tuawtia. People were people, and money was money.

"Halfak's gates be shoved up my own arse!" Tassi barked. His men laughed as they drank. The bard winced but kept playing, though he did liven up his melodies a bit. Other patrons, too, began to relax as the Huntsmen seemed not to be on the hunt this night.

"So, what brings you to this sleepy town?" Darkknife asked as he raised his own cup again.

"Ah, coin lad!" Tassi said with an unsettling laugh, like a bullfrog being squished under an iron boot. "Eight bars to track a single man down. Said to have stolen some important letters or such from the Patriarch." He took a long drink and slammed the cup down hard, saying, "Ah, damn them too! Bunch of self-righteous prunes. Sitting in their marble chapels, robed in silk and taking coin from the poor for a spot of fake land in the fields of Vanherran."

"So, I take it you aren't the religious type?" Darkknife laughed.

"Two facts in this life, driver," Tassi said as he pulled a thick, single-edged knife, the length of which could have almost named it a short sword, from his belt and slammed it into the table. "Life leads to death. And a Huntsman always gets his prey." He bobbed his head in satisfaction with the depth of his words, his darkly clad men nodding and agreeing.

"Well, it's been a pleasure talking, but I have a long ride in the morning. We're off to Livithia in the morning."

"Livithia?" Tassi's voice hardened as his eyes drew in on Darkknife in contemplation.

"Aye, delivering a letter from the High Seat. Urgent business," Darkknife replied hastily, sweat beginning to form on his palms.

"Why, then, did you come to this forsaken spot? You are over five leagues past the road to Livithia from Tur'Mor," Tassi asked as he ran his fingers over the black leather handle of his knife.

"I don't question orders, sir. Especially when they come from the Rising Star," Darkknife said in hushed tones, trying to regain control of the situation. He knew Huntsmen didn't fear much, but surely, they wouldn't act out against one who carried orders from the head of the High Seat of the Republic, would they?

There was a chill silence. The lute had stopped, and the serving girls had not come by for a while now. Alessandro Tassi measured up Darkknife. They were dressed not too dissimilarly, save that the driver had less chain and leather as those whom he shared the table with. And far less weaponry.

"Ahh, right you are," Tassi breathed out. "No questions asked. No questions asked," Tassi added, winking at Darkknife. "It's a shame I couldn't hire out that cart of yours. I could use it. But I wouldn't dare stand between a messenger boy and his lord."

Darkknife grimaced at the words. They cut his pride like a hot knife. But now was not the time to act on that. His own rapier was upstairs against his bed; he had naught but a boot knife and a cup of ale. Tassi smiled a cruel smile as he saw Darkknife's reaction. However, he did not do anything but lean back into his chair and pull out a short black pipe, stuff it with tobacco, and light it.

"Well, lads, I think I'll head to bed," Darkknife finally said after several more moments of awkward silence.

None of the Huntsmen even regarded his statement. Grateful for the lack of concern from the dark-clad men, Darkknife rose and headed up the stairs. And though he could hear the group beginning to talk once he left them, he could not help but feel like one of them was following him up the stairs. The hairs on the back of his neck rose, and his hand wanted to reach for the small blade that was strapped to his right calf. But when he reached the top step, he could clearly see all six still sitting around the table talking and drinking. He walked into the open floor bedroom and shut the door.

***

Dawn's light brought welcome warmth. The room held little heat, despite the bodies that cluttered the several beds. Some of which, the large ones, had two men to a bed. Darius had not slept well but had slept some. Darkknife did not seem to sleep until well past the high moon. Billtooth took the longest watch, though there had not been a stir.

To everyone in the room's great relief, the Huntsmen had left late into the night. Apparently, they had cursed the owner of the Fourth Eye Inn and left some time after decent hours. The owner was complaining about this to everyone as he wiped glasses and helped set tables for breakfast. That being said, he couldn't deny that they had paid him well, though the manner of which was not regular currency. There were golden galleons, red chips, and carved gemstones in an animal hide bag, which the innkeeper proudly showed off to all who came to eat.

266

Darius and his drivers ate quickly and left as soon as they could. The stable hands had taken well enough care of their horses, and they were prepped and ready for the last stretch of the journey. Billtooth urged Darius into the cart with a grunt and shove, and then hoisted himself in behind. Darkknife and Ironclaw climbed into the driver's box. And with a snap of the reins, they were off.

The arduous journey finally came to an end when they reached the outskirts of Ranok Outpost, which was the farthest point of the Ordiatian nation. Ranok Outpost was a small fort that housed no more than fifty soldiers, most of which were volunteers from the neighboring villages and townships. The Outpost sat atop a small, stony hill and bordered the dark trees of the forest. A stacked stone wall with wooden ramparts jutting out of it surrounded the bleak buildings inside, and at the center of the fort, a simple tower peered over the valley and tree line.

The two men who stood outside the simple timber gate, wearing loose chainmail and iron, nasal-styled helmets, became visible to Darius as the cart came to a halt. They held long spears, and simple arming swords hung from their waists. Darius could tell these were no royal guards, though they bore the insignia of Ordiatea across their tattered and fading surcoats. Their gait was loose, and the armor did not quite fit, causing their appearance to seem lackluster. Darius also noted that these men shifted too much in their stances and steps, and he thought to himself, *these are no trained soldiers.*

"Listen, these guys here, it's their job to check anyone leaving Ordiatian soil," Ironclaw whispered down to the carriage. "Produce that envelope the High Patriarch gave you, and there shouldn't be any trouble."

Darius reached for his satchel and dug through the contents. A spare shirt folded inside, stockings, and a few apples he had replenished at the Fourth Eye rustled as he dug. There was also the crystal vial of effervescent blue liquid that Alyn had given him, which was wrapped in white cloth. He quickly found the large, leatherbound envelope which bore the Seal of Ordan on it. He pulled this out and held it in his hands, ready to be free of the carriage and off on his own again.

But to what end? he thought bleakly to himself. *Perhaps clarity will come in the trees of Ranok, perhaps on my own I will have a better connection to these visions.*

Darkknife had hopped off the top of the carriage and was making his way around to the door. The two guards who had been at the gate had begun to make their way forward.

"Greetings, lads!" Ironclaw called out in a rather unusually chipper voice. "How fares the Far Quadrant?"

"Nothing fares here more than the rest," a gruff voice replied.

Darius caught the scent of something off. A whiff of fear mixed with perspiration. There was something wrong.

"What business does a royal emissary have this far east of Ordiatea?" the other soldier called out, his voice uneasy. "You don't come guarded enough to be hauling a member of the High Seat with you. And there has been no word of any legislation needing taking to Daneland or Cogadh. State your business true, and you'll not have a worry."

Darius leaned forward towards Billtooth to warn the man, but he had already begun to run his fingers along the hilt of his rapier. Darius wondered how adept these men truly were with the blade. Would it come to that? Why? The stench of fear hung heavy in the air.

"We carry naught but a man with a letter sealed to go into the capital of Dane." Ironclaw's response was drawn out; Darius could tell he was uncomfortable.

"Strange you should say that, lads," the larger of the two soldiers replied as he peered through the iron-barred window of the carriage a good ten paces away. "Men came early this morning bearing the seal of House Adelmo, the lord Alec, brother of the Mayor of Tur'Mor."

"Did they now?" Ironclaw continued as his weight shifted in his seat.

Darkknife, as silently as possible, unbolted the carriage door. Then, with a facade of nonchalance, walked on around the lacquered carriage and waved to the soldiers. "Oy, been at it days. Just making the final stop here. Got coin to pay the fee to access the forest, and the letter is sealed. You can inspect it with your own eyes, lads."

"Tassi had said there was foul play in hand and warned us of such nonsense," the soldier replied grimly as he pointed the tip of his spear at Darkknife's chest, who raised his hands openly with calm eyes.

Damnation! Tassi? What in the blazes of Halfak is he doing here? Darkknife took a deep breath, then spoke softly and reassuringly, "We mean no trouble, men. Just doing our jobs."

The taller of the soldiers, who was far darker in complexion, a Telnorian by the looks of him, called back towards the gates of the Outpost, "Bring Tassi and his men. We'll have them take a look." Several men had gathered near the opening and hurried away at the command. "If what you say is true, Master Tassi can clear this up real quick like and you can be on your way."

Darkknife swallowed hard.

"See here," Ironclaw called to the guards. "We are in quite a hurry and don't want trouble. I believe we could reach an agreement that could be mutually beneficial to both of us if you could just let us go on our way."

"We are appointed royal guards here, driver!" the more lightly copper-toned man spat, as if overcompensating for something.

"A simple bag of twenty silver pieces, and I can be none the wiser," said the driver as he raised an eyebrow. "Besides, I don't want to deplete this fort of too many resources."

"Understood," the Telnorian guard responded as he ran a finger over his patchy beard.

"Get him out, then!" the other called into the carriage.

Billtooth shot Darius a hard look, and he subtly moved his head. He then took him by the arm, pushing him roughly out of the cart. Darius stumbled onto the ground, rolling over onto his stomach. The Outpost soldiers had made their way around the cart by now, and the Telnorian reached down and grabbed him by the hair, pulling on it as Darius rose to his knees.

Up to this point, Darius had had all intents and purposes to escape without causing too much damage. This action, base and uncalled for, had wiped away those chances. He was not a dog and would not be treated as such.

He turned quickly on his knee, bursting the bands around his hands and shrugging the chains off his arms. Darius jumped up quickly, headbutting the guard full in the face just below the wide-brimmed helm. In doing so, a stream of blood splat across the ground. Darius grabbed the chains that had been intended for him in both hands. He swung them rapidly in a circle, wrapping them around his hands, forming an impromptu pair of gauntlets. The second guard thrust his spear at Darius's head, which he barely dodged. He grabbed the shaft of the spear between his bicep and forearm, and then, using his other arm, snapped it like a twig. The driver yelled to his men to run, and they got on their carriage and departed as a flood of twenty or so men began to run out of the fort.

Darius landed a single punch in the stomach of the second guard that he had just disarmed. The man crumpled to the ground in a moan of agony. Darius looked to the northeast where the hills of grass turned into a thick line of dark green and grey. He grabbed the satchel that Billtooth had thrown onto the ground by his head and began to run.

"Call for the Huntsmen!" another guard yelled out towards the fort. "Run him down! Run him down! Sound the alarm! Call for the Huntsmen!"

Darius was running with all his might towards the trees when he heard the sound of horses' hooves pounding behind. He did not look back but pressed onward, knowing that if he did not do something quick, he would be run down. The sound of Darkknife urging Billtooth into the carriage and Ironclaw commanding the team of stallions was distant but still sharp to his ears. Still, he did not look back. He knew that if he could just make it to the trees that they could never find him. The sun was setting, but the warm embrace of its rays could be felt, reaching out, caressing him. Darius felt the desire rise, the raw emotion of need welling within.

With a sharp inhale, Darius opened himself, extending his will beyond his body, and pulled on the burning rays of the sun, Binding them to his essence. Flames of liquid rushed through his veins. A pounding as loud as kettle drums sounded within his chest, his heart surging from the untapped flow of light. A shout of pained exhilaration bellowed from his lungs, followed by tendrils of golden light that poured from his mouth and into the air around him. His honey-yellow eyes burst into orbs of brilliance, and the world around him became as clear as crystal. Great, leaping steps took him from the field, running faster than man, horses, or any other being. Into the trees he vanished, a streak of light scarring the vision of those who pursued him.

Second Caesurae:
Betrugyn, Bloodbound of Khadais

A sound like glass shattering filled the dark room. Betrugyn fell from a mist of sticky smoke onto the floor. He landed on all fours, blood streaming from his mouth. He coughed. It was a gurgling, grinding cough. More blood spewed from his lips. He rolled over onto his back with a cry of pain. A spear with a broken haft was protruding from the lower left side of his abdomen. The chosen woman had not died easily, but she had died all the same. Just as all the others before her had. Their impure bloodline severed.

Betrugyn wailed hoarsely as he pulled the metal tip from his gut. Blood splattered across the dirty wood floor he was lying on. He ran his finger over the stone eye of the hawk pendant and whispered, "Master, heal me. . ."

Five breaths.

The hawk's eye of his pendant lit with an ominous black anti-light. A swirling sound like rain on the ocean mixed with that of a flame being doused filled the wounded assassin's ears. It was an all-too-familiar sound. One that both relieved and terrified Betrugyn.

The droplets of blood on the floor and his clothes began to vibrate.

Five more breaths.

The blood began to slowly roll towards the open wound on his side and up his neck, back into his mouth. He lay there, eyes struck with anguish and horror, as wisps of black smoke emanated from within his eyes and wounds, drawing the blood in. After all the blood, even that which had stained his attire, was back in his body, tendrils of dark mist sealed his wounds. Betrugyn writhed in pain at this last part. And then, in an instant, all the pain was gone.

Betrugyn was healed.

He rose from the floor. The only sign of injury was that of his torn garments and a thin white scar on his side. The scar shone like a dragon's scale in the dimly lit house. It was glassy and unnatural, shimmering against his pale flesh. He ran his fingertips over the mark. It was cold like ice yet had no feeling to it. He shuddered.

The assassination had not been without its issues. But the deed was done. Betrugyn looked at his shaking hands. He drew in a deep breath. His heart sank a little lower, for he knew he was now tangled even deeper into the web of his master. The Khadais had saved him again. And if Betrugyn knew anything, it was that magic always came with a price.

THIRD MOVEMENT

The Son, the Daughter, the Intellect, and the Healer

CHAPTER 26: WITCHES AND BEARS

Ranok Forest smelled of old and rot, the scent assaulting Darius as he fumbled through the trees. The density of the trees blocked the waning rays of the sun from reaching the forest floor, causing the lower levels to be practically pitch black. This alone would not have been so bad if Ranok's underbelly was not so overgrown with brush and bramble.

Darius, in his haste, had not chosen to flee on the trail that cut through Ranok but had run wildly into the deep of the wood in an attempt to shake his pursuers. At that moment, it had seemed like the most obvious idea. Now, he cursed as he tried to maintain his hold on the light, flesh beginning to burn from maintaining the power within. Yet, the light was draining from him far faster than he could restore it.

With eyes that no longer burned with iridescent light or muscles that surged with untapped strength, Darius began to falter, stumbling about wildly. Having lost his footing, he attempted a sudden halt. This harsh stop, or failure to do so, sent him crashing through the underbrush, flailing about like a ragdoll tossed down a hill. Countless animals scattered at the noise, bounding away in different directions.

When the world finally stopped swirling, or more accurately, when his body ceased rolling, Darius pulled himself upright with a groan of pain.

"My head!" Darius growled loudly as he rubbed his temples with his forefingers. A trickle of blood was running down his ear, mixing with the dirt that muddied his face. The silver ring on his third finger had a soft glow to it and burned slightly; the itch to touch it, however, had subsided. At least for now.

After gathering his senses, Darius began to stumble across the forest floor. He felt hollow. He had always felt hungry, weak, and tired after Binding for such a long time. But hollow? No, this was different. However, hollow he felt from the lack of energy, the lack of hunger was creeping up as well. He chuckled mirthlessly to himself. *Well, there's the hunger you were missing.*

Darius could hear the soft murmur of a stream bubbling over smooth rocks. He could also hear animals of all kinds, several of which were totally unfamiliar to him. Looking about in the twilight hours, he could see green birds with great plumes of feathers, strange deer-like creatures with white coats of fur and golden spots, which darted off here and there as they sighted him. He saw odd reptiles disappearing into the murky pools along the forest floor. And the babbling brooks housed small crustaceans that blended into their environment perfectly.

Darius knelt by a small fountain of water and dipped his hands into the cold liquid. With three large splashes, Darius washed away the soil from his beard and face, and with a steady hand, he plucked the branches and vines from his hair. A bush with large purple berries and flat leaves was growing over the edge of the stream.

Taneberries! Darius thought excitedly. It had been years since he had eaten the tart, wild fruit. Through a mouthful of juicy goodness, he laughed out loud. It had been over a thousand years, to be exact. He still wasn't used to that. The laugh dissipated and a pang at his heart soured the mood as he thought once more of those he had lost.

Darius looked up into the darkened canopy. Thick branches, gnarled and twisting, reached towards each other, as if they were attempting to choke the life from one another. A murder of crows was sitting atop one of said branches, staring down at him. Darius shuddered. He wasn't one for superstition, but a murder of midnight crows was never a good omen. He decided it was high time he moved on.

The deeper into the strange and dark wood Darius delved, the more mystical the creatures became. He began to slow his flight, and in doing so noticed that on the forest floor there were prints of animals he did not recognize. And while curious, he did not take the time to study his findings. Finally, he came to a stop near another of the many large pools of water that sprouted from the numerous natural springs. He knelt beside a clear pool to drink some water and rest. As he did so, he noted several patches of green foliage.

Odd weather for green growth, Darius thought as he lay against a large rock. *Though, it is unseasonably warm.*

Though it was dense in Ranok Forest, Darius could tell the sun had long passed and the moon was rising high into the sky. *There is no way they could still be behind me. I can't hear a thing*, Darius thought as he listened motionlessly to the wood. The sound of running water drew his attention back for another refreshing drink.

It was in this moment of peace, while Darius sat, that the questions began to form in his mind. What in Ordan's throne were these Huntsmen after him for? What had he done? The thoughts swirled around his tired mind, and he could not make sense of any of it. He had done nothing in Tur'Mor save help repair an old bread-house and some stonework for the Sanctuary. Were there enemies of the Church that were so corrupt that they would send Huntsmen to take down a simple mason?

Darius shook his head as he picked up a smooth rock from the creek bed. He thumbed the rock absentmindedly as he tried to draw any sort of conclusion. Nobody but the Holy Council knew of his visions, save Ranun.

He grimaced. Ranun was dead, and he had not had two seconds to grieve. Darius had not known the man well, but Ranun had been kind and pure, a good man who had cared for the needs of many. Darius threw the stone and then folded his arms in agitation. Something was not right about any of this.

He reached into his satchel and pulled out the leatherbound envelope. As he studied the seal, he began to speak to himself aloud, "High Father, I swore oaths to you... oaths to obey your will and protect the people, and I have always striven to do so. A little direction couldn't hurt, could it?"

Darius sat there, dumbly waiting for his plea to be answered. He laughed a hollow laugh. "Beyond the ways of men..." Darius mocked the words of Elcon, and suddenly, he missed that man too.

***

After a night of uneasy sleep, filled with images of Brei and Alyn surrounding his naked body, speaking in words he could not understand, their eyes burning with blue light, Darius awoke. He ate an apple from his sack, took a piss, and then left his spot against the rock. Darius wandered northward through the moss-laden trees, and despite the humidity, there was a chill in the air. *Warm at night and cold in the morn? What is wrong with this place?* A heavy fog made it nearly impossible to see and the sounds of squawking birds filled the dense air. Yet, despite all this, he did not stop.

Darius ambled onward, searching for the trail into the twilight hours, stopping here and there to climb up a tree to see if he could see anything, but to no avail. And as the sun began to set, the thought of bedding down for the night seemed to be the best idea.

He found a small thicket where the roots were not so heavy and the rocks not so sharp. Beds of green plants with winding vines and crumpled leaves dotted the hillside. He laid his satchel down as a pillow and used his foot to push pine needles into a heap for a mattress. It would not be as nice as the beds in the monastery that he had become accustomed to.

What have I become? Years I spent in the woods and slept on the soil without a second thought. That city softened me. I need this more than I thought.

Darius stared into the night sky. It was cold, but that did not matter. He enjoyed the cold, and he had a heavy enough overcoat to use as a blanket. Food was what he wanted. Lazily, he reached behind his head into his bag and pulled out a bruised apple and his flask. Darius grimaced. *Food, too? I have gone soft.*

He ate his meager meal, and then drank two drinks of his syrupy tonic. Now that warmed him to the core, bringing a slight twisted smile to his stonelike face. He placed the flask back in the bag and threw the core of his apple against a tree. It exploded upon impact, adding satisfaction to the mirth he was feeling.

Darius rested his right boot over the left and folded his hands on his stomach. Owls calling and small animals scurrying about in the branches of the trees were his melody. And crickets chirped the songs of night, which soon brought sleep.

***

Dawn woke Darius with a start. He sat up sharply, eyes flashing about him. He closed his eyes and drew in two deep breaths, and then went totally silent. He felt the earth, the air, the trees. He reached his hands into the dirt, feeling for motion. There was nothing near, save a nest of squirrels above that were bickering over an acorn and a few small swallows chirping about.

Satisfied that he was relatively alone, Darius rose from the ground. He drew his satchel over his shoulder, took one final look about himself, and began again in a northward direction through Ranok.

Onward he pressed, stopping only briefly for water at one of the many cold streams that ran through the forest floor. Streams were not the only things that covered the earth. Many small plants, fungi and fauna also grew about the ancient forest, most of which Darius knew, and several of which he was totally unfamiliar with.

Darius walked over the space of many miles, all the while trying to find his way back to the roadway from which he had strayed. But night was coming on fast, and he was growing weary. The prospect of another soft apple for a meal was not appetizing, Darius decided to look for a place to bed down and then try his luck scavenging for food, or perhaps even taking down a rabbit or squirrel with a heavy stick.

However, as he was searching through the trees for a decent spot to settle in, he smelled something not far off in the distance. He sniffed the air twice.

Fire!

Darius moved swiftly and cautiously through the trees, drawing closer to the smell of charred wood until he could see the flickering of flames in the distance. Smoke filled the twilight air, smudging the pink and purple shades of the evening sky with a gruesome grey-black haze. Cautiously, Darius crept forward, staying low and keeping to the thicker parts of the underbrush. As he drew closer to the flames, he began to hear something that horrified him.

Sounds of screaming and chaos, mixed with shouts of angry men and gunfire, filled his ears. Darius was no stranger to warfare, but these were not the cries of battle, but a sound that haunted him to his core, a sound he knew all too well. Darius, in dread, looked left and right for something to use as a weapon. Across the forest floor, he spotted a thick piece of old hickory which looked to have been broken off from the downed tree nearby due to lightning. Grabbing the large straight stick, he moved hastily towards the noise, climbing to the top of a nearby hill. At its peak, Darius could now clearly see what was causing the great disturbance, and disturbing it was.

In a circular clearing of twisting trees and winding streams at the base of the hill, an encampment lay in mayhem. Dozens of colorful tents were ablaze, and strangely dressed people were lying face down in the mud while others fled, screaming in terror. Men in long, black cloaks armed with guns, nets or crude polearms were hunting the men and women of the encampment. And those who resisted the cloaked men were either shot down or beaten to the earth.

"No!" Darius muttered aloud. Pain wracked his consciousness as he saw the people of the camp fall and die, screaming in agony. Guilt like a knife dug into his heart and dropped him to his knees.

Whether it was true or not, it did not matter; Darius placed the blame of this on his own shoulders. He looked down and saw men who would surely not have been here had they not been tracking an assailant who struck a guard outside the Outpost. Sure, they would not have come this far had they not been sent from Tur'Mor to apprehend a man who dabbled in things which they could not understand. It did not matter that Darius did not believe what he had done in the city was appropriate, or that his actions at the Outpost weren't without warrant. All he could see was people suffering, burning, dying, and it consumed him with grief and rage.

Darius looked to the sky and found a sun past setting. He could not soak in her rays of added strength; it was too late. He gazed back at the camp, re-witnessed the harrowing screams of the people. He could smell a wrongness down below, a rank scent of evil, a scent of darkness and vile hatred. There was no way he could take on that many Huntsmen at once, not as he was. Darius snarled, and then the sound of his father's voice flooded over him, words which now echoed through his memories.

As long as a Feromage stands, the wicked, cruel and unjust shall fall.

Do you pledge on your blood that you will care for the weak? Will you protect the helpless and defend those in need?

Remember the Second Oath and the power it brings.

Remember these words, my son, and may they bring you power in the darkest of nights.

'I will always fight to preserve those who walk in the light of truth, to protect the weak and guide the lost.'

Remember those words, my son, and you will find your inner strength.

"I remember..." Darius muttered to himself. A tear from the pain of the past and of present circumstances welled in his eyes. He knew what he must do. He had to turn himself over to the power within. To trust in the might of the Ellitheor and rise anew as their Guardian.

Sighing deeply, Darius ran his fingers over the rough-hewn silver ring on his left hand. He paused reluctantly and then rose resolutely to his feet. Weeks with Elcon had passed where he had openly demonstrated the First Binding, that of the sun, bound to him by the First Oath. He took off the long overcoat that hung from his body, and then removed his shirt, boots and pants. The moonlight, at full brilliance now, beamed down on his powerful, bare body. The Second Oath, and its accompanying Binding, was far more conspicuous than Binding sunlight.

Darius stood boldly atop the hill, taking one final look at the encampment aflame, and then dropped viciously to the ground on one knee. He drove his left hand powerfully into the dirt while yelling, "*Bursus-fortae uet Feromage!*"

The moon seemed to send a radiant beam of light, far brighter than the sun at high noon, directly down from the heavens. This ray struck Darius straight in the burn mark on his back, illuminating the Mark of the Claw. His yellow eyes ignited with a blaze of light and the silver ring on his hand scintillated with a vibrant energy, which coursed up his very veins and flesh, radiating his body from within. Then, in an instant, the transformation began.

The hair on Darius's head lengthened and began to spread rapidly across his body, becoming coarse and thick. The growth happened swiftly, moving from the scalp past his shifting torso, until it had travelled all the way down his vastly expanding back. His hands swelled into massive paws, each brandishing razor-sharp silver claws. His teeth formed into large, menacing fangs that protruded from his displaced jawline. A large strip of silver fur ran from where his beard had been down to his midsection. Darius's shoulders and arms grew furry and animalistic, bulging in size and might.

When the dust settled, a low growl escaped his lungs. Glowing yellow eyes glowed from behind a black snout. In the place where the man Darius had once stood, a colossal black bear rose upon his hind legs, towering over fifteen measures tall. The bear let out a roar that cracked the sky like thunder.

In his Fero-form, Darius's mind was somewhat warped, nearly feral, and his view reddened with righteous indignation. Yet, Darius was still in there, where he remained in control, mostly. Normal thoughts did not fill his mind's eye, but an instinctual drive to destroy the wicked was enhanced exponentially. As a matter of fact, all of his natural senses were doubled, his sense of smell, hearing, taste, and sight magnified.

The cries of the people rang in his furry, pointed ears, almost as if he stood amidst them now. The scent of wrongness was almost overbearing; there was no denying that now. There was an evil out this night, and he would wrench it from existence with silvery tooth and claw. For this purpose was he born. It was what he was made for, destined for. In a fury, he dropped to all fours and rushed down the hill at full speed toward the camp.

The Huntsmen turned in surprise, having not heard him approach due to the screams from the encampment and blasting of their guns. Terror struck in their wide eyes. There was no escape now, and they knew it. Some attempted to jump away in fear, while others turned their weapons towards Darius. It would all be in vain. Through Darius's savagery, they would all atone for the errors of their ways. And though they braced themselves for the fight, it would be a fight that would only end in the pitiless release of death.

And so it began.

Darius rushed towards the largest group, ten or eleven cloaked men in mail or gambeson, all of whom were holding either billhooks or war hammers. Their gambeson tunics, though extremely effective against a regular blade, were shredded like parchment by Darius's enormous claws as he struck with rage. Screams and blood gushed out of two of the Huntsmen, who then fell lifeless to the dirt. Four stepped forward, thrusting their weapons as a unified group at Darius's left side, but none pierced his thick hide. And though it was still extremely painful, the pain surged in Darius like a refiner's fire, fueling his rage. He swung a massive paw into the Huntsmen, breaking both weapon and bone at once

After a few more screams and failed attempts to stop Darius, he had eradicated the group of accusers. Yet, to his dismay, he saw something truly terrible ahead. Women and children, who had been tied to pikes atop pyres, were being set alight, lit with yellow flames.

Enraged, Darius leaped over the remaining Huntsmen and rushed across the encampment to try and save the lives of those poor people. Fury burned at his eyes, which seemed to leak mists of yellow flame. He was not Blessed. No, he was the Damnation of the Wicked.

The Huntsmen, who were burning the forest dwellers, fled before him, using the murder of the innocent to pull the attention away from them as a means of escape. However, even as they ran, they threw their torches at tents, sparking wild flames, masking their flight in the burning chaos.

Darius rushed to the pyres as fast as he could, disregarding any Huntsman that shot an arrow or threw a stone at him. He had one focus: to save the people. However, when he arrived at the flames, the screams had stopped. He had been too late; they were dead.

Disgust turned to rage and hate. He could feel his heartbeat rise and his senses focus. Wildly, he flung his head about, spotting two men fleeing from the camp. Darius tried to chase them, but several hidden men with guns began to fire at him. The shots tore through his flesh, stinging like molten lead being poured down his body. Yet this only angered him more. A massive roar blasted through the camp, causing the Huntsmen to lose their composure. Darius swooped down on two men. He could feel their bones break under the weight of his mighty paws, and as much as he hated to admit it, it brought a sick pleasure to him to hear the crunching of the enemy. He bit violently at another, shredding his flesh.

And then, from behind, a shot hit him in the hind leg, causing him to fall to the ground. He turned his head. Another man stepped out from the shadows and lifted his firearm to his shoulder, aiming at Darius's head.

CAZAP!

A flash of emerald light struck the gunman, whose body crinkled and contorted as if it was being folded into itself before falling lifelessly to the ground. Through the flames, Darius made out the silhouette of a woman holding some kind of rod in her hand. Her face was encased in shadow, save two eyes that pierced the night. They were raging tempests of green, flames of power and majesty. The woman then yelled something as an emerald stone in the handle of the wand, which matched her eyes in color and vibrancy, began to glow as a green beam of light hit another Huntsman with the same effect as the first.

Darius had no time to wonder at the specter as another two Huntsmen rapidly approached with a large net of linked chains held between them. They cast it over his body, eyes filled with indignation as they trapped the beast who had brutalized so many of their own.

This, however, was of little consequence. Darius tore through the binding with brazen claws. The Huntsmen gaped at him with unnatural eyes as he began to limp towards them, the wound in his hind leg fountaining a steady stream of hot blood. Darius had not truly seen the faces of the Huntsmen before this moment, and what looked back at him appeared less human than he. Ink black eyes with red irises gazed maliciously. Veins that looked like charred rock coursed with magma trailed from the black pits, scarring their faces in horrid patterns.

One of the dead-eyed men, taking a pistol from his belt, fired a round into Darius' shoulder. The other pointed his billhook at Darius's muzzle, the tip shaking in apparent fright, though his eyes showed no such anxiety. Both Huntsmen's motions were lethargic, and there were trails of black mist emanating from their limbs and mouth as they lowered their weapons into place.

It was in that moment that Darius, despite all his abilities and powers, faltered. His hind leg crumpled, and his front gave out. A searing pain writhed in his chest, like a branding iron being pressed from the inside of his bosom to the flesh. He teetered unsteadily, and then stumbled to the ground. Streaks of red and specks of black filled his vision. Blood, char, and gore filled his nostrils in sickening wafts. And the drive to fight, to continue, vanished. He was just too tired, his body too far spent, the pain unbearable.

Heartened by the fall of the beast, the Huntsman rushed towards him, black eyes wide, mist streaming with every step. Darius saw them coming but could not move. He closed his eyes and attempted a growl of defiance.

What came out was a pitiful bellow of a broken bear with no strength left to give.

Just as the two men were raising weapons of brutality, a woman shouted something Darius could not quite make out. Her voice sounded airy, deep, and horrifically powerful. What looked like tentacles of black smoke wrapped around both Huntsmen, binding them about their midsections. They screamed out in pain as burn marks formed where the wispy, yet solid, appendages of black mist dug into their smoldering flesh, burning away clothes and flesh alike. They were pulled violently backwards and then thrown across the campground into a burning tent. And as they crashed into the blazing cloth, they erupted in black flames.

Disoriented and badly wounded, Darius beheld the destruction strewn about him. There was no life, just blood and dead bodies. There was no sign of the enchanting woman nor shouts of the Huntsmen. He pushed himself up onto all fours, all the while wincing under the strain and pain of battle and transformation. After taking a few measured breaths, he limped off into the night. The surge of the fight was lessening from within, and his mind began to form thoughts of normalcy. Darius felt himself Turning back again.

How long had it been?

And as he slunk away, he slowly began morphing back into the form of a young man. He crawled slowly, on all fours at first, as steam drifted from his flesh. As he dragged himself back up the hill from whence he had come, patches of thick, black hair fell from his body, leaving his skin bare. Several small lacerations, carved by the Huntsmen's spears and polearms, covered his body. However, it was his leg and shoulder that burned with a searing pain. Every motion forward caused agony he had never before endured.

The transformation back from beast to man was even more terrible than the reverse. His body let off rivers of hot mist in the cool night air, and wisps of translucent smoke rose from his haggard frame. The lead shot that had been embedded in his left thigh had started working itself out. It was terrible. And when it finally popped out, sinews and flesh stretched to close about the gaping wound, a wound that leaked blood and yellowish light. As for his shoulder, that shot had gone straight through, and blood dripped down his chest and back.

Frantically, Darius began to search about the forest floor, looking for an herb he had seen growing earlier on the hilltop. Vynatxion Leaf, a natural antiseptic and coagulant. Darius's mind recalled his training as a youth. The leafy purple and red plant grew in small tufts near water. Darius pulled himself up next to a small stream, having spotted a bushel of Vynatxion growing next to it. He plucked and chewed the bitter herb into a cud that he pushed into the gaping gun wound in his leg. He let out a sharp yelp as the oils from the leaves stung.

A Feromage, sworn to protect Ordan's creation? Ha! Darius laughed cynically as he rolled over onto his back, looking up into the night sky in exhaustion. *And what good am I now? How am I to stand against such new weapons?* A darker thought filled his mind. *Perhaps it is best if we are gone; the world doesn't need my kind anymore.*

However, it was in that thought that he recalled the strange eyes of the Huntsmen, void of life or emotion. He had seen eyes like that before, but not on any man. A pit formed in his stomach. Only creatures had eyes of black and red and exhibited the strange burning lines around their sockets. Itheanam and Morreans – Morreans through their pagan worship and blood rites to their heathen goddesses, the Fallen Ones, and Itheanam, having never had souls of their own, bound to the Terral Plane only through the same black magic the Morreans sought to control.

That's impossible, Darius thought to himself as he rubbed his forehead. *I must have been seeing things. The Morreans are all dead and their queen cast down. I drove her own blade through her heart.*

Why the North? Why this trail and why this need? Brei had been so specific in her incantation that he would need to choose a path, and that he would need to leave another. What if this was part of the journey he had to take on? But he could not believe it. He simply could not accept that they were back, that such beings could have somehow survived the burning of the Black Isle of Morr. His entire tribe, all his people, sacrificed everything to destroy those creatures of darkness. And if any had survived, surely Elcon or the Church would have known of it or stopped them.

Another voice, though not a voice at all, called into the back of his mind. A low rumble, a distant quake of thunder moaning lowly, "Find them…"

The thunderous voice vanished as quickly as it had come, clearing Darius's mind of all else but that incessant need to find. Addled, but coherent, Darius slowly found his way back to where his gear lay strewn about the hilltop. He found a few loose rags in his pants pockets, which he had used to wipe sweat from his brow when he was working the stones in Tur'Mor. These he used to bind his leg. After dressing the wound, he attempted to make himself somewhat decent. However, after having just barely pulled his pants about his waist, he crumpled over in exhaustion.

Darius just lay upon the hilltop for a moment, struggling to regain his breath and steady his nerves. The process of Turning hurt like Halfak. It took so much energy that it could leave him weakened for hours afterwards, and without a full night's moon to restore his strength, he would be vulnerable. So, he lay there, silently looking at the stars. With the moonlight bathing his body, he began to feel a warmth flow through him. It was not the same as the sun's rays, but it did help. He would not be able to go through the Turning again tonight, he could tell that much. Ever since awakening in Tur'Mor, his strength seemed to be lessening. But the moonlight was nourishing, like warm soup after a cold night of hunting.

He could feel it restoring his body, slowly binding up the wounds that marred him.

After several long minutes, perhaps an hour, Darius sat up and breathed in a full breath of cool night air. It brought no satisfaction. In fact, the taste of foulness and gore from battle lingered upon his tongue. He sat up and retched. Blood, cloth, and other chunks spewed from his mouth, an unsavory side effect of fighting as a bear. He pushed his silver ring to his lips, rocking back and forth, trying to ease the nausea. As a Feromage, while he still maintained most of the control, his primal instincts were often too hard to overcome, and he gave way to them in battle, causing him to do things he considered regrettable.

Darius rose slowly; his body, though healing, was not entirely whole. Yet he did not want to linger any longer. He pulled on his heavy boots, and after a struggle to get the left one over his foot, he twisted the brass gears to tighten the laces. Darius then took up his white shirt from the earth, pulling it slowly over his torso, wincing as he raised his shoulder. He frowned as he looked down at the water that was bubbling from the spring. Though most of the cuts were completely sealed, leaving tiny purple and blue scars across his body, a few of the larger lacerations trailed lines of blood that stained his nice shirt.

Something in the distance shuffled.

Darius snapped his neck quickly to the left while leaping backwards, grabbing the hickory stick in one swift motion. He landed in a three-point stance, his toes and left hand digging into the dirt, ready to pounce, and his right hand behind him with the rod held tight. He smelled the air. It was a human coming towards him, or at least... Something strange caught his attention, a scent he did not understand.

Violently, he bounded towards the being's silhouette, short staff of hickory held high. He was met with what felt like a burst of lightning, striking him out of the air. A green flash arced across the night sky. Darius yelped in pain as his body crashed into a small tree, causing it to snap like a twig.

Darius grunted as he pulled himself up from the dirt, shaking his head to get his wits about him. He looked about, spotting the hickory branch a ways off. Shakily, he rose and began to stumble towards the rod, left arm hanging limp and bloody, torso smoking with an acrid smell.

"Wait!" a voice called towards him frantically. "Please, wait." Her voice was soft yet shaking. It trembled and broke as she tried to gather her words.

The distant silhouette shifted from shadow into that of a woman. A soft glow emanated about her, appearing both alluring and dangerous. Darius squinted his eyes against the light as emerald tendrils wisped from her body, coiling upward into the night sky. The woman held a long, black wand with an emerald on its pommel. Her large eyes were gleaming with a wild, beautiful green, which stood in stark contrast to her dark flesh. The wand cast an eerily similar green light to that of the bearer, illuminating her path up the hillside. Her path directly towards Darius.

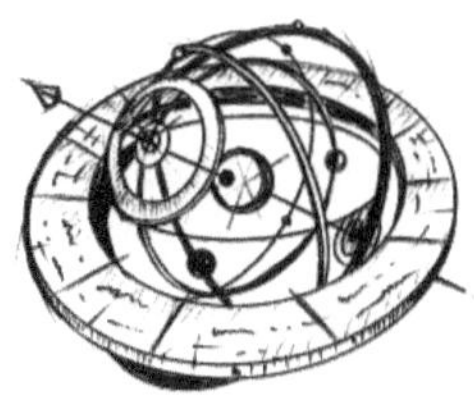

Chapter 27: Tel'un Aund

Elcon watched, eyes reddened from tears, as the procession of green-robed monks adorned with golden aprons carried a wooden casket up the winding path towards the Royal Crypt. He stood at the top, next to the steps of the monolithic resting place of the forefathers of Tur'Mor. There was no rain, but a dull sky. It had been three days since his companion, brother of the cloth, and friend had fallen. Elcon sighed as the incense burners walked past, swinging the silvery dishes at the end of long chains. The smell was sweet, a worthy offering to Vanherran.

Ranun would not be buried inside the Royal Crypt – that honor was reserved only for the bloodlines of Tur, the Line of the Patriarchs, and the High Houses of Tur'Mor. Rather, he would be buried in the earth in the Papal Yard underneath the shadows of the dogwood trees. For generations, all of the holy priests, priestesses, monks and other members of the Parsonary were buried in the Papal Yard. Thousands of smooth river stones, with two golden coins atop them, sat in that yard, each marking where a holy man or woman lay.

Elcon's address was short. He did not have many words to say, and the few that came, came painfully. None, other than the monks that carried Ranun's body and a few loyal patrons from the bread-house, were present at the meager ceremony. The hole had been dug and the coins laid upon the stone to pay for passage at the Gates of Vanherran.

As the last mounds of earth fell over his friend's coffin, Elcon made a vow. He swore to seek out who had done this. He swore he would find who was responsible, and make sure that they would pay. It was not the way of the Church. But Elcon had long done things his own way, and he would not change that now.

***

Aellia stood in a world of falling waters, purple hues, and grandiose scenery. A single tree grew on this island, whose branches and roots were gold and leaves were each a fine gemstone. The stars in the heavens ebbed and flowed, falling only to rise again.

Then suddenly she was in a castle, or a cathedral of sorts, with towering spires of crystal that punctured the clouds and glistened in the rays of two suns. The floors were solidified flames of azure, and the ceiling was endless pools of gold. Endless rows of statues adorned the halls, each of which were holding a rod that looked exactly like the one she had found.

***

"Paper! Get your paper!" a dirty-faced lad called out to men and women who bustled along the streets, waving a large sheet of paper in his hand, a sack full of the same over his shoulder. "Read it here first! A siglat for the news! Hear, hear! The King's Jewel reclaimed! House of the Mayor in shambles! Death in the streets!"

Aellia awoke in the middle of Tinker's Square. It was a quaint place, located in Northend, where the artisans and craftsmen created strange items and unique gadgets to be sold by the merchants of Tur'Mor. It was a place Aellia frequented often, an easy place to find a loose purse or a gullible lord or lady who needed a mistress for hire. Despite her familiarity with the location, she had no recollection of how she had come to find herself on the street.

She sat up gingerly, head throbbing with a dull pain. She brought her hands up to rub at her aching eyes, though only realized as the cold silver of the strange scepter brushed her cheek that she was holding it in her hand. Startled, she jumped up from the ground, scanning her eyes about her surroundings. Callers, the boys selling the papers, were crawling all over the place.

"What happened?" Aellia mumbled as she tried to force herself to remember. However, as she did so, a sharp pain attacked her mind. She winced and squeezed her eyelids shut. A flash of blue light erupted in her darkened state, and she felt a gust of wind pull at her hooded vest. Air rushed past her flesh, and when she opened her eyes, her heart nearly stopped.

Aellia looked out over Tinker's Square, hovering high above the tallest buildings. Her would-be scream caught in her throat as a great lump of fear struck. She was not afraid of heights, or at least, she never thought she was. That being said, she had never found herself floating helplessly in the air. Whipping her head downward, she fixed her eyes on the glowing azure gemstone set in the sinuous silver rod. Fear nearly caused her to drop the scepter, though a greater fear of plummeting to her death caused her to cling to it with whitened knuckles.

In her panicked state, Aellia could not form a coherent thought. She just clung to the scepter and pleaded to the gods to find her way back to the ground. A gale seemed to push her from behind, thrusting her laterally across the sky at incredible speed. Buildings blurred in her eyesight as she rushed past them. Then, despite the soul-wrenching terror, a grin began to form across her tight lips as a pulsating thrill overtook her. Aellia began to focus, somehow forming a pocket of air around her head, causing the blurs to form into crisp images, eyes now shielded from the battering winds, and the world opened before her.

Buildings, factories, courtyards, and people, despite the height, were crystal clear in her vision. Colors swirled and became shapes and figures so quickly she did not even have to think but immediately saw them for what they were. High above Tur'Mor she soared, above the smell of char, waste, and mud. She was so high in the sky that she would not even appear a speck to those who walked below, and yet all was visible to her. A gleeful laugh escaped her lungs after she drew in her first breath of air. It was sweet, crisp, and clean.

Aellia did not get the opportunity to relish in the sweet release that the gale brought her. Like an arrow loosed over the side of a towering wall, she began to plummet to the earth. The smile was ripped from her face, replaced with the terror that had gripped her so tightly. Tumbling through the clouds, she tried with all her might to straighten herself, direct the motion of her fall, but she could not, nor could she release the silver scepter. It felt as if the strange rod had fused to her flesh, and as the stone pulsated with azure light, so did her heartbeat in perfect unison.

A feeling like that of a rope yanking about her navel pulled Aellia downward. She stopped tumbling and flailing and jetted straight down in a streamlined form. Beyond her own thought, the silver scepter, still firmly clutched in her fingers, shot out in front of her. Thunder boomed and dirt surged upward from the ground.

Surrounded by a perfect sphere of whirling air, Aellia hovered a hand's length from the ground, eyes gleaming with effervescent blue. Her heart was pounding and her chest heaving as she stood mid-air over a patch of broken land, as if it had been blasted by a cannon shot. Dirt, grass, and debris swirled around the base of Aellia's case of air, though none penetrated the translucent orb.

"Enough!" Aellia yelled out in a commanding voice.

Her eyes flashed with a bright blue beam, and the stone in the scepter went dull. Just as suddenly as the gemstone lost its gleam, the barrier of air that surrounded Aellia dissipated, and she dropped to the ground. She barely managed to stick the landing. Her feet tingled in an unusual way; the blood flow to them had been decreased during her flight.

"You are strong..."

Aellia jerked her head around, searching for the source of the voice that filled her ears. No one was near. She was alone, standing on a small spit of land a league out in the Western Sea.

"You are very strong..."

"Who's there?" Aellia said, wide eyes darting about every inch of the small island. "Show yourself!"

"I see you..." The voice was eerie, cold, and distant.

Aellia dropped to her knees with a scream. She tore at her ears with panic, trying to get the voice from her head, but it would not leave her. She could feel it, like a splinter in her mind, wedged deep within, festering about.

"I feel you..."

"What is happening to me?"

"We are you now...and you are I... We are one," Iaenora said definitively, her voice satisfied.

"Iaenora?" Aellia gasped as the name slid from her lips. *How do I know that name?*

"You have spoken the Oath," Iaenora mused in the back of Aellia's mind. *"We are bonded now, Ancient One."*

"What are you talking about? What happened to me?"

"Even now, we grow together in unison." Iaenora hummed. *"I have awoken at long last in you."*

"Get out of my head!" Aellia thrashed, trying to throw the silver scepter from her grasping fingers; it was to no avail. She could not open her hands; her flesh was entwined with the sinuous metal.

"The bond is formed, but the fusion must finish... Patience, Ancient One, we awaken together. It has been too long."

A jolt of pain rushed through Aellia's hand, searing through the veins of her forearm and then across her chest. It caused tears to well in her eyes and a scream to fill her lungs. Doubling over her knees, Aellia raised a hand to her vest, pulling away the strings which held it together. Azure light that matched the stone in the scepter was erupting across her flesh, cutting lines and symbols into her body, lines that swirled and symbols of winding patterns that were etched from her wrist to her bosom.

"I am Iaenora, Spirit of the Winds. We are the Sage of the Sky and Tempests," the once disconcerted, now more lucid voice, said in the back of Aellia's mind.

Through staggered breaths that caused her body to tremble, Aellia focused on the sound of Iaenora's voice and asked, "What has happened to me?"

"We have Bonded," Iaenora's voice was now almost sweet, yet authoritative. *"You took upon yourself the Ada'eha El-dached."*

Ada'eha El-dached? Aellia's heart seemed to skip a beat as the words crashed over her memories. She was in a dark room, hiding from the Kh'ar... She had not remembered saying the words, but somehow, she knew exactly what they meant. *Ada'eha El-dached* roughly translated to *bind soul to spirit* in the Daulkaefarean Tongue. The Oath of the Seven. The Seal of the Sages.

More shock and terror flooded Aellia. Her mouth went dry, and a gaping pit began to form in her gut. "How do I know that?"

"We know many things." Iaenora laughed melodically. *"We are shared now."*

"What does that even mean?"

"There is much to learn, Ancient One," Iaenora stated, though her voice lost its gentler sound, turning somewhat sad. *"Our bond will help you learn many things, but there are so many more that you must come to know first-hand. Let us begin with the beginning. I am Iaenora. We are the Sage of Air, the first awakened to herald the return. And it is our duty to bring about justice to the world."*

***

Elcon von'Harr of House Harr, lineage of the First Kin of Tur, High Priest of the Church of Ordan, and the Elder of Tur'Mor, sat in his study, secluded from the rest of the monastery, as he did so many times before. For years he had come to the Office of the Elders to clear his mind and focus his intentions. Lady Adoline's portrait, having been the high priestess before him, hung above the shelves of books to Elcon's back.

Elcon von'Harr was an inquisitive man, a man of science and learning. He loved the Church, and his devotion to it was lifelong, his faith infallible. Despite this, his desires to understand the secrets of the universe were unrelenting.

A silver goblet rested between his aged fingers. Only a few droplets of a strong drink remained at the bottom of the chalice. In front of him, a small book laid open on his table. Next to it, the globe of his own construction rotated slowly, stars and planets moving in perfect form. The Yyhanzmar, the Cosmos of Men, the Cycle of Life, was the accumulation of his life's work. Hundreds of hours poured into charting stars, researching scrolls of both ancient and modern astrologists, tutelage from men and women ranging from the burning sands of Tuawtia to the island nations to the east and west of Ethrea. Now, it was all that Elcon could do to stare at it. Anger and guilt welled deep within him. Despite a lifetime focused on conviction and enlightenment, Elcon could not bury the emotions within.

What was life if it ended only in death? What was understanding if lost to the grave? What was the purpose without something beyond? These questions plagued Elcon. A lifetime of learning and devotion, and he was still afraid.

He rose from his seat, eyes puffy and reddened from tears, and walked past his contraption towards a small figure of Ordan in a shrine of stone and candles. Elcon stared at the image of the High Father in solidarity, the hurt of his lost friend tearing at him from within.

As a young man, Elcon was considered handsome. As an old man, he was considered wise. As a young man, he was known as a great swordsman. As an old man, he was known as a notable scholar and holy man. Yet, on the inside, he still felt hollow. His entire life, he had searched out truths, knowledge, and enlightenment, for his fear of death had harrowed him from his youth. In his middle years, he had found himself in the ranks of the Royal Knights of Tur'Mor. A proud moment for himself, a moment of shame for his family. The von'Harr family had always been of the Parsonary, dedicated servants of the High Father and the Holy Mother.

Elcon moved like mist past the edifice of his god towards the rear of the room. He pulled forth an amulet, blue Everlight swirling gently around the azure stone. The wall was tooled with a beautiful pattern of twisting lines and shapes, imitating vines crawling upward with thorns and flowers populating the reaching tendrils of stone. Placing the jewel into an inconspicuous slot, the stonework cracked down the center, revealing a secondary doorway in the octagonal room. With a steady push, Elcon opened the secret passage and began to make his way down the granite steps that spiraled into darkness.

With each step downward, a series of blue stones began to catch with tranquil light, lighting the pathway into the hidden chamber. The air was cool and still and harbored a sweet smell of clean, floral notes. Elcon sighed as he marched down the steps of speckled stone, a path he had trodden so many times before.

At the base of the lengthy stairwell sat an old oaken door with heavy iron latticework covering every inch. A tumble-styled lock was fastened to the red oak, heavy iron bolts holding it in place. Elcon produced a key from his robes, heavy and worn, much like the mechanism that sealed the door. With no small amount of strain – Elcon's aged body was significantly weaker than when he had taken on the mantle of High Priest of Tur'Mor – he turned the key inside the keyhole. A low rumble of metal sliding on metal creaked as Elcon slowly rotated the circular, multi-knobbed lock. With a final heave, Elcon pushed the oak door inward.

The secret chamber was all white marble, down to the very shelves which were hewn into the walls. A throne-like seat was gilded with gold, as was a thick table, whose legs were scrolled and ends formed to look like lion's paws. The domed ceiling was bare, not a painting upon its glossy surface, though there was a crystal chandelier studded with glowing stones of sapphire that hung from a silver setting in the white stonework. And the floor was checkered in white and off-white squares of polished marble.

There were two statues, twice the height of Elcon, standing on either side of the Holy Seat, each with an intricately carved hand on the back of the seat. The statue on the right depicted Ordan, though more powerfully built than generally shown in the chapels and other paintings of the Church. The haft of mighty Ethra was in his right hand, the head, set with a large emerald, rested on the ground near his bare feet. His eyes depicted a solemn knowing that was masked behind orbs of endless sight. To the left of the chair, slender and beautiful, stood the Holy Mother. Her long hair was carved in a way that was so lifelike that every time Elcon saw it, he had to stop and admire the workmanship. About her neck was a series of slender chains, seven silver chains of slender tooling. Her flowing dress was carved so perfectly it seemed nearly transparent about her body. Her beauty was unmatched, though much like her husband, she had a fierceness etched in her serene face that told of a woman who was more than even tales could tell.

Elcon moved reverently across the checkered floor. The span of the room was nearly forty measures across, and his eyes focused on the desk of gilded marble. The vaulted ceiling must have nearly touched the underside of the monastery's sublevels, though the high priest paid it no heed. Nor paid any mind to the dangling pans of silver which held burning incense; plum blossoms from the orchards of Livithia, his favorite scent. He was hurting; powerful emotions of loss and anger welled within his battered soul. He was determined. Determined to find the answers that had evaded him for nearly eight decades.

Upon reaching the high-backed seat, Elcon sat, his body melting into the cold stone. He laid his hands upon the desk and stared at what rested atop the white surface. A strange silver rod, twisting like muscle and sinew around an emerald no larger than the end of his thumb, was the focus of his gaze. Hundreds of books, dozens of charts, and a handful of trinkets had been the focus of his studies within the endless libraries of the Asterivae, yet none were as esteemed compared to this.

In truth, Elcon had not expected those who guarded the secrets of the Asterivae to allow him to depart with the strange silver scepter. He knew of the cult of the Asterivians, practitioners of the hidden works. They were not known for violence but for their never-ending search for knowledge and understanding, something Elcon could not fault them for. Yet, their methods were often strange and bizarre, standing in stark contrast to the teachings of the Church of Ordan and the laws of Ordiatian providence. However, the Asterivians esteemed themselves above law, above religion; their only purpose was the pursuit of enlightenment. They did not subscribe to the ways of man or god and placed themselves outside of the touch of either. They had only their doctrine, ruling class, and means whereby to enforce them. Members of note in both society and religion were members of the secret cult, passing laws and establishing bylaws to protect the organization from any formal search or seizure. They were, in truth, more powerful than any deigned to admit, a hand in every branch of government, every route of trade, every union or guild formed, and it was even said they held positions in the hierarchy of the Church.

Elcon ran a fingertip over the cold silver of the rod. It felt too smooth, too precise, as if impossible to craft with the daft hands of humanity. There was a feel of life, something within, though he did not understand. When he had found the strange scepter, it had been sealed in a chamber room, away from the main series of shelves in the uppermost section of the Asterivae. It had taken considerable leverage and promises to convince the Curator of Histories that he would bring the strange item called a Tel'un Aund back to the tower once he had finalized his studies.

Tel'un Aund, a strange name, Foreteller of Gods. Or at least, that was the closest translation Elcon could make out, having only found bits of the Ancient Words in the endless libraries of the Asterivae. He had known Ra'el Aund, Light of Gods, the endowed amulets that the Church used to harness flows of Everlight for the Blessed to use. He had even heard of Sy'ey Aund, Force of Gods, items that were crafted for the sole purpose of defending humanity from the onslaught of evil that at one time plagued the Terral world. Of Ra'el Aund, little was spoken amongst the commoners of Ordiatea. To them, magic or powers were a myth. The only true power was directly from the Ellitheor, given to the Blessed and High Patriarch of the Church. Of the Sy'ey Aund, none spoke, though few in high places knew of the secret weapons forged under the direction of the Ancient Ones to fight the shadow of the Fallen Ones. Yet, of Tel'un Aund, none knew. Or at least, none remembered. Elcon sighed. This had to hold the answers, to life and death, and the great beyond. Foreteller of Gods. He would have to find out just what that meant.

CHAPTER 28: IN THE DARK OF RANOK

"You, you saved me," a shaky voice called out from the darkness.

The young woman stepped into Darius's view, her wand showering her with effervescent emerald light. The beams danced on her flesh of amber like starlight on a still ocean's surface. Loose curls of liquid black fell down her back and over her shoulders, tied back by a green headband that matched her low-cut dress. Around the headband, which kept her locks out of her almond shaped face, a series of golden chains and disks were affixed. Her green eyes stared uneasily at Darius, reddened with sadness and tears. Splotches of blood and dirt tarnished her formfitting dress, more so near the cutaway leg portion, which revealed black britches and high boots that hugged her thighs.

Darius could not form words, captivated by her beauty in the moonlight. He did, however, take note of the sweat that beaded at her forehead and the worry that marred her distant eyes. He could also make out a subtle tremble of her full lips, stained with a rosy red. His gaze then fell from her face to a golden necklace which bore a pendant, a necklace that sunk between her ample breasts.

She noticed, apparently.

Quickly, she brought her left hand to her chest, a blush forming across her freckled cheeks. "That was you, was it not? In the camp?" she asked with trepidation.

Darius wracked his brain, striving to think of something to say. Anything. He could not.

"You're hurt," the young woman said with a sniff as she drew in even closer to Darius. Her voice seemed to flow, rhythmic and strange.

She lowered her wand, the light fading away as she did so, and then placed it into a sheath at her side as she walked towards Darius. She outstretched a hand, her long fingers adorned with ink lines of golden vines, and softly touched his arm where a particularly large gash lay open in his flesh, the blood having seeped through his shirt. Her hand, though gentle, was slightly calloused and very firm. This was not a weak woman in any sense of the word, and Darius could tell.

Darius winced, drawing in a sharp breath as she touched him. A rush of lilac and a spring morning's rain filled his nose. The scent was unlike anything he had ever experienced before, calming and peaceful. And then it hit him. He jerked back, shuffling away on the palms of his hands and heels of his feet, eyeing her with concern.

"I followed the trail of blood you left." Her words were strained, and it did not sound like this tongue was her first language. "Let me help you," she continued. "It is the least I can do to repay you."

She retrieved a small crystal vessel which contained a light purple potion from the brown satchel that hung across her body. She extended the bottle, saying, "Drink this, it will help with the pain and healing."

Darius gave her a look of mistrust. He then raised a hand and pushed the bottle away while stating, "I can manage."

"Don't be a fool," the young woman stated as she wrapped her fingers around Darius's, closing his hand around the vessel. Her hands were warm to the touch, and when she spoke again, her rhythmic voice was less intense. "I promise, it will help you. My people are healers, gifted in the arts of exotic herbs."

Darius's eyes narrowed on her, his fist resisting as she pushed the crystal vial towards his mouth.

"You do not need resist. You can trust me, Mah'kau."

"Mah'kau?" Darius grunted. His throat was still sore from his fighting and roaring. Stupid bear. "What is that?"

She cocked her head when he asked, and then smiled softly. "Friend. I mean no harm to you."

"I saw what you did to those men," Darius said darkly, pulling his hand away, bottle in his white-knuckled fist. "You're a witch, aren't you?"

"What *I* did?" Her voice cracked. Tears then filled her tormented eyes, which bled emotion from an open wound of the soul. "They hunt us for sport! They were burning us alive! If I am a witch for defending myself, then they are the very spawn of Halfak!"

She knelt there, trembling. And in that moment, she lost some of her beauty. Her face looked dead, drained of life and color. She stared into nothingness, through Darius and on into the Beyond. A lump formed in Darius's throat as he looked upon her. He in nowise meant to cast blame on her for her actions. No, he was simply trying to connect the dots.

Curse it all! Why would you say that? Darius swore to himself; he was just so bad with words.

Awkwardly, he opened the vial. A tinge of bitterness rushed through the air and into his nostrils, causing his eyes to narrow on the frothy liquid. It was thick and smelled like old socks and bad citrus. His brow furrowed deeper, but he committed to the task. In one large swallow, he drained the vessel of its contents. Besides, he could heal from poisons. Well, most of them anyways.

The taste was that of wildfire and soured wine, with a kick of something that made Darius's throat burn like he was trying to swallow pure lightning. He let out a gasping cough in shock. Darius's eyes shot directly to the woman who knelt across from him. She was smiling, though not a joyous smile of merriment, but one that seemed to say, "Serves you right."

"See, you will not die," she said as she took the vial from the ground where Darius had dropped it, then placed it back into her side bag. "It is very good."

"If I die, I die," Darius said as he coughed violently; the viscous tonic he just swallowed seemed to crawl uneasily down his throat.

"You won't die, that I can assure you. Besides, killing the man who saved me does not seem to be the most appropriate way to say thank you." Her voice was now calm, and the sweet allure returned. She laughed softly, her tongue clicking against thick, stained lips, and then said, "I am Izebal Knight of the Diju family."

Darius, eyes still watering from the putrid brew, could not seem to form any words at all. Not even poor ones.

Izebal laughed again, still soft and quiet, as she shook her head. She then ran her eyes over Darius, looking at his battered body. "You did not look so manly earlier."

Somewhat insulted, and a little embarrassed, though he didn't know why, Darius croaked out the only response his muddle brain could form: "What do you mean?"

"I know what I saw," Izebal said as she shook her head and ran a hand through her hair. In doing so, it revealed a golden-hilted dagger at her left side that had been covered by one of the many sash-like belts around her waist. "You are more than a man."

"I don't know what you think you saw," Darius said sharply. "I was taken and beaten by one of those men down there. I just managed to escape."

"Do not play me for a fool," Izebal pressed. "Tell me, Mah'kau, how do you do it?"

"I am telling you the truth," Darius said, frustration building in his voice. "I am with the Church of Ordan –"

His words stopped abruptly as he pressed his finger to where the pendant of Ethra was on his vest.

She turned and reached for his coat, which still lay folded. As Izebal twisted about, he noticed a black tattoo on the back of her neck. It was of three small swirls that formed a triangle and a winding line that formed a knot around them, ever winding, never ceasing. However, the ink that formed the black lines seemed to flow, like water running through a canyon.

Darius was unsure as to what he could say. He just knew he did not want to talk about his abilities with a stranger, especially one who could wield magic. The last time he had had a run-in with a witch, he had been blasted in the face, leaving him with his silvery patch in his beard.

Hadn't Elcon said that magic was no more? Darius rubbed his brow. He had nearly begun to believe it himself, hoping almost, that if there was no true magic, there was no true evil. The Blessed made sense, as they drew their abilities from an omniscient, endless well of power. There were limitations and rules there, bloodlines and oaths. But magic – pure, unadulterated flows of unnatural power. The implications were terrifying.

Izebal, face strewn with sorrow, had to have thousands of questions within her. But Darius knew she had to also be experiencing crushing emotions of loss and trauma. Part of her needed to know who this man was who sat across from her and that he was not a danger to her wellbeing...as long as she didn't try to cast a hex on him.

"So, what do we do now?" Izebal finally asked, realizing the other would not make a move.

"I do not know," Darius said sheepishly as he looked to Izebal. "Is there anything I can do?"

Izebal's controlled face cracked like a pane of glass, all the pieces there, just fractured. "They're all dead," she whimpered and then, in a moment of shock, she threw herself around Darius's neck and wept.

Darius, unsure what to do, wrapped a steady arm around her as she buried her face into a stranger's chest and cried like a child. He held her for quite some time, though he knew not how long. It seemed like ages, and at the same time when it ended, only a moment. Izebal arose, wiping tears from her freckled cheeks. Her eyes then rose to his; a spark of green flashed through them. The amulet that hung from her neck also seemed to flash. There was a green stone set in it Darius had not seen before, and it seemed to glow with the light of a thunderstorm, wild and untamed.

"My grandmother gave it to me," Izebal said as she ran a finger over the jeweled necklace. "Nanna was the last of her kind. A powerful wielder, unlike any other." Her voice held a sense of wonder and adoration.

"I have seen such gems in the Church," Darius said as he looked to the amulet, intrigued by the mystic object.

"Church?" Izebal said with a raised eyebrow. Then, she smirked as she looked down at the hammer pendant on his vest and back to Darius. "Oh, right. You are one of them then, aren't you?"

"I am just an emissary, a messenger, you know?" Darius replied awkwardly, fumbling his words as she stared at him. He was thankful, however, that she was no longer talking about his transformations. He really did not want to talk about anything, but anything else was better than that topic.

"And what is a messenger boy doing this far in the woods? There are no chapels near here," Izebal pressed.

Darius did not answer, just shrugged his shoulders.

"Well, at least tell me your name, won't you?" Izebal inquired firmly as she spun on her heels to face him.

Darius sighed as he dusted away a few stray leaves that clung to his satchel. "Darius."

"Thank you, Darius," Izebal replied. "You are a good man, the Earthmother grace you."

"I didn't do anything anyone else wouldn't have done," Darius said without looking up. He had all but forgotten his story from before.

"You risked your life for me," Izebal said quietly. "Darius, no one risks anything for a Diju, ever. You could have died, but that did not stop you."

"I am fine," Darius said shortly. He paused and looked to Izebal. She could not have been much younger than him, if at all. Well, younger than him in terms of looks – he had a thousand years on anyone alive. He sighed, squatting down next to her, and then asked in a softer voice, "You aren't hurt, are you?"

"I'll be okay. But..." Her voice broke. "They are dead."

Izebal hugged herself around the knees and bowed her head.

"There is nothing more you could have done." Darius's voice was barely a whisper. "You nor me nor anyone else. You can't blame yourself."

Izebal lifted her head, eyes still fractured by pain but ablaze with hate. "I do not blame myself. It was those bastards in black! They hunt, kill, and steal. They destroyed everyone and everything I love." Tears began to stream down her face once again.

"Maybe some survived?" Darius's words did not bring much hope. He saw the flames and death. He knew it, and he knew that Izebal knew as well.

"No," Izebal said shortly, "I wandered the whole camp before finding you. There were none left. None of my family nor the Huntsmen."

Darius licked his lips. He was, yet again, in a place where he did not know what to say. So, he did the one thing he knew how to do and prepared to move on. However, as Darius went to grab his hickory walking stick, something inside stopped him. From deep within, he felt a sudden instinctual need to protect Izebal.

Yes, she was beautiful, and she was scared and in need, yet this was more than attraction or raw emotion. His heart hurt for her and her loss, but there was nothing he could do about that now. No, this was something else. Something deeper.

Darius stopped in his tracks and closed his eyes as he breathed out, "Where will you go?"

"The rest of the Diju live up north, above those of the Blackwater Clan, in Eastern Dane," Izebal said, her voice growing surer. "I will make my way there."

"A little company not trying to kill me would be a nice change of pace," replied Darius, half joking and half serious. He then shook his head and picked up his walking stick.

A smile, warm as a summer's evening, fluttered across her lips. Her eyes widened and her spirits noticeably lifted. When she rose to her feet, she extended her hand and asked, "Your stick, may I see it?"

Darius handed over the gnarled piece of hickory. Izebal pulled out her wand, and as she rotated her wrist, her irises glowed a vibrant shade of green, mirroring the glowing stone at the base of wand's handle. The staff's broken edges softened, and a rounded handle formed at the top. She drove the base of the stick into the ground, raising her left hand while doing so. Green runes of light formed around her hands and vines began to crawl up the shaft, weaving themselves into the rod of hickory. After a brief inspection, Izebal smiled, looking at her craft.

"You'll find this quite suitable now, no more splinters," Izebal said as she handed the rod back to Darius. "See, not all 'witches' are bad. Well, at least, not that bad," she added with a wink.

Darius took the cane from Izebal with a simple thank you. It felt lighter, yet somehow sturdier and harder, almost like glass or metal. He tightened his grip about it. *Feels good*, he thought to himself with an almost indiscernible smile.

CHAPTER 29: REVENGE AND CLARITY

"You must go to the Ancient One, the youngest of us," Iaenora said into Aellia's mind. *"Do not resist it. It calls to you. It is your duty."*

Aellia pressed a tired finger to her mind, attempting to silence the ever-present voice of Iaenora. She was tired, having walked nearly three days to get back to Tur'Mor after a subconscious flight had taken her from the city. She was hungry – there had been little to forage along the roads of Telnor's hills.

The Holy Temple of Ordan perched atop her solitary hill, a beacon to the righteous. A waste of stone and mortar to Aellia. Gold, jewels, and marble formed that building, and tens of thousands of Ordiatians went hungry in the province.

"You have a duty," Iaenora urged.

"I have friends," Aellia snarled through gritted teeth. Though, it was not friends that urged her forward. True, she did care for Felik and the crew. But Tomo – she could not lose her.

"You have a duty, ancient that is new!" Iaenora pushed harder, nearly turning Aellia's step.

"Halfak burn you!" Aellia cursed. "I don't give a damn about you or this duty. I have to get back into the city." *I have to kill that bastard Aldorian.*

"Murder is wrong, child."

"Great," Aellia scoffed, throwing her hand up. "You can hear my thoughts?"

"I am your thoughts, Aellia of Livithia, daughter of –"

"You shut up! You do not know me!"

"I am only showing that I do! I need to help you find your way."

Aellia took a breath, clenching the scepter in whitened knuckles, and jumped.

She soared into the air, bounding past the spires of the temple, sailing over the crescent-formed Templetown. The wind licked her cheeks and fluttered her archer's cloak. The silver vambraces glistened in the moonlight, veins of sapphire contrasting the hallowed light.

"Aellia," Iaenora pled. *"Do not do this."*

Aellia shoved the voice away, forcing the control, the total control of her body back into her own grasp. With that recapturing of her own self, she dipped in the sky, faltering slightly. She could not fly well when she did not allow the link between Iaenora and herself to flow openly. But this time she did not need that link, for she had something better to fuel her flight.

Rage drove Aellia now.

***

Midcouncillor Aldorian walked proudly, and why shouldn't he? Felik, the greatest thorn in his side, sat in the dungeons bound in shackles. And his pathetic crew, they were crushed, all the pesky worms dead. The city guards had been very clear – he had made sure. Every member either in chains or dead, and the only one wearing chains was that damned traitor, Felik. Proud indeed. What a wonderful day it was.

The salty air was warming now, though a mild chill still hung about in the early morning breeze. Aldorian breathed in deeply as he ambled forward, his two lackeys directly behind him. Remus and Tiberius had been with Aldorian for nearly ten years now, both having served under him when he had held the rank of Captain in the Ordiatian Army. They were the best of the best, deadly swordsmen and even better ears. They knew the channels and the backstreets of Tur'Mor like the backs of their hands. And now that Aldorian held the title of Midcouncillor, they too had received in his good fortune.

"It's a good day, boys," Aldorian said with a smile, his cane tapping the cobblestone with a rhythmic *click, click* as he walked. "Regent of Southend has a nice ring to it, doesn't it?"

Tiberius, the taller of the two lackeys, who was characterized by the ebony-handled kemghana – a wide, flat-bladed hunting knife with a crooked tip – that he wore at his side, spoke first, "That, it is. But been word in Southend about distaste towards you, my lord."

"What?" Aldorian scoffed, not even turning his head back to look at his men.

"It's true, my lord," Remus continued. "Been a lot of talks about overthrowing the whole damn government."

"Preposterous!" Aldorian laughed. "Wishful thinking of gutter-scum. And what do they think? That they would rule in our stead?"

"I don't know, my lord," Tiberius answered. "But that don't change the facts, which is that there is unrest in Southend. People are hurt'n there, my lord. Don't do us no good if there is a revolt."

"I have worked far too hard to have my plans upset by the squabbles of peasants and miscreants." Aldorian sniffed. "It took forging a botched attempt at the King's Jewel to even get Adelmo to remember my name. And now that I have returned it to him, alongside capturing the traitor

302

who took it, I have finally cemented myself in the upper echelon of Tur'Mor. No more will I have to wallow in the mire of midcouncillors, self-righteous prudes. Regent. I am a regent now, even if it is over Southend, lowest of the Quadrants."

"And what of the rumors, my lord?" Remus asked.

"What rumors?"

"Of the Kh'ar, my lord?" Remus answered, grey eyes looking troubled.

"The Kh'ar? Ha!" Aldorian laughed. "That misguided lot of ignorant buffoons. They are little more than a speck of dust, a mote in the eye at worst. No real threat."

"Beg your pardon, my lord," Tiberius cut in, his voice low and grave. "But word on the street is that them Kh'ar are quite a bit thicker than we'd thought. Rumor has it they are even funded by King Karanos of Calun, that they even got someone close to the High Seat."

"Preposterous!" Aldorian laughed even louder than before, though there was little mirth present. "Our good mayor may be a worthless airhead, filled with notions of false equality, but the true leader of this nation, our glorious Rising Star, the only true noble-blooded man in this faulty government, would never allow such nonsense."

"Only saying what I hear, my lord."

"It is all well and good to listen, but don't concern yourself with such," Aldorian said, fixing the wide brim of his hat against a sudden gust of wind. "The Kh'ar are –"

Remus screamed in pain as his body lurched backwards, soaring widely through open air. The source of his scream: a silver dagger protruding from his chest.

"What in the name of the gods?" Aldorian shouted in shock and rage, twirling about wildly.

Another flash of silver shot through the air, but Tiberius knocked it away with a swift move of his own blade. He jumped forward, standing in front of his lord, sword at the ready. The sound of shattering glass filled the air. What fell from the sky was something that no amount of training could have prepared the man for.

***

Aellia landed on the cobblestone street outside the charred remains of the place she had called home for years. She had been a child, destitute and starved, when Felik took her in. Her hair had faded with the White Fever, hence the name, to a color that she had never sought to cover up since. Felik had told her to be proud of it, that it proved her strength. She did not feel strong now as tears streamed down her ashen cheeks.

She rushed into the rubble, taking no thought of danger or harm. She flipped over beams with unnatural strength, though some crumbled to ash as she tried to move them. The wood was either rain-soaked so badly that it was dilapidated or charred into unrecognizable pieces. Only one of the fireplaces remained upright, and her tower was little more than a mound of muck, nails, and scrap.

To Aellia's immediate relief, there were no bodies in the ruin. Though that relief turned to distress quickly as thoughts of capture and torture filled her mind, or worse, death. Without anything else to pull from for clues as to the whereabouts of the crew, Aellia left the place that was once the Loft.

"*Aellia, listen...*" Iaenora's voice was so quiet, pressed to the darkest recesses of Aellia's mind, that she could barely make out the pleading. "*Please.*"

"Shut up, damn you!" Aellia choked as she yelled the words. Bitterness filled her bosom and a lump had formed in her throat. But she would not cry. Not yet. "I will find them!"

"*You are meant for so much more. Destined for greatness! We must go to our brother at the Silver Gates.*"

"I will not leave until I find her," Aellia snarled, holding her left arm in a pained attempt at comfort.

"*Where will you go? Who shall you seek? There is nothing here for you.*"

"I said shut up!"

"*You are only going to hurt yourself further, Aellia. Let go and be free to the winds and skies where you now belong.*"

I belong with her, Aellia thought to herself in defiance of the voice in her head. *I belong with Tomo. She needs me.*

The Twisted Stool was not a far walk from the Loft, a walk Aellia had taken many times before. She hurried down the road, each step furthering her anxiety and fear. She did not stop to look at the dull-clad Southenders who gaped at her in her steel vambraces and white cloak. She had to look like a painting, though the mud and ash had to have marred that image distinctively.

To Aellia's horror, the brothel was in no better shape than the Loft. Little more than a heap of rubble lay wet and singed where the building had once stood. Other shops and houses that surrounded the Twisted Stool bore damage, though still remained erect and mostly intact. The only sight that brought any source of consolation was that of Lady Phaedra, who was standing with hands on wide hips, staring crestfallen into the charred remains of her bar and home.

Others surrounded the busty barkeep, strongmen and barmaids alike, rifling through the wreckage. Three men in black uniforms, silver stars on the chest, were talking to Lady Phaedra, one of which was taking notes on a pad of paper. They did not wear the regular City Guard uniforms, however, but long overcoats with broad lapels and squared shoulders. The sleeves were ornate with silver embroidery and their hats were not steel, but brimmed gentlemen's hats. The one taking notes had a monocle squished into his left eye and a thick black mustache that left his chin bare but twisted into his chops.

"And like I said to the others, sirs," Phaedra was stating, her tone exasperated, "they were wearing masks. I didn't see nothing. Came in the night, they did, burning and yelling. Barely got my girls out, many in less than their knickers!"

"The masks, what did they look like?" asked the monocled man with the pad of paper.

"Looked like some demons out of a monk's story to scare children straight," Lady Phaedra answered, throwing her hands up. "Teeth like fangs, carved from ivory, red eyes and strange markings. Others were like skulls, stitched and inlaid with copper or other metal. And one, it was only over half the face, and he had so many rings on his fingers I was surprised that he could hold his twisted knife!"

Aellia felt her anger swell at the description, and in her mind, she began to connect the dots. Aldorian had been the one at the Twisted Stool, confronting Felik with some gods-be-damned task to steal the King's Jewel. Kh'ar robbers had been about both nights. By chance? *No one is that unlucky*, Aellia thought as she hid herself in the shadows of an alley, listening to the conversation. The only question that remained in her mind was of little consequence – was Aldorian a Kh'ar or were they manipulating him as well?

Aellia turned from the scene of destruction, pulling her hood over her head so as to hide her face. The last thing she needed was one of Phaedra's girls, or the mistress herself, to notice her. Once clear from the sounds of interrogation, she gripped the silver scepter from her belt and soared into the air, blasting gusts of wind through the cramped and dirty street.

***

Aldorian sat in a dark room, hands and feet bound, his mouth gagged. The side of his head screamed in pain where something hard had struck him directly in his temple. He could tell a nasty welp had formed, probably bluish-purple and bleeding. He itched to massage the wound but could not due to the cords that held his hands behind his back.

"Remus?" Aldorian tried to call out over the gag that choked him. "Tiberius?"

The words were little more than a mumble. He leaned his head back against the wall and drifted back into unconsciousness.

Despite the consuming darkness, when Aldorian awoke the second time, his sight was far more focused. He could see the white walls, gilded with gold leafing. He could make out red flooring with black marbling. He could even see pictures hanging on those white walls, pictures that depicted his own facade. A rush of terror roused the rest of Aldorian's senses. He realized the gag had been removed from his mouth.

305

"What in the name of the gods?" he shouted lucidly, anger beginning to boil in his veins.

"You recognize this place?" The musing voice came from the shadows.

"Do you know who in Halfak's gates I am?" Aldorian barked. "I'll have you gutted for this! Do you hear me? I will –"

Something hard struck him across his cheek, causing stars to swim in his vision. Pain seared at his flesh where the strike had landed, though no visible source of the affliction could be seen.

"You pitiful, weak, useless little man," the voice from the shadows sneered. "You have no power here."

"Damn you!" Aldorian screamed. "This is my home. I am the master here!"

"You are a worthless bastard. Not even worth the coppers you throw at whores."

"What?" Aldorian's voice nearly cracked in rage, his entire face reddened nearly to bursting. "I'll f-"

A blast of air struck his gut, knocking the wind from his lungs and driving the breath from his body. Aldorian doubled over, gasping and coughing violently. His bound hands kept him from catching himself, and his fat face smacked into the red flooring with a grotesque mixture of bones crunching and skin splatting.

Cold laughter, without mirth, filled the dark room.

***

Aellia hurried down a dark alleyway, a long dagger in one hand and the silver scepter in the other. A faint blue light emanated from the gemstone, casting a foreboding glow on the rain-slicked stones. Shops were closed, iron bars pulled down over windows and heavy wooden doors sealed tight. Aellia rarely ever came into Darhdall Alley, knowing that this particular part of Southend was not a safe place for even one as deadly as she. A feeling of darkness hung over the buildings. Not that of the lack of light, but that of the lack of hope. Buildings were reconstructed, though the old bones were still there, their doors and windows covered with iron and steel. Granite gargoyles sat on several of the roofs and eaves, staring ferociously at those who walked below. Sharp-edged, wrought iron fences surrounded several of the homes and shops.

Aellia moved quietly until she finally found what she was looking for. Down the street, standing two by two, four men stood talking. They wore masks that covered the lower portion of their face, from their nose to the bottom of their jaws. A symbol was raised in the leather masks: a crown wreathed in flame. These men were beefy men, with broad shoulders and arms that looked like they were forged from steel. Cudgels hung from wide, black belts and the toes of their boots were capped with thick iron plates.

"Gallea's breath!" Aellia swore to herself as she looked at the mountainous men.

"*Language, Aellia!*" Aellia jumped, forgetting that she now had another voice loitering in the back of her mind. "*Do not speak of the Godmother in that way!*"

"You have got to be shitting me," Aellia scoffed. "You are going to have to get over that real quick."

"*Get over what?*"

"They're just words. Words don't hurt people."

"*Was it not words that bound us together?*"

Aellia didn't answer. She just rolled her eyes as she plotted how she could possibly take out four men without getting her own neck snapped. They were just words.

"*You are not focusing on the right things, Aellia. If you would just listen, we could get you trained so that you needn't risk yourself with such petty things.*"

That was it. That was the straw that broke the camel's back. The final shove that pushed Aellia over the edge.

"Petty?" Aellia screamed out loud, taking no thought of the four men that stood just down the street.

"*You are being childish!*"

Aellia did not hear the men shout, nor did she care. "You need to understand one thing and understand it well. I am in charge. This is *my* body, my mind, my decision! I'll go where I want, say what I want, and do what I want. And if I choose to raze this entire city in search of Tomo, so help the gods who stand in my way. I'll rip their heads off as well!"

It was the first time she had said Tomo's name out loud since she had awoken with Iaenora in her mind. The name left a taste of metallic guilt on her tongue. She hadn't found her yet, and she hated herself for fear that maybe she was dead. No. She couldn't be.

"*You are a child.*" Iaenora sounded exasperated. "*You do not care for anything but yourself and your own feelings.*"

"What is that supposed to mean?" Aellia snarled.

Heavy footfalls were rapidly approaching. Just seconds away.

"*Strike.*"

Aellia threw a punch in that very moment that Iaenora spoke. Her vision seemed to swim as she did so. She saw the world in two separate shades. One in colors and forms, the other...ebbs and flows of energy. Her hand met flesh as bones crunched. A thunderous crack filled the air, snapping Aellia back to reality, and only the world she had always known remained.

The leather-masked man she had punched soared through the air and then crashed into a fence. Blood oozed not only from the fist-sized puncture in his chest, but also from where two iron barbs protruded from his gut.

Three very wide-eyed men in leather masks stared at a very shocked Aellia.

And then they ran away.

"Are you trying to get yourself killed?" Iaenora seemed to scream.

"What was that?" Aellia said as she held her fist in front of her eyes. Still clenched around the sinuous scepter, her shaking hand was covered in the blood of the masked man she had launched through the air. "What did you do to me?"

"You want a fight? Fine! But I have waited countless years to find a host. I will not have you kill yourself. Especially not in facing such weak opponents as these."

"I think I fractured his sternum and spine," Aellia said, horrified. "I felt everything inside him break."

"You've killed before."

"Not like that."

"The others are getting away."

"You didn't answer me," Aellia countered, eyes now on the fleeing men. Strangely, they seemed to be moving in slow-motion.

"Your brain sees things so much faster than you can perceive. When we are connected, you can make out more of your surroundings, understand more complexities, and comprehend more than you can possibly know."

"I mean, what was that I saw?"

"Oh, you saw that too. Makes sense."

"For the love of Gallea's tits, just spit it out!"

"Language, Aellia! Learn respect in your words. This is most unbecoming."

"Tell me what that was!"

"I no longer exist in the Terral Realm. To put it simply, I died. But I secured my soul in the scepter, linking my essence to this plane. My cognitive self exists in the Aethereal Realm. This is what you glimpsed."

Aellia felt her heart miss a beat. Despite her usage of swearing, she had never really considered the Ellitheor to exist. She figured, just like mystical creatures and magical beings, that they were little more than children's tales. Figureheads used to control the masses into obedience. The fact that she was now linked with a being that didn't even exist in – what had she called it – this *realm*, made her feel dizzy.

"Aellia, focus! You are fast, but they are almost gone!"

Aellia snapped her eyes open as a rush of lucidity washed over her. The masked men were just turning down an abandoned side street, about twenty measures away. The few men and women who had been out had now vacated the area. Aellia, subconsciously, thrust a hand behind her. Her irises ignited with a brilliant blue as she bolted forward through the air. The force of the launch cracked the air, making a thunderclap that shattered the glass in the windows around her.

Her landing was not graceful. On the contrary, it was extremely messy. Aellia slammed into ground next to a lagging member of the men, sending him, along with chunks of cobblestone, crashing into the third story of one of the buildings, not to be seen again. The other two turned with dumbstruck expressions, and to their credit, reached for their cudgels, which were tied about their belts.

"Stop right there!" one of them commanded, though his voice lacked all authority. Somehow, his extremely muscular body looked frail now, like a giant glass vase that, if tipped over, would shatter.

When Aellia opened her mouth to speak, she could see tendrils of blue light leaking outwards. Though unsettling, she ignored it for now. "Where is Rahnaluz?" Aellia commanded. Her voice sounded distorted, as if it were not just her speaking, but two unique voices fused into one, an echoing, thunderous voice.

"Who?" the other whimpered, body shaking.

"By the gods, you're all pathetic!" Aellia snapped. She tried to clench her teeth, but the flows of blue light leaked out ceaselessly and her tongue was bitter with the metallic taste of energy.

"Do not kill them. You can't find answers without them!"

Aellia slapped away the cudgel of the lead man, breaking the head of the weapon, sending splinters of lacquered wood spraying into the man's face, chest, and outstretched arm. He screamed out in agony. But none of the splinters were lethal.

"Where is Rahnaluz?" Aellia bellowed.

When neither answered, she wrenched the busted cudgel from the bleeding hands of the Kh'ar Talker. Aellia, having grown up on the streets of Tur'Mor, was familiar with many different subgroups and gangs. That being said, none were more complex than the Kh'ar. She also knew that none were more devious, dangerous, and secretive. These snakes had infested the streets of this city for years, at least since the fall of the aristocracy. Maybe even longer. Unable to calm her nerves, Aellia did what she knew best and continued to inflict pain.

The man screamed as Aellia shoved the splintered shaft into the man's thigh. The other winced in shock and abhorrent disgust, frozen in place by fear. Aellia stifled a dark laugh as she looked at the two men pissing their pants in fear.

"I take it you two aren't used to being on the receiving end?"

"What in Halfak are you?" the bloodied one cried out.

Aellia struck him across the face, perhaps harder than she had meant to. She still was not used to this newfound strength. The strike sent him toppling over unconscious, though still breathing. She snorted in frustration and turned to the other. "Well, it's just you and me now."

He vomited.

It was one of the most repulsive things Aellia had ever witnessed. Bile spewed out the mouth grates and the sides of the mask. Tears began to stream down his eyes, just like the piss that ran down his pant leg. It was a disgusting scene. And a dark part of Aellia reveled in it. These were the men responsible for the death...no, the capture of Tomo, and she would make them pay. Every last one of them.

"Pull yourself together, you little bitch," Aellia scoffed as she looked up into the man's quivering eyes.

Shaking, the man pulled away the soiled mask from his face. Chunks of his last meal were pressed into his twisted mustache and black beard. He raised his other hand, dropping his weapon to the ground. "Please, I don't want to die."

"Well, then tell me where the man called Rahnaluz is," Aellia sneered, her voice barely above a whisper.

"I don't know," he whimpered. "You have to believe me."

"Then, you're worthless," Aellia muttered. Her voice was void of emotion now. It was worth a shot. She would just have to find someone...

"No!" he scrambled, pleadingly. "I know where his man is, called the Squire he is! Please don't kill me!"

"Squire?" Aellia looked back to the man, who was now kneeling on the ground, hands open in front of him, begging for his life. The word, well, she knew what it meant, but who used that kind of word?

"Yes, spirit! Please, just don't kill me."

"*Spirit?*" Iaenora laughed in the back of Aellia's mind. "*Well, he's not totally wrong.*"

Aellia swatted at the air, trying to drive the unwanted voice from her head. The kneeling Kh'ar looked confused, but only for a slight moment, reprising the facade of a terrified man. Well, perhaps it wasn't a facade.

"This Squire, who is he? How do I find him?" Aellia asked, refocusing on her prey.

"Last I heard, there was a big haul going down today," the man answered quickly, eyes filled with earnestness. "He'll be there, I'd bet."

"He'll be where?" Aellia was losing the minuscule bit of patience she had harbored for the sniveling thug. "Who is he? I need a name!"

"The regent's house," he answered. "The Squire will be there! I don't have a name. No one has a name! Not a real name amongst the Kh'ar!"

"The regent?" Aellia snapped. Her patience was now gone.

"Aldorian, ma'am! Aldorian was named Regent. Rahnaluz wasn't too thrilled, said the man Aldorian owes him for some deal. Sent the Squire to get the payment. That's all I know, I swear."

"I believe you."

Aellia struck the man in the forehead with a clenched fist. The punch was not nearly as hard as Aellia could have made it. But it shut the sniveling weasel up. And praise the Ellitheor for that.

"*Praise the Ellitheor?*" Iaenora mused in the back of Aellia's mind. "*Are you becoming religious, Aellia?*"

Aellia didn't answer, not out loud anyways. Truth be told, she had no idea. Two weeks ago, she didn't believe in anything, no higher power, no life after death. This was it. And that belief had fueled her hate towards the Uppers because they had ruined her life. They had taken her family from her. That would all have to wait now. She would have time for religion later. She would have time to sort out all of this later. Now, she needed to pay a visit to that fat bastard, Aldorian.

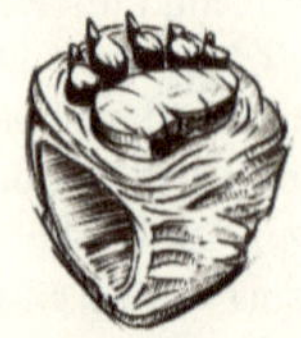

CHAPTER 30: THE DIJU

The sun was just beginning to break over the trees when Darius finally stopped walking. It had been hours since he and Izebal had left the hilltop, and both were feeling the strain of the arduous meandering. Darius had always prided himself in his sense of direction; however, this forest was so dense that he really couldn't make out where they were headed. Izebal had been utterly silent, only allowing a few sniffs and subtle sobs, and those had long since passed.

Unlike directions, Darius had never been good with women. When Darius looked back on the bleary-eyed woman, who had just lost her entire family, it hurt him, and he longed to be able to comfort her. However, he dared not say anything. He was a gruff, blunt warrior. He knew his strengths and talking through loss was not one of them. He had not even taken the time to unpack his own emotions. What he had witnessed in the encampment was nothing short of a horrible nightmare. He had spent his entire life facing soulless demons, evil witches, fell beasts, and blood-worshipping Morreans. None of those compared to the screaming faces of the people, now burned forever into his memory.

"We should rest," Darius finally said. As he spoke, he looked back on Izebal's tired face. Lines ran down her cheeks where tears and ash met. But, at the sound of his voice, her eyes seemed to brighten slightly.

In the light of day, Izebal's features were more clearly visible. She was curvy and tall, more so than any of the Ordiatian women Darius had seen. That being said, she had a strength to her frame and lean, hard muscles could be seen on her arms and through her tight britches. Her hair was refreshingly undyed and natural. Loose locks of inky black were pulled back from her face by a green bandana that wrapped around her forehead. She wore golden rings on her fingers and several hoops in her ears. The flowing sleeves of her dress revealed her shoulders and cinched tight at the wrist. Gloves of black leather, without the tips of the fingers, were stitched with vine-like patterns to match her green dress. The torso of the dress was formfitting, accentuating her curvaceous bust and hips. Izebal's hands were much larger than a typical Ordiatian woman's own, and they lacked the porcelain fragility that so many of the Uppers sought after.

Izebal found a large rock and sat, her right leg sticking out from the split front of her dress. Her black boots were laced up the side, weaving through several brass facets. Darius realized a strange imprinting on the boot that he hadn't seen the night before. A thorned rose wound up through the leather of the boot, starting at her slender heel and ending over her lean but muscular thigh.

Izebal caught Darius staring at her leg. "Perhaps you should rest your eyes," Izebal said coyly. "They seem to wander."

He had meant nothing by it; he was just intrigued by the patterns and make of her vibrant outfit. Everything was so bright and colorful. Unsure what else to say, Darius shook his head with embarrassment. A blistering wave of heat rushed over his face, and he stammered out, "I meant nothing by it, I promise."

Izebal laughed. It was the first real laugh he had heard from her. It was rich and loud. She followed her bout of laughter with a shake of her head, saying, "The pious devout have no fun."

Darius's eyes fell to the earth in shame.

"Ah, come now," Izebal said. "You will not be burning in Halfak for looking at a woman's leg, priest."

"I am not a priest," Darius mumbled, still unable to look up at her. He could feel the blood throbbing in his ears and reddening his face.

"Ah, even better." Her voice rang out, thick with her unique accent, which sounded more like a song than normal speech patterns.

"What do you mean?" Darius said as he cleared his throat, attempting to regain some of his composure.

"The Diju do not run into priests often, friend Darius," Izebal began, her voice seemed to craft words with an unnatural fluidity. "The Diju travel the woods, selling our tonics and fabrics to towns from lush Livithia to rural Cogadh. And at times, all the way up into the Blackwater Clans of Druid. The religious types do not take kindly to our peoples though. They say we drag their devotees down unrighteous paths of sin."

"I am only an emissary," Darius replied, slightly distracted by Izebal's liquid eyes and flowing words. "Just a messenger, that's all."

"I half believe you, you know." Izebal laughed. "Your eyes break your lies, Darius."

"My eyes?"

"People of Ordiatea don't like our type, you know." Izebal's smile faded somewhat as she spoke. Her eyes dropped to the ground where she found a long shoot of grass. She plucked the green blade, then waved her hand over it while speaking a single word, "*Ablaea.*"

A flash of light surged from the stone in her amulet. Her eyes, which had glowed softly with emerald light, burst into vibrant brightness. Wisps of energy began to flow around her hands, forming into runic symbols, ones which Darius did not recognize. The stalk of grass was consumed in an instant by arcane flame, leaving nothing but ash drifting slowly in the wind.

Darius jerked backwards, nearly falling over. His eyes widened, though not with fright, but astonishment. Darius had not had the best history with witches and dark fiends, that was certainly true. And the simple display reminded him that this was not just any young woman, lost and helpless, but a mysterious, powerful being, whose strength and limits he did not even have the slightest perception of.

"Don't be frightened," Izebal said confidently. Her eyes dimmed back to a normal green hue, no longer dancing with wild light. "We must watch out for our own kind, you and I."

"They said there were none left . . . That only the Blessed remained," Darius stammered, more to himself than Izebal.

"Blessed? Ha! More like the Cursed!" Izebal spat with a roll of her eyes. "If your Church had it their way, we would be no more. *Ulka'jika!* Stealing away young girls who are born with the Spark and forcing them into their cult!"

Darius glared at her with a steadiness that was perhaps sterner than he meant it to be. These people she was insulting had taken him in. They clothed, fed, and sheltered him. Offered him relief and solace during one of the worst experiences any man could ever imagine. And now, this woman was acting as if they were worse than the Fallen Ones themselves. True, they had their issues; hiding the truth about magic and the aftermath of the Fallen Ones wasn't necessarily ethical. But their belief systems were no reason to speak with such hostility, especially since it did not actually hurt anyone. It just kept the people of Ordiatea happy and unconcerned.

"Save that stare for someone who hasn't seen what your Church does," Izebal snapped at Darius. "I have seen first-hand the fruits of your religion."

"As have I," Darius responded in defiance to Izebal's claims. "They took me in as a stranger. They saved my life."

"Did they?" Izebal questioned sharply. "And are you free now? Do you walk these woods of your own accord?"

A quiet stalemate took place between them. Neither spoke, but their eyes stayed fixed upon the other. Studying, searching. Darius could tell, by the beat of her heart and the measure of her breaths, that Izebal was not lying. And yet, if both were being totally honest, how could that be? How could two individuals have such polarizing experiences with the same thing?

Darius, not wanting to extend the confrontation, as such things caused him too much discomfort, decided to break the silence. He drew a slight breath, softened his face, and simply stated, "I can't do what you do. Nor do I understand what you have experienced. I am different and will see things differently."

"But it does not change what I say," Izebal said firmly.

"Perhaps not," Darius replied, "but I try to see the good in people."

"That can get you killed, messenger boy," Izebal scoffed.

Darius sighed and shrugged his shoulders. He did not want to argue. He was hungry and tired, and he knew this conversation was going nowhere. *This is why I just keep quiet*, Darius thought as he turned away and opened his satchel. There was only one apple left, that and his flask, which was nearly drained.

"I am sorry."

Izebal's voice startled Darius. He turned to see her standing behind him. She hadn't made a sound as she drew close to him.

"You don't need to be," Darius replied with a half-hearted smile. "I did not mean to start anything."

"Men never do." Izebal raised an eyebrow, a smirk forming across her lips. She then quickly dropped her eyes to the ground.

Darius did not reply. He felt heat rising in his face and his palms began to sweat. He cleared his throat and went to stand. Izebal's eyes shot up from the ground and locked onto his. They were so clear, beyond beautiful. Her irises looked like things of art, patterns within patterns, swirling about endlessly. They held him in place, and he sat back down willingly, if only to look deeper into the emerald pools.

"You never answered me." Her words were firm, yet kind. "I would know whom I travel with, and what you are capable of. I could force it from you, you know? But I do not think this thing is necessary."

"What I do is not tied to the Church or their Blessed. It is older, far older," Darius replied, unsure as to why he was speaking. *Maybe she is forcing me? Some kind of charm or spell?*

"My kind." He breathed out a laugh as he spoke, driving the thought away. It seemed foolish. "Well, I am the last of my kind. Born before the days of the Church and the Great Desolation. I am a Feromage, a Guardian of Ethrea. The sword that strikes the hardest." His voice cracked just as he broke a twig between his fingers.

Izebal's face was filled with a soft understanding. There was empathy written in the wells of her emerald eyes, and kindness on rosy dark cheeks. She sighed as he spoke, a sigh that seemed to drift comfort to Darius. Her next response came after a long silence.

"I have never heard of Feromages, my friend. But I do know of sorrowful loss and of great hurt. For whatever fate has befallen you and your people, I mourn with you for them as I mourn for my own kindred dead."

"I speak of scars, while you have open wounds," Darius said as he shook his head. "You have borne hurt enough for one lifetime. Do not take my pain on with your own. That is my burden to bear."

"So stoic." Izebal chuckled mirthlessly.

"My duty is my own, as is my pain," Darius answered with a false resolve, though he could not bring his eyes to meet her own.

Izebal asked, "And what you do, the laying low of those who walk in darkness, do you find fulfillment in that?"

"It is not my place to seek fulfilment," Darius responded, the words of his own father filling his mind. "I have sworn oaths. Oaths that I must fulfill."

"So, not only stoic, but steadfast to a fault," Izebal mused as she looked at Darius in contemplation. Her eyes seemed to dance with a subtle mirth.

"Do you mock me?"

"I do no such thing," said Izebal. "I only speak what I see and seek to understand. Is it then duty that binds you to these woods? What are these oaths you speak of? I mean no insult, only to understand."

"The oaths..." Darius's voice was unsteady. He truly could not tell if Izebal was genuine or not. However, he saw no reason why he shouldn't tell her. He hadn't withheld from Elcon, so why not Izebal? "Each Feromage takes upon them three oaths. These are more than just words. They are a binding of soul, blood, and body to the will of the High Father. Through these oaths, we are granted certain abilities. It is in this that our fate is sealed, from the first to the last. I seek now only to fulfil my oaths."

"Sounds boring," Izebal replied with a smirk. But, upon seeing Darius's frown deepen, drew her own lips to a thin line and asked, "And how do you receive such will from a being who has no words with the children of men?"

Darius's mind flashed with visions and memories of radiance and thunder, lightning and endless woe. But he blocked those as swiftly as they had come to him. "The Oaths are passed down, from father to son, from generation to rising generation."

"So, these oaths are what take you through Ranok, messenger boy?" Her eyebrow lifted with intrigue as she prodded at Darius.

"I was asked by the High Patriarch to deliver a message to one of their own in Dane," Darius replied.

"And what does the message say?"

"I don't know," he lied, unwilling to share in the more intricate portions of his journey. That being said, there was a measure of relief in his voice due to the shift from his past and of the Oaths to something else. He rummaged through his back, producing the sealed envelope and said, "I was just asked to take this to the capital of Dane."

"It is a long and dangerous road through Daneland, Darius." Izebal's voice seemed troubled. "And the people who live there, they are not so kind to foreigners."

"I can manage," Darius answered nonchalantly.

"Oh, I don't doubt that." Izebal smirked. "You got a little of their fire in you yourself. Stubborn and unyielding, like a great bear!"

Darius's eyebrows furrowed.

"Just a messenger boy?" Izebal mused. "You think me a fool, and that I saw not what I saw, messenger boy?"

"And what is it you saw?" Darius replied slowly.

"I saw you," Izebal said as she stared into his eyes. "I saw your eyes that night, deep within the form of that bear. Do not think you can dissuade me from this."

Darius drew a breath, shaking his head in frustration. *Careless!* He cursed at himself. He had hoped to avoid delving further into this topic. "Listen, you cannot speak of this to anyone, ever. Under any circumstance."

"So, you do not deny it, then?"

"Would it matter if I did?"

"No." Izebal's smile returned, intoxicatingly warm and sweet.

"Each of the Three Oaths that are taken grant a different ability. These changed us from mere mortal men into something different," Darius began to explain, trying his best to keep his explanation simple. "What you saw at the camp stemmed from the Second Oath, the Oath of the Moon. It was from this Oath where our name, Feromage, is derived. It grants me the ability to Bind moonlight to my essence, shifting me from a man into a form designed to decimate beasts of darkness."

"So, you admit then" – her voice was somehow both condescending and playful – "that you were the bear?"

Izebal's sly remark did not go unnoticed. However, Darius just shrugged his shoulders and continued, "Few mortal men outside our tribes know of this ability. And none have moved in their Fero-form for over a thousand years."

"None of the Diju who Touch the Spark are able to do such things as that," Izebal added quickly upon noticing Darius's downturned lips and saddened eyes. "It is quite remarkable."

"I wouldn't think so," Darius said as he rubbed the silver ring on his finger. "There is more to it than just harnessing the moon's rays. It is a blood oath of sorts. A covenant. Two must form such an oath, and if either were to falter, that power would break, along with the ring of the bearer. Blood of Ellitheor sealed with blood of man, bound in the silver which I wear." Darius held up his hand as he spoke, thumbing the ring in a circle around his finger.

"So, your ring is your bond?" Izebal questioned in confusion.

"Yes and no. The ring was forged from the blood of my ancestors, mixed with the blood of the gods." He left out the fact that he was no longer sure if it was Ordan's or Fenron's blood. And honestly, he still did not seem to really care either way. "There were twelve made by those who had sworn the oaths. Never more. It was said that there could be less, as only a true descendent can bond with a ring and take the oaths."

"That seems strange, don't you think?" Izebal asked, seeming to be genuinely invested.

"What does?"

"That there should never be more. What if a bearer died before having child? Who would assume the ring? A cousin? Kin?"

"No one," Darius said. And he felt another, deep twinge in his soul. "Only a direct descendant can Bind, as his blood is already forged in the covenant."

"So..."

"So, if a Feromage were to die without offspring, their ring would lose its luster and the abilities that were crafted into it would be severed."

"Oh," Izebal muttered, sensing Darius's downcast demeanor, apparently putting together the pieces rather quickly.

"Once the oaths are broken, they cannot be reformed," Darius said, still looking at the ground where the broken stick had fallen.

"Just because something is broken does not make it useless," Izebal said, missing the point Darius was trying to convey. She did, however, notice that he was not comfortable continuing down that path of conversation, and thankfully, asked another question, "So, Darius, you said that the Second Oath allotted you the powers of skin walking. What do the First and Third Oaths lend?"

Darius sighed out a subtle laugh, realizing he was still looking down, and shook his head. He looked up, meeting Izebal's eyes and continued trying to explain, "The First Oath, the Oath of the Sun or the Oath of Enlightenment, is the beginning of the journey to Feromage, and it is not an oath that can be taken lightly."

"So, does one just recant words or is there a ritual? What does it feel like? What does it allow you to do?" Izebal pressed. She was leaning forward with wide eyes of intrigue.

Darius blinked at the barrage of questions. He had never been a talker, especially not with women he had met just the night before in a forest. And yet, something seemed to compel him forward, allowing him to open up completely for perhaps the first time in his life. He felt comfortable. Oddly so. Yet, as he looked into those beautiful green eyes, it was not a spell that compelled him, but her earnest intrigue.

Maybe it was the trees, the forest, the scents of nature and freedom he had not felt while in Tur'Mor. Perhaps it was the beauty of the woman who sat across from him. Or maybe, maybe he just needed someone to talk to who would just listen for once, not trying to piece together and draw conclusions. He had been on this journey for so long now, waking and searching every day. Seeking for truths in the shadows of the past and in the hidden places. Even now, he was running through Ranok, sent to deliver the words of a vision that he had witnessed first-hand to a man far away for reasons he could not totally understand. He felt the ebb and flow of purpose washing over him, the unceasing need to seek out and find some unknown thing.

All of this had consumed his mind, body and spirit for so long that now, in these trees, sitting with a woman who had lost just as much as he, that Darius could not help but open up and divulge parts of his past that he had never shared before. He was tired of always guarding, always defending. He was weary, and this was the boon his mind had sought. And so, he continued to speak, unable to hold back the floodwaters.

"A Feromage's oaths are taken with great sacredness and honor," Darius began, recalling words his own father had told him when he was just a young boy. And as he spoke, his mind was transported to that small mountain village where he had been raised.

The still air of Ranok seemed to open up to the crisp winds of the Iron Hills, memories rushing through Darius's mind as the wind rushed through the leaves of the trees around him. He could see his mother holding his baby brother, standing over the fire in the center of their home, smoke rising through the hole in the ceiling. He could smell the sweet scents of venison cooking and of tubers boiling with spices in the blackened iron pot. And he could see his father, sitting across from him, his axe-blade running methodically over a whetstone as he told Darius of the importance of his birthright.

"We are responsible for the peoples of this world, but we cannot do it alone. That was why the Ellitheor gave us the Oaths, so that we could stand against the torrents of darkness that rise and fall. The First Oath is that of the rising sun, and through it we are able to harness the powers of light and strength. When you are of age, you will begin the journey, my son. You will be tested, but you will prevail, for you have the blood of greatness in your veins. It is your duty to do so." Darius's father explained.

"How will I know where to go?" a young Darius asked with wide eyes.

"You will be led by the Spirit of the Land," his father answered. "Each of the Twelve has been led back to the Origin where the First Oath was sworn for the first time. It is a place of sacredness beyond all others. There you will find the Spirit of the Land, who will lead you through the journey, teaching you the Oaths, preparing you for the day you shall wear my ring, my father's ring, and his before him to the swearing of that same First Oath."

"When we, the Feromage, take this First Oath, we must do so in a place no mortal man can go on their own," Darius said, recalling the mysterious pool that he had stepped through, guided by a spirit not of this realm. "There, we swear on the blood of our ancestors to uphold the precepts of our forefathers, to live by the Oaths, and to be faithful to those who granted us strength. We marked, then and there, the symbol of our heritage seared into our flesh. Though, we do not seal the Oath until the ring of our father is passed on to us, which is how the Second Oath is sealed. We mark the ring with our own blood, swearing the First Oath again and the Second Oath for the first time. It is then that we are

transformed into true Feromage, Guardians of the Ellitheor, the fist that strikes the hardest." Darius clenched his fist as he finished, the cold, familiar feel of the unnaturally bright ring brought forward as a testament to his words. "And so it is until the last line breaks."

Darius stared at his hand. Izebal stared at Darius. Neither spoke, not for a very long time. Slowly, Darius lowered his fist, allowing his fingers to relax.

"That is incredible," Izebal said quietly. And she seemed almost upset to have broken the silence that had ensued.

"It is not nearly as incredible when it is your own life," Darius said with a shrug.

"Perhaps not," Izebal said in an upbeat tone. "But it is better to know you are meant for something than to wander about in uncertainty."

Darius glanced at her, brows furrowing slightly. Had she not heard him? Did she not understand? He had thought he had been clear. He was wandering, lost and unsure. He was supposed to be this great Guardian, a Feromage, that knew what he was and understood his purpose. But he didn't feel that way. His people were dead and gone. His life was a mess of confusion and misdirection. Truly, he wanted more than anything to feel the reassurance he had once known, over a thousand years ago. He wanted to know that he was on the right path, that he was doing something of great worth. But he didn't feel that way. He felt lost and alone.

"Your Second Oath allows you to become a bear, drawing upon the moon," Izebal contemplated out loud. "The First, then, must allow you something similar?"

Darius shook his head and cracked a weary smile, forcing away the dark thoughts that had begun to creep upon his mind. When he spoke, his voice was solid, firm and clear, despite the feelings of insecurity and anxiety he felt within. "Not really, no. You see, each oath allows us to face our enemies in the best way possible. Creatures of darkness and shadow can only be truly slain by Ellitheor's Silver. Sure, decapitation will cause them to mist away or falter, but only the holy silver can truly destroy them, burning away their essence completely, both from the Terral and Aethereal. When I am as a bear, my claws and teeth are mixed with the silver of my ring, allowing me to rend and tear away such beings. And those fiends cannot exist in the light of day, forced to flee to the shadows and dark places of the world."

"So, there are no abilities with the First Oath?" Izebal questioned. "I am confused."

"No, there are. It is just very different. The First Oath and the Second's given abilities are both created to make us as effective as possible against our enemies. While creatures of shadow and darkness can only be destroyed by Ellitheor's Silver, the other evils of the world need less specific means of destruction. The First Oath allows us to harness the power of the sun's rays, granting us great speed, heightened senses, and increased strength and healing capabilities."

"Like a Spark Dancer," Izebal said with an excitement in her eyes.

"A what?"

"Spark Dancers can touch the light of the Earthmother, and are in turn granted strength, speed and healing, just as your kind are," Izebal replied. "Though they must have some kind of sacred totem or crystal infused with her eternal light."

"Like the Blessed?" Darius asked.

"We are not the heathen Blessed, conscribed to the worship of men," Izebal scoffed. "The Spark Dancers and Lifesingers, what I am, are granted their abilities from the Earthmother, whose source is endless. They must travel to the sacred place of the Diju, Yhnzan'ahr, to refuel their crystals, so that the Earthmother can grant them more light."

"Storms and shadows lessen my abilities to draw on the sun's rays, but only the setting of the sun can cut me off from utilizing this," Darius stated. "The High Priest of the Church spoke of Touching the Source, but it is different for me. I Bind the power of the sun into my being. It is not a stone or orb that I draw upon. As long as there is sunlight, I have a well to draw upon. Though I must be careful, so I do not burn myself out."

"Odd. Our Spark Dancers can harness the Spark in gemstones, reserving the light to draw from their wells at will," Izebal stated as she thought. "Though I have never heard of them, how did you say, burn out?"

"Burning out," Darius began, feeling a bit of wary recollection from his explanation with Elcon. Both seemed so abashed at the idea. *Well, what did you expect to happen when you Bind the power of the sun to your very essence?* "Happens when you hold onto the sun's flows for an extended period of time. In simple words, it cooks you from the inside out."

"What?" Izebal yelped. Her shocked expression caused Darius to chuckle. When she continued to speak, her words were rushed and her melodic tone uneven. "Why would you ever do that? Surely it hurts, doesn't it?"

"Oh, it hurts," Darius said wistfully, leaning back as he spoke. "It also feels amazing. The longer one Binds the sun's flows, the more enhanced your senses become. You feel everything, and it is beautiful. It is easy to lose yourself in the limitless surge of power. It is more addictive than anything else I have ever encountered. It utterly consumes you, both physically and mentally."

"Doesn't seem worth the risk," Izebal said, shaking her head in apparent awe.

"What about you? You said you were a Lifesinger? What is that?" Darius asked, taking the opportunity to change the conversation from himself to Izebal. As oddly satisfying as it was to open up and share with someone, the awkward, concealed side of Darius was becoming weary of speaking.

"To understand those that are connected by the Earthmother's Lifeforce, you must understand the Diju as we truly are. Not the lies that are spread by those who fear, but to hear the songs we seek and listen to the Words we sing," Izebal began. She settled into a comfortable position, and then drew her leather satchel into her lap, a small, dark bag with a bone clasp and a rune of three twisting lines. Izebal withdrew an old book, bound in leather-wrapped wood. Thick letters were worked into the leather of the small book, delineated with a silvery dye. Under the letters was the same emblem that was tattooed on her neck. "This is Glhadaskae, Book of the Ancestors. This script contains many of the last known Words of the Earthmother."

"What do you mean by Words?" Darius asked as he looked at the ancient text.

"Others believe they live and die by actions and consequences, each made by your own accord and unconnected from anything else," Izebal started. "A Diju's life is a tapestry, woven by ten thousand threads and tens of thousands more. Every thread a Word, stitching together the reality we live in. My ancestors learned how the pattern was woven and committed it to song. This changed the way they saw the world, and with this change, a Spark was lit within their souls. They were called the Lifesingers. They could touch the realms on both sides, and commune with the very essence of life through the Words. This song was passed down from generations until it was lost and tattered." Izebal smiled a sad smile as she nearly sang the words, her voice enchanting and baroque.

"What happened to them?" Darius asked. "The Words, how did they lose them?"

"Same as any song that has ever been sung," Izebal said with a bow of her head. "Some found ways to corrupt the Words, bending and twisting the songs of old. The Spark was taken from mankind. Now, only few are ever born with the Spark. And of those, even less know the Words of the Life Song."

"So, there are others like you?" Darius inquired, leaning in as he listened.

"Like me, no." Izebal sighed. "No, I am alone in this. There are those who are the Spark Dancers, my near kin. They are those who draw upon the Earthmother's Lifeforce, perform great acts of strength and stamina – they are the warriors of our people. Then there are the Earthshakers. They can push and pull on the earth, moving stone, soil, and living vines and trees. The Earthmother entrusted in them her most sacred of duties, that of preserving nature itself."

"That is incredible."

"In the days before iron and steel, when the land was free from the taint of industry, the Diju walked Ethrea freely, sharing in the goodness of the Earthmother. We sang the great songs, shared in the richness of her Lifeforce, and we were one with all the realms. We cultivated the grassy fields, we nurtured the flowing waters, we tended the beast valleys and the fowl of the air, and we strengthened the deepening roots of the great forests. Those were days of great joy and happiness. Days when we were seen not as devilish fends that lurk in the trees, but as guardians of nature and a people of peace and life," Izebal sang mournfully. "Now, we are persecuted and hunted, threatened for merely existing."

"Izebal, I am so sorry," Darius stammered. He felt guilt wash over him as he stared into her tear-reddened, glassy eyes.

"Ah, Darius, you are too sweet, but you cannot blame yourself for the plight of my people," Izebal said with a weak smile. "You saw only a normalcy. It was not your fault what happened that night."

Izebal's words did not bring comfort, but twisted the knife of guilt even further in. The feelings of shame and anguish were nearly unbearable. He had been the one who had brought those Huntsmen into Ranok. They had been searching for him. Had he not fled, they would not have found the Diju camp. Had he kept his abilities concealed, they would not have been sent after him. Had he just listened to Elcon, focused on his research into the words of his vision, not gallivanting about each night and fueling his desire to fight for others, maybe he would not have gone after the robbers in the street. Maybe Ranun would not have died.

"Darius, are you okay?" Izebal's words broke through the consuming feelings of despair and guilt. And when Darius looked up, everything was blurry and out of focus. The episode had come on so fast, he hadn't had time to steady himself. "You are shaking, Darius. What is the matter?"

"It's nothing," Darius grunted, steadying himself where he sat. His thumb coursed over his ring and his breathing slowed to rhythmic inhalations and exhales.

"It is not nothing," Izebal said tenderly. "Something is wrong. What is it?"

Darius's mind raced, unsteady and unfocused. Thoughts pounded at his psyche, racking his brain with overbearing torrents of emotions and questions. *How can I tell her? Does it matter? If I leave now, it would be better for her. Those Huntsmen are after me, not her. Besides, she said she has family in the north. The Diju, they can protect her. But how far is that? Don't be foolish. Asking a lone woman to wander alone for leagues in forests filled with wild beasts and Huntsmen? It doesn't matter how powerful she is, what she can do...*

Darius went to open his mouth, to utter some semblance of an answer. But when he did, a familiar chill crawled up his spine. His pupils dilated and his stomach lurched. He tried to stand, but all his crumpling body could do was let out a strained gasp for air.

Thunder rolled over ink-black sky. It was night now, though the stars were not in their correct places. A bone-rattling lightning strike illuminated the sky, the great crash forming what appeared to be a face, if only for a brief second.

Vapors of smoke rose from Darius's translucent flesh once again. And he heard the endless voice bellow out the familiar refrain:

Find them!

Find them!

Find them, or blood shall rain!

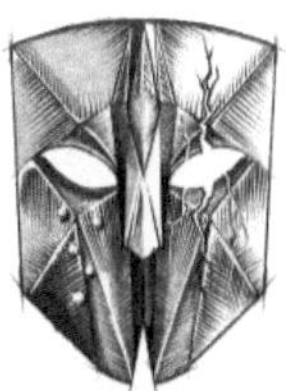

CHAPTER 31: DEMONS AND SHADOWS

The man called Rahnaluz sat in a wingback chair. He curled his lip in disgust at the chair's arms, which were worn, the threads turning white where heavy arms had slumped on them day after day. There were small stains on the fabric as well. Wine. But he did not dare to move. His hands were locked in his lap, ringed fingers intertwined. His face was slick with sweat beneath his fanged mask of red and blue with intricate carvings that were inlaid with gold. The mask gave Rahnaluz the appearance of an ancient demon. However, he did not think demons ever feared for their lives the way he did this night. Salty sweat stung the cut that lined his neck, seeping under the high collar of his shirt and through the white bandage he had tied about the unhealable wound.

"You're nervous," the shaggy-haired man that sat across from Rahnaluz scoffed. He had an odd voice, his accent broken and uncommon. His outfit was as strange as his voice, though it was his mismatched eyes that caused Rahnaluz the most disconcertion. Those, or the cruel dagger that he held. The man apparently had noticed Rahnaluz's uneasy stare. "You like my knife? It is quite precious to me, her properties particularly unique."

"What do you mean?" the man called Rahnaluz asked, trying his best to mask the fear in his voice.

"You see, there are strange beings in this world, twisted, wicked, evil things they are," he said, leaning back and crossing his high leather boots over the knee of his dark green pants. "This is crafted of a silver that fell from the heavens, immersed in extraterrestrial illumination. See how it catches the light?" he asked as he turned the blade. The flames from the large, open-faced fireplace danced off the glimmering blade. It was actually mesmerizing, beautiful really.

"Very nice," Rahnaluz stated obtrusively. "I too have a sharp knife." He drew his wavy-bladed dagger from its golden sheath. The pattern-welded steel boasted a beautiful pattern, and the flame-like curves in the dagger were a work of expert craftsmanship. "You do not scare me with your bewitched blade."

"Bewitched?" the man responded, laughing mirthlessly. "No, not bewitched. Invested!"

The strange-haired man pointed to the two bodies that lay face down on the floor with the tip of his glistening dagger. The young women's backs both bore a single penetration, directly into their spine. Crusted, red blood soiled their fine dresses and stained the tips of the white hair on their head. The mark of one who had survived the White Fever that had ravaged the city years ago. Their frames were slight, their build petite.

"My blade isn't something that merely cuts and kills. No, it is the final destination for those whose blood is tainted with the curse to draw upon the Eternal Lights."

"Eh," Rahnaluz scoffed. But he could not totally suppress the gulp he took afterwards, staring at the lifeless bodies on the floor, feeling the waves of dread washing over him, battering him like a ship lost in a stormy sea.

"Come now, little man. No need to be rude, I am not here for you." The laugh that ensued was more horrific than the bodies and the blood, colder than ice and sharper than steel.

The firelight wavered, warping unnaturally in sporadic directions. Sparks popped and flames jutted onto the floor, though they did not singe or burn. Through the distorted air stepped out a man whose face was shrouded by waves of what could only be described as heat.

The man called Rahnaluz stood swiftly from his chair and then fell immediately to his knees, proffering himself in a subservient bow to his master. His dagger clanged awkwardly to the ground in his hasty rise, though Edous took no notice of it.

"Rise, Khall'ah Kh'ar," Edous commanded, extending a deathly white hand. A ring sat on the hand, the stone of which was cut onyx, wrapped by two iron serpents whose mouths bit into the sides of the gemstone.

"My lord!" Rahnaluz proffered, kissing the stone. It was as hot as the flames, and he winced as the rock seared his lips.

"I see you are not dead yet," Edous scoffed, looking at the wrapping that poked out under Rahnaluz's stiff, white collar. His left hand rested on the jewel-encrusted pommel of the sword that had left the wound on the man's neck. "It must truly bring agony by now. Tell me, Khall'ah Kh'ar, how deep?"

"My...my, mu-" Rahnaluz muttered.

This was the most humiliating thing that had ever happened to him. He had spent his entire life striving for greatness, reaching for power. And in every endeavor, he had failed. Even in this, he was failing. All he had to do was get that stupid rod from his brother's house, and that little white-haired bitch took it. All he needed was that to rise out of the shadow of his oh-so-pious and younger brother, Xander. It was his birthright to rule, to lead men, not lick the boots of these freaks.

All had gone so well. He had done everything right. Placed the right people in all the right places, taken over the Kh'ar, a useless bunch of wannabes with tainted bloodlines. He had bought the court, owning their allegiance. He had even secured Aldorian's loyalty, one who knew the underground, so that he could keep eyes in all directions. And it was ruined.

Alec Adelmo, Eldest of House Adelmo, was a direct descendant of the Tur House. His own cousin sat upon the highest throne in all the land, the Rising Star, Lord of Nations. His brother was the Mayor of Tur'Mor, the grandest city in Ordiatea. He had been promised all of these, command of the nations if he were to deliver but one, single, simple thing. Years of planning, the distraction of the King's Jewel, all of the countless hours, ruined in one singular moment. Humiliation and dread were all that he could feel. It was all that he was.

"That bad?" Edous laughed hollowly, and then turned to face the other man in the room.

He had not risen from his chair or proffered himself upon the floor. As a matter of fact, he looked even more relaxed than before, his golden-specked eyebrows rising in an emotion that could only be described as amusement. This baffled Rahnaluz. *Who is this man that smirks at a god? Or a demon, to be more accurate, for no god would subject anyone to the pain that this deepening cut brought.*

"Betrugyn," Edous leered. "I see you have performed your duties well." His eyes drifted to the young women who lay face down on the floor.

"These are not her," Betrugyn answered with a shake of his head. Not a motion of horrid realization that he had murdered two innocent women, but of utter indifference for the loss of life.

Edous stepped up to one of them, placing his boot into her side and flipping the lifeless body over. Her eyes were burned out of her head; only orbs of cracked ash remained. They looked like magma had solidified where eyes had once been. It was the single most disturbing thing Rahnaluz had ever seen. And he had just seen a man walk into a room through flames from the gods know where and he bore a cut that steadily grew in length and depth, eating away at his neck.

"So, they could Touch?" Edous asked, seeming surprised.

"I have no reason to kill otherwise, as commanded," Betrugyn answered lazily. "That's why you had me come, was it not?"

"Bah! You are as useless as that man." Edous's insult dripped with disdain.

Betrugyn twisted his knife outward, as if making to thrust it into Edous's face from his seated position. It was a fast motion, ultimately pointless however, as his target was much too far away from the tip. A sharp clash made Rahnaluz jump, a sound that was like thousands of panes of glass shattered simultaneously rippling through the still air. There was no possible way that Edous could have drawn his blade in the time it had taken the other to thrust his own. But there Edous stood, stance perfect, arm true, with rapier in hand, blade crossing Betrugyn's. Tendrils of black mist undulated from where the two blades crossed. The steel seemed to scream out in anguish, continuing the torrent of glass-shattering, until Betrugyn pulled his dagger back.

"You would do well to remember your place, Cogadh half-souled swine!" Edous spat. And for a brief moment, Rahnaluz thought he could just make out the pale face of a beardless man with red spheres for eyes behind the veil of haze.

Betrugyn rose angrily, driving his dagger into its sheath in a fluid motion. The steel sung as it slid, until it was silenced with a subtle clack of steel against the polished throat, engraved with a hawk that matched the pendant on his cloak.

The two men faced each other, neither uttering a word. One, a demon who could walk through flames and kill with a simple scratch. The other, a shadow, a silent killer who had fetched Rahnaluz from his bed, ignoring countless guards and soldiers who had been set to watch over him. The feelings of dread thickened, and the consuming thought that he was powerless to protect himself nearly drove Alec mad before Edous finally broke the terrible silence.

"So, they awaken?"

"It appears so," Betrugyn returned spitefully.

"Then, you have failed."

"Seventy-three."

"What?"

"Seventy-three," Betrugyn spat. "Besides these two. I have killed seventy-three who have been born with the curse. I have sought out every single birthed daughter who could have spoken the oaths required. Every one of them has fallen to my blade. The fact that one esca-"

"I do not require your excuses," Edous said with a finality, slamming his own sword into its scabbard. "You were tasked with a simple thing. Slay those who could speak. That is all. In this, you have failed. Killing these Ordiatian witches does not mitigate that."

Rahnaluz's mind spun. He was trying his best to piece everything together, but he was coming up short on answers. He had known that that scepter had been important for some reason, before Edous had come to him. When he had learned of the abilities that could be derived from the strange rod, he lusted after the power with uncontrolled desire. He had plotted for years, making plans and movements, aligning everything so that he could command. The war with Calun, sparked by the rage and deceit he had fueled amongst the Kh'ar and the aristocrats who had felt distinguished by the more democratic direction the nation was headed.

The steady placing of loyal Kh'ar amongst his own brother's council, poisoning his decisions and eroding his vision.

Alec had thought his brother's insufferable goodness and his love of the people were going to be the greatest hurdles to overcome. When Edous had come to him, promising him godhood in exchange for the scepter, his scope had changed from the hope of leading a nation to the tantalizing lure of ultimate power and immortality. But now, he just wanted to make it through this day alive. To escape and hide where none of these, these *creatures* could find him. They were nightmares, capable of doing inhuman things. Impossible things.

"Khall'ah Kh'ar," Edous barked, causing Rahnaluz to crane his neck upwards to stare into the abyss that should be a face. "It is in your best interest that the girl come."

"She will, my lord! I know she will!" Rahnaluz replied. "She'll come. She will want the midcouncillor. She believes it was his fault, she has to. You see, he knew them, well, their leader anyways, he was always talking about-"

"Stop your incessant prattling, it is beneath me," Edous stated. "She will come, and we will sever the Oathrod from her or you will die, your usefulness extinguished."

Rahnaluz swallowed hard.

"Let us go then," Edous mused, waving a hand to Betrugyn and Rahnaluz. "I would meet this Aldorian. He seems to be quite the character. We shall see how he fares against my blade."

CHAPTER 32: THE SQUIRE

Aellia found her way into the house of the one known as the Khall'ah Kh'ar. Like most of the houses of high nobility, the outside was of ancient design, the doors, windows, and eaves modernized with steel and painted wood. Mosaic paths and a marble fountain made up the inner courtyard of the Khall'ah Kh'ar's estate, and the interior was floored in fine woods from exotic forests. The magnificent mansion was located at the back of Darhdall Alley, and shops and other estates of lesser grandeur lined the cobblestone road, funneling towards the wrought-iron gates that guarded the towering building.

The lack of movement or sound caused Aellia's skin to crawl. There was an unnatural, foreboding feeling in the air that she could not seem to shake. Like a biting cold after a winter's rain once the warmth had vanished, and only grey, dreary skies remained. Surely the vacancy was due to the spread of the attack on the 'Talkers' of the Kh'ar. But even still, it was eerily quiet.

The front door had been unlocked and no lights lit the massive estate. Paintings of women, warriors, and hunts lined the walls. Immaculate floors were carpeted with exotic rugs hailing from the Tuawtian Nations, carried on camel's backs over burning sands and then by caravans over the Eduth Grasslands. Hundreds upon hundreds of swords, ranging from single-handed bronze sickle-like halfmoon blades to modern rapiers and backswords, with hilts as verified as the weapons. Halberds, war-hammers with a large spike known as Crow's Beaks, popularized amongst the elite of Un'Mor's savage vanguard, and other variations of polearms were held by suits of armor from days gone past, when knights wore gleaming armor from head to toe. Now, knights wore more practical armament and crisp, clean uniforms beneath.

The advent of gunpowder had changed many things, but Aellia knew a good sword, a well-placed knife or a powerful polearm was hard to be replaced. Guns were too slow and too loud for her liking. But as she walked past an array of over a dozen rifles, crossed over one another in an intricate pattern, she could not deny the feeling of dread. One day, her swift feet and coarse mouth might not be enough to escape such destructive power and range.

A sound alerted Aellia to the presence of another living body, thrashing her mind from the thoughts of conflict and firearms, refocusing her on self-preservation and anger. The noise came from up the double stairs at the front of the estate. It was a shuffling, nearly silent. But Aellia's senses were far keener than they had ever been before. She could swear that she could almost taste the other human that loitered in the house.

Aellia drew a dagger in one hand, the other gripped the scepter. Pulsating flows of heat surged through her veins, and the cracks in the silver vambraces shone with blue light. Had Aellia been more focused, she would have contemplated the oddity of the flows of energy. Why had they not done this outside? What caused the light? And why in the name of the forsaken gods did it burn her chest so badly?

Blue light shone from the scepter's stone, lighting the long hallways and vacant corridors of the Khall'ah Kh'ar's estate. Though, Aellia did not think she needed the light anymore. She could see the dust particles floating, she could see the thread in the rugs, she could make out every color in the tapestries and paintings, and she could see waves of heat, radiating from a body through the walls atop the stairs and to the right.

As the heat from the sun cleared away the mists of dawn, so did Aellia's presence burn away the shadows and darkness of the grandiose estate. Every step forward further eradicated the blackness that had been creeping behind walls and corners, festering like an ancient wound. The smell of salt and body odor clung to the air, far more potent than it should have been. Aellia could hear the unsteady heartbeat racing in the next room over as she topped the steps.

The person on the other side of the wall was crouching low. His stance, despite his pounding heartbeat, was steady. He did not flinch or move. Aellia's lips drew up into a wicked smile. She was happy to know that this one was ready, waiting to strike. She liked it. It had a familiar edge. She had spent her life slinking in the shadows, striking out against those who should have easily overcome her. But she had won. She always won. And now, she would gut this Squire, make him scream out the location of his master. Then, after he had fulfilled his purpose, she would dispose of him.

Aellia struck quickly, without hesitation. She kicked in the door, busting it from the hinges with legs surging with untapped power, spraying the inner room with chunks of red-lacquered wood. The squire, to his credit, who had hidden off to the side of the door, did not falter in the explosion of splinters and light.

He drew a blade. The soft ring of steel sliding from its sheath reverberated through the darkness. In her state of heightened senses, Aellia recalled that sound. It was specific, exact. A sound she had heard a thousand times, and a thousand times again, though had never truly noticed its exactness before.

Masked in a silver cover that hid his entire face, lined with jagged streaks of black, the squire rushed at Aellia, swinging the Di'kha with a red cloth-wrapped hilt and a golden hoop for a pommel. Aellia's stomach lurched as she saw the curved blade slice through the air, and she barely escaped its edge as it slashed out. It was Tomo's sword.

Aellia struck out in a frenzy of manic thrusts and slashes, using both the scepter and her dagger in perfectly synced motion. To the Squire's credit, and Aellia's burning frustration, the man handled the blade expertly, and sharp clangs and crashes of metal rang out in rapid succession. The Squire was lean of frame, tall and well-muscled, though his loose cloak and Kh'ar tunic hid that from eyesight. But Aellia knew, she could tell by the feel of each strike, every parry, feint, and counter-feint, firm and true.

He moved unlike any normal fighter, with a grace that did not speak of military training, but of urban warfare. Each strike was subtle but deadly. Clearly this man had trained with the Di'kha and against the knife. And as the fierce duel continued, a more horrifying realization came to Aellia's mind. Clearly this man had trained against *her*, for he knew every single move she was about to make before she did so.

A light-infused strike sent the squire sliding back, chipping the edge of the Zau'fi Di'kha. Instead of stepping forward, battering the man, Aellia lowered her weapons and studied the Kh'ar in the dim blue light. Tall, lean, well-equipped and able to fight.

The pieces of the puzzle slammed into place in her mind, and Aellia could not help but gasp out loud as the horrific truth manifested itself. "Tornak!" The name, like a curse, leapt from her lips.

The squire stood tall and pulled back the hood, revealing red-blonde hair. Next, he reached up and removed his silver mask. The scarred face that stared back at Aellia was not the kind, mild face she had known. His eyes were hard and focused, yet somehow vacant, devoid of the life and mirth they once held. Three brand marks caused his flesh to rise, red and flaking skin festered, and Aellia knew these were not old wounds.

"Why?" Aellia stammered as she stared in shock, rage, and sorrow.

"I did not want to die," Tornak answered simply. His voice was raspy, as if he had screamed for days without end. His eyes, dead as they were, did not falter though. They stared lifelessly into Aellia's.

"What do you mean?" Aellia snapped, rage beginning to swell within her breasts. "What do you mean, Tornak?"

"Tornak did die," he answered icily. "I am all that remains."

"You're not making any sense. None of this makes any sense!"

"Felik damned us all when he got in bed with Aldorian," Tornak spat. "I just chose my own form of damnation."

"By the gods," Aellia gasped. "You betrayed us! That night, in the mayor's house. It was you. We thought you died."

"I told you," Tornak answered bitterly. "I did die, in a way. It was, however, the only way that I could live."

"You sold us out to save your own skin!"

"I did what I had to," Tornak cut in bitterly. "Felik would have done the same. He did the same."

"What in Halfak is wrong with you?" Aellia roared. "Felik didn't betray us. You did!"

"He betrayed us when he chose to align with Aldorian, rather than admitting to us what he was. A traitor." Tornak's lip curled into a snarl, revealing chipped and missing teeth. "He chose our lives over his secrets. He chose pride over truth. I only sought a means to escape what everyone else seemed to believe was a viable plan. You were all blasted idiots with your heads shoved so far up his arse that you couldn't see the truth. I told you that we couldn't forge the right signatures, that we would be noticed. But he didn't listen. *He* never listened, to me, to you, to anyone. So, I found a way out."

"You call Felik a traitor," Aellia said, aghast and disbelieving of what she was hearing. "But you, not he, doomed us all to die."

"Well," Tornak said with a roll of his neck, which made a terrible cracking noise as bone and muscles ground against each other. "Apparently you didn't die, and you seem to have found what the Khall'ah Kh'ar was searching for." He eyed the scepter in Aellia's hand as he spoke. "He will forgive my shortcomings when I return it to him."

Aellia blinked. Utter shock washed over her a second time, as the words and realizations crashed into her again. Then, in a mad rush of steel, Tornak leapt forward, swinging the Di'kha with expert precision. Aellia jolted backwards, pulled by an Aethereal force.

"You are distracted."

Aellia tried to refocus her eyes, but something was causing her vision to blur. Tears. She was crying. Tornak had said that they had all died. But that couldn't be true. It could not be true. Aellia lurched to the side, hovering just above the red carpeted floor, the Di'kha of her lover barely missing her neck.

"Aellia, please! You cannot die."

Numb, Aellia seemed to be propelled by an external force, not of her own accord. She shifted left and right, each time only narrowly escaping the slashing edge of steel. Something inside Aellia broke. A dam of emotions, fears, and doubt came crashing down on her. She couldn't breathe. The room closed in around her as the shadow in green and black swung viciously at her.

I can't do it. I can't go on. The thoughts raced through her clouded mind, desperate and uncontrolled. She saw her brother, so young, so frail, lying in her arms. He was dead, and she couldn't save him. She saw her father, being beaten with clubs and hauled away in a black wagon with iron bars, only for saving his son. She saw her mother, body a wisp of translucent flesh and bony angles, looking down at her hands.

"Aellia, you must fight! I cannot do this on my own!"

Felik stood over a table strewn with papers as he had done dozens of times before. His mischievous smile lit the room. Belthazer and Felohme were arguing about dragons or gods or something.

Tomo was lying there next to her. Her curves and sweet scent, so warm, so inviting. Her back was to her, and Aellia ached to reach out and trace the line of her spine. She wanted to feel the warmth of her Mirano'ko, her lover, her friend.

"Aellia! PLEASE!"

Tomo was gone. Felik and the crew were gone. Her mother was gone. Her brother and father. Everyone, everything was gone. All that was left was the gaping pit of despair that ate away at her core. Blackness engulfed her.

And Aellia fell to her knees. There was just nothing left to fight for anymore.

*****

Tornak rushed forward, seizing the opportunity of Aellia's despair. However, to his dismay, her body dodged his cut. It moved like a puppet on a string. He rushed again, and the same happened. Aellia, whose face showed no sign of coherent thought or presence, was somehow being propelled through the air. He swore in rage, the scream burning his throat. Weeks of conditioning had left him little more than human, and the scars on the outside were nothing compared to those he bore within.

Manic rage twisted his face, contorting his scarred features into demonic lines. His dead eyes now burned with fury, fueled by the hatred he had for all things connected to Felik. He had trusted the bastard. He had looked up to him. By the false gods, he had envied him. He still envied him. He hated him. He hated Aellia. He hated them all for letting him go down this path of pain and Halfak.

Yet every strike was evaded. Every blow dodged. This caused the anger to boil inside Tornak, marring his ability to think and perceive. Hatred seethed from his body. His scarred flesh screamed for revenge. He had been the one to kill Felohme, the only member of the crew who had ever really listened to him. He had been forced to do it as a sign of loyalty. Belthazer was easier; the pompous Tuawtian had always looked down his crow's beak nose at him. And though he had not been the one to loose the arrow on Tomo, he had told the Kh'ar where she would go. Pointing her out to them from the top floor of the Asterivae, sealing his fate as the newest member of the Kh'ar.

The puppet body of Aellia suddenly crumpled to the floor in front of Tornak, as if the strings had been cut by invisible shears. She fell lifeless to her knees, and her fingers lost their hold on her weaponry. The sinuous rod made a sharp, glass-shattering noise as it struck the floor. Her dagger clacked twice, then fell silent. Her head was down, and her chest heaved. He never really understood what Felik or Tomo saw in the petite, flat-chested girl. Her white hair was a sign of sickness, and her blue eyes made her a freak.

A surge of emotions swelled within Tornak as he stepped forward. He placed the edge of the Di'kha under her bony chin. The girl's sunken cheeks were stained with mud, blood, and tears. Yet, as he raised the girl's head up to stare into her eyes as he dealt the killing blow, a blue light erupted from her chest, eyes, and hand.

***

"Aellia, can you hear me?"
Aellia was drifting somewhere. It was quiet. It was still and peaceful. Purple lights swam amongst the clouds, and radiant beams of warmth reached out and stroked her flesh.
"Aellia, please. You must get up. Please."
Looking down, Aellia realized that she knelt in a field of green grass, far more vibrant than anything she had ever seen. The sweet smell of air – fresh, clean air – wafted about her. She breathed in deeply. If this was what death was, then perhaps she had fought against it far too long.
"Aellia . . ." The voice had grown too distant, not even a whisper.
Mountains, jagged like the teeth of massive creatures, rose before her. Their spire-like formations of brown stone were capped with lush greenery. Aellia had never seen mountains like this before; they were strange and foreign to her. And yet, they were somehow familiar.
"Beautiful, aren't they?" Tomo sighed as she too stared at the rising peaks.
Aellia turned in shock and saw the face of her beloved. She could not form words, and bitter sadness lumped in the back of her throat. Tomo sat facing the rising landscape, her translucent flesh letting off a dim light that twisted and curled into the air like steam. Tomo's glass body was covered by a white robe-like gown with golden dragons curling about the hems. Her hair was long now, pulled back in a more traditional style.
"I always wanted to bring you here," Tomo said wistfully. "To see them, to show you the beauty, the raw majesty of the Yexhu Xar."
"T- Tomo?" Aellia sobbed. And she reached out a hand to touch her face.
Tomo smiled, a simple, warm smile. Aellia's fingers did not quite touch her radiant flesh. Golden light swirled about Aellia's outstretched hand, and a gentle pulse flowed through Aellia.
"I am here, now, Aellia," Tomo said, still looking to the peaks, the purple sky shimmering behind them. "I am at peace now."

335

"Tomo." Aellia fumbled the name.

"Do you come to me?" Tomo asked, not looking at Aellia.

Aellia dropped her hand into her lap; the warmth vanished from it. Her hands were stained and bloodied. Her clothes were tattered and frayed. She did not appear beautiful but was plucked out of reality, somehow transcending the realms. That lump that had formed in her throat felt like it would burst. She felt like she would burst open as thousands of emotions battered her from within.

"Mirano'ko?" And Tomo still did not look at her. "Are you there?"

This was all she had ever wanted. She had peace. She had Tomo and endless sunsets with her. She only had to stay. But Aellia was bloodied and soiled. She did not belong here. She did not belong in the warmth of this sunset. She did not belong with the innocent and the loved.

"Aellia . . ."

Tomo turned to face Aellia, and she gasped. Cracks like that of fractured glass spiderwebs dotted Tomo's translucent flesh. There was one over her left eye, one through her right breast, three through her stomach, and a final through her leg.

"What happened, Tomo?"

"What do you mean?" Tomo asked in a voice that was so soft, so sweet, that it caused Aellia's insides to wrench in agony.

"You are broken," Aellia said. "How?"

"I am not broken, Mirano'ko," Tomo said, turning back to face the mountain range. "I am at peace."

Deep feelings of guilt, shame and anger battered against Aellia's already broken walls. Tears formed yet again in her eyes, and she wept long, mournful sobs. Tomo said nothing. She just stared into the eternities, smiling peacefully into the purple sky.

"Aellia, I need you!"

"I have to go now," Aellia whispered.

"I know," Tomo answered.

"Will you wait for me?" Aellia asked, doing her best to build her resolve.

"I will always be waiting," Tomo said, and then quirked her lips into a slyer smile. "I am not the one who must go. I am here, for when you need to find me. Always."

"Tomo," Aellia said, choking on her words. "I never told you. I should have told you."

"Told me what, Mirano'ko?"

"Told you that I love you. I did love. I do love you." The words cut deeper than any wound Aellia had ever felt. They were the words she had feared to say for so long. They were also the end of this chance to be with the one she did love.

"I knew you did, Mirano'ko," Tomo said with a close of her crystal eyes. "I knew."

"I'll find you again," Aellia said. "I promise!"

"Do not search for me," Tomo said. "For I am found. Seek out those that are lost. Do not mourn for the fallen, for we are at peace. Search out the living, for they need you, Mirano'ko. Ethrea needs you, Aellia."

"What do you mean?"

"You know what I mean." Tomo laughed softly. "You are connected to us all now. We can feel you, and I will always be with you."

Tornak swung the Di'kha towards the bare neck of his former crew member.

The sinuous scepter shot from the floor towards Aellia's open hand, fitting perfectly into the scorched flesh where the Oath had taken hold on her.

The blade sung as it cut through the air.

Aellia's body ignited in a fury of blue light. A gale blasted outwardly from within Aellia, sending Tornak flying backwards just before the blade caught her neck. Squire slid across the floor while carpets, pictures, and tapestries were flung in all directions. The winds howled wildly as a vortex began to swirl about Aellia, casting stray items flying wildly about, including Tomo's Di'kha, which lodged itself into the wall.

"You killed her!" Aellia's voice was not her own, but a mixture of her own, Iaenora's, and roaring winds.

Tornak, having lost the Di'kha, pulled a curved dagger from his belt and gripped it in an underhand hold. Aellia stepped towards him, eyes crackling with torrents of blue lightning. She thrust her hand outwards, towards the blade. A rush of wind ripped it from the wall and sent it flipping, end over end, until it slammed into her outstretched hand, making a satisfying sound as cloth-wrapped hilt met flesh.

"What in Halfak's blazes are you?" Tornak bellowed over the raging winds.

"I am the Sage of times long past, of times come again, of prophecies fulfilled. Mourn now, mortal man, for today is the day of your reckoning."

"Like f-"

Aellia threw the blade, impaling Tornak through the gut and nailing him to the wall. He let out a grunt of pain, and blood began to pool from his mouth. The sword punctured the left side of his abdomen, severing many of his internal organs, but not quite killing him. Not yet.

"Where is Rahnaluz?" Aellia's thunderous voice was more terrible than the sight of her frenzied hair, flashing eyes, and light-leaking mouth.

"I'd die before telling you," Tornak snarled through the pain.

"You'd die for him, but not your friends?" Aellia scoffed, and then took the hilt of the blade and ripped it out of his side, tearing cloth, flesh, and wood from the wall behind him.

Tornak fell to the floor with a scream. Blood pooled on the jostled rug, soaking his extended hand and the fabric upon which he landed. Aellia stepped closer, placing the flat of the pattern-welded blade against Tornak's cheek.

"Where is Rahnaluz?"

"You bitc-"

With a flick of her wrist, Tornak's right ear was sheared from his head. Another cry of agony rang out. Aellia squatted, meeting his eyes with her own. His eyes quivered with pain, but his scar-laced face showed no signs of fear.

"Tell me where he is," Aellia commanded.

He spat blood at Aellia's face. The flurries of air swept it away, splattering it against the walls. She smirked, and then swung the blade into his left shoulder. The skin split and bones crunched as a fountain of red drenched his cloak.

"I will kill him, with or without you," Aellia snarled. "I will end your suffering if you tell me though."

"You're a burning witch, you are!" Tornak whispered through gritted teeth.

"Maybe," Aellia said, the winds beginning to die down and the light ebbing slowly into a low glow of soft blue. "But I promise, if you tell me, I will let this pain end."

"I just wanted to live," Tornak said. "I just wanted to live."

"You tell me where Rahnaluz is, and I'll let you walk," Aellia answered.

Tornak's hand, which had been pressed to his side, lifted slowly, so that it was directly between their faces. "I am dead."

"I can heal you," Aellia answered, somehow knowing that she could do that.

"What?" Tornak asked. "How? Why? Why would you?"

"I want the man who planned the deaths," Aellia answered placidly, lowering the sword to the ground and taking Tornak's hand. "I don't want his gutter rats. I want the head of the Kh'ar. I want him to suffer."

Gentle streams of light flowed from her body, starting in the vein-like cracks through her vambraces, pulsating forth from her hand and wreathing Tornak's own. Slowly, like the fall of fog, the light slid down his arm, taking the blood with it and focused on the gaping wound on his side. And then, in an instant, it sealed itself shut, leaving only a scar that looked like a branch of lightning.

Tornak gasped in a full breath of air, coughing and spluttering. The blood had left his mouth, and only spittle remained. His ear, however, still laid upon the ground, severed from his head, and blood stained the hair and flesh where the appendage had once been. Aellia touched the hole, and just like with the side wound, sealed it.

"Now," Aellia said as firmly as she could, having to take measured breaths due to the sudden exhaustion that assaulted her being. "Tell me where to find him."

"He..." Tornak said slowly, as if unsure how he was even speaking. "He is at the Aldorian estate. He is me-"

Tomo's Di'kha removed Tornak's head in a motion so fast that it caused the air to crackle, trailing streams of blue light. The spray of blood that issued forth from the severed neck soaked the green-black cloak anew. And Tornak, called the Squire, the traitor, fell motionless at Aellia's knees. The deed was done.

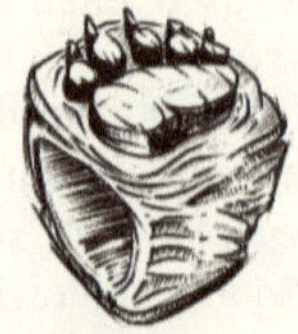

Chapter 33: Plight

Ranok Forest was old, very, very old. She was an ancient and mysterious place, filled with mythical creatures and arcane allure. For over the last hundred and fifty years, few men, of either Ordiatea or Daneland, had braved the winding path that cut through the primordial trees. And those who did traveled swift and spoke little of the foregone images they witnessed within. Most would say it was the great cats of the woods that they feared, or the Diju, with their strange practices, or the wolves and bears that lurked about. None dared to speak the truth – that there was a magic this place, a deep, dark, ancient magic that lay not so dormant beneath the leafy eaves of the forest. There was also a smell of earthy rot, an aroma of decay and death, that lingered heavy on the air. A darkness permeated the trees, dense and gnarled, blocking out the light of day and obstructing the soft glow of the stars and moon at night. However, there were also sounds of living things and swiftly running waters. Wild things grew here, and ancient things thrived. Powerful sensations, spectacles, and species, all found in this place a refuge from the steady march of time and industry that had begun to sweep across the land.

It was within these trees that Izebal had learned to speak the Words of the Diju. It was upon these hallowed, root-tangled and leaf-strewn forest floors, that Izebal had taken her first steps, cast her first spells and received her first runes. Powerful emotions flooded over Izebal as she gazed out into the deep, dark, green of Ranok.

Tears began to stream down her face and her hands trembled. Images of flames and death flashed through her mind. However, it was not these that caused her current disarray. Darius lay upon the earth, and though his body was now still, his chest still heaved up and down, struggling to capture breath.

He had fallen so swiftly, overtaken by some unknown force. She had tried to bring him to, chanting the Words of healing and revival, but to no avail. She had done all she had known how to, but nothing had worked. So, she sat there, watching over him, praying to Ethenealal, the Earthmother, that this stranger would not pass from the Song this day.

The tears and whimpering eventually subsided, and after a time, Izebal turned her thoughts upon the Diju who had fallen. It was not right to let them pass without prayer, and in their haste to flee from where other Huntsmen might strike, she had not offered up the Words of Passing.

Izebal's eyes were reddened, streaked and puffy. Her cheeks flushed and tear-stained. She pulled a rag from her pouch and wiped the dirt and ash from her face, cleansing herself for the ritual.

She burned the cloth with a Word, "*Ablaea!*" And while still kneeling, scooped up a handful of dirt. She looked over at Darius's motionless body as she rose, making sure he was still unconscious before continuing. It was not that she feared him or distrusted him, but these were sacred rites, not to be observed by outsiders.

"*Yinyuran, ryu onwae Valenaela,*" Izebal chanted while dropping the earth into the wind. As the dirt fell, it began to sparkle with emerald light, as did the rune markings on Izebal's neck, arms, and though hidden from sight, back, stomach, legs, and chest. The wind carried the dirt skyward, glistening trails of light wisping away into the eternities. The leaves on the trees chimed in the wind and a soft tinkling reverberated throughout the forest. Izebal, in perfect harmony with the winds and sounds, moved her body. The dance was subtle, though each motion exact and in form. Tendrils of green streamed upwards, reaching to the dark canopy above. And when she opened her mouth to sing, flows of tranquil green misted forth. "*Yinyuran, ryu onwae Valenaela. Duni'le muk'ora Lal Ethenealal.*" *Depart now, gone to Valenhalle. Rest well within the Heart of Ethenealal.*"

When the song ended, the Words spoken, the light dimmed from within Izebal. And as that light waned, a resilience began to form, a hardened shell around her heart. It was not that she had never faced death or pain before – she had. So much of it. But never in such a manner as this. Never had she been so bitter and angry at the hatred of mankind as now. Izebal knew the way of the Valean, the religion of the Diju, was not one of malice or revenge. But in this moment of grief and pain, that did not matter to Izebal, not anymore.

Izebal rubbed her hands together, gathering her senses and searching the dark trees with keen eyes. The forest was still. Deathly still. And this unnatural stillness sent something crawling beneath her skin. A sensation that she was being watched. A coldness had set within the trees, causing Izebal's breath to frost as she exhaled cautiously.

The forest darkened suddenly, as if the very sun had been doused. Izebal's heart stopped, though she held her poise. The amulet around her neck began to glow, and she drew in a deep breath through her nose, inhaling the emerald light. Her eyes brightened with streams of green energy that swirled within her irises. These flows were not the gentle, mist-like tendrils that had encompassed her before during her Ritual of Passing. No, these were bold streaks of lightning, arcing from amulet to flesh, and from flesh to her hastily drawn wand. Crackles of energy leapt about her, connecting randomly and sizzling wildly upon contact.

Rolling thunder sounded in the distance, terrible and long, both rhythmic and tempestuous. Hues of greys and blacks bellowed outward, as if the sky had wrenched its guts of all the darkness it could find. Gales blew suddenly through the forest, thrashing away branches and vines. Izebal raised her wand to the storm and shouted.

"*Derdralsul*!" Silver runes flashed around the tip of the outstretched wand, forming a barrier between Izebal and the storm.

Tendrils of blackness whipped around her, slamming against the silver shield of rune-formed light. Thousands of shadows rushed through the trees carried upon these black winds of fury. It was worse than any nightmare Izebal had ever dreamt. The trees leaned and grabbed at Izebal, as if possessed by the shadows, twisted and corrupt. And in the darkness, blood-red eyes peered through the shadows, far brighter than natural eyes should be. They burned as waves of heat, piercing and unblinking.

The color drained from Izebal's face and sweat beaded about her brow as she fought against the blackening current. A sickness gnawed at her gut as she pulled ever harder upon the Spark from within, forcing every bit of strength she had into the shield. Specs of flame leapt, and mists curled about as silvery light met raging blackness.

Then, as suddenly as it came, the tempest of shadow and blight vanished. The eyes blinked out and the mist vanished. But the destruction remained. Ash and char ravaged the ground around Izebal. The trees were scarred and broken, blasted in a straight line towards her, a path carved by an arcane darkness that haunted Izebal to the core. But it was gone, and she was alive.

Exhausted, Izebal lowered her wand. The silver light vanished from before her, the runes dissipating like fireflies into the night. Falling to her knees, Izebal let out a sigh of relief. This surge of relief, however, was short-lived as lucidity cleared her mind. *Darius!* Izebal's eyes widened with concern and her heart pounded. The air seemed to swim about her, just out of grasp. She had pulled too hard on the Spark and her strength was spent. But Darius, she had to make sure he was okay.

Turning about, she found him lying motionless upon the earth, her wedge-shaped shield having protected him from the onslaught of darkness that scorched through the forest. Leaning back and sliding the wand into its sheath on her thigh, Izebal let out a tired laugh.

"Men, they would sleep through the end times."

A bemoaning grunt from Darius caused Izebal to look back to the man prone on the forest floor. He had a hand to his head and a look of confusion in his eyes. And why wouldn't he? There was a scar of dearth that cut through the trees nearly thirty measures long. Black specks drifted from the sky and ash coated the snapped branches.

"So, the sleeping bear awakes."

***

342

A dull ringing was the first sensation Darius noticed, like distant bees buzzing aimlessly. When he tried to open his eyes, specks of black and white danced in his vision. The ringing grew louder, and he winced in pain as he tried to focus. Something smelled like singed flesh mixed with scorched wood and the bitter tinge of sulfur.

"What..." Darius stammered as he began to look around, the scene finally clearing before his bloodshot eyes. "What happened?"

"I would like to ask you the same, messenger boy!" Izebal said pointedly. "Do you often find yourself convulsing uncontrollably?"

Darius's face soured, his lips turning into a bitter frown. "Those... Well, those are something I am learning to deal with. Nothing to worry about."

"Nothing to worry about, Mai jianab?" Izebal swore in disbelief. "Do you not see this forest? Do you not see? And what good were you? My big, strong man, no? You lay there, snug as winter's night, you do! Bah! Men!"

"Glad to see you are feeling better," Darius grunted as sourly as his face looked. He reached for his satchel and pulled out his flask and drank deeply.

"Bah!" Izebal yelped. "What in the Yjup is that?"

"Stout," Darius muttered before placing the lid back on. It had taken him a long time to find a liquor hard enough in Tur'Mor to cut through his Binding abilities. The radiant heat within him had a nasty, unwanted habit of always burning the alcohol away before it ever set. But this stuff, it was nearly as strong as the gunruk juice his grandfather had brewed, fermenting for years on end before being drinkable.

"Gah! And it does not fog your mind?" Izebal asked in utter disbelief.

"Well" – Darius chuckled – "it's about the only thing on this blasted rock that can."

"But how?"

"How what?" Darius asked, feeling a little confused now.

"Alcohol – those who feel the Spark, well, it does harsh things to our minds," Izebal stated, as if Darius should know this intrinsically. "How can you stomach it?"

"Easy enough." Darius smirked before taking a long, deep dredge from the flask. He sighed as the hot liquor slid down his throat, and with a noticeably steadier hand, secured the lid.

"By the green and the skies, you are a strange man, Darius," Izebal said with a shake of her head. "Though, you did not answer my first question. What happened to you?"

"I don't want to talk about it," Darius answered gruffly while he shoved the drained flask into his bag.

"I would like to know, Darius, that the man whom I travel with is stable enough to make the journey," Izebal pressed gently.

"I am fine. What I would like to know, is what happened here?"

"Ah," Izebal said with a click of her tongue. "It does not look good."

"There is something wrong here," Darius said as he looked about the charred forest, having risen from the ground, his satchel over his shoulder and the enchanted stave in his hand.

"Obviously," Izebal snorted as she too rose from the forest floor.

Darius rolled his eyes and shook his head subtly at the Diju's remark. "More than this, this... well, whatever this is. There is something wrong in this forest. A darkness I felt the moment I stepped foot inside."

"Is that what caused you to faint?" Izebal asked.

"I didn't faint."

"It looked like fainting to me," Izebal said, nudging Darius in the arm.

Darius looked abashed. Red heat crawled up his neck and flushed his cheeks. The knuckles that grasped the hickory stick whitened. And his back went stiff.

"Well, if it was not a faint, then what was it?" Izebal asked, dropping all pretense of timidness.

"I –" Darius started, but then seemed to stumble over his words. "They are, well, not normal. I don't know what they are. I just... see things."

"What kind of things?"

"I can't explain. But I just, I think I am being directed to do something, find something. And I think it has something to do with what is in this forest. Whatever is causing this plight," Darius stated with a heavy voice, holding an open hand out towards the earth.

"But this only just happened," Izebal continued. "You said you had premonitions before?"

"Izebal," Darius said softly. "I don't think those Huntsmen were there by chance. I –" His words caught in his throat, his tongue twisting unnaturally, betraying him. He couldn't say it. He couldn't say he led them into the trees. So, he changed back to the darkness he had seen within their eyes. "Did you look at them? See their faces?"

Izebal did not answer, but her face was troubled.

"It was dark, I know, but did you see their eyes?" Darius asked. "Something was wrong with them. They weren't... normal."

"They are Huntsmen," Izebal said scornfully. "They kill for sport. Something is very wrong with them. But no, I did not look into their eyes. What was it you saw?"

"Izebal," Darius said, now looking directly at her with steely eyes. "There is something you need to know about me, something that will sound very strange."

"You can trust me, Darius," she answered, giving a reassuring nod of her head. "Whatever it is, I promise, as a Diju, I have heard stranger."

"I told you I am what is called Feromage, a Guardian," Darius began. "Well, I am not just a Feromage – I am the last son of the Feromage. I am the last to swear the oaths. I was cursed a thousand years ago by one called the Blood Queen of Morr, Mireya, who sent me into a state of oblivion, where I neither knew nor existed. When I awoke, I found myself a stranger in a strange place, in a world that had left me and my kind in the past, utterly forgotten. Since my awakening, I have been plagued with these visions. And when they hit, well, I guess I do just black out."

When Darius finished speaking, he realized that he was looking down at the ground, not meeting Izebal's eyes. She, on the other hand, was staring at him with a look of confusion and concern. Her deep, emerald eyes were focused, her breath held, as if she was hanging on to every word that fumbled clumsily out of his oafish mouth. Darius hated how he spoke; the grunts and halted words, the awkwardness of it all sent waves of embarrassment through his mind. Not to mention he had just shared more with this stranger than he had with anyone else alive.

A terrible realization that was, to know, to understand that you were utterly alone. He was unlike anyone else. Even the Diju, hunted and cursed as Izebal had made them out to be, still had roaming bands that wandered in the Northwood. The Blessed, secluded and mystified by years of propaganda and collusion, had their conclaves and sisterhoods. Knights and city guards, priests and monks, merchants and paupers, all of them had their place. But he, he was alone. Lost to time and out of touch with the world in which he wandered.

A doleful silence fell upon the wood, and neither Darius nor Izebal disturbed it for a long time. Both had suffered insurmountable grief. Both had seen horrible things. Things that would cause even the strongest to falter. Neither seemed to care that the other was somewhat broken, and though they had just met, Darius was beginning to feel a bond with this woman. Something beyond a physical attraction or a lust for more carnal pleasures. But a closeness, a connection that went deeper than flesh.

"By Ethenealal's bosom," Izebal stammered, finally breaking the hollow silence.

"I told you." Darius chuckled mirthlessly. "I'm not normal."

"Ah." Izebal's voice was regaining its melodic notes. "But who desires normalcy when one can obtain extraordinariness? You, Darius, are something that is beyond. And that is nothing to be ashamed of."

"Right," Darius answered. He then cleared his throat and more sternly asked, "Now, can you tell me what in the blazes of Halfak happened here?"

"This?" Izebal's lips quirked into an enchanting smile as she rolled a shoulder at the charred path of ash and destruction. "Tis not but what you saw in the eyes of those men. The Plight."

"The what?"

"Something has been wrong in these trees for a long time now, I think. We had begun to call it the Plight. Creatures turn into darkness, trees rot, and waters sour. It is a sickness caused not by nature. It is the work of Nkuaue."

"Who?"

"Nkuaue," Izebal said bitterly. "The Stone Man. Last son of Ethenealal. The bringer of Death. He who stands in opposition to the Earthmother. Father of the Hoards, Sire of Dragons, whose ancient flames ravaged the lands. He is a demon of shadow and flame, whose core is corrupt and whose face is a shroud of death."

"Sounds like a real piece of work," Darius scoffed.

"He was one of the Huyenyu'Vana, the children of Ethenealal. He was consumed by envy and lust and pulled upon the Unspoken Words for his dark powers."

"Sounds familiar," Darius grunted. "I was taught that my God was Ordan. That he crafted the world and all that is in it with the swing of his hammer. That my people, the Feromage, were called to protect by his own authority. I was also told that he sacrificed his own daughters to seal them away to save the world.

"When I awoke in Tur'Mor, I was treated to another tale, not so dissimilar to the one I was raised on. It was filled with many of the same names and trials and ended nearly as the other did. Blessed instead of Feromage. A light that could be harnessed only by the chosen ones.

"So, why not another story from another people? Why not another god, or goddess," Darius added with a shrug of his shoulders. "Another light, another darkness. Another evil and another fight. My whole life has been a fight. Demons, shadows, darkness. It's all the same. And me? I am just the tool sent to strike."

"Are you okay?" Izebal asked apprehensively.

"I am fine," Darius answered coldly, eyes hardening.

"You don't seem fine," Izebal returned, drawing closer and looking him directly in the eyes.

"This Nkuaue," Darius asked, turning his face from Izebal's studious gaze. "The Stone Man. Why would he strike here? Why now?"

Izebal tried to recapture Darius's eyes, but she failed to do so. Her answer stung with a hint of exasperation. "Who knows?"

Darius let out a sigh, and then, while pulling his mane of hair back with his hand, continued, "Listen. I am sorry I was blunt. I just..."

"I get it," Izebal snapped coolly. "You are a fighter. A big, strong man who just needs to bash something."

"That's not –" Darius began again but was cut off a second time.

"I don't know why Nkuaue is here, not now anyways," Izebal said, turning away from Darius to look over the ruin. "He is a creature of chaos and destruction. My people have long been collectors of hidden things. Maybe he feared us recovering the Words. Perhaps we were closer than we believed."

"Why would he care about your people finding these Words?" Darius asked softly, trying his best to regain some semblance of concern for anything. Trying his best to fight off the inner darkness, the feelings of anxiety and dread that crept along the back of his mind. Pulling him ever down into the abyss of doubt and guilt. Guilt for surviving when others died. Guilt for doubting what others had held as truths. Guilt for living when his people did not.

"The Diju were the sacred keepers, entrusted with the secrets of the eternities. The Words were given by Ethenealal to ensure the survival of her greatest creations, daughters and sons of her own heart. Living things that could think, perceive, and create. Immortality was what was lost, for it was the first Word."

"What do you mean? Humankind was never supposed to live forever."

"I mean, Darius, that the Diju were never supposed to be mortal. We are the children of the Heart of the Earth. Descendants of the Daulkaefar. The First Born of Ethenealal, the Immortal Ones."

"Wait a minute," Darius realized, taking Izebal by the shoulder and turning her about to face him. Not forcefully nor swiftly. His hand trembled as it rested on her soft skin, but his eyes locked hard onto hers. "Daulkaefar? *U'halkal y'nu Vanherran?*"

"*Y'nu Valenhalle,*" Izebal answered with a subtle smile, along with a corrective tone and wide eyes that spoke of the obvious surprise that streaked across her face. "You know of the First Ones?"

"Elcon called them angels," Darius answered. "Well, the Church called them that anyways. Our tribes, the Guardians, we knew them by their True Name, Daulkaefar. I didn't think anyone else was aware of their true nature, or at least, knew them by their True Name."

Izebal crooked her head to the side and placed a hand on Darius's. She removed his hand, gently but assuredly. "Names, Darius, true names are the Words we seek. So many are lost. So many are gone. And with that loss, their true nature is lost with them. *Diju,* descendant. *Daulkaefar,* the First Ones of Life. Feromage. *Fero,* of beasts or animals of nature. *Mage,* wielder or holder."

"Binder," Darius answered slowly. "It means Binder."

"Well, that makes sense." Izebal laughed subtly. "Though, Fero-hallahndar would be more appropriate. Though, admittedly, it does not flow as smoothly. Feromage has a nice ring to it."

"That's, fine. Just –" Darius stumbled as he tried to turn the conversation back to where it had been. "The Daulkaefar – they all left Ethrea. Sailed back to Vanherran with the departure of the Ellitheor."

"Seven remained," Izebal said nonchalantly, as if everyone should have known this. "Seven stayed behind to preserve the world and guide her peoples. And while time has changed their names, their purpose has remained the same. A purpose that Nkuaue cannot abide, for while there is light, darkness cannot stand."

"This Nkuaue sounds a lot like Mireya," Darius grumbled thoughtfully. "She was bent by Halfak's flames with the urge to kill and destroy, not for the sake of conquest, but for the sake of death alone. It fueled her, made her...stronger somehow."

"The Diju do not recall this Blood Queen," Izebal said. "Though she does sound rather horrid. Nkuaue, however, is a ceaseless evil, a cancer upon the land that corrupts all."

"And it is here?" Darius asked. "In the forest?"

"He is in all places and nowhere," Izebal said forebodingly.

"Well, I've killed unkillable atrocities before," Darius scoffed. "It's my purpose. Besides, I don't find it a coincidence that, in the very moment this plight strikes, I received my first vision in days. No. I am here for a reason. I have been propelled forwards for months, unknowing of what I should do. Seems like killing a demigod of death and shadow is what I was called back to do."

"And you draw this from my mention of the First Ones?" Izebal queried with uncertainty as she stared at Darius, confusion riddling her face.

"No," Darius answered flatly. "I draw it from a lifetime of the same. The Blood Queen and her priest, Diabhail, or Nkuaue and his shadow hoard. It's all the same. Another fight."

CHAPTER 34: WHAT LURKS BENEATH

By the time twilight cast her amber beams onto the treetops of Ranok, Darius and Izebal finally admitted to being utterly lost. Despite Darius's keen sense of direction and Izebal's intimate knowledge of the forest, the two had wandered hopelessly until their feet grew sore and their bodies weary. Izebal had insisted that she knew where she was going, but the longer they had ventured forward, the more concerned her face had grown and the less talkative she had become. Darius was far more thankful for the latter, as he was both mentally and physically exhausted from talking more than he had in his whole life combined.

"I do not understand," Izebal said, voice bitter and tired.

"I told you," Darius grunted. "Something's not right in these trees. I can feel it."

"*Ablaea*!"

A crackling fire burst into existence as a flash of green light emanated from the stone backdrop against which Izebal sat. Her pendant ebbed out slowly, and Izebal replaced her wand.

"Your magic," Darius asked as he squatted next to the gentle flame. "Is it stored in the stone at your neck or from your wand?"

"It comes from Yhnzan'ahr," Izebal answered with only the slightest hint of annoyance in her voice. "I told you, we store our light in crystals to be drawn upon later."

"So, why the Words?" Darius asked. "Why do you need to say the Words if you've harnessed the power already? The Blessed just 'do'."

"Your Blessed, messenger boy," Izebal leered, "are not able to do more than one blood-bound thing. Blessed can heal or can see. That is all. And only what they are born to do. I can draw upon the Spark and speak Words, command nature itself to do my bidding. Your petty Blessed can do no such thing."

"If they knew Words, could they?"

"Ha! They are like our Spark Dancers, though less skilled. Born with a singular purpose. How could they speak the Words of a deity they do not believe in?"

"So, only a Diju can speak the Words?"

"Right," Izebal said proudly, lifting her chin as if to dare Darius to disagree.

He did not. On the contrary, he chuckled softly and shook his head in amusement.

"You still find our ways silly, messenger boy, even after all I have said?" Izebal asked, turning a querying eye on him.

"Not silly," Darius answered honestly. He didn't, however, mention that in order for him to Turn, it required him to speak Words. Words that he, until meeting Izebal, did not realize anyone else besides his people knew of.

Darius let the conversation die as he folded his arms about themselves, huddling into the warmth of his heavy overcoat. Izebal looked to him as if she were about to speak again, but apparently thought otherwise. She rose and walked away from the flame, stating that she was going to look for something other than bruised apples to eat.

The fire inside Darius, fueled by the continual, pressing sensation to find whatever the gods-forsaken thing or person or whatever it was, was dying out. The fear that his whole life would amount to nothing more than death and violence replaced the drive to continue.

Ever since he had awoken, Darius had witnessed miracle after miracle. The invention of steel, of foundries and machinery. Steam-powered devices and mechanical systems that moved people, produce, water and other resources across vast distances or up towering heights with ease. Gunpowder and explosives, though he thought far less of these percussive inventions than others. Fashion changes and architectural wonders had met him. And yet, despite all the grandeur, the world had seemed hollow.

Darius looked into the trees, spying a green bird with plumes of purple feathers that bore resemblance of eyes staring back at him. A slow smile slid across his lips as he watched a second, far less colorful version of the bird land next to the other. Darius gazed at the two, nesting together, and let out a sigh of... Well, he didn't know what it was. He stared at them for a long time, studying their colorful feathers, their strange song, and peaceful resting.

Darius missed moments in nature like these. As a young boy, his father had taken him and his little brother into the woods numerous times. He had taught them to hunt and forage, to survive and to thrive in the wild. Darius's father had been, to many, the stoic leader, the powerful warrior, and the vigilant guardian. To him, the young boy, he had been his dad. A loving man, who, much like Darius, spoke more with actions than words. It was his little brother who had inherited their mother's gift of speaking. Darius recalled long nights in front of the fire as his sweet mother would sing along with her youngest son, whose tenor voice, even near infancy, was beautiful and strong.

Without his family, his tribe, his people, Darius felt empty. He knew deep down that he could not just give up, roll over and quit. Not when there was so much wrong in the world. And yet, it was just that very thought that caused him to shrink before it all. Despite all he had done, all he had witnessed, there was still evil. Despite all the death, the wars and conflict, there was still darkness in the world. People still chose corruption over compassion, vice over virtue. Tolerance and generosity had once been the currency of the realm. Decency the law and honesty the way. Or at least, that had been what his father had taught him. However, the world was not like that, not anymore. And perhaps it never truly was. That sickened him to the core.

A scream rang out through the trees, loud and shrill.

"Light blind it! Will this night get worse?" Darius yelled as he jumped up in apprehension and reached for the enchanted hickory stave.

"What was that?" Izebal asked from the darkness.

"Great gods on high!" Darius yelped as he grabbed at his chest, eyes wide. He had not heard nor smelled Izebal approaching; he had been far too lost in thought. "Where the blazes did you come from?" Darius asked, railing on Izebal manically.

"I went to find food," Izebal answered levelly, though a hint of frost nipped at her words.

"Well, what was that scream?" Darius fumbled. "Did you hear it too?"

"Obviously," Izebal answered dourly. "Why else would I have asked what it was?"

Had Darius looked embarrassed half a second ago, he looked doubly so now. His large shoulders, however, were squared to a harsh line and the hair on the nape of his neck stood alert. Despite his embarrassment, there was still that shrill cry to account for.

"It came from that way," Darius said, nodding off into the darkness, white-knuckled fingers clenched too tight around his rod to point with.

"What do you think it was?" Izebal asked as she tugged her wand free and loosed the clasp that stayed the golden hilt of her long dagger.

"It sounded like a child," Darius growled as he peered. The moonlight seemed to glance off the golden rings that formed his irises. And though he did not draw upon her beams, the moon provided ample light for his enhanced eyes to see far into the woods.

A wolf pup slunk between two trees, far from where Darius and Izebal had bedded down. It was small, and had it not been for a peculiarity, Darius was sure that not even his eyes could have picked out the pup. The wolf was glowing, ever so faintly, a dim silvery-blue light. And not only that, now that Darius could clearly see the animal, it seemed to him that the beast moved with a peculiar grace. Its tiny paws seemed to never quite touch the earth, and at times, the wolf pup moved through solid objects, like trees and rocks. Despite its seeming lack of adherence to the laws of nature, the pup did seem to be limping and bore an almost human look of concern upon its tender face.

"Do you see that?" Darius asked, doubting his own eyes for perhaps the first time ever.

"See what?" Izebal asked, straining her eyes in an unfruitful attempt to pierce the darkness.

"There is a wolf pup," Darius said as he gestured deep into the trees.

"Darius," Izebal mused. "There is nothing there."

When she turned to look at him, Darius nearly toppled over backwards. Unlike his gentle moonlit eyes, hers blazed with spiraling cords of emerald light. He did, however, manage to steady himself quite swiftly, and answered, "Out there. It must be some kind of apparition. I've only ever seen something like it one other time."

"What do you mean?" Izebal asked, lowering her voice to match his subtle tone.

"I don't have time to explain," Darius whispered hurriedly. "We need to go, now!"

"Wait, what? I'm confused."

"Doesn't matter. We need to hurry. That spirit looks hurt."

"Spirit? I thought you said wolf pup?" Izebal questioned in defiance to Darius's command to move. "What is it that you see?"

"I told you," Darius answered, his voice nearly pleading. "My people, we walk as kindred spirits to the forests and the beasts. That out there, that is a spirit in need."

"I don't see anything," Izebal countered stubbornly. "How do you not know if Nkuaue plays tricks upon your mind?"

Darius let out a slight breath of air, releasing the frustration that had begun to build. The wolf sat on its haunches and bayed into the moonlight. The shrill, blood-curdling cry sent shivers up Darius's spine. The pup then bounded deeper into the darkness, taking three long steps forward, and then turned and looked directly at Darius with eyes of white flames.

"We need to go, now!" Darius said as he slung his satchel over his heavy coat. He stomped on the firepit and extinguished the flames.

"Darius, you are too tired," Izebal argued. "We need to rest."

"No, Izebal. We are leaving."

"How can you be certain this isn't a trap? I still see nothing!"

"You're going to have to trust me, Izebal," Darius stated emphatically. "Will you trust me?"

The brief silence that stretched out immeasurably filled the dark hollow where they stood. Darius, whose hand was outstretched in a sign of good faith, stared pleadingly into Izebal's concerned face. A heartbeat, unsteady, was the only sound that broke the silence as Izebal nodded in agreement.

"We'll need to move fast," Darius said as he turned on his heels. "Whatever is wrong with these woods, Stone Man or shadow-spawn, that spirit is trying to guide us." *Or*, he continued in his own mind, *is leading us directly to whatever is cursing this forest.*

Darius took off without another word. He ran with speed far faster than man. This was not evil, not this light. However, the closer he drew to the wolf-form of light, the further it moved through the trees, winding and floating, always just faster than the two could manage. However, as they ran further, the forest began to change. The trees thickened, long tendrils of moss hanging from their warped branches. The ground dampened, becoming a sludge of muck and rot. But Darius did not stop running, leading Izebal deeper into the mire.

Hours seemed to pass, yet the stars and moon were so far obscured by the swampy trees that none could tell the hour. The glowing specter, which had diminished from the form of a wolf into a small orb of nearly translucent light, came to rest at the trunk of a gnarled tree.

It was a great banyan tree that sat at the top of a stone hill, her mass of roots digging through the stone and deep into the black soil. The hill looked as if it had been hewn into with spikes and hammers. The rock was scarred and twisted. A cruel cave split open at the base of the hill, gaping like an open wound. A heavy fog seeped from the mouth of the cave, drenching the air with heaviness and gloom. The small ball of light sunk into the cavern, and then evaporated.

The hair on the back of Darius' neck and arms rose. His stomach churned and his eyes locked on the entryway. He tightened the grip on the hickory rod, clinging to it as if it were the only thing holding him back from falling into eternal darkness.

He knew this place. He had visited this very spot time and time again in his dreams.

Blood!

Blood!

Blood shall rain!

"No!" Darius's voice faltered as he spoke the word in horror.
"What have you seen?"
"Heard..." Darius mumbled. *Find them!* "Is this it..."
"Darius, you're scaring me! What is this?" Izebal's voice trembled as she spoke. Her hand was outstretched to touch him, but she pulled it back quickly, placing it on her breasts.
"I must go in... This is it, this is my purpose, why I was brought back." Darius said the words but lacked the resolve. Months of searching in Tur'Mor, days on the road, and even more in the trees. Endless nights of torment, being consumed by the unanswerable questions that plagued his mind. All had pushed him in this direction. Each step now seemed predetermined from the one before. A lump formed in his throat. The terrifying sensation of dread crawled unwantedly up his spine.
"I will come with you!" Izebal exclaimed. "I can help."

"You do not know what is down there. It's not safe." Darius's reply was cold and calculated; his mind was focused. He was ready to face his trial and earn his peace.

"And you do?" Izebal sounded more aghast and offended than afraid for her wellbeing.

"Well," Darius began.

"Well, nothing! Whatever is down there is dangerous! And unless you have the Spark and can conjure the Words, then there is nothing you can do to stop me!" Izebal chided. And then added, "Men!" with a humph.

"I may not be able to protect you down there," Darius began again.

"I can take care of myself, messenger boy." A sly smile formed across her thinned lips, though her voice held little amusement. "Besides, I fought off a hoard of Huntsmen while you incapacitated just two. Or were you mistaken?"

"Fine," Darius growled in frustration, unwilling to wait any longer. If Izebal wanted to go and get herself killed, what business was it of his? "We go now!"

Izebal drew her wand with a smirk, an expression that did not last as she stepped into the dead mist of the cave. She closed her eyes and began to chant, "*Mata Ethenealal, Ablaea! Ablaea! Ablaea!*" Runes of vibrant green light ignited around the tip of her wand.

The mist seemed to part in the presence of the gleaming spell. However, the toothy crevasse did not brighten at all. No, it was dark and lifeless. And the more Darius stared at the black hole, the more like a still lake it looked, almost liquid in nature.

Peeling his eyes from the gaping darkness that loomed before him, Darius looked up to the full moon. It hung low this evening, silver and vast. Beams of grey light cloaked the forest in transcendency. Was it enough time? Had he recovered enough strength for another Turning? Did it matter? No, he would face whatever was in that abyss regardless of any strength he could muster. *I can be free of this, this voice. I can be at peace and go back to the lands of my people. My people...*

That last thought stung to his very core. He knew they were gone. Dead for generations, and yet he had not had a moment to reflect and to grieve. And this was not that time. No, he could do this. He could do this last good thing and then fade away from this place. Darius drew himself up tall and walked past the green light of Izebal's spell and into the darkness.

Nothing physical barred the entrance to the cave; the liquid black opening gave no indication of resistance. However, Darius could feel something as he stepped down into the shadows. Something he had known before. His body shuddered. Izebal followed closely behind him, casting green light down the deep crack in the hillside. The slant that led downward was harsh, forcing the two to lean back as they walked so as to not tumble forwards into the dark. The walls of the cave were as scarred as the entryway had been. Something akin to refuse dripped down from the ceiling and coated the walls, a viscous mess of putrid grey and brown. The cavern's height was twice that of Darius's own and looked to be of natural stone, save a few long gashes that cut deep into the rock, like claws being dragged along its surface.

"This is an evil place." Izebal shuddered. "Death lurks here."

"Something worse than death." Darius's reply was less than a whisper. His heart beat a slow thump in the back of his mind and his thumb ran over the etchings of his silver ring in melodic succession. He felt every curve and line that was forged into his forefather's ring. *Ordan, give strength...* It was the first prayer he had uttered, if only in his mind, in a very long time.

The descending pathway came to an abrupt stop, blocked by something forged of man, not nature. A large door of heavy brass was bolted to stone, rising from floor to ceiling and spanning the width of three men. The bolts that fastened the metal door were as large as a man's arm and the hinges a man's thigh. In the middle of the dull brass door, a single hand was etched into the brass. Each finger on the outstretched hand had a ring about it, a different design upon each. And in the center of the palm, an upside-down eye wreathed in flame was carved. The eye had seven lashes which reached down towards the wrist, and at the base of the eye, which pointed to the ringed fingers, a strange marking had been painted with what looked to be blood.

"Damnation take us!" Izebal hissed.

"You know this symbol?" Darius inquired hesitantly. His attention was not on the door but something behind it. A slumbering sickness of evil and hate lay dormant. He could feel it as if it were touching him even now.

"I know it. Aehn Un'Bhais it is called, the Burning Hand of Nkuaue. This is a great evil to see." Izebal's voice was both distant and fraught with terror.

Darius did not hear Izebal at all. He just stared at the enormous door. A faint blue light flickered underneath the frame, catching Darius's eye. "We must get through now." He clawed at the door in a futile attempt to open the behemoth but found no purchase. He beat the door with the base of his fist, pounding at the metal. It did not budge.

"It is sealed from within," Izebal called out over Darius's insistent pounding. She retrieved that old book from her bag and rifled quickly through its ancient pages. "I can try and open it, but I do not know what resistance I will face from the other side."

Darius turned and faced her, his eyes wild with a primal fury. "Do whatever it takes. Rip the damn wall down if you must."

"I'm not sure it is that simple," Izebal countered, her focus not on Darius but the turning pages of ink-marked parchment. "Here it is!"

Darius, unbidden, stepped away from the door.

Izebal held her wand outstretched with one hand, and with the other she held the spine of the tome. Her eyes burst with light, streams of green energy flowing from her amulet up into her nostrils. Her hand trembled under an invisible strain as runic characters lifted from the pages of the book. Izebal's mouth began to move wordlessly, though with each motion another symbol rose and began to swirl around her hand. Terrible, grinding sounds of metal twisting began to swell within the confined space. The brass door began to moan under the arcane light and, ever so slightly, creased at the seams. The hinges wailed and the bolts screamed in failing resilience. And a small stream of blood began to drip from Izebal's nose, running over lips that muttered silent spells.

Then, in a sudden jolt, the door lurched open, sending sparks of red and green dancing through the darkness. Izebal let out a scream of agony and Darius wheeled about to see her now kneeling on the cavern floor, sweat drenching her brow.

"I can't hold this open," Izebal cried. "Do what you must, now!"

Darius, without hesitation or second thought, dove between the rock and metal, the gap barely wide enough for his broad chest to fit through. He had no sooner cleared the entryway when the brass door slammed back into place, sealing Darius away from Izebal's presence with a deafening thud.

Dazed, Darius searched about himself, trying to regain his bearing. His eyes were unfocused, the brilliant emerald light that had blazed from Izebal leaving specks of black dancing in his sight. However, after a not-so-gentle massage with his thick fingers, they began to refocus. And what they beheld was nothing short of amazing. Terrifying, but absolutely astonishing.

Darius stood at the top of a stone-cut series of steps that led down into a massive cavern. The ceiling was covered with stalactites, whose cold, wet arms reached down to join with stalagmites, slick masses reaching up with unyielding persistence. A path on the floor leading to the center of the room had been hewn smooth. Along either side of the wide path, crevices with black water running beneath them scarred the floor, and at the center, a monolith had been erected. Statues of stone holding ancient weapons surrounded a dais of obsidian. And atop that dais, an altar of black-veined crimson marble rose. Four dead torches rose from the dais, forming a square around the altar.

As Darius approached the altar, the blue apparition vanished and the torches that surrounded the monolith ignited with an eerie red flame. The ghastly light revealed two things: the insignia of the ringed hand wreathed in flames cast in gold on the face of the altar, and a body bound in tight cloth. He could tell by the contours of the body beneath the binding that it was a female; however, no part of the body was visible. A horrific realization caused Darius's knuckles to whiten around the hickory stick.

By Gallea's grace, she is a child!

Enraged, Darius's eyes darted around the room, searching for the source of this monstrosity. And they were met with a dreadful sight.

Dozens of mangled bodies littered the floor. Each was wrapped in the same binding as the girl on the altar, though some looked to be in the earliest process of decaying. Each girl had her chest torn open and her torso covered in what looked like teeth and claw marks. Darius felt his stomach wrench. The smell of the room, which had somehow escaped his notice until this very moment, mixed with the horrid sight, causing a visceral reaction. He fought down the urge to vomit.

Something drew Darius's attention back to the lifeless body that was bound atop the crimson altar. Something so quiet, so minute that none save one born with the enhanced senses of a Feromage could have even hoped to notice. A faint heartbeat. A single, lone *thump*. And then another. *Thump.*

She's alive! Darius's bushy eyebrows rose in unwarranted hope. *I can still save her!*

However, as he turned to head back to the altar, something terrible became all too apparent. The walls were covered with hand-painted images in blood, each depicting a ritual of sacrifice to some kind of horned beast surrounded by flames. His eyes widened as he studied the crude markings. Where there was a hint of doubt, or at least a hope of doubt, there was now surety.

A loud bellowing erupted from the back of the room. The sound was terrible and caused all the blood to drain from Darius's face. He turned slowly and faced the direction of the noise, peering into the darkness with eyes that needed no light to see.

Two men, whose bodies were completely nude and pale as ghosts, stood at the far side of the room. Men was not the right word, for these were no longer human. No, these were something different, something stranger, something darker. Their too-small eyes were sunken, black as coal and unblinking. Veins of black rose from around the sockets of their eyes and trailed up to their shorn heads, save a single braid at the back. Blood was used to paint their bodies, which was amplified by the bony protrusions on their chests and foreheads. They looked frail, but Darius knew better than that.

"Morreans!" The exclamation was as much a question as a curse. *How could they have survived? Morreans only existed because they were bound by blood-magic to Mireya or one of her predecessors. They could not be here! Mireya was dead. I killed her.*

The two bone-white fiends had not noticed Darius before his roaring exclamation, and they did not seem to care in the slightest that some stranger had penetrated their dark sanctuary. They looked at him through hollow, decaying eyes. His whole life, Darius had faced, fought, and slain Morreans. And still Darius feared them. Not for what they could do, but for what they represented.

A burst of pain seared his body, knocking Darius to one knee. Invisible flames licked his flesh and what felt like molten glass was poured directly onto the handprint branded into his chest. A yelp of agony fled his tongue as he fought against the raging pain that debilitated him. He had not felt a pain like this since the first night of his awakening, and it was all he could do to remain conscious.

The Morreans both pulled on a chain of blackened iron, lifting a gate that bore an emblem of an animal's skull with three horns, two curling ram horns and one straight, covered in flame. Hooves clopping against stone reverberated through the tunnel. A grating sound, like stone being pulled over stone, followed the hoof falls and a bleating, mixed with an oxen's bellow, shrilled from the depths.

Darius, gripping the hickory stick for support, rose slowly from the damp floor. Fighting the burning pain in his chest, he focused his eyes, steeling himself in front of the shaft. Its gaping maw flickered with deathly tongues of flame, whose light cast shadows in all directions. Unperturbed, Darius began to make his way towards the behemoth that was marching forward.

With a bound aided by a rush of adrenaline, Darius soared through the air towards the two men, staff raised overhead. He was met in mid-flight by a blast of red flame originating from the gateway. The torrent crashed into Darius's chest like a cannonball, sending him sailing backwards, then crashing helplessly to the stone floor. The Morreans, who had secured the chains to anchors hewn into the walls, dropped to their knees. They bowed their shorn heads before the doorway and began chanting in their dark tongue.

From out of the pit a demon of shadow and flame emerged. The beast was part man and part beast, merged together in some unholy manner. Two ram's horns grew above each of its long ears, and a third horn jutted from the center of the beast's forehead. The third horn was long, straight, and ablaze with some form of mystic flame. The beast was over ten feet high and black as night. Large fangs pierced out of its gruesome, elongated jaw. Its eyes, three to each side of its long face, burned with the same fire that emanated from its central horn. Spirits seemed to phase in and out of the beast's body, as if trying to escape from black tar, but were pulled back into the creature. Black hair covered the body of the beast, claws adorned its hands, and bull hooves held the cursed creature upright. It lifted its head and let out a mighty roar that echoed through the room, and then began to make its way towards the girl upon the altar.

Darius gathered himself up off the floor. Dazed and vision blurred, his ears ringing wildly, he was having trouble realizing what just happened. Pain brought back clarity. He looked down at his chest and stared at the circular burn mark where his skin was nothing more than a melted mess of oozing flesh. Where his clothes had once been, there were charred rags.

"Damn, this was a new shirt!" Darius swore as he flung off his coat, tossing it to the side. He then ripped away his shirt and vest with ease, dropping the ruined cloth to the ground.

Despite the lack of sunlight, Darius still healed at a much faster rate than a normal man, and the gruesome burn was already beginning to seal. This, however, led to an even more troubling sight. The scaly scar of Mireya's curse now stood out, wreathed in muddied and charred flesh, crisp and white.

Darius looked up, just in time to see the beast looming over the small girl atop the altar. He ran full speed at the beast, covering the distance in six long strides. He cried out a roar of rage and swung the hickory staff into the back of the beast's head. The rod landed with an awful crack, sending the creature toppling over. Darius rolled into a three-point landing, his momentum far too much to land softly.

"You're gunna die now, Itheanam!" Darius grunted as he rose to his feet, spitting blood out of his mouth with a curse and raising the end of the stave to point at the beast. His bare chest was heaving, and all but the white handprint was a reddish blur of flesh.

He was terrified, true. But admittedly, he was also a little surprised. That blow would have splintered any normal rod. Halfak! It would have bent iron or shattered steel. Whatever Izebal had done to the stick, it was working. The wicked smile that was little more than a snarl curled in cruel understanding of what this fight would descend into. And, unfortunately, he now knew what he faced, and he knew he could not falter in the slightest.

CHAPTER 35: THE LIGHT WITHIN

Tomo's Di'kha rested on Aellia's shoulder as she climbed the steps of the Aldorian estate. Her clothes were tattered and bloodied. Her eyes were downcast and her spirit drained. She was tired, sore, and spent. She paused, looking up at the arched double doors that formed the last barrier between her and her final revenge.

"Iaenora?" Aellia asked out loud, though she knew it didn't matter. The ancient being was bound to her mind and could read her thoughts, with or without her permission.

Iaenora did not answer. A profound silence hung in the air. Aellia did not take another step forward.

"Iaenora," Aellia continued through struggling breaths of both exhaustion and dread. "I know you can hear me."

"And what does that matter? Do you listen to me? No! You almost got us killed. And for what?" Iaenora's telltale haughty, impertinent, condescending voice sounded in the back of Aellia's weary mind.

Aellia's first instinct was to rail against the authoritative prick that had sealed itself, unwantedly, to her subconscious. But a single drawn breath allowed her to calm her nerves and continue levelly, "Iaenora. What I saw, the dream, was that you?"

"Me? Showing a vision? I was too busy keeping your corporal form from being eradicated, thus ensuring both our survivals in the process! Do you have any idea how hard it is to find a comparable bound, especially one who was born with the ability to Touch?"

"That place." Aellia sighed, focusing her eyes on the door, hardening herself against what she was about to do. "Was it real?"

"I don't know how you got there. It should not have happened."

"So, it was real?"

"There are so many things, Aellia, that you need to know. So many things I can teach you. You have only barely touched the surface of what you can do. We must go to the youngest of us, he who is ancient of all. He can show you the way, he can help you unlock your potential. Without his guidance, we are incomplete."

"So," Aellia stated icily. "She is dead, then."

"Who?"

"It doesn't matter now," Aellia snarled as she shrugged the Di'kha off her shoulder. "I promised her we would be together. I'll either avenge her or keep my promise, maybe both."

"Aellia, you don't have to do this. You can still walk away. Be the better person."

Silence was Aellia's response. She did not want to be the better person. She wanted blood. And blood she would have.

The Aldorian estate was a large house, well-built and respectable. It was in no way a comparison to the colossal Mayoral Residency but was adorned with all the appropriate frivolities that accompanied wealth and prosperity, down to the marble and brass busts of the Aldorian House. Long tapestries hung from the lofted ceilings, covering the papered walls, whose patterns were swirling shapes that hurt Aellia's eyes when she tried to focus on them.

To her surprise, Aellia had made her way through the entire ground floor of the estate without meeting so much as a rat, much less a butler, or better yet, Aldorian or Rahnaluz himself. Her wanderings, however, were cut short when she heard muffled whimpering coming from below the floorboards. Quickly, Aellia searched the lavishly decorated parlor until she found a concealed door in the wall paneling. It was slightly ajar, allowing the muted sounds from below to creep unwarranted into the vacant parlor.

"Something is down there."

"No kidding," Aellia mumbled sardonically.

"Aellia, stop! Please. There is something very, very wrong down there. We are not ready to face what lurks beneath this house."

Aellia used the butcher knife-like tip of the Di'kha to pry open the paneling. A waft of sweet alcohol swirled up from the dark stairwell, nearly taking her breath away. Tears began to form in her ducts, and then rolled unbidden down her cheeks. Her head grew light, and her vision swam.

"What in Halfak's blazes is wrong with me?"

"Alcohol muddles the senses."

Aellia steadied herself against the doorframe. The iron bar railing that lined the stairwell seemed to warp and twist like water winding down a mountain stream.

"I've drank my whole life, and I've never had this problem."

"Except at the masquerade . . ."

Wait... what? Aellia questioned inside her head, realizing it probably wasn't a good idea to be having a one-sided argument out loud in a house that potentially held one, perhaps two, killers.

"Do not tell me you did not feel her tenuous touch that night? The blissful corruption of sense and sensibility."

So, Aellia worked it out in her head, *I wasn't drugged? No, not drugged... drunk! Off of one measly drink? Well, two or three if you counted the small vials of amber drink Felohme had shared with me before. But wait, we weren't bonded yet!*

"No, not yet. But we connected that night, and our paths became one. A part of my soul was spliced to yours, so that you would seek me out once more. I had hoped you would take me from that drab glass prison I was in that night."

You can see your surroundings?

"How else would I have kept you alive when you were off drifting in the Aethereal Plane?"

The what?

"Listen, either we go down those steps or we leave, now! Before it is too late."

"Burn it all," Aellia groaned aloud as she used her free hand to rub her temples. She then stood up straight and began to make her way down the stairs.

The steps were cut into stone, this basement carved into the earth beneath the Aldorian estate. Wrought iron lamps with glass faces and yellow candles lined the walls, though none were lit. The sinuous scepter cast a blue light that provided enough clarity that Aellia did not stumble too badly as she made her way down into the cool cellar.

At the base of the steps, there was a small, oval landing with a wooden table and a three-legged stool. Atop the table was a leatherbound book and an inkwell.

"His wine log," Aellia whispered as she turned through the pages. "It's a wine cellar. Just my bloody luck. I guess I get to kick his arse drunk."

"Aellia. Be ready."

I've been ready for this moment for a very long time, Aellia thought to the voice in her head as she slid the silver rod into an inner pocket of her hooded vest. *It's about damn time one of them suffers for once. It's time for them to feel what every downtrodden and despised lower-caste member of society has felt. And I promise it won't be pleasant. I'll make sure of it.*

Aellia was not sure what was going to meet her when she flung open the door to the cellar and burst in with her raised Di'kha, but it was definitely not at the top of her assumptions list. On the floor across the room sat three men, each stripped to their undergarments, gagged and bound. One of them, whose massive nose and broad gut made him distinguishable as Aldorian, was separated from the other two and leaned against one of the massive wine barrels. While the other two were out cold, Aldorian had wide, tear-reddened eyes.

The door slammed shut behind Aellia, who stood dumbfounded in the room with a blade held over her head like an idiot. Aellia swore as she whirled around to face none other than the man who had tried to rob her of the scepter. He had greed in his eyes, but also desperation.

"You!" Aellia shouted. "I knew I should've put a knife in your gut."

"Silence!" the man called Rahnaluz barked with a raspy voice. He then sneered and said, "And put your sword down, it will do you little good here."

"I'm going to cut that eel tongue out of your face, you wiry little-"

Glass shattered within the darkness.

The sudden clamor drew Aellia's attention away from Rahnaluz, who didn't seem to want to move towards her in the slightest, despite her open stance. He just stared at her with snake-like eyes, filled with venom and hatred, and also dread. A man stepped forward, and Aellia was certain he had not been there before. He had matted hair of blond speckled with red, green-brown clothes that did not look like anything Aellia had seen before. He held a dagger in his hand, or at least, a dagger floated about his open palm, twisting and turning slowly.

A candle flickered, sitting on an obscure table. A gust of wind swelled the flame, which increased in size rapidly until it consumed the table in a blaze. A second shattering filled the room as a well-dressed man with a jeweled rapier stepped out of the flame, whose face was obscured by waves of heat.

"Who..." Aellia questioned with squinted eyes that darted back and forth between the two men who now stood at either side of her, just out of arm's reach. Confusion was apparent on her drunken face. "The Halfak you come from?" she slurred.

"Put the sword away," the strangely dressed man scoffed. His words were a slur, he pronounced all the wrong letters, and his accent grated on Aellia's nerves. "Before you get hurt."

In response, Aellia sliced the blade through the air in a swift motion, stopping it inches from the man's nose. He had been ambling carelessly forward. This stopped him dead in his tracks. Though it was a look of frustration or annoyance that tinged his oafish smile, Aellia had been hoping for fear or doubt. It didn't matter. She had been up against big men who had thought they could have their way with her before. This would be no different.

"Ah," sighed the veiled man with what could only be described as excitement. "A sword is nice. A worthy weapon, for a rather unworthy foe. Put the blade down, child. You're needed."

"I don't know what you think this is," Aellia snarled as she tried to focus, which was hard to do when the whole cellar felt like it was adrift upon waves. "I don't know who you are. But I'm here to kill that sour-faced lump," Aellia spat as she nodded to Rahnaluz. And then, turning her head to Aldorian: "And then, I think I'll cut his manhood off, and shove it up his own arse!"

"Colorful, aren't we?" the second to appear said, resting a gauntleted hand upon his pommel. His fine overcoat was expertly fitted, and despite his slenderer frame, hard muscles pressed against the taunt fabric.

In that moment, Aellia decided that she literally despised everything about this man. His pompous attire, the stupid jeweled sword, his leering voice, and the simple fact that he was another useless, entitled man who thought he could walk over her. She decided then and there that this one would die first. The only redeeming factor about the man was that at least she didn't have to look at his stupid, condescending face.

"I'll show you color," Aellia slurred, turning to face him. "Red, when I spill your guts all over your nice, fine suit."

"Is that right? Well, I hate to disappoint such an ambitious young woman, but I am afraid that won't be possible," the man scoffed.

"Sure it will," Aellia snapped and moved in a fluid motion, slinging a dagger from her belt towards the suited man and following up with an overhand blow with Tomo's Di'kha.

The dagger struck metal and was sent sailing through open air where it struck an oaken barrel with a thud. The Di'kha met the rapier of the suited man in a bloodcurdling noise that could only be described as shrill. The reverberations threatened to empty Aellia's stomach, but she remained focused. Shocked, but focused.

"Not bad," the man mused, pushing her back with ease. "But, as I said, we are here to collect you. Not to fight you." He slid the rapier back into its sheath with an ease that could only have come from performing that motion countless times.

"What are you?" Aellia snarled as she swung the Di'kha in front of her, holding it outstretched with both hands.

"What I am, Miss, is of little importance to you."

"Lord Edous," proffered Rahnaluz as he bowed quickly. "Be warned. She does have the-"

"Silence, cur! You had your chance," the man snapped. "Now shut up and let me work."

"I don't know what kind of back-alley, brothel-like business you three indulge yourself in." Aellia laughed, though without mirth. "But I came here to kill that spineless excuse of a man, and you best get out of my way unless you mean to talk me to death."

"I've had enough," the speckled haired man said coldly. "I will cut the light from within." The dagger that had been twisting about dropped into his palm with a thud that spoke of something that weighed much more than a dagger should.

"I didn't come here for you two," Aellia said, sidestepping towards the body of Aldorian, away from Rahnaluz who stood by the door and the other two who flanked her. "But Halfak is always hungry for another soul. Who am I to deny the flames?"

"Who are you? Why, you are nothing," said Edous in a voice that was thick with insult.

"Strange," Aellia snarled. "Looks to me like there are three too many people here for nothing... especially since two of you just popped in out of thin air. You get fused to some crazy rod too?"

The silence that fell was deafening.

"Khall'ah Kh'ar," Edous finally growled.

"My lord?" the shaking robber answered feebly.

"Did you neglect to tell us that the bloody girl has already begun the bonding process?" Edous's voice was like nails sliding down a mathematician's blackboard. The waves of heat around his face seemed to flare at the question.

"Betrugyn, now!" Edous screamed.

Both men rushed towards Aellia. Edous's rapier was out of its sheath in a motion too swift for any normal mind to comprehend. Betrugyn's dagger had been turned tip-down in an underhand grip and was whistling towards Aellia's face. Aellia's Di'kha swiped towards Edous, and with her left hand she pulled the sinuous rod with the blue gemstone forth from her vest.

Radiant blue light erupted from the scepter, momentarily blinding Betrugyn, causing him to miss by no less than a hair with his dagger. The Di'kha's edge sparked with lightning, which flowed through her vambraces and into the outstretched black, sending volts of electricity arcing through the room. Edous, seeming unable to feel the volley of crackling energy that assaulted his body, held his rapier in perfect stance, blade meeting blade as Aellia began to lift into the air. The volts did, however, manage to pierce his veil of haze, if only for a moment. Dead black eyes stared at Aellia. A shorn head with markings, like that of tattoos, though red instead of the common black, ran like rivers of blood over his face and scalp. As fast as the veil parted, it solidified, obscuring Edous's face from view.

Aellia did not have time to think about tattoos or lightning; she had three men that were apparently just as enhanced as she was and eager to kill her. Well, two that were enhanced and eager – Rahnaluz appeared to be neither. Actually, Rahnaluz appeared to be unconscious. And a look upwards at the ceiling told her how a misdirected bolt from the clash had knocked a brick from the cellar, which had fallen and knocked into his head.

"Aellia, can you go to the place where you were?"

Iaenora's voice could barely be heard over the crackling of lightning, despite the fact that that voice was in her own head. Aellia, focused on keeping two different assailants from cutting her down, struggled to make sense of the question. Alcohol and violence, two things Aellia had become intimately familiar with over the years, betrayed her.

A swell of black mist spewed from Edous's free hand, pressing back the crackling lightning and darkening the room once more, save Aellia's silvery-blue aurora. The mist curled about, like ink ejected from some strange sea creature that Aellia had only heard of in stories. It was cold and lifeless. It not only dampened the lightning but seemed to quell the very power from within.

Betrugyn struck next, a whirl of silver metal and shattering air. He jumped from place to place, leaving refracting scars of anti-light where he had been only seconds before. Deep, ugly scars, a blackness so vivid, with a beating heart of wine-dark maroon. The portals where Betrugyn just jumped through did not twist and curl like Edous's ink-like magic, but looked like mirrors smashed to pieces.

However fast Betrugyn moved, Aellia seemed to know where he would be, as if she could see a second or two into the future. She just knew. And somehow, her mind, drunk as it was, was able to make calculated movements to block and parry every strike. Tomo's Di'kha swung wildly about her with deadly grace and precision, sending sparks and pangs out as it met its foes in blinding combat.

What seemed like endless hours of adrenaline-fueled moments of mayhem passed. Two against one in mortal combat. Aellia fought with a vigor she had never known before. She could feel her muscles screaming in protest with each swing of her sword. She could feel her heart beating so hard that it neared failure. Worst of all, she could feel every knicks and slice from either of the two men that pressed against her. Aellia had to admit, she was impressed with herself, more so than she should have been. She had trained with the sword, spent hours on end sparring against Felik, Belthazer, and Tomo, but none of them merited half of either of these two men. She also had to admit when she was outmatched. And she was clearly outmatched now.

Suddenly, Edous pulled back. He raised a hand to his head, as if something had struck him. Aellia saw no such thing happen, nor did she take the time to try and figure it out. His negligence towards the ensuing fight left Betrugyn alone to face the streaming blows of Tomo's Di'kha. And while Aellia managed to strike the latter, if only shallowly, across the right arm and then the left thigh in quick succession, Edous had regained his presence of mind.

Something very sharp caught Aellia in the right shoulder, which she had left open after her flailing attack on Betrugyn. A seething flow of venom crept into her body from the shallow puncture. She looked at the glistening blade, which was so black in that moment that it did not seem to be metal at all. The veins around the wound began to darken and with every tormented heartbeat, the poison spread. Edous grunted with scorn as he wrenched the blade from her shoulder. Aellia fell to her knees, grasping at the bloody wound.

"I trust you'll play your part this time?" Edous snarled at Betrugyn. "I have...more pressing concerns that draw me. Do what you must now. You have little need of me, I have done more than necessary for you." Edous then turned his veiled face on Aellia, "As for you, little cur, you'll get what you deserve. You should never have dabbled in these affairs. You are beneath them in every way."

A red ember on the ground, the only ashen remains of the table that had once stood, blazed alight. The now familiar sound of shattering glass sounded once more as Edous was transported away into the flames. And, as suddenly as the flame had ignited, it burned away, leaving the room with one less occupant.

Betrugyn lifted his head, his mismatched black and green eyes staring daggers at Aellia. His own blade, which had been knocked from his hand in Aellia's last attack, flew to his open palm. He grunted, rolled his shoulder and twisted his neck, which made several bone-crunching pops, and said, "Your life is forfeit. Relinquish the Bound One, little one, and die gently. There is no need for further pain, comrade. You are marked by Edous's blade, neht. I promise you a swift demise, and an end to the burden you carry."

"What in Halfak's seven levels are you going on about?" Aellia snarled as she tried to rise. Her whole right side was on fire with flames of icy death.

Betrugyn drew himself up and mumbled something strange in a language Aellia did not recognize. Time passed, five or six seconds, in which Betrugyn drew very measured breaths. The gashes on his arm and leg began to flare with a white light. The assassin bared his teeth in a pained grimace, though he did not let out a sound of protest or agony. And, in an instant, each of his wounds were healed, knitted together by some incorporeal light that left nothing more than a crystalline scar.

"This deed, it must be done," Betrugyn stated without emotion. "It is the will, and the will must be obeyed."

"It ain't my will," Aellia countered boldly, though she could not help but feel the gloom that had entered the room, the pressing sense of hopelessness that Betrugyn seemed to now embody. It was soul-crushingly cold, unbearably heavy, and it was forcing itself upon her with unyielding weight. "Apparently it wasn't the other guy's either."

"What my comrade does, it is his own commandment, ya," Betrugyn said as he moved his thumb down the edge of his knife. "My command is clear. A soul for a soul. And I have finally found you."

"Finally?" Aellia questioned. "What do I have to do with you? I don't know you, and you sure as Halfak don't know a thing about me if you think I'll just keel over and die."

Betrugyn smiled. Not a wicked smile nor a cruel one. It was almost thankful, as if Aellia's defiance brought some measure of gratitude to the man. "Then, little one, I will allow you to die well, and I shall remember you until the end."

"You won't need to worry about remembering long," Aellia countered, raising her lover's blade in weakened arms. "I came here to kill the man who took away my life. And I'll kill anyone who dares to get in my way."

"Strong words from a very strong woman," Betrugyn said. "But they mean nothing to me."

"Aellia, we are not strong enough to face him. He is one tainted with the darkness. Can you find the way into the other realm?"

Aellia shut the sound of Iaenora's plea away. She had come here to kill, to bring justice down upon the heads of those who had cost her dearly. And she would dole out that justice, right, wrong or against all better judgment. There was no turning back now.

"Two of you couldn't kill me," Aellia scoffed. "What makes you think you have a chance now?"

"It is not a matter of chance, little one. It is a matter of command. I will cut out the light from within. This thing, it is my purpose."

"Shit on you and your bloody purpose!" Aellia swore. She hauled herself to her feet and rushed forward.

A flurry of swings and slashes met open air, every strike cutting through rippling air where Betrugyn had only just been. Aellia screamed in rage into the open darkness. Her hatred boiled in her veins. The frustration of failure berated her mind and seared her psyche as she spiraled further out of control. Tears, salty, burning, bitter tears streamed down her cheeks as she jabbed and slashed. Images of Tomo's face filled her eyes. She had not seen her body. She had not laid her to rest. She had not said goodbye. She would not let her go without vengeance. She could not let her go. She would not let Tomo go.

Betrugyn, who had apparently been holding back before, allowing Edous the chance to lead in the fight, was now moving with such speed and expertise that Aellia could not even track where the man was. She did, however, take note of the strange tendrils of pain that were creeping into her flesh from where Edous's blade had nicked her, not to mention the gaping, gruesome, putrid wound in her shoulder. Those unpleasantries, mixed with the blurring motion of the assassin and the incapacitating fumes from the wine barrels, were quickly proving too much, even for Aellia's insatiable thirst for blood and revenge.

A strike to her face blinded Aellia. Whether it was a fist, a dagger's edge, or some incorporeal flow of dark magic, she could not tell. All she knew was that it hurt. It hurt badly. And when her hand touched her brow, hot, sticky blood stained her fingers. *So, it was the dagger then*, she thought as her fingers traced a long gash from her forehead, across her left eye, and to the middle of her cheek. *Gods be damned. He's cut out my eye.*

"You, little one, have fought well," Betrugyn said sympathetically. "You should be proud. None of the other ones had your strength. They died weakly, pitifully. Like lambs from the hills, eaten by the wild cats. But you, you are the lynx, aren't you, comrade?"

Betrugyn was thumbing his blood-soaked dagger, sitting on a barrel, right leg crossed over the left. His eyes were not focused on the flamberge blade, but locked onto Aellia, who was kneeling on the floor. The Di'kha was out of arm's reach, its edge chipped in several places.

"Why?" Aellia asked weakly. She was spent, her body broken and her energy depleted. She could not keep fighting, not physically. Words. She could still, maybe, talk her way out of this, right? Felik could always talk his way out of shit places. Maybe...

"Why?" Betrugyn echoed with a sigh. "Why would a farm boy be asked to commit atrocities, neht? Why would a man steal the life of one's lover, holding her for ransom?"

Well, he's talking.

Aellia's muddled head was barely functional, but she had to keep him talking. "What?" The world was spinning, closing in on her. It took every ounce of strength to mutter a single-worded question.

"I don't blame you, little one," Betrugyn answered, his voice nearing wistfulness. "I don't blame your kind, neht. You were born this way, with this curse in your veins. It was not your fault, comrade. But it is my commandment to cut out this thing from you. It is not personal, and you will not live to hate me for it. If it's any consolation," Betrugyn said as he rose from his perch. "You are the first one to die with honor. You will rest well in Yhah'ka once the evil is cut from you, amongst the Line of Warriors."

"I don't know what you think I am," Aellia seethed. She then spit out a mouthful of blood and looked Betrugyn in the eyes with her one whole eye. "But you got the wrong girl. I ain't what you think I am. I am just a thief. I don't belong in this mess. You want the light, whatever that is? Take it. Take this rod. It ain't done nothing but betray me."

"Aellia, no..."

"Get out of my head!" Aellia snarled to the voice, hers barely a whisper.

"Take it," she said, standing and thrusting the rod outwardly towards the assassin. "Take it and leave me be. I don't want this or any part of whatever it is you're a part of."

Betrugyn looked at the sinuous rod like a child would an adder. A fear welled behind his mismatched eyes. A hatred formed there, dark and deep. He stepped back, raising his dagger between him and the rod. The blue jewel pulsated dimly, weakly, casting ebbing waves of light outward.

"Take it!" Aellia yelled, finding some form of strength. "Take it, damn you! Leave me be and take it!"

Betrugyn's contemplative face morphed into that of a cowering, hateful, fearful man. He shied away from the scepter, not daring to close the gap between him and Aellia. And for some reason, this alone caused an anger to burn within Aellia's chest. A confusion and rage she did not, could not comprehend.

"If you don't want it, then why are you here?"

"Put that down!" Betrugyn commanded. "Relinquish it!"

Aellia, overcome with ten thousand emotions, an overabundance of fatigue, pain, sorrow, and misery, gave way to something primeval. She phased from one reality to another, from one plane of existence to another. She saw both purple light and dim darkness. Her dead eye saw not the corporeal world but the Aethereal one. Betrugyn too was torn. A soul was bound to his own. A half soul anyways, for how else could Aellia describe what she saw? A blackness leeched upon him, tendrils of inky darkness had barbed into the translucent, crystal like being. With her physical eye, Aellia saw a man who was realizing he had been seen for the first time. Truly seen for what he was.

"No!" Betrugyn shouted. "It is unnatural! Stop!"

Tomo's Di'kha slid across the floor, the steel screaming across the stone. Swirling gusts of wind lifted the blade into Aellia's outstretched hand, the other pointing the scepter at Betrugyn. Iaenora was there, despite Aellia's futile attempts to vanquish her from her mind.

"You are there, Aellia. Hold on to this. We can fight him, together."

I can't, Aellia answered the voice in her head. *I am spent.*

"Let me help you."

Four words. Four simple, meaningless words. Four words that penetrated the iron cage around Aellia's heart. Somehow, in the mixture of hatred and rage, in some way inexplicable to her, Iaenora had found a way to bond with Aellia. Not the physical bond that had fused their beings, their essences, together. But something deeper.

Aellia let Iaenora in. And the light within consumed her.

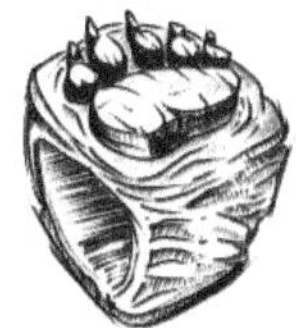

CHAPTER 36: THE COST OF IT ALL

The Itheanam let out a beastly roar and charged towards Darius with his head lowered. Darius jumped to the side with a speed unnatural to mortal men. He brought the enchanted rod down right into the center of the beast's back. The creature let out a yelp as it crashed headfirst into the floor. Darius was a mess of sweat, blood, and muck. He had been beaten, tossed, and rammed by the unholy creature. That being said, his fury for what the creature had done, and had been attempting to do again, urged him to rise after every strike, fight after every blow, and continue on despite the pain.

"So, you like to eat the hearts of little girls, do you?" Darius's voice was filled with malice and venom. He slapped the rod into his hand with each step towards the tar-slick beast. "Guess I am a little more than you're used to!" He swung his staff into the side of the beast's body, sending it rolling back towards the iron gate from whence it came.

"Gulad!" cried one of the pale Morrean slaves.

"Gulad, rise," whimpered the second.

The beast rose onto its terrible hooves, letting out a deafening bellow. It then plunged its wicked claws into the backs of the two Morreans. Gulad's center horn went from burning red to a chilling blue flame. Then, to Darius's horror and surprise, the souls of the two slaves were ripped from their bodies and forced into the beast's churning flesh. Gulad's eyes burned with blue flames, and he increased in stature.

"I eat you next!" Gulad's voice boomed, his speech foul and broken, as if two voices were being blended into one, asynchronized tone.

"So, you get bigger, eh?" Darius said as he rolled his head from side to side, cracking it twice. "Let's see if it helps."

Gulad's flames melded back into the crimson red they had been, and he dropped on all fours to charge at Darius, moving far faster than before. Darius tried to move out of the way, but a ram's horn caught him by the hip and flung him into the air. He crashed into the cave's rough wall and then fell to the mud-caked floor with a thud.

"Yep...it helped," Darius moaned to himself as he rolled over. His staff was lying several yards away, and he knew he could not get to it in time. *I am moving too slow...far too slow.*

Gulad was already charging again before Darius could rise. He planted his feet into the wall and pushed himself out of the way just in time to escape the horns of the beast. Gulad's head cracked the wall, lodging its straight horn tight. Darius slid on his knees in a circle, rising to his feet with unexpected grace. He removed his leather belt, spinning it quickly, wrapping it around his right fist. He grabbed the beast by a tuft of hair with his left hand, and then landed three heavy uppercuts into the ribs of the creature with his right. Each blow cracked ribs; Darius could feel them breaking with each strike. But that was not what drew Darius's attention.

The tuft of greasy black hair that Darius held with his left hand had begun to smolder. Gulad roared with fury and swung a massive fist backwards. Darius lifted his hands to block the strike too late and was sent soaring through the air.

Darius stumbled as he lifted himself back to his feet. He could tell through blurred vision that Gulad was still stuck on the wall, horns embedded deep in the stone. He looked at his left hand where his silver ring was. "I guess it's gunna be the hard way with this one," he groaned as he unlatched his boots and slid them off. The beast Gulad broke free, the stone giving way around his massive horn. Darius turned to face the beast as it charged towards him. He quickly jumped to the side, throwing off his trousers as he did so. As Darius landed, he shouted, "*Bursus-fortae uet Feromage,*" driving his fist down into the floor.

His hand struck hard. The sound of meat slapping stone sent out a reverberation through the cavern. That was the only thing that happened.

"Burn it all," Darius cursed, kneeling awkwardly with one first driven to the ground. He was barefoot, shirtless, without pants, and both wet and battered. And most noticeably, he was not a bear. Not even in the slightest. "No moonlight." The feeling of stupidity that followed the obvious did not help his sour mood.

"Gulad eat! Gulad feast!"

"Would you just shut up you overgrown, slimy, sack of putrid scum!"

"Ha! Ha! Ha!" Gulad's laugh was a broken, forceful thing that sounded more like stones grinding than mirth. "Gulad think he will enjoy you!"

Darius, without other options, rose to face the creature in naught but his small clothes about his loins. He was, though no one would notice, extremely well built now. The nights training with the Aluth had paid his body no small reward. He had always been big and thick, but now his muscles were tight and riddled with veins. His flat stomach sucked in and out as he tried to steady his breath and his barrel chest heaved. Hair, black and coarse, hid the well-defined lines that contoured his torso, but there was no mistaking the near statuesque build he had attained.

All those muscles did little good in the ensuing moments. Darius, unfortunately, found himself thrown thrice, kicked twice, and gouged once in the thigh with the central horn. The last wound would have been far worse had the searing red flames not cauterized it upon puncture. Blood flowed freely from his nose, broken for the umpteenth time. Cuts and scrapes turned his body into a maze of blood and gore. His healing factor could not keep up with this brutality much longer, and the cynical words he had told Elcon weeks ago crept into his mind once more. "If you die, you die." And suddenly, Darius realized, quite emphatically, that he did not want to die.

The dread, the anxiety, the lack and loss of purpose that had berated him for months now seemed like a distant thing. There, but not pressing. They were replaced, replaced with a fear far more powerful, far more terrifying. The fear of death.

Darius's heart raced. His breathing quickened to a state near hysteria. He trembled with the shock of realization that, if he did not survive this, he would die. In hindsight, it was a rather obvious realization. But, in that horrific moment, Darius knew had to survive. He couldn't fall back to the darkness. A thousand years of nothingness, an endless abyss without thought or comprehension. It had passed in an instant. And he knew that if he were to fall again, he would not awaken a second time.

Gulad raised two meaty fists over Darius's head and began to bring them down, fingers locked together, with a bone-splintering speed. It was not fast enough. Darius pushed the beast's swinging arms, thrusting his body towards the hickory rod. He rolled three times and scooped the staff with deft hands from the floor. From his crouch, he found the Itheanam and lunged forward.

The first strike caught the beast in the neck. The second, its groin. Darius did not know if the beast was male or female, or if it even had reproductive organs. But if the guttural yelp that escaped from the beast's throat was any indication, Darius would have to assume it was a male. Three more strikes with the rod broke Gulad's arm, which he had raised to defend his head. The fourth strike landed squarely across its mouth, shattering teeth and spraying tar-black blood across the cavern floor.

Gulad, wounded, was not immobilized for long. A barrage of fists struck Darius, one after the other in such quick succession that he was knocked flat on his back. Gulad's torso had sprouted two additional arms on each side, and though one hung snapped at the forearm, the other five were clearly functional. The beast rushed towards Darius, who, from his prone position, was unable to evade.

A shockwave of agony rippled through his body. The focal point? A blood-soaked, silvery horn, wreathed in flames, impaling his abdomen. Darius screamed in pain, or at least he tried to. No sound came out, no air filled his lungs. Only blood came forth, a gurgling pool that trickled over his lips like a crimson waterfall. Gulad hoisted Darius from the ground, bleeding body still impaled upon his gruesome horn. He charged towards the wall in an attempt to bash Darius to death.

Darius, with only a fleeting bit of lucidity left, made a terrible choice. Just before the beast drove him into the wall, Darius shoved one hand on the slick surface of Gulad's broad shoulders and the other between its feral teeth, and twisted himself about, snapping the beast's neck with his own momentum and the weight of Darius's skewered body. The sudden movement tore the horn free from Darius's guts, misting the air with entrails and blood. And, in a moment of agonizing pain, Darius tumbled over the back of the beast and fell helplessly to the cold, hard floor.

Gulad struck the wall with a bone-crunching thud. His already twisted neck snapped back into a right angle and a jutting bit of rock found its way through the beast's chest, puncturing out his back. Tormented screams, two-toned and dissonant, bellowed out of the snout of the beast. Souls of inky black tried to wrench themselves free of his mass but were perpetually sucked back in. Gulad, the soulless, was defeated.

Long moments passed while Darius lay upon the cavern floor. His eyes found no focus nor did his breathing return to normalcy. Trembling fingers touched his side, or more or less where his side had been. Strange. It did not hurt. As a matter of fact, nothing did. Not that wound, nor any other wound from the fight. The world seemed to have gone quiet; it was eerily peaceful now, lying in the muck and blood. He couldn't smell or feel, so why would it bother him where he lay?

Gulad, whose body was broken and bloody, let out a yelp of pain. The body of the beast began to shake violently. Darius tried to lift his head, to see what was causing the beast to move, but could not find the strength to do so. Gulad managed to rise to his feet, roaring in agony as the souls within the beast began to tear at its body. The neck of the beast then snapped backwards with a loud *crack* so that its eyes of red flame stared directly into Darius's own. Gulad's lifeless body began to float in mid-air all the while a whirlwind of flame and smoke filled the room, consuming the beast's body. The tormented souls trapped inside his flesh screamed in terror and pain.

What followed next shook Darius to the core.

From within Gulad's chest, whirling flames began to burn blue, as before when he had harvested the souls of the priests. A cold and unfamiliar voice echoed from its bestial maw, "I see you!"

There was a long pause. Terrible eyes, six of blue flame that morphed into two, stared lifelessly at Darius. The structure of Gulad's face crumpled, the skin splitting in horrific patterns of red, patterns Darius had known before. Then came a leering voice, not that of the Itheanam. It was proper, every word well pronounced, and very conceited. "So, one does remain from the line of old."

"Diabhail!" Darius gasped weakly through bloody lips. The face was horridly distinct now.

"We shall meet again, Son of the North," the creature that was Gulad asserted with disdain. "You have cost me much this day. Though this corrupted form was always a lesser vessel, I had higher hopes for another. That too shall come to fruition soon enough."

Darius could not answer. His body was broken, his stamina gone. He could do nothing, not a thing more. *Not such a bad way to go, attempting to save a life,* Darius mused to himself in a final, bitter thought. *But I'd have rather survived. Oh well.*

Gulad tried to step forward, but the creature faltered. Beneath its crumpled head, near the base of what would be considered its throat, a silver flame penetrated the inky flesh. Gulad screamed out in pain, flesh beginning to melt from his body as Darius watched from the ground.

"What have you done?" the phantom face of Diabhail cried out. "What have you done to me?"

Darius did not answer. Only a weak smile creased his crimson-stained lips. He did not want to die, but it was worth it to save the child. It was a price he was willing to pay. It was the cost of it all.

An awful smell began to emanate from the creature. The silver forks of flame tore away the neck of the beast. The body, having fallen to the floor, melted as if acid had been poured over the inky mass. Plumes of grey-green smoke rose into the air, swirling about the screaming head from the lifeless body beneath. And when the smoke settled, there was no trace of the Itheanam left save for a pile of ash and bones. The beast's skull hung mid-air, suspended in the ether for a singular moment, as blue eyes of flame locked onto Darius one last time. Then it dropped to the ground, shattering upon impact. The beast Gulad was no more, save for its silver, spiral horn.

***

Elcon moved swiftly through the Sanctuary's catacombs. The labyrinth of the chapel was vast, far more than anything he had shown Darius. Levels upon levels descended and rooted out in a myriad of different directions. Statues of the fallen kings, rulers, leaders, military men, and scholars were carved into small alcoves here and there. Blue light from mounted Fragtorches lined the varying pathways, providing ample light to see. Elcon knew his way well, and he had little time to stop and admire the mosaic works of art that lined the walls between the crypt and cavern.

A vaulted room with nineteen doors besides the one Elcon just walked through, was lit by perhaps the largest Fragtorch ever made in the form of a great chandelier hanging from the painted ceiling. At the center of the room directly beneath the chandelier was a pedestal atop a spiraled set of stone steps, nearly twice the height of a man. Atop the stunningly blue quartz pedestal was an object of brass rings and crystal spheres, bound together to mirror the device that sat in his own room, save only much, much larger.

Avajan'Aluth stood at the base of the steps, a look of deep concern on her face. When Elcon made his way towards her, she slid an object from a sheath at her hip. Had there been another individual in the massive, octagonal room, they would have most likely thought her about to assault the elderly priest. But there were no others in the rather empty room and Avajan'Aluth was most certainly not out for blood. At least, not his.

"Micaela, thank the gods, you're here!" Elcon said as he hurried forward to greet her.

"A sword, Father von'Harr?" Avajan'Aluth answered as she studied his approach, the brass item in her hand still.

It was an odd look for him, one that he had not taken upon himself in many years. Elcon wore a fighter's coat, padded at the breast and cut close to the body so as to not tangle in advanced movements. He wore tight trousers and high boots, thick leather boots, vastly different than the short, buckled shoes he had grown accustomed to. His blade, a weapon he had not carried since the loss of his wife and son. It was a beautiful yet practical blade, just as he had been. Effective, deadly, and unremarkable at first glance.

"A blade speaks volumes of intent, even sheathed," Elcon answered through measured breaths, for he had been moving quite fast for his age. "And Harr is well enough. I am afraid I am no longer worthy of the title *von*.'"

Avajan'Aluth handed over what could now be seen as a massive skeleton key, nearly the size of a dagger, forged of brass and whose handle was wrapped past the ring to a hand's breadth from the head with blue cloth. As Elcon took the key from her, she replied softly, "No one could ever take that title, not one so hard-earned."

"I did what I thought was right at the time," Elcon said as his hand touched hers. He let out a short, remorseful breath, then took up the key and stated, "I have since learned that I was a particularly vain and foolish young man. I could have been so much more without the sword. But that is not the reason for our meeting now. Hurry, Micaela, we must move swiftly."

"As commanded," she answered, bowing her head in reverence.

"Hundreds of years have passed, Micaela," Elcon started as he began to climb the spiraling steps. "Not a whisper, not a motion. Then, only a matter of weeks ago, all reality as we have come to define it has changed. Or will."

"I do not understand, Father," Avajan'Aluth asked, following two steps behind. "Please, enlighten me. Does it have to do with that strange young man you had me train with my Aluth? What is it you are not telling me, Elcon?"

"In due time, Micaela," Elcon huffed as he rounded the top steps. Over eighty and still able to move with the agility of a sixty-year-old. This thought caused him to chuckle, though it was short-lived.

"My duty is to keep you and the Church safe and secure," she countered, a tinge of frustration showing through her tight lips. "I cannot do that if you do not let me know what is going on."

"Things are in motion," Elcon said as he slid the massive key into a keyhole at the base of the apparatus. "Things that have long slumbered begin to stir. Shadows that were dormant have started to creep and move. And legends that were lost walk amongst us once more. The time has come for the return of the Sages, who, in great glory, will usher in a new era."

Elcon twisted the brass key. The several spheres and hoops of the mechanism began to shift and turn. Dozens of crystals, both blue and green, began to glow faintly. A soft humming sound emanated from the motion of the spring and shifting rings, along with a rhythmic chiming that seemed to be emerging from the crystals themselves.

"Where do we search this time, Father?" Avajan'Aluth said as she stood next to the elderly priest, unfazed by the workings of the strange device. And why would she be fazed? She had seen him use this machine hundreds of times in search for those born with the ability to Touch. Those who, when found, would become Blessed of the High Father and Holy Mother.

"Do you recall the child's fable, that of the six, sleeping sheep?" Elcon asked, slightly raising his voice to be clearly heard above the increasing volume of the device.

"The what?"

"The story of the sheep who slept and their brother could not find them," Elcon stated with slight confusion. *Hasn't everyone heard that tale? Or am I that old now?*

"I do not recall such a story," she replied. "Nor do I see the relevance."

"An allegory, Micaela, an allegory!" Elcon's voice was rising in excitement as the whitewashed walls began to catch the light from the mechanism. "Six lambs slept while the seventh remained lucid. It was a short story, meant to teach children to be watchful and observant. Funny things, children's stories, how they so often stem from more factual events."

"I am afraid I still do not understand."

"We search for more than sheep," Elcon said as he pulled forth a wrapped article from within his topcoat. It was a stonemason's hammer, engraved by a friend.

Did he know? How could he have? Elcon thought as he took the hammer and held it near the whirling disks. A small hair lifted from the hammer, floating inches above the metal head. *He had hoped I would give this to her to bring recollection to their chance meeting. Little did he know it contained what I had needed for so long. Had I only looked closer and not gone in so many other directions first.*

The snow-white hair was sucked into the machine. Three crystals of sapphire and three of emerald spun around the strand in a double helix, never intersecting, but ever moving. Swirling lights burst outwards, painting the white walls with a map of the nation. The humming increased in volume and the lights brightened. The map morphed into the region, then the city of Tur'Mor. Ten thousand specks of white light sparkled over the plaster. Then, slowly, pinpricks of blue popped up in various locations, most of which were clustered three or four together. When a green light flashed here or there, Elcon's eyes narrowed, but he shook his head. There would be time for those later. Tur'Mor seemed to be drawing itself closer, though it was only becoming more focused on a single area.

"By the gods!" Elcon gasped as he stared at a bolt of blue light which crackled and sparked, directly in the middle of the map, which was drawing ever closer.

"What on Fenron's holy hilt is that?" Avajan'Aluth exclaimed.

Next to the blue source of light, there were two other lights, if one could call them that. One, a deep black mist which seemed to suck the light away from the mural. The other, a bit of what looked like fractured onyx with deep veins of maroon. This one seemed to flicker about, moving about the room in random motions.

Suddenly, the misty apparition vanished from sight. Elcon gasped. Avajan'Aluth swore, and the whole mechanism seemed to creak in pain as the lights attempted to refocus and reform a proper image.

"We need to go," Elcon gasped. "We need to go now!"

"Of course," the Avajan'Aluth answered with assurance, though the slight tremble in her voice did not go unnoticed.

"We make for the Avenue of Estates of Northlane," Elcon said, turning the key and effectively cutting out all lights, save the hanging chandelier, which seemed so much dimmer than before. "And let us pray to Ordan's holy throne that we are not too late."

CHAPTER 37: PERSPECTIVES

Ash and smoke swirled violently around the room, along with bouts of red crimson flame and blinding flashes of blue lightning. A howling cry of wind reverberated against the cellar walls and the glass-shattering sounds of realm-splitting.

Aellia hovered inches above the floor, a tempestuous gale holding her up. Her white archer's cloak billowed in the wind; her hood cast off her so that her icy white hair was clearly visible. The vein-like flows of blue energy that emanated from her chest and webbed along the silver vambraces gave off a terrible light, a brilliant light. Blood trickled from her face and her now dead eye burned with a blue energy that matched the crackling of her armor.

Betrugyn looked to be a demon of shadow and blackness. He warped reality around himself, the air appearing distorted due to his many jumps from portal to portal. Aellia had noticed that he did not simply create a portal to step through, but he rent the air, the bridge between the Aethereal and Terral, and moved through it. She discerned this not with her natural eyes, but through the bonding of herself and Iaenora.

Iaenora, one of the ancient Sages who, to Aellia's prior knowledge, were no more than child's tale or religious bollocks. Apparently Aellia was in need of rethinking her own personal theological belief system. For here she was, floating in air, bonded to a myth from scripture, battling some arcane being who could step between realms. Realms Aellia hadn't believed existed until only hours before. Well, she believed now. Whether she wanted to or not, she had to. There was no denying any of it anymore. Now, she only had to live to try and figure it all out.

"We must get out of this cellar! We cannot continue here; we can achieve no advantage."

Obviously, Aellia thought, frustrated. They had been fighting for at least ten minutes now, and neither had gotten the true advantage.

Admittedly, had Aellia not opened herself to the aid of Iaenora, she would most certainly be dead now. But she would never admit that to her.

"I know, young one. But thanks are for survivors. We need to drive him out. Too much darkness, too many shadows and crevices to lurk and hide in. We need open air and wide skies. That is where we thrive." There was a swell of excitement and belonging in those words, along with longing that Aellia felt personally.

As much as Aellia hated to admit it, the two were more alike than she had first perceived. They both loved the chase, the thrill of the fight, and though Iaenora had her obnoxious moral compass, they both seemed rather practical when it came to the need to survive. And right now, that was the only instinct that mattered.

Betrugyn was not slowing. His hands blurred with animalistic speed as he twirled his daggers about. The fight had seemed less than fair when he had only held his flamberge blade, but now that he had drawn a second weapon, a straight, kinzhal style knife, he was untouchable. Aellia, on the other hand, was tiring swiftly and felt as if the floor would swiftly be greeting her face if she could not find an edge.

Something out of the corner of her eye caught her attention. A blur, a motion. Something green-grey lunging towards the assassin. Betrugyn turned just before the man called Rahnaluz found his mark. He caught the head of the Kh'ar robbers' face with his straight blade, the tip finding its mark through his gaping mouth, opened with a cry of misused vengeance.

"Galk!" the guttural noise choked out of his mouth.

Aellia blasted Betrugyn with a surge of gale winds, flinging the assassin across the room. She then darted for the stairs that led out of the blasted and charred cellar. Her feet carried her swiftly, though her legs screamed in protest, every step a burning mixture of exhaustion and agony. But she was now out of the brick wine cellar and in the upper rooms. Next, she was through the spacious estate's sitting rooms, not stopping to look back, not slowing in the slightest.

Purple-gold twilight met her eyes as Aellia stumbled out of the house, having smashed through a window onto the cobblestone path that led to the front of the manor. She fell on her hands and knees, gasping madly for air. Fear, crippling, terrorizing fear, ate at her consciousness. It forced her to her feet. It forced her to turn about. And it did in fact herald the bitter truth that stood facing her.

Betrugyn stepped through the fractured air onto the cobblestone in front of Aellia. He held Rahnaluz by the skull in his left hand, dragging his body as if it was a paper doll, lifeless and pale. Dead eyes, filled with shock, stared out to meet Aellia. Blood ran like a crimson river from his mouth, staining his rich clothes and dribbling onto the road. Betrugyn looked unfazed. His green eye caught the light, sparklingly beautifully. His black eye, however, seemed to draw light in, suffocating it, snuffing it out of existence. The stone in the eye of the diving bird on his cloak seemed like liquid, matching his onyx eye, the two swirling harmoniously.

"A pity, little one," Betrugyn said with a shake of his moppy hair. "This could have been a good comrade. Ha! He will still serve the Dorr A'Gadah. Frail man, not useless after all. Just needs reconditioning."

The assassin dropped the body to the ground. It crumpled pathetically. Aellia seriously doubted that that man would be of any worth to anyone. A pang of frustration gnawed at her. Frustration and anger at Betrugyn for taking her revenge from her. She wanted to kill that man more than anything. Or, she had. But now, now there was something else there, inside her. A new need that seemed to consume her. A swinging pendulum within, a harsh motion of emotions.

Iaenora's voice filled Aellia's ears.

"He is cursed. He has Touched that which is not of light nor creation, but of corruption. You are not strong enough yet. You have done well enough to survive this long. But we must flee, seek out he who is youngest of us all and most ancient of days."

Aellia hefted Tomo's Di'kha. It felt so heavy now. She held it in one hand, the scepter of silver in the other. The gemstone was nearly dead, the light diminished to a small spark at the very heart of the sapphire. That spark pulsated weakly and Aellia knew her time was short. Her shoulder screamed. The whole of her flesh looked like a maze of dark, blackish-green lines that were her veins, corrupted by whatever enchantment resided in Edous's blade.

"You have fought admirably, little one. You could follow and find much in the hand of my master."

"I could bloody cut your hand off," Aellia snarled. "I'd have no part of whatever it is you're mixed in."

"Ha! Comrade, do you think you have a say in this thing now?" Betrugyn laughed dryly. "You have chosen this thing already, when you made bond with Sage."

"So that's it, then?" Aellia scoffed, side-stepping slowly. The two were now moving like a dance once again. Each footfall subtle and exact. Each sizing up their opponent in the new, open arena they stood in. "I am some Sage or some such? And you're here to carve that out of me with your knife then?"

"Ah," Betrugyn sighed pleasantly as he ran a finger over his flamberge blade. "Due'shalesh. She is my salvation. She is my penance. She is my burden and my joy. Her work is of great importance."

"Do you always talk this much?" Aellia snapped. Though, to be fair, his stalling was perhaps the only thing keeping her alive. And every moment he spoke was another she drew breath. And she very much wanted to keep doing that.

"No," Betrugyn said, almost sorrowfully. "I do efficient work. But I have never met a Lightbound who could stand against me alone, much less

Edous and myself in mortal combat. I respect that, little one. But you're right. I must carve from you what I came for, or you can agree to come willingly, dah."

Aellia rushed the man, swinging an overly telegraphed downward slash that would have caused Felik to cringe. Well, Felik was dead now, and she would be too if she didn't find some way to get a lethal strike on this man, if that was even possible. Aellia had witnessed so many impossibilities over the last few days, that when this was all said and done, she was going to need years to sort it all out. If she survived. Too many ifs.

Betrugyn side-stepped the swing and thrust his dagger towards Aellia's side. The tip nearly bit into her flesh, but a resounding crash of steel on silver rang out as she caught the curving blade with the head of the scepter. The dagger sliced through her cloak but missed her flesh by a hair. Aellia brought the false edge of the Di'kha backwards, her body enhanced by Iaenora's light. The overly telegraphed motion had been a decoy for the far more lethal return strike.

When the steel cut into the assassin's flesh, tearing at muscles and cloth, Aellia felt her blade vibrate unnaturally. As she tore it free, blood spewed forth from the man's back and neck, blood that was black as ink. Betrugyn reeled in pain, screaming as he stepped away from her. And, to Aellia's grim satisfaction, she felt Iaenora pulsate in surprise and what could only be described as adoration for the hazardous move. One didn't live on the streets of Tur'Mor without taking risks, and Aellia had been on the streets for a very long time.

Betrugyn sagged to a knee, a grimace on his face. He breathed slowly, carefully. His left arm hung limply at his side. Aellia looked down at him, having taken two steps back after landing the fatal blow, more so out of instinct than fear.

"Your master abandoned you," Aellia said, then spat at the ground in front of her foe. "I didn't get to kill that bastard. But I guess I'll settle for you tonight."

Aellia stepped forward, raising the Di'kha, ready to take the assassin's head from his shoulders, when a shockwave took her feet out from under her. She felt the world tilt, slowing almost to a stop, and from her vantage point, she witnessed all things as if she were not seeing from her own eyes. She saw Betrugyn roll across the cobblestone towards the body of Rahnaluz. She felt her flesh slam into the cold, hard earth. She heard the glass-shattering tell that was the realm being torn asunder. And then all went black.

***

Darius groaned as he tried to lift himself from the floor with shaking limbs. *How have I become so weak?* They weren't words, thoughts. His memory drifted to the words of his father: "Feromage are strongest together. In unity there is our greatest strength." But it had been over a thousand years since he had last been with another of his kind. Darius's strength was faltering, he had realized that fact what seemed like a lifetime long ago. And there was nothing he could do about it.

He was dizzy, blood loss would do that to a man. In fact, he was so dizzy that he could not make out anything around him at all. Colors and shapes swam in his eyes, lucidity fleeing rapidly. He heard a strange moaning. Perhaps it was himself. Anyhow, it was distant. He couldn't swallow, he tried. Blood gurgled out of his mouth instead. He had slain the beast, but at what cost. It was his purpose, right? To find and slay this thing, stop this creature before blood rained, wasn't it? Then, why the apparition at the end? That terrible, cruel, specter of one whom he had cast down a millennia ago.

The moaning grew louder.

Darius gritted his teeth. He would not die crying; he couldn't even feel the pain anymore. His whole body was numb. What had he to moan about? But that moaning, it seemed to be coming from –

An ear-splitting crunch of stone and metal resounded throughout the cavern. A flash of emerald light illuminated the muck-covered floors and mineral-soaked walls. The *cling-clack* of the heavy door, that had once sealed the cave, rang out wildly as it tumbled down the steps. Then swiveled and turned about, like a coin on a table, before it fell silent at last, resting at the base of the stone steps.

"Damn," Darius murmured. "That was loud."

***

Izebal choked on acrid fumes as she strained her eyes to see into the enormous cavern. The deafening crash of the door, a bloody stubborn thing it was, had shocked her facilities to full alert, but the smoke was so thick she could not make out anything. She had worked on the incantations that had sealed that door for what seemed like an eternity. And then, out of nowhere, it had just given way. As if it had lost all interest in being a door at all. Whatever was harboring the enchantment was gone, or at least weakened to a state that it could not focus its strength on sealing the cavern.

Disregarding the stench, Izebal rushed down the slick steps, her wand held in front to light the cavern. The stalagmites and stalactites were massive. The threadlike rivers of water that ran through the fractured floors were endless. The maw of the cave seemed to open into a vast terrarium of stone and earth. Luminescent algae hung like drapes and phosphoric crystals jutted out randomly from mineral deposits and drips. It was spectacular, breathtaking really. But Izebal had no time to stop and admire the structure, though she could not force back a fleeting thought of the wonders that lurked in this place.

A gasp echoed throughout the cavern, emanating from her own mouth. A sound that surprised her nearly as much as the scene before her filled her with terror and worry. Desolation. Destruction. Devastation. There was charred stone and there was rent stone. There was ash and there was blood. So much blood.

"Darius." The name dropped from her mouth. He lay there, unmoving, bleeding, dead. His whole body was torn, his insides strewn about him. His face was turned, as if he were looking to the stairs in some hope of salvation, but his yellow eyes were sightless.

Izebal scrambled to his side, dropping to her knees and placing two fingers on his neck. There was no pulse. She looked at the torn flesh of his torso, the blood pooling dark red around him but no longer flowing from his body. Izebal tore open her satchel and drove her hand inside, fumbling with shaking hands through vials, bottles, crystals, herbs, and other such healing things. She withdrew another wand, this one gnarled and thorny, with a tiny white crystal threaded into the tip. Next came two vials, corked things with red and purple liquids in them. She took out the stoppers and poured them over the wound and then waved the smaller wand round and round, chanting, "*Usaylun, usaylun, usaylun.*"

The crystal in the tip of the wand glowed faintly, and the potions puffed colorful smoke. Darius did not move.

Again, Izebal reached for her things. Herbs came next, herbs and ointments from her travels to the East. Strong herbs filled with healing properties. She could not allow him to die, not her. She chewed the large, bulbous leaves into a cud and then spat them onto his side, massaging them into the wound, soaking her hands in blood, gore, and spittle. And Darius did not move.

She threw her head back, tears leaking from her eyes. She tossed her hands up in frustration. She had witnessed so much death, why did she have to see him die too? Why? Why? Why did it have to be this way? He was a good man. An honest man, wasn't he? Truly, she had not known him long, but he had saved her life that night when her world burned. He had been helpful, offering to travel with her through the wood. He had spoken with her. He had been kind, something not many men had ever been to her.

A glint of blue light caught her eye. It came from across the cavern, a faint, but very real, beam of pure light. Izebal rose slowly, her trembling fingers pressing onto the cold, damp floor for support. The gnarled and thorny wand rolled from her lap, clattering to the ground, though she did not hear it, she could not. All of her focus was on the source of that light.

At first, Izebal's steps were slow, cautious, but they quickly morphed into a run, carrying her swiftly to the source of the sapphire light. And as she drew closer, she recognized the shoulder bag as Darius's. It laid open, its contents spilled out on the dirt and stone. A loose sock, a once-clean shirt, an empty flask, a bruised apple and something else wrapped in white linen. She reached in, the light seeming to scorch her fingers as she touched the crystal vial, though she paid that pain no heed.

"By Ethenealal's green heart!" She gasped as she took the cylindrical container into her hand. The many facets felt like razor's edges on her flesh, but that too she shrugged away. She knew, if not exactly, what this was. It was a portion of the gods. Not of the Earthmother, but the sensation was unmistakable. She herself had traveled to the Farlans, had visited the Fountain of the Great Tree, and had touched those waters of eternity. That was where she had come into her own as a Diju, and more importantly, a Lifesinger.

Without a second thought, Izebal ran back to Darius's side. She pulled the cork from the vial. The ensuing nausea made it hard to focus, but she pressed through the discomfort. She poured out the majority of the contents on the bloody torso of her friend and waited.

Nothing happened.

Izebal pressed the vial to his lips, tilted his head back and poured more into his mouth. The light from the mixture soaked his lips, stained his teeth, and coated his tongue. But he did not stir. He lay there, lifeless as when she had entered.

"Damn it all!" Izebal screamed. And she flung the vial across the cavern where it struck a stalactite.

A plume of blinding light flashed as the crystal vessel shattered into a thousand pieces. Light bathed the floors, washed the walls, and drenched the ceiling. It struck outwards, downwards, and upwards. Beams of white cut the floor, sliced the walls, and punctured the cavern's vaulted roof.

The blast knocked Izebal on her back, casting her a few yards from where Darius had lain. When she landed, something sharp jabbed at her back. A silver, twisting horn. She pulled it from under her. Her eyes, spotty from the flash of light, couldn't make out what kind of creature it had come from. Yet, as she stared at the unnatural, swirling thing, a glinting of light drew her attention away. On the floor, lying bare, was a rough-hewn ring that glistened in the light of the sun. The light of the sun that streamed in from the perforated ceiling. Darius's words seemed to blare in her mind. He healed through the light of the sun. He could still make it!

Izebal picked up the ring in her other hand and ran back, once again, to his side. She forced the ring onto his finger and then dragged his body towards the closest ray of light. She heaved as she grappled with his lifeless mass, every step a struggle, but she did not give up.

At last, Izebal managed to pull him into the light. She stared at him, studying his face, his features. They looked weak now, unlike they had ever appeared before. She wanted to do more, anything, but exhaustion finally took its toll, and she dropped to the floor, lying next to Darius, staring up into the blinding light.

Two dozen Aluth, all dressed in their titular white garments, faces wrapped and swords ready, marched hurriedly in the open streets of Tur'Mor. They moved unabashed through crowds of merchants and peddlers. It was a sight to see, or that was what Elcon would have thought had he not been leading them to what could only be their impending doom. They were not ready. No one was ready. The prophecies were not fulfilled. This should not be happening. Where was the Keyholder? Where were the Sages of Old? They could not be left to this fate, not alone.

Men in fancy suits scoffed as Elcon waved them out of his way. The Avajan'Aluth barked at women in floral dresses who, to hide their disdain, raised colorful fans and scurried back from the militia in white. City guards, who roamed about in packs of twos and threes did not seem to have any desire to get involved. They simply turned their heads or vacated the premises. Whatever the feelings were between the city and the Church, neither seemed eager to make the first move. It also didn't hurt, Elcon mused as he watched a particularly scared lot jump into a pub to be ignored, that everyone knew Aluth were the best trained warriors in Tur'Mor. Them and the personal guard of the High Seat.

"This way!" shouted Elcon in a voice far firmer and louder than any man in his eighties should be able to muster. "We must be vigilant. All eyes open!"

The Aluth followed in perfect step, not one uttering a single word in reply. The Avajan'Aluth did not unsheathe her sword, but her white-gloved hand rested eagerly on the pommel. It was the only emotion she showed on her stern face. Her features were carved from granite. Elcon admired those hard lines with an adoration forged from an understanding of their crafting. Countless hours of swordplay, endless days training, all to be pronounced the Avajan'Aluth. And what a spectacle she was. He, too, had trained but had long since turned his days to the service of the Ellitheor. But those hours were hard to forget, and those skills, well, they had never truly seemed to dim.

The body moved towards Northlane Alley in swift procession. The houses were slowly morphing to mansions. Ancient architecture made modern with glass and steel. Great statues and square gardens formed a straight line, cutting the massive roadway into two distinct lanes, one for going and the other for coming. With all the carriages and carts in this richest part of town, traffic had to be diverted and managed in such unique ways as had never before been necessary. Men in high-collared coats that buttoned up the side, who carried truncheons looped around their belts and goofy hats on their heads, patrolled these streets. These were not the City Guard, but a hired force of men to keep these Uppers as safe as possible.

The Aluth, in one fluid motion, drew their swords. Each blade was the same. A hand-and-a-half sword, dual-edged, with a white, leather-wrapped hilt and a pommel of dull steel. This motion invited the so-called Enforcers, with their clubs and hats, to part. Elcon did, however, nod politely towards them, as if to say, "Never mind us, gentlemen. We are just an armed force of trained killers walking openly through your streets. We mean you no harm. Have a pleasant day now and do enjoy this lovely weather we're having." They looked at the lot of them with eyes filled with shock and rage but did not engage.

The streets forked every few estates, which were steadily growing larger and more luxurious. Elcon led the body down one of these side streets, which angled back towards the center of the city. It was down this road that the smell of something very particular could be scented. It was not a stench, nor was it foul. It was actually very pleasant to the senses. Light, airy, like a gentle rain, though more extensive, volatile. It tantalized Elcon's memories for the thousandth or so time. It livened his step, invigorated his body. It was a Spark of the Everlight; he would know that power anywhere.

"Avajan'Aluth," Elcon barked, raising a hand to halt the body. "You and your Aluth await me here. If I do not return in ten minutes' time, strike hard and fast, for our whole world may depend on you and your Aluth."

"High Priest, it is unwise-"

Elcon cut her off without a word. His hard eyes glared at her until her lips formed a thin, bloodless line.

"As you command," she spoke, nearing a whisper.

"And I do," Elcon replied. He drew the sword from his side. The blade was so much heavier than he had remembered, and yet it was so familiar. It was a piece of him that had been missing for over thirty years. A subtle smile tugged at the corner of his lips, but he turned his head before anyone could see it. And then he headed towards the source of the Everlight.

High walls rose around each of the mansions so none could see inside the courtyards of the lavish estates. Elcon did not need to see, he only needed to follow the feel of the Everlight. It was a sensational thing, the Everlight, a source of endless power. He had spent the last thirty years engaged in holy work, serving the Ellitheor, and in doing so, had spent thirty years in the presence of the strongest source of Everlight in all of Ethrea. The first Temple of Ordan, and subsequent, most grandiose Temple, had been built over the fissure in the earth where the Light shone the brightest. He had basked in those rays for decades. And while he was not a Blessed, for he was neither Healer nor Vision Blessed, nor was he the High Patriarch, he had benefited from its bounteous flows. They had given him health, vitality, strength, and wisdom. He was not about to let them, if the prophecies were correct, become corrupted and lost. He still had too many unanswered questions. He still had too much life to live.

He was close now. Very close. He could feel the power ebbing and flowing. *How could this be?* Elcon thought to himself. He had never before felt anything like this, and he had traveled through these streets many times on personal and religious engagements. The wealthiest of Tur'Mor would never degrade themselves with the baser citizens and would therefore hold private ceremonies and studies at great cost to themselves and benefit to the Church, of course. Whatever was causing this had attracted very dark things, very dark indeed.

Elcon reached into his swordsman's coat and pulled forth a hammer-shaped amulet with a sapphire set in the head. He held the heavy jewel-set golden amulet for a short moment. Only one thing, as he had known before meeting Darius, could destroy dark creatures, and that was concentrated Everlight. Cut out the heart, place an amulet within the wound and the creature would be consumed by light. For where there was light, there could be no darkness.

Elcon was now nearing a towering gate of wood and iron, a plaque with golden, raised letters spelled out, "ALDORIAN." It was the last house on the street. This house was an old house, with high blood indeed. However, just before he reached the gate, something within the courtyard erupted. A blast of some unnatural form. A blast which, for some reason, he recognized. He had heard that same sound before, but where?

It had been at the Mayoral Residency, when the King's Jewel had been nearly taken, Elcon realized. That night had been a catastrophe. It had taken hours to Mend the minds of all those who had witnessed what had taken place. Dozens of Vision Blessed sisters correcting the memories of each of those in attendance, and many Healing Blessed covering the wounds of those injured. But here, how? There was no way that –

A sharp sound, like glass shattering, resonated, cutting Elcon's thought short. The old priest rushed to the gate, sword in one hand and amulet in the other. When he reached the gate, he found it open, the lock having been broken by what appeared to be brute force. Once inside the gate, Elcon's eyes bore witness to a very disturbing scene.

Trees were uprooted, tossed violently about. Statues were broken and scattered, and flowers ripped from their beds. There had been a fountain in the middle of the front courtyard, at the center of a circular drive. It was broken, and water spewed and gurgled in all directions. And on the drive lay a figure in white, unmoving.

Elcon moved cautiously towards the body, eyes darting this way and that, searching for any signs of motion, any hint of an attacker lurking in the rubble. But he saw nothing, he heard nothing, so he continued forward. When he reached the body, his stomach turned. It was a girl, no older than her early twenties. She had snow-white hair, straight and short. The left side of her face bore a nasty cut, fresh and deep – her eye was dead. The right shoulder had a terrible wound that oozed a vile black liquid. The poison seemed to have permeated through most of her body, for her veins were all dark and her skin taking on a sickly hue. However, something strange caught Elcon's eye. He outstretched a hand to turn over her body to see the emblem inked into her chest of vibrant, shimmering blue.

Her hand shot up, clutching his wrist with a vise-like grip, cold as ice. Her left eye blazed alight and her head turned to face Elcon.

"I am Iaenora." Her voice was strained, as if she spoke through breathing in, though it was loud and terrible. "I am One of Seven, awoken again. Oathbound. I require the Light."

The hand of the wounded shoulder reached out and tore Elcon's amulet from his neck. The girl breathed in so deeply, gasping, rasping in pain and agony. The Everlight flowed from the hammer into the girl's open mouth. It washed over her flesh. It soaked her eyes and twisted up into inhaling nostrils. And when she was done, the stone was dull.

"Impossible!" Elcon gasped as he wrenched his arm free, all the while staring wide-eyed at the girl.

"I need to replenish," Iaenora said in her terrible, booming voice. "I must recover this body. It is weak. Please, take me to where the Source Touches this Realm. Surely you know of this place."

"I...I..." Elcon could not form words. This was impossible, wasn't it? Well, wasn't it what was prophesied? The Sages would return, and she was of the Light; he could feel it emanating from her. And the way she drained that gemstone? A healer could have healed a dozen men with that much light and not even dimmed it in the slightest.

"There is little time, Priest of Ordan. Take me to the place I have spoken. The body of this one is strong, but weak. She has suffered much since the Bonding. The Keyholder chose well with this one, but there is little time."

"Of course," Elcon muttered. What else was he going to say? "But it is a long ride from here."

"There is no time for the ride, show me." And with that, she reached out a hand and touched Elcon's forehead.

Elcon saw himself, though out-of-body. He saw himself awakening this morning and getting ready. *Flicker.* He saw himself below the city with the Avajan'Aluth. *Flicker.* He saw himself beneath the monastery. *Flicker.* He saw himself in the Chamber of the Oracles, sitting amongst the Holy Council, staring at the crevasse on the floor. And then he saw a brief glimpse of Darius as the vision folded in upon itself.

"So, you knew of him, did you?" The air split with a boom and Iaenora soared into the sky, leaving Elcon on the ground staring upwards in bewilderment amidst a cloud of swirling dust.

CHAPTER 38: ENDINGS AND BEGINNINGS

If Darius was being honest, death was not so bad after all. It was a peaceful feeling; far less painful than the life he had known. There were no wounds nor aches or pains. The fear was gone; that terrible, gnawing thing. He could breathe easily, and so he did. A wisp of golden mist whirled before his eyes, flowing from his open mouth.

Darius cocked his head.

Well, that's not natural... He let out a long, deep, guttural laugh, one he had not allowed in many, many years. *None of this is natural. I'm dead.*

He looked at his hands. Translucent flesh, like millions of individual shards of glass, refracting light in all directions, formed his body. Veins of golden light could be seen beneath the glassy flesh, like tiny yellow rivers, pulsating.

A rolling peel of thunder sounded in the distance.

The earth beneath Darius was scarred, blasted by some powerful thing. The trees about him were shattered shafts of wood, uprooted or snapped like twigs. The sky was a dark purple and the stars shone like gemstones, each a different color.

Instinctively, Darius rose from the scarred earth and headed to the edge of a cliff he knew would find himself upon. And so it was, like a sail furled over the sea of land below, Darius looked out over oblivion, except it was not oblivion this time.

Endless fields of vibrant green rolled out before him. Thousands of beings conversed as they walked to and fro on the grassy plains. Their bodies looked like his own, translucent and glittering. Veins of gold under their skin, pumping the eternal blood of light.

As Darius stared at the hosts of resplendent beings, he began to pick out faces from amongst the multitudes. First was Angenthor, his white-haired and wizened old friend. He had been a counselor to Darius from the day his father went back to the earth. The next was the Lord of Tur, Tareth. His face was peaceful as he talked with his son, Tarish. A single tear streamed from his eye as picked out his brother and then his mother, both walking together, speaking in words he could not hear. And how he longed to hear them, to stand with them. A lump formed as he saw the towering figure that was his father, standing proudly amongst the Great Ones of Old, the ancient chiefs of the Twelve. His face was clear of scars, his body whole once more. His eyes shone with the same brightness of all those below, and he appeared at peace.

In the dark and rolling clouds that spanned the heavens, a face formed. The eyes were stars, the brows lightning. A mouth of gaping winds revealed a tongue of fire. Eternal was the being, and endless was its presence. And it gazed down upon Darius with all the weight of existence.

Are you the High Father? Are you his son, Fenron? Darius pleaded into the skies. *Do you even hear me?*

Do you hurt?

Darius started to answer, but then stopped short, unsure as to how he could.

You were chosen, Last of the Sons of the Feromage. Last Guardian. Last of the Oathsworn. You were to find them!

Find who? Find what? What is all of this? I slayed the beast, didn't I? I saved the forest from its darkness. I saved the people from the creature that would have slayed all. What more do you want from me? Darius screamed into the endless skies. There might have been no hurt, not physically anyways, but his emotions were still raw in this place. And he had found his voice, and it was strong.

You are what you are, Denathurias of the Iron Mount Tribe. And I am what I am!

Darius's golden heart nearly stopped. Denathurias, his True Name. It had been given to him by the Spirit Guide. He had never uttered that name to any man, save his father alone at the Passing of the Ring. He felt his mouth go dry. An odd sensation, as there was no saliva there in the first place. His thumb jerked to his finger, seeking out that familiar silver ring. It was not there.

I know you, Son of the Forests, Son of the Mountains, Son of the Guardians. You are the Last of the Sons of the Feromage! And your oaths are not yet fulfilled, nor is your duty!

Am I not dead?

Seven! the voice thundered, sending a surge of wind and a spattering of frigid rain from the darkening skies. *Six slept while One remained. You have Bonded the Daughter of the Skies, who is precious to me, and thus begun the Return.*

What do you mean? Darius called out, nearly overcome with emotions. First of these being shock and awe – incomprehensible were the feelings of communication between him and this unearthly being. But the greatest emotion was fueled by that of need, a burning, seething need to understand.

Find the others! Bind them! You are called upon to fulfill the Final Oath. This is your final obligation. This is your birthright.

How? How can you ask this of me now?

A low rumble echoed through the skies, a thunderous booming that crawled slowly across the winds. A smile, if it could be called that, seemed to spread across the eternal face in the heavens.

Darius felt a jolt, as if something reached into his stomach and pulled hard at his organs. It tugged on him, ripping the scene from his eyes, pulling him from the reality in which he stood.

A path has been chosen, once more to be trod. Another you must abandon. Guard our Light with all your might. But mind you the night, for desolations gather. The Sages Return once more to the land. They must be found.

How will I know them? What must I do? Darius pleaded into the night sky. His family had already vanished, as well as Angenthor and Tareth. He longed to look upon them, but the pulling sensation would not allow it. Bright beams of light began to penetrate the face in the clouds, shining blindingly into Darius's own.

It is the end of an era, but another must rise. You must find them!

Don't leave me like this!

Find them! Thunder rolled, growing ever distant as the face faded away into the wind.

Please! I have questions! Don't do this to me!

Find them, or blood shall rain!

Blinding, all-consuming light seared Darius's eyes. And the pain was back once more, and it was terrible. There was something else, something distant. A voice? Yes, that was it, a voice. It was a woman's voice, though the accent was all wrong. Or perhaps, it was all right. Whatever it was, it was not of the Iarainn Tribes. It was rich, melodic, and very worried.

Darius raised a hand to his eyes. Something sticky touched his face. He could smell the iron of blood, along with other strange smells. *Is that goat piss? No... of course not, right?* Something else rubbed on his cheek as fingers ran over his beard, nose, and eyes. It was cool, hard, and felt very, very right. *My ring!*

And the memories flooded him.

He was in a cave. He had been traveling with a woman. What was her – Izebal! That was her talking now. And was she laughing? But the cave... there had been an Itheanam. Where was it? Did his stupid stunt work? By the gods on high, it had, hadn't it?

He had shoved his ring into the beast's mouth, forcing it down Gulad's throat as they crashed into the wall. Darius knew only two things could kill a soulless one. And those were light, pure light, and Ellitheor Silver. The latter of which just so happened to be what his ring was forged of.

Darius let out a laugh of realization. And then let out a subsequent cry of pain.

"Gurgha huhlg!" he roared, but then choked on a lung-full of blood, which sent him into a fit of raspy hacking and coughing. He had meant to scream, "What in the flaming pits of Halfak?" but his mouth could not form the words. This episode of violent heaving and jerking motion, however, did not help the pain that had caused his swearing, the greatest of which was emanating from his side.

Darius's eyes were still unfocused, though blurry shapes and forms were now beginning to coalesce into blobs of grey. The voice from before floated about him, originating from a particularly curvaceous grey blur, which was slowly focusing into emerald cloth and liquid black hair that curled as it flowed over the shoulders and around the almond face of Izebal.

"*Bjornhak rahsfadan*, Darius!" Izebal's voice echoed through the cloud of incomprehension that clogged Darius's ears.

Growing more and more lucid with every passing moment, Darius pushed himself up on his right elbow. The twinge of pain that shot through his body caused him to wince, but he did well to stifle the desire to cry out again. An action that had not helped in the slightest before.

"*Dhande'lal yhelna vra.*"

Izebal's harmonic voice, despite tremulous quivering, washed over Darius. He smiled, whether towards her or off in some other direction, he did not know. He could not help it. Something about her voice just seemed to make everything else seem less important, less painful. He relished in the sound, if only for a moment, before the terrible realization of what he had seen in the cavern came crashing through the trance.

"The girl." Darius forced the labored words out of his trembling lips. The muscles of his jaw were tight with bruises, his tongue heavy and coated with blood and bile.

"Darius." Izebal sounded astonished.

What happened?

"You can speak, how?"

"The girl," Darius grunted, finding more and more strength with every moment. The room too was growing clearer, what was only just foggy blurs now appearing as sharp features in his eyes. And then he saw his side.

Shocking was not a strong enough word, nor was *disgusting* appropriate either. *Grotesque* could be used to describe the current state of his body. But then, one would also need to evoke the word *miraculous* to further describe the nature of the restorative process taking place.

Darius, who had seen himself heal from a thousand wounds, stared in utter bewilderment as tendrils of light stitched his flesh, retracted his blood, and mended his organs. He gawked at the speed at which it was all taking place, and then nearly laughed as he felt the pain ebb away, like a falling tide being lost to the sea.

No grievous scar marked his body; only a single, circular mark. This had been where the central horn of the Itheanam had punctured his flesh. All the tearing, disembowelment and hemorrhaging was gone, erased by a source beyond what Darius knew he himself was capable of producing. He had once told Elcon that there was no healing death. He had resigned himself to his fate. And yet, here he was. Sent back from the grave to find these mystic Sages of whom that high priest had only spoken of in hushed tones.

That being said, those Sages would have to wait, if only a little longer. Questions, purposes, and memories could all wait, for there was a far more pressing matter at hand.

"Careful, Darius," Izebal cautioned as she laid a gentle hand on his bare shoulder, urging him to stay down and rest.

Darius, feeling the touch of flesh on flesh, suddenly became acutely aware of his lack of clothing. He had been so caught up in the moment he had totally forgotten he wore naught but his undergarments, and only those that covered his crotch. A flash of heat turned the tips of his ears and the back of his neck scarlet.

"Ah," Izebal chortled. "Do not be embarrassed, my friend. I have seen all manner of bodies. Besides, you have nothing to be ashamed of." She winked at him with the last remark, which sent a secondary flush of heat up his neck and into his cheeks and ears.

"There is a girl," Darius said after clearing his throat. "Please, I am fine. Go, tend to her. I'll be right there."

Izebal, looking rather unconvinced, finally conceded to Darius's plea. She rose and made her way across the cavern to the dais where the red-veined marble altar loomed.

With a grunt, a snarl, and a silent curse, Darius picked himself up from the floor. He felt strangely invigorated. True, the pain had washed away, but the echo of it still haunted his nervous system. Ghost pangs sent shudders down his spine, and he winced as he walked, though nothing actually hurt him.

He found his pants first. To his delight, they were nearly unmarred, and he once again gave thanks to the old priest Ranun, whose kindness had provided for him once more, even in death. His boots were not far, but his socks had not survived this fight. He sighed, but then remembered he had a spare pair in his bag.

Darius looked around the room and spotted the satchel. It was open, its contents spilled. He hurried over to the leather bag and began shoving things back in, taking little thought to what he was doing. It was in this moment he realized that the crystalline vial was gone. The vial that that Blessed had given him. He looked around the cavern, which was pinpricked with rays of sunlight, but he did not see it.

Strange, he thought as he wondered what had caused that. But he hadn't the time to stop and ponder. Urgency filled his mind once more.

Quickly, he slid his feet into the thick wool socks and then laced up his heavy boots with a turn of the cogs on either side. He was reaching for the crumpled shirt when Izebal called out.

"Darius! You need to see this!"

Without a second thought, Darius scooped up the bag, his shirt, and the long overcoat from the ground. He rushed across the cave towards Izebal and that horrid altar. However, when he stopped next to Izebal, he dropped his load onto the dais in shock.

The little body had been cut free of its bandages. Darius had never been one to get squeamish, but the naked body of the young girl was a horrific sight to behold. Her curly, red hair was pasted to her face, the bandages having been pressed tight to her flesh. Blots of blood and filth matted her hair and blemished her freckled face. Lifeless eyes bore a greyish, yellow tinge. And her flesh, pale as moonlight, was riddled with veins and bones pressed close to the surface in starvation.

As Darius stared at the girl, his eyes stopped on the only article of adornment upon her slender frame. A necklace hung about her, the emblem resting on her undeveloped chest. It was silver and bore the face of a wolf whose eyes were set with two, small sapphires. He gasped as he saw what that silver was. Not normal silver at all, but Ellitheor Silver. The selfsame silver from whence his ring had been forged.

"She is alive... But there is a darkness over her," Izebal said as she ran her hand over the unresponsive girl. "She is beyond my abilities to heal."

"What do you mean?" Darius asked without looking away from the pitiful sight.

"We must take her to her clan," Izebal answered. Her voice then turned sour. "There is a powerful mage amongst the Bordermen. I fear he is her only hope."

"Mage?" Darius asked, finally tearing his eyes away from the girl and facing Izebal. "Bordermen?"

Izebal let out a long sigh, and when she spoke, her voice was troubled, "In Talahmnas, amongst the Ruthvin Clan, there is a mage, powerful enough my own people know of him. He is called Tyree. It is said that he is a master of healing and spirits. A practitioner of the arcane ways."

"And you think he can help her?"

"I am not sure," Izebal answered. "But I do know that this little one has not much *ma'lahana* left. If she is to survive, we must try this thing."

"Then we must take her there at once!" Darius said as he turned back. He dropped the leather satchel and took the white shirt and pulled it over the girl's naked body. He then pulled his coat over himself, concealing his own bare torso.

However, as he swooped the girl up in his arms, Izebal spoke with a pained hesitancy.

"Darius, there is something you must know. The Bordermen, the Danes as they are known, despise my people. They believe we Diju are lesser, an abomination."

"Izebal, you said it yourself, we must help this girl," Darius replied forcefully.

Izebal sighed and nodded her head in begrudging agreement. He was right, she thought with a sigh of deference. *The more I see this man, the more awed I am. How is it he is so good? How is it he has such hope, such trust?* She smiled as Darius carried the little one in his arms. So gentle, so tender he was with her. However, the smile faded fast as the realization of what would come next crept back into her mind.

The Danesmen. A proud and cruel lot. They had long been a scourge to her kin. They hated the Diju, and the Diju despised them. For hundreds of years, the two groups had been at each other's throats.

Izebal wanted to cry and laugh. She would just have to trust this man in front of her once more. Trust that he would be able to overcome centuries of discrimination, seemingly uncompromising hate and venom, and for what? All to save this little girl. She winced as an admonishing impression pierced her melancholy mind. *Had he taken a second thought to save me? He did not even know who or what I was, and he just rushed in with no thought to himself.* If there was one who could achieve such a feat, Izebal could think of none more suited to the task.

Izebal hurried after Darius, who was now nearly to the steps that led out of the cavern, when something caught her eye.

The horn rested on the floor, glittering with an ominous light that did not mirror any direct beam of sun. She hurried over to it as Darius was heading up the stairs.

"Now this is odd," she mumbled to herself as she ran a finger over the twisted silver. It was hot, very, very hot. She jerked back, the feeling of something still very dark and evil bound to the thing.

Izebal craned her head about, making sure Darius was not looking, and then hefted the horn from the floor and snuck it into her rucksack. It disappeared from sight without a sound, and she quickly lashed her satchel shut.

Realizing that the delay might cause questions and feeling quite uncomfortable for some reason for taking the horn, Izebal gazed about the room with a hurried glance. It was in this final overview that she spotted Darius's hickory staff laying on the floor. She chuckled when she recognized the rod. A self-lauding laugh. She knew she had enchanted the bit of wood well, but the thing had taken a rather harsh beating and it had held up better than she could have hoped.

She hurried forward, taking up the staff and then turning towards the steps. A feeling of unease crept at the back of her mind. She did not like hiding things from Darius. As she passed the crumpled door, she assured herself that it was of little consequence. And by the time she emerged from the jagged mouth of the cave and into the forest, Izebal had put away any feelings of guilt or deceit. She had always been one to collect odd and strange things.

Darius stood two paces from the cave's entrance. His tired face turned bright as he saw her emerge. Izebal felt something she had never experienced before as the man before her smiled at her, despite his pain, despite all that he had faced. He smiled a gentle, tender smile that could not be mistaken for anything other than relief.

"I found your stick." Izebal fumbled the words. Since when did she struggle with speaking?

"Thank you." Darius laughed as he tilted his head just so.

The sunlight beamed off his face in the clearing. *Hadn't this been a dreary, swampy place?*

The two stared at each other for another moment, and then the big man's eyes fell downwards. Izebal felt heat rise in her chest as he did. He looked so noble, so good, so kind and strong. True, he was dirty, bloodied, and missing his shirt. Well, she smirked, perhaps that last part was helping his appearance after all.

"I do not know the way from here," Darius mumbled as he stared down at the earth like a lumbering imbecile. *Isn't he literally holding a girl's life in his hands? What in the blazes is coming over him?*

"I do," Izebal answered. Her voice was uncharacteristically breathy. *She must have run up those stairs. And for what?*

"Good," Darius answered, perhaps a little too hurriedly.

"I'll lead the way then," Izebal continued as she walked past him. "It is a long way still, but I do believe Ethenealal has blessed us with good sun and clear passage. I can feel the earth, her rhythm and her tones once more. This way, Darius, we must be off."

Darius nodded in agreement and fell in step behind Izebal as she headed northward through the forest. Yes, purposes and plans would have to wait. Sages and songs as well. Darius would fulfill his duty, that much, he was sure. But until this little one was safe. Well, he would do the right thing by her, even if it meant putting off his duty for a short while.

A laugh tried to find its way out, but Darius stifled it. And what had caused such an emotion? One thousand years he had slept beneath the crypts of Ordiatian soil – what could a few days' march change? Besides, was it not the land of the Danes where he was commanded to go? Perhaps this truly was all part of a bigger picture, part of a masterful plan that had been crafted by the High Father in his infinite wisdom.

Well, whatever it was, Darius would meet it face on. He would never lose himself again, and he would never be without purpose. He knew what his duty was, even if the path was still unclear.

The Final Oath. The Unspoken Oath. All Feromage had sworn this oath. And yet, never once had any had to fulfill its terrible fate. Darius was ready to accept that fate, if not quite yet. This little one, he would save her first. He had to. Darius snorted. Then... well, then he would figure out the rest.

End of Book 1

"Thank you for reading."
David A. Trotter

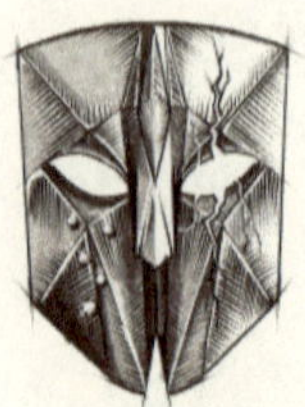

EPILOGUE

Clump, drag. Clump, drag. Clump, drag. Clump, drag.

Pain seared the nerves with every limping step. Agony, dulled by the years but ever-present, ever-persistent, gnawed at Tassi's body as he pushed himself to continue, as he had always done, forward. However, it was not his old, familiar pain that discomforted him this evening. No, it was the chamber he found himself in. Dimly lit and far too garish for his bleak taste, the Chamber of the Illuminated One was the one room Tassi never felt comfortable entering.

"Welcome, Master Huntsman," a man in long, purple robes stated.

The shrouded man had his back to Tassi, something the Huntsman found rather unsettling. No one turned their back to him; they were all too afraid of what he might do. But this purple-clad man seemed to not even care. The golden trims of his robes rested easily on the mosaic floors, covering the slippers Tassi knew the powerful man to wear.

Tassi knew his wardrobe. He knew his mannerisms, he knew his title, his reach, and his power. But he did not know his name, not truly.

"Illuminated One," Tassi's iron voice creaked in reply as he tried his best to offer a bow, the metal plate in his hip sending a jolt of pain while doing so.

The man stared at a painting that was three times the height of a man, towering from floor to ceiling. It depicted a war, but not of mortals but of gods. Tassi knew the painting, he had seen it here a dozen times. It was of Ordan, Gallea, Fenron, Morgana, and Moranna fighting, clawing, tearing at one another. Tendrils of power, depicted by vivid greens, blues, and black-tinged maroons writhed and flowed from each of the beings. Muscles, far too large, far too sculpted for any human to possess, wound themselves around the mighty Ellitheor, who were locked in mortal combat with one another. Ordan wielded Ethra, in whose head was set the great Stone of Ria'Elahm, showering his physic in streams of emerald brilliance. Fenron hewed at the body of a Soulless One, an Itheanam, with his mystic blade of Godslight. From Morgana's bare chest a flow of blackness inked the portrait, casting unnatural shadows across the others.

"The Fight at the Dimdreal." The Illuminated was said, still staring up at the colossal painting. "Did you know that up until this point, it is said that mankind had never Touch the Lights of the Celesti?"

"No," Tassi's answer was frank. He did not know, nor did he care. Tassi had never liked those that could. Unnatural things, dark things, and twisted humans; hence his occupation. Tassi killed those corrupted by the so-called Lights. He did not care if it were blue, green, or the anti-black-maroon color. Unnatural was unnatural and damn any who thought otherwise. Besides, it paid well, killing nightmares and stories, and that made up for it. A jolt of pain surged to the tip of the bone wrapped in leather that was set into his steel leg. Well, it made up for most.

"This world, this land that we live upon, it was not made for magics." The Illuminated on continued, hands locked behind his back, the long sleeves of his robes covering them. "No, this was a world barren of any such things before the coming of the Elder Ones and the Ellitheor. We do not talk of it, we do not teach it, but there are texts, verses lost to the eyes of mankind that tell of a people virgin to mysticism. That the only source of power was held by the ancient protectors of this land, the dragons."

"Dragons?" Tassi could not conceal the scoff in his question.

"Is it so strange?" The Illuminated One snapped in response, whirling around while speaking to reveal a face completely masked in gold, save for two eye holes and barred slits for breathing over the mouth. Strange runes were etched into the fitted mask, eerie and unnatural, that made Tassi want to reach for his pistol. He did not, and the Illuminated One continued his high-winded rant. "You, you have slain hundreds of beasts, dark and incorporeal. Draugr, gaukal, goblin and troll. You have burned wraiths and bested skerrak. But you disbelieve in dragons?"

"I disbelieve anything I have never seen," Tassi replied. "But Wise One, I never discredit the chance of something new. Or, in this, very ancient."

"And what of the Zau'fi peoples, the Tuawtian tribes, who worship the great beasts?"

"What of them?"

"Do you not think that their religions pull from some truth?" The Illuminated One questioned, the rage extinguished from his voice.

"Does not the Ordaitian people's own religion point out that Touch is only a gift from a god?" Tassi countered, and to his surprise, the cloaked leader of the Asterivians was silent for a span.

"You are wiser than you give yourself credit for, Alessandro Tassi," the chuckle that followed The Illuminated One's words chilled the Huntsman to the core. "Not the mindless brute the orators paint you to be. A thinker I see before me."

Tassi cleared his throat, not chancing a reply. He did not like others to know him, observe him, or speculate about him in any way. He had built a brand for himself, a name. Tassi was hard, far harder than any other man in all of Ethrea. He would kill, cut, burn, or blast any that stood between him and his contract.

"Ah," The Illuminated One sighed. "But you did not come to speak of dragons and gods, did you?"

"No."

"To the point. Very well then," replied the masked man. "Did you complete your commission?"

Tassi growled slowly as he scratched the scruff of his chin with gauntleted-fingers. His dead eyes lifted to face the Illuminated One and he spoke in short, gruff tones. "He was at the Fourth-Eye, as you said he'd be, I could smell'em, got a stink to him like no other Light Toucher male I've ever met."

"I don't pay you to question," the Illuminated One said, noticing Tassi's trailing remarks. "Did the boy make it to Ranok?"

"Boy? He is nearly my size and looked to be hewn from an old oak. He ain't no defenseless boy," scowled Tassi. His eyebrows then climbed, and he laughed aloud. It was a gravely, harsh laugh. "Ha! He knocked one of those tin heads real good. Crumpled'em like a boned fish and bolted straight to Ranok."

"Anything else to disclose?" The lack of patience was beginning to show in the Illuminated's voice, so Tassi cleared his throat.

"Sent a fifteen or so head after'em, to trail'em. Told them to stay far back, don't get seen," Tassi's smile went sour. "Truth is, ain't heard a word from them since then. Not a peep. Strange of Horace to hold silence, and it's been over a week."

"The boy should have made it through Ranok in a week," the Illuminated One did not seem to be addressing Tassi, least not that he could tell. That damn golden mask made it impossible to see facial features and the blue lenses screened the eyes. It made the Huntsman very uncomfortable indeed.

"You commissioned me to get him to the woods, not through it." Tassi found his backbone again, taking a step towards the Illuminated One. "Anything extra I did was of my own free will, to show my gratitude. But had you wanted him to arrive, I could've slit the necks of Orrum's goons and taken him to the Borderlands myself."

"You are right, Master Huntsman," replied the robed man without emotion. "You did your part, and you shall have your reward, as promised."

The Illuminated One clapped gloved hand together thrice.

A door opened, and then two curtains were drawn apart to reveal said door. Three personages in robes deep red and masks of silver, molded to look as if they were weeping, appeared through the opening. The first wore a grey apron over his robes with a large cog stitched over an open scroll and from the borders hung long, braided bits of blue fringe.

Tassi knew there were several Orders and Levels, or Lights as they called them, to the Asterivian Cult. That being said, he did not know what any save the purple robes denoted. Only the Illuminated One and Its Eyes and Hand wore the purple and gold, only they were ever permitted to speak in Tassi's presence.

"You're payment, Master Huntsman," stated the Illuminated One, gesturing to the rather plain-looking box. Strange for Alessandro to care about how something looked on the outside, things were things. But in a place like this, everything held meaning, everything was crusted with symbolism and secrecy.

The two carrying the long box set it down without a sound. The leading Asterivian produced a key from his neck and knelt to unlock the box. As he did so, the other two hurried across the room and lifted a chair, bringing it to rest behind Tassi. There was a sharp click as the tumbles of the lock fell into place, and then cling as the melt bolt opened. A red-gloved hand was placed on either shoulder, ushering Alessandro Tassi into the seat as the lid of the box opened.

"This took the Order of Understanding much effort to craft, Master Huntsman." Again, the Illuminated One spoke with all emotion devoid from his voice.

"It looks, spectacular," stammered Tassi, unable to lift his eyes from the gleaming contents of the box.

A mechanical leg lay on black velvet. Not like the one he currently wore. No, this looked almost organic. There were pistons and tubes, sockets and cogs, but all so meticulously crafted that it did not seem humanly possible.

"Will it do as you say it will?"

"Let us find out together," replied the leader of the Asterivians, a slight rise in his voice, a subtle hint of curiosity.

One of the robed individuals grabbed the cuff of Alessandro's pant leg and pulled it up until it was above mid-thigh, or at least where mid-thigh should have been. A skeletal prosthetic of dull metal was strapped to the stump of scared meat that made up what was left of his leg. There was a joint with two cogs where the knee should have been and something similar for the ankle, which was being revealed as his boot was removed from the mechanism.

"It's got toes," Tassi did not mean to speak out loud, but when the leg had been lifted from the box, he saw the detailed work, the physiology of it.

His own contraption, which had once awed him to look upon, now appeared even more foul and inhuman than it had this morning when he had strapped it to himself, just as he had done every morning for countless days, years. Tassi's reminiscing was cut short, and he swatted the hand away that was reaching for the buckles that strapped the damn thing to his leg. "I still have my dignity still."

"Gentle, Master Huntsman," chided the Illuminated One. "None shall lay a hand upon my own."

The old leg was discreetly done away with, one of the red-robed individuals diseasing through the doorway with it, never returning. The other who did not wear the apron hefted up the other leg, and despite their apparent effort, Tassi would have thought the leg to be near impossible to lift. It appeared to be solid metal, with only the apparatus on the backside of the leg, mostly covered by smooth caste metal to resemble human muscle and tissue.

"Now, Master Huntsman," the Illuminated One said as the leg was turned so that the socket was facing the stump of Tassi's femur. "I have been told that this part may cause you some discomfort."

Before Alessandro understood what the man meant, the apron-wearing Asterivian twisted something at the head of the metal leg. There was a small popping noise, like a thumb being quickly pulled from the mouth, and then a cavity was revealed. A cavity filled with long, sharp needles and tubes.

The two Asterivians in red jammed the metal leg into Tassi's thigh stub.

Tassi screamed.

The two continued turning paper-thin rings, which seemed to snake up the leg and wrap around the meat of Tassi's thigh, binding the metal leg even tighter. Searing pain coursed through Tassi's body and he screamed as the needles were forced deeper and deeper into bone, flesh, and muscles. One of the cultists retrieved three blue stones from a black sack, which shone with vibrant light. Unable to think, Alessandro tore at the arms of the chair upon which he was sitting. He bellowed in agony, but the cultists did not cease their work.

The three stones were set into the leg, each placed in a compartment that seemed to materialize out of nowhere as a finger was pressed and then turned in quick succession. The openings, once fitted with a stone each, then closed without command.

Tassi's mouth was filled with bile. He could taste a bitterness he could not explain. Something had been in that leg, something unnatural. It burned at his tongue, it ate at his lungs and esophagus. His gut felt as if it were being filled with molten lava, and his thigh itched from pain. It itched as if a thousand ants were crawling about the metal hoops that sealed his thigh to the prosthetic. It itched from the top of his hip down to his knee.

Tassi's eyes went wide.

Despite the pain, the horrible, gut-wrenching pain, he could not deny what he just felt.

His knee, the back of it, itched.

His calf tightened, and his leg kicked outward in reflex.

Alessandro Tassi leapt from the chair. And he landed on his own two feet, awkwardly, but on two feet. He could feel the floor, the cold, the hardness of it, the slight creases and uneven portions. His toes moved, one by one. Up and down. He lifted his leg, and then, for the first time in a very, very long time, he took a step. He took a step, without that cursed clump, drag.

"It appears to work."

The words caught Tassi off-guard. He had forgotten everything. Where he was, who he was with. His heart took a spiraling dive downwards.

"Well, it seems you are beginning to understand without me even saying," sighed the Illuminated One in a pleased tone. He waved his hands and the other two quickly grabbed the old leg, threw it in the case, and hurried from the room without a word. "Your leg is quite the marvel, isn't it?"

Tassi stared back dumbly.

Tassi had always had the upper hand. He had always been the only one to hunt, to take advantage. He had the sinking feeling that that paradigm was about to shift out of his favor.

"I have spent years gathering the best and the brightest to my Court," said the Illuminated One as he turned away from Alessandro and back to his painting. "I have spent fortunes beyond your meager comprehension. And for what? What purpose?"

"I..." stammered Alessandro stupidly, tears and snot running down his grim face. "I don't know."

"Silence!" Barked the Illuminated One. He then drew a steadying breath. "I did all this for a glorious purpose. For the gods, they do not die. So neither shall I. Purpose beyond comprehension. Life without end."

"I did what was asked of me," Tassi growled, albeit weakly. "What more could you want?"

"What more?" Laughed the Illuminated One as he turned away from his grand painting. "Why, everything! You will be my hound. You and your Huntsmen shall be the dogs leading the hunt for immortality. You shall go where I won't, do what I cannot be seen to do, be the knife in the dark that I must have. These Kh'ar have been a thorn in my heel for too long. It is time we aid the good people of Ordiatea and exterminate these so-called Robbers."

"I hunt tainted bests and Light-sick men, not street thugs," Tassi replied, finding more and more of his spine. "Find someone else. You've paid for my work, that's all that was guaranteed."

"Oh? Is that what you think? I do not think it is. You see, I know that you know. I own you now, Huntsman. That leg of yours needs Everlight and there is only one source known on this continent. So, you can either serve me or that contraption will slowly poison you once the light fades away. Our studies showed that it is a very horrific end. The flesh is eaten away much like acid."

Tassi stared at those blue lenses that hid the eyes of his new master. He wanted to be defiant, he wanted to lash out. But what would happen? What other safeguards were put in place on this thing. He had seen how just running a finger on certain areas of it had opened secret compartments, what if there were explosives or poison, just as the cultists had admitted there was. Had walked straight into this. He had gone against his better judgment, and now he was trapped in a prison of his own body.

"What would you have me do?" The question came from a defeated man, not the great Alessandro Tassi, Head of the Huntsmen, Terror of the Night.

"First, I need to know what happened to your men," stated the Illuminated One. "Secondly, have you, in all your dealings, ever stumbled across the name of one called Edous?"

***

Time meant nothing. There were only the hard walls of a dark box, barely large enough to lay flat in, with three holes drilled on either side. And when the caravan would stop, smoke from some hallucinogenic plant would be bellowed into the box, turning vision into nothing more than swirling colors. That was until the sack was forced on, obscuring all light once more, and brutish men forced him off the trail to relieve himself. Such had been the past several days or so, he did not know how many.

Men shouting, horses whining, and metal clanking loudly outside broke the monotone monotony of two mules, four men, and two women three horses and oxen pulling his cart. He had become so used to the repetitive sounds of the men grumbling, the mules braying, and the women carrying on, that the sounds of newness nearly overwhelmed him. And yet, he knew those sounds. He understood them in a deep, dark part of himself, a part of himself he had sealed away too many years ago.

"Halt! State your business!"

"Letters of Writ, Sargent," exclaimed one of the men, accompanied by a ruffling of parchment being pulled from a leather tube. "I'm Captain Del Maltiso, of the Four-o-Five. I have urgent business as stated!"

"Have to check, sir. No offense, sir!" replied the first.

There was the briefest of pauses.

"Are we clear?" barked out Captain Del Maltiso.

"Aye, sir! Command Tents are towards Centerfield. The tower there, he'll be near there, sir. Shall I send an escort?"

"No, Sargent. You're to look after my company, as I ride alone, save my two officers. Lieutenants, this way."

There was a crack of reigns and then the oxcart creaked forward. When the cart finally came to a stop, there was another exchange of papers and titles. But then a strangely familiar voice, like a ghost from the past, and barely audible from inside the box, began ushering commands. All others fell silent.

The box was lifted from the cart and set on the ground, surprisingly gently this time.

"Everyone out!" commanded the man with the voice of a forgone memory.

There were several complaints, but they were quelled with a ferocity of a man who had earned the title of The Lion of Ordiatea rightfully, there was no mistaking it now.

The tent they were in was quickly evacuated with begrudging, "Yes, sirs!"

The Lion drew a breath and the lock on the box fell away.

"Hello, cousin," Mikel Thanadius, the Lion of Ordiatea said with his same old crooked smile. Though, his curly beard now had streaks of grey in it, where it had once been midnight black. "Strange, reality is, isn't it? You had to die to escape me all those years ago. And now, in your recent death, you come back to me."

"I...I don't understand."

"You never could see the bigger picture, could you, Marcel?" Mikel laughed with a shake of his head.

Mikel looked good. His thick, curly hair had not started to grey as his beard had. He wore his officer's jacket well; the golden epaulets were a nice touch to the purple coat that had not been there the last time he had seen his cousin. Mikel had broadened across the shoulders and chest, though he still maintained that slim, warrior's build.

"Marcel died, I don't know that man anymore," was the only response that he could offer up, his eyes watering with thousands of emotions; guilt, love, hate, betrayal, envy, hurt, embarrassment. It had been he, not his cousin, who had led those men to their death. It was not Mikel's fault; it had never been.

"True, but so did, was it, Felik?" Mikel crooked an eyebrow as he said it. He then extended his hand and took Felik by himself, pulling him upright.

"I am a disgrace to you and this military," Felik replied with a grimace. "You should not have brought me here."

"Do you take me for a fool, cousin?" The whip-like snap from compassion to stern reprimand struck Felik harder than the question itself. He had spent the last thirteen years or more playing burglar and bandit, thieving and stealing for a living. Mikel had been commanding an army, leading the Ordiatian forces against the Calun and their Tyrannical King.

"No," muttered Felik awkwardly. "I just, I just don't see what you could want with me. Except to humiliate me further. But then, why not just let me be hanged for trying to steal the Jewel."

"Put that behind you, cousin, and think for once in your life, for something other than yourself! You were one of the best Captains Ordiatea had to offer. You lead over two dozen campaigns, winning every one of them."

"Not my last-"

Felik's vision blurred with white light and black specks as a hand struck his cheek.

"I said to put it behind you," Mikel growled. "I paid a handsome fee to bring you here."

"You knew I lived?" Felik said with surprise, both for the blow and the knowledge of his survival from his infamous Folly of the Fourth.

"You were engaged in petty theft, cousin," Mikel said as he walked away from Felik and towards a large, oval table. "That is until you got the brash idea to steal the King's Jewel. Why?"

"How... who told you?" Felik just could not connect the dots.

Mikel poured a cup of steaming tea from a painted kettle. He lifted the small cup, along with the accompanying saucer, with all the dignity of a nobleman... like an Upper. As youths, they had dreamed of making it to Academy, becoming Lieutenants, being what none in their family could have ever imagined. Neither would have imagined that they would have both risen to Captain, despite their blood. And now, Mikel had progressed so much further. Felik suddenly felt very small, foolish, and undignified.

"Marcel, and I do expect you to get used to that name once more, do you think I lack resources?" Mikel asked as he set the white cup with blue veins of ink and golden rim back onto the saucer. Placing his hand onto the antique hand-and-a-half sword on his hip. It was his grandfather's sword, and Felik had heard the story of how it had been awarded to him a thousand times. It was out of regs, obviously, but who would tell a Battle Hero-General he was wearing the wrong sword?

"Why?" Felik pressed.

"You failed one time, once," Mike said slowly, firmly. Felik moved to speak, but Mikel cut him off abruptly. "You failed one time. Do you think I have not known failure or loss? Do you not think I know the pains of remorse, the guilt of survival? I was content to leave you alone, to live your life in obscurity."

"I deserved to be hung for my crimes, if not for abandoning my men, then for stealing the King's Jewel."

"Did you think your actions that day would have gone unknown?" Mikel asked. "Did you think I would not have sent men to aid your company?"

"I betrayed my men," Felik countered. "I left them to die!"

"Don't lie to me, cousin. Don't lie to yourself!" Mikel thundered. "When my men arrived, do you know what we found? What we saw? Let me tell you. Hundreds of dead, both in purple and in the olive of Calun. But do you know what we did not find? Your body. I allowed the lie to spread that you abandoned the men so as to lure the Calun to strike once more at a supposedly weakened and frightful militia. The lie had to stand so that we could."

"It was no lie."

"Oh? Was it not? Do you think we only found the dead?" Mikel mused. "No cousin. There were whispers amongst the prisoners we took, whispers of a demon with two swords, hacking and cutting any who came near the men of the Fourth. A man who stood against many, until the Calun broke down their rear barricades and slaughtered the few remaining men who the two-sworded demon protected. I have known that demon, I have seen him in action. You do not fall lightly, cousin. But your moment of weakness, your moment of flight allowed for a much greater victory. I am sorry that you suffered for it. That you have borne the shame all these many years, but your shame can be expunged. You can return and the world can know what truly happened that day. That a single man stood against dozens. That a single man fought to exhaustion, and then when his foes were distracted, he chose life. There is no shame."

"Why bring me back?" Felik asked, having resigned that memory to the very darkest parts of his own mind, feeling unworthy of any sense of solace that it might have brought. His cousin had a way with words that was undeniable. But Felik did not wish to move on, not now, not until he knew Mikel's ulterior motive. He could have come to him any of 'these long years' before. So why now?

"Because you were betrayed," Mikel stated bluntly. "I do not mean that battle all those years ago, no. You and your band of thieves were betrayed by one of your own. He sold you and yours to your deaths."

"What are you talking about?" Felik's mouth had gone dry, and his stomach lurched.

"Let me ask you something, cousin," Mikel countered. "Do you believe in magic?"

"Mikel, I asked you a question," Felik growled. "Don't toy with me right now."

"Or what?" scoffed Mikel as he folded his thick arms across his torso.

Felik bit his tongue, stifling the desire to lash out at Mikel. Thirteen years. It had been over thirteen years, and still, his older cousin could get under his skin just as quickly as he could when they were youths. The only difference now was a simple truth that was this- thirteen years ago Felik, or Marcel at the time, was a young man who trained daily with the sword and lance. Now he was washed-up and old, and his older cousin looked younger and healthier than he, despite his two years in seniority.

"That was crass, Marcel, I am sorry."

Did Mikel just apologize? By the Fenron's lost blade, what had happened these last thirteen years?

"Anyways, I meant my question in earnest," Mikel continued, noting that his cousin would not answer. "Strange things have been happening, cousin, things I can't explain with reason. You know me. You know I have always been devout. But, the things I've seen, Marcel, I have seen demons and monsters. I have seen men and women cast flame and darkness from their very hands. Marcel, I don't mean to say that the Church has lied to us, but, it is not a coincidence that you were brought to me now."

Felik's mind swam. He had felt strange things, seen inexplicable things, heard- the explosion at the Mayoral Residency. That had been no cannon shot, he had known it, he had heard far too many in his years as a military man.

"Your team, your 'Crew', I had them watched all these years, once I finally found where you had settled," Mikel pressed on, whether ignoring or not noticing the confusion and concern on Felik's face, Felik did not know. "Well, one of the members of your team was spotted after your hideout was burned to the ground. I saw him talking with Kh'ar Kingsmen... and he did something...strange."

Felik's gut dropped. Tornak? "No..." the uttered word escaped Felik's mouth without him even realizing it.

"You were betrayed, cousin. You and your team. My men went to take him, but they were burned by a flame from that bastard's hand. Only the retainer survived, having stayed concealed during the confrontation. When he relayed the message, I sent my top men to find you and bring you here."

"What about my Crew, Tomo, Belthazer, Felohme...Aellia?"

"I'm sorry, Marcel," Mikel replied somberly, placing a gentle hand on his shoulder. "My information didn't find anything else, not in the limited time allotted. I was lucky to find you, all with that fat pig Aldorian screaming for your head."

Felik's world tilted. It was too much; it was far too much. Magic, that was impossible. A traitor? Tornak, why? He had been hard on the boy, true, but nothing that would call for the death of his team. And his crew, his Crew...they couldn't be dead. It just couldn't be. Felik's knees turned to jelly, and he fell to the rugged floor of the tent.

A long moment passed. And in that prolonged nightmare, reality crashed over Felik in ceaseless waves. He did not want to believe it, but it made sense. It had been so hard to get those forged invitations. The boy had just vanished that night, no sign, and they had all mourned for him, cried tears of comradery and loss. But it made sense, how else could everyone have known where everyone would have been positioned at the parade. That little rat must have snuck in and spied on all their plans, handing it over to the Kh'ar of all people? He did not want to believe it, but it was too perfect, it made too much sense.

"Cousin," Mikel said softly, extending a hand. "I cannot change the past. But I can offer you a future. I need you here. Felik is dead. Marcel can live once more. I need you to fight, not as a thief or mercenary, but as a Knighted Captain. What do you say?"

What say I? Felik stared at his regal, proud cousin. He looked into those steel eyes and felt a swell of pride, a swell of anger, a swell of hatred. Felik knew, no, Marcel knew that his old life was dead now. He was given a chance to be something more. A second chance, a chance he did not feel like he deserved. But, perhaps, this chance would come with a side of revenge on those that had wronged him. Tornak, the Kh'ar, and those damned Calun. "Aye, cousin, I could do that."

"Then rise, Captain Marcel Moretriou. Rise and accept your place as a Knight of Ordiatea once more."

Marcel rose, leaving Felik dead on the floor. He shucked off that weak, sniveling, coward of a man. For what he would do next, he knew there was no place for weakness nor regret. Marcel would face the world as he had once done, with a straight back and firm hand.

"What would you have me do first, Lord General?"

"First," Mikel said with a smile. "You need a bath and a shave. Second, we need to discuss these Kh'ar and what they are actually trying to accomplish. I believe it goes far deeper than overthrowing Ordiatian law and establishing their king over all free peoples. I believe they have found something, access to some dark power damned by the Forsaken Ones themselves. And you and I, we are going to cut out the heart of the Kh'ar once and for all."

Acknowledgements

First and foremost, I have to say a massive thank you to my wife, Heather. She has been by my side since we were in High School, and supported me every step of the way, reading the same chapters a thousand times, and listening to me monologue for hours. I cannot say I love you enough. Secondly, is to my mother. It was due to her influence that I fell in love with reading at a very young age. She opened the doors of my imagination and inspired me to seek the mystical and wonderful things of this life. I cannot say thank you enough for this. And last, but not least, to Grandma Val, who has read and helped from day one, offering editorial advice and opinions on the plot.

Now, please bare with me as I go through a whole list of names, as for anyone who has completed a book knows, there are often far more hands than are ever seen, and I could not have completed this without them. Stephen Tate, who has seen me whiteboard more plotlines, outcomes, names, and places than any one human should ever have to endure. To Jesse Watson, who befriended me as a freshman in college and inspired me to follow my passions, even if they were not always 'cool'. She was also an excellent beta-reader, providing much needed feedback. To my artist, Aaron Moschner, who has gone through countless cycles bringing color and shape to my black and white dream, you are amazing, and I look forward to our future. To my amazing editor, Clara Abigail, without your aid, my dyslexic self could never have produced a coherent work. Each one of you have been so integral in the culmination of this work, that I honestly believe it is as much yours as mine. To each member of my family who openly supported me, I love each of you. To Ciara Devine and Nathan Baxter, for your input and ideas, they were much appreciated.

And to end, for each one of you have read my work, you are allowing the childhood dream of one person blossom to life. Thank you.

About the Author

DAVID ANDREW TROTTER was born in a small town in rural Arkansas. His mother provided much of his childhood education, and in doing so, instilled in him a love of reading and of learning. As a young man, David courted, and then married, the love of his life, Heather Scott. They now have three beautiful children, Oliver, Lily, and Theodore. David graduated from the University of Arkansas – Fort Smith with a degree in Business Administration.

David currently spends most of his time juggling a job, an active gym life, and his true passion, writing. This book was a culmination of years of hard work, effort, joyous moments, and bitter sorrows. This story, while you will never know, got him through some of the darkest times of his life, and he hopes that it will inspire and entertain each who dare to explore the wild, mystical world of his imagination.

https://www.facebook.com/david.a.trotter.3

https://www.instagram.com/datzme16/

Glossary

CHARACTERS:

Aellia - *A-lee-a*
Orphaned after her father was imprisoned for assaulting an Upper, which he did not actually do, and her mother died of the White Fever, Aellia turned to the streets for survival. It was there that she met Felik and his Crew. Like her late mother, Aellia also contracted the White Fever, making her skin pale like porcelain and her hair straight and white. Despite her petite size, Aellia has spent most of her life running rooftops and fighting with knives, leaving her lean, muscular, and spattered with scars.

Alec Adelmo – *Al-ek A-dell-mow*
Mayor of Tur'Mor, appointed and loved by the people. He is handsome man with intense features and a powerful build. He dresses well, but not too ostentatious. He, being of pure bloodline and lineage, has the titular olive skin, dark eyes, and curly, black hair that bespeaks an Ordiatian.

Alessandro Tassi
Head of the Huntsmen. He has been brutally injured numerous times in his craft, resulting in a missing leg which was replaced by a prosthetic crafted by the Asterivians

Alyn Candius – *A-lin Candy-oos*
Is twin sister to Brei Candius and is a Blessed. She has the ability to Touch Aetora, which allows her to heal others of physical wounds and injuries.

Arrius Aldorian – *Are-E-oos Al-door-E-an*
A Midcouncilor of Tur'Mor and a pain in Felik's neck. He is responsible for maintaining civility in Southend but uses his power to abuse and coerce people into his bidding. He has become fat of power and wealth, his name being one of the oldest and 'purest' in Tur'Mor.

Aurelius Hallock – *uh-rail-E-oos*
Chief Inspector of Tur'Mor and friend of Alec Adelmo. His mutton chops and no-nonsense attitude are his defining features.

Avajan'Aluth – *ah-von uh-loo-th*
Also known as the Voice of the Aluth. This is a title appointed to the leader of the Aluth organization. The Avajan'Aluth is the only Aluth allowed to speak.

Belthazer Haadura – *bell-th-u-z-ear HA-d-er-uh*
Belthazer was a Zealot of the Dragon God Uuradan. He is a tall, darkly complected man who wears traditional Tuawtian garb as often as

possible. He is one of the members of the Crew.

Betrugyn – bet-reh-geh-N
An assassin from Cogadh with one green eye, one black eye, and
blonde hair speckled with red. While not a large man, Betrugyn is very
deadly, and has a brooch that allows him to Touch Iodaba, granting
him the ability of Metaphysical Transportation.

Brei Candius – *br-E candy-oos*
Is twin sister to Ayln Candius and is a Blessed. She has the ability to
Touch Aetora and receive visions of the future.

Darius
Darius, True Name, Denathurias (den-ah-there-I-as), is a Feromage.
The Feromage were called as the Guardians of Ethrea, instructed to
protect the land against dark creatures, evil beings, and those
perverted by the dark Touch of Iodaba. Darius is of the Iron Mountain
Tribe and bears the branding of the Bear upon his right shoulder. He
has the unique ability to Bind direct sunlight, something that no other
person save a Feromage can do. There are three Bindings
accompanied by three Oaths, each allotting Darius a unique set of
abilities, though each come with increasingly severe consequences.

Diabhail – *Die-buh-hail*
High Priest of the Blood Queen Mireya, Diabhail is hell bent on
serving his dark queen. He was tainted by the Touch of Iodaba from
the Blood Queen's hand, granting him unnatural strength and speed.
He fell by Denathurias's hand at the Battle of Morr, ultimately failing
his queen and allowing her body to be cast into Dimdreal.

Edous – *E-dose*
The man with a face shrouded of flame. He is a master swordsman,
trained in the arts of warfare from an early age. He is a noted leader in
a secret organization, whose purposes are less than clear. He has the
ability to both Decay and Metaphysically Transport. As part of his
ensemble, he shrouds his face with Antilight, making it look like
waves of heat are constantly engulfing his features, disguising himself
from all who look upon him. His sword is tainted by Iodaba's power
and if cuts anyone with it, the cut will continue to spread until it kills
the inflicted.

Elcon Von'Harr - *L-Cone v-O' h-are*
High Priest of the Church of Ordan and Steward of the Congregation
of Tur'Mor. He is old man who wears fine clothing and fancies himself
a scholar of many studies. He is an extremely intellectual man who is
in a position of vast power and control.

Felik – *Fee-lick*
The charismatic leader of a group of thieves and scam artists called
The Crew. He is a muscular man with a scared face from a long
forgone battle. He holds a dark secret, one which Midcouncilor
Aldorian uses against him many times.

Felohme Yhzan – *fell-home yu-z-ah-n*
A fat Tuawtian man who escaped slavers and fled to Tur'Mor, where
he joined Felik's Crew and became the negotiator and transporter of
the Crew. He is also an excellent cook and has an all around jovial
personality. He bears brandings on either temple of a dragon, the
mark of the slaves.

Iaenora – *I-A-nora*
This is the name of one of the Sealed Sages who were prophesied to
return to Bind the Forgotten Ones once more and forever.

Izebal – *is-uh-bal*
She is a Diju Speaker and knows many Words. She is a beautiful
woman who is extremely powerful, as she can not only Speak Words,
but also has access to Ria'Elahm through not one, but three Ra'el
Aund. Her tokens of power are her dagger, her wand, and her amulet.
These three sources allot her near limitless access to the Lifesource.
Izebal has ink-black hair, dark, rich skin, and vibrant emerald eyes,
whose irises are wild with green arcing flows of Ria'Elahm's touch.
She has a tattoo on her neck of three emblems and a sinuous line
winding between them. She is tall for a female, even of the Diju.

Khadais – *k-I-d-a-iss*
The Head of the Dorr A'Gadah.

Mikel Thanadius
Lion of Ordiatea, a General of the Ordiatian Army.

Mireya - *meer-E-yuh*
Blood Queen of Morr
Mireya was the last known descendants of the blood of the Fallen
Ones. She professes to be a descendent daughter of Moranna, who
was said to have birthed seven daughters, as did her sister, Morgana,
who of each birthed seven additional daughters, and thus filled the
earth with the dark Touch of Iodaba. The Feromage spent most of
their existence hunting and slaying the spawn of the Fallen Ones. It is
also said than many of these descendent daughters would seek out
their kin and slay them, using their Lifeblood as a means to Touch
more of Iodaba's dark light.

Orrum Caldurius – *ore-um cal-dur-E-us*
High Patriarch of the Holy Church of Ordan. Caldurius is an old
name, dating back the earliest days of the Republic. The title of High
Patriarch is one of the only hereditary callings in all of the Republic.
Orrum can trace his bloodline directly back to the first Patriarch of
the Church, who, it was said, was to be touched by the finger of Ordan
and the Holy Mother, Gallea, whispered into his ears all things that
were, that are, and that would be. The High Patriarch is the only male
Blessed.

Rahnaluz - ran-uh-law-z
The leader of the Kh'ar Robbers, also called *Khall'ah Kh'ar*. He wears a mask to hide his true identity.

Shanavaral Lynak – *shawn-uh-var-all lin-ack*
High Priestess of Un'Mor, member of the Holy Council, Overseer of the Infirmary and Keeper of the Ancient Secret. She is a grey-haired woman of high poise. Priestess Shanavaral's features are sharp and angular, with no hint of humor or amusement.

Talendeal Un'Dar - *talon-deal oon'dar*
High Priest of Telnor and member of the Holy Council. He is primarily responsible for managing relationships with the Nation of Galacia. He is tall, dark skinned man, with thick brows that are salt and peppered with age.

Tomokorash Yukysa – *toe-mo-core-ah-sh U-ki-suh*
Also called, Tomo, is from Zau'fi.

Tornak – *tore-nack*
A rarity, he is pale skinned with freckles on his face a head full of red hair. He is the youngest member of The Crew and is exceptional and forging documents and writs.

Xander Adelmo – *zan-der A-dell-mow*
Xander is the mayor of Tur'Mor, elected for his charisma, progressive ideals, and his apparent love of the people. He was also a war hero and the second son of a rich noble house. His family is well informed and is an ancient name in Tur'Mor. He has broad shoulders, curly black hair, the titular Ordiatian olive skin tones, and a sharp beard with tight ringlet. While he does not talk much about it, he is an expert marksman, being the former Captain of the 34th Musketmen. He is also more than adapt at rapier fencing, saber fencing, poetry, dancing, wrestling, and the throwing of the discus.

Yemera Haldwen – *ya-meer-uh hal-d-when*
A member of the Holy Council and the High Priestess of Livitha. She is of Ordiatian blood and lineage, but is more reserved than her fellow Council Member, a Livithian trait, due to their negotiations with foreign dignitaries from outside the Republic.

<u>**THE ELLITHEOR:**</u>

The Ellitheor are the gods of Ethrea, or at least, are recognized as the gods of several major nations, excluding the Zau'fi and Tuawtian Nations. The Ellitheor towered over mortal men during their time on Ethrea. They stood between eight and twelve feet tall, Fenron being the tallest of the Ellitheor. They are immortal beings, whose true origin is a topic of fierce debate amongst the devout worshipers and the theologians of Ethrea. What we do know, is that they came down from their dwellings on Vanherran upon silver sky ships, manned by the Daulkaefar.

Ordan
The High Father, Lord of Creation, Wielder of Ethra, the World Forger. He commands the power of Aetora and holds the Hammer, Ethra, in whose head is a fragment of Ria'Elahm itself. He is the only being able to access both Aetora and Ria'Elahm. He is a powerfully built, bald man with a great beard. He is often depicted in loose robes, with feet shod in golden sandals that wrap up the calf.

Gallea
The Holy Mother, the All-seeing, Mother of Crows and Sparrows, Mother of all Living, Vessel of Ria'Elahm. No physical description could be made that would not pale in comparison to her beauty. She had rich skin and liquid black hair and eyes the color of Ria'Elahm itself.

Moranna
Once Daughter of Fates, now Daughter of the Lost. She was gifted the ability to Touch Aetora. She forsook that ability to Touch Iodaba, whose corruption leeched the Light from her, replacing it with corrupted darkness. She took on the name, Fallen One.

Morgana
Once Daughter of Love, now Daughter of Lusts. She was gifted the ability to Touch Ria'Elahm. She forsook that ability to Touch Iodaba, whose corruption leeched the Light from her, replacing it with corrupted darkness. She took on the name, Fallen One.

Thaellan
Shepherd of the fields and steward of the seas. He is known for his fiery red hair and green eyes, a unique feature that none of his fellow Ellitheor share. He is also very quiet and almost followed his older sister's path, becoming a Fallen One. He was the first to return back to Vanherran and was not heard or seen from since his departure.

Fenron
The Honorable One, the White Knight, Zaufuine's Bane, Wielder of the Godsblade. Fenron is everything noble, grandiose, confident, and proud. He is the most skilled warrior of the Ellitheor, even surpassing

his own father, Ordan. His sword is made of Endun'gar and Ellitheor
Silver, with a peculiar white stone set in its cross-guard. The blade
burns with white flame when in the presence of Iodaba's darkness. If
he slays something with the blade, it becomes indestructible to that
thing. He was last seen fighting Zaufuine, the Green Dragon of
Galacia over three hundred years ago.

Organizations and Religions of Note

Aluth
A group of secret warriors, vowed to silence and the protection of the
Church of Ordan. They were a special wrap about their heads called a
Lo'Phandrak, a vest called a Han Ru Dhar, and boots made from a
secret plant that grows in the Swamplands that muffles footfalls to
absolute silence called Zhanrak.

Asterivians
A group of scholars, engineers, scientists, and theologians who have
sworn to secrecy and fealty to their leader, known as The Illuminated
One. Their main purpose is finding the key to immortality.

Church of Ordan
The Church's hierarchy is as follows: First comes the Holy Patriarch,
who is the only male Blessed and has his own Sy'ey Aund, which
allows him to receive Visions from the High Father. The Holy
Patriarch sets as the Head of the Church and the Voice of the Holy
Council. The Holy Council is comprised of the sitting High Priest or
Priestesses from each of the major cities of Ordiatea and the Holy
Patriarch. These council members oversee several priests, priestesses,
and monks, each who have their own responsibilities in their given
city and conclave. The Church is the oldest organization, with the
Holy Patriarch being a blood descendant of those first men who
fought alongside Ordan and Gallea in the Fall. The Church has
massive amounts of wealth, power, and influence.

Diju
The Diju are a group of vagabonds who follow the Valean faith and are
ever searching for the Forgotten Words of Lifesong, true names of
things as given by their Goddess, Ethenealal, the Earthmother. They
mark themselves with inks to show their Path. They believe that
Nkuaue, or the Stone Man, is responsible for the Breaking and for all
the evils and sorrows of the world. They believe all life is a woven
tapestry, knitted by the hand of Ethenealal herself. Lifesingers can
Speak the ancient Words. Sparkdancers and Earthshakers can Touch
Ria'Elahm, the first allowing for the ebbing forces like water, fire, and
air; the later can manipulate earth, plants and foliage, metal, wood,
and ore. The Diju are not of Ordiatea, though they are known to
wander its forests, seeking out the forgotten Words. They are despised
by the Danesmen, due to superstitions.

Huntsmen

A group of contractors who discreetly hunt and exterminate unwanted creatures of a mythic or paranormal nature, helping to uphold the current societal standards and belief systems. They are almost as obscure as the creatures and beings they hunt, more myth than men.

Kh'ar Robbers

A group of Noble-born individuals who seek to overthrow the democracy of Ordiatea and align themselves with the King of the Calun Nation. They were masks and meet in private, so as to hide their identities and ideals from the democratic government of Ordiatea.

Hierarchy of Ordiatian Government

Major City-states

Tur'Mor – Capital City and heart of the Republic's Government. It houses over two million citizens, structures older than the Republic itself, and hundreds of tradesmen and thinkers who continually push the boundaries of what is possible.

Un'Mor – The city farthest south, bordering the Calun Nation's borders. This is where the primary force of Ordiatea's military resides. It also is where the infamous Infirmary is located.

Livitha – This city-state is located in farthest southern reaches of Ranok, though not considered a part of the forest itself. It also is near the Dogtooth Mountains and is on the Potamae river. It is a primary producer of dyes, wools, and spices, as they are first on the Potamae and run steam powered barges up-river to trade with the other nations.

Telnor – The farthest city-state north, bordering the Iron Mountains. The people of Telnor are strongly akin to the Tuawtian and the Galacians who, during earlier periods of history, were not as welcome in Ordiatian society.

Minor Cities of Note

Templetown – A quaint town formed around the base of a high hill in a half-moon pattern. This town is responsible for maintaining the Temple of Ordan. It is only a few miles northward of the Outer Walls of Tur'Mor.

Harbortown – Directly eastward of Tur'Mor, set on the Potamae River, Harbortown is where the Ordiatian Navy docks their fleet.

Outpost of Tur'Mor – A garrison is stationed here, bordered next
to the Old Marsh. They are responsible for keeping guard of the
eastern reaches of the land.

Ranok Outpost – A garrison is stationed here, bordering Ranok
Forest. They are responsible for keeping guard on the road to
Daneland, which cuts through the forest.

Furrow's Gap – A small town with only one inn. Often used by
travelers heading to and from Daneland, though not many traverse
that road anymore.

Government Officials

Rising Star
Head of the Republic of Ordiatea, which comprises of the Nations of
Ordiatea, Galacia, and Daneland.

High Council
A group of dignitaries, each representing their home countries, that
discuss all the geo-political intricacies that go into the running of a
Republic.

Mayor
Each City-state of Ordiatea is overseen by an elected official called a
mayor. They hold office for set term limits and are replaced via vote
by those who own land.

Regents
Regents are unique to Tur'Mor, as the Capital is far larger than any
other City-state in Ordiatea. There are four regents, and they each
oversee a portion of Tur'Mor four quadrants.

Midcouncillors
Midcouncillors are voted upon officials, but typically only come from
Houses of Name, high-born nobles. They are primarily responsible for
different aspects of the city's functioning, schools, taxes, prisons,
water supply, and so on. Tur'Mor has eighty-three Midcouncillors
across the Four Quadrants and the inner court, known as the
Valamour.

Royal Guard
The Royal Guard are responsible with the guarding and defending of
the Noble Houses, the Valamour, Mayoral Family and the reports
directly to the Rising Star. These are often referred to as Knights or
Royal Knights, as they were once actual Knights, before the
modernization of Ordiatea.

Inspectors

A subset of Royal Guards are those call Inspectors, who specialize in deduction and solving of high profile cases, including but not limited to, murder, rape, theft or harassment of any noble-born member of society.

City Guard

These are the policing body of Tur'Mor. They wear black jerkins with Silver Stars on their chests. They are charged with keeping the peace and promoting a city of harmony and cleanliness.

Artifacts and Items

Ra'el Aund

These were crafted for those born of the blood, but not powerful enough to directly access the True Source. They are unique in the fact that they are only bound by one Oath and only allow the wielder to use one of the Light Sources' three powers. The Blessed are most commonly known for using these.

Sy'ey Aund

Directional Items of Power. Rarer than Ra'el Aund, but less so than Tel'un Aund. The only thing that makes these lesser than the Tel'un Aund is these too, like the Ra'el Aund, can be forged by man. Though the process is far more complicated and dangerous. One must swear an oath of Unbreakable loyalty to craft such a weapon.

These require 3 things;
1. An Unbreakable Oath
2. A direct source from one of the Stone Keys (A perfect imbued gemstone to harness it)
3. Either Ellitheor Silver, Dragon's Bone, or Endun'gar (white gold of Vanherran)

Tel'un Aund
Scepter of Sages / Oathrod

These Scepters, Tel'un Aund, were crafted in secret for the Seven Sages of Ordan, half endowed with the Everlight and half with Lifesource. Upon each are etched the words Ada'eha El-dached, the binding words of the Sages

Ellitheor Silver

The rings of the Feromage are the only known source of true Ellitheor Silver, though there is a near exact match of ore that is found in Talahmnas. What makes the difference? When Ellitheor Silver is forged, it must be mixed with three things; ore that can *only* be found on Vanherran, the power of Aetora and Ria'Elahm fused together, and lastly, the blood of an Ellitheor, dripped onto the billet while white hot. Once Ellitheor Silver is hardened and cooled, it cannot be broken or re-melted, unless unbonded by the blood of the

Ellitheor who sacrificed and all three Celestial Lights fusing into one
destructive channel.

Fragtorch

Ra'el Aund with the specific use of shining blue light, but the users do
not have to be Blessed, as they continually shine until the light dims
and needs to be refueled at a Source.

The King's Jewel

A large amethyst that has been in the Royal Treasury since the
founding of Tur, before it was Tur'Mor and only the Valamour existed,
though it was only called Tur at the time.

<u>Buildings and Locales</u>

Asterivae

The above ground part of the tower is a cylindrical building with a
domed ceiling of brass, with great sheets of glass allowing for light.
Beneath the dome is the Star Gazer, a massive telescope. Under that is
the Library of Ages, where the Globe of Galaxies sets, tens of
thousands of books gathered from seven nations and three ages fill
this multi-leveled library.

Temple of Ordan

The Temple of Ordan is located atop a high hill overlooking
Templetown. The temple is one of the oldest structures in Ordiatea,
though it is constantly renovated and kept up. It is said that the
temple was plotted out by a Patriarch who was given a vision from the
High Father himself, which is why it does not look like any of the
other buildings in Ordiatea.

Valamour

The Valamour is the name used for two separate things. Firstly, it is
the name of the oldest structure in Tur'Mor, the tower at the heart of
the city, which atop is carved the likeness of the First Three, the
Founders of the Republic. The Valamour is also the name given to the
Inner Court of Tur'Mor, a walled portion of the city where the ruling
class resides. There are also grand gardens, expansive courtyards and
gorgeous statues strewn throughout.

Darhdall Alley

Perhaps the wealthiest portion of Tur'Mor outside of the Valamour.
These are permanent estates, owned by the upper echelon of
Ordiatian society. It is located in Northend and is a gated community.

The Sanctuary

This is the largest Chapel of The Church of Ordan in Tur'Mor, located
near the gateways from the Market District and Southend. It is a

massive building with a domed ceiling, and four spires rising from the sides of the building. Its large, open-front doorway, is covered by a massive stone eave with dozens of carvings telling of the Ellitheor and the early Ordiatians.

The Loft
Once an academy of fine arts, the Loft was commandeered by Felik and is used as the Crew's hideout and base of operations.

The Monastery
The compound where the monks and priests of The Church of Ordan reside. It is located at the farthest portion of the Market District, butted against the dividing wall of Southend. And while it is a rather plain, stucco complex, it hosts its own courtyard, study, and private bathhouse.

Mayoral Residency
Located within the Valamour, this is where the sitting Mayor resides. It is a colossal estate, with expansive courtyards, viewing galleries, winery, and baths.

<u>Mythical Creatures</u>

Daulkaefar
Known as Elves, Angels, or Heralds, depending on who you ask. They have greyish skin, black eyes with star-like spots that act like pupils, granting them far-sight and night-sight, thus they prefer darkness as much as possible. They are immortal, super strong and fast, and can utilize a type of magic from Speaking Words.

Itheanam
Dark creatures created from the dead bodies of humans, fused to beasts by the souls sucked from living mortals. They come in all types and styles, depending on what beast(s) were used to form them, but they all have one thing in common, a central spike, driven through the skull, marked with runes, which tethers Iodaba's darkness to the beasts. Their skin appears almost tar-like, and if you look at it, you can see the souls of those trapped trying to escape from its body.

Morreans
Once human, Morreans are corrupted beings who have given up a portion of their soul to Touch Iodaba. This grants them unnaturally long life, enhanced speed and strength, but it comes with an insatiable bloodlust. It also turns their eyes black, extends their limbs, and causes various bones to protrude from their bleached flesh. Female Morreans are also said to release a pheromone that can cause males to become extremely aggressive and lustful.

The Three Celestial Lights

Aetora

Known as the Everlight or the Cognitive Light, the Light of Understanding. It is perceived in the Terral Realm as a brilliant blue light, wisping about like a fine mist. This light resides on Vanherran, sitting upon the throne of the House of Or. Its three attributes are as follows:

- *Healing*
- *Vision*
- *Aethereal Projection*

Iodaba

Known as Antilight or the Source of Death, Decay and Destruction. It is perceived in the Terral Realm as black in color with a maroon tint to it, flowing like liquid ink, but fracturing as cracked obsidian. The ultimate source of Iodaba is located in Halfak in the Seventh Level. Its three attributes are as follows:

- *Decay*
- *Vision Casting/Nightmare Trance*
- *Metaphysical Transportation*

Ria'Elahm

Known as the Lifesource or the Source of Material Creation. Ria'Elahm is seen in the Terral as a deep emerald color, vivid and wild. It sparks and jumps, like arcs of lightning, crackling and flowing. It is the power of nature and creation. Its three attributes are as follows:

- *Elemental Control*
- *Repairing*
- *Shielding / Warding*